A MARK OF KINGS

by

Bryce O'Connor & Luke Chmilenko

Bryce O'Connor & Luke Chmilenko

"A Mark of Kings"

Book One of The Shattered Reigns series
Bryce O'Connor & Luke Chmilenko
Copyright © 2019 Bryce O'Connor, Luke Chmilenko

ISBN: 978-0-9988106-9-0

Cover Art by Billy Christian
Cover Design by Shawn T. King, STK Kreations

BOOKS BY BRYCE O'CONNOR

The Wings of War

Child of the Daystar
The Warring Son
Winter's King
As Iron Falls

BOOKS BY LUKE CHMILENKO

Ascend Online

Ascend Online
Hell to Pay
Legacy of the Fallen

Bryce O'Connor & Luke Chmilenko

For Mike Faltraco.
For the tough love
in which confidence took root.

… and because whenever I was distracted at practice,
it's probably because I was working on this story
in my head…

-Twinkle Toes

ACKNOWLEDGMENTS

Writing acknowledgements for a single person is hard enough, but when a book has *two* authors, this section has a tendency to become its own chapter. For that reason, we have decided to keep things short, and settle on thanking *you*, the reader who currently holds this book in their hands, for your purchase and support. *You* are the reason—in many ways the *sole* reason, in fact— that we get to do what we love to do for a living.

In particular, we would like to thank our beta readers, who answered our call for help, and gave us so much incredible feedback and assistance when we needed it most. Thank you all.

BETA READERS:

Adam Siefertson, Adarsh Venkatesh, Amy Lizette Davalos, Andie Wilson, Andrew Miller, Anthony Gallo, Ronni Adams, Bruce L Hevener, Barbara Ryan, Brandon, Bryce MacTurk, Carole, Daniel Crain, Daniel A. Shay, Damian Ryan, David A Hammer, David Lubkin, David Nott, David Smith, Cherry Obsidia, Mr. Derek E. Larson, MMus, Med, Devin Fuoco, Drake Vato, Einar Nygård, Elise Woodfolk, Emi-Jo Smith, Master Seamen Walsh, Emily-Ann, Emma Ellen Clor, Professor Ethan L. Alderman, Fuchsia Aurelius, Gary Sather, Gilbert Dumas, Alexandria Strutton the legacy, Iain Hare, AFCBJane&AMAP, Jacques Smit, Jacob Greer, Jedediah, Jennifer, jayjay, Jerri-Lee 'Sprinkles' Bickley, Joe Jackson, Johnny Ayers, John Gerlak, J Henninger , JoJo, Joli, Jonathan Williamson, Joshua Burns, Juan, TuFF GoNG, Kate Churcher, Katie, Ken Reeser, Khendarian, Krystal S, Lening Gonzalez, Mackenzie King, Ares Wolfe, M.B.Schroeder, Matt Gorsuch, Michael Matthews, Michele L. Metzler, Nathan Fears, Nicholas Rocan, Noel Townsend, Robert J. Mosentoff, Roger " chainsaw " Harris, Imabookworm, , Ruth C. Jones (ruthiejones.com), sally b, Sargash, Shawn A. Dressler, Shawn Sharrah, Si Richards, Simon "MORT" Evans, Simon Sheanon, Stephen Neal, Steve Thomas, Struan Findlay, Theresina Lloyd, Todd Ponto, Tony M, vena thunderbird, William Alexander, AJ Larson, Alex Gallegos, Amanda Jimerson, Andrew Jones, Brady West, Brandon Kennedy , Brenden Stopher, Brittany Adams, Caleb F, Cameron Londergan, Casey Munger, Chela-Rene Spaargaren, Chris Moore, Connor McPherson, Curtis S, Daniel Boyce, Daniel Prince, Daniel Vick, Daniel Womack, Dave K, David Durand, David Muir, Daylan Ethridge, Dennis, Devon Jolly, Doug Grimes, Edmund Milne, Elias Dantas, Emilie Fostvedt, Erik Borgstrom, Gus Blackmer, James Dillard, Jamey Sultan, Jamie Collins , Jared Bodewig, JC McIntosh, Jeff Kohlbeck, Jesse Morin, Jesse Reynolds, Jim Stojkov, John B. DeBlanc, Jon Johnson, Jonas Talley, Jonathan Campbell, Josh Spagnuolo, Justin Ballew, Kaztith Dundar, Kelly Flynn, Kendon Holtz, Lee Anderson, Linda Wilson, Mari Krugel, Michael Hackett, Michael VanderMeer, michael walker, Mike Pratt, Morgan Douglas, Nathan Lindeman, Nathaniel, Micah Stoops, Nick Johnson, Patrick McQuoid, Paul J, Paul Smith, petey waple, Pierre Larsson, Rebekah Wilpon, Rich Parker, Richard London, Rick Sebrite, Rick Ulshafer, Rickie Brown, Robert Pratt, Ryan Gurr, Ryan O'Malley, Selena Banales, Seth Morgan, Stephen Kutz, Stephen Reynolds, Tammy Krause, Thomas Sigman, Victor Rasky, Weston Bohannon, Zach Veckov

We would also like to take the time to thank our Patreon supporters for their support, assistance, and enthusiasm over the month and years they have been with us. You guys are seriously the best, without exception. If interested, you can check out **Bryce's Patreon** at (**patreon.com/bryceoconnor**), and **Luke's Patreon** at (**patreon.com/LukeChmilenko**).

PATREON SUPPORTERS:

Andrew Cheng, Daniel Bacon, Dawn Horn, Dennielle, Ithamon, Jordy, Kaladin_Paran, Luka Tisus, Noctifer, TheDwiin, Kevin Chan, LunaLagoon, Neil Davis, William A. Riley, Daedakus. Devin Fuoco, Ethan Alderman, Karneth Kenitharian , Luca Raven, Nargoth, Corgikong, Jacob M Bruner, Adam Billingham, Agustin Olide, Alex Donovan, Alex , Athy192 , Austin Hartt, Benjamin Pryer, Benjamin

Bryce O'Connor & Luke Chmilenko

A MARK OF KINGS

by

Bryce O'Connor & Luke Chmilenko

Bryce O'Connor & Luke Chmilenko

PROLOGUE

1052p.f.

"This 'Accord' of man's creation seems—in my humble opinion—a pathetic thing. To this day I question Tyrennus' wisdom in having allowed our kind to be bent to its will, the one and only time I have ever faltered in my faith in the primordial line. After all, while it may well hold sway over the races of man and elves and dragons, there are other dangers lurking in this seemingly peaceful world of ours.

Dangers, regrettably, that are as yet beyond the reaches of even that greatest of magical treaties..."

-Arrackes, High Chancellor of Ysenden, c. 500p.f.

Around Abegale Idrys, the world burned.

There was nothing to be done as the fire rose up around her, swallowing the walls of the small nursery she was trapped in and choking away the air from her lungs in a constant wave of heat and smoke. For a time she had tried to scream, tried to make her voice heard through the inferno, but eventually she lost the strength to do even so little. Her body was weakening. She struggled to stand, but staggered, her breath coming in shallow, panicked heaves. Against her bosom, the bundle of brown cloth squirmed, and it was that feeling which was all that kept her upright, that knowledge that her child still lived which helped her cling to hope.

Desperation, however, was fervently clawing at that hope, scratching it away sliver by sliver.

"...GALE! ABE ...GALE! DEC... LAN! ABE... GALE!"

Abegale's vision was just starting to grow hazy when she made out the voice, faint against the roar of the fire. She blinked and coughed, gulping as she tried to draw breath enough to call back. She managed only to take in a lungful of soot, and what little will left to her failed all at once. As she crumbled to her knees, though, her arms barely managing to hold on to the writhing, squalling infant in her hands, she heard the voice again, stronger now.

"ABEGALE! ABEGALE! DECLAN!"

Abegale wheezed, wanting desperately to respond, to yell that she was there, *there*! No other sound escaped her, however, and instead it was the room itself that replied, a resounding *crunch* snapping over the sound of the flames. Abegale doubled over, shielding her child with her body while a

1

shower of embers and twisting sparks rained all around them. She tried to stand again, tried to get a foot under herself. She wouldn't die there, she *wouldn't*. Even if she had to face the cruelty of the flames that blocked her path to the door. Even if she had to meet the heat that raged all around her, wicked and shimmering. She *wouldn't die there*.

Most unfortunately, conviction can only hold at bay for so long the callous realities of the world.

Abegale's leg gave out the moment she tried to put weight on it, and she tumbled to the ashy floor, falling not feet away from the closest edge of the fire. There she lay, shivering despite the broiling heat, unable to do more than blink at the outline of the room's framed entrance through the blaze, hardly two body-lengths away but oh-so-far out of reach. She cursed herself, cursed the Mother and Her Graces, cursed her home of wood and straw and the beasts who had set it ablaze in their savagery. Her vision grew dark around the edges, and she thought it perhaps a trick of the light when a shape appeared in the doorway, shifting like a mirage in the heat.

Then the form lunged for her, bellowing her name and that of her son, and Abegale felt her hope blaze for the briefest moment even as she dropped into nothingness.

■■■

She came to as the icy air of the winter night blasted across her bare face and neck, drawing her back into consciousness with a painful gasp that stung at her boiled lungs. She began to cough again at once, every breath raw and stinging, every exhale tasting of ash and smoke.

"Abegale," a voice wheezed near her ear, exhausted but relieved. "Thank the Mother. You're alright. You're both alright."

She turned. Ertus' bearded face was inches from hers, and she realized then that she was in her husband's hard arms, already some dozen yards from the burning remnants of their home. All around them, most of the other buildings of Estwyn were ablaze, the flickering, growing glow blackening out the night sky. Dozens of shapes rushed by in the chaos, many panting and swearing as they took in the devastation, while others called out in distress to loved ones lost among the panicking crowd. Not far off, the harsher sounds of steel screaming against steel could be made out among the village homes and shops, cutting across the pained cries of the injured and dying. Through the haze, Abegale thought she could make out the violent shadows of battle against the light. The forms were indistinct, her vision muddled by the smoke, but what might have been men bearing swords and spears looked to be making their stand in the streets, holding firm against darker, crueler shapes. Abegale shivered and looked away from the violence, registering instead that it was cold, so cold, the trampled cobblestone around them peppered with scattered frost and muddied snow.

It didn't matter. She was out, freed from the flames, and with a thrill Abegale realized that bundle of cloth still squirmed in the hook of her hips, quieter now, but yet moving.

Alive… Her son was alive…

Tears welled up in Abegale's eyes, and she tried to speak. The effort only made her chest ache, and produced nothing more than a harsh choke of noise.

Ertus' face twisted with shared pain without looking down at her, moving as quickly through the rushing people as he could under their combined weight. "Don't speak," he told her over the shouting of the throng, his own voice rough from the fire. "Save your strength. We need to find Ryn. He'll get us away from here."

A flame of reassurance sparked in Abegale's heart at that, and she instinctively pulled her child tighter against her with one hand. With the other, she reached up, wanting to take the man's face and guide it down to meet her eyes, but Ertus winced as her fingers touched his cheek, finding it raw and sticky.

Burned, she thought in horrified realization.

"It's fine," her husband answered her silent question, turning his head away slightly to hide the wound. "Others have suffered worse." He looked at her sidelong. "Can you stand? More than a hundred made it through the old gates before the Vigil's men managed to shut off the pass. Most of them are still around, and I can't fight like this."

Abegale felt a shiver that had nothing to do with winter evening, registering suddenly the sensation of the cool pommel of Ertus' longsword knocking against her ankle from where it hung from his left hip. She considered the question, feeling her limbs still shaking, but the night air had returned some measure of strength back to her body, so she nodded. With a grunt Ertus stopped and eased her down. She winced as her bare feet found the frozen stone, sending a tremble coursing up her spine, but her legs held her weight. She steadied herself, one hand on the man's shoulder, the other holding tight to Declan, cradling his small, swaddled form against her breast. Before she could make a sound to stop him, her husband kicked off his boots, then stripped out of the singed remnants of the heavy pelt cloak that had been draped across his shoulders.

"Don't argue, just put them on," he told her, bending down to place the boots at her feet before draping the mantle over her body. "I'll be fine, and you two need them more than me right now."

Hesitating only briefly, Abegale did as she was told, grateful for the warmth of the oversized footwear and the weight of the charred furs. She'd run to Declan the moment the fires had started to glow through the frosted window of their bedroom, and hadn't had time to dress before the flames trapped them inside the nursery.

"Better?" Ertus asked, looking her up and down only briefly before returning to scan the dancing shadows all around them. He didn't wait for her to nod before continuing. "Good. Let's get out of here. Ryn shouldn't be far." He motioned up the way, towards the east end of the closest road, in the direction many of the fleeing villagers were coming from. "He chased off the ones that set the house ablaze. Probably the only reason I managed to get you out. He was hounding them past the Toytes' place last I saw." He looked west, towards the farmlands everyone was evacuating into, then turned to her again. "Can you walk on your own?"

Abegale grimaced and shook her head. Standing was taking a toll on her enough as it was.

Ertus looked torn, chewing on a corner of his beard. His blue eyes were bright in the firelight, and his loose shirt was damp with sweat, clinging to muscled arms and a broad chest. She caught a glimpse of the burn as he glanced over his shoulder nervously, towards the sound of fighting, and felt her stomach flip at the sight. It covered most of his left cheek and had eaten away a good portion of the short-cropped hair along his temple and ear. Still, she made no attempt to comment on it.

Now was not the time to worry about anything but the immediate and present danger she could hear snarling in the village around them.

Just then, Ertus seemed to make his decision. Drawing his sword from its sheath, he waved it towards the east road, in the opposite direction everyone was running. "Come on," he told her, starting for the mouth of the street. It led deeper into town, towards the continued howls and commotion, but Abegale was relieved all the same.

The sooner Ryn was back by their side, the better, no matter what trouble they had to face in exchange.

Together they moved as quickly as Abegale could manage, she holding as best she could to Declan and Ertus' off arm with one hand each, her husband keeping his eyes on the alleys and side-roads, sword held bare and ready at his side. Dozens passed them heading west, the residents of Estwyn shouting in fear and despair as they fled with their children and valuables clutched in their arms, and several times they were shouted at to turn back, turn *back*! But Ertus ignored all such warnings, pressing forward, calling out Ryn's name himself as best as his lungs could manage in the burning haze. Around them, the boiling fires that consumed the thatched roofs and timber walls illuminated their way all-too-clearly despite the lateness of the hour. As they pressed further into the village, the crowd started to taper, the numbers dwindling around them, and Abegale found herself having to focus on her husband's back, forcing herself to concentrate on Declan's kicking against her chest. It was all she could do, really, to stop herself from gaping in horrified fascination at the gruesome details the thinning crowd was now revealing, the evidence of savagery's ill-willed passing.

The dead, after all, are often far more disquieting than those still left to live.

Corpses were scattered where they fell, mostly villagers and townspeople. Of these, Abegale was horrified to find she could recognize only a handful of their number, a disturbing fact in-and-of itself. Estwyn was—before today, at least—generally considered an obsolete, unremarkable outpost guarding the long-sealed eastern pass that was said to have once crossed through the Mother's Tears into the wild tundras of Eserysh beyond. It was not a large community. Abegale didn't think the town's population had ever risen above a thousand souls in her lifetime spent at the foot of the mountains. She ought to have been able to name every man, woman, and child they passed, living or otherwise.

The mangled remains of the bodies, though—so clearly torn asunder by dirty claws and rotting teeth as often as they'd been struck down by rusted blades and crude clubs—left little to be known by...

There were others, too, among the dead. The King's Vigil, those soldiers unfortunate enough to be garrisoned in Estwyn, had not died quietly either, having fallen in ravaged groups of threes and fours. To their credit, not a man or woman among them looked to have failed in putting up a fight. Around their still forms, crueler, harsher shapes lay equally unmoving, some burly and mountainous, others lithe and sinuous, and still more somewhere in between. These silhouettes, dark against the glow of the flames, Abegale avoided looking at too closely, glancing away the moment she made out the outline of sharpened horns or antlers or matted fur across the melting snow.

The wereyn and their warg were terrifying creatures to behold, even slain and silenced, and she thought her courage could only weather so much.

While it felt like hours, it couldn't have been more than a few minutes on the road before the last of the stragglers of the evacuation passed them in the form of a baker rapidly towing his wife and three daughters away in a hand-drawn cart, wooden wheels clattering desperately against the stone. After that, Abegale and Ertus moved more cautiously, no longer calling out for Ryn, careful to peer around each corner they took and glancing over their shoulders every few seconds to make sure no sinister presence might be creeping up on them from behind. For a time Abegale suspected the Mother was making up for her lack of mercy earlier in the night by watching over their movements with a careful eye, guiding them around the correct turns and into the shadows at all the right moments. The fighting continued, more north of them now, the shearing sounds of cutting steel mixed with the bellows of men and the wild calls of their more beastly opponents. Every so often they would catch a glimpse of outlines darting against the lit end of one pass or another, usually chased by a handful of men waving swords and axes, but nothing ever crossed their own path.

Then, while they were nearing the village's center square, the Mother must have blinked.

It happened as they were edging along the low half-wall of old Adus' smithy—one of the few buildings in Estwyn made of stone rather than timber, aside from the ancient gates at the mouth of the pass to the north. Of the blacksmith himself, Abegale glimpsed only a single booted foot sticking out of the narrow mouth of the shop's great clay furnace. The sight, coupled with the horrid smell of cooking flesh, nearly had her emptying the contents of her stomach onto the road, and her momentary pause as she heaved nearly cost Ertus his life. He must have felt her slow, must have looked around at her instinctively, alarmed at the sound of her retching, and turned his back on the road ahead.

By the time they heard the throaty sounds ahead of them, like the growling of a pack of hungry wolves, it was almost too late.

Ertus cursed, spinning so fast Abegale lost her grip on his arm and stumbled to her knees. She looked up in time to see a humanoid, furred form barreling at them from where it must have been lurking in the space between two burning homes across the way, howling as it ran. Her vision had cleared, but against the brightness of the blaze mixed with the constant whirl of smoke the wereyn was nothing but a black outline against the heat. She made out the shape of an old, chipped sword and what looked like a torch clutched in its off hand, but the details of the figure were lost to the fire as it launched itself at them.

Fortunately, Ertus didn't wear his own steel for show.

In a flash the man was between Abegale and the charging creature, bare feet set in a fighter's stance, blade shrieking diagonally upwards even as the wereyn brought its own weapon down at his head. The swords met with a *clang* that made Abegale's teeth shudder and set Declan to screaming again, but her heart leapt as she saw the rusted iron blade spinning away, its master having lost its grip on the hilt. Instantly Ertus reversed the slash, bringing his razored metal down in a savage, two-handed chop, and the fires swallowed the wereyn's dying shriek.

They did nothing, on the other hand, to hide the pitching bays and snarls that rose up in a rumble all around them even as the dark shape of the beast fell to the cobbled stone, split half-in-two.

"UP!" Ertus roared, spinning on Abegale and hauling her to her feet by one arm. "UP! RUN!"

Abegale didn't have to be told twice, seeing the forms and shadows split off from the fires all around them, converging on them from ahead and behind.

Adrenaline beat away the fatigue in her legs, and Abegale suddenly had no issue keeping pace with Ertus as he led them, full-tilt despite his bare feet, north down the nearest alley. He still held her in an iron grip, pulling her forward through the blazing remnants of the town, taking every turn they could. They skirted the edge of the center square, passed the charred remains of the *Snowy Joy Tavern*, and even leapt clear over the smoldering remnants of the barracks stockade where the Vigil had once kept their mounts, the horses now dead and ravaged as any of the other corpses. Behind them Abegale could hear the panting of their pursuers, the *clacking* sound of claws on stone and the howling of the warg mounts, and her blood ran cold. She wished she could scream, wished she could shout in fear and hopelessness. Never before had she felt so helpless, so useless, unable even to voice her terror. As Ertus turned and led them up the wide side-road between the burning husk of the Ferens' former home and the still-standing wall of the town brewery, Abegale felt tears streaking along her face, unbidden and unwanted.

Unfortunately, all it took for her to forget about them were the trio of ghastly outlines who appeared at the end of the way, cutting off their flight.

Ertus swore again, halting so suddenly he nearly tumbled forward, but he found his feet in time to get his sword up once more, hauling Abegale so that she and Declan were between him and the searing timber of the brewery wall.

"BACK!" her husband howled, swinging his weapon to the left and right, alternating between threatening the lumbering forms who had barred their escape and the four or five pursuers, approaching more cautiously from the other end of the alley now that their prey was trapped. "BACK, YOU BASTARDS!"

Abegale, for her part, clutched at Declan while he screamed, pressing herself against the wood behind her even though she could feel the blistering heat of it through her borrowed furs. She shut her eyes tight, praying to the Mother above for Her mercy, for Her assistance. She fought to keep at bay the horrid sounds of snorting, huffing breath, of gnashing teeth and iron blades being dragged across the stone.

"BACK!" Ertus howled again, but Abegale could hear the fear in her husband's voice now, could make out the desperation with which he yelled. "ON MY LIFE, IF YOU COME ANY CLOSER I'LL—!"

Before he could finish his threat, a beast to the left, one of the wereyn who had blocked their way, lunged with a snarl.

Ertus spun to meet it, and Abegale saw in terror what would happen as the figures on the right—still some four or five paces off—launched themselves at the man's exposed back, taking advantage of the opening. She tried to scream, tried to beg, holding Declan so tightly to her chest he screeched in discomfort. She saw Ertus' black outline knock away the wooden club of the first charging form against the flames, saw him sweep his blade up, lodging it squarely in the creature's throat in a spray of dark blood. She saw the others' clawed hands reach for him, saw dirty blades rise in the heat, and the maws of the warg opening wide.

And then, over everything else, a roar, as loud and terrible as the layered howl of the living hell blazing around them, shook the very stone beneath Abegale's feet.

From the left side of the alley a massive, four-legged shape came hurtling over the heads of the paired wereyn still barring the path, black as the darkest night, white fangs bared. It half-flew, the momentum of its leap carrying it past Ertus' own silhouette, and slammed into the charging line of beasts to Abegale's right. The thing was so big it bore the leading warg and its rider to the ground in an instant, slamming them back into the cobblestone as they screeched in terrified surprise. There was a flurry of action, terrifying against the blaze, then a wrenching, ripping sound, and what looked like a head bounced back up the alley, torn loose of its body. A moment later there was another scream, and the thing pulled open the warg's chest with a strain of its neck, wrenching most of its ribcage away and leaving it to die, shattered and jerking on the stone.

The horror that followed would keep Abegale from ever sleeping soundly again. Unable to tear her eyes from the scene, she watched as Ertus, on one side of her, danced with the two remaining wereyn along the left side of the alley, while on the right the hulking form of the creature who had saved their lives ripped into the remainders of the pack. Her husband's blade sang over the cacophony of the fire as blood splattered the ground and walls around his opponents, blade severing a twitching limb, cleaving open an abdomen to spill acrid entrails over the ground, then ramming through a wide, furred throat. At his back, the action was nothing more than an engine of slashing and tearing and roaring, the great black *thing* as indomitable as an avalanche as it shredded its way through its opponents with tooth and claw. The screams were horrible, the dying wails of the wereyn and the sheer terror in their shrieks as nightmarish as their calm approach had been moments before. No mercy was spared for them, no blow measured, no death withheld. Seconds stretched into a minute, then two, until the last of the beasts finally fell, or turned and fled. When the scene was quiet again, when nothing moved but the shimmer of the blaze around them, Ertus and the creature still stood ready. He was heaving, drawing in staggered breaths with his reddened sword still held before him, while it padded back and forth across the lane, bloody hackles raised and rumbling a constant, threatening growl that shivered through the air.

Finally, when it became clear that the fight was indeed well-and-truly over, Ertus sagged, falling to one knee, blade tumbling to clatter to the stone from his shaking hands.

"Mother's *bloody* hells," Abegale heard him say, looking over his shoulder at the creature still prowling behind him. "To compliment you on your timing would be an understatement, Ryn."

At his words, the beast looked around at him.

If she'd had to, Abegale Idrys would have called the creature a wolf, except not even the *er'enthyl* trackers of the Vyr'en would have been fool enough to hunt *this* wolf. Its shoulder measured higher than Ertus' elbow, and its head rose to just below the man's chin. Its fur was black as a bottomless pit in a lightless room, carrying a sheen to it that was something like glass, or melting ice. Its curved claws were similarly dark, but the tips of its white fangs, exposed as it panted steam into the winter air, were reddened by the fight. If all that wasn't strange enough, though, it was Ryn's eyes that always stood out the most to Abegale. Matching amber orbs, they gleamed like gemstones in the light of the flames, their uniform gold marred only by a dim, vertical paleness where irises might have been, centered by faint white pupils. To the common passerby, those eyes would have been nothing short of eerie.

To Abegale, in that moment, they were the fitting emblem of everything that was warm and safe in the world, and she sagged, sliding down to sit on the cobbled floor of the alley, not even feeling the heat of the wall still burning at her back.

At her movement, the wolf's great head turned towards her, and Ryn loped forward, bringing his black snout close to sniff at her and the baby still crying in her arms.

Be at ease. They've gone for now.

The voice, deep and resounding, came—as ever—from nowhere in particular, rising rather from the depths of Abegale's own mind. She looked up, meeting the beast's bright gaze, and felt again the tears against her cheeks as she nodded in ascension, hoping Ryn would be able to sense the gratefulness in her understanding.

Whether he did or not, the wolf looked around at Ertus. *You should have stayed by the house*, the voice chided, speaking to both of them now. *I could have met you there just as easily.*

"It was a gamble," Ertus conceded with a pained expression, picking up his sword. With a grunt, he used it to leverage himself to his feet. "You only chased the two off who'd set fire to the house. There were more close by, and I thought the fleeing crowds would attract what numbers the Vigil wasn't able to handle."

Ryn considered this, then bobbed his head in acknowledgment. The faint paleness of his pupils scanned the three of them, lingering on the squirming bundle that was Declan, still held in Abegale's arms. She might have been mistaken, but she thought she saw something like relief pass across the creature's features at that, a moment in which the wolf, too, relaxed infinitesimally.

We have to get the three of you away from here, Ryn said, looking up and down the alley quickly. *The remnants of the garrison are being pressed at the gates. They won't hold long. It's a miracle they managed to shut them before more got through.* He glanced back at the gruesome, scattered remains of the wereyn with what might have been distaste.

"What's happened that would make them attack like this?" Ertus asked aloud. He was a bloody mess, but a long, narrow cut below one eye looked to be the worst of his injuries, apart from his burn. "Where did this come from?"

Ryn hesitated at this, and not for the first time Abegale thought she caught something in the creature's gaze that hinted of words left unspoken.

Then the wolf shook his great head. *Questions for another time. We need to leave, Ertus. Now.*

In answer, Abegale watched her husband hesitate, looking north, towards the sound of continued fighting.

"Yes," he said after a moment, seeming to shake himself before looking around at her. "Abegale can't walk on her own. Can you carry her?"

Of course.

There was shifting in the corner of Abegale's vision, and she looked around at Ryn. Where a moment ago there had been a massive wolf, however, a tall, handsome stallion now stood, its coat as pitch as the night sky above them. The only flash of color in its form, in fact, came from those same golden eyes that were the only thing the two animals shared. Hooves clomping over the stone, Ryn stepped closer to Abegale, dipping his head low in obvious suggestion. She nodded her thanks a second time, looping her free arm over his thick neck, and allowed herself to be hauled to her feet. The stallion's hair felt strange beneath her fingers. It was wet, slick with the same blood that had coated the wolf's fur, but beyond that the coarse hair was stiff, almost rigid, like no hide she'd ever felt on any other animal. This was nothing new to her, of course, and—as Ertus moved to help her clamber up onto Ryn's strong back—she patted the beast's newly grown mane gratefully.

They made their way west, then, back in the direction she and Ertus had come. Ryn plodded along as smoothly as he could, conscious of Abegale huddled over his shoulders, babe yet held to her chest. They took the widest road, avoiding the fires and the bodies that still clung to the edges of the street, and within five minutes they reached Estwyn's western edge, where a trickle of villagers still fled into the farmlands beyond the town limits.

The entire time, Abegale watched Ertus, studying her husband, taking dreadful note of how often his head turned back, towards the audible chaos of ongoing battle at the pass gate.

Her worst fears came true when they reached the edge of Ulrot Theron's tilling fields, now frosted with a crust of snow.

"Ryn," her husband said in a voice of forced calm, stopping at the edge of the plot. "Take them away from here."

For what must have been the hundredth time that night, Abegale Idrys cursed her absent voice. His words pulled at her heart, twisting her stomach into a heavy knot, and she spluttered and coughed as she tried to protest. Ryn, too, snorted in anger, and there were several seconds of silence as Abegale could only assume the horse berated Ertus privately.

"You said yourself the gate won't last," her husband answered in a tone of false calmness. "Look at that." He indicated the train of fleeing villagers passing them with a shaking hand. "If the pass opens again, how far do you think these people will manage to get? A mile? Maybe two? Aletha's a hundred leagues from here. Mathaleus won't even *hear* of this for days, much less mobilize a response any sooner."

And you think you can change that? Abegale thought to herself, wishing desperately she could demand so aloud as she clutched at Ryn's mane in cold panic.

Fortunately, the horse apparently asked the man something similar.

"I don't know." Ertus' face hardened, and the sword in his hand trembled slightly as he gripped it too tightly. "But every man is going to count." He looked up at Abegale, and his expression grew torn as he saw the way she was staring at him. "I'll catch up to you as soon as I can, I swear it." He stepped forward, reaching up to her, and she took his hand desperately, clinging to his fingers with her own. She tried to tell him, tried to plead with him with her eyes. She attempted to speak yet again, even knowing how little good it would do, but a faint croak and a pained rasp was all she could manage.

"I'm sorry," he told her with a heartbroken smile that twisted the cruel stain of his burned cheek, and she could see a wetness in his eyes that frightened her more than anything else in the world. "I have to. No one will make it if some of us don't stand here, now."

That only made her grip harder, refusing to let go.

"Abegale, please," he pleaded, and this time the words came broken, his resolve clearly fraying. "Please. You need to go. Take Declan and go."

She wouldn't. She couldn't. She refused, abjectly *refused* to release her husband's hand. She had him, here, now. She wouldn't let him go for all the world and all the wonder and misery in it.

Abegale.

Ryn's voice was gentle across her mind, a soothing spell that pulled at the tension in her soul, drawing it out slowly. As he spoke, the tightness faded, the fear receding gradually as if guided away by some unseen hand, but she still wouldn't release Ertus' hand.

Abegale, let him go. This is a choice he's making for you. He's right. Not even I can do much if the entire mountainside gets overrun by the beastmen.

Abegale shook her head in violent denial. She squeezed her eyes shut, trying to block out the voice, feeling the tears leak from them and trace her jaw as she buried her face into the folds of Declan's blanket.

Abegale, he's doing this for us. For you. For both of you. Let him go.

For a long time, Abegale did nothing. She sat there, atop the stallion's back, clinging to her husband's calloused fingers, feeling their son squirm and cry against her bosom. She could sense the shaking in Ertus' touch, sense the fear there, just as present as the conviction. For a second more she held on, begging that the Mother and Her Graces would allow the moment to last for eternity, would let them stay like that, together, forever.

Then she slacked her grip, and felt Ertus slowly draw his hand from hers.

She didn't look up until he said her name again.

"Abegale."

She lifted her face, knowing that she could not stop herself from crying now. The ache twisted in her throat, in her cheeks, as she fought off a sob and met her husband's blue eyes. With a *thunk* he planted his bloody sword into the frozen ground, using his right hand to fumble with something around the index finger of his left. Pulling it loose, he paused, staring at the thing in his palm for a moment.

Then he held it up slowly.

"For Declan... When he's old enough..."

With shaking fingers, Abegale picked up the plain, cold band. It was an old, worn ring of battered gold, with little ornation to its face other than a simple black stone, wide and flat, set into the thickest part of the metal. Ertus had worn it for as long as she had known him, had *never* removed it, even on their wedding day.

To have it now, empty and solitary in her shaking fingers, brought the reality of the moment crashing down on Abegale in a way even Ryn's voice wouldn't have been able to.

With a gentle press, Ertus closed her hand around the ring, then gripped her wrist and pulled her down towards him, as low as she could come. On bare feet he stood on tiptoes to kiss her, his lips meeting hers hungrily, desperately. She closed her eyes again, feeling the sadness grip her once more. They stayed like that, seconds ticking into each other, neither willing to separate from the other.

Finally, in the end it was Ertus who pulled away.

"Take care of them," he told Ryn, using one hand to pull the horse's head around and press his forehead to the animal's cheek, still not letting go of Abegale's with the other. "For me, will you?"

Even Ryn, it seemed, could not gather the right words in that moment, because he only closed his white-gold eyes in response, nodding into the embrace.

Then, at last, Ertus released Abegale's closed fingers, yanking his sword from the ground.

"I love you," he said hoarsely to her through glistening eyes, backing away with blade bare. "Both of you."

And then he was gone, turning to run headlong back into the blaze of the village limits, leaving behind his wife, child, and the dead, dull ring of lifeless gold she kept clutched in her palm.

CHAPTER ONE

1076p.f.

"Beware the idle scoundrel, friend. It is not the cautious or the wary warrior you must need guard yourself against. Rather, it is the indolent and the lax, the swordsman whose blade is lifted only when necessary. In this, our profession of blood and violence, there are only two types of men whose souls are calm enough to smirk down the length of sharpened steel: the mad, and the truly dangerous."

-Cassandra Sert, Iron Wind Guildmaster, 1072p.f.

A cool breeze blew through the forest, stirring the summer leaves and gently persuading Declan Idrys to open his eyes. He'd been dozing under the shadowed eaves of a maple tree, the soft rush of the creek below soothing him better than any lullaby ever could. Shaking sleep away, he shifted to sit more comfortably against the mossy trunk of the maple at his back, stretching with a groan before gazing up at the speckled patches of blue sky he could distinguish between the entwined branches overhead. All around him sunlight poured through the woodland canopy, coloring the hill in a pattern of glowing amber and green grass. The wind ruffled his dark, shoulder-length hair, and he reached up to free a wild strand from his stubbled cheeks with a loose hand. Below him, the broad stream ran its course, winding gracefully through the woods as it flowed eastward, towards the distant sea, churning and bubbling in the song that had lulled him so effectively some hour or so before.

Ryn, once again, had been displaying his ever-present knack for knowing things he shouldn't when he'd suggested they make camp nearby. It made for a good spot, ideal to hole up in for the job.

A small splash resounded from below, catching Declan's attention. He turned back to the makeshift net now stretched across the creek down the hill, ends lashed to a pair of branches staked firmly into the sandy riverbanks. So far all the fish he'd made out beneath the shimmering waters were too small to get caught in the knotted vines, but it was doubtful any of them would have made good eating regardless. He scratched at his day-old beard with the edge of the old gold ring on the middle finger of his left hand, watching yet another slim, silvery form slip through.

Life of a wanderer, he thought with a smirk, leaning back against the maple again with a satisfied sigh.

Despite his content, after another quarter-hour Declan began to wonder if he might have been wasting his time. The bounty papers felt hot in the breast pocket of his sleeveless traveler's vest, and Ryn was off foraging for other supplies as it was. Maybe Declan should have been doing some scouting, or at least getting to know the surrounding forest. They'd stopped that morning at a nearby hamlet—one of several local municipalities who'd thrown together the coin needed to post the notice— and the villagers had been quite eager to point him towards these parts of Viridian's western woods, saying it was the direction the tracks always led and disappeared into. Frowning down at the stream, Declan reached out to absently pluck a blade of grass from the hillside, setting it between his teeth to chew.

Just a little longer, he told himself.

Fortunately for their supper that evening, his procrastination paid off.

Creak.

The sound of straining wood, not two minutes later, dragged Declan's thoughts out of the clouds and earthward again. He leapt up, finding the net suddenly stretching inward, the water at its center churning as fin and tail thrashed about. In an instant he was rushing down the hill with a triumphant exclamation befitting a boy ten years young, holding tight with one hand to the longsword at his hip, keeping it from catching between his legs. The moment his already-bare feet found rocky bank he unsheathed the hunter's knife on his belt. Reaching the branches, Declan slashed the supporting vines loose, holding them tight so the net wouldn't be swept away in the current. With a shiver he waded across the thigh-deep flow, gripping the knife between his teeth and stepping high over the water, hauling the meshed ends with both hands alongside him. The rush was cool about his knees as he moved, and his feet guided him to the far side with practiced ease. Checking that his catch was still secured in the tangles, Declan began to reel it in, struggling somewhat while the heavy fish did its best to get loose. When it reached the shallows of the bank, he yanked sharply on the vines to drag it free of the stream. Declan found himself grinning when his prize began floundering against the stony ground, recognizing the blood-colored stripe running down the animal's back.

Redfin was widely considered a particularly sumptuous roadside feast.

Pulling it away from the water's edge, Declan took the knife from his teeth and sliced through the mass of tangles until he'd freed the thrashing fish. Tossing aside the now-useless net, he pinned his meal to the damp ground with a free hand and slid the blade into the base of its slim skull, finishing the job quickly. Once the redfin was still, Declan wiped his blade clean and sheathed it again, then carried the limp catch over to wash off in the stream's clean flow. He'd just finished, and was in the midst of standing up again, when a voice in the back of his mind caught him by surprise.

Anything good?

Gaining his feet, it took a moment for Declan to shade his eyes and find the speaker against the late afternoon sun. Ryn stood behind him, having appeared along the ledge of the steep embankment at his back, looking down from some ten feet above the scene. Completely black from nose to tail, the stallion's coat shined almost metallically in the day's light, looking more like smooth, sleek skin than fur. His long tail swept from side to side, batting away the pestering flies that insisted on accompanying a wave of late-season heat, and his narrow ears flicked this way and that with every subtle sound of the forest around them.

In answer, Declan hefted the fish above his head, showing it off with a laugh. "Caught this guy just a minute ago. Any luck on your end?"

Ryn's mouth twisted into what Declan had grown up knowing to be a pleased grin. Craning his neck back, the horse bit down on one of the leather flaps of his saddlebags, lifting it up to reveal a healthy assortment of large, red apples.

There's a sizable tree between here and the camp. Plenty of nice ripe ones, too.

"I take it you mean there *were* plenty of nice ripe ones?" Declan asked with a snort, throwing the fish over his shoulder and making his way towards the horse.

Ryn let go of the flap and turned to help his friend up the sharp incline of the bank. *I saved enough for you, don't worry*, he promised humorously, bending down so Declan could grab the side of his halter before hauling him up and onto more even ground.

Declan raised a curious eyebrow at the creature as he found his footing, but the horse said no more, a smile playing at his dark lips that made his strange eyes—their faint, white pupils vertically slit through a pool of gold—shine mischievously. Instead, Ryn turned and trotted back in the direction of their campsite, leaving Declan to follow and repress his own chuckle. When it came to this horse and food, it was best not to get in the way lest you be trampled to death by the ever-famished animal.

Declan gave up trying not to laugh, though, when he passed the tree in question. Sure enough, barely a single decent apple was left.

Not even—to his great amusement—amongst the topmost branches.

■■

Ryn looked up when Declan Idrys finally strolled into camp a minute or so after him, redfin still hung over one shoulder. His companion was a broad, handsome youth, and taller than most men had any right to be. His dark brown hair hung loosely around his wide shoulders, and his blue eyes—so much like Ertus' and his mother's before him—shined cheerfully while he whistled some old tavern yarn, heading for a stump near the center of the clearing where they'd left their things a couple of hours before. From

Declan's waist hung both his hunting knife and longsword, lashed to the leather belt he'd strapped at a rogue's tilt around his hips, his free hand—one finger of which glinted with a plain gold ring adorned by a single black stone—resting comfortably on the pommel of the larger weapon. The rolled-up sleeve of his left arm revealed a scarred, well-muscled forearm and a faded arrow tattoo, hinting at the swordsman's body that had been forged by years on the road and staggered employment among the Alethan mercenary guilds. His strong fingers were long and rough, callused by the practice and training that had been part of his daily routine from the moment Abegale had allowed Ryn to talk her son through how to handle a sword properly.

Herst would have been proud of this one, Ryn often found himself thinking privately.

Declan was grinning as he approached, but didn't offer any reason as to why. Ryn watched his friend unlatch his sword from his belt, resting the weapon against his pack near the unlit pile of kindling they'd gathered earlier, before taking a seat on the felled tree. Drawing his knife, Declan slapped the large fish down across his lap and began scaling and gutting it as he set about preparing dinner for the both of them.

Satisfied that a meal was on the way sooner rather than later, Ryn turned back to his own tasks.

He'd been able to gather plenty of extra wood around their little clearing—fallen branches that had died and dried out in the summer sun—and everything was stacked nearby within easy reach. Checking that the flaps of his saddlebags were securely pinned down, Ryn undid the harness straps with his teeth and pulled the satchel off his back, depositing it on the ground beside Declan. Finally free of the load, he trotted back through the trees to the stream for a quick drink.

By the time he returned, Declan had finished with the fish and was already slicing up several of the apples, as well as a handful of wild onions and edible mushrooms Ryn had found while foraging. The smell made his mouth water, and he let out a groan of anticipation when a teasing waft played with his nose, fanning the flowered scent his way. Looking up, Declan laughed and tossed half an apple to him, which Ryn deftly caught.

"Ease up," the man said, returning to his chore and wiping thin layers of mushroom into their traveling pot set between his feet. "At least let me cook the stuff before you wolf it down."

Ryn huffed at that. *I'll take it raw*, he snorted, trotting over and sniffing at the emptied fish beside the stump. *Not like it will bother me.*

Declan made a face, picking up another apple and starting to dig out a bad spot. "It'll bother *me*, and my mother would have had *both* our hides if she'd ever caught me letting you eat uncooked fish. Patience. It won't be long."

Ryn grumbled a concession under his breath, and settled in to wait.

■■■

An hour later, Declan was turning the fish over a healthy fire as Ryn lay down lazily nearby, snuffling at the grass, his tasks done for the evening. Declan smiled, watching his friend doze off in the dimming sunlight of the fading afternoon. With his eyes closed, Ryn might almost have been any other horse lounging about, waiting for night to fall. Declan had long since given up wondering at the beast's origins, having figured out at an early age that it was better not to voice such curiosities aloud, especially since Ryn himself consistently seemed to go mysteriously deaf at such questions. Declan's own mother, too—when she'd still lived—had always scolded him for asking, and in the end he'd learned to take Ryn's presence in his life in stride, finding himself caring less about the strange creature's past as time went on.

Giving the fish another quarter roll, Declan turned his attention back to the papers he held in his left hand, reading them over again with a grumble of frustration. The notice was the sort of bounty he'd always hated taking, and the kind Cassandra Sert—or any of his other old employers— would have laughed at him for so much as considering. It was vague and unspecific, largely lacking in any of the details he would have preferred to have on hand before starting a contract like this. Still, the money had been paid up front—not to mention ten gold levers and twice that many silver lehts would add nicely to the accounts they still held with the Iron Wind— and the locals had at least been able to give he and Ryn a place to start, pointing them towards the woods they now camped in.

"We've done more with less," Declan muttered to himself, glancing at the fish absently to make sure it wasn't burning.

It was true, but that didn't make the current situation any simpler or surmountable...

Missing villagers. That was largely the extent of what they had to go on. For the last several months there had been odd disappearances in and around the region's municipalities, dozens over the course of the last half-year, all with frustratingly little consistency between them. The first had occurred at the end of the past winter, when a boy was taken while clearing the family fields for tilling after the season's late snows. The next, though, had been a grizzled hag of ill repute from a village a mile to the north of the farm from which the child had been stolen. Then the third had been a grown man, a barkeep at a merchant's outpost a half-hour to the south. It had continued like that, apparently, up until the most recent vanishing not a week before, in which a young woman had been taken on her way home from the baker's shop where she worked as an apprentice.

This girl, however, had been the granddaughter of one of the town elders, and the old woman had pulled every string she could to gather the funds they needed to get a bounty posted in every major town and rest within three days ride of the area. Declan and Ryn had stumbled across the listing not two days before, tacked to the wall by the inner door of an inn on their way north from Kanrys, and it hadn't taken more than the absent weight of their near-empty coin purse to convince them of looking into the matter. Now, there they were, a pair of fools out in the middle of the wilds, about to go on a likely fruitless search through some of Viridian's densest forests in order to pick a fight whose odds they didn't even know.

Fortunately for them both, Declan had already figured out where to start their hunt, and Ryn offered them one or two unique advantages all his own…

The fish sizzled and popped, and Declan swore as he realized he'd drifted off with his thoughts, forgetting to turn the make-shift spit. One side of the meat had dried and darkened over the flames, and he spun the redfin over quickly before it burned beyond saving. The sound of his cursing roused Ryn in turn, the horse blinking and looking up, eyeing the fire with distinct anticipation.

Finished? he asked hopefully. In answer, Declan tucked the bounty papers back into his breast pocket, then drew his hunting knife to check the fish with the steel blade. The underside—the side that *hadn't* lingered too long over the heat—was still pinker than he would have liked.

"Just another minute or so," he answered with an apologetic look in his friend's direction. "Can you get the plates?"

Ryn nodded, heaving himself onto all fours again before ambling over to their travel pack and rummaging through it with his snout. By the time the horse had pulled out two battered tin platters with his teeth and set them by Declan's feet, the fish was cooked to satisfaction. Giving the spit a final roll, Declan grabbed one plate and sliced off a large portion of the meat onto it, along with the majority of the apples, onions, and mushrooms sitting already steamed in their pot just within the warmth of the fire. When it was well laden, Declan carried the meal over and set it down between Ryn's feet.

The ravenous animal started in before the food had a chance to touch the ground.

Grinning at what anyone else would think of the sight of a horse eating fish—cooked or otherwise—Declan returned to the fire and served himself, then kicked a little dirt over the flames to burn it down. Sitting on the stump he'd claimed earlier in the day, he dug into the simple meal happily enough, using his knife like a crude fork.

Together the pair ate in silence, enjoying the growing sounds of the forest evening rising up around them. Night was fast in coming, the woodlands darkening about their camp with each passing minute, and with the failing light came the throaty croak of frogs among the trees, the chirp of crickets in the undergrowth, and the call of owls and other nocturnal birds in the branches overhead. The air cooled, teasing of the approaching fall, but even after Declan and Ryn had both had seconds, finishing the fish, neither moved to rekindle the flames of the dying coals.

No sense in spoiling their night vision if they could help it.

On a satisfied stomach, Declan rinsed clean the plates with a hefty splash from one of their waterskins, then took a quick swig of it himself before offering it to Ryn. The horse shook his big head, though, already peering off into the woods, more alert now that the moment to get moving was approaching. Declan could see the focus in his bright eyes, the gilded white almost glowing in the night, and he knew the beast was searching, reaching with that strange sense of his into the darkness, far beyond what either of them could see through the trees.

"Anything?" Declan asked once the stallion relaxed again.

Again, Ryn shook his head. *Nothing, but I think you're right. The stream is as good a place to start as any.*

Declan nodded with a resigned sigh. "Would have been too easy, I guess." He squinted into the shadows of the forest floor, one hand on the strap of the skin he tossed over one shoulder, the other resting loosely on the pommel of his longsword. Looking around again, he met Ryn's eyes in the dark. "Ready?"

There was a flurry of motion, a twisting of body and limb. Black against the evening twilight, Ryn changed as a shifting of shape and silhouette, shrinking slightly but growing wider as he did. In a pair of heartbeats the horse was gone, replaced by the hunched, hulking form of an oversized wolf.

Ready.

With that, the two stepped quietly back into the thickness of the woods, making for the faint gurgle and rush of running water to the west.

The hunt was on.

CHAPTER TWO

The screams echoed shrilly over the wooden walls of the dark house, pitching, then fading, leaving the air empty and cold. A weary nurse rushed past, the wavering candle in her hands casting hard shadows across her bloody robes as she vanished once more around the corner of the hall. At once the shrieks started again, terrible in their pain, and this time didn't wane. Minutes passed, the sounds an inescapable nightmare in the empty blackness of the winter night.

Then, abruptly, they died away, giving leave for silence to reclaim its grip in the chill, horrid stillness.

Motionless as the stone statues that flanked the wooden bench he sat upon, Declan strained to listen, strained to make out any hint that might tell him if life still flickered in the room down the hall. Hearing nothing, he reached out, seeking with his mind's eye the imperceptible bond that tethered the soul to one's mortality. White robes and black armor gleamed in the faintest light of the moon through the nearby window as he shifted in his seat, pressing callused palms to his bearded face and taking in a single, ragged breath as he felt the coolness of the signet against his cheek.

Nothing.

No light, not even the faintest glimmer, held sway in Brilyn's consciousness now. It had sputtered and died, draining away with the screams to carve away and leave an empty well into the depths of Declan's heart. Though he did not cry, something within him shattered, a fragment of his existence carried away by the Mother with the woman's passing.

It was a long time before the nurse reappeared, the glow of her candle dancing around the corner ahead of her as the echo of her footsteps called out to him. With reddened eyes he looked up, longing to witness some hint of joy on the woman's face, some glimmer of hope, of anything that might release him of the wrenching ache that threatened to consume him.

What he saw instead was the small, shifting bundle of pale cloth she held in the crook of one arm, clutched to her breast, squirming and crying out in anguished need.

Getting up slowly, his black armor shining burnished gold in the light of the flame, Declan moved to stand over the nurse, his grief and sorrow suddenly numb. Before him the child continued to wriggle, twisting in the bundle as its tiny hands reached out, futilely seeking the grasp of the mother they would never find.

"It's a girl," the nurse said quietly, half-turning to offer forth the infant.

Slowly, tentatively, Declan reached out to take the child. Gently he rested her against the dark steel of his chest, rocking the newborn girl in a daze of realization, whispering words of comfort into her small ears. At the command of his King's blood the cold air of the room grew suddenly warmer, and after a minute or so she calmed, snuggling deeper into the folds of the cloth. Not long after, the girl had fallen asleep, breathing quietly and deeply, content and comfortable in his arms.

When he was able to take his eyes away from the bundle, Declan gazed over the nurse's shoulder, into the room he could just see down the hall. The bed was cleaned, the bloody linens having already been replaced. The woman lying there might have been simply resting were it not for her pale, lifeless face. Brilyn's blonde hair lay spread about her shoulders like a golden wave, and he glimpsed her hazel eyes for the last time as a midwife closed them respectfully with a careful hand.

Then a white sheet was pulled up, over the woman's head, settling across her features like a veil to hide her forever from the cruelties of the world.

It was all Declan could bear.

With as much of a nod of thanks to the nurse as he could manage, he turned away from the still figure in that far room. Silently he made for the door he had been waiting beside for much of the night and all of the previous day. Gently he pushed it open, his daughter cradled carefully in his arms, ignoring the grate and squeal of the old hinges calling out into the empty cold of the surrounding trees. Without looking back he stepped into the snowy night, heavy boots crunching against the hard, icy ground, calling out a name to the darkness of the sky above.

The familiar beat of heavy wings seemed to swallow the hopelessness, leaving nothing behind but the joy of the child in Declan's arms for that one, priceless moment.

CHAPTER THREE

Declan woke to a cold nose shoving lightly into his shoulder and hot breath against his face.

Your watch. Ryn's voice cut into the lingering drowsiness. He was standing against the night, still in the wolf's form he'd maintained for the last week. *We've got another hour of light at most. I'm going to sleep while I can.*

With a tired nod and a yawn, Declan stretched and blinked, trying to recall the details of the strange dream he'd been having as Ryn padded off to find a comfortable spot to lie down. He recalled a house, and a man in armor, but the other specifics escaped him. It had felt familiar, and as he sat up, running a hand through his hair to get it out of his face, he wondered if he'd had it before.

Looking blearily around at the clearing of their camp, Declan shrugged off the curiosity.

For eight days now they'd been searching the forest, finding little of interest and even less of relevance to the villages' troubles. Once or twice they'd come across hints of the passing of men—dead campfires, knife-cleaned animal bones, discarded torches, and the like—but such signs were often days old at least, and there was never any evidence to indicate they pointed to the kidnappers he and Ryn were looking for. More likely they were the remnants of passing travelers, or the trappers that made their living in those woods. Twice such men set off false alarms as Ryn's hackles had risen and he'd informed Declan of their presence, only for the pair of them to be disappointed both times when the wolf was able to make out more details of their persons after they'd gotten closer.

Unless the culprits in question made a habit of setting up rabbit nooses and bear pits, it was doubtful these men were the ones they were hunting for.

Grumbling at the memory, Declan took his sheathed sword up from where it lay by his bedroll before gaining his feet and rolling his neck to loosen it. While his frustration grew a little with each passing evening, he wasn't at all surprised by their lack of progress. The disappearances *had* grown more frequent of late—or so the townspeople claimed, at least—but it had hardly been more than a fortnight since the last woman had been taken. It was very well possible that whatever was responsible for the vanishings, be it creature or man, might not strike again for days, or maybe even weeks, if it did again at all. Not ones to renege on a job once paid, though, he and Ryn had settled into their nightly rhythm of scouring the trees by the light of the moon and stars, sometimes delving deeper into the woods, but usually sticking close to the banks of the wide stream.

Declan suspected, after all, that the heavy flow of the current—churning almost river-like in some narrower parts—was key to the skillful vanishing of the kidnappers and their victims.

Still, Declan thought to himself, rubbing a sore spot on his back with his free hand as he made for their packs along one edge of the small glen, *eight days in the woods without a proper bed leaves something to be desired.*

Stealing a fistful of leftover venison as his evening meal—Ryn had downed the animal in the early hours of the previous morning—Declan chewed on a mouthful of the meat as he settled down to wait, his back to his habitual stump, sword against his shoulder. The remnants of the day's fire smoked lightly not far to his right, and to his left Ryn had curled up between two ashwoods, lying in a carefully chosen patch of sun that would last until the fading of dusk.

Smirking, Declan turned away from the wolf and chose instead to gaze up at the dimming, cloud-spotted sky. He'd always enjoyed the sunset vigil. Everything—stone, moss, and tree alike—became dusk's painting with the day's end, bringing a final bit of warmth to whatever the light touched. The greens and browns of the forest in the afternoon always faded steadily to orange and yellow and purple, transforming the world with a muffled stillness. Declan remembered when he'd first noticed the colors, one of their earliest nights away from home, sitting on a cliff overlooking one of the great woodland lakes to the east. He and Ryn had gone the night after his mother died, her passing leaving the pair alone in the world with nothing but a battered family ring to remember her by. Declan fidgeted with it absently, now, spinning the black stone slowly about his finger with his thumb as memory drifted back.

It had been over a decade since his mother's death, the autumn following his thirteenth birthday, and his recollections of her had started to fade of late. She'd been young, *too* young, he knew, but a fire in the year or so after his own birth—in the incident that had claimed the life of the father he had never known—had left her weak of body, and often of mind. In the months before she'd finally passed, his mother had started confusing him with ghosts, frequently calling him "Ertus", and asking Ryn if he knew if her husband would be returning home in time for supper. When the day had come, when Declan had woken one morning to find his mother unmoving in her bed, the thing he remembered most was the slight smile that lingered on her lips in the peace of death.

He often prayed to the Mother and her Graces that the woman had found the one she was searching for, somewhere in the realms beyond the grave…

Declan. Someone's coming.

Declan jerked and nearly swore out loud as Ryn's voice lanced across his thoughts, jarring in its own fashion. It had been all of ten minutes since he'd taken over the watch. Despite this, he was up in an instant, sheathed sword held at his side and right hand on the hilt, ready to draw. Sparing a glance to his left, he saw that Ryn had lifted his head to peer west through the trees. His ears, each larger than Declan's hand, were twisted in the direction he was looking, and in the colors of dusk his black fur burned a darkened-orange against the green of the clearing's grass.

Declan didn't have to ask for details. They had weathered more than enough fights together for habit to hold rule.

Five men. Ryn pressed himself up onto all fours quickly, golden eyes never flinching from the direction of the stream. *A woman too, but she's bound and gagged. Looks to be putting up a fight.*

Declan grimaced at that and started stepping quickly towards the trees. "Are they armed?"

The wolf nodded, loping up alongside him as the shadows of the branches claimed them. *Knives on the two carrying the woman, another on a third. The last pair have a club and sword respectively, as well as torches. Seems like they're leading the way.* Out of the corner of his eye Declan saw Ryn's ears twitch. *They've just waded into the stream. You were right.*

Declan grunted, picking up his pace. "Bad luck you taking first watch, I guess."

More like good luck they're about as quiet as a boulder rolling through this underbrush.

That got a snort out of Declan.

Ryn's uncanny ability to know things he shouldn't—typically in incredible detail—was generally as much a mystery to Declan as most things about the beast, save for a few details. There appeared to be a range, for one thing—about a half-mile in any particular direction as far as he had been able to make out, with some lesser ability for a way beyond that—and it seemed to require no small amount of concentration from the wolf, or whatever form Ryn was taking in the moment. Declan had learned *that* the hard way, a decade back, having the scars to show for an incident in which a group of bandits they'd been tracking with the Iron Wind got the drop on them in the night after Ryn's watch had ended.

Still, Declan thought, leaping clear over a fallen tree in their hurry, scabbard and sword still loose in hand, *this is good. Now we have them.*

He was relieved that his suspicion had come true. It had been odd that the kidnappers they were now chasing had consistently been able to cover their tracks upon reaching this particular neck of the woods, but as soon as he'd seen the stream Declan had had a hunch as to the means by which they managed it. The flow—as he'd discovered himself—was hardly more than knee deep, but strong and quick.

Perfect for hiding one's tracks.

As the forest ahead of them thinned, opening up into the wide way through which the water cut, Declan and Ryn slowed to a careful walk, approaching the embankment they knew dropped off not far from the edge of the trees. Getting nearer, Declan gestured questioningly to Ryn, not speaking as he pointed first left, to the south, then right, to the north.

The wolf indicated the right with a jerk of his head.

Downstream, he said, taking the lead and padding silently through the gnarled trunks. *A hundred paces up the way. We can take our time. They're not moving quickly.*

Declan tailed the wolf, more careful now that they were closing in. The afternoon light was starting to fade, the brightness of the full sun beginning to deepen into the dark red that was the last desperate call of the day. He had to watch his footing, avoiding fallen branches and noisy underbrush as best he could. After five minutes of careful maneuvering, the glow of firelight started to press its way through the descending dark to his left. Not long after, Ryn shifted his course to slink towards the riverbank again, staying low and hunched, looking back only long enough to indicate with a twitch of an ear that Declan should follow.

Together they left the cover of the woods, crouched and silent, still a ways behind the flickering light of the torches. Reaching the edge of the steep embankment, they peered together downstream, eyeing the backs of the men that made up a small group some twenty paces ahead of them now.

Just as Ryn had said, there were five of them, all dressed in the common garb of the rural peasantry, their cotton pants soaked to the groin as they sloshed through the churning current. It was a common enough trick—one that Declan himself had used at least a few times in his life—serving both to hide their trail and help mask their scent in case hunters came after them with hounds.

Small wonder the townspeople couldn't track them, Ryn said, his voice achieving a whispered intonation even though Declan knew he was the only one who could hear it.

Declan, in turn, nodded, then pointed towards the rear of the group, indicating a writhing figure slung across the shoulders of two of the men, hands tied behind her back and a rough-spun sack pulled over her head. Despite her disadvantage, the woman looked to be doing her best to make things difficult for her kidnappers, flailing and butting and letting out muffled, angry yells that spoke to the fact that she was very likely gagged under the bag. Even as he watched, the two trying to keep ahold of her staggered, splashing about in the water when she bucked with particular violence.

At the sound of their struggles, the other three, walking ahead, slowed and turned, forcing Declan and Ryn to shrink away from the shifting torchlight.

"C'mon!" the largest of the group barked, a balding, bearded man with a broadsword sheathed at his hip. "Ol' bastard's not gonna wait all night for us!"

"We can't hardly hold 'er, Darb!" wheezed one of the smaller men, still struggling to keep his grip on the woman. "She's slippery as a corner'd fox!"

The man called Darb laughed gruffly at that. "Y'er tellin' me you's two can't hold on ta' *one* little lady?!" He sneered, watching the paired men wage their war against the fighting woman for a moment longer before looking to the third, empty-handed man between him and the pair. "Gravin, give 'em a hand."

Gravin grumbled in answer, but started wading back up the current, making for his struggling companions. Unfortunately for him, he had the foolish instinct upon reaching them to take the woman about the ankles, trying to get ahold of her boots and keep her feet from thrashing.

He realized his mistake as she flailed the instant she felt his hands around her shins, catching him squarely in the side of the face with both feet.

"Ahg!" Gravin cursed, stumbling back and tumbling into the water with a *splash*. When he resurfaced, his face was contorted in fury. "Bitch bloody *kicked* me!"

He got up unsteadily, still glaring at the woman and reaching for the knife tucked into his belt. Before he could draw the blade, Darb lunged forward, slushing through the flow, his heavy fist *thudding* into Gravin's other cheek. The blow put the man down a second time, his body flailing as he crashed into the stream again. When his head came up, he found the larger man standing over him, livid.

"Are ya' mad?!" Darb raged in Gravin's face. "Ya' want 'er guts spillin' everywhere before we get there?! Damn thing'd be on us 'afore we could fuckin' *blink*!" He looked around, speaking to the other torchbearer, a squatter man with arms as thick as Declan's thigh. "Calm 'er down, Rolan. I'm 'bout sick a' all this noise.

The comrade—Rolan—made no response aside from pulling a short wooden cudgel from the back of his belt. Wading forward until he was even with the struggling woman, he raised the weapon. It fell, delivering a *cracking* blow to the back of her covered head that made even Ryn wince at Declan's elbow. Stowing the club away equally silently, Rolan took the now-motionless form from the smaller pair, tossing her over his shoulder like a limp doll before heading downstream again, torch still held high. Gravin, meanwhile, had gotten to his feet a second time, and was trying to squeeze water out of his thoroughly-drenched shirt.

"'Ere now!" he exclaimed, bloody phlegm flecking his wet chin with every word. "Why couldn't ya' just've done that in the firs' place?!"

"Shu' up," Darb muttered, turning to follow Rolan's illuminated form with long, churning strides. The remaining three exchanged glances, then splashed after them, not wanting to be left alone in the coming dark.

As the torchlight slipped away, Ryn turned to look at Declan.

What do you want to do?

Declan didn't answer for a moment, eyes on the men as they disappeared around a bend in the stream, blood boiling in anger. He and Ryn had the element of surprise. Even without it, judging by their clumsiness he was pretty confident the pair of them would have been more than a match for the group. If anything, the trickiest part would be making sure the woman didn't accidentally get dropped into the stream and drown if they came to her rescue.

On the other hand, something bothered him. Something Darb had said. It sounded like the group was *delivering* the woman somewhere…

"We follow," he said as quietly as he could, standing up again and moving silently through the woods.

The light crunch of Ryn's paws behind him told him the wolf had no qualms with that plan.

The group walked for longer than Declan would have expected, trudging painstakingly up the stream for well over a mile before finally clambering out of the water and up onto the east bank, the side he and Ryn already trailed along. After that, their pace quickened, and the two of them started following from even farther back, using the light through the shadows of the trees to their advantage. The five men moved along some invisible path with a familiarity that told Declan they'd come this way more than once before, though *where* they were actually headed, he couldn't venture a guess at. He and Ryn, unfortunately, had to be more cautious, watching their step in the faint light as night fell in truth. It was a tedious stalking, the sunset winking through the branches as minutes stretched into an hour, then almost two. Finally, after what must have been ten miles through the thick woods, the men finally started to slow. To Declan's surprise, the hints of starry heavens began to shine through the canopy overhead, the half-moon of the late summer night glinting more and more frequently between the leaves to the south. They were approaching a clearing, he guessed, and one much larger than his and Ryn's some leagues back.

Wait.

Declan's quick stride faltered to a halt, and he looked around to find Ryn had stopped several paces behind him. The wolf was now sniffing at the air, eye's shining gold as they shifted about, scanning the forest around them

"What is it?" Declan asked in a hushed voice, slipping toward him through the shadows. "What do you sense?"

For a long moment—*too long* a moment—Ryn didn't answer. Eventually his gaze settled on the thinning branches overhead, and Declan thought he saw something like concern play across his animalistic features.

Nothing, he finally answered, taking a careful step forward, then another, still watching the sky. *That's the problem. I sense nothing at all.*

Declan gaped at the wolf's haunches, utterly taken aback. Never—not in more than two decades of knowing the beast—had he *ever* known Ryn to admit such a thing. It was the equivalent of an expert archer blankly stating that he couldn't see the hay target set five feet in front of him.

"What do you mean '*nothing*'?" he repeated in a hiss of disbelief, hurrying after the wolf. "How can't you sense *anything*?!"

Again, Ryn didn't reply, and after several steps more he stopped again. They were in the last layer of trees now before the clearing proper, and his hackles were on end. For the first time in his life, Declan thought the wolf might have looked frightened.

It was among the most disconcerting things he had ever witnessed.

Draw your sword. Even Ryn's voice was sharp. *We go to the edge of the forest, but no further. Understood?*

The command, beyond anything else, settled upon Declan the potential gravity of their situation. It had been a long time since Ryn had ordered him to do anything. When he'd been younger, it had been different. Then, Ryn had taken the lead, working him through learning the sword, leading them to Aletha, finding the right companies to join and guiding him through the process of doing so. Eventually, though, Ryn had stepped away from that role, allowing Declan to lead with his own decisions, almost like a parent bowing to the growth of their child.

If he felt the need to go back on that now…

Without a word, Declan drew his blade with the quiet rasp of steel grating over leather.

Ryn nodded, understanding the acknowledgment of his order, and started forward again slowly. It took them almost half a minute to edge through the last dozen yards or so of shaded pines, so careful was their approach. Declan felt his heart start to thud unbidden in his chest, and he slowed his breathing, trying to calm himself.

When they reached the lip of the woods, he saw at once that Ryn's fear was anything but without reason.

The clearing was wide, perhaps fifty paces across, and ringed by a thicket of towering evergreens that encircled it like a dark crown against the night sky. The grass had grown high, here, where the sun reached the ground all day long, and flowers of a dozen different colors dotted the swaying field, barely visible in the torchlight and shifting in the evening breeze. It would have been a calm, peaceful glen, Declan thought, except for paired oddities that broke the serenity of the place.

The first of these was a cave, its entrance formed by a space between two large boulders that jutted up into the night, apexes resting against each other like an angled roof of stone. Declan might have thought little of it, but the great rocks looked somehow out of place, like someone had deliberately set them there, leaning one against the other and tunneling down into the earth between them. How a man could achieve such a feat without the assistance of cranes and pulleys that would never have made the trip this far into the woodlands, Declan couldn't begin to guess, but the sight of the grotto itched at him, his instincts telling him it wasn't natural.

Whatever concerns he had about the *cave*, though, paled in contrast to what stood in the center of the clearing...

In a rough circle, each about a pace or two apart, a number of tall, heavy timber columns had been planted firmly into the ground. They were old, worn things, cracked and smoothed by weather and time, bleached by the sun and spotted with moss and lichen. Forms were lashed to them, bound to the wood with leather and rope, some so tightly they stood tall against the stakes, some more loosely so that they sagged in their restraints. For several seconds the light of the torches—bright now against the evening darkness as the five men gathered around these forms—stole Declan's night vision away, and the figures were obscured by shadows and the white flash of blindness every time he blinked.

Then his vision cleared, and Declan felt his stomach turn.

"Mother's Mercy..." he couldn't stop himself from muttering, the words muffled as he brought his left hand up to cover his nose and mouth, attempting to stem the stench of death that wafted through the trees.

Corpses.

There were dozens of them, the ones tied to the columns apparently only the freshest of the gathered collection. The remnants of a score more were scattered about the feet of those secured upright, ribs jutting from the torn, rotting flesh of broken chests, empty sockets staring into the sky from drawn, horrid faces. Weeks in the wilds made it hard to tell, but Declan suspected there would be no sense to the bodies. The husks of men buzzed with flies beside the corpses of women and children. The old had died with the young, their remains as scattered as the rest. The bodies were ravaged, sundered and ripped, a grisly display of cruelty and violence in the breathtaking stillness of the night. Something had torn them apart, shredding them limb from limb, bone from bone.

A few even looked to have been split in two, bodies rent and cast apart with terrifying strength…

Declan, fearing he would be sick if he stared any longer, turned his attention on the kidnappers, channeling his horror into something more useful to the task at hand.

Anger.

The five men still hadn't noticed he and Ryn, well-hidden as they were within the trees, and now seemed too preoccupied with their task to give much thought to anything else. Rolan—the one with the club—lingered beyond the strewn dead, the woman still thrown over one shoulder, while Darb gingerly managed the bodies to examine the closest staked corpse in the light of his torch. With a building fury Declan watched the large man draw his sword to saw through the bonds securing the carcass to its post. It fell to the ground in a ghastly tangle of limbs, and was promptly dragged out of the way by Gravin and the two other, smaller men. His gruesome task complete, Darb stepped clear to allow Rolan through, and the two men thrust their torches into the ground before working together to tie the woman to the post with fresh bindings they retrieved from somewhere within the carnage.

Suddenly, there was a quiet snarl at his side, and Declan turned to find Ryn looking eastward, teeth bared.

"What is it?" he whispered, alarmed.

I don't know. Ryn scanned the tree line along the east side of the clearing before them. *Someone else, I think…*

"You *'think'*?" Declan demanded in a forced hush. He still couldn't wrap his mind around the fact that Ryn's senses were failing him, now of all times.

Ryn held his silence. His golden eyes had settled across the space from them, lingering on the strange cave Declan had first noticed upon arriving. Something seemed to click, in that moment, his wolfish features twisting in what could only have been horrified realization.

Then he was gone, ripping away through the trees to the east before Declan could even think to call after him.

Stop them! Ryn's voice reached him even in the wolf's absence. *Stop them NOW!*

For two whole seconds, Declan stared after his friend, watching his inky form vanish in a flash into the woods.

Then the desperation in Ryn's words overpowered his confusion, and Declan launched himself out of the underbrush, crossing the clearing with swift, calculated strides.

The kidnappers were lingering, muttering to one another or casting about the tree line absently, like they were waiting for someone. Declan closed more than half the distance between them before he was seen by Gravin and one of the smaller men, and even then they were so surprised that their shouted alarm came almost too late.

Almost.

The other three spun on their heels in surprise. Rolan was closest, and had drawn his cudgel free the moment the yell arose. There were no words exchanged, then, no parley for reason or surrender. The instant he caught sight of Declan, the large man launched himself forward, bellowing as he brought the heavy club down in a massive overhead blow. It was a practiced, confident move, one that looked to have ended many other fights before they even had a chance to begin.

Unfortunately for the kidnapper, it was also the easiest sort of strike to read.

With a plant and pivot Declan changed the angle of his momentum, deftly sidestepping the downward arch of the weapon. Before the cudgel even had time to hit the ground, the steel of his longsword snapped up, lopping off the hands that had been attempting to drive the assailing club down on his head with a *shlunk* of severed flesh. In the same motion Declan twisted and kicked, catching Rolan in the back of his forward knee just as it accepted the weight of his rush. The big man's leg gave in before he knew what had happened, taking him to the ground. Finishing the turn, Declan ran the length of his sword through Rolan's ribs, skewering him from side to side, piercing heart and puncturing both lungs in a single practiced thrust before the kidnapper so much as had time to scream.

In all of five seconds from the moment he'd drawn his weapon, Rolan died with no more sound than a wet gasp and a shudder.

The fight had been so quick, so brief, that the other four hadn't had time to shake themselves of their shock at being discovered. Putting a foot on Rolan's limp neck, Declan drew the blade back out of the man smoothly, then swept the bloody steel at them in invitation.

"Anyone else?" he spat through bared teeth.

For half-a-second they stood frozen—even Darb—all eyes fixed on the body of their fallen companion.

And then they came in a rush, drawing weapons as they howled and lunged.

Fine by me, Declan thought, unsheathing his own knife coolly.

With a quick step, he met them halfway.

He dispatched the leading man quickly with a thrusted blade through the eye, wrenching it free even as he ducked and pressed up with his legs, flipping the corpse over his shoulder. Twisting, he got his sword up just in time to block a heavy overhead swing from Darb's own weapon, the steel blades shrieking against each other as they met. Almost at once the large man recoiled, howling as he clutched at the long cut Declan's knife had sliced across his unprotected neck and face, getting in over the man's guard. Turning back again, Declan gutted the thinnest assailant as he tried to sneak up behind him, carving the kidnapper open from hip to hip so that the man tumbled, dead from shock, into a pool of his own entrails. Whirling finally, Declan leapt away, expecting a blow from Gravin, the last of the group.

To his surprise—and partial amusement—he instead found the man barreling westward, running full-tilt towards the edge of the clearing, making a desperate bid for the cover of the pines.

With a sigh Declan switched hands, taking up his knife in his right and his sword in his left. Judging the distance carefully, he cocked his throwing arm back and counted Gravin's paces. When the moment came, he hurled the weapon end-over-end with a grunt, listening as both the spinning blade and its fleeing target disappeared into the darkness. A *thud*, paired with a brief shriek of horrified pain, rewarded his ears a second later.

Silence fell as the echoes of the battle faded into the blackness of the swaying forest. Declan grimaced, looking at the scattered bodies tumbled about the ground around him, their number adding to the horrid scene. It was hardly his first time amongst the dead, but Ryn had long since convinced him that any man who could become accustomed to the violence and mayhem of battle had lost a vital part of their soul.

Briefly, Declan offered up a prayer to the Mother, wishing his fallen enemies better circumstance in the next world.

Then the moment was broken by the sound of heavy steps and the keen of slashing steel.

"Bloody *BASTARD!*"

Adrenaline coursed cold through Declan, and he threw himself sideways just in the nick of time. All the same, a burning sensation enveloped his left arm, and he felt his sword slip from weakened fingers before rolling to his feet several yards away. Standing, he winced at the blood trickling down the limb, staining the slashed sleeve of his shirt to drip from his knuckles onto the already-splattered grass.

"Stupid," Declan muttered to himself, watching Darb approach him.

He'd misjudged the wound he dealt, assuming it to have been a killing blow across the throat. It probably would be before long—the man's chest and neck were covered in blood, his plain tunic soaked in crimson streaks— but for the time being he was very much alive. He grinned like a madman, the expression maniacal through red-stained teeth and the great gash across his face, but Declan was more concerned about the sword still held in the kidnapper's twin grip.

"I'll kill ya', ya' damn shit," Darb was muttering, almost to himself, breathing hard with eyes wide and locked on Declan's face. "I'll cut ya' limb from fuckin' limb, then do it all over again!"

Declan ignored the taunts. Darb was clearly in shock, which he could use to his advantage. It meant the man wasn't thinking straight, and was prone to wild, unpredictable attacks. Declan held his ground, watching the blade-tip in front of him as it swayed slightly. With no weapon to his name there would be little opportunity to make the first move. He had to wait, had to bide out his opponent's delirium.

"I'll kill ya'," Darb was still grumbling through his bloody smile, continuing to stare as he approached one step at a time. "I'll kill ya'. I'll cut ya' up and leave ya' with the bitch. I'll chop ya' ta' pieces and let 'im make soup outta ya."

With every move the man made to approach, Declan retreated. It might not have seemed brave or honorable, but survival was more important than pride in a fight to the death.

Just then, with a furious yell, Darb finally leapt forward, thrusting the blade ahead as he did.

His triumph was short-lived.

Declan sidestepped, avoiding the direct attack. In the same motion he looped the madman's elbow in the crook of his aching left arm, right hand taking firm hold of the sword's hilt over Darb's own grip. The kidnapper's eyes broadened even further, registering surprise when his steel met nothing but air. Unfortunately for him, he only had time to gasp before Declan broke the stiffness of his thrust, forcibly bending Darb's arm under the lunge's own momentum, shoving the razored edge of the blade up and back. This time Declan made sure the blow was true, feeling the metal slip through the muscle and tendon of its master's neck before scraping against the rounded bone of the spine. He didn't fight to hold onto the weapon once the damage was done, releasing the sword's hilt and darting sideways, out of reach of any last, panicked flail. Darb fell to his knees, choking and clutching desperately at his neck as blood spurted through his grimy fingers. Soon it began to spill from his mouth, and he hacked and coughed, bending double to spray the grass with red, the very sword which had slain him tumbling uselessly at his side. Declan watched from several paces away, breathing harder than he would have liked, gripping the leaking gash above his elbow tightly.

Then Darb keeled over, twitched for several seconds, and stilled, becoming just one more body among the strewn, putrid corpses.

Finally, Declan allowed himself to feel the pain.

"*Shit!*" he half-keened, half-groaned, briefly doubling over himself as he grit his teeth against the burning wash that consumed his left arm. He stayed like that for several long seconds, hissing out more curses and shutting his eyes tight until his body adjusted, coming to terms with the bone-deep ache. When he could stand up straight again, he examined the wound through watering eyes. It was a deep cut, a jagged slash about five inches long along the outside of his upper arm, and would require cleaning and stitching. Trouble was that all their herbs, wraps, and poultices were back at the camp, safe in Ryn's saddlebags. Settling for tearing a strip off the sleeve of his ruined shirt, Declan bandaged the injury for the moment, at least managing to staunch the flow of blood. Satisfied that he wasn't about to lose the limb, he moved to retrieve his own sword from where it lay in the half-trampled flowers behind Darb, cleaning it on the man's trousers before getting back to his feet.

Picking through the carnage was a distasteful affair. Declan set his eyes resolutely above the ground whenever possible, studying the woman as he approached the post where she still stood bound between the dead lashed to their own columns. She wore a simple cotton-and-leather tunic, not so different from his own, and the empty knife sheath at her hip made him think she must have been another hunter or trapper. Her head hung slack against her chest, ever hidden by the bag, and Declan feared the worst before reaching her and seeing the gentle, uneven rise of her shoulders as she breathed.

Still unconscious, he realized in concern, taking the ridge of the rough-spun sack and pulling it free of her face. Sure enough, she didn't so much as flinch at his touch, but this realization was only one of several Declan made as he registered everything about the woman in untethered astonishment.

Her shoulder-length hair fell in a shifting sheet before her face, hiding her features from view, but the color of it was what had Declan do a double-take. It looked almost blonde in the glow of the low-burning torches behind him, but in the light of day he thought it might have been a cooler shade, more silver than yellow. She had a slender figure that hung heavily against the ropes around her waist and chest, and the shirt beneath her leather tunic had torn at some point in her struggles, revealing more than she would probably have deemed appropriate had she been in any shape to voice her opinion. Averting his gaze, Declan fixed her clothes as best he could without looking before he reached up to lift her chin, hoping to wake her before cutting her lose.

He almost swore again, taking her in. He'd had his suspicions after the hair, but gaping at her face, he knew for sure, now.

Definitely a half-elf.

The woman had been gagged, as he'd suspected, but the loop of damp cloth between her teeth did little to mar the fragile features of a breathtaking face. Her skin was pale and smooth over high cheekbones that framed a delicate chin, her nose small and straight. Her ears were rounded, lacking the distinctly pointed tips some of her breed bore to their pride or shame, and her eyes were closed. Declan found himself wondering what they looked like, almost hoping that they might blink and flutter open, meeting his. As it was, he couldn't help but take a slow, steadying breath at the sight of her.

He regretted it the moment the stench of the dead and the iron reek of blood filled his nostrils.

Brought roughly back to the present with a retching cough, when his stomach stopped heaving Declan reached up to shake the woman lightly by the shoulder, still holding her head up with his other hand. "Hey," he said quietly. "Wake up. Wake up."

Nothing. He tried again, louder this time, but the woman was all but dead to the world. Suddenly fearing his earlier assumption, Declan felt for a pulse, and was relieved to find one along the side of her throat, feeble but present. Pulling his hand away, however, he frowned as his fingers came back bloody. Peering closer, the frown deepened when he found a thin trickle of crimson running down her neck, and he followed it up to the back of her head. Moving aside a bloody mass of matted hair, he whistled at a long, spattered gash that adorned the base of her skull.

Abruptly, Declan wished he hadn't made Rolan's death so quick...

"Let's get you some help, shall we?" he muttered to the incoherent woman, reaching for his sword again.

The oversized blade, coupled with his injury, made cutting her loose and heaving her up into both arms a more difficult—and painful—affair than it might otherwise have been. After several slips and further curses directed at everything from the ground to the ropes to the Mother and Her Graces, Declan managed it, carrying the still form of the half-elf clear of the carnage and back towards the trees. He'd intended to make straight into the woods, having no interest in lingering another second amid the horror of the scene, but as he passed out of the light of the still-flickering torches, something stopped him.

Over the crackling of the flames, Declan thought he could make out the subtle sound of quiet breathing.

He whirled, facing the direction the noise had come from. He found himself staring into the darkness that was the mouth of the strange, boulder-wrought cave, which he'd utterly forgotten about in the aftermath of the fight. For several seconds he paused, waiting, straining to hear the sound again.

Eventually, when nothing reached his ears, Declan took a tentative step forward, curiosity getting the better of him.

Don't. Stay back.

Declan stiffened and looked over his shoulder at Ryn's sudden voice, finding the form of the great wolf trotting towards him like a shadow against the firelight from the east, the direction he'd vanished in.

"Where'd you run off to?" Declan asked, a little annoyed, as his friend settled in beside him.

Ryn's eyes didn't leave the cave as he answered. *I thought I sensed… something. I had to make sure.*

"What was it?"

Ryn grimaced. *I don't know. It was gone before I could track it down, if it was ever there at all.*

Declan hefted the woman up more carefully in his arms, still unsure what to make of this sudden change in his perception of the wolf's abilities. "Did it have anything to do with that?" he asked, indicating the cave with a jerk of his chin. "What's down there?"

Nothing, as far as I can tell, Ryn answered, eyes narrowing at the shadowed entrance. *But that doesn't make me feel any better right n—*

He stopped abruptly, sniffing at the air, his head turning slowly until his snout was practically pressed against the leg of the half-elf Declan was carrying in his arms. Abruptly, the wolf jerked back, gilded eyes wide in the light, taking in the woman with very obvious surprise.

"What?" Declan asked, alarmed, looking between the pair of them. "Do you know her?"

For what must have been the tenth time that night, it took a moment for Ryn to answer. He still stared at the woman, and Declan didn't know what to make of the very clear shock painted across the beast's wolfish features.

Not her, no… he finally managed cryptically, bringing his head forward again to sniff at her once more.

"Then *what is it?*" Declan demanded, definitely getting irritated with the lack of answers the evening's events were offering for all the questions they had produced.

It's nothing. Ryn was quicker in responding this time, stepping away from them. *Probably just a mistake. She smells like someone I knew, once.* There was a blur of shifting shape, and the wolf was replaced by the towering form of the great black horse. *You're both injured. Let's get back to the camp and gather our things. You need stitches, and she needs a proper healer, by the looks of it.*

Declan grit his teeth, less than pleased by the empty answer, but he knew Ryn was right. With a dissatisfied grumble he hefted the woman up over the horse's back, then said he'd be right back. Jogging off into the woods, it took him a minute or so to find the cooling form of Gravin in the dark, the kidnapper's body collapsed facedown upon the forest floor,

Declan's knife buried to the hilt in his back. Retrieving the weapon with a wrenching jerk, Declan flicked the blade clean of blood and sheathed it before returning to the clearing.

When he passed near the mouth of the cave once more, he forced himself not to look, fearing what his imagination might form from the shadows of the jutting entrance. Reaching Ryn and the unconscious half-elf again, he clambered up onto the stallion's back without pause.

Only once Ryn had taken off at a full gallop—fearless despite the dark in the rugged and uneven undergrowth—did Declan brave glancing back one last time.

As the black outline of the trees swallowed the ghastly clearing, he wondered if the glint of eyes following their departure from the cave mouth was a trick of the dying fires.

■■

From the shadows of its den, the drey watched the intruders leave, taking with them its promised meal. The creature had been woken from its slumber by the shouts of man, crawling out of its hole to investigate. It had watched, intrigued, as a single figure had cut a swath through its caretakers, bringing them down in quick, skillful succession.

The smell of blood had been so enticing, the drey had wanted nothing more than to join in the fight.

Now, watching the strangers go, the urge to follow them, to hunt them, to rip them part from part was so strong that it began to salivate, slaver dripping from its fanged maw to splatter the bone-riddled ground about its taloned feet. The need had grown with every passing moment, shivering through the thing's powerful limbs especially when the second figure had revealed itself, masquerading in a skin that was not its own. Despite the charade, the drey had recognized its nemesis, sensed the truth of its being. The desire to kill, then, to streak from the dark shelter of its cavern and strike, had been nearly overpowering.

But no. It wouldn't. It couldn't. The need was strong, true.

But not as strong as the compulsion to follow its master's command to stay hidden, to stay away.

Minutes ticked by, though the drey had no real sense of time. It crouched, hunched at the mouth of the stone archway, careful to stay within the shadows. Patiently it waited, occasionally reaching out with its simple mind to test the imperceptible restraints that held it in place.

Then, abruptly, the bindings fell away.

"They've gone. You can come out now."

While the words themselves meant nothing to the drey's broad ears, the intent of them rang clear within its mind. Quietly it stole forward, out into the night, tucking its wings tight to its back as the cool air shivered across their leathery membranes. Before it, the scattered remnants of its past meals glowed in the faint light of a pair of torches that had been stuck into the ground. Around these, the warm bodies of its caretakers were left where they'd fallen, so fresh they still smelled of life.

And between them, fur-lined cloak shifting in the shadows of the dancing fire, its master waited, watching it come with calm patience.

The drey hurried towards the smaller figure eagerly. The man stood hardly half its height and not a fraction its weight, but the pull was there regardless, drawing it forward like some great, dragging gravity. When it reached the man, the force led it down, onto all fours, so that he could raise a wrinkled hand up to stroke its muzzle lovingly. Long grey hair spilled in waves from its master's raised hood, and the drey met pale green eyes as he spoke.

"Brave child," the man said, the words little more than empty sound. "That was difficult, wasn't it? But you did well. So, so well. Patience. Your time will come. I had to hide, too, as much as it pains me. That *thing*... For such a creature to come here, of all places..." The man paused, fingers halting in the drey's coarse hair. "It matters not. Look." He stepped aside, sweeping his hands to indicate the scattered bodies of the men who had been its feeders. "They've left you more than enough to last. Go. You will be called on soon. For now... *feast*."

The last word rang as a command in the drey's mind, and one whose design it readily reveled in. With one massive hand it grasped the body of the largest man, sniffing at the gruesome wound in its neck before opening its wide maw to latch its teeth around the corpse. The warm, wet taste of iron flooded into its mouth, and with a snarl of delight the drey picked up another body in each hand, then turned to retreat once more for the darkness of its cave.

When it looked back, its master had gone, vanishing between the dancing flickers of the flames.

Within the huddled safety of the cavern, the drey sat among the broken bones and rotting flesh of older suppers, ripping mouthfuls of meat from the corpses even as it thought. In its mind's eye a picture played itself over and over again, flitting across its consciousness in endless repetition.

Golden eyes, split by pale white pupils, unchanged even as the beast shifted from form to form.

While it dwelled on this, its master reached out once more, his brushing touch against its mind gentle and amused.

Soon, he promised. *Very soon.*

CHAPTER FOUR

"It is not often that mankind pauses to take stock of the repercussions which often come with the passage of time. Age, certainly, our kind is familiar with more so than any other race, but senility and death pale in consideration of the greater consequences the passage of years, decades, and centuries may have. There is a reason the elves frequently refer to their longevity as the 'curse' of immortality. Even for them—some of whom have lived long enough to witness the world change in ways we humans cannot fathom—time distorts. Time warps. Who is to say if the histories are true? Who is to say if the records are valid? Can we honestly—any of us—truthfully attest that the history of our world is as we believe it?"

-private journals of Mathaleus Kenus al'Dyor, King of Viridian

"Ryn, what in the *Mother's name* was that all about?!"

It was the third time Declan was attempting to broach the subject of the previous night's events, voicing the question again as the first light of dawn made itself known over the treetops to the east. He had tried twice already as they'd ridden through the night after collecting their things, the half-elf held carefully to his chest in the same manner she was now, but Ryn had claimed both times he needed to focus, to stay intent on the uneven ground that made footing precarious in the dark. Now, however, morning was upon them, breaking grey and dismal, a steady rain had started up even as they'd left the woodlands behind in favor of the north-running thoroughfare. Rivulets streamed along the sides of the hard-packed road, sweeping away dead leaves and loose earth, and before long Ryn's hooves were sloshing through puddles and mud while he ran.

With the light returned and the day's mood bleak, the horse must have sensed Declan was out of patience.

I don't know, he answered this time, adjusting his gait slightly to avoid a particular impressive pool that had formed in the center of the path. *Nothing good, to say the least...*

"No shit," Declan muttered, reaching up to pull the hood of his traveler's cloak a little higher over his face, clearing his vision. "Have you ever seen anything like that? What were they *doing*?!"

I don't know, Ryn answered more firmly this time. *Whatever it was, I don't think it's anything to dwell on. We've got our coin for the job, we'll find a healer for the girl, and we'll move on. There are sick people in this world, Declan. You and I know that all too well already.*

"'Not something to dwell on'?!" Declan echoed in disbelief. "Ryn, did you *see* those bodies? They looked half-eaten! How am I not supposed to

40

dwell on that?! And are you going to tell me those men seemed like madmen, to you? I'll bet my *left arm* they were being paid. They practically said as much."

At his words, Ryn partially turned his large head, fixing Declan with a single bright eye.

There are wolves everywhere in woods like these, he said evenly, not looking away. *Bears, even. Anything could have done it. More importantly, how* is *your arm?*

For some reason, as he spoke, Ryn's words made more sense to Declan than he thought they probably should have. He found himself nodding along in quiet agreement, grunting in answer to the horse's question.

"Hurts," he admitted, pulling the half-elf tighter to his chest and wincing as the movement made his elbow throb. "Nothing to be done about it now, though." Declan had earned enough blade wounds in his life to know how to thread a decent line of stitches, but between the unsteady light of a hasty fire and the hurry they'd been in the previous evening, his closing of the gash could hardly have been considered his best work.

Ryn looked back to the road, but bobbed his head sympathetically. *Hold out another half-hour. The village isn't far, by my recollection.*

Declan just nodded in reply, trying to shake off the odd haze that had settled over his thoughts, blaming the muddling on fatigue and too many hours without a decent meal.

Sure enough, not long after, they thundered into the crossroads of one of the larger communes that had posted the bounty, a hamlet whose name Declan couldn't recall. Unfortunately for their little party, however, it turned out the village healer had left the morning before for the city of Ebadon, two weeks' walk to the north, to purchase supplies for the coming winter. The best the local elder could do—a wizened old man who looked as though a healthy breeze might have sent him sailing into the overcast sky—was mutter about some hermit out in the woods, and tell them that the owner of an inn a half-day's hard ride north used to work as a surgeon in the King's Vigil.

Trying not to roll his eyes at the idea of hounding *back* through the forest in search of some sylvan hack, Declan turned them northward again with a frustrated groan.

Ryn, on the other hand, galloped on almost anxiously, setting himself back into a heavy pace that would have winded any other horse, which Declan found all the more odd. More than once throughout that morning and the remaining day he caught his friend glancing over his rolling shoulder with a worried expression, eyeing the woman in Declan's arms. It became so frequent, in fact, that Declan ended up calling the horse out on it, but Ryn—in what seemed to be a developing fashion—denied any excess interest in the half-elf. All the same, even after they'd fallen silent again the horse seemed unable to help himself from stealing a look back every quarter-hour or so, like he was searching for something in the woman, studying her face, her form, even the empty sheath at her hip.

Eventually, Declan, too, found himself glancing down, wondering what in the world it was about the woman that had captivated his friend so thoroughly.

Droplets of water streaked in lines along the pale, smooth cheek he could see, streaming down her neck and into the folds of her shirt. In the light of the day he had indeed found that her hair was a clean, silvery-gold which no pure-human would have ever been blessed with, and he was almost sad to see it soaked and plastered against his arm. More embarrassing, though, was the fact that every time he took in her face, Declan found himself again wondering what eyes looked like. Once or twice throughout the ride he'd caught the woman muttering nonsensically through her absent delirium and thought he'd seen them flutter, thought he'd caught a flash of brilliant green in the grey of the day, but whenever he'd glanced down to check he'd noted no further indication that she wasn't still out cold.

Half-elves were a rarity in Viridian, and for good reason. The *er'enthyl*—the wood elves of the Vyr'en, the expansive forest realms to the south—were notoriously territorial of the boundaries of their lands, not to mention largely disdainful of their human neighbors as a whole. Declan himself had had a handful of run-ins with their kind, working with Holden's Guard along the border as a younger man, and the encounters had always left him with a bad taste in his mouth. Despite being something of a wild, tribal people, the *er'enthyl* were also haughty and dismissive, looking down on him—and even the more grizzled veterans of the company he'd been a part of at the time—like parents might look down on poorly behaved children. They'd been dependably unhelpful, even when the Guard had spent several weeks hunting down a band of highwaymen who'd been causing trouble on both sides of the border, and hadn't given so much as a word of thanks or appreciation when the job was done.

All in all, Declan wasn't enamored with the elves he'd known in his time, and could understand the distaste many Viridians felt towards the older, long-lived race.

Still, no dogma is absolute within any people, and laws and traditions might often be flaunted as easily as they might be upheld. Half-elves *could* be found within the boundaries of the country, if one was willing to look for them, or at least what most would consider "half-elves". Oftentimes such examples were actually fourth or fifth generation bastards, bred along until hardly a drop of their ancestral blood remained, but the traits of their forbearers were powerful, and usually lingered on. The woman in Declan's arms, on the other hand, was first-generation, second at most. He'd *never* seen hair like hers on anything but a pure-blooded elf, and he might have thought her one herself were it not for the conspicuous absence of the tell-all ears. She was breathtaking, even limp against him, strands of that silver-gold hair streaked across the wet skin of her face.

Still, none of that explained Ryn's obvious interest in the woman, and Declan thought his own patience wouldn't suffer another snub if he asked and was denied an honest answer yet again.

As the hours pressed on, noon passing into early afternoon, the rain began to fall harder, the showers turning into a full-blown summer storm. The woods around them began to dance and lash, the wind picking up to howl along the road, buffeting first this way, then that. Speaking became impossible aside from Ryn's soundless warnings of sharp bends in the road or leaps over the occasional fallen tree across the path. The day dimmed, and soon the sun was so distant beyond a thick swath of clouds that Declan began to lose track of time, which was probably for the better. He had a good cloak, but between trying to keep the woman covered as best he could, the endless rain, and the splashing pound of Ryn's hooves beneath him, it wasn't long before he was soaked from head to boots. By the time he thought early evening had arrived, Declan was fairly sure his temper couldn't have grown any blacker.

Then, like a reprieve sent by the Mother Herself, Ryn's wonderful words surged across his mind.

Ahead. Less than a mile out.

Declan squeezed his knees together in excited understanding, holding the half-elf to him even tighter as the horse drove forward with a burst of speed through the lashing rain.

Three minutes later the glow of well-lit windows announced the presence of the promised inn, and Declan almost whooped in relief into the storm. Coming to a halt under the swinging sign that read *The Woodsman's Rest*, he dismounted in a hurry, boots splashing down among the trickling streams that ran away into the woods before turning to carefully slide the woman off the saddle and into his arms. The moment they were both clear of his back, Ryn began to change, shrinking rapidly. Having anticipated this, Declan managed to catch the straps of the saddle and bags awkwardly in one hand just as they started to fall, almost dropping the half-elf in the process. He stood straight again in time to feel a heavy weight settle down on his right shoulder, digging into the leather of his traveler's cloak. Glancing sidelong, he had to blink rain out of his eyes to make out Ryn's form against the storm.

A black hawk, slightly too large to be any bird of prey Declan had ever seen otherwise, looked back at him evenly over a gleaming, hooked beak.

Its white-gold eyes glimmered in the sheen of its pitched feathers, over which water ran like oil on glass. Its narrow talons, curved almost cruelly as they clung to his shoulder, might have made him wince had it been the first time he'd born witness to them. Despite its fierce appearance, though, even as he blinked at it the bird extended one broad wing over his head and shoulders, momentarily shielding Declan and the woman from the rain.

Put our things down by the door, Ryn told him, indicating with a thrust of his beak a dry spot beneath a slate awning near the entrance of the inn. *I doubt anyone who might pilfer from us is fool enough to be on the road in this weather, and I can see to them later.*

With a shake of his head in an attempt to clear his vision of wet hair, Declan knelt and dropped the saddle and bags as instructed. This done, he stepped forward and shoved his way through the slightly-ajar door of *The Woodsman's Rest*, shouting even as he half-tumbled into the warmth and clamor of the room beyond.

"Innkeep!"

A respectable throng of customers—many looking as though they, too, had been seeking shelter from the rain—all turned at his voice, and the clatter and chatter that had filled the space with noise died down almost at once. Occupied tables filled the large common room, and a raised bar extended the length of the left wall, beyond which the sounds of an active kitchen could be made out through a door in the far corner. Clean straw was spread over the old wooden floor, and the place smelled of food and ale and the smoky haze of the lit candles bracketed overhead every few feet, dousing the space in dim orange light. At Declan's shout, a squat little woman with a kindly face looked up from the table she was clearing of dirty plates, her natural smile freezing as she caught sight of the girl hanging limply in his arms.

"Oh!" the woman exclaimed, dropping the dishes at once and hurrying forward, shooing away a number of patrons from the table nearest Declan and Ryn. "Away! Away, you lot!" The group clambered up and out of the way at once, taking what dishes and tankards they could grab with them. The rest fell to the floor with a *crash* as the woman swept the surface clear with a quick arm. "Here, boy. Oh, dear."

Groaning a world of thanks, Declan laid his unconscious charge carefully across the table, ignoring the continued pain in his left arm. He felt Ryn's weight leave his shoulder as the hawk spread his wings and leapt gracefully to perch on a nearby chair, causing a half-dozen nearby customers to gasp and flinch back in surprise.

To her credit, the plump tavern worker hardly gave the great black bird a glance as she looked over the sopping half-elf draped across the wood before her.

"Graces…" the woman hissed as she checked the girl's pulse, brushing the silver-gold hair away from where it clung to her pale face. "What happened?"

"Took a blow to the back of the head," Declan explained wearily, collapsing down in the chair Ryn already sat atop. "A nasty one. Are you the innkeeper?"

He thought it was rather a fair question, given that the Vigil recruited the able-bodied of Viridian's men and women both to the King's ranks. The woman, though, shook her head, catching the eye of a serving girl who was standing nearby, staring open-mouthed at the half-elf with a stunned expression.

"Dora, get Brohn," she said urgently. "He'll be in the kitchen. Tell him we've got a wounded—" she glanced at Declan, gaze flicking to his arm before correcting herself "—*two* wounded customers. Quick now!"

The girl—Dora—started as she came to her senses, then rushed off, slipping behind the bar and disappearing through the kitchen door already shouting. As she did, Declan looked down at his own arm, wondering what had caught the older woman's attention, and groaned when he saw red mixing with the dripping lines of rainwater still trickling from his fingers.

His shoddy stitch-work hadn't held up to shouldering his way into the inn, it seemed.

Apparently thinking the half-elf could survive without her attention a minute more, the plump woman hurried over as Declan gingerly slid himself out of his traveling cloak. As soon as his soaked shirt was exposed—the fabric of his left sleeve now dyed a blotchy burgundy—she took hold of the slashed remains of the bloody fabric and ripped it further open, revealing the ugly, torn threads winding into the bleeding gash above his elbow. Pulling what looked like a clean dishtowel from some pocket of her rough-spun dress, the woman tied the cloth above the cut like a makeshift tourniquet.

"You're *sure* you're not the innkeeper?" Declan asked of her, impressed as the blood quit flowing at once.

She gave a short laugh in response, lifting his arm to examine the injury more closely. "I'm *an* innkeeper, but not the one you're after, I think. I'm Dia. My Brohn and I are the owners here, and I've picked up a thing or two from him over the years." Satisfied, Dia let Declan's hand down carefully, standing up again and eyeing Ryn as she wiped her hands on the side of her skirts. "Is this a hunting bird? I've never seen one like it…"

"He is," Declan answered automatically, gingerly pulling at his wound to exam it further. "A cliff falcon, from the Tears to the north. No need to fret. He's harmless."

It was a brief, practiced story that he'd repeated an untold number of times in the last decade. The hawk—according to Ryn's own *repeated* declaration—was the least favorite of the transformations Declan had ever seen his friend take, but it was a useful one. It *did* have a semblance to the large grey raptors that hunted the bluffs of the Mother's Tears, the great ranges that capped Viridian's northern border, and it allowed Ryn to stay at his side no matter the circumstances. Despite whatever reservations the beast might have for the form—Ryn had never told Declan *why* he found it so distasteful—the beast had admitted on more than one occasion that it was easier to room with a hawk than a horse on the road.

Or a wolf, Declan thought with a private smirk, grimacing as the pressure of the cut-off blood flow began to build in his arm.

"Is he... uh... trained?" Dia asked, glancing from Ryn's sleek black form to the straw-covered floor beneath his perch.

Despite his fatigue and discomfort, Declan couldn't help but laugh, doubly so when Ryn himself swelled in silent indignation as he caught on to the matron's concerns.

Before Declan could answer, a broad, bearded man wearing a stained burlap apron over an ample stomach appeared in the frame of the door behind the bar, drying his hands on an old rag and casting about with a worried expression. Catching sight of them, he hurried over at once, already eyeing the unconscious half-elf. With hardly a glance at Declan the man tossed the cloth over his shoulder and bent over her, listening for breath.

"Back of the head, dear," Dia guided him quickly, returning to the table now that she was sure Declan wasn't about to bleed out in her common room. "He says she took a blow to the back of the head."

With a grunt the bearded man—whom Declan assumed to be Brohn—tilted the woman's limp head gently to the side, peering under it. It was at this point that Declan noticed the scene had drawn something of a crowd, a good score of the *Rest's* patrons lined up in a half-circle around them, many standing on tiptoe and craning their necks in an attempt to see what was going on. The closest were the four or five individuals who'd vacated the table for them, but others had rapidly crowded in, including several rugged looking woodcutters, an older man with lank grey hair and a fur-lined cloak, and a stout woman in the regalia of a King's messenger.

Unfortunately for them, Brohn apparently had no patience for onlookers given the circumstances.

"WHAT ARE YA' ALL GAWKIN' AT?!" the innkeeper thundered suddenly, standing straight and making everyone except Dia jump. "GET BACK TA' YER OWN MEALS AND LEAVE THESE TWO BE!"

At once the customers scattered like mice, fleeing in all directions. Brohn, in turn, looked to his wife. "Rothwort, Dia, if ya' please," he requested much more calmly. "Should be some in our room." His eyes moved beyond the woman and found Declan's bloody left arm. "Damn... And yer sewin' kit, when ya' can."

The woman nodded and hurried off at once. Recognizing the herb, Declan groaned.

"Rothwort?" he asked tentatively, grimacing. "Is that necessary?"

His question earned him a dry chuckle from the innkeeper, who moved to stand over him, extending a large hand.

"Brohn," he said by way of greeting. "And aye, it is, for *you* at least. By the looks a' it, ya' been riding all day with that shite stitchin' job, meanin' you'll be lucky ta' avoid infection if'n we don't do somethin' 'bout it otherwise." He gave a wry smile. "It's the rothwort, or I can cauterize it for ya'...?"

Declan gave a pained grin in return, accepting the hand. "Declan," he answered the introduction. "And you offer that like cauterizing *wouldn't* be preferable."

Brohn gave a quick, booming laugh that seemed almost to make the candles around the room shiver and dance. "Ya' musta' seen yer fair share a' battle, for ya' ta' know rothwort so well," Brohn said, his smile holding for a moment. Then his face grew somber, and he looked over his shoulder at the unconscious woman. "Wha' happened, lad?" His eyes fell back on Declan's own wound. "I'd stake me inn on the fact tha' one's been clubbed, but tha' arm a' yers' been carved up by a blade, sure as the night is dark."

Declan nodded slowly, a bit of the weariness that had weighed him down during the ride returning. He leaned back, feeling Ryn hop sidelong across the head of the chair behind him to give him a little more room.

"Contract job," he told the larger man simply. "Bounty that could have gone better."

"Bounty?" Brohn frowned, tossing a thumb back at the limp form of the half-elf. "For her? *She* cut ya' up like that?"

Declan shook his head quickly, clarifying. "No, no. A notice put out by some of the villages south of here. Same ones that recommended *you*, actually. They've been dealing with disappearances for the last couple seasons. Turns out they were kidnappings." He gave a dry, humorless laugh, then winced as the act made his arm shift, lancing pain through the tourniquet. "Doesn't matter, though. Won't be a problem for anyone anymore."

Brohn's eyebrows rose together, at that, and he looked between Declan and the woman for several moments, putting two and two together.

"How many?" he asked with a sad, angry growl, gaze lingering on the unfortunate half-elf pityingly.

"Five," Declan answered with matching coolness, also watching the woman. "They're in more pieces now, though."

Brohn started to nod sanctimoniously, then jerked and turned around sharply. "Five?" he repeated, clearly taken aback, and his eyes lifted to the door. "Ya' got partners waitin' for ya', out in this storm?"

Declan shook his head, reaching around with his good hand to start gingerly pulling the snapped twine of the now-ruined stitches from the flesh of his arm. "No—*ngh*—No partners," he grunted, freeing several inches of bloody string and tossing it on the table. "Just Ryn and I." He gestured at the hawk before grabbing the end of another frayed length.

Brohn blinked, looking at him in disbelief "Ya' took on *five* men," he started tentatively, "with barely a scratch ta' show for it?"

Declan barked a harsh laugh as another two inches came loose. "I'd hardly call this a 'scratch'," he said, lifting his left arm to make his point.

Brohn stared at him, momentarily at a loss for words. Before he could get anything out, however, there was a *clunk* and a curse, and Dia appeared at the top of the long set of stairs along the back of the chamber, a simple bag in one hand as she clasped a heavy clay pot in both arms.

"Yer sharin' the story while we work," Brohn said in a hurry, giving Declan a sharp look before sliding through the tables to help his wife. When they returned, Brohn was carrying the pot and Dia was red in the face from the strain.

"...and next time, if you want me to go faster," she was thundering in annoyance, "you'll remember to put the herbs on the *bottom* shelf, rather than the *top!*"

Brohn, for all his superior size, was cowering under the smaller woman's berating, which got another smile out of Declan. For a moment, he was reminded of his mother, and a time long before her mind had started to fail.

"Sorry, love," Brohn mumbled apologetically, setting the pot down on the table beside the half-elf before uncapping it and reaching in. The moment the cover was removed from the container, a pungent, unpleasantly familiar smell wafted through the air, making Declan's stomach clench.

This should be a good show, Ryn told him privately, sounding all-too amused as his golden eyes followed Brohn's hand retracting from the pot, carefully withdrawing a number of small, black seeds.

"Shut up," Declan told the hawk under his breath, clenching his teeth involuntarily as the innkeeper approached him, crushing the seeds together in a clenched fist. At once the sour smell grew more pronounced, and Brohn opened his fingers to reveal a green, pulpous mess coating his palm.

"You first, lad," he said with an apologetic smile at Declan, motioning for his arm. Hesitating only briefly, Declan offered up the limb, unable to help himself from turning to look the other way as Brohn took him by the elbow with his clean hand.

"So ya' were tellin' me about this bounty a' yers," the innkeeper said, examining the wound himself. "Five kidnappers? Ya' sure about that?"

Declan just nodded, trying not to speak, eyes fixed on a window along the top story of the spacious room, left open to help keep the air from growing stale. From behind him, he heard Dia inhale sharply.

"Kidnappers?" she repeated, and he made out her leather shoes thumping across the floor towards them.

Declan winced as Brohn pulled at the gash, opening it wide to draw out the remaining threads he hadn't been able to free himself. Deciding it might be for the better to have something else to think about, he briefly filled the couple in on his and Ryn's previous night, omitting the more gruesome details of the bodies they'd come across. They'd informed the village that morning, giving them directions as best they could manage, and could only hope the locals would find the clearing so they could bury and mourn their dead properly.

"To the south?" Dia confirmed after his quick explanation. "Is *that* what was going on?"

"Ya' heard about this?" Brohn asked his wife in surprise as Declan felt the last of the twine pull free.

"Aye, a couple of times. Three weeks past there was the better part of a family in here, on their way east after losing their boy. Poor things. And they weren't the only ones. Heard there's been lots of—"

The rest of what Dia said was lost to Declan as he felt Brohn wipe a thick finger into the cut, spreading the rothwort paste along the ridges of the exposed flesh.

Immediately Declan saw stars, his jaw clenching, the nails of his right hand digging into his palm as it balled into a fist. The pain bloomed like a shock, building into an agony at his elbow, then washing up his arm and into his neck, head, and chest like a crashing wave. As it peaked he let out a hiss through bared teeth, closing his eyes against the burning ache. It ripped through him, digging into his bones and tearing at his skin like a hundred thousand boiling needles.

It was nearly half-a-minute before it finally started to ebb.

"I swear by *all* the damn Graces," Declan managed to get out eventually, opening his eyes again and blinking away tears as he looked around, "if I went a thousand years before having to see that shit again, it would be too soon."

Brohn chuckled darkly, giving him a nod. "Aye, I hear ya'. Still," he stood up with a grunt, allowing Dia to wipe his hand free of the leftover plant paste, "ya' did far better than most. Between that and takin' on five men on yer own, you've got the blood a' Kings in ya', boy."

Declan frowned at the words, watching Brohn wipe his fingers on his rag again before kicking a chair closer and sitting down to fumble through his wife's sewing bag.

"'Blood of Kings'?" Declan asked as the innkeeper pulled a couple needles and a length of fine twine from the sack, eyeing them critically. He'd heard the term on the road before, he was sure, but only ever in passing.

Brohn looked surprised at the question, glancing up as soon as he'd threaded one of the—mercifully—smaller needles. "You weren't an army man?"

Declan shook his head, equally bemused. "The Vigil? Never. Thought about it when I was younger, but a friend talked me out of it." He did his best not to glance towards the black hawk over his shoulder. He'd forgotten about that discussion, somehow. It had been so long ago, not a year after Declan's mother had died, and Ryn had put his foot down on the idea with absolute finality.

Why was *that?* Declan found himself trying to recall, with no answer coming easy to mind.

"Ah," Brohn said with an understanding nod, returning to his task as he scooted his chair closer. "Sellsword, then? I won't believe yer *not* a swordsman, looking at yer hands and the wear on tha' hilt." He indicated the sweat-stained grip of Declan's longsword with a brief tilt of his head before taking his left arm up again.

Declan nodded, saying nothing more, watching the needle slip into his flesh and across the wound. Silently he prayed to the Mother that that would be the end of the questions.

Of course, it wasn't.

"What company?" the innkeeper asked, sounding nonchalant, though Declan knew better. He was being tested, now. He regretted having told the man of the fight, thinking he should have known better. He wasn't the *most* skilled swordsman he'd ever met—Cassandra Sert alone had drilled that particular knowledge into him more times than he could count—but there weren't many he'd come across in his life who'd proven able enough to best a decade of Ryn's tutelage and critical eye. Declan was young, sure, but he'd spent more than half his life now with a blade on his hip.

As a result, he was used to having his claims questioned.

"The Iron Wind," he answered Brohn, who continued to work slowly and carefully, stopping now and then to let his wife dab new blood away with her towel. "The Seekers before that, and a few between them."

"The Wind?" Brohn paused in his threading to glance up at Declan, sounding torn between impressed and suspicious.

Internally, Declan sighed, unsurprised. Cassandra's company was largely considered the most sought-after of Aletha's mercenary guilds. At the very least, it was certainly the most successful. They had outposts in every major city in the country, and in the capital itself frequently took on work for the varying levels of the nobility. They'd even been known to accept tasks passed down from the al'Dyors themselves, though that hadn't occurred in the three years Declan had spent with them.

Fortunately, the Wind—like all the Alethan companies—made proof of employment rather simple.

With his free hand Declan reached up to tug back the collar of his shirt, revealing the skin underneath to Brohn and Dia. The former whistled, genuinely impressed now, as he took in the simple black tattoo under Declan's right collar bone, a plain sword flanked by feathered wings. Every guild had their own mark, and the Wind's was only one of several emblems inked into Declan's body. Stonewall's simple, crenelated band—meant to emulate the ramparts of Aletha—circled his right upper arm. The Grey Shield's starred kite shield covered his left shoulder, while Holden's Guard's spears crossed his right. Oldest of them all, the plain arrow of the Seekers was fading along the inside of his left forearm, gone understandably unnoticed by the innkeepers under several trails of drying blood.

"Good on you, lad," Brohn said, continuing his careful work, apparently familiar enough with the companies to know the Wind's mark on sight. "I don't peg ya' as more than—what?—twenty-four? Five? Explains why you don't know the army yarns, ta' be sure."

"Yarns? The blood of Kings? What does it mean?" Declan asked, eager to keep the conversation going. Any distraction from more talk of his mercenary work—not to mention the throb of the needle—was more than a welcome diversion.

Brohn chuckled, drawing yet another stitch through. "Jus' an ol' camp quip. Somethin' we used ta' say whenever one a' our own would survive a tussle they probably shouldn't've. They got 'the blood a' Kings' or 'King's blood' we'd tell 'em."

Declan frowned. "Why? Seems an odd thing."

"Not in the Vigil, dear." Dia was the one who answered him, this time. She, too, was watching her husband work. "The al'Dyors are a hardy bunch. A thousand years they've been in power, almost without fail. The stories I heard this one's company share, back in the day." She patted Brohn's broad shoulder fondly. "Wars. Kidnappings. Poisonings. Nothing seems to touch them the way it would you or I."

"'Blood of Kings'..." Declan smirked. He'd heard say that Mathaleus al'Dyor and his ilk were something beyond common men, but he'd always chalked it up to the peasantry fawning over a sovereignty that seemed—by all accounts—to treat them well enough. "I'll have to remember that one."

"Makes ya' a lucky man, lad," Brohn said with a laugh, reaching the bottom edge of Declan's wound. "Our lot think it means tha' about the only thing yer gonna have to worry about in life—" he tied the stitches off with an artful twist of the needle "—is a dragon."

CHAPTER FIVE

Declan blinked, not sure what to make of that as the innkeeper accepted a small pair of scissors from his wife. Of the two of them, only Dia noticed his confusion.

"Old history," she explained sympathetically. "A war from a very long time ago. Dragons attacked Aletha, killing the old King and stealing away his heirs as ransom. Or so the story goes, at least."

Declan's brow shot up, his interest piqued. "*Dragons?*" he asked, astounded. "Attacking *Aletha?*"

He'd never even heard of such a thing. It was common knowledge, even among the gentry, that dragons had once ruled the western fringes of Viridian, nesting in the highest peaks of the Reaches, the mountain ranges that ran perpendicular to the Mother's Tears to form the country's western boundary. Still, whenever there'd been mention of them, Declan had always thought of dragons as part of ancient, extinct history. To have them referred to in conjunction with the politics and wars of man was altogether unexpected.

In truth, it sounded like a scary story mothers told their children to get them to behave.

"Oh yes," Dia answered with a bright smile, apparently happy to keep talking. "This was hundreds of years ago, mind, but yes. After the attack, the nobility rallied the army and laid siege to the Reaches, trying to rescue the prince and crown princess, taken prisoner. It was a bloody conflict, but man prevailed, wiping out the dragons and retrieving the eldest, Elysia al'Dyor. Unfortunately, they couldn't save her... her brother... who..."

Dia trailed away, her expression suddenly fearful, her eyes on something over Declan's head. Surprised, Declan sat up and twisted, almost inadvertently pulling his arm free from Brohn's grasp, the innkeeper having noticed nothing as he finished his work.

What the...? were the only words to come to mind as Declan stared, dumbstruck, at the sight behind him.

Ryn's white-gold eyes were fixed on Dia with frightening ferocity, burning into the woman like twin candles in a dark room. Within them, shining across their amber hue, Declan was shocked to find what he could only describe as fury; abject, fathomless anger that seemed to come from nowhere and everywhere. What's more, the hawk had *bristled*, his black feathers on end, each sticking out like a knife against the warm glow of the surrounding light. It gave Ryn the impression of growing, of swelling even as he sat perched there, on the back of Declan's chair.

Then there was the subtle *creak* of straining wood, and Declan realized with a start that the bird *was* growing.

Thinking fast, he did the only thing that came to mind in the moment. "Oy!" he snapped at the hawk, trying to appear like nothing more than an owner bringing his animal to heel. "Where's this coming from?! Feathers down!"

At once Ryn appeared to come to his senses. He sunk back down into himself, his rigid wings settling, his form shrinking to a more appropriate size. As he did so, the room around them grew brighter, and Declan had to partially squint at the sudden glow, like the hawk's mere presence had been absorbing the candlelight.

All the while, Ryn didn't look away from Dia, fiery depth meeting the woman's frightened gaze with almost cruel determination.

I'm going to see to our things.

His friend's voice was strange as it shivered over Declan's mind. It was hoarse, angry, but also somehow sad. Before he could think to say anything in response, however, Ryn finally looked away from Dia and spread his great wings, taking flight in a *whoosh* of wind. Declan followed the hawk's black shape, watching him circle the room once, then settle on the sill of the open window high above them.

There, Ryn paused, facing the lashing storm outside for a moment.

Declan... he started to say without looking around, then stopped. For a long few seconds Declan could only stare up at his friend in baffled silence, unable to call after him in public.

When Ryn finally found his voice, however, it was hardly helpful.

I'll be nearby if you need me, he said, half-turning to briefly fix Declan with a single golden eye. *Take care of the girl.*

And then he was gone, vanishing in a blink into the rain, leaving Declan with the numb, empty feeling that words had been lost between them with the hawk's hesitant silence.

His attention was quickly brought back to his surroundings as Dia let out a gasp behind him. Shifting around again, Declan was astonished to find the woman looking—of all things—concerned, her eyes on the window through which Ryn had just departed.

"Is he going to be alright out there?" she almost squeaked. "It's not looking to let up anytime soon!"

For a second, Declan gaped, completely at a loss of words. The fear Dia had demonstrated seconds ago was utterly absent, and she'd clearly noticed nothing of Ryn's momentary growth as he'd stood perched before her.

What in the Mother's name is going on? he demanded of himself, looking between the two innkeepers. Brohn hadn't done more than glance up when Ryn had taken flight, and was just finishing clipping the tie-offs of Declan's new stitches.

"He…" Declan finally started, looking to Dia again, who was still watching the window. "He'll… be fine. He's used to worse than this, on the road."

Dia looked unconvinced, biting her lip nervously, but nodded in resignation before finally dropping her eyes from the storm.

Just then, Brohn let out a quiet exclamation of triumph. "Done," the large man said proudly, sitting back to examine his work. Declan, too, looked down, and through his confusion had to admit at being impressed by the tight, clean sutures.

"My thanks," he said briefly as Brohn reached to undo the makeshift tourniquet, keeping one eye on Dia while trying to understand. He couldn't think of a time he'd ever witnessed Ryn appear so…. upset? Much less a time the beast had taken his leave so abruptly. Declan felt a chill, recalling the savage anger in the hawk's eyes following the woman's recounting. He'd never even *imagined* Ryn could respond like that to anyone, and certainly not following what Declan would have generally qualified as barroom banter.

What was that all about? he asked himself again, more calmly this time, before deciding he would try to get some answers.

"Dia…" he started hesitantly while Brohn got to his feet and moved quickly over to the unconscious half-elf. "What was the rest of that story? You didn't finish it."

"Hmm?" Dia looked at him in quiet confusion, like she didn't know what he was referring to, moving to help Brohn turn the woman over. "What story was that, dear?"

Declan stared at her blankly for a moment before finding his voice. "The history? About the old King's death, and his heirs…?"

And dragons, he thought privately, not wanting to bring it up and sound ridiculous.

"Oh!" Dia said at once, her gaze clearing while Brohn bent over across from her to examine the half-elf. "Yes! Of course… Where was I?" She pondered it a moment, looking like she was struggling to remember.

"The nobles?" Declan offered helpfully, standing up and flexing his arm experimentally, watching her with a frown. "Are you feeling well? We were just talking about it…"

"Oh, yes," Dia said with another smile, motioning to the half-elf. "Just a little distracted, I think. But yes, the nobles." She gathered her thoughts for a second or two more. "After they'd eradicated the dragons, they managed to find Elysia al'Dyor, somehow alive. Her brother, Amherst, on the other hand…" The woman gave a sad shrug. "Still, Elysia was the eldest, so her safe return was likely what mattered most. She was returned to the city not long after, if I recall correctly, and her line has thrived ever since."

"The al'Dyors're a hardy lot," Brohn echoed his wife's earlier statement even as he continued his examination, proving he'd been listening all the while.

Declan blinked at this anti-climactic finish, having expected—for no particular reason, he conceded—something much grander. Then again, the story essentially amounted to a history lesson, so he supposed he shouldn't have been surprised. Declan had only ever learned to read and write at his mother's insistence, and it had been Ryn who'd taught him his numbers in the year after they'd left home for Aletha. The men and women of the Iron Wind and the other companies had rarely been of the stupid sort—stupid swordsmen didn't tend to lead long lives, after all—but Viridian's past and the events that had shaped their country weren't exactly favored topics in the mess halls.

All in all, history was a subject in which Declan thought he could readily admit to be sorely lacking.

"Lad, help us out, will ya'?"

Brohn's addressing of him brought Declan out of his ponderings as he realized the large man was waving him around the table, beckoning him towards the end over which the half-elf's soaked boots hung. Looking at the innkeeper questioningly even as he did as instructed, Declan saw that Brohn had retrieved the leftover rothwort paste his wife had saved for him, the greenish concoction lathered over a hand he kept well away from his face.

Declan put two-and-two together quickly. "Need help holding her down?" He eyed the paste with distaste.

"Aye," Brohn said, his face tight as he looked over the woman sprawled before them. "Her legs, if'n ya' think ya' can manage it with that arm'?"

"No problem," Declan said with a shrug, bending his elbow again in demonstration. The stitches held. "You do good work."

Brohn managed a smirk at that, but Declan could tell his attention was elsewhere as the man tugged away at a few stray strands of silver-gold hair that clung to the wound on the back of the half-elf's head. Looking down at it, Declan couldn't help but worry. The wound was uglier now than it had been the night before. The skin around the gash was black and blue, the bruising having drained down her neck and into her shoulder. The heavy scab that had formed wept, and a crust along the edge of the exposed flesh was pale and dry.

He didn't like the look of it one bit, and nor, it seemed, did Brohn, the former surgeon's drawn expression not helping Declan's fear.

"Did ya' clean this already?" the big man asked, letting Dia take over the task of freeing the wound of hair.

Declan nodded slowly. "As best I could, but all we had on hand were some basic herbs and drinking water. It's boiled, and I used a fresh bag. I flushed it before we left the forest."

Brohn nodded silently, the answer apparently doing little to quell his concerns. "We can cut the scab free, and I can apply the rothwort, but I don't know how much it'll help. She's been unconscious since this mornin'?"

"Last night," Declan corrected, feeling his stomach twist at the realization. "I thought she came to once or twice on the ride, but I can't be sure. I heard her muttering, at the very least, but that's about it." He cursed himself. The day had been so grueling, it was only hitting him now how poor the woman's condition might be…

"That's long," Brohn muttered, echoing Declan's own thoughts. "*Too* long. If she came to at all, even jus' mumblin', tha's a good sign, but still…" He looked to his wife, pointing at the scab with his free hand. "Are ya' alright to open that?"

The woman didn't hesitate, mumbling something about going to get a clean knife before hurrying off for the kitchens again. While she was gone, Brohn explained his fears to Declan.

"There's more going on here than tha' cut," he said, still indicating the back of the half-elf's head. "Probably swellin' in her brain, if I had ta' guess. Likely fractured her skull, but I can't tell tha' for sure either way…"

Declan felt another chill. "Can you do anything about it?"

Brohn shook his head slowly. "Not me, no. Might've been able to if'n I had my old tools, but the Vigil kept those, an' hardly anyone survives that sort of thing anyhow, nor always for the better when they do."

"There's *nothing* we can do?" Declan asked in distress, his fear deepening.

"I didn't say that," Brohn answered quickly, meeting Declan's eye sidelong. "I said *I* couldn't do anythin' about it." He pointed towards the door. "You came from south a' here, right?"

Declan nodded slowly.

"Good, then ya' might already know the woods. There's an ol' man, lives in the forest east and south a' here. Don't ask me where exactly. I don't know. Never met 'im. All I can tell you is I know men who have, and it makes me think he might be yer best option—hell, yer *only* option—right now."

Declan groaned, a twinge of annoyed regret flicking at his tired mind. "I've heard of him," he muttered. "The village we stopped at this morning told us about a hermit we could try. I didn't think it was worth our time."

The innkeeper gave a humorless chuckle just as Dia reappeared out of the kitchen, paring blade in hand. "I don't blame ya', lad, but I been in these parts long enough ta' tell ya' otherwise. Had a couple loggers in here last summer, tellin' me how one of them got half-crushed by a tree they felled, and yet there he was, right as rain. A month later there's a hunter sittin' over there"—he motioned to a corner table of the room "—swearin' by the Mother and all Her Graces that he got good an' torn up by a warg come too far off the Tears. Passed out holdin' his insides in his hands, then woke up feelin' like nothin' had ever happened with the ol' bugger standin' over him"

Declan almost rolled his eyes, but Brohn stopped him.

"I *know* how it sounds," he told him as Dia reached them. "But ya' hear enough tales of miracles, and ya' start to wonder. Ya' want to save her?" He motioned to the woman, then waited for Declan to nod. "Then ya' take the bloody risk that I'm sendin' ya' on a wild chase through the fuckin' woods. Ya' hear?"

Declan hesitated, glancing out of the open window as he listened to the rain continuing to lash at the walls and roof. He was exhausted, and his arm hurt despite the stitching.

Still, it didn't take him long to sigh and nod, giving in to his own conscience.

"Good on ya'," Brohn said quietly before looking around to watch Dia work. The plump little woman didn't balk at the task at hand, taking the edge of the small knife she'd retrieved and using it to pry away chunks of the scab on the back of the half-elf's neck with quick, slicing flicks. The prone figure flinched and groaned as this happened, washing Declan with the briefest sense of relief every time she did. In less than half a minute Dia was done, taking yet another damp rag she had slung over her shoulder to clean off the flecked scab and new blood.

By the time she stepped away, the wound looked fresh again.

Brohn didn't dally. "Legs, lad," he reminded Declan, moving to take up the space his wife had vacated, his clean hand pinning down one of the half-elf's shoulders while Dia herself leaned into the other. Declan, in turn, took each ankle firmly, then motioned that he was ready.

Brohn pressed his rothwort-covered palm to the back of the half-elf's head, smothering the newly open wound.

The expected effect was immediate.

Like someone had driven a knife into her back, the woman gasped and began to convulse. At once Declan had to bear down harder on her shins, almost losing a leg completely before catching it and shoving her more securely into the wood. The woman jerked and thrashed, and Declan again thought he caught a flash of brilliant green as her eyes blinked in pain. After about fifteen seconds or so her movements lessened and her breathing became steady again, though she remained as dead to the world as ever.

After another ten, she was finally still, whimpering and mumbling inaudibly, but still unconscious.

"So sorry, darlin'," Brohn murmured soothingly into her ear as he stroked her smooth hair with his free hand, allowing his wife to one last time wipe clean the remaining paste from his other. "It's done now. It's done."

The woman, of course, gave no response.

"Tha's all I can do, lad," Brohn grunted, looking to Declan again. "Can't stitch it up and risk increasing the pressure. I admit I was hopin' the rothwort might see her awake, but..." He let the words trail away in disappointment, allowing Declan to finish the thought for him.

"No luck. Of course... If that didn't do the trick, I don't know what would." All the same, he sighed, glancing at the door. "South and east?" he confirmed aloud.

"The old man?" Brohn asked, thanking Dia with a nod when the woman started gathering up the mess the evening had left the space in, bending down to collect the plates and dishes she herself had swept onto the floor what could only have been ten minutes earlier. "Aye, if ya' take a trailhead south a' here and ride through the woods."

"How do I find him?"

"Like I said, couldn't tell ya'." The innkeeper shrugged apologetically, he himself gathering the bloody towels, scissors, and knife from the table by the half-elf. "I think it'll be pretty obvious ya' need help, though, so there's a good chance he'll make 'imself known."

"*He'll* find *us?*" Declan asked in disbelief, looking around again. "How?"

The large man shook his head in answer. "Wish I had more answers than stories for ya', lad."

This did nothing to solidify Declan's confidence in the situation, and he was tempted to say so. Still, he had no better ideas, so he turned his grumbling into a word of genuine thanks, gathered up his damp traveling cloak before heading for the door with the intention of finding Ryn.

"Oy!"

Declan jerked to a stop, a big hand having taken him by the shoulder. Looking around, he found Brohn staring at him like he'd abruptly gone mad.

"And jus' where in the Mother's name do ya' think yer goin'?!" the innkeeper demanded.

Declan frowned, under the impression that the answer was fairly obvious. "To get the old man," he replied after a moment.

Brohn shook his head, pulling him back. "Not like this yer not. It's dark out, it's still pourin' ropes, and ya' said yerself ya' ain't slept in Grace's knows how long."

"Or eaten," Dia offered helpfully from the floor, not so much as bothering to look up as she finished gathering a set of battered silverware.

"I'll sleep when I get back," Declan muttered, even as his body fought this statement with its lugging heaviness. "She doesn't have *time*."

"She's speakin', which is better than some in her condition." Brohn was staring him down, unmoving. "She'll live the night, I'll wager. Regardless, how do those chances change if ya' can't find the man tonight? Or if ya' break yer neck or lame yer horse lookin'?"

"That's not going to—" Declan started, but Brohn cut him off.

"I can't say for sure, but there's a fair shot the man's not likely ta' help ya' if ya' go out there on yer own as is." The innkeeper waved over to Dora, the serving maid, even as he continued. "Yer gonna have ta' take the half-elf ta' prove to him ya' need his help, and if ya' think I'm gonna *bloody well* let ya' move this poor girl in this weather, yer mental, boy. She's wet, she's sick, and she's cold enough after yer day's ride as is."

Dora reached them, looking a little flustered, her eyes continuously straying to the still form of the unconscious woman beside her.

"Find a room for these two," Brohn told her at once, not even giving Declan a chance to argue. "Two beds, if ya' can."

"And a bowl of whatever's still hot, dear!" Dia called after the girl as she hurried off again before making back to the kitchen with her arms full of platters and cups.

Declan, foreseeing his reasonings being run over, felt what willpower he managed to hold onto begin to fray. "She might not survive the night," he tried one last time, though even he could hear the absence of resolve in his voice.

"Aye," Brohn admitted solemnly, his face softening. "But if tha' were the case, she'd be gone 'afore ya' were able to come back with the ol' fella as is. She's made it this long, lad. The Mother's lookin' out for this one."

With that, Declan felt the last of his arguments fall away, and he nodded with a slow sigh. His body ached for sleep, and the prospect of a *real* bed before trekking back south in the morning was more than minimally enticing.

"Tha's my boy," Brohn said with a mirthless chuckle, wrapping everything he'd picked up in one of the dirty towels and tucking it under one arm. "Can you carry her, or should I?"

"I'll manage it," Declan said, approaching the table and hearing the exhaustion in his own voice now that he knew sleep was soon in coming. Brohn helped him turn the woman over onto her back again, allowing

Declan to carefully hoist her up into his arms, doing his best to keep her head still. He felt the stitches above his elbow strain under her weight, but hold. When he was ready, he followed Brohn through the common space towards the back of the room, and up the set of solid stone stairs leading up to the *Rest's* second floor. Trailing the innkeeper, Declan found himself turning sideways in a cramped hallway. Dora waited for them halfway along the left wall, a lit candle in hand as she held open a narrow door, and Declan nodded his thanks to her before slipping past Brohn and into the room. Light flickered in the chamber from a second candle sitting on a small, shared night table set between two narrow beds. There was no window to speak of—*Which means Ryn will have to suffer the storm,* Declan thought regretfully—but the mattresses looked comfortable and the room was warm, likely over the kitchens built below.

All in all, it was as welcome a sight as Declan could ever recall experiencing.

Sliding between the beds, he set the half-elf down on the furthest mattress just as Dia reappeared, shuffling into the room with an armful of what looked like clean clothes. When she shooed him out and told Brohn to close the door behind him, Declan took the hint, stepping back into the hall quickly. Mercifully Dora wasn't long in returning with the promised meal, and Declan waited in content silence with the big man, wolfing down a hearty stew of spiced lamb, potatoes, carrots, and onions.

Finally, Dia opened the door again.

"All done," she said in a whisper, giving Declan a half-warning, half-teasing look. "Mind you keep your hands to yourself tonight."

"I don't know if I'll muster the energy to undress, much less fondle anyone," Declan answered with the best smile he could manage. Then it fell away, and he looked between Dia and her husband. "Thank you both. I'll remember this."

"Get some rest," Brohn answered, clapping him briefly on the shoulder. "Ya' got more ridin' ta' do in the morning, it seems."

Declan nodded, feeling that knowledge weigh on him as he repeated his thanks, then stepped into the room and closed the door at his back.

The half-elf's wet hunting tunic was hung over the worn rail of the bed frame at her feet, and she'd been tucked in on her stomach beneath several thin blankets—likely to keep her wound from sticking to the pillows—hiding the clean clothes he knew she now wore. Her face was peaceful, still and calm, and Declan found himself one last time wishing he could see her open her eyes, if only to sate his curiosity.

The weight of his own eyes, though, told him he doubted he would have had the presence of mind to appreciate such an occurrence regardless of whether or not it happened.

Quickly Declan peeled off his own soaked clothes, dropping his sword belt unceremoniously to the floor by his bed before pulling off his boots with a damp *squelch* that made him pray they would dry out by morning. His shirt and pants came next, but his small clothes he left on, unable to bring himself to strip down completely with a strange woman in the room with him. Taking just enough time to lay the wet garments out to dry, he collapsed atop the mattress with a sigh of exhausted bliss. Lulled by the sound of the rain hammering against the slate roof overhead, Declan was asleep before he could even think to extinguish the candle, which burned lower and lower as the night wore on, finally going out with a last guttering glimmer.

The room was dark, therefore, when his dreams were interrupted early the next morning by his own knife being pressed against his throat.

CHAPTER SIX

Declan sat tall in the saddle, dressed in his full regalia of smoke-blackened armor. Gold gleamed along the fringes of the darkened steel, shifting in the distant light of the sun through storm clouds that lingered over the quiet of the world. The thick leather was hard beneath him, the padding new and unaccustomed to his frame, but he doubted it would stay so for long. The air was clear, the vast expanse of the horizon reaching out in an endless roll of mountains to the very furthest reaches of the earth. His plate mail shifted, moving fluidly with him as he looked down. In one gauntleted hand he held a longsword, a plain thing of unadorned beauty, but peerless quality. The fingers of his other were knotted into a pair of long, braided reins, the tethers hanging slack for the time being.

And there, beneath him, was the beast.

Declan's newly-made saddle straddled a lithe, reptilian body of gargantuan proportions. Black scales twisted and shifted with every move the creature made, roped muscle beneath them flexing in waves like wind across an open field. It had come to rest along a rocky outcropping, hunched over the edge of the icy cliff on four powerful legs, black-and-grey talons finding easy purchase among the uneven stone. Behind Declan's knees, leathery wings shivered, folded against the creature's monstrous sides for the moment, their dark membranes flecked with white scars and red arteries. Behind him, the tail, a three-foot-thick lash of scaled brawn, curled back and forth with anxious steadiness through the gathered snow.

And before him, suspended on a stout neck as it overlooked the scene below, was the head.

Large, webbed ears protruded outwards from its skull, rippling slightly in the cold blow of the mountain breeze. A blunt snout crowned a wide mouth lined with pale teeth, each one as long and broad as Declan's whole hand. Great gusts of vapor formed briefly in the creature's every exhalation, and he could feel its steady breathing below him as it peered down the ridge, following the movements of a scattered line of soldiers crossing the stone-speckled valley.

Declan gave a short tug on the reins. At once the plated neck twisted, bringing the beast's face around. Large, white-gold eyes bore into his own.

Ready? it asked. No sound issued from its half-open mouth. Instead, Declan heard the voice ringing clearly from within the depths of his own mind.

"It's past time," he acknowledged sadly, those words far gone from anything he would have preferred to utter. The creature nodded, turning to look back down the cliff at the approaching army of men in red and black uniforms. Sheathing his blade temporarily over one shoulder, Declan reached down to grasp a hollowed horn that hung hooked from his belt. Shaking it free of the flecks of snow that clung to its smooth surface, he brought it to his lips and drew a single long, resounding note. It hung in the air for a time, reverberating over the rocky cliffs.

And then, shaking the very ground beneath their feet, the peaks erupted with the roars and screams of a thousand black forms.

The beasts plunged off the mountain, diving towards the oncoming forces in graceful, low-sweeping arcs. Declan felt himself squeeze down into the saddle with his knees, and the great wings on either side of him unfolded, each well over twenty feet in length. Replacing the horn on its hook, he took hold of the reins with both hands, checking one final time to ensure he was firmly lashed in place before turning to his mount.

"To war, my friend."

Then they leapt off the cliff, plummeting towards the rocky ground, iron-colored smoke chasing them as white fire bloomed in the dragon's maw.

CHAPTER SEVEN

"Be vigilant, child. You are worth more than this world might think of you. Prepare yourself for that. Steel yourself. This land is often as cruel as it is kind."

-Bonner yr'Essel, to his daughter, Esteria

At first, when Ester came to, the utter darkness she awoke in nearly had her convinced she'd gone blind. For almost a minute she lay still on her stomach, her breath catching in her throat, willing herself not to panic. Trembling, she lifted a hand to her face and waved it in the air beside her. Relief rushed in a hot wash through her limbs when she realized she could just make out the faintest outline of her fingers, barely distinguishable— even to her sensitive eyes—against the limited light slipping under what must have been the jamb of a nearby door. As her vision adjusted further, she realized she was lying in a bed, tucked away in the corner of what appeared to be a small, plain room. The fear returned suddenly, and Ester instinctively scrambled for the knife usually belted at her hip, which she discovered to be missing.

Missing, along with every other article of the clothes she'd last remembered wearing…

The thrill of horror that followed this understanding was unlike any fear Ester had ever experienced in her life. Her hands went cold as she slowly moved them up and down her body, feeling what could only be a rough-spun wool shirt and pants in the place of her hunting garb. Her heart thundered in her chest, the pounding blood lancing an aching discomfort with every beat across the back of her head. Pushing this aside, she forced herself to take a calming breath, seeking other pains, other signs that might explain why she wasn't in her own garments anymore. Feeling nothing, a little of the tension left her, and something like perverse gratitude momentarily flit across her thoughts.

At the very least, the men who'd caught her in the woods seemed to have *some* decency about them.

Still, the fact that they'd stripped her of her gear wasn't a good sign. For a minute more Ester lay there, warm in the soft bed, struggling to piece together the last events she could recall. She remembered tracking the men, stalking them through the woods, only to have them turn on her like some whisper in the wind had told them she was there. She remembered fighting, remembered struggling with her captors in the rushing flow of what must have been a stream or river, then a blinding pain that had dragged her down into blackness. After that, all she had were brief flashes of consciousness, clouded memories of firelight, of the stench of rot, of the back of a black horse and a strong arm pinning her to a man's chest. It had been raining, and all she'd been able to make out through the fog of semi-consciousness was the pounding of the hooves and the dim sounds of her kidnapper speaking, seeming only to himself.

I have to get out of here.

The thought welled in Ester's mind, consuming her as the panic of potential violation faded. She didn't know where she was, much less how precisely she'd gotten there, but that mattered little in the moment. The men she'd been tracking were up to little good—if the local rumors were to be believed—and she couldn't imagine what sort of trouble she'd managed to get herself into. Making a decision, Ester kicked away the blankets she'd woken up under, rolling over and sitting up with the rapid intent of standing and getting a sense of her surroundings.

She didn't even make it completely off the mattress.

Letting out a barely-stifled cry of pain, Ester fell onto the bed again, clutching at the back of her head. The base of her skull—originally just aching—felt like it had been pressed against a hot brand, any abrupt twist of her neck triggering a searing jolt that left her weak and nauseous. Beneath her fingers she felt a long, fresh scab, wet even to the touch. Ester retched, allowing herself—despite the obvious danger of her situation—to roll onto her side, curling inward. She lay there for a long time, breathing carefully as the agony slowly eased, fading second by second. When it had finally waned to a manageable throb, she pushed herself back up gently onto all fours, then carefully back onto her feet. She waited there for a time, relieved when only a fleeting wave of dizziness returned.

Given her father's skills, it had been some time since Ester had suffered pain like that...

Reaching out, she found the wall nearby, and with careful steps began making her way towards the outline of the door in the far corner. When she reached the end of her bed, she paused, confused, blinking down at the outlines of what could only be her own leathers and clothes dangling over the frame, like they'd been hung to dry.

"What the...?" she started to say under her breath, reaching out, completely perplexed by the sight of her thought-lost things within easy reach.

Then Ester froze, hand inches from her pants, her sharp ears catching the soft, rhythmic sounds of breathing in the otherwise silent room.

There was someone there. There, alone with her in the dark.

Straightening again slowly, Ester cast carefully about the small chamber, grateful—not for the first time in her life—for her mother's *er'enthyl* blood as her eyes worked the faint light of the jamb to her advantage. The first thing she noticed were clothes scattered across the room, hung to air much like her own. Among these, Ester's heart leapt when she made out the distinct shape of a weapons belt, complete with sheathed sword, knife, and purse, outlined in long shadows by the light of the door.

Then she found him.

The man was lying barely clothed on his back on a second bed she hadn't noticed initially, his bare chest rising and falling in the steady pattern of sleep. Ester stood stiff, contemplating this new complication, undecided on what to do. Assuming the man was dangerous, rousing him might be the worst decision she could make.

Still, she knew she could only be in an unfriendly place, and if her chance of escape were any better with a hostage…

Ester made her decision with a blink, stealing forward as rapidly as the growing ache in her head would allow. She winced with every step, the creak of the floorboards beneath her feet screaming, but didn't hesitate when she reached the sword belt. Sadly she had little choice but to leave the longer blade sheathed where it was. She knew well how to handle the weapon— her mother had seen to that long before the Matriarch's court had called the woman back to the Vyr'en—but, under the circumstances, she was in need of something less unwieldy.

Drawing the hunting knife with a *snick* of metal on wood, Ester took a moment to get a feel for its weight before straightening up again and creeping forward.

Even in the faint light of the closed door, Ester could tell the sleeping figure had a handsome face, his strong, stubbled jaw framed in long brown hair that fell loose just short of his broad shoulders. She would have marked him as a young man, maybe twenty-five or twenty-six at most, except that the scattered pattern of scars that marred his bare skin—marking his chest, arms, and legs alike—looked to have been gathered over a healthy lifetime spent with steel in hand. He even had what looked like a freshly-cleaned wound, stitching tracing up from his left elbow. What was more, there were tattoos, too, emblems she recognized only indirectly, from tavern talk and travelers who'd visited her father in years past.

A city mercenary, Ester realized, wondering what it was she had gotten herself tangled up in. The man had a swordsman's body beneath the scars of his trade, lithe and strong, and she ventured a guess that he was over six feet tall judging by the way his bare feet stuck off the end of his bed. She intended to take all of this in critically, gathering what information she could before she did what had to be done, but Ester couldn't help but find herself wondering what color the stranger's eyes were…

Ugh, the more sensible part of her consciousnessgroaned, shaking her out of the momentary distraction.

Cursing under her breath, Ester did her best to focus through the throbbing in the back of her skull. Carefully she bent over, bringing her stolen blade down lightly.

The moment the cool metal touched the stubbled skin of his exposed throat, the man's eyes snapped open, a dark, marine blue that betrayed only the briefest instant of fear before flicking to meet hers. Almost impassively as he lay perfectly motionless, recognizing the situation he was in at once.

Ester felt her confidence wane upon witnessing this rapid assessment, any hope of taking an oafish coward as prisoner dashed, but she couldn't falter now.

"Get up," she spat, driving every ounce of venom she could into the order. The man complied, taking great care to leave his spread hands in the open where she could see them. As he got steadily to his feet, Ester realized she'd underestimated his size. When he stood to his full height, the man had to have been almost a full foot taller than her. It didn't bother her. She had the upper hand, and the larger they were, the slower they moved.

"Who are you?" the stranger asked in a surprisingly calm voice, squinting at her while his eyes adjusted to the darkness of the windowless room.

"No," she snarled, pressing the blade upward ever so slightly to make her point. "*You* don't get to ask the questions, right now. Answer me. Where am I? Where are your friends? The last I remember there were at least five of you."

To her distinct bewilderment, the man's expression relaxed at her words. "The woman." He sounded relieved, and he continued to peer into her face, though Ester could tell he still couldn't see her clearly. "You had us worried, but I'm glad you're awake. As for the men you're talking about, I think they'd consider me anything but a 'friend', if they still could. They're dead." Something like a grim grin played at his lips. "All of them."

Ester's head stabbed angrily, and she did her best to keep the pain from showing on her face. "Dead?" she demanded. "You're implying *you* killed them? On your own? Do you take me for an idiot?"

The stranger shrugged. "You don't have to believe me," he said.

"I don't." Another pulsing ache, but this time Ester ignored it. She eyed the man suspiciously. "Next you'll be telling me you took their ears as trophies, or something equally horrendous."

For some reason, she was relieved when the handsome features before her twisted in revulsion.

"Their *ears*?" he said with a repulsed laugh. "Do I look like some sort of savage?"

"Caught practically naked in the same room as a woman you don't know, scarred and tattooed, all while claiming to have killed five armed men single-handed," Ester drawled sarcastically. "You tell me." She would have rolled her eyes, but she was pretty sure that simple movement might have been too much for the headache that was now moving forward, up her skull. "Enough. You're going to get me out of here. Lead the way, and if any of your friends try to stop us, you'd best tell them I'll carve you a new smile collar to collar."

"I'm happy to show you out," the man said with a crooked smirk. "Not at knife-point, though. We're in a tavern. *The Woodsman's Rest*. It's about a half-day's ride north of where we found you."

"'We'?" Ester repeated with a snap as her fears were confirmed, jerking the knife upward a fraction of an inch more. There were more brigands somewhere beyond the room door. "Who's 'we'? How many of you are there?"

In response to the press of the blade, the stranger's hands rose a little higher. "Just me and my… uh… horse," he told her, looking for the first time a little thrown by her question. "Ryn. He's outside."

"A horse?" Ester demanded eagerly, remembering the black mount from her short fits of wakefulness. "Good. I'll be taking that." She put a hand on his shoulder and stepped closer, hoping the stranger would be intimidated enough not to notice her leaning on him as she fought not to fall over. Her vision was darkening again. She needed to get out, needed to get as far away as possible before she fainted. "Lead me to the stables."

The stranger frowned. "As I said, I'll be happy to show you out," he repeated. "But *not* at the tip of a blade. A blind man could tell you're still not well. One slip, and you're liable to slit my throat on the way down."

"Well wouldn't *that* be a pity?" Ester answered rancorously, wincing and squinting as her view of the mercenary's face shimmered. "All the same, I think I'll be keeping the knife where it is, thank you."

The man's face darkened.

"So I can't convince you otherwise?" he asked, his voice abruptly harder.

Ester sneered, starting to pull on him. "No," she told him firmly, twisting the blade into his neck for emphasis. "You can't."

"Well…" the man grunted, as though in regret. "Then… sorry."

Wham.

She may have been right about his size, but Ester discovered in that moment that that was *all* she'd been right about. His eyes clearly having adjusted to see enough by, the man's hands moved faster than she could follow through the limited light, one snatching up and pressing the wrist that held the knife away, the other catching her by the other hand and twisting her around. The snapped turn pulsed agony through her neck and head, and she gasped as the darkness rushed upward. For all of a second she realized she was pinned in the man's grasp again, pressed against his bare chest with her own arms held harmlessly in a cross over her breasts.

Then, though, the nausea roiled up, and Ester spasmed forward, her stomach heaving.

The last thing she saw before falling away into the blackness again was her own vomit splattering against her captor's bare feet, immediately followed by the man's muttered curse of "Dammit…"

CHAPTER EIGHT

"That is the foul reality of magic. It destroys as easily as it creates. It hides as simply as it reveals. For every great wonder the arcane provides us, there is an equally vile horror. What other reason needed I for outlawing the practice, upon my rightful reclamation of my father's crown? Weaving is a magnificent, terrible power that must be wielded with care, lest its master become seduced by the darker marvels spellwork can produce..."

- Elysia Enus al'Dyor, on the banning of magic in 328p.f.

"Dammit..." Declan grumbled, feeling the sick spew over his toes and the wooden floor. The woman herself went limp, the knife—*his* knife—falling from her hand as legs gave way, and he barely caught her weight in time to keep her from falling face-first into the pool of vomit. Bending down, Declan lifted her gently into his arms before moving to lay her on the bed he had just been forced to vacate. She didn't stir again, even when he shook her gently, and he eventually gave up and took the liberty of wiping the half-elf's mouth and chin clean with a corner of what had been his blanket. Doing the same to his own feet, he considered that he was going to have to tip Dora *very* well to make up for the mess the poor tavern maid was going to have to deal with. It almost got a smile out of him.

Then Declan's mild amusement turned to annoyance, his eyes on the discarded blade still laying on the floor nearby.

That was *twice* in only a little more than a day he'd been taken by surprise because of own his reckless mistakes.

I'm getting soft.

He stood and stooped to snatch up the knife and sword belt, shoving the blade roughly back into its slender sheath while wondering if he and Ryn hadn't spent too long away from the discipline and structure of the guilds. Cursing himself, Declan gathered his still-damp clothes and started getting dressed, pulling his pants, socks, boots, and bloody shirt on in quick order. Choosing not to don his heavy traveling cloak just yet, he slipped his arms through the holes of his sleeveless jerkin, then checked on the woman one final time before turning and shoving his way through the door impatiently, sword belt in his free hand. Taking the stairs down to the common area, he found the room bright and cheerful, illuminated by a mid-morning light that said the storm of the previous night had long-since faded. A scattered assemblage of patrons had claimed seats about the room, including a few Declan had seen the previous night. Some of the loggers were chatting over tankards of mead to his left, the old grey-haired man was gnawing on a lamb bone in the corner, and even the group whose table

Dia had commandeered were among the other quietly eating customers. Inclining his head in this latter foursome's direction in a quick sign of thanks as he reached the bottom steps, Declan turned the corner of the banister and headed for the bar. Brohn stood behind the raised counter, polishing the stained wood with a worn rag, but looked up as Declan approached.

"Late riser, eh?" the bearded innkeeper asked with a chuckle, pausing in his work to toss the cloth over his shoulder and reach under the bar as Declan took a seat opposite him. Tossing his cloak on a stool to his left and setting his sword and belt on the counter, Declan watched the big man pull out a dented brass pitcher and fill a chipped wooden cup with water, which he promptly handed over.

"Would have liked to be later," Declan muttered in answer, accepting the cup with a grateful nod. "Woke up to a nasty—"

A flutter of wings from behind cut him off, and he didn't even have time to turn before a comforting weight settle on his left shoulder.

"Ryn," he said in half-surprised greeting, looking up at the large shape of the hawk who had descended from somewhere in the rafters. "Over our tantrum from last night?"

Hardly, Ryn quipped back privately, stretching his wings out and "accidentally" catching Declan in the back of the head. *I've just decided I have better things to do than pick a fight with a tavern wench.*

"That one's been waitin' up for ya' since 'afore dawn, I think," Brohn said before Declan could formulate any subtle reply, watching the bird with an impressed expression. "Well trained animal ya' got there."

"With some exceptions," Declan nodded, glancing at the hawk sidelong. "Otherwise I'd have roasted him for a road-side supper a long time ago."

Ryn kept a dignified silence at that, but Brohn cracked a grin before gesturing towards Declan's left arm.

"How's the elbow? Is that what woke you?"

Declan shook his head, rolling up his reddened sleeve to show the innkeeper the clean stitching. "Unfortunately not. Like I said yesterday, you do good work. *I*, on the other hand, was fool enough to leave my sword belt out of reach last night."

Brohn looked confused at this, but Declan saw Ryn's head turn sharply towards him. Before either could get out a question, he gave them the long and short of the story. By the end, Brohn was practically crying with laughter. Clutching at his sides, the innkeeper gasped for breath.

"So *ha-ha-ha,* y-ya got he-held *ha-ha,* held up in y-yer *hi-hi-hi,* yer own *bed ha-ha-ha* with your own *knife?!*" he roared, struggling mightily to speak through his mirth. Declan nodded, smirking himself. Brohn's amusement was infectious, and pretty soon Declan was chuckling along, unable to keep it in as he covered his face with both hands in amused exasperation.

Is she awake now? Ryn's voice managed to reach him. Declan shook his head in silent answer. The hawk said nothing more, and as Brohn continued to laugh uproariously—repeating his favorite parts of the story to himself—Declan glanced up. Ryn's head was turned upwards, eyes on the ceiling in the direction of the room the half-elf still remained, and Declan knew the bird was extending his senses. He frowned, unsure if his imagination was tricking him into thinking that his friend looked worried, anxious even.

"What's all this?"

A woman's voice rang clear across the common area, and Declan looked around in time to see Dia poke her head out of the kitchen, undoubtedly drawn by the sound of her husband's booming guffaws. She stared in bewildered astonishment upon catching sight of Brohn, who even at the appearance of his wife didn't seem to be able to get ahold of himself. It took several seconds before he managed to catch his breath enough to repeat Declan's story through wheezing laughs.

By the time he finished, Dia looked anything *but* amused.

"So you're telling me," she began coldly, "that the two of you are down here, having a merry old time, while that poor girl is lying all alone on a bed in your room, *unable to be woken?!*"

Brohn stopped laughing abruptly.

"We was jus' havin' a bit of fun, dearie," he tried to explain before promptly withering under his wife's glare as he mumbled again. "Jus' a bit a' fun…"

Dia, for her part, let out a loud "*hr-umph!*" and stalked out from behind the bar, making for the stairs, undoubtedly off to check on the half-elf. As soon as she was gone, the two men exchanged a look, grinning hesitantly at each other.

"Best be on yer way, lad," Brohn said. "Don't want ta' prod tha' one's patience much more, or she's like ta' serve *us* in the soup tonight."

"Wouldn't want that," Declan agreed readily, standing and lifting his weapons belt from the counter. Cinching it around his waist, he paused, then reached down to fish through his pouch.

Pulling out a single gold coin—almost a tenth of the advanced payment he and Ryn had made on the village contract—he set it on the bar between himself and the innkeep. It was likely worth five times the cost of the meal and room, which Brohn seemed to recognize as soon as he took in the piece.

"Lad, that's—" he started, eyebrows rising, but Declan cut him off.

"It's less than your and Dia's help has been worth to us," he said, gesturing to himself and Ryn as he slid the coin towards the man. "If you think it's too much, then you can gift me a room next time I'm in the area."

For a second or two more, Brohn hesitated. Finally, he took the gold piece tentatively, held it for a moment, then slid it into the pocket of his apron.

"Glad I was careful with those stitches, now," the innkeep grumbled, eyeing Declan's left arm as he proffered a grateful hand.

Declan laughed, accepting it with a firm shake of thanks before turning and heading back for the stairs. "Let's hope I won't need them much longer, if this old man you're sending me out after is half as gifted as you say."

■■■

From his table in the corner of the room, Gonin Whist watched al'Dyor's whelp briefly clasp hands with the innkeeper, exchanging a few last words with a laugh. As the man turned towards the room, the horrid great bird still on his shoulder, Gonin dropped his eyes and pretended to go back to chewing on the soup bone of his lamb stew. When the pair started up the steps, though, he again lifted his gaze, studying the black hawk with particular care.

The creature, though, didn't take notice of him. The woven wards held, the imbued bone talisman about his neck—strung to the same frayed twine from which hung his crystal speaker's charm—hiding his power from the beast, just as the Queen had promised it would.

Gonin took a steadying breath, then settled in to wait, pale grey eyes never so much as flinching away from the landing of the second floor he could barely make out from his vantage across the room. He'd had to calm himself every time he'd seen the man and his monstrous companion. He'd wanted to strike immediately, to cast the two of them into fiery oblivion then and there, but his mistress' words always held his hand, guiding him as they had seen him to the inn ahead of the pair the previous night. It raked at him, tore at him, being shackled as he was, but his trust in her greater wisdom outweighed his confidence in his own abilities. There was a reason she dissuaded him, he knew, a reason she tethered him with her commands. It frightened him, if he was honest with himself.

As strong as Gonin was, and despite the added power of her bone charm, the Queen still feared that *that* was a fight he was not guaranteed to win alone…

There was the *clunk* of booted feet, and Gonin watched silently as the woman innkeep—Dia, he had heard her called by the other patrons—reappeared, leading the way down the stairs in front of the man and his beast, the former of which now carried the limp form of the half-elf they'd arrived with yesterday in his arms. Gonin had to keep his face in check as annoyance welled up in his chest, seeing the unconscious woman again.

Months of preparation to see his mistress' pet was fed, all gone to waste in the course of a single night…

Shoving the irritation aside, Gonin's long, lank hair shifted over the edge of his grey-brown mantle as he followed the group's descent, then watched them navigate the length of the common area until Dia opened the inn door for the man and his burden. There the two held a last brief conversation, the plump woman apparently offering directions before they exchanged their farewells, and the door was closed again.

Gonin didn't bother watching the woman return to her husband behind the counter, his interest in the couple having dissipated the night before after he'd come to the conclusion the two were nothing more than pawns in this game the Queen was playing out. Instead, he stared at nothing, extending his senses only slightly, straining to feel through the thick timber walls of the inn.

He didn't have to be patient long. A brief shiver of magic told him the creature had changed forms, and not two minutes later the rapid strikes of hooves fading down the forest road reached his ears.

With a nasty smile, Gonin drew back his power, gathering it to himself, and began to weave.

The Purpose formed quickly, the shifting blue-black light of the spellwork invisible in his gnarled hands to any but his own eyes. Quickly he threaded the simple command into the magics, forming and shaping it. When it was done, he shattered the ethereal entity with a thought, cracking it into a score of smaller shards, each carrying their own will. With a flick of his wrist, he banished the fractured spell through the wall to his left.

Getting to his feet, Gonin's smile lingered as he dropped a couple copper pieces on the table and made for the door, feeling his enchantments chase the distant sound of galloping, bearing with them their hungry, singular need.

Devour.

CHAPTER NINE

"There is a stock misunderstanding among the gentry of our country that all who practice the arcane arts can and should be classified as one and the same. It is an understandable confusion, to an extent. To the simple mind of the commoner, any display of magical ability must appear something along the lines of miraculous. To them, there is little difference between a mage who diverts a river to assist in watering dying crops, and one who summons up a three-day storm. These examples, likely, are equally astounding to the uneducated eye, and understandably so.

We who have had the fortune of that otherwise lacking education, on the other hand, know better. Beyond the classification of arcanic affinity, beyond the labeling of auramancy, verdamancy, pyromancy, and the like, it is to our benefit to equally be aware of the tiers of ability in our kingdom's spellcrafters. One should not, after all, confuse a college acolyte in their first year of study with the King's own court magus, less the former die of embarrassment and the latter strike one from the face of the earth with little more than a thought for such an insult..."

-*On the Study of Magic*, author unknown, c. 300p.f.

When Bonner yr'Essel was troubled, the entirety of the forest shivered in mirrored concern.

Three days, now. Three days his daughter had been absent from their home. Ordinarily Bonner wouldn't have been so worried. Esteria had left their clearing a hundred times before, sometimes taking to the outside world for weeks at a time. She enjoyed exploring the deeper woodlands and farming communities nearby, occasionally going so far as the High and Low Roads to meet and speak with travelers from all across the nation. It was her way of understanding the wider nature of the land, and she only steered clear of the larger nearby cities of Kanrys and Ranheln at his and her mother's insistence.

Still, on those occasions, Esteria had always left word of her departure, as well as some indication of when she would return. This time, if anything, had been even more deliberate, as she had taken leave bearing the responsibility of a grim task. For months she had been returning from her excursions with tales of disappearances, of vanishing villagers from all the nearby hamlets. At first, they had chalked the trouble up to wolves and the occasional wild warg that strayed too far south.

Then Esteria had come back with tales of a third child being taken, and Bonner yr'Essel had decided it was time to intervene.

It had taken them two weeks of searching, of his scrying and weaving whispers into the forest and her putting her mother's training to use before they'd pieced together even some trail of the kidnappers. It proved a more troublesome task than either had been expecting, and Bonner regretted now having chalked up their difficulties to any particular skill on the criminals' parts. Still, they had agreed together the work shouldn't have claimed more than a day and a night.

Three days, the fearful thought came again.

Bonner's weave trembled as his concentration faltered, and he pressed the distraction aside with the iron discipline he had instilled in himself too many centuries ago. Being worried was a father's right, to be sure, but it would help Esteria little if his magics failed under the strain of something as base as parental sentiments.

Bonner cursed himself. Perhaps if he had been less diverted in his *initial* search, he would have sensed the tinge of power flickering in the trail they had been hounding, the near-invisible hint of a dark, guiding hand in the action of the kidnappers...

Perhaps he might not have been so foolish as to allow Esteria to set off on the hunt on her own...

The weave shook again, and Bonner clenched his jaw, solidifying it once more. This time he did not allow himself to be drawn away, did not allow his thoughts to disturb the spellcrafting he had been at since the early hours of the morning. He stood with his eyes closed in the smaller clearing some ways west of the glen in which he had first made a home for himself and Arathia, built beyond the reach of common man and all his follies. His hands were outstretched, and he knew without seeing that a dozen tendrils of power undulated from every finger, faint in the light of the fading day. They snaked their way into the trees, connecting him to the vital aura of the forest itself piece by piece. It was a spell that was neither as accurate nor quick as scrying would have been, but given enough time Bonner's consciousness would be connected to the uniform life of the western woodlands. If his spirit held, by tomorrow night he would share a presence with the earth itself for some hundreds of miles in every direction. His senses would be weak, practically useless to search for much of anything, but Esteria was of his own blood. He was confident he would find her, in this fashion.

After that, whoever or whatever had taken part in her disappearance would know the wrath of powers from an era in which magic was *anything* but forgotten...

Already Bonner's awareness extended a dozen miles in every direction, and he willed it further, feeding the spell with all the magic he could provide. The largest details of the forest opened up one by one, revealing themselves to his weave. Here the churning force of a river. There the rising swell of a great hill. He ignored them all, focusing, seeking his daughter's presence with all his might.

Bonner was so intent on doing so, in fact, that when he suddenly found it, the sheer presence of the being that accompanied her nearly shattered the fragile weave into nothingness.

Bonner staggered and gasped, barely keeping to his feet. Relief took him first, feeling Esteria's wavering aura approaching, but the creature she was with was like a weight on his mind even through the indistinct sensations of this weaker spell. It brought him down, pulling him towards the ground like it needed nothing more than the force of its monstrous existence to crush his will into nothingness.

What's more, Bonner *knew* this presence, and knew it well.

Ryndean?

There was a third with them, he realized then, and the moment of closer examination Bonner spared the person—the *man*, he registered—confirmed his astonished inner eye. A seed flickered inside this one, he could see, an echo of the greater power of the beast accompanying him.

Blood did not lie.

Bonner let out a wheezing laugh of relief, straining to cope with the torrent of information that had taken hold of his mind all at once. Esteria was in good hands, and a friend from a past life looked to have made himself known once again. Something like anticipation bloomed where worry had only seconds before taken hold, and Bonner made to release the spell little by little, intent on scrying out the trio's more specific position.

Before he managed to do so, however, yet another force broke the boundaries of his extended mind.

The black smell of death filled his nose and mouth, and Bonner retched, unable to stop himself. He watched, horrified, as the chasing Purpose hounded his daughter and her strange companions. He felt, too, the familiarity of that banned magic, the notes and tenor of the weave that marked its maker.

In it, he saw the very hand which had played a part in Ester's initial disappearance.

Dispensing with safety, Bonner banished his spell with a snap of his wrists, opening his eyes. The sudden severing of the link he'd held for more than twelve hours was reeling, and he fell on all fours to the clearing floor, but that suited him just fine. Even before his vision had stopped spinning Bonner was reaching out, two fingers tracing rapid shapes across the earth, leaving the grass smoking and charred like he'd run over the blades with a burning stick. With the practice of ten thousand repetitions the spell came into being under the dimming gaze of a slowly setting sun. Slamming a palm into the weave he activated it with a pulse of power, feeling his consciousnesssoar skyward like his soul had taken wing. The useless speaker's charm he always kept on his person slipped from the folds of his robes, and he clutched at it with one hand for comfort. More than ever, in that moment he wished that he could yet have had the comfort of Arathia's words through the crystal.

All the magic in the world, after all, didn't stop Bonner yr'Essel from knowing he would be too late.

CHAPTER TEN

"I recall—distinctly—the day my eyes were opened to the harsh truth of my reality. I see my father's spilled blood in my dreams, smell the fires of my burning home in my nightmares. I thought I was aware, thought I was informed. I was ally to elves, mages, and even dragons. I was the confidant of many, and the friend of more. I thought myself awoken to the strife and hardships of my people, to the desperate needs of the gentry and the jealous desires of the nobility. Forward, always, I looked. Forward at the simple, plain realm I thought was the extent of my world. I never saw the knives that lingered behind us, those cruel, covetous blades which cut my father down before me and cleaved through the veil of blissful oblivion which had previously covered my eyes.

I do not envy any man who might suffer a harsher awakening to the foulness that lingers in our world..."

-Amherst Sehren al'Dyor, First Prince of Viridian, c. 350p.f.

It took them an hour or so to reach the trail Dia had directed them towards as they'd left *The Woodsman's Rest*, Ryn galloping back south along the muddy, leaf-strewn road, Declan back to holding the half-elf tight to his chest in the saddle before him. The previous day's rain had indeed ended, and he breathed easier for it, wondering if his sanity would have withstood another stormy journey. The bright, cloudless day that had replaced yesterday's grey gale was a welcome change, and the cool breeze that shivered through the trees around them did wonders to dry his still-damp clothes. All the same, he worried the entire time they rode in relative silence, only speaking up occasionally when Ryn queried about some detail or marker Dia had mentioned.

After all, even when the innkeeper had gone in to dress the half-elf once more in her hunting tunic, she hadn't stirred…

Finding the head, they turned due east, Ryn taking the uneven path through the undergrowth faster than any horse aught, and before long they were cantering across the denser parts of the woods, deeper and deeper into the maples and pines and oaks. The forest rapidly thickened around them, the sounds of the wind and birds and larger animals crashing through the bushes settling over everything. The humidity of the long-gone rain clung to the air, but an early front of fall chill had overcome the late-summer heat, balancing the staggered beat of the sun through the leaves overhead. It was a pleasant morning, to say the least, and any traveler would have been in his right mind to slow his mount and breathe in the wonder of the verdant, rolling undergrowth around him.

Declan, instead, couldn't help but glance down every few minutes or so, taking in the smooth, slack face of the woman whose name he hadn't even been able to catch during their morning's brief altercation.

You should worry less.

Declan looked up at Ryn's words. The horse was still moving at a brisk pace, sleek head forward, but all the same he seemed to have sensed his rider's trepidation.

Indeed, even without looking back, he kept on.

She woke up once. That's a good sign. At the very least we can assume she'll survive long enough for us to find the hermit.

"You're awfully confident," Declan said with a doubtful snort. "I'm still not convinced this old man exists, much less can meet the expectations Brohn was hawking. And where do *you* get off telling me not to worry?" He eyed the back of Ryn's mane with a raised brow. "Don't think I buy for a *minute* that you weren't as concerned as me the whole ride yesterday? You checked on her so many times I thought you were going to lame yourself."

That was before she demonstrated enough vitality to threaten your life, the horse answered, finally looking back with a teasing gleam in his gilded gaze. *With your own blade, I might add.*

Declan grunted, still none-too-pleased with the morning's events. "It'll teach me to sleep with a knife under my pillow…" he muttered, half to himself.

It should *teach you not to leave your weapons laying around for anyone to pick up,* Ryn retorted, looking ahead again. *I thought I'd taught you better than that.*

Declan snorted this argument away. "I hadn't slept in a full day, I'd barely eaten, and I thought this one—" he jostled the half-elf lightly to make his point "—had one foot in the grave. I wasn't exactly expecting an ambush."

Despite his pace, Declan could have sworn Ryn shrugged. *Expect the worst, and you'll be prepared for any situation.*

"I'm starting to feel thirteen again," Declan grumbled, using his free hand to brush aside the low bough of an oak tree that would have caught him in the head. "Back when you had me swinging at branches with a stick and yelling at me to stand up taller and move my feet more."

I never yelled *at you,* Ryn said indignantly, taking a dipping bend in the path before splashing across a narrow stream. *Cassandra, on the other hand…*

Declan winced internally, imagining what his former mentor and superior would have said if she found out he'd allowed himself to be caught with his pants down. The Iron Wind emblem on his chest itched suddenly, and he had to consciously keep himself from scratching at it.

"It's a good thing you don't talk to anyone but me," he said dryly. "Otherwise I might have had to sell you to a glue maker to ensure this is *never* spoken of again."

He heard Ryn's light laugh echo in the back of his mind, and he smiled, relaxing ever so slightly.

They spent the remainder of the morning riding in comfortable conversation, making up for the silence they'd been forced to hold in the lashing storm of the previous day. As the sun crested its peak in the clear sky, they stopped for a quick rest along the edge of a small, nameless lake, breaking just long enough for the pair of them to grab a drink, lunch on several handfuls of nuts and berries Ryn scoured out nearby, and for Declan to try and trickle a little water between the half-elf's dry lips. Succeeding only in making her choke and cough, he gave up quickly and called for a return to the trail, heading further into the woods.

As the afternoon came and went, the sunlight sweeping through the shifting branches above starting to dim, Declan's skepticism began to bloom in full. With no better plan, he'd been willing to follow the trail as Dia instructed, but with night fast approaching he couldn't help but begin to wonder *how* in the Mother's name they were supposed to find the old recluse, much less how *he* might find *them*. He considered saying so aloud, but Ryn was very clearly unperturbed by the lengthening shadows twisting and crossing over the path before them. The horse drove forward with an almost-irritating confidence while the forest shifted from bright green to somber orange in the early setting of the sun. As the sun began to slip behind the canopy to the west, Declan studied the land around them, half-hoping that some wizened form might come hobbling out from between the gnarled trunks, beckoning them mysteriously to follow as it leaned heavily on a gnarled walking stick. It was a stupid expectation, he knew, but all the same he couldn't stop himself from starting to see outlines forming beneath the low-hanging branches, his mind twisting them into being from the descending darkness. He sighed audibly, giving up as they started to run out of daylight, and was about to turn towards Ryn, thinking to suggest that they start searching for a campsite for the night.

As he did so, a passing shape caught the corner of his eye, and Declan stiffened as they rode on.

Beneath him, Ryn must have felt the sudden change in his body language, because he looked around in concern. *What is it?* the horse asked, slowing down ever so slightly.

"I'm not sure," Declan answered cautiously, his eyes behind them, back in the direction he'd thought he'd seen the figure. This far in the woods it wasn't uncommon to run across wolves or deer or even bears, but the outline he'd caught distinctly belonged to none of those animals.

Still, it could have been anything. Maybe a twisted sapling or a—

Declan cursed. A second form flit by, half-hidden between the darkening trees, but this time he was sure he'd caught a glimpse of it.

"Is there anyone around us?" he asked over the clomp of the horse's hooves. In answer, Ryn reduced his pace even further, dropping from a quick trot to a walk, then finally to a stop. His head didn't move, his eyes fixed on the ground before him, and Declan knew he was focusing, reaching out to feel the world around them. In the absence of the hoofbeats the stillness of the evening took over, eerie in its silence.

Its silence…?

"It's quiet," Declan said under his breath, making Ryn's ears twitch. "Why is it so quiet?" Instinctively he shifted his hips, making sure the hilt of his sword was free of the woman's hanging arms.

Beneath him, it was Ryn's turn to tense, and the horse nodded slowly even as he peered around into the trees. *Agreed. But there's nothing there…*

For nearly a minute they waited like that, Ryn continuing to scan the woods around them, Declan still looking back, in the direction they'd come. Together they listened, taking in the frightening absence of woodland noise as the sun continued to fail.

Nothing. Just like Ryn had said.

"Maybe I'm still tired," Declan finally grumbled, feeling the tautness leave him as he took a breath. "Sorry." He turned to Ryn with an apologetic look. "Light must be playing tricks on—"

Declan. Draw your sword.

The way Ryn gave the order eliminated all inclination to hesitate. Dropping the reins, Declan reached around the women between his legs and drew the blade with a quick tug, wincing as the scrape of steel against cork and wood cut like a bell-toll across the quiet.

"What is it?" he asked in a low voice once the weapon was free. "I thought you said there was noth—?"

A noise from behind them, in the direction he'd thought he'd seen the forms, made him stop. A shuffling, scraping sound, like that of feet being dragged through brush and leaves.

Declan whirled as best he could with the half-elf against his chest, sword held high. Through the deepening red and yellow of dusk he peered, studying the woods as the top of the blade trailed from trunk to trunk before him. At first, yet again, only the empty silence answered his steady eyes. Nothing moved except the leaves in the wind, kicking up and tugging at his long hair. All the same, the sound kept on, growing ever closer, and Declan finally settled on a narrow space between the bare bodies of two pines, some dozen feet away.

Then the creature dragged itself into view, and Declan recoiled in horror.

Out of the woods stepped a woman, or what little was left of a woman. The thing was skeletal in appearance, the sharp angles of its frame outlined in old rags, clothing that had rotted and torn away in slivers with time. What skin and flesh remained clung to the body like a putrid sheet, drawn and tight over its form, colorless and decaying. Yellowed bone could be seen clearly where insects and animals had torn into the thing, and its horrible face gaped in what could only be described as a soundless scream, jaw half-hanging from its head, dead sockets filled with translucent, milky eyes.

A walking corpse.

Ghoul! Ryn snarled in a very un-horse-like fashion, half-rearing to turn about on the thing. *Whatever you do, don't let it get ahold of you!*

Declan barely heard him. He was staring, open-mouthed, at the shambling, dead woman, his mind unable to comprehend what he was seeing. The cadaver moved towards them with hunched, stumbling steps, like it only possessed the faintest concepts of how to use its limbs. Its gaze was empty, transfixed on the pair of them, utterly ignoring the uneven ground even as it approached. It walked on legs that were mostly bone, feet dragging along the ground with every step it took. As it inched closer, flashes—like someone else's memories—dashed across Declan's mind, filling his head with glimpses of scenes he didn't comprehend. Snowy fields choked with corpses. The bodies of his enemies rising to turn on their former comrades. Iron-cold hands reaching out to—

DECLAN! BEHIND US! ON OUR REAR!

Ryn's mental bellow ripped Declan back into reality. The warning gave him just enough time to turn and block the clumsy blow of a rusted broadsword from a second undead man, one that had come fumbling out of the woods at their back. Their weapons met with a *clang* of metal on metal, and Declan turned the strike aside with surprising difficulty, the corpse's swing carrying a strength he wouldn't have imagined possible. A grinding thrust, and he locked hilts with the tarnished weapon, finding himself staring into another pair of opaque eyes, his stomach roiling as the stench of the creature filled his mouth and nose. Forcing himself into the moment, Declan ripped the sword out of the creature's hand with a practiced twist, sending it spinning into the trees. Before he even heard the blade hit the ground, he reversed his swing to bring his own weapon about in a horizontal slash from above, aiming at the thing's neck, putting as much force in the strike as he could, given his awkward positioning. He felt wet flesh give and the remnants of old bone shatter, and he shouted in victory as the steel made a clean blow of it, cleaving the head right from the cadaver's skeletal shoulders.

An instant later, the shout died in his throat.

The undead man still stood, unfazed by its sudden decapitation, and began to reach for him with claw-like fingers, the skin having rotted away long ago to leave nothing but pale tendons clinging at its stained bones. With a grunt Declan sheared off both hands with another blow and kicked out, landing a boot in the thing's ribs and knocking it to the ground.

Strike at the chest! Ryn's urging rang through his head, and he felt the horse sidestepping as he attempted to get away from a third corpse that had appeared off the trail just east of them, cutting off any easy escape. *At the chest, Declan!*

With no better advice to go by, Declan brought his sword around reflexively, ramming the better half of the steel's length through the breast of the first corpse, which had finally reached them. The undead woman's head jerked back when the blade impaled her, and she reached up, clutching at the weapon with dead hands. An unearthly wail echoed through the trees, tearing at the relative silence of the implausible fight. Looking down at the sword, Declan yelped in alarm, nearly releasing the hilt as blue-black flames licked out of the undead's pierced flesh, trailing along the weapon's edge. Wrenching it free of the splintering bone, he watched in horrified fascination as the creature tumbled to her knees, clawing at her chest and the hole from which the inky fire was rapidly rising. The ghostly scream held, rending the air, then pitched. As it did, the cadaver erupted into a dark inferno, collapsing to the ground to thrash violently while the flames consumed it.

In a handful of seconds, all that was left of the corpse was an uneven, charred patch in the moss and grass of the forest floor.

By now, though, the shock of the moment had been replaced in Declan's heart by a cold need to survive, and his eyes didn't linger on the blackened stain. Turning back to the front, he faced the third corpse. The creature was shuffling steadily closer, empty hands held out, clawing at the air. Letting go of the woman for a moment, Declan grasped the reins with his left hand, sword still clutched in his right, and gave his knees a signaling squeeze. Immediately Ryn reared back onto his hind legs, kicking out at the undead. Though his view was now blocked, Declan heard the distinctly hollow *thumps* of hooves striking rotten flesh, making out a decayed head flying off into the woods, white hair whipping about it. A heavier *thud* told him that the creature had fallen to the ground, but before it had a chance to get up Ryn came down hard, driving both front legs through its fragile ribcage. The mournful wail came again, and the stallion leapt nimbly aside as flames bloomed out of where the corpse's heart might have been, devouring it from the inside out.

Not bothering to wait, Declan brought Ryn around to face the last creature, the one he had already partially dealt with. The headless undead was struggling to rise now, pushing itself up with the rotting stumps he had left it for hands. When it found its feet, it immediately shambled around and began staggering towards them once again.

This time, neither Declan nor Ryn were willing to grant it the opportunity to threaten them again.

Not a word had to be shared between the companions as Declan squeezed his knees again. More than a decade on the road together proved itself when Ryn launched forward at a full gallop, trusting the rest to the man on his back. Declan's blade flashed downward in a sweeping arc when they thundered past the corpse, hewing its body half-in-two as it ripped all the way through, splitting the stained fabric of its clothes and brittle bones beneath with ease. The flash of blue-black flames lit up the darkening forest once more, and Declan flicked his blade clean of the greyish blood splattered across the steel while Ryn cantered to a stop some thirty feet up the path. Together they turned to watch the creature thrashing about on the ground as the flames consumed it.

When the vile scream had finally echoed itself into nothingness, Declan turned his attention on his friend.

"Ryn," he managed to get out through heavy breaths, "what in the MOTHER'S *BLOODY NAME* WAS THAT?!"

For a long time, Ryn didn't answer. Eventually, though, the horse twisted his big head around, fixing Declan with a single white-gold eye.

If he'd been about to say something, though, it was forgotten as his entire being went rigid.

BEHIND YOU! the stallion bellowed, trying to twist himself around again. *LOOK OUT BEHIND Y—!*

Too late.

With the creaking sound of old joints and straining flesh, Declan felt something take hold of his jerkin, dragging him back and out of the saddle. Letting go of the woman more out of instinct than sense, he barely managed to get out a terrified yell before hitting the ground with a heavy *thud* that knocked the wind out of him. His sword left his grasp. Cold hands tightened around his waist. In a panic Declan scrambled to draw his knife, but the handle slipped through his shaking fingers and the blade tumbled to the ground. As he felt about in terror, trying to find it, he became aware of shapes looming up around him. From some distant place he heard Ryn's animalistic screams, the stallion's voice ringing through his head in panic even as the corpses descended. Declan tried to answer, but in that moment the creature that had pulled him to the ground lurched upward and came into view. Its dead features were wet and white, its empty sockets devoid even of eyes. Declan howled in angry fear, ending his desperate search for the knife in favor of pummeling the corpse with his bare fists. Knuckles struck moist flesh, sloughing it off. The thing's jaw *cracked* and fell away. Overhead the other forms bore down, clawed, skeletal fingers reaching out. Declan shouted in terror, his will to fight redoubling. He felt the icy touch of death against his skin, felt bone start to scrape and dig at his cheeks. He screamed one last time, kicking and thrashing as his view of the dusk-lit forest become obscured by cold, lifeless faces.

And then, seemingly out of nowhere, a roaring torrent of sound ripped across the dusk like a lingering thunderclap.

WOOSH!

With all the power of maelstrom, a searing eruption of brilliant white light devoured the humid coolness of the evening air. It rocked the world with the strength of a battering ram, colliding with the throng of corpses hovering over Declan and blasting them into bone and ash. Even several feet below it, the billowing force was enough to catch him in its grasp, and Declan had just enough time to make out a spewing column of roiling ivory *fire* before he was sent tumbling across the ground, landing heavily on his stomach. Shutting his eyes tight against the blinding light, he held still, covering his head with his arms, howling against the pain and shock of the heat, not understanding what was happening. Several blistering seconds the roaring flames held, screaming overhead, sounding like some wild beast that had been let loose to devour the earth and heavens whole.

Then, abruptly, it was gone.

For half-a-minute Declan didn't move from his spot on the forest floor, coughing and blinking through the sudden smoke that hung thick in the air around him. Finally, a crackling sound told him that fire flickered nearby, which was enough to get him staggering up onto his knees, then his feet.

Looking around, Declan blinked in astonishment through the heavy haze.

"All Her Graces…" was all he managed to get out.

Before him, in an expanding wedge that extended some hundred feet westward, the forest was gone. Completely, utterly, absolutely *gone*. In its place, succeeding the life and lush greenery that had been trees and brush and woodland, nothing but charred ground and the blackened husks of thick stumps held sway. Flames still licked along the edges of the destruction, residue of whatever it was that had turned the scene to soot and smoke. Of the undead, nothing remained. It was as though they had never been, any hint of bone or flesh or cruel, decaying faces vaporized in the heat.

For a long time Declan gaped at the destruction, his mind struggling to comprehend. It was too much. Too much. The corpses. The fire. His consciousnesscouldn't handle it. He could feel something strain within him, something begin to stretch at the seams.

That, unfortunately, was also the moment he became aware of the presence looming behind him.

It started as tingling along the back of Declan's neck, like he was standing in the residual charge of a lightning strike. Something was there, something powerful and incomprehensible. The knowledge turned his skin to gooseflesh, and there was a heartbeat in which Declan stood petrified, the sensation redoubling when he made out heavy, billowing breath from somewhere above him.

Above...? A small, frightened voice spoke up nervously from the back of his mind.

Slowly, moment by moment, Declan turned, every inch of his body telling him not to, telling him to stop, to flee. All the same, his need to know overpowered his fear.

Overpowered, that is, until he saw what it was that stood behind him.

His mind still reeling, Declan barely had time to register a monstrous black figure towering before him, almost indistinct in the thick smoke. Rising up some fifteen feet above his head, the thing's inky scales he could make out gleamed blood-red as the true colors of the sunset poured over the scene in the absence of the heavy blanket of branches and leaves that had been swallowed by the all-devouring fire. Declan's gaze, unbidden, climbed upwards, noting little of the titanic creature as he sought the beast's face, hoping and fearing at the same time.

Then he met its eyes, and the world bottomed out beneath Declan's feet.

A torrent of memories, none of them his own, erupted across his consciousness. He staggered, gasping for air as a thousand images of skies and lands and blood-soaked battles crushed him. Mountains and fields, forests and rivers. Everything passed by far below as he felt the wet coldness of mist and clouds whip across his face. To either side of him the great wings of the beast thrummed against the winter air as they traced the horizon together.

"You..." Declan chocked out, feeling the world continue to twist beneath him, and he started to have trouble distinguishing what was real and what was dream. "It... *You...*"

At his words, the massive creature before him blinked in surprise, bringing the colossal, indistinct form of its head down through the smoke and haze.

You know me? it demanded with that all-too-familiar voice. *How?*

As its shocked questions rang through Declan's head, though, an entirely new wave of images crushed into him like the words had opened the floodgates. Buzzards spiraling down over fields of beastmen and armor-clad corpses. A pretty woman with brown eyes much like his own—*his own?*—cursing his cowardice. A delicate ring, its carved black stone engraved with a coat he couldn't distinguish, set into a golden band formed in the shape of twin swords slotted behind matching shields.

That was when everything started to fade, darkness beginning to churn at the edges of Declan's vision as more memories sped by in a blur.

"Too much..." Declan heard himself mutter, losing the battle to the distant recollections of what felt like another reality. "Too much..."

And then he was falling away, the ground rushing up to meet him, the shining, white-gold eyes of the beast above fading into blackness, the first two twinkling stars of the coming night. As his mind gave in, he heard that voice—that familiar voice—calling out his name, the shouts echoing in the infinite darkness of a blissful oblivion.

Declan! DECLAN...!

CHAPTER ELEVEN

It was snowing again, as it so often did in the depths of winter. Declan loved the snow, but after any length of time amongst the grey of the peaks, the endless curtain of white tended to get dull. They were patrolling high above the mountains in the earliest light of the new morning, circling the Reaches in search of lingering Vigil soldiers that might have been overlooked. This most recent wave of Aletha's men had been led by Sevus Kant himself, and had taken three days and nights' hard battle to rout. They'd failed to take the noble's head, and despite the darkness, Declan and Ryndean both had needed the emptiness of the skies to vent their frustrations at the missed opportunity.

That being said, they'd been making passes for over two hours now, and even dragons got bored.

Taking a break from scouring the wind-swept bluffs, Declan chuckled into the snowy wind when he looked to his friend. The beast was gazing up at the clouds, distracted for the moment, wings beating absently and automatically at his sides. Even without words Declan knew where Ryndean's mind had gone, and he gave a short pull on the reins with one gloved hand. The tug got the dragon's attention as intended, and when he turned his great head about to look questioningly over his shoulder, Declan pointed upward, making the suggestion plain.

The dragon's face broke into a ferocious grin that showed off every one of his fire-bleached fangs.

At once Declan pressed himself flat in the long saddle, tapping Ryndean's side with an open palm when he was ready. Immediately the beast twisted into a plunging roll, tucking his wings, and for five wrenching seconds they plummeted earthward, turning like a top. When they had the momentum needed, the dragon quit the spin, spread his wings, and arched so that the force of gravity slung them into a pendulum arc from a fall into a great, soaring ascent. Declan felt hard muscle and black scale stretch and pulse with each beat behind his legs. They rose, climbing at a near vertical angle, faster and faster. The wind whipped by in a howl. They were in the clouds now. The freezing vapor soaked Declan through, its chill forcing its way into his armor and clothes. He didn't complain. Bonner could see him dry later, and he knew the temporary cold was well worth the treasure they were hunting.

And then, in an explosion of clinging mist, they were through.

As usual, Declan was forced to hold a gauntleted hand up before his eyes, shielding them until they could adjust to the blinding light. Once they had, he brought down his arm to stare out at the wondrous world so few of his kind would ever have a chance to be privy to.

Below them, a sea of clouds stretched out endlessly in all directions, shifting with the fathomless patience only nature could provide, tinted orange and purple and red by the distant eastern glow of the rising sun. Even the usually-black dragon beneath him reflected the thousand colors of autumn leaves as they hovered there, Ryndean beating his great wings steadily to stay level with the far-off horizon.

A Mark of Kings

Smiling at the sheer beauty of that realm beyond man's knowledge, Declan tapped his companion's side once again, and with echoed roars of pleasure they shot off over the clouds together, chasing the infinite painting of dawn.

CHAPTER TWELVE

When is he going to wake, Bonner?

Ryn's muffled voice gently lifted Declan from his dreams. His head spun as he blinked, trying to get his bearings.

"I don't *know.*" A different voice this time—an older man's, and one he didn't recognize—grumbled in response. "And I wish you'd stop asking! That's got to be the third time in the last ten minutes."

"Ryn, leave him alone." A woman's, now, and one Declan *did* know, though the last time he had heard her speak it had been with much less amiable tones. "You know Father's doing the best he can."

There was an audible—if reluctant—grunt of ascent, and Declan decided it was time to shake off the grogginess of a sleep that felt like it had been almost *too* deep.

Then again, when his vision started to come into focus, he froze, abruptly questioning whether or not he was still dreaming.

Gone were the dusky tones of the trees in sunset. Gone was the fire and smoke and the ashen ground of the ruined forest. In their stead, the bright light of a sunny day streamed through an empty window frame in the wall to his right, illuminating the small room he found himself in. Overhead, a ceiling unlike anything he could have ever imagined hung, its belly jagged and green, with dancing patterns that looked like spined leaves. Declan squinted and blinked in confusion, reminded of the body of a heavily-grown evergreen.

Half-a-second later, he realized with a hiss of disbelief that it *was* an evergreen. *Several,* in fact, a number of narrow spruces growing at an angle over the chamber so that their spindly branches intertwined to form verdant rafters.

Declan sat up so sharply that the room started to whirl around him again.

He was seated in a comfortable bed, fully clothed except for his boots and belt. Several heavy furs fell away from him as he jolted upward, slipping onto the feather-stuffed mattress beneath him. Kicking them free, he made to swing his legs off the bed only to register with another shock that it was raised a foot or so off the ground by a delicate cage of what could only have been thin, entwining *roots.* With wide eyes he took in the plants, which looked to be growing right out of the floor, and he gave a choke of amazement when he saw that said 'floor' wasn't a floor at all, but rather a carpet of lush, rich grass. Instinctively he pulled his bare feet up, like the blades might try to snare his toes, his heart thundering in his chest.

"W-what the...?" he stuttered in incomprehension, looking around.

Aside from the unbelievable ceiling and floor, the room was a plain sort of space, furnished only by the bed he sat in and a simple, three-tiered dresser along the far wall that had a wide, hammered bronze mirror hanging over it. Noting with a wash of relief that his weapons belt sat innocently atop the dresser—complete with sheathed sword and knife—Declan forced himself to take a moment, to allow his heart to settle.

When he was ready, he lowered his feet again, tentatively easing them into the grass.

The ground was soft, almost like down, and it might have been delightful had Declan not been so perplexed by his surroundings. Steeling himself, he stood slowly, edging his weight onto the floor little by little, half-fearing the incredible illusion would shatter and he would tumble down into nothingness at any moment. Once standing, he hesitantly let go of the bed, tensing instinctively, only for nothing extraordinary to happen.

Taking a steadying breath, Declan finally started to gather himself.

The still-murmuring voices were coming from the room next to his, reaching him through an unremarkable wooden door set into a distinctly more-remarkable arched frame. It, too, appeared to be made of living trees—a pair of saplings this time—growing parallel about three feet apart before tapering and twisting together to corkscrew up through the leafy roof.

Seeing this, Declan officially started to wonder if his encounter in the woods had driven him mad.

Shaking that disquiet concern, he moved quickly to take up his weapons from the dresser, belting them on with practiced ease. Finding his boots on the floor nearby, he bent down to pick them up, leaning against the dresser as he pulled them on one after the other. This done, he was about to make for the door when something odd caught his eye, and he glanced towards the mirror, frowning at his own reflection.

His shirt sleeve had been repaired...

Sure enough, looking down, Declan saw with some surprise that the left sleeve he'd torn to make a tourniquet two nights prior—if it had indeed *only* been two nights—had been expertly cleaned and mended, the missing cloth replaced and threaded in carefully. In the same moment, Declan noted abruptly that his arm didn't hurt. Puzzled, he started rolling the sleeve up, wondering if Brohn's stitches had been so tight he'd lost feeling around the wound.

He stiffened when he revealed his elbow, gaping for a full five seconds before managing to pull up the rest of the cloth, exposing his upper arm and the remainder of the cut.

Or, rather, what had been a cut...

The injury was gone. Vanished, stitches and all. In its place, a thin, narrow scar line that might have been nothing more than a poorly-healed scratch remained, pale against his tanner skin. Declan choked as he looked at it, uncomprehending. His mind reeled, trying to make sense of it—of *everything*—as he looked again around the room. For nearly a minute he stood frozen, eyes flicking from the grassy earth to the canopy ceiling to the root-bed.

Finally, they fell on the strange frame of the door again.

There was only one way to go, if he wanted answers…

Letting the sleeve fall again, Declan's feet stuttered beneath him as he made for the room's exit, nearly tripping in nervous trepidation. Reaching it, he took hold of a plain rope handle set along its edge, hesitating yet again as he made out the voices taking pause in the next room, likely hearing him move.

Unable to keep himself from putting a hand on the hilt of his sword, Declan pulled the door open with a nervous jerk.

The chamber he stepped into was much more spacious than the one he'd just left. It was an even rectangle, the longer walls—made of stone and timber—broken up by several more doors undoubtedly leading into other rooms, while the shorter walls—at opposite ends—rose only knee-high before opening onto a view of an expansive glade surrounded by forest in all directions. Overhead, the angled trees that comprised the ceiling interlocked in an unbroken pattern, reminding Declan of the Mother's Word cathedral in Aletha.

What drew his attention most, though, was the wide, uneven table that took up the center of the chamber, carved from the split trunk of what looked to have once been a single old oak.

That, and the trio seated around it, all watching him expectantly, making Declan stop short to take them in.

One of the figures was distinctly familiar. The half-elf met his gaze with a smile that might have made his knees weak in any other situation, her brilliant green eyes bright and wide, her silver-gold hair gathered in a braided plait along the top and back of her head. She looked clean and content, right at home in the strange house, to the point where one would never have guessed she'd recently spent the better part of at least two days unconscious and bleeding.

Countering the woman's familiarity, at her left an older, unknown man sat patiently watching Declan in quiet contemplation, his own shining emerald eyes a mirror image of the half-elf's, and Declan registered that the woman had called someone "Father". Clearly the human side of her parentage, the figure looked to be in his late sixties, maybe seventies, his face weathered and wrinkling, lined by time and what looked like too many smiles. His long, greying beard was strung with narrow braids, each streaked with a peppering of brown that matched his heavy eyebrows. His head itself looked to be bare, slick and bald, but it was hard to tell beneath the hood of the strange, patterned robes he was dressed in. The leather thong of a necklace hung about his neck, strung with a clear, thin crystal, but other than that the man was unadorned and unremarkable.

Declan, however—despite the strange presence of the odd pair—hardly managed to give either of these two a glance.

It was the third figure, instead, that he couldn't look away from, its dark, inhuman frame more shocking than anything he'd seen thus far.

The creature's skin was a uniform pattern of smooth black scales, with long, lithe arms extending from a similarly corded chest that—setting aside the curved claws which tipped the slender fingers of its hands—seemed to be modeled after those of a man. The creature's legs, tucked under the table, appeared only a little less human, scaled thighs, knees, and shins ending in feet that looked to be managed on the balls of taloned toes. A heavy, ridged tail poked out the space in the back of its chair—it bore no clothes to speak of, and seemed unperturbed by this fact—to slink slowly over the grassy floor behind it. Its head, unlike the rest of its body, was distinctly inhuman, blockish and serpentine, a little like the blunt skulls of the caimans that dwelled in the swamplands along Viridian's southeastern coast, if caimans could have torn a man's head from his shoulders in one snap. Not helping the image, the creature's jaw hung slightly agape, revealing pointed white teeth the size of Declan's little finger.

But it was the being's eyes where the truth could be found. Its eyes, burning the same gilded shades he was so familiar with, watching him as silently as the others.

The same eyes that had gazed down on him from the smoke-filled sky of the burning forest as he'd remembered dreams of flight and endless skies…

"… Ryn?" Declan managed to get out, barely keeping his voice from catching in his throat. "Is that you?"

The creature's face, originally so anxiously still it might have been dead stone, twisted in what could only have been described as relief. After a moment's hesitant delay, it slowly got up, pushing itself onto its feet, and approached Declan around the table cautiously. Only when it stopped just within reach of him did Declan realize just how *big* it was—an easy head taller than even he—towering at least seven feet high in all.

It took every fiber of will he possessed not to draw the blade at his side.

Give me your hand.

The voice was familiar, even and calm within his head, but all the same the shock of it made Declan start and take a half-step back, gaping at the beastly *thing* he just couldn't convince himself was his life-long companion. Again his mind struggled to keep pace. He had witnessed Ryn assume the form of a horse. Had seen him hunt as a wolf. Had watched him take flight as a soaring black hawk. Those transformations he had lived with all his days, hardly questioning the abilities when Ryn had chosen not to speak of them himself.

But *this*... *This* was something altogether different...

What are *you?* he tried to get out, transfixed by the creature's reptilian features, only to have his voice fail him.

"Give him your hand. He won't hurt you."

The gentle words made Declan jump and look around. Unbeknownst to him, the half-elf had come to stand by his elbow, her footsteps muffled in the thick grass. She was smiling at him again, almost sadly, like she understood something of his confusion, of his fear.

It was disconcerting to witness, in a way, after the impassive glare which had been all she'd allowed him when they'd last been face-to-face...

When Declan did nothing, the woman laughed softly and—before he could think to protest—took his hand in hers. Her fingers were warm against his palm, soothing even, but just the same he couldn't help but tense at her touch, earning another light laugh.

"Give him your hand, Declan," she said again, her smile brighter this time, lifting his arm up slowly.

Declan didn't bother asking how she knew his name. Instead, he resisted her instinctively, glancing back at the towering humanoid that stood before him, who'd now extended its own open hand expectantly. Declan couldn't *help* but hesitate, couldn't *help* but pause even if it *was* Ryn's eyes that stared at him from that frightening face. The woman squeezed his palm, though, coaxing him on.

Finally—all the while asking himself once again at what point he'd left his sanity behind in the last few days—Declan allowed her to guide his arm forward, settling tense fingers against the cool, smooth scales of the creature's waiting palm.

For a moment, nothing happened, and Declan wondered what was going on.

Then the dam broke for a second time, and the images came in a rush that almost brought him to his knees, and his body spasmed against the discomfort of the mental plunge.

Once more, he smelled the smoke and blood, heard the shearing sound of steel, the screams of the dying and the roar of disgorged fire. He gasped, legs weakening beneath him as he saw the corpses of soldiers and beasts alike scattered across the cliffs once more, and he hardly registered the still-unnamed half-elf taking him about the waist with her other arm, bearing part of his weight. Mercifully, in that moment of panic, the visions suddenly slowed, the memories coming easier, more carefully. They leafed across his mind with deliberate care, imprinted over the world he stood in, like someone was meticulously thumbing through the pages of a book.

"W-what are you doing?" he stammered, voice coming out strained, unable to think straight as whatever the presence was delved deeper his mind. The creature before him held its silence, and the recollections began to stream by faster. Declan saw the snow-capped ridge of the mountains, taking in the world from high above. He made out the pounding of wings and the echoing calls shivering through the winter. Lands and plains moved by below in bursts, lakes and rivers changing shape and form in the space of an instant. The brown-eyed woman. The ring. The dead rising from where they'd fallen. The world was a blur, and soon Declan was once more having trouble distinguishing what was present, and what was past.

Then, just when he thought he was going to faint again, the visions stopped. Declan realized he was thinking, unbidden, of the dream he'd had the previous night, poised above the clouds, bearing witness to the new day and the rising sun.

The bestial being before him stilled suddenly, its eyes distant as it, too, undoubtedly, took in the images. After several more seconds, it carefully pulled its hand away from Declan's, who sagged as he regained control of his own thoughts. The woman at his side helped him take a step back, leaning him up against the open doorway behind them, and he mumbled his thanks as his body slowly recovered from the intrusion.

That last memory was your own. How did you get it?

Ryn's voice again. Declan had been expecting it, but still couldn't keep himself from flinching.

"A dream," he replied breathlessly, looking up at the monstrous figure. "Last night. I've never had it before."

A look passed across the creature's face that told Declan this news was not remotely welcome. It stared at him almost angrily, but he could tell the thing was looking beyond him, its mind taken by other concerns.

"You... You *are* Ryn... right?" Declan asked again, standing straighter as his legs finally found and reclaimed their own strength.

The creature's eyes cleared, and it studied him for a long moment, like it was sizing up whether or not he could handle the answer.

Finally, it nodded.

Yes, Declan, the voice said quietly. *I am Ryn.*

And then it began to change.

The reptilian head grew, and its muscled arms thinned out as it fell on all fours in the grass beside the table. Its neck lengthened while its tail shrank, pulling into its body even as the scales of its skin seemed to crack and split into a thousand slivers, forming sleek hair. Within seconds, the black horse stood before them again, and Declan couldn't help but breathe easier, seeing his friend back in a form he could wrap his head around, at least for the moment.

All the same, the shock of the situation was far from dissipating. He didn't even notice the woman still holding on to him, supporting him up while he struggled to comprehend. Fortunately, this time he managed to get the question out, his voice as even as his hammering heart would allow.

"What *are* you?"

At this, the old man at the table blinked, turning in confusion to Ryn, his strange robes shifting over what looked to be a short, stocky frame. They made Declan think of physician's mantles, complete with a multitude of pockets and linings, but were colored very oddly. Rather than the stark-white or blue of the trained surgeons of the capitals' medical colleges, *these* robes were stained in a myriad of greens and browns and reds, like a scattering of turning leaves. Even the hood, pulled high over his head despite what felt like a return of the summer warmth, was stained in such a fashion.

Abruptly, Declan rather suspected he knew whose incomprehensible home he was standing in.

"What is he talking about?" The stranger's slow question was addressed to the black stallion. "Have you never…?"

Ryn threw the man a quick glare. *Of course I never told him! What good would it have done, aside from invite in trouble I couldn't control?* He shook his wide head in a disgruntled fashion. *I don't think any of this has made that remotely easier to do so, either.*

The old man stared at him. "But… his parents? You said he carries it through his father? Surely *he* must have thought to—?"

Declan's father passed when he was very young, Ryn cut the man off. *Even if that hadn't been the case, it wouldn't have changed anything. Ertus knew nothing of this either.*

"*What?*" the stranger hissed in disbelief, eyes widening. "How long have—?" He stopped himself, apparently coming to some realization as his mouth dropped open. When he found his voice again, the man's questions were tinged with something between sadness and anger. "How many generations of this family have you been watching over? Twenty? Thirty? And you never told *any* of them…?"

Ryn nodded slowly. *Elalyn knew,* he said, sounding like he wasn't altogether pleased to admit even this much. *Herst told her, against my better counsel. She was the last. Sehren, her son, wasn't even five when she died…*

"And you never told him yourself…" the old man finished for the horse slowly, leaning back in his chair heavily, clearly following Ryn's words far better than Declan was as he stared blankly between the two of them. Apparently sharing something of a similar thought in that moment, the old stranger met his eyes. "Well… I think it's about time you changed your ways…"

Apparently, was all Ryn answered with, turning, too, to look at Declan. *Apparently…*

After that, though, there was only silence.

"Oh. come *on*," the half-elf at Declan's side finally cut across the awkward pause, distinctly annoyed and finally sliding her arm out from around his back, stepping towards the other pair. "The last thing he probably remembers is the disaster in the woods! You bloody owe it to him, Ryn."

It's not so easy, Ester, Ryn answered her pointedly. *Telling you was one thing. Bonner has exposed you to this world your entire life. Declan has not had the same opportunity.*

At that, Declan mouthed at the air, trying to put his bewilderment into words, but the woman—Ester, it would seem—threw her hands up in exasperation.

"Only because *you* shielded him from it!" she insisted. "The man just survived a *ghoul* attack! The least you can do is buck up and tell him why!"

"Esteria…" the old stranger Ryn had called "Bonner" started warningly from his seat by the table, but the half-elf cut across him, too.

"*No*," she snapped, glaring between the robed figure and the horse. "Even leaving the draugr aside, he—" she waved furiously at Declan "—just lugged me around for the better part of two days, saved my life at *least* twice and almost died as many times, and killed five men in the process. Can you blame me for thinking he's earned the right to know his own history?"

Almost a millennia of history, Ryn answered, still not looking away from Declan, but his tone hinted that the woman was testing his patience. *Of which—I would remind you—you've been around for hardly a fraction.*

"Which puts me in the best position to speak for him when I say he *needs* to know." Ester seemed to sense that she was pushing her luck with the horse, her voice no longer edged with impatience. Instead, it was closer to pleading. "Things are *happening*, Ryn. You know it, and Father knows it. Declan should as well."

"She's not wrong…" Bonner chimed in with a sing-song voice, earning himself yet another glare from the horse.

"W-wait…" Declan finally managed, stumbling over the word while his thoughts raced to keep pace, trying to make sense of the jumbled conversation. "Herst? Elalyn? Wh-who are they? And what are ghouls? A-

and draugr?" He struggled to keep track of all his questions. "And what do you mean my 'history?'"

At this last question, the other three fell quiet, all eyes on him once again.

Finally, Ryn spoke up. *What do you remember of yesterday, Declan?*

Declan blanched at the question, not so sure he wanted to think more about the events of the previous evening than he had to. All the same, he swallowed, and did his best to answer steadily. "We... We left *The Woodsman's Rest* in the morning, looking for the hermit like Brohn and Dia suggested." He paused to glance at the old man, who had "*harrumph*"-ed at his words and muttered something that sounded like "hermit, my foot."

After that, Ryn pressed Declan, ignoring the robed stranger. *After we followed the trail. What do you recall?*

Declan grimaced. "The attack. I remember the attack. The bodies... They were... moving..."

Ryn nodded steadily at that, meeting his eyes carefully. *Ghouls,* the horse told him. *A type of draugr, though you can call them whatever you like: lurchers, walkers. The elves call them 'yn'feri'. In the end, whatever name you choose amounts to the same thing: corpses, reanimated with black magic, bestowed with a Purpose that drives them ceaselessly towards their given goal.*

Declan felt his hands go numb. "Magic?" he repeated faintly. "'A-a purpose'?"

In answer, Ryn shot an angry look at Ester, who'd stepped closer to Declan again, anxiously watching him like she was afraid he might need her arm once more. *I said it was too much,* the horse half-snarled in clear irritation.

Before Ester could respond, Declan interrupted. "N-no," he wheezed, watching his friend with wide eyes. "Tell me... Tell me more... How do you know this?" He glanced at the others. "How do you all know this? And who *are* you?"

"Apparently, I'm a 'hermit'." The old man's grunted response was something between amused and resigned.

How else would you describe yourself? Ryn asked him with a raised eyebrow. *Even I didn't know you were out here. I only started to suspect when I smelled you on Ester when we first found her.* He looked back at Declan, bobbing his head in the direction of the half-elf. *You've already met Esteria, of a fashion, I believe, so I'll let her make her own introductions later. This, however*—he indicated the old man at the table with a flick of his muzzle—*is her father, Bonner Fehn, a very old friend of mine, and the reason the two of you are standing here with nothing more than a few scars to show for the last two days.*

"yr'Essel," Bonner corrected with a smile, bowing his head briefly in Declan's direction. "Bonner yr'Essel, now, as I have been for more years than I can count. Remind yourself that the *er'enthyl* are a matriarchy before you go and marry an elf, boy." He chuckled at his own joke before waving a hand at his daughter. "As for how we know these things, Esteria has been fortunate enough to have learned through study and explanation." He glanced at Ryn. "As for the pair of us..."

Bonner and I—the horse picked up for him—*have a more hands-on experience. When it comes to the ghouls...* He paused shortly, studying Declan's face before continuing. *We helped throw what we thought were the last of them over a cliff, more than seven hundred years ago.*

For a long time, Declan stared at his friend, wondering if he'd misheard the statement. When Ryn did nothing more than meet his gaze evenly, he finally choked out the obvious question that came to mind.

"S-seven hundred *years*?!" he demanded. "How can you be seven hundred years old?!"

Ryn gave him a sad sort of smile, at that.

Oh, I'm older than that, Declan. That's rather young, in fact, for a dragon.

CHAPTER THIRTEEN

Thump.

Declan saw himself slide down the frame of the door as though from a great distance, not even registering the cushioned thud of his rear hitting the grass, or Ester's scrambled attempt to catch him as his legs finally gave up on trying to keep him standing. From his place on the floor he stared up at Ryn, taking in the horse's form as he fought to come to grips with his friend's words.

"What...?" he started unevenly. Ester crouched down at his side, putting a hand on his shoulder to keep him steady. "What... did you say?"

You heard me fine. Ryn sounded resigned, taking a step closer. *I don't need to repeat it.*

Absently, Declan nodded, watching the stallion come to stand over him. He remembered vividly the indistinct shape of the colossal head towering above him in the smoke-choked air of the ruined forest. He recalled the gleam of those known eyes shining down on him through the smog. First ghouls, then magic...

Now... this?

Declan didn't know what to think, much less what to *say*. It was like two parts of his mind were battling against each other, one half screaming that he should have known all along, the other half fighting with all its might to cling to the concept he held of this oldest friend.

"You're not..." were the only words he managed to get out, unable to look away from Ryn. "You can't be..."

After a moment, common sense won out, and his mind cleared, articulating a single, fervent belief.

"That's impossible."

For the first time since entering the room, he thought he saw something like amusement flashed across Ryn's feature. *Is that so?* the stallion asked dryly. *In that case, I'd offer the argument that dragons are about as much an impossibility as the dead rising from their graves...*

That took some of the wind out of Declan's sails, and his distraught mind scrambled for another explanation.

Unfortunately, he found he had only straws to cling to.

"But... dragons are extinct." He blinked up at Ryn in continued disbelief. "The war... The attack on the capital..."

From his place down the table, Bonner yr'Essel snorted. "Yes, yes," he said with an impatient wave of this hand, like he was shooing away Declan's words. "The ransoming of the heirs. The nobility's all-too-altruistic siege of the Reaches to retrieve them." His tone dripped with sarcasm. "We've heard it all before, and too many times at that." He paused, looking Declan up and down with a critical eye. "Do you always believe everything you hear, boy? The way Ryndean speaks of you, I wouldn't think you nearly that much of a fool…"

The history lesson can wait, Ryn tried to cut in with a quick look at Bonner before turning his attention back on Declan. *For now, I have to ask you to trust that—"*

"Ryndean."

Declan repeated the name quietly, interrupting the horse, his mind suddenly pulled away as it returned to him, absent from his recollection until that moment. It came back, ringing now, the subconscious knowledge of it suddenly roaring into life, as it had in his dreams.

Once it settled, setting into his understanding as though it had always been there, Declan slowly blinked at Ryn. In his mind's eye the horse's gaze shifted before him, turning into the steady, calm stare of the great black beast he recalled perched over the edge of the icy cliff.

The dragon with which he had leapt into nothingness, diving into a war he didn't remember…

"It was you…" he almost whispered in realization, eyes wide. "From my dreams… It was you…"

He didn't know if he imagined it, then, but he thought the horse's hair stood on end as he spoke.

Dreams? Ryn demanded, emphasizing the plural and taking yet another anxious step forward. *You have more of Herst's memories?*

Declan began to nod numbly. Then, abruptly, a twinge of irritation returned to him, momentarily shaking him from his shock. "Again, *who* is Herst?" he demanded, looking between the trio that surrounded him. "Is someone going to tell me, or am I just to be left wondering? I can't imagine it could be a bigger surprise than walking corpses and a… a…"—he waved towards Ryn, unable to bring himself to say the word.

To her credit, Ester did her best to answer.

"Amherst Sehren al'—" she started to say, almost like she was reciting a passage of text she'd memorized, before Ryn stopped her gently.

Ester. Allow me, if you would.

The half-elf stuttered to a stop, flushing suddenly. Looking mortified, as if she'd just participated in some great trespass, she nodded at once.

In the short silence that followed, Ryn took a slow breath, giving Declan the impression that the horse was having about as hard a time getting everything out as *he* was taking it in. All the same, he knew he couldn't let up now.

Not when he was finally getting somewhere.

Herst, the horse got out finally, *was a very, very old friend of mine, as old as Bonner here.* He motioned to the robed man again. *Of a fashion, you could say the two of us spent our most formative years together, though I was already nearing my first century in age by the time we met.* He paused, and Declan thought he saw the hint of another smile flash across his features. *Eventually, events led Herst and Bonner both to the Reaches, to live among my kind, where they earned their respect and trust to a greater extent than any human—or any being, for that matter—before them.*

"The... dragons'?" Declan clarified hesitantly, looking towards Bonner and earning a nod of ascension from the man even as Ryn kept on.

That was not a peaceful era. In their time among the mountains, they had to fight to keep our home safe. Herst in particular gave up much to do so. Ultimately, he became integral to our defense against the enemies assaulting us, and our primordial line—our 'royalty', I supposed you'd call them—chose to reward him for his sacrifices. At this, Declan thought he saw Bonner glance sharply at Ryn, but he was too ensnared to pay the old man any mind as the horse continued. *It wasn't until his daughter, Elalyn, was born some years later, that I realized the gift was one that passed on from parent to child, confirming so again and again over the centuries.* He met Declan's eyes evenly. *Not until now, though, did I know that his* memories *appear to have followed his bloodline as well...*

For a long time after that, there was silence, Declan taking in his friend's words.

"My... My ancestor?" he eventually choked out, head spinning once more.

Ryn nodded again. *Yes,* he answered simply, *and one who lived in a time far bloodier and terrifying than anything this age has seen, long before Viridian cast aside its magic. That's why these dreams of yours are so concerning.* His bright eyes shined fiercely. *They may be a portent, a sign of things to come. Please. Will you show me?*

For ten seconds more, Declan stared at the creature that had been his most cherished friend, his mind an ugly jumble of confusion, denial, and comprehension. It took Ester ultimately standing up and offering him a hand to shake him from his stupor, and even then it was a moment before Declan could accept it and allow himself to be hauled to his feet. Standing before Ryn, he took in the horse, forcing himself to see the white-gold eyes as he'd always done, as he'd always known them. He did his best to press aside the image of them set into the beastly head of the creature that had loomed over him like a titan in the setting sun.

When he'd steeled himself, he offered a shaky hand, palm up.

Ryn met him half-way, pressing his nose down between the open fingers.

Declan felt the presence at once, the subtle attendance of a second consciousness along the borders of his own, but it was *he*, now, who willed the memory forth. With as much detail as he could muster, he recalled the snowy cliff, the scattered armies of man against the white and grey of the valley, and the shrieks of a thousand winged terrors launching themselves off the mountains, into the open sky.

After a moment, Ryn pulled back, breaking the link. He didn't look away from Declan, but addressed Bonner in a low, worried tone.

He remembers the first charge...

At once, Bonner paled, all the blood draining from his face, one hand clenching into a fist on the table while the other jerked to the clear crystal strung about his neck almost reflexively, clinging to it. He looked between Declan and the horse several times, mouth moving without sound.

Then abruptly, he seemed almost to deflate, sinking back into his chair like a loose, wet rag.

"Why *now*, Ryndean?" he asked weakly. "What's bringing these dreams now? Is it the Accord? And the *ghouls*? What's happening?" He paused, taking a shaking breath. "If this is the Queen's doing..."

Inexplicably, Ryn bristled. *She died. I witnessed it myself.*

"As did I," Bonner insisted. "I watched Elysia burn her to ash in front of my very eyes. Unless by some trick of our side, there's no magic I know of that could have saved her. But Sehranya was beyond my power. It took the two of us to defeat her, and that was *after* Elysia accepted your blessing, not to mention you and Amherst spending hours wearing her down! I checked us all, after the fight. I even examined every damn soldier left of the *Vigil*, and not one of us carried the mark of possession." He looked pained, the thin braids of his beard twitching as he grimaced. "But I can't promise there isn't *some* way she could have tethered her soul to the world. You said yourself you were never convinced we'd seen the last of her!"

Ryn nodded like he had heard this all before. *Herst and I both,* he confirmed slowly. *We spent most of the next fifty years hunting for her. It cost him his relationship with Elysia...*

At his words, a memory flashed like a brief reflection on water across Declan's thoughts, recalling again the brown-eyed woman screaming at him in fury. He brought a hand to his head as the recollection was echoed by a brief wave of dizziness, but it was gone as fast as it had come.

Ryn, meanwhile, had continued. *Still, after so long... I admit it's been centuries that I've thought that danger long passed.* His voice was faint in their minds, almost half to himself, but then he turned to Bonner and spoke more firmly. *Regardless, whatever the cause, the presence of the ghouls alone tells me we have trouble on our hands. Even if Sehranya isn't involved...*

"Then there's a necromancer in Viridian," the old man finished for him with a morbid nod. "Aye... I've been thinking the same thing ever since you spoke of the clearing you found Ester in. Bodies everywhere, like that? If I didn't know better, I would have said it was a feeding ground for something nasty. Wights, or a drey, even."

The two having again slipped into topics Declan couldn't even begin to follow, he looked to Ester almost pleadingly. The half-elf did her best to help, despite the fact that her own face was paling with every word her father and the horse exchanged.

"A-a necromancer is a sort of mage," she said shakily, speaking under her breath to him while the other two continued to discuss. "A magic user who specializes in black arts, like the 'Purpose' Ryn was talking about earlier. I-I don't know what drey are, but I think wights are another, more dangerous type of draugr…"

"Who's 'Sehranya'?" Declan asked her quietly.

The woman lost what little color she had left at this question. "A witch," she hissed back. "The Endless Queen. An *er'endehn* who spent more than her natural lifetime gathering so much power, she could raise an entire army from the dead."

Declan shivered at the thought, imagining hundreds of ghouls—or possibly worse, it sounded like—gathered in lifeless ranks. Still, something else the woman had said caught his attention, and his brow creased in confusion.

"An 'er'endehn'?" he repeated. "You mean an *er'enthyl?*"

Ester shook her head, and had just opened her mouth to answer when Ryn's voice cut off whatever she'd been about to say.

Declan, have you had any other dreams you haven't shown us? he asked pointedly. *Any other memories?*

Declan thought for a moment, considering the question.

"A-A house?" he started tentatively, the image coming back to him. "There was a child, I think? And… a woman?"

Ryn's face stilled, and Declan saw true sadness in the creature's face, then.

The woman. The horse spoke like he was afraid of an answer. *Was she alive?*

Declan blinked, recalling the figure's still face and the nurses who closed her hazel eyes before covering her with a sheet.

He shook his head.

Ryn nodded slowly, clearly expecting this. *Brilyn. Herst's wife. She died giving birth to their only child, Elalyn…*

The darkness of his words hung over the room for a time, a moment of grief passing for events that had transpired over half-a-millennia ago.

No more, though? Ryn asked eventually, shaking the somber mood. *No other dreams?*

This time, Declan was ready with a response. "Not that I can remember. They only started recently."

"Unfortunate." Bonner was the one to respond, now leaning back in his chair again as he studied Declan for what felt like the hundredth time. "Or fortunate, depending on how you look at it..."

"Look at *what?*" Declan grumbled dryly, crossing his arms over his chest. "Ester was just trying to catch me up. You two—" he glared between Bonner and the horse "—seem more intent on each other than you do on helping me understand what's going on."

"That's largely because *we're* not sure what's going on, boy," Bonner answered heavily, sounding suddenly tired. "These dreams of yours do not bode well, particularly when coupled with the events of the last few days. At best, practices and knowledge that were banned even before *my* time have fallen into the hands of someone they shouldn't have. At worse, we have a powerful enemy of old at our gates, with this ghoul attack and those kidnappers Esteria was after being the only warning knocks we may get."

Well that explains why she was in the woods that night, Declan thought, giving the woman a sidelong look without turning away from Bonner. "The Endless Queen," he confirmed, wanting to demonstrate *some* semblance that he was catching up. "Sehranya. Who is she? Where did she come from?"

If he didn't know better, Declan would have said that Ryn actually groaned, then.

What little we know is history for another day, the horse replied. *For now, we have more pressing concerns. We need to get a better sense of what's going on. Even if it is nothing more than a rogue mage, the fact that they attacked you and I specifically can't be coincidence.*

Bonner nodded darkly in agreement, drawing a frown from Declan.

"Because you're... a dragon?" he asked slowly, the concept still feeling too foreign to accept just yet.

Ryn, in response, gave him an uncomfortable look. *Possibly*, he said at first, before appearing to catch himself and answering again more confidently. *Quite possibly. At the very least, whoever they were, they knew what I was. The clearing two nights ago was masked from me, as were the ghouls. It's not so hard to do, for an experienced caster, but in this day and age, spellwork like that is nigh unheard of...*

Declan blinked at him, not understanding. "'Masked'?" he said again. "What do you mean? They hid the clearing from you? Is that even poss—?" he stopped himself, bringing a hand to his face and rubbing his temples as his head began to hurt. "Never mind. Of course it is. Why wouldn't it be?"

It's more than possible, Declan, the horse confirmed gently. *My kind is capable of a great many things, but we are as far from infallible as any other living thing.*

"I wouldn't know," Declan muttered bitterly. "I feel like I suddenly don't know anything about you, anymore…"

The look of hurt that flash across the stallion's face then was so genuine, it dug at Declan's heart. He wished to take the words back, but before he could think to do so, Ryn looked to Bonner.

Weaving and binding a Purpose to us couldn't have been done haphazardly, he said. *We had to have crossed paths with the necromancer at some point in the last few days. I'll return to the villages and The Woodsman's Rest and see if I can find anything. Can you adjust the wards? I'll need to locate you again, if I'm to return.*

The old man nodded without hesitating, getting to his feet. "Not a problem." He glanced at Declan before making his way around the far end of the table, heading for one of the doors set in the opposite wall. "You'll leave the boy with us, I suppose?"

For two or three days, yes, Ryn acknowledged. *If your barriers were powerful enough that even I couldn't sense you, I'm not so concerned about some novice caster. Barring the worst, he'll be safer here, for the time being.*

"Wait," Declan interrupted, addressing Ryn as Bonner nodded and put a hand on the door he'd moved to, about to open it. "You're leaving me behind? Why?"

Not just yet, Ryn assured him, motioning to Bonner that he could go. The old man disappeared into the room without another word. *I understand that you have questions, and it will take some time for Bonner to make changes to the weave around this clearing.*

"The… weave?" Declan asked in confusion.

Ryn sighed, and his eyes shifted to Ester. *My point exactly. Furthermore, there are some things you* both *need to see. Follow me.* He turned and trotted towards the low west wall at the end of the room that opened up directly onto the clearing outside. *It's too cramped in here.*

An image of a colossal mass of black scales and golden, blazing eyes flicked across Declan's mind.

"Couldn't imagine why," he mumbled sarcastically to no one in particular.

Ester, at his side, gave a short laugh at that, then made after the horse. "Come on," she said with a smile, motioning Declan to follow, an action which required little coaxing. Together the two of them trailed Ryn over the knee-high wall and started out across the field. The strange transition brought the astounding nature of the place back to the forefront of Declan's mind, and the moment he was clear of the morning's shadows he turned around, walking backwards beside the half-elf across the high, uneven grass, shading his eyes against the sun in the hopes of seeing how the magnificent home was built.

He almost tripped over his own feet as he sucked in a shocked breath.

The stock and body of Bonner's house looked exactly as one might expect any woodsman's cottage would appear, though perhaps a little larger. Four long walls, each roughly eight feet high, were comprised of layered stone and mortar supplemented by staggered timber studs that were brown and green with forest moss. The low-cut space they had just cleared was odd, but it stood in stark contrast to the plain wooden front door set in a carefully cut archway, complete with a simple, iron handle and an unassuming brass knocker. All in all, Declan was rather reminded of his mother's home, the humble little hut he and Ryn had left behind so many years ago, now...

Or would have been, rather, if it weren't for the roof.

On either side of the structure, a short line of four or five tapering spruces indeed grew at an angle over the western and eastern walls. From there, their bent branches interlaced, thickening the spined, blue-green foliage several-fold until it formed a dense canopy that Declan suspected worked as well as any slatted or slated covering. From within this verdure, *more* trees made their appearance, protruding upwards through the living roof. These smaller evergreens were just as strange as the larger spruces, each trunk growing in a bare, spiraled pattern, utterly leafless until the very top, where the foliage grew naturally. They gave the home the impression of a castle, stone walls complemented by a handful of turrets and towers.

The doors, Declan realized, completely mesmerized by the sight.

"Like it?"

Declan tore his eyes from the wonder. Ester had stopped not far away and was watching him with a knowing grin, making him realize he'd inadvertently halted in his tracks to take in the house.

"I do," he answered at once, stepping backwards to rejoin her, looking back up at the roof one last time before turning and walking alongside the woman as she made for Ryn again, who was waiting for them in the open expanse of the glen. "There's more to your father than meets the eye, isn't there?"

"Much," Ester conceded, her smile faltering a little as they walked. Declan watched her bring her fingers up, touching the back of her head tenderly. "More than I could explain, to be honest. He's the one who healed us, my head and your arm." She brought her hand down to gesture at the sleeve of Declan's left arm, which hid the nearly non-existent scar of what had been a newly stitched wound not a day before.

Declan nodded at her words, having figured as much already judging by Bonner's earlier commentary. "Is he... He's a 'mage' as well?" Declan asked, trying to inject some confidence in his voice as he posed the question.

By that point, though, they'd gotten near enough for Ryn to overhear them, and it was he who answered.

Calling Bonner a mage would be much like calling the ocean a "large lake", the horse said with a chuckle. *You might not technically be wrong, but to say it was an understatement would be putting it mildly. He's always had an uncanny talent with the arts. Still...* he paused, suddenly thoughtful, and looked to Ester. *Even I'm surprised to have found him doing so well. He doesn't seem to have aged more than a decade, maybe two, since I last knew him. Your mother's doing?*

Ester gave a noncommittal shrug as she and Declan came to a stop before the creature. "Partially. Old marital magics, from before the *er'enthyl* closed off the borders of the Vyr'en. I don't really understand it, but it apparently allows the two of them to share their lifespans? Given Father's affinity for auramancy, though, I don't think it's as big a sacrifice on Mother's part as it might have been."

Yes, your father's always been long-lived, to say the least, Ryn agreed. *He's older than I am, if you'll believe it, and I found that out long before he and Arathia were wed.*

Declan, who was finally starting to get used to these incredible asides, did his best to let the idea that the old man in the house behind them was nearing a thousand years in age roll off his shoulders. "Auramancy", too, he decided likely meant some kind of "healing" branch of magic.

Magic... The word was as alien in his thoughts as "dragon" had been on his tongue...

Shaking off such thoughts with surprising ease, he instead looked back to Ester. "Is your mother another mage?"

"Not much of one, no." The half-elf shook her head and gestured to the sword at Declan's side instead. "She knew enough to help my father with the conjugal rituals, but if you gave her the choice between magic and a blade—or a bow, rather—she'd choose the latter in a heartbeat. She used to be a member of the *Aveer al'En*—Father calls them *er'enthyl*'s "High Guard"—before she... lost the position."

These last words trailed away as Ester met Ryn's eye, and Declan couldn't help but suspect some private exchange had happened between the two he wasn't privy to. It irritated him, scratching at the building anger that had been welling in his chest, unaided by the confusion and frustration that had permeated the morning's conversation. He had no idea what the "High Guard" were even after the translation, but in the moment he didn't care. The underhanded silencing of whatever the half-elf had been about to say brought more pressing matters back to mind.

"I'm getting tired of these secrets, Ryn." Declan allowed some of the growing resentment to leak into his voice. "If you're done trying to create more, how about giving me some answers, for once?"

I intend to, the horse told him, choosing to ignore the subtle reference to the exchange between he and Ester. *Before you ask me anything else, though, there's something you need to know. An admission, of sorts, and one I think will go a long way in helping you come to grips with... everything...*

"Oh?" Declan asked, the anger drying up in a heartbeat to be replaced by a mixture of excitement and trepidation. An admission? What sort of admission?

Ryn nodded, but it took a moment for him to continue, clearly steeling himself for what he had to say.

I told you masking a presence was simple magic, and that's true. However... there are more complex methods that one can use to hide themselves, often in plain sight.

Declan frowned, but Ester, beside him, nodded like she already knew this. Not wanting to come off as more a fool than he already must look before the woman, he held his tongue.

I've discovered that I make for a poor teacher in the ways of the arcane, Ryn continued morosely. *I find I tend to explain things with needless complexity, so I'll leave it to Ester and her father*—he inclined his head towards the woman—*to explain the greater nuances of what it is exactly to 'weave' magic. For now, think of it merely as a spell. Masking is a simple weave, and one that can be threaded and cast upon most anything.* Here, he hesitated again, giving a sound that might have been the horse clearing his throat. *The more complicated magics, on the other hand, can manipulate the mind directly. They form something less than reality, but more than illusion, for the afflicted.* Ryn met Declan's gaze steadily. *I'm going to release you, now.*

"You're going to wha—?" Declan started to demand, alarmed, before feeling something he hadn't even known was there give up its hold on his psyche. As it did, the world before him shimmered momentarily, like an impossibly thin veil were being cast from his eyes. He blinked at the sudden distortion, taken aback. As his vision cleared, he heard Ester gasp at his side, and was about to turn towards her in concern when he caught sight of what it was that had surprised her.

"Mother's Graces..." The curse came out in a half-whisper, and for the second time that morning Declan couldn't help but take a step away from Ryn, mouth wide as he took in the horse.

No, he knew now. *Most certainly not 'the horse.'*

Ryn had largely kept the rough form of a stallion, but where before had stood a proud and perfect charger, a far-less ideal beast now took up its place. Instead of the smooth, silken coat Declan had always known, large patches of scales the size of his thumbnail patterned portions of the creature's hair. Ryn had kept his mane and tail, but instead of hooves, two thick, reptilian toes with blunt, stubbed talons adorned each leg. His body had kept its proportions, as had his neck, but his head was subtly different, the high-boned structure of a pure-bred charger having shifted into a lither skull that harkened to the smooth features of a snake.

Of the two of them, Ester managed to speak first.

"What... happened?" the woman asked, torn between confused and concern.

Ryn laughed dryly at this. *Nothing has happened*, he assured them, glancing back at himself. *You two are merely seeing me as I actually am, in this form. The way Bonner sees me, or anyone else untouched by the weave I surround myself with always.* He grinned hesitantly at the pair of them, revealing short, pointed canines that looked more suited to tearing at flesh than grass as his eyes fell on Declan.

You said you felt you knew nothing about me, he spoke quietly. *I don't believe that. You likely know me better than any living soul. Perhaps even Bonner, in your own way. Still. I won't pretend that there is much you* don't *know, which pains me to admit.* The horse—*No*, Declan finally admitted to himself. The *dragon*—took a slow breath. *For that reason, I'll hear your questions, and Ester's, too, if she has any. I cannot promise to answer all of them now, but those I can I will do my best to. This is what I am, in truth.* Ryn gestured back at his warped form with his scaled muzzle. *Even magic can only do so much when it comes to transforming a physique like my own. If you can handle this, then I don't think there's anything I could say that would really surprise you from here on out.*

Again, Declan felt himself mouthing at the air, his mind working against itself as he struggled to come to terms with what he was seeing and what Ryn was saying.

"This... This is what you are?" he finally managed to echo, continuing to take in his friend's warped body. "Not... more?"

Ah, Ryn answered quickly, like he was catching on to Declan's confusion. *I should have said this is how I am* now. *No. As you're getting at, this is not my natural state. That transition requires an enormous amount of energy, of magical power, you might say. I'm hardly recovered from yesterday's transformation, so doing so again as a mere demonstration would be unwise, given the situation we have found ourselves in.* He grimaced. *The ghouls took me by surprise. Truthfully, it's my greatest hope that you—any of you—will never have to see me like that again.*

Declan nodded, almost understanding this logic. Still, there were other concerns.

"And you've... been in my head?" he asked after a moment, unable to look away from the heavy, clawed toes that had replaced Ryn's hooves. "... For how long?"

From the moment you were born. The answer was prompt, the question obviously expected. *And always since. Herst was the last to see me as I am. Even Elalyn, who knew what I was, never witnessed this.*

And always since...

The words resonated in an unpleasant way, making Declan meet the dragon's eyes sharply. "What about now?" he asked, more coolly than he'd probably intended. "Are you *still* in my head?"

Beside him, Ester frowned. "Declan, are you not seeing what I'm seeing?" she asked him quietly, herself clearly having a hard time looking away from Ryn. "I don't think——"

Yes, Ryn answered flatly, interrupting her. *I'm still in your head, Declan.*

This response shut Ester up, and she closed her mouth with an audible snap, looking confused. Declan, on the other hand, felt furiously victorious. His suspicions had been building from the moment he'd taken the dragon's hand in Bonner's house and had his mind so easily sifted through.

"*That's* why I've been having trouble remembering things," he seethed, glaring at Ryn. "*That's* why I couldn't recall talking about joining the Vigil. It's how you calmed down Dia, too, isn't it? At *The Rest.*" He recalled seeing the woman's terrified face as Ryn had started to grow behind him. "You scared her half-to-death, but the moment you left it was like nothing had happened."

It is, Ryn confirmed regretfully. *I lost control, and allowed her a glimpse of something she shouldn't have witnessed. If she'd gone around telling her patrons about what she'd seen, it could have meant trouble.*

"So you wiped her mind?!" Declan demanded, feeling the fury build. "What gives you the right to do that?!"

I'm hardly capable of 'wiping' anything, Declan, Ryn responded with a sigh. *I'm a dragon, not a god. The mind has its own protections, and—as I've said—my kind is hardly omnipotent. I can only suggest a different course of thought, when need be. In Dia's case, all it took was bringing the suspicion that it was a trick of the candlelight to the forefront of her consciousness, coupled with the trust she put in you when you said I was harmless. As a result, the fear and certainty were pushed to the back, where they will eventually fade to nothingness.*

This answer did nothing to improve Declan's mood.

"I ask again," he almost snarled. "What gives you the right?"

"Declan, I don' think——" Ester tried to cut in once more, but again it was Ryn who answered first.

Would you like me to show you? he asked of Declan simply.

At this question, Declan took pause, wondering what the dragon meant. Before he could answer, though, he felt something else detach itself from his being.

Then, in the space of an instant, he shuddered, staggering backwards, clutching at his head.

Then his mouth opened, and Declan screamed.

Fear, unlike anything he had ever experienced in his life, raged upward out of some distant hole in his own mind. It was a terror of such proportions he couldn't fathom its depth, an all-consuming horror as images seared themselves on the forefront of his thoughts. The dead, cold stares of the ghouls, the incomprehensible roar of what he suddenly understood to be dragonfire laying waste to the woodlands, the gleaming of Ryn's great golden eyes in the smoke, framed against the indistinct form of his petrifying features. Intermingled with the fear, too, were other emotions. A drowning sense of hopeless bewilderment as Declan's mind took in the *truth*, the depths of what he had seen and learned, dwelling on Bonner's home, his healed arm, Ryn's strange, humanoid form. An insatiable itch of curiosity he understood to have existed all his life, questioning everything from his own skills with a blade to the strange friendship with the beast he now knew was a dragon. A need to know raged within him, a need to understand all these things which he had always been aware of but never seemed to care for as much as he should have.

Despite everything else, though, it was still the *fear* that nearly took him to his knees.

And then, from some distant place, Declan felt something settle back into place in the depths of his consciousness, and everything ceased as abruptly as a river flow cut off by a closing dam. At once he was left standing, gasping for air with his hands still pressed across his face, gaping at the ground through his fingers with little sense of *why* it was he had been so terrified.

Before today, I have never *sifted through your mind*, Ryn's voice said firmly from nearby, and Declan heard the shifting of grass as the dragon approached. *Had I, then I would have known of these dreams much earlier, and perhaps even saved us both a great amount of trouble. Consider that.* He stopped within arm's reach. *Yes. There have been times I have guided you away from certain paths and decisions, but I can only swear on your "Mother" that I've never done so without the utmost cause. The Vigil was not a place for you and I. You may not recall, but I didn't even want to go to the capital, only allowing that choice because it was manageable, and it was your own. What I* have *done, on the other hand, is shielded you, protected you. Sometimes from curiosities and questions that would have strained our relationship and perhaps even put you at risk, but most often from greater cruelties. You are a strong soul, Declan. Not since Herst himself, truth-be-told, can I think of a forefather of yours with greater potential. But the human mind, even tethered and secured in the gifts passed down in your blood, is a fragile thing. You don't find it strange that you've hardly asked about the clearing, and the corpses? Or that you haven't mentioned the fact you were nearly* eaten alive *by men who should have been dead?* He paused there, as though giving Declan an opportunity to respond.

When no reply came, the dragon continued quickly. *Could you have handled it all on your own? Probably. I have little doubt, in fact. But not easily, and not without such a struggle bringing with it its own damages. You have been thrust into the hard truths of the world at a speed that would have killed a lesser man, and nearly killed you all the same. My right, as you called it, comes with the fact that I am your greatest friend, and love you like a brother. Do not ask of me not to help you, not to safeguard you when I can. I won't respect that request. Rather, trust me. Trust that I have my reason, and that I have your best interest at heart. Allow me to alleviate some of that burden.*

Slowly, as Ryn finished speaking, Declan looked up. He found himself face to face with the dragon's serpentine, horse-ish head, standing closer now than they had all morning. Ester had also approached, lingering at Ryn's side with wide, scared eyes, and Declan realized what he must have looked like, howling for no apparent reason.

"That's what I should be feeling?" he asked, his voice stronger than he would have expected. "*That's* what you're holding back?"

Ryn dipped his head in confirmation. *Even when we are separated, my weave holds that at bay. You won't need it forever. I hardly think you'll need it for long, in fact. Ester has no bindings, for example. She knows this world, has lived in it for many years. She feels fear of dragons and ghouls and other such beasts as you might feel fear of an armed opponent, or the wereyn, or whatever other familiar enemy you already know. Once understanding settles in, once you have a sense of what it is you are* actually *facing, you will have no need of me in your mind again.*

His words, perhaps meant to be assuring, ironically sent a shiver up Declan's spine as he thought of bearing the weight of that horror again. As though reading his concerns, Ryn almost smiled.

There's nothing to worry about, he promised gently. *Like I said: you're a strong soul. You'll manage it well, when the time comes.*

Declan nodded shakily, understanding and appreciating the dragon's faith in him, but doubtful all the same. Seeking further reassurance, his eyes shifted to Ester's. In their blooming green depths, he found his comfort, his solace. Ryn was right. The woman had spoken of the undead, of the wights and the Endless Queen, with obvious—but natural—fear. Giving himself a moment to consider it, it occurred to him that he should most certainly have been more scared. He'd nearly been devoured alive by shambling corpses, and yet he'd woken that morning with his greatest lingering concern being where his sword was and why the ceiling he'd found himself under was crafted from living trees.

Then again, the latter was probably a valid consternation, he allowed himself privately.

Abruptly, Declan felt like changing the topic, deciding he didn't want to dwell on the confusing deliberation that was happening in the back of his mind. He knew well enough he would struggle plenty as it was in the coming days to deduce whether Ryn's actions were a betrayal unlike any other, or the greatest gift Declan could have been offered...

"What else can you do?" he asked, realizing how abrupt the question seemed only after it had left his mouth.

You mean other than flying and breathing fire?

For the first time all morning, Declan felt something like a laugh tug at him, the humor—as forced as it was—a small step towards reminding him that it *was* the Ryn he knew, standing before him.

"Yes, other than those," he answered with the least-strained grin he could manage.

To his relief, the dragon smiled back, albeit tautly. *We're capable of a good many things. Alteration of our physiology, for one, as you well know. We can take a form at will, using it to our advantage as needed.*

"Any form?" It was Ester who asked, sounding eager to keep the conversation now that some of the tension had passed. "That seems a potent talent…"

Ryn scoffed wistfully. *If only. Our magic has limits, as our bodies do. We have to learn the anatomy of whatever it is we wish to take on intimately, practicing and developing our ability to shift into that particular appearance. How long that takes depends on the form, and the one learning it. Even then, there are almost always imperfections.* He lifted a flawed foot in example, letting the blunt claws swing pointedly. *Still, there are those who persevere. There's a story, among my kind, of an old primordial who took most of two centuries to learn the shape of a sea serpent, all so she could explore the oceans as readily as the skies. It isn't easy, to say the least. Many don't ever bother with it at all.*

"So, there *are* more of you?" Declan followed up with.

Ryn gave him an exasperated look. *Of course. We weren't completely destroyed by the war, as Dia would have had you believe, and it's been seven-hundred years. Even dragons don't reproduce that slowly.*

"But why, then?" Ester asked, clearly having trouble wrapping her head around the reasoning. "Why wouldn't they try to learn how to use their power?"

Too much of a burden, Ryn answered with a shrug, stepping around Declan and starting to amble north, clearly expecting them to follow. *It takes time and energy in amounts a lot aren't willing to sacrifice, particularly among those who have little interest in exploring the outside world. Even among those that do, most learn a single additional form, maybe two.*

Declan was surprised at that, joining Ester to walk on either side of the dragon. "And you know three?"

On his right, Ryn chuckled. *Four,* he reminded them proudly.

Then his body began to shrink.

In the opposite transition they'd witnessed earlier, Ryn's horse-like legs retracted, his neck shrunk, and his head pulled into itself. His tail thickened and extended, and Declan watched in amazement as the dragon smoothly counter-balanced himself into a standing position, not even missing a step while he completed the transformation and reached his full height. In a matter of seconds, the twisted stallion had been replaced by the lithe, towering humanoid who had been waiting for him as he'd left his room that morning.

In our language, this is my 'rh'eem', Ryn said before Declan could ask, the name garbled and guttural. *You could translate it to 'form of lesser', in Virisian, but Herst always found that pompous, and not without reason seeing as it's a body modeled after that of men and elves. He called it a 'dragonling'. It was a common-enough form in his time, when the races mingled much more openly.*

Declan stared, finding his words gone for the moment. With some odd measure of relief, he noted that the muscular, lissome body of the dragonling appeared the same now as it had earlier, Ryn moving along on the balls of his clawed feet between he and Ester. It helped Declan register that the dragon hadn't been hiding *everything* from him with his 'weave', at least…

"Four forms?" Ester asked from his other side, sounding surprised as she echoed Declan's early curiosity. "Even though most others only know one or two?"

Ryn shook his head. *Not unlike Declan, I have my own gifts.* He led them in a slow, ambling circle around the glen as he spoke, clearly keeping no apparent destination in mind. *I was raised as an ambassador, of a sort. Dragons are capable of more than a few things the average human would consider impossible or unnatural, even hundreds of years ago. Transformation, flight, magics of mind and body. We can communicate across an extensive distance, and we can produce dragonfire so hot, it can turn bone to ash and melt steel.* Ryn gave a pained huff of a laugh. *All that was well known, though, and my kind required their representative in the courts of the other races to be able to demonstrate something more, something that would make them truly question any action against the Reaches or its surrounding lands.* He waved a clawed hand down at his scaled form. *Given that… I was chosen, young as I was. To be fair, I'd only learned how to take on this shape, in addition to my natural form, then. A hatchling of less than a hundred years learning any foreign transformation— even a rh'eem—was a rarity.*

"'Hatchling'," Declan quoted under his breath, again mesmerized by the distinct separation in their sense of time.

"Is that when you met my father?" Ester asked brightly, clearly excited to hear an old tale from another perspective.

It is. Ryn looked from her to Declan. *And Herst as well.*

Declan blinked at that. "At court?" he asked, perplexed by this revelation. "How did that happen?"

A roguish gleam suddenly shined in Ryn's eye, and he looked skyward, taking in the cloudless day as he gazed back in time with obvious fondness.

That's a story I hope I enjoy telling you one day. Unfortunately, for now—he looked back over his shoulder at the house—*I believe Bonner's just finished with his adjustments.*

Declan followed his gaze. Sure enough, even as he glanced towards the house, he saw the simple front door open and the old man poke his head out, peering about. Catching sight of them, he began jogging in their direction, waving in clear confirmation even as he approached.

"You're leaving, then?" he asked quietly of the dragon, not looking away from Bonner's home.

Not for long, the dragon assured him. He, too, was watching the old mage approach. *I'll have to take my time searching, but I'll move faster on my own.*

Declan caught a shift of motion in the corner of his eye, but didn't look around even when the old weight settled on his shoulder, the wicked claws of Ryn's hawk's form digging into his tunic.

We have a moment more, though, the dragon said, and for some reason Declan had the impression this time the words were for him, and him alone to hear. *There's one question I'm surprised you haven't asked, yet…*

Declan didn't respond for several seconds, his eyes still on Bonner yr'Essel, watching the man cut a path through the wind-blown grasses. Nearby, Ester still stood eyeing he and Ryn, clearly sensing that some exchange was happening between them that was not for her to interrupt.

"…Why didn't you ever tell me?"

It came unbidden to his tongue. The inquiry whose answer he needed most. With it finally out in the open, he turned to face the dragon.

Ryn's hawk's form was—to Declan's relief—not so far different in its true state than it had been beneath the illusions of magic. His body was much the same, though his talons were thicker and even sharper than before. His black beak was unchanged, but above his eyes a narrow pair of what might have been horns curved delicately back, beyond the end of his skull. Of the entirety of the transformation, only his wings were truly distinct now, dark feathers hardly scattered in patches over leathery membrane stretched between narrow lines of bone ending in clawed tips.

The dragon shifted his weight on Declan's shoulder, adjusting as his lighter body was caught in the hard breeze. Only when Bonner wasn't more than a dozen yards away did the dragon answer, his voice almost regretful but firm all the same.

How much easier do you think you slept, ignorant of dead things walking in the dark? How much brighter were these woods—he extended a warped wing to indicate the nearby tree line—*before you stepped into that clearing, two nights ago?* The dragon's eyes lifted skyward again, taking in the blue-white brilliance of what might have been the season's last glorious morning, drinking in the warmth and the sun with an expression across his hawkish features that took some time for Declan to place.

Heartbreak, he realized abruptly.

To drag you into this world before you had to be, if you ever had to be at all... the dragon said with agony in his voice. *I see now it wasn't impossible this day would eventually arrive. But just the same*—he looked down then, meeting Declan's gaze with cold, grim stillness—*in the weeks to come, I've an unfortunate feeling you and I both will come to miss the time where our greatest concerns were hunting for our evening supper and what split in the road to take.*

And then, with that, Ryn spread his wings, leapt from his perch and took flight, circling once high above Declan, Ester, and Bonner's heads before streaking off west, back in the direction they'd come from the previous day.

Back, before fate had seen fit to turn their futures upside down.

CHAPTER FOURTEEN

"There is power in the unknown. One could argue—given the vastness of our own world and the endlessness of the heavens above—that there is more power in the unknown than the known. What sort of secrets lie in the mysteries of this ever-infinite universe? What hidden fonts of potential linger beyond the mere dregs of our understanding? Man has largely mastered himself and the material, the physical laws of our world. But beyond that, what have we managed to harness? What have we managed to control? Perhaps one day the stories we tell our children of magics and wonders will be our reality. Perhaps one day we will hold the reins to mystery, having mastered everything from the inconsequential details of the mundane to the secrets of our very dreams and nightmares..."

-A Study of Modern Advancement, Terean Bord, 992p.f.

Rehna Toyte shivered as she watched her breath mist in the air, framed against the empty grey and white shades of the mountains before her. Clutching at the winding layers of scarves and shirts she'd swathed her small frame in that morning, she took in the ranges with detached distaste, frowning up at their peaks. By all rights it was really only nearing fall in Viridian, but this far north, sidling up against the Mother's Tears in the foothills Rehna had spent all of her life in, the brief warmth of spring only ever lingered a few weeks in the course of a short summer. After that, the weather gave way—with depressing predictability—to the cold winds falling from the cliffs above, spilling down on Estwyn in a frigid deluge.

Hardly for the first time in her life, Rehna cursed the King or Queen whose name she did not know, whatever ancient monarch it was that had deemed it necessary to build a *town* at the very foot of the treacherous ranges, all to protect a pass into the untamed, unknown lands of Eserysh, beyond the mountains.

A pass that's been blocked off and useless for as long as anyone can remember, Rehna thought bitterly, grey eyes trailing the pale outline of the monstrous corridor before her, a sharp, winding break through the mountains that looked like some god had dragged their sword along the face of the earth to cleave a rugged path through the unforgiving heights.

"Rehna? What are you doing?"

Rehna blinked and brought her eyes up from her observation of the canyon. Her mother was some thirty feet away, looking down on her in concern from the incline of the hills, having climbed up a bit farther in search of the thistle and thornweed they were there to reap.

"Is everything alright? You haven't caught cold, have you?"

Rehna quickly shook her head. Like her daughter, Lara Toyte wore layers of grey and brown wool, and her head, nose, and mouth were wrapped in a heavy shawl to stave away the bite of the harsh wind. Her hands were gloved, partially to safeguard from the stinging herbs, but more so to ward off the chill that would numb her fingers in minutes, even this many weeks before true winter loomed. Looped in the crook of her elbow, the woman had a gathering pannier, and Rehna flushed when she saw that the basket was already brimming with narrow, rooted stalks.

Glancing down at her own nearly-nonexistent yield, her embarrassment redoubled.

"I'll look by the stream!" she called back over the distance, catching sight of a generous patch of thistle twisting about by the narrow creek not far west of them, one of many bare flows that trickled down from the Tears as the snows slowly melted higher up.

If her mother responded, it was lost to the distance and the breeze that rushed over Rehna's own garb, whistling through her ears as she hurried towards her prize. For a time she was able to focus on her task, moving and plucking, careful not to slip on the loose shale and sink a boot into the icy stream while she separated the plants she found into two piles. Her father had studied medicine in Aletha, in his youth. The herbs were for him, for the poultices and potions he concocted to ease the aches and pains of the elderly that descended with the approaching frosts. He was a good man, one who had returned from the comforts and warmth of the south some twenty-odd years prior to aid Estwyn after the town had been nearly razed to the ground by the wereyn they only saw occasionally now. Rehna loved her father, and had been thrilled when her mother had decided she was of an age to assist her in gathering for his practice.

All the same, she cursed *him* too, sometimes, for not having had the sense to take them all back to the southern lands, after her birth.

Rehna sighed, reaching out to rip yet another thornweed from the tough ground, meticulously claiming it roots and all. Placing it in her basket, she couldn't help but glance over her shoulder, southward, taking in the town of Estwyn from high enough now to see over the great, gated wall that blocked off the wide mouth of the eastern pass.

For as long as she had remembered—which she was smart enough to grant wasn't any great span of time, given her twelve years of age—the town had been a cold, hard place, made only slightly warmer and softer by the people who called it home. Estwyn was a stronghold, a garrison for nearly a thousand of the Vigil's soldiers, which Rehna had heard the older girls at school say was more than ten times the number it had once been. A high, wooden palisade that had been erected two decades prior encircled its borders, ringing the maze of houses, shops, and other such structures whose tile and slate roofs she could make out from where she stood. It was an impressive defense for any mountain town, but the north wall—the one Rehna was peering over now—was even more imposing. While the timber ramparts of its original build could still be seen when one took it in from within, from the exterior it was nothing more than a flat monolith of somber, plain stone. She'd commented on this once to her father, saying she would have much preferred the simple wall of wood, like the rest of the palisade, but that had only earned a nervous sort of chuckle from her parent. He'd told her that the town defenses had had to be fortified, that the wall and gate had been strengthened with granite carted up from quarries to the east on the orders of the previous King, Malythus al'Dyor, who'd feared further assaults that never came.

Rehna remembered telling her father that the old King must have been a fool, which had gotten her a more honest laugh.

Of all the things Rehna hated about Estwyn, that wall was easily the crowning jewel of her list. Running almost perfectly east to west in parallel with the mountains, the great blundering contraption didn't even have the decency of providing any shade in which to bask in summer. During the winter months, Vigil soldiers were often either kicking piled snow down on the heads of passersby below, or not uncommonly toppling down themselves as the overly-smooth stone grew slick with slush and ice. Its greatest crime by far, however—in Rehna's budding opinion as a young lady—was that the thing was *ugly*, a colossal eyesore easily spotted from any part of the town when not blocked by a wall or roof, making it a central fixture in Estwyn.

Rehna sighed, her breath once more gusting out into a wash of mist as she took in the unadorned stone, lingering on the massive double-gates and heavy portcullis that formed the only entrance or exit from the town northward. The way was ajar, now, as it had always been for as long as she could remember, deliberately kept open to allow the easy flow of individuals with special permission—like Rehna and her mother—though more commonly for the sake of the miners coming to and fro from their day's work in the excavations higher up the crags. Across its parapet, from some hundred yards away she could distinctly make out the shape of the King's men and women in their red-and-black uniforms, some standing watch at staggered intervals behind the crenellations, while others moved in pairs up and down the walls, completing their pointless, cyclical rounds. It all made her feel constricted, even as far away from the gate as she was, and for the hundredth time that year alone Rehna swore to herself that she would leave Estwyn the moment she was of an age to—leave it, and never look back.

She couldn't help but wonder, on the other hand, if she would be able to convince her mother and father to join her when that happy day finally came…

At the thought of her parents, Rehna started as she realized she'd allowed herself to be distracted again. Looking around, she exhaled in quick relief when she didn't catch sight of her mother, her fear of being scolded abating. She wasn't surprised, of course. Lara Toyte was as diligent a worker as any woman in Estwyn. More often than not she ended up climbing high enough up the mountain so as to make the first outcroppings of jutting boulders and cliffs, amongst which there were ample obstructions behind which one could inadvertently slip from the eyes of others. Still, Rehna's basket was getting full, her arm was starting to tire, and the cold was finally clawing through the worn soles of her boots. Deliberately putting her back to the great wall of Estwyn in the hopes of forgetting about it and its obtrusive unsightliness for a little while, she began to scale the incline, making for the spot she had seen her mother last.

The ascent took her longer than it should have, after a particularly brutal gust blew the top layer of herbs from her basket and sent Rehna scurrying after the scattering plants. After recovering most of them, she'd taken a stone and placed it atop the pickings, making her load even heavier, but at least ensuring she wouldn't lose half her yield to the wind again. After that, she took her time, distracting herself from the cold and barren land around her by allowing her mind to drift to a future in which she persuaded her family to move south, to set up her father's practice in one of Viridian's bustling inner cities, bright and warm and cheerful under a handsome sun that blazed year-round.

Finally reaching the outcroppings, Rehna leaned against the closest slab of jutting stone for a while, pulling the scarf from her face in an attempt to catch her breath. After a minute or so she pushed upwards again, calling out as she did.

"Mama? *Maaaama?*"

No response.

Again, though, Rehna thought nothing of it. The wind was crueler now, blowing and lashing more fiercely with every passing minute, and was easily angry enough to steal her words away, or any answering reply. She could tell a storm was brewing in the heights far above, and with a miserable chill wondered if they would have their first frosting of the year's snows that night.

Deciding to move east, Rehna carefully clambered up and over the rocky shelf, continuing to hail after her mother while she did, cupping her mouth with her gloved hands whenever she had the opportunity. After a minute or two more without so much as a hint of the woman's presence, something finally began to stir in her chest, a twinge that was more than an annoyance, but less than fear. Eventually, Rehna reached the edge of the pass itself, the walls of the canyon far too steep to brave, forcing her to descend a bit, back down towards the town.

It was as she was gingerly maneuvering her way between two slanted boulders, careful not to let her herbs spill from their basket, that an oddity caught Rehna's eye.

There was something dark against the stone, to her left, splattered markings clear amidst the grey of the rocks and colorings of the few plants that thrived in the arid earth. Frowning at the stains, Rehna found her footing and approached them, heart hammering after she drew close enough to make out what they were. Even then a child's mind can be deceptively resilient, and so only after she had knelt down and touched the black-red splotches, the tips of her gloves coming away wet, did Rehna understand in truth what she was seeing.

Blood.

Streaked in splashes and stripes, dark crimson painted the cliffs in a thrashing, linear pattern, like something had been wounded and dragged off and over the nearby ledge leading treacherously down into the pass. Rehna felt fear wrench at her throat like a vice at the sight, the first and most obvious possibility coming to mind immediately, but she was a level-headed girl, and it didn't take long to remind herself that man wasn't alone in these ranges. There were animals, here; spotted deer, wild sheep, and all their like, as well as the grey wolves and brown bears that hunted them. As much as Rehna *didn't* want to encounter any of the latter while she was some two hundred yards from the safety of the town walls, it was preferable to the alternative, and she clung to that possibility, unwilling to allow the other option to take form just yet. Still holding tight to her basket, she edged herself forward, little by little, making for the angled ledge. Reaching it, she peered down.

Immediately, her breath caught in her throat.

Some fifty feet below her, a grouping of dark, furred forms were writhing along the steep incline of the canyon wall. To her great relief, the first thing Rehna made out among them were the arching twin horns of a large mountain goat, twisting this way and that among the huddle. The wind kicked up again, then, pulling the edge of her scarf before her face, and she thought she could make out the agonizing screams of an animal in pain as she reached up to free her eyes of the fabric. With a grimace Rehna began to scoot away from the edge carefully, thinking to find her mother quickly and set off back for Estwyn, intent on warning the Vigil of wolves in the slopes.

Then, just as she was about to turn away from the scene, Rehna saw the ruined basket.

With a lance of horror she took in the shredded wicker remains, recognizing them at once, unable to look away. A sound, a choke of incomprehension and denial, formed in her throat as she noticed the collection of nettles and thornweed, the carefully gathered plants tumbling about the bloody ground in the wind. Ice welled up, living and pulsating, in Rehna's gut, and despite the shrieking voice in her head telling her not to look, not to bear witness to what she knew she would find, she dragged her eyes from the herbs back to the shifting shapes she'd assumed was a pack and their prey. Only then, taking the time she needed to distinguish the forms and bodies of the creatures, did Rehna realize what they *really* were.

Only then, as two of the beasts shifted to provide a space between their bodies for her to see through, did Rehna make out the torn and savaged form of her mother, shattered and convulsing as claws and teeth ripped into her still-living flesh against the loose stone.

There was nothing else to be done, after that sight.

All Rehna could do was scream.

The shrill shriek, even over the wind, echoed down between the walls of the pass, making the monsters freeze, then slowly turn their terrible heads about and up, glinting gazes scanning the ridgeline with hungry intelligence. Before they'd even caught sight of her, they rose, standing on humanish legs, and with another gasp Rehna took them in, recognizing the trio of twisted forms in truth. The evils that were the center of so many stories she had heard, of the accountings the soldiers told in her father's treatment rooms and the scary tales the children at her school shared amongst themselves.

Cold eyes found her then, still and feral in the frame of their warped heads. Something greater than grief took hold of Rehna, something more powerful than terror. A desperation, a bottomless, infinite *need* consumed her, devouring her as a single word rippled in the depths of her mind.

RUN.

With a yell Rehna hurled the basket down the slope, not waiting to see if she caught any of the beasts with its weighted contents before bolting southward, down the mountain. Stones and earth slipped and shifted beneath her feet, shale and pebbles flying in all directions as she hurtled away from that horrible scene with a speed she would have never thought possible. Behind her she heard the raking sounds of clawed hands and feet scrabbling at the hill, chasing after her while howled brays and snarls replaced the empty silence of the suddenly-absent wind. Rehna hardly even noticed when the edge of her scarf caught on a sharp ridge, tearing it from her head and neck. She didn't care when she stumbled and nearly fell, didn't feel the ground giving way under her boots, or the bite of the air anymore. Nothing mattered to her, then, nothing existed to her but the monsters she knew would be chasing her up over the ridge of the pass.

The monsters, and the great grey wall of Estwyn.

For the first time in her life, Rehna saw something *more* in the boring, unadorned stone. Where only minutes ago it was nothing to her but a scar on the landscape of the foothills, now the striking paleness of the granite shone as brightly as a signal fire before her, a beacon drawing her home. A stinging on her cheeks surprised Rehna while she hurtled towards the defenses, and with a detached jolt she realized that she was weeping, terrified tears streaming down her face.

Descending at a breakneck pace took only a fraction of the time she'd needed to climb the mountain's base, and before long Rehna hit solid, softer earth and grass, the uneven shale and hard-packed ground giving way to the richer loam of the Viridian wilds. Instead of relief, however, she felt her stomach twist as she slowed, gravity no longer aiding her in her flight. Her body seemed to grow unexpectedly sluggish, the headlong hurtle from high above stiffening and stuttering as she found herself all at once moving forward on nothing more than the meager power of her own two legs. The wall was closer now, though, a mere sixty or seventy yards away. Behind her Rehna heard the scraping of shifting stone and a snapping growl, and she sobbed even as she pushed herself to go faster, faster. Fifty yards, now. She could see the scrambling of the King's men atop the walls, the sentries having long noted their approach. Forty yards. She saw bows appear, arrows being knocked over the ramparts. Thirty yards. She could hear shouting, though what orders were being given she couldn't know. Twenty yards. Rehna's breath rasped in broken relief as she made out the outline of the streets and buildings beyond the narrow opening in the wall's great double-doors.

Then, however, she finally made out the shouts from the top of the wall.

"SEAL THEM! SEAL THE GATES!"

Something unlike anything Rehna had ever thought she could feel washed through her limbs. An empty absence of all sense, of all reason. With numb disbelief she watched several forms clad in the white and red of the Vigil appear in the space between the massive doors. For the briefest of moments she met the eyes of one soldier in particular, a young man maybe ten years her senior. What she expected to see there, in his eyes, she wasn't sure. Pity perhaps? Maybe even hope? As he and his comrades threw their weight behind the heavy timbers, she would have at least thought to witness sorrow, or regret.

Terror, though, was all that welled in that gaze. A fear she couldn't understand, given the ever-praised strength of Estwyn's defenses.

Then the gate closed with an echoing *boom* that crashed like a physical blow over Rehna's small body.

"NO!" she screamed, sobbing and howling, reaching the wall not five seconds after, slamming into it and pounding at its weather-worn surface as if she could knock it down with her own small fists. "NO! PLEASE! LET ME IN! LET ME IN!"

She didn't understand, *couldn't* understand. She cried and pleaded, clawing at the wood until her gloves broke and splinters cut into her fingers. Just then, a myriad *twangs* of released bowstrings rippled from above, and a number of *thuds* and yelps not so far behind her made Rehna whirl.

In an instant, her confusion was wiped away.

Rehna was a level-headed girl, after all. With no more than a trio of the creatures running her down, she hadn't understood why the Vigil would have seen fit to close the gates, sealing her outside the safety of the walls. It had made no sense. In the stories, the soldiers always won in the end, always cut down the foul monsters and rose triumphant with swords held high. Sure enough, as she turned, the first thing Rehna noted were the tumbling forms of the three beasts who'd killed her mother, each falling and rolling under the momentum of their mad chase, corrupted forms bristling with half-a-dozen arrows each. She might have been happy, then, might have been relieved.

On the contrary, Rehna felt her water run down her legs when she lifted her eyes, looking back to the pass where she knew her mother's body lay, and saw with a wash of horror and awe what it was that had frightened the soldiers so.

The three creatures hadn't been alone, it seemed. Not alone at all…

Then there was a *clunk* and the rattling of churning chains, and Rehna Toyte had just enough time to glance up, to blink in surprise a single time, before the portcullis of Estwyn's great wall thundered down upon her.

CHAPTER FIFTEEN

"A dragon is not some beast to be trifled with. It is not merely some greater animal. A dragon is a mind, a terrifying consciousness, one whose knowledge, power, and awareness would certainly put the common thoughts of man to shame. Do not be fooled by its bestial appearances. A dragon possesses will, and is just as capable as you or I of wielding it to its own substantial advantage."

-Tryvean Morne, High General of Aletha, c. 315p.f.

Despite Ryn's continued absence, Declan spent the next four days in a state of unexpected content. He had been briefly concerned—as any stranger would be when thrust into the care of unfamiliar acquaintances— that his presence might be unwanted in the yr'Essel's home, maybe even burdensome. Ester had been friendly enough, but Declan had had a hard time distinguishing at first if her amiability was genuine, or merely born of gratitude for the role he'd played in saving her life, or perhaps regret for having put his own knife to his throat. More distressing, of the half-elf's father he'd known even less, save for the brief introduction and revelations presented to him by Ryn and Ester herself.

Fortunately, it didn't take long for his concerns to be alleviated.

Bonner yr'Essel, it transpired, was a buoyant, cheerful man when not laden by worries and premonitions brought on by dreams and ghoul attacks. Within a quarter hour of Ryn's departure, the mage—another concept Declan was still struggling to come to terms with—had demonstrated more than once how he'd earned the crinkling laugh lines about his eyes. He took every opportunity to chortle at one comment or another while giving Declan a succinct tour of the rest of his home, to the point his daughter—who'd accompanied them—started rolling her eyes anytime he broke a smile. He'd also insisted Declan keep the room he'd woken up in, and then, over a filling lunch of roasted boar, spiced tubers and roots, and chilled water flavored with lemon and strawberries, suggested that Ester show him about the dense woods that surrounded the house. The woman had been quick to agree, flashing Declan a smile that had made it impossible to even *begin* to think of a reason he might refuse.

After that, the days ticked themselves off in a pleasant blur. It became a habit, waking up each morning well before dawn to watch the sun make itself known over the eastern rise of the clearing's surrounding trees. Often Declan was the first up, even before the master of the house, and he enjoyed feeling the world come to around him, rising from its slumber while the cool nights of the ending summer fled from the sky. Ester tended to sleep in, but Bonner always rose in time to join Declan before dawn turned to true day, the two of them breakfasting on fruit, jams, and fresh bread, talking and laughing over their meal as the air warmed outside. The old man had more stories to share than any living person Declan had ever met, which he supposed shouldn't have surprised him. The mage stayed clear of his history with Ryn, for the time being—following the dragon's lead, undoubtedly—but all the same his tales were always grand and intriguing, not to mention—when his daughter wasn't around—not uncommonly bawdy to the point of blushing. It turned out Bonner—when he'd yet been Bonner *Fehn*, rather than yr'Essel—had been a court magus in Aletha under the purview of Kings who'd lived so long ago, Declan couldn't recognize a single name among them. As a result, there were plenty of tales to be shared about the ludicrous extravagancies of the nobility. The time one particularly odd lord had thought it a good idea to attempt to tame a peacock and carry it around on his shoulder. Or the time when a lady of one of the minor noble families had induced a scandal—and trend, shortly thereafter—by appearing before the royal family wearing little more than blooming sunflowers over her breasts and womanhood.

This latter story had had Declan spitting his morning's drink over the common room table, coughing and laughing and choking all at the same time.

Still, despite his charm and pleasant nature, Bonner yr'Essel was certainly not without his peculiarities. He never made a demonstration of his power—and Declan was far too overwhelmed by the very idea to make any such request—but the old man exuded a presence of not-so-quiet confidence in all things, striding about with a boisterous spirit that was much at odds with the somber, pensive image the tales spun of sages, wizards, and knowing men. Stranger, however, were the sporadic interruptions Declan had come to attribute to the wards Ryn had referred to, the spell-wrought barriers "weaved" about the mage's home. It wasn't uncommon for Bonner to pause mid-sentence, twitching in one direction or another, pulled by a distant sense towards something Declan couldn't feel or see. When this happened, his eyes tended to lose their focus—or rather, perhaps, train on the imperceptible—flicking about in the air as though reading letters only he could make out in the currents of the wind. Odder still, of course, was the muttering. There seemed to be no such thing as even companionable silence to Bonner. Even when left to his own tidings, he could often be caught speaking to no one in particular, typically under his breath, and usually grasping and tugging at the clear crystal around his neck like an old habit. Declan never quite got the impression Bonner was conversing *with* anyone in particular, what little of the conversations he overheard being very obviously one-sided. Then again, he never went out of his way to linger around these dialogues long enough to be sure.

Eavesdropping on a man whose power *Ryn* clearly bowed to seemed to Declan—to put it mildly—a poor idea...

Where the father was odd and exuberant, the daughter was simpler, more reserved company. The fire Ester had shown their first morning in the yr'Essel's home occasionally reared its head around Bonner, but it was generally subdued in favor of a cooler, pleasant exterior that was so at odds with the dangerous woman who'd held Declan up with his own knife. Ester always joined them an hour or so after the sun's full rising, breaking her fast late while listening to the other two continue in whatever direction the morning's meandering conversation had taken them. She rarely joined in on their talks, though—given how often she shook her head and muttered a sardonic "men" into her toast—this might have been more due to the subject of their discussions than anything else. On the other hand, the woman grew animated enough whenever Declan found himself alone with her, which happened more often than he might have hoped. Every day, in the hours before noon, Ester led him into the woods about her father's home. There in the underbrush, she rapidly proved herself to be as knowledgeable in a great many areas as the old man appeared. In a surprisingly short period, Declan learned a vast amount about the verdure that could be found within Viridian's deep forests. Ester had a keen, knowing eye that never ceased to impress him. After their first casual amble beyond the glen he could tell the age of a buck by the length of its legs and darkness of its coat, and name a dozen different birds by the color of their wings and the sound of their song. By the third, Declan could even track a few of the larger animals' paths through the undergrowth, and usually guess correctly what beast they might have been. More useful still, Ester taught him to identify some score of herbs he'd never noticed before, all incredibly useful to a man who lived by the sword. She showed him horse-chestnut and black-mallow for poultices, gumroot and sarrow-back for bindings, and even pointed out rothwort, whose blade-like stalks, heavy with its distinct black seeds, were much more commonplace than Declan might have expected. After that, he learned to identify hemlock and belladonna—both deceptively pretty, flowering things—along with a half-dozen varieties of poisonous mushrooms he might have eaten without a second thought, and probably had, at some point.

Ester's talents, of course, extended beyond her simple knowledge of the bounties of the forests. It was she, it turned out, who downed most of the game that graced Bonner's table. She had a marksman's shot, and was hardly ever without a shortbow and a quiver of goose-fletched arrows on any of their morning jaunts. This hadn't surprised him, given her parentage.

Aside from the sharp eyes and keen senses that lent themselves well to an archer's countenance, the *er'enthyl* were a people of the wild land, a culture that worshipped nature as the living embodiment of divinity, the earth itself a god. They sought out the plenty of the Vyr'en for their grains, fruits, and vegetables, and hunted for their meat. The idea of cultivation would have been unsettling to the few elves he'd met in his time, likely bordering on blasphemous, a fact Declan had known even before Ester explained it to him. He learned too, in the same conversation, that her mother had spent a great deal of time with her in these very woods, showing her how to nock and aim from the moment she was tall enough to draw the string to her cheek.

What *had* taken him aback, on the other hand, was his discovery that the bow was hardly the sole weapon the woman had drilled her daughter in.

Declan already possessed some small sense that the woman knew her way around a blade already, of course. All the same, it still came as a surprise to him—as the three of them had lunched on the first afternoon after Ryn's leaving—when Ester offhandedly asked if he would be willing to spar with her. Less doubting her ability and more concerned that they would be a poor match, it had required a knowing wink from Bonner before Declan tentatively agreed, earning himself another one of Ester's brilliant smiles.

It hadn't taken long—the two of them wielding a pair of well-worn practice swords the woman retrieved from her room—for Declan to understand why the old man had seemed so confident. As it turned out, of the two of them, he *was* the more skilled combatant, but by a much smaller margin than he might have expected. From the moment their blades first met, Ester fought brilliantly. Her wooden weapon swept in graceful arcs about her lithe form, her footwork through the swaying grasses of the field tempered in almost perfect resonance with the movements of the sword. Declan had been impressed from the go, and found himself working far harder than he'd anticipated in order to keep her at bay. She *danced* more than fought, the rapid patterns of her strikes as fluid as silk let loose on the breeze. He knew of the style, had read on the elven forms he found her going through now, but it was the first time he'd ever had the opportunity to observe its grace in person.

Still, Ester's patterns were yet patterns, and though she caught him a few good blows in their initial encounters that first afternoon, Declan discovered just as quickly that he had experience on his side. It was an advantage he pressed as soon as he'd started to discern the rhythm of her movements. A swordsman did not live long if they couldn't adapt, and Declan would have wagered—after a handful of matches that left both of them bruised and sweating—that Ester had never had much need to adjust her forms. Whether she was aware of this or not he hadn't yet perceived, but he proved himself right not ten seconds into their next meet, reading the feint from the left he had seen three times already. Playing into the move, he bluffed a step back, seeing at once the look that passed over Ester's face as she pulled her practice sword back and instead sent it slicing up at his right shoulder.

The *crack* of wood meeting as Declan planted and parried the blow had taken her by distinct surprise, though not half as much as his free hand gripping her over-extended wrist, pulling and twisting her over his body. She yelped as he brought her swinging down—as gently as he could manage—onto her back, stripping her sword with the worn crossguard of his own even as he did. She'd landed with a heavy *thump* that very obviously knocked the wind out of her, gasping from the blow, so abruptly disarmed and defeated Declan could see the confusion play across her face while her mind struggled to figure out what had just happened.

Her expression stilled when he brought the tip of his blade down to hover over the space between her eyes. For a moment she met his gaze, looking up the length of the weapon. Then, together, they grinned at each other, unable to keep from doing so while listening to Bonner guffaw from where he'd been watching them, in the shade against the east wall of his home.

Ester improved, in the days after that, seeking his thoughts and advice and taking them to heart almost *too* thoroughly. Often Declan found himself on the receiving end of his own lessons, the repetition in the woman's attacks breaking up, the predictability in her positioning steadily fading. Ironically, the bruises he received as thanks endeared her to him all the more. He *liked* having an opponent that could challenge him in a fight. Not since Cassandra and the grizzled bastards of the Iron Wind had Declan had adequate opportunity to train with a partner, much less one that actually pushed him. More than once he'd caught himself smiling like a mad dog, trading blows with the skilled half-elf, who never spoke a word as to whether she noticed this.

Declan suspected she knew that doing so would have opened her up to commentary on the hard excitement that always flared in her green eyes whenever their swords met.

It was in this fashion that the days eased by, one after the other. Mornings breakfasting with Bonner, then out with Ester in the endlessness of the western woodlands before training after lunch. When the sun began to dip down from its crowning heights, it was the signal for leisure, or doing chores about the mage's home. Declan did his best to earn his keep where he could, which he suspected Bonner found diverting more than anything. It was on one such errand, in fact, mid-afternoon of the fourth day after

Ester had gone off to track down their evening meal, that Declan was out gathering wood with the old man, and Bonner spoke up suddenly.

"You've led a hard life for someone your age, boy."

The comment was stated as fact, and not a disapproving one. Declan stood straight from where he'd been snatching up a dry branch to add to the teetering pile of kindling already precariously balanced in his right arm. Looking around, he saw that the old man was studying the inside of his left arm from around his own stack, where the Seeker's arrow was plain even against Declan's scarred skin.

"No harder than some," Declan said with a shrug, tossing the branch atop his collection. "I might even argue the opposite, given some of the stories I heard from others while I was part of the companies."

"And how many of them weren't even fifteen when they joined, I wonder…"

Bonner spoke more in suggestion than in question, raising an eyebrow at Declan, who offered half-a-smile and a laugh in return.

"Sure, I was on the young end of things wherever I went. But I had Ryn to help me. In hindsight, I can say now his presence was probably worth more than I could have ever imagined."

"I'm sure it was." The mage skillfully tucked a booted toe under a twig, and with a deft flick of his foot kicked it up onto his own pile like a boy not out of his adolescence. "Then again, don't give that oversized lizard more credit than he's due. I'm sure you have some sense of your own potential."

The choice of words had Declan take pause, midway through reaching up to peel a sheaf of loose bark from a nearby pine. He had an awareness of his own abilities, sure—what swordsman of any skill didn't—but he wouldn't have been so quick to say he still had "potential". Ryn had been an excellent teacher, and he'd been lucky enough to practice the blade under several masters after him—not the least of which had been Cassandra. He'd taken to the profession quick enough, even earning himself a position among the top captains of the Iron Wind in the short years he'd spent with them.

Still, a man could only learn so much in one lifetime…

"I'm fortunate enough to have some skill with the blade, sure," he answered, thinking modesty was the best route to go if he was to glean out Bonner's meaning. "It's been some years since anyone told me I had 'potential', though."

If it had been Ryn's eye in which the knowing gleam shown then, rather than Bonner's, Declan knew he probably would have been irritated. He still wasn't quite sure if he was going to forgive the dragon, or even if he had it in himself to do so at all.

For some reason, however, the look the mage gave him then only made him curious.

Of course it was best not to let *Bonner* know that, given how mischievous the old man could be.

Declan feigned a sigh of indifference, returning to his task. The bark came loose in a solid chunk, and he shook it free of dirt, ants, and pine needles. They would need these gathered stockpiles of wood soon, if the nights continued to cool. Ester had told him in confidence that her father typically used something called "firestones" to cook and keep the home well-lit and warm, but the mage had—in what was likely consideration of Declan's already overwhelmed understanding—returned to the common ways of maintaining a comfortable home for the last few days.

Declan was not unappreciative of this accommodation, and so felt almost guilty at the leap of victorious excitement in his gut when Bonner pressed on behind him.

"You're not aware of anything more? You think you've achieved all there is to achieve, in your ability?"

"With the sword?" Declan asked over his shoulder, working hard to keep his voice nonchalant despite the quickening of his heart.

"Amongst other things."

Unable to help himself at this, Declan glanced back at the old man.

He found Bonner with his back to him, imitating Declan in an obvious display of showing that the mage knew *exactly* what he was about.

Declan almost laughed, but thought he would at least get out of his host whatever he was willing to share.

"All I know is the sword. I get the impression Ester would love to put a bow in my hands, but I've never had much talent for archery."

"Yes... Not surprising. Herst lacked any ability as a marksman too, from what I recall."

The words brought Declan up short, and he half-turned to face the man now.

"Herst? What does he have to do with anything?"

It was Bonner's turn to shrug, and Declan realized with a wrench that he had just been played at his own game. He was about to abandon slyness and press the mage for more when Bonner stiffened, his attention abruptly diverted, head shifting westward. Declan, who'd grown accustomed to these disruptions, waited a moment, then carefully bent down to scoop up a spare twig that had tumbled from the top of his pile when he'd turned.

He was mid-way through the motion when the mage spoke, making him halt.

"Ryndean..."

It wasn't Ryn's name itself that had stopped Declan cold. It was the *way* Bonner said it. Surprise mixed with a distinct concern, accented by the frown that suddenly marred the old man's face.

"What is it?" Declan asked, straightening up again, mind suddenly on anything but their conversation. "He's back?"

"Yes," Bonner confirmed at once, eyes lifting to the sky they could see between the entwined canopy of the trees. "And coming fast, too…"

Again the worry was there, and Declan felt a knot form in his stomach. He considered dropping his gathered kindling and loosening his sword in its sheath, but hesitated as a shadow passed across the sun overhead, the familiar silhouette dipping down silently towards them, dancing and dipping through the layered foliage. A moment later the twisted black hawk was above them, shifting and changing even as it pulled up, growing heavier while its leathery wings shrank.

Ryn landed at half-a-run not far from them, clawed feet breaking his momentum, having skillfully completed the transition into the body of his *rh'eem*—his dragonling's form—even as he dropped. He barely paused to look between the pair of them before speaking without preamble.

Estwyn has fallen. Wereyn, out of the Tears. Apparently their numbers were in the tens of thousands.

For once, Declan understood the context of the dragon's rushed tidings, as well as he understood the paling of Bonner's face beside him.

"*What?!*" the mage demanded. "When?!"

Nearly five days ago, if the rumor is to be believed, Ryn answered while looking over his shoulder, the motion almost nervous. *I overhead a group of the Vigil's soldiers discussing it at the Rest. The town sent birds to every corner of Viridian in warning before the walls were overcome.*

"Wereyn?" Declan spoke this time, yet numbly clinging to the bundle of branches in his arms. "You're sure? Again?"

That's what they said. The dragon was still scanning the trees behind him, like he was searching for something hidden beyond the dense shifting of the leaves. After a moment or two more, he finally turned his attention back on them, looking to Bonner. *And I'm worried that's not all. Can you scry the woods west of here?*

The old man's brow creased. "In the direction you came? Is something wrong?"

I don't know… I thought I sensed a presence a few times, but it always faded before I could focus on it. It could be nothing.

"Or it could be something," Bonner muttered, letting his gathered kindling tumble from his arms before brushing himself off. "Given recent events, I'm unfortunately inclined to consider the latter more likely than the former. Come. I'll need open sky."

With that, he started off at a quick pace south, back in the direction of his home. Shaking himself from his moment of disbelief, Declan followed suit in casting aside his own day's bounty, joining Ryn as they made to follow Bonner back through the woods.

"What's going on?" he asked the dragon, walking side by side. "Wereyn haven't made a major push for any of the northern towns for more than twenty years."

All I can do is guess, which doesn't help much right now, Ryn answered, ducking under the lowest limbs of a young pine as the glen came into sight through the trunks. *The fact that they've targeted Estwyn twice, though... That's telling.*

Declan grunted in ascension. "The pass."

He didn't need to see Ryn's dipping head to know he was right. It was the only thing that made sense.

Still, the dragon's answer affirmed his thoughts. *Karn's Gullet, it used to be called. Don't ask me why. I couldn't tell you. It's been blocked for more than six hundred years, now. One of the last things Herst and I saw to before he died.*

"*You* blocked it?" Declan demanded in astonishment, looking around sharply. "How?"

He registered, then, taking in the alien form of the dragonling, that Ryn's sudden return had been less jarring than he'd anticipated. For the last four days he'd thought often of the conversations they needed to have when he saw the dragon again, but with this more pressing news those concerns had been shoved to the back of his mind. Now, given this sudden admission, Declan was reminded once again of all the things that still sent his head spinning when he thought of the world he had stepped into so abruptly not even a week ago...

A landslide, Ryn responded with a strained smirk. *More your ancestor's doing than my own, believe it or not. It doesn't matter now. If the wereyn found a way to clear the pass, and were allowed to gather on the other side of the ranges...*

He let the thought fade, and Declan, too, said nothing more. He was curious as to how Herst, his own forefather, could have been responsible for the collapse of a mountainside, but he let that thought slide given the current circumstances. The two of them needed no more words shared. If the pass—the Gullet, apparently—was clear, and there were *more* of the beasts waiting in and beyond the Mother's Tears...

And Estwyn gone, too... Declan thought privately. *The first line of defense, overtaken in a blink...*

He felt a twinge of nostalgic discomfort. The town had been his birthplace, even if he didn't remember it. He'd been less than a year old when the last assault had come from the wereyn, the twisted people of the ranges and—it was commonly believed—the frozen, uncharted lands of Eserysh beyond them. That scattered offense had been repelled only barely even then, beaten back by the small garrison of Vigil soldiers who'd held residency in the village. They'd been joined, too, by those men and women of Estwyn itself who'd been brave enough to rally behind the black-and-red banner bearing the King's mark, the frame of a shield emblazed by a crowned stag. Hundreds had died that night, Declan's mother had said on the only occasion he'd cajoled her into telling the story, and the sadness in her eyes had been plain to perceive. He'd never asked for the tale again, the pain there, written clearly across Abegale Idrys' pale features, enough to sear her understanding of that atrocity into his memory forever.

His father, after all, had been among those who'd stood so dauntlessly against the savage tide of the beastmen, and among those who'd fallen to it.

But now? Declan thought to himself, finally stepping out into the clearing with Ryn some dozen feet behind Bonner. The mage was already busy easing himself down to kneel in the swaying grass. *Why now?*

He'd been to Estwyn once on Iron Wind business, and twice before with Stonewall, then Holden's Guard. If he'd had to describe it, Declan would have called the place more stronghold than valley town, shielded as it was by the twenty-foot palisade that encircled it to the west, south, and east, a defense Ryn had told him had not been in existence in his father's time. Also new had been the reinforcement to the north gate and its surrounding walls—built from stone and mortar, now, rather than wood—as well as some thousand of the Vigil's numbers, refreshed every two years according to the locals he'd asked. Those changes had been made over two decades ago, of course, and Declan might have written the town's fall off to laxity borne from too long spent without a sign of the threat the defenses had been built to thwart.

But *tens of thousands* of wereyn? As far as he knew, the creatures were uncommonly seen as it was. For so many to have gathered and coordinated such an assault…

Unbidden, Ester's angry words to Ryn rang in Declan's ears in that moment, echoing back to him. "Things are happening," she'd said simply.

"And fast," he muttered to himself, gritting his teeth as a hint of the frustration he'd largely pressed aside over the last four days came trickling back.

The crackling smell of fire dragged his irritation away again.

Declan looked up, alarmed. Still a few feet ahead of him, Bonner was on all fours, now, his back largely hiding whatever it was he was doing, his right hand moving about in rapid, practiced patterns through the grass before him. Smoke was rising around him, curling up from the field to be whisked away by the breeze, and Declan shouted out instinctively, closing the short distance at a run. He reached out, ready to drag the old man away from the burning ground by the nape of his multi-colored robes, when he caught sight of what it was the mage was working on.

Almost four feet wide starting at Bonner's knees, several nearly perfect rings of blackened earth had been burned into the grass, the charred blades still smoldering and curling over themselves. Within these fuming circles, an intricate tapestry of shapes and symbols had been similarly branded into the earth, as though written out with a bar of white-hot iron. They trailed together, penned out like the fine curving script in some educated noble's hand, half-a-dozen layers of them banded inside one another. Even as Declan watched with an open mouth, Bonner put the finishing touches on the very center of the arrangement, the index and ring fingers of his right hand twisting through the grass with a final flourish of smoke.

His *fingers*?!

The realization barely had time to gain a foothold in the wash of confusion that overtook Declan, because in the next instant Bonner brought his hand down again, palm flat, slamming it into the ground in the very center of the circle. There was a flash of light, a rippling glow like the man had just struck the surface of an incandescent water pool, the arcs whisking outwards to the edge of the circle in an instant.

That was when the rings began to spin.

"Mother's Mercy."

It took a second for Declan to realize it was *he* who had sworn, staggering half-a-step back at the sight before him. He felt a hand—a *clawed* hand—reach out to steady him, but he hardly noticed as he watched the shifting mosaic twist about the grass in awe. The runes—for that was all they could be, Declan knew—turned this way and that before his eyes, each layer racing clockwise, then the opposite, while the one below it followed its own course. *Within* the rings, too, the symbols themselves shifted and repositioned, glowing like red embers and raising new plumes of faint smoke as they seemed to lift from the ground, hovering a moment before settling down in some new position in the line of shapes.

"What *is* this?" Declan barely got out.

Scrying. The familiar tenor of Ryn's words did much to bring Declan back to himself, and he felt the dragon release his upper arm. *Bonner is searching the woods to the west of us, looking for anything abnormal.*

There was an irony to that statement Declan rather thought Ryn didn't catch, as well as a potential amusement that was lost on both of them.

"He's… searching?" Declan distantly realized he was growing tired of being rendered speechless by this unearthly pair. "For what? For something you couldn't see?"

Exactly. You've had the unfortunate chance to observe the limits of my ability more than once, in the last week. Bonner's wheel is less encompassing, but more precise. If there's something there—even something masked from me—he'll find it.

Declan lapsed back into silence after that, allowing himself the incredible experience of watching the mage do his work. Magic. The word tolled like a bell in his heart, overwhelming him in more ways than one.

He was seeing magic, clearly now, for the first time.

For a minute or so he and Ryn stood quietly, looking down over Bonner's shoulders, watching the "wheel"—as the dragon had called it—spin in its myriad of directions. At first the fascinating warmth that had built up in his chest held, pulsing in breathless wonder each time a rune flashed and resettled itself. As the seconds passed, however, Declan felt his captivation begin to ebb, shrinking and tightening into nervous anticipation. Something was wrong. The shifting magics, gracefully flowing through the burned grass, were alien to him, beyond his comprehension. All the same, Declan didn't miss the tensing of Bonner's form below him, nor the muttered curse as the old man's hand traced the rings like one might use a finger to follow the lines of a book.

Ryn, it seemed, didn't either.

What is it? The dragon's voice was low, like he was afraid of drawing unwanted attention to the three of them. *Do you see something?*

Bonner's head tilted beneath his hood at the query, and Declan saw with a thrill that the green in the man's eyes was gone. In their place, an opaque film of white, like the gaze of a blind man, had overtaken his irises. The mage wasn't reading the scripts at all.

He was spying on some distant part of the land with his *own eyes.*

"Something, yes…" Bonner answered Ryn's query slowly. "It's too far, though…"

Is it approaching?

Bonner nodded.

How fast? By land or sky?

This time, the mage took a moment, clearly struggling to discern the answers. "I can't tell from where yet. I can only feel it. But fast. *Too* fast."

This was, very apparently, *not* what Ryn wanted to hear. He spun on his clawed toes to look westward, white-gold eyes scanning the shadows of the distant forest, deep in the midafternoon light. Turning himself, Declan took firm hold of his sword, and he imitated the dragon's scrutiny, lifting his gaze to study the heavens above the tree line. For a time the two of them waited like that, the clearing about them silent save for the faint whistle of the wind and crackle of the spell.

Then Bonner gasped behind them, scrambling back from the rune wheel onto his feet.

"Gods! Ryndean! The sky! The *sky*! It's—!"

SCCREEEEEH!

Before the old man could finish, the shrill, otherworldly cry cut him off, flooding their ears like shards of broken glass as it tore down from above. It reminded Declan of the sound steel made when dragged over stone, shivering and horrible. Desperately now he scoured the horizon, having heard all-too-clearly the distress in Bonner's attempted warning.

It didn't take him long to find the source.

High, high above the shifting pines of the forest, far above where he'd been vainly eyeing, a dark blotch plummeted from between the clouds, small in the distance, but growing larger by the second as it plunged towards them at a steep angle. A second shriek shattered the day, and behind him Declan heard Bonner finally spit out the name like it was something foul he'd been holding between his teeth.

"DREY!"

CHAPTER SIXTEEN

GET INSIDE!

Ryn's roar ripped across the momentary bewilderment that had held the three of them fast, and Declan had the briefest glimpse of the dragon beginning to change at his side, body swelling and limbs thickening even as his friend fell on all fours. Before he could demand what was going on, Bonner had taken him by the arm and—with what seemed supernatural strength for a man his age—started to drag him towards the house, pulling him along at a full run.

"Bonner, what's—?" Declan tried to get out once his feet found their pace in the sudden rush, but the mage cut him off.

"Not now!" They'd reached the door, and Bonner wrenched it open, shoving Declan through without ceremony. "Inside! *Get inside!*"

Declan half-stumbled over the threshold into the house's narrow entrance hall, catching himself barely on the rough stone of the closest wall. By the time he turned around again, Bonner had followed him in and slammed the entrance shut behind them. He was backing away from the door, face intently lifted, like he expected the entwined, living rafters of the ceiling to cave in on them at any second. At his sides his hands shook, and he was muttering what sounded like strung prayers to some foreign god under his breath in rapid succession.

Bonner yr'Essel, Declan realized then, was frightened.

Declan wasn't all too sure why, but this understanding brought the gravity of the situation down on him in a way even Ryn's thundered order had not been able to. His questions died in his throat, and he stood there in the almost-eerie silence that followed, ears ringing in the dreadful quiet. Every sound, every scratch of the spruces' branches overhead and muffled step of Bonner's slow retreat from the door made his heart jump. He *wanted* to speak, *wanted* to ask what in the Graces' names a "drey" was, or why they had had to run from it, but no matter how hard he tried, he couldn't manage to get the words out. Fear held his tongue, and there was no stopping himself from lifting his own eyes to the ceiling as Bonner reached him, finally quitting his withdrawal when they stood side by side. For almost half-a-minute there was nothing, the two of them waiting with bated breath, the house creaking and groaning with feigned placidity around them.

Then the shrill scream came again, infinitely closer now, ringing through Declan's nervously clenched teeth almost painfully.

This time, however, it was echoed by a monstrous, guttural roar that tremored through the cool grass about their feet as Ryn met whatever it was that had fallen from the sky.

Though hidden from him, Declan could largely picture the battle raging outside on nothing more than the terrible sounds of the two combatants' clash. He made out the frantic beat of wings—more than a single set—and knew that Ryn and this opponent were both struggling to stay airborne. He heard the pair throw themselves against each other, bodies crunching into one another, heard the tearing sound of ripping flesh and the keen screech of claws rasping over steely scales. All the while the pair snarled and bellowed in pain and rage, Ryn's growls coming in booming blows, the unknown creature's rising in terrible shrieks of defiant bloodlust. Both Bonner and Declan winced as the trembling *WOOSH* of what could only have been dragonfire ripped over them, making the doors of the house shake in their frames. More thuds of mass against mass followed, and together they craned their necks ever upward, following the sounds that faded while rising and rising some more, dwindling almost to nothing.

For a time, the peace of the summer day began to return. The sound of the breeze through the trees overhead could be heard once again.

Declan's own heartbeat, though, was the loudest thing to his own ears. "Is it done?"

His voice was raspy, hoarse in his throat. Beside him, Bonner winced at the sudden query, but shook his head.

"Can't be," he muttered, not dropping his eyes from the direction of the now-vanished battle noise, and said nothing more. He seemed to be waiting, tense and uneasy.

A moment later, he was proven all too right.

OUT OF THE HOUSE! OUT!

Ryn's words erupted into their minds like a rockslide, so abrupt and so jarring Declan almost fell to one knee. He staggered, clutching at the side of his head with one hand, but Bonner caught him with a curse, and once again Declan felt the smaller man hauling him along. The mage shouldered his way back through the door with a *bang*, the pair of them tumbling over each other to spill out onto the grass. The moment they were outside, Declan heard the fluttering, rippling sound of something large and loose plummeting through the air, and this time it was *he* who reacted first, taking Bonner by the collar of his robes and practically lifting the old man off his feet as he sprinted further afield. Five yards. Ten yards. Fifteen yards, he managed.

CRASH!

The impact was so tremendous behind them, the earth actually quaked beneath their feet. Debris—wood splinters, broken stone, and scattered mortar—flew over and around the fleeing pair like shrapnel. A chunk of rock struck Declan in the lower back, bringing him down with a yell of pain, but he managed to pull the old man under his body as he fell. Throwing his free arm over his own head for protection, he curled atop the mage, shielding him from the pattering detritus that rained down about them. The *thumping* and *thudding* of heavy rubble made him wince with every impact, and he grit his teeth in terrible anticipation of their own death tumbling down upon them. Mercifully, the Mother must have been watching, because no crushing blow came, the scattered sounds of destruction steadily dwindled over the course of several seconds, then finally ended. Still, it took a moment before Declan managed to convince himself to lift his head, inch by inch, then his body, allowing Bonner, too, to sit up. Together the pair of them gained their feet, turning to face the sad ruination that made up the scene before them.

The old mage let out a piteous, heartbroken moan.

Bonner's house—his wondrous, serene home of magic and nature—was in ruins. Each of the angled spruces had either snapped in two or torn up at the roots, and most of the walls had shattered and collapsed. They tumbled into loose patches of rock, layering the remnants of the building in a thick cloud of dust as it came to rest. Declan fought to find something to say, some words that would comfort the old man through his daze. Before he could think of anything, the haze began to settle.

That was when the two of them saw the writhing, dark forms twisting about each other in the center of the wreckage.

"Gods…" Bonner got out at Declan's side.

Hardly more than a heavy outline and a hint of scales in the dust, Ryn was the first to free himself and stand, wrenching up out of the remnants of the house with a raging snarl to send shattered wood and stone flying again. Even fifty feet away, Declan felt himself forget to breathe. For the first time he took in the dragon's true form for himself, experiencing the sight not from the depth of distant memories, but in the moment, then and there, as the creature had been intended for the world. Wide wings, each at least thirty feet across, flickered over the destruction, black, leathery membranes stretched between narrower, jointed bones. Despite being on all fours, stepping away and knocking aside what was left of the south wall, the ridged, raised scales of Ryn's back towered some fifteen feet above the ground, his horned head another five over that. His iron-black body had to be forty feet long, his ribbed, snaking tail almost that over again, and his gaping mouth, lined with savage, eight-inch fangs that gleamed white in the afternoon sun, was an easy five feet wide. Sliced gashes tore through the dragon's dark hide, weeping across the silken scales, and Declan didn't miss the myriad of older wounds that marked his shoulders and side, long-healed injuries he didn't recall seeing in those mysterious memories. The dragon's eyes burned gold and white, and as he watched, Declan saw Ryn rear and take a deep, devouring breath, corded chest swelling, mouth beginning to glow.

"Look away!" Bonner howled from beside him, taking Declan's shoulder and twisting him only just in time.

WOOSH!

Declan caught hardly a glimpse of brilliant, broiling white flames aimed into the remnants of the house at Ryn's feet, but even that was enough to leave him cursing and blinking for several seconds afterwards, fading afterimages of the light seared across his vision. Heat, billowing and brutal in its intensity, struck them from behind like a physical blow. When the roar of the fire had ended, the two of them wheeled around again, Declan fully expecting to find the dragon standing victoriously over the indistinguishable corpse of some charred beast.

Nothing so fortunate awaited him.

Ryn, instead, was snarling in frustrated fury, gnashing his teeth, trying to fight off the horrible *thing* that had somehow managed to escape his fire and wrap its long, strong arms around his head. Partially obscured by the newly billowing smoke and writhing flames that largely consumed the devastation around the pair now, Declan could barely see more than Ryn's neck being wrenched this way and that, his opponent doing its utmost to wrestle him to the ground. For a time the two were little more than silhouettes, outlined shapes in the flickering light, and all that could be caught of either was the thrashing end of a tail, a clawed hand digging into a ridged snout, or the glint of eyes through the grey.

Then, though, the winds shifted, casting aside the curtain of smoke, and Declan felt his stomach flip as the beast Ryn so viciously fought against was revealed in all its horrible depravity.

Almost fifteen feet tall in all, the thing had massive, bat-like wings extending from a body that was almost a man's, complete with lithe, muscular arms ending in clawed, cruel hands still wrapped about the dragon's head. Its legs, too, thrashing around in the burning debris in an attempt to find good purchase, were humanoid, but its taloned feet and scaled skin looked more to have been stolen from the bipedal form of a dragonling. Unlike Ryn's, however, the beast's scales were a sickly hue, grey-green in color, bringing to mind the sheen of dead, rotting flesh. At its back, a long, thin tail lashed and stabbed at the dragon's side, tipped with a wicked, barbed end that stuck and retracted with alarming dexterity, spraying blood into the raging fires with each blow.

It was the beast's own head, though, that drew Declan's eyes, a horrible bastardization of all that was terrifying in the world.

An enormous wolf's features were set upon a man's shoulders, grey-white fur matted and slick with crimson wetness. Over each pale, colorless eye that reminded Declan of the ghouls who had attacked them only four days prior, a curved horn twisted, almost a mirror to Ryn's own. Its teeth were bared, an uneven row of cruel, broken things, its front-most canines easily the length of Declan's longest finger. It was shrieking again, its unnatural, keening tone like a dagger to the mind.

A drey.

The name had seemed so inconsequential, even when Bonner had spat it out with fear in his voice. Now, looking upon the chimeric corruption, that atrocious conglomeration of scales and fur and fangs, Declan didn't know if he would ever bear hearing the word again without feeling his mouth go dry.

"Declan, get behind me."

Bonner's voice drove Declan out of his stunned gauging of the beast. Looking around, he found the robed mage, inexplicably, on all fours again, hands splayed through the grass, staring at the ground like a man mesmerized.

"What are you doing?" Declan demanded in a panic, fearing Bonner had been struck by some flying lance of timber or stone after all. He made to grab the mage, made to get him back on his feet, but when he took hold of the robes he found—to his disbelief—that the man wouldn't budge.

It was as though he was rooted to the ground, entrenched as firmly into the earth as a tree.

"Get behind me," Bonner said again, his strained voice barely audible over the renewed sounds of battle. "Please, Declan. I fear Ryn might be losing this fight."

Declan blinked at the words, momentarily not comprehending. As he turned his attention back on the ruined house, however, he saw with a thrill that the man was right. Sure enough, despite its smaller size, Ryn seemed unable to throw his opponent off, like the thing was anchored in place by more than muscle and will. Worse, the drey was in the process of forcing open his mouth, wrenching at his jaws with both hands even as it screeched triumphantly. Declan gaped at it, trying to fathom what sort of strength it must take to pry open a *dragon's* maw. The beast was large, granted, more than twice as tall as Declan and proportionately as thick and broad, but it still couldn't have been more than an eighth of Ryn's weight, pound for pound.

Magic.

The realization clicked into place, and Declan's skin turned to gooseflesh. The ghouls had been one thing. Horrible as they were, they'd been slow and easy enough to dispatch if one didn't allow themselves to be overrun by their number. *This*, though… Declan didn't know if he could wrap his head around *this*. The drey was terrifying, unfathomably powerful, but clearly as equally quick if it had managed to free itself of the collapsed structure in time to dodge Ryn's last exhale of dragonfire. It wasn't just holding its own against him, either. It was *winning*, still tearing at the dragon's shoulder and side with its tail all while managing to pry open a gap between the foot-long teeth.

Despite himself, Declan did as he was ordered, stepping away and behind Bonner, who was still kneeling in the earth.

"A moment more..." he heard the old man mutter. "Just a moment more..."

Before them, the drey screamed in atrocious, near-childish delight again. Ryn's strength was failing, now, the dragon scrabbling about and tossing his weight like a trapped animal, fighting with everything he had to get free.

"Bonnerrrr...?" Declan let the alarm in his tone linger. The mage didn't answer. A second passed into two, then five, then ten. Ryn's jaw finally gave, mouth heaved wide by the drey's clawed fingers, and Declan saw the drey's cruel tail come around, poised and ready, set to strike at the soft pale pallet of the dragon's gullet.

Then, before him, Declan heard Bonner give a triumphant grunt, and he looked down just in time to see the old man drive his hands *into* the earth, fingers, palms, and wrists sinking through the grass like water, burying themselves up to the elbow. There was a dull throb of light, as though from below the ground itself.

That was when, with a rumbling sound like the stampede of a hundred wild horses, the field came alive before them with an explosion of earth and grass.

Massive, tendril-like shapes writhed in the dozens from the broken ground, lashing upwards in a wave of brown, twisting forms. They raced, more and more rising up with every passing second, towards the wreckage and the two struggling opponents, crashing and whipping around each other as they curled and snapped. In less time than it took Declan to gasp at the sight, the strange, slithering summonings reached the house, and the drey's gleeful sounds shifted into a shriek of ire. The writhing things drove upwards at it, wrapping themselves about its legs, wriggling up its torso, and even entwining its arms and neck. With a strangled scream the drey released Ryn and leapt away from the dragon, needing both hands to rip at the brown, cord-like creations, pulling and tearing at them. It was quick, *too* quick, and within a handful of seconds it had torn itself free of the strange restraints, dashing back several long paces only to find the things following it, more and more erupting from the earth to ensnare its feet with every step.

With a howl of animalistic frustration, the drey made the only decision left to it. Leaping back a final time, it bent its scaled legs and launched itself upwards, taking to the sky before the tendrils could ensnare it again. Wide wings extended, and it beat at the air once, twice, three times, that trio of powerful strokes all it needed to get a hundred feet above the glen, hovering high over all their heads. The writhing shapes attempted to chase it, a hundred massive snakes baring their fangs in warning as they lifted their thin forms from the ground, but most could only reach so high before falling back or even breaking under their own weight.

Breaking? Declan thought to himself in confusion, watching one particularly wide mass rise and rise and rise, nearly snaring the drey by the foot only to *snap* in two and tumble earthward again.

Then it hit him.

"Roots," he mumbled to himself, not believing his own eyes. "They're bloody *roots...*"

He could understand why he had missed it, initially. The things moved like they were *alive*, flailing and bending to chase their prey. Looking at those closest to him and Bonner, on the other hand, stilling now that the drey had climbed beyond their reach, Declan saw them for what they were. The rough, damp surfaces. The thread-like extensions that protruded like veins to hang limp in the air. It was as if the grass had come alive all around them, their submerged stems swelling and bending to the command of the man who still knelt, arms submerged into the earth.

Like he could feel Declan's eyes on his back, Bonner awkwardly turned his head to look up at him. His hood flopped awkwardly off his neck and his clean-shaven head shined with sweat and exertion, but he still managed a strained smile that gleamed humorlessly through his peppered beard.

"More useful a trick than making the trees grow queerly, eh?"

In response, all Declan could do was ogle the mage, comprehending at last why Ryn had been so firm in his acknowledgment of Bonner yr'Essel's capabilities...

WOOOSH!

Declan yelped, blinking furiously again when the unexpected blast of brilliance stole his vision away for a second time. Ryn had gathered himself and reentered the fight, roaring in pure rage up at the drey still circling above them. His massive form stamped around the wreckage, flattening walls that clung to their shape and snapping smoldering trunks like dry twigs beneath his taloned feet. Twice more jets of white fire spewed from his mouth into the air, trying to catch the creature while it flicked back and forth with uncanny speed. The drey screamed its own anger back at it, rising higher still, staying well clear of both the fire and the magical roots that continued to claw at it from below.

With a flutter and snap of rushing air, Ryn's wings extended and flexed. Showing incredible agility for a beast his size, the dragon maneuvered his way out of the ruins in three quick steps, breaking into a graceful, bounding run that reminded Declan more of the great mountain cats of Viridian's northern forests than any reptile he'd ever seen. With a leap and a heavy beat of his wings, Ryn was airborne once more, and Declan felt his breath catch yet again when the dragon's black scales caught the bright sunlight of the day, rippling across his hide while he streaked upward.

The drey, seeing its chance, dove to meet him.

The pair collided with another mind-numbing *crunch* of limbs and bodies. They roared and shrieked, sometimes clinging to each other to tear and bite and rip at chests and shoulders and abdomens, sometimes breaking apart to gain altitude and circle one another before coming together again. Slowly they climbed higher and higher, forcing Declan to squint upwards against the day's brightness, the details of the fight becoming steadily more difficult to make out.

There was a *squelch* of sound, like a booted foot pried loose from muddy water, and Declan glanced down just in time to catch Bonner when the man made to stand up beside him, staggering as he did.

"Many thanks," the old man said weakly, finding his balance. He looked exhausted, but shaded his green eyes with a hand so clean it might have just been washed, trying—like Declan—to make out how the fight was progressing. Around and before them, the animated roots trembled, holding their form several seconds more before collapsing to the ground, losing all semblance of life as their source of power was taken from them. Even so, the two men hardly took notice of the tumbling tendrils. Together they stood, eyes on the heavens, shared breaths held while the dragon and drey—little more than shapes among the clouds—wheeled about in their vicious battle.

Finally, after what seemed a small eternity in which blood and fur and scales pattered around them like some grim rain, Declan just made out Ryn's massive jaws clamp down on the drey's right arm, finally catching his nimbler adversary.

"He's got him!" he whooped with a jolt of cold adrenaline. "He's got— Oh, Mother above."

Even as far below as he was, Declan thought he could hear the rip of muscle and torn flesh as the *drey*, horribly, bit into its own shoulder, tearing the limb loose with a wrench of its wolfish head. It broke away from Ryn just as an explosion of dragonfire flashed across the sky, a blast that would have incinerated the monster had it not ripped itself free. The sacrifice paid off, but only for a moment. At once the dragon released the scorched remnants of the limb, blackened and smoking bones tumbling to the earth, and dove at the drey. The beast dodged sweeping claws and gnashing teeth, but the wound obviously slowed it, because it didn't manage to avoid the heavy blow from Ryn's tail that caught it full in the side, knocking it out of the sky. It tumbled, screeching as it tried to stabilize itself in the rush of passing air.

This time Ryn's dragonfire struck much closer to the mark.

The flames, tumbling from the dragon's mouth like a waterfall of molten light, chased the drey earthward. The monster managed to right itself, but evaded too slowly to avoid the fire entirely. It shrieked yet again as most of its left wing was engulfed, and when the blinding heat faded Declan and Bonner peered up again to see the thing plummeting towards the ground, clawing and kicking at nothingness as its remaining wing whipped uselessly about its body.

THUD!

The sound the drey made as it struck the earth reminded Declan of a time he had seen a man take a mace to the head. The wet, hollow resonance of breaking bone and crushed flesh. It hit the ground at an incredible speed, just east of the remains of Bonner's house, and when the dust and grass settled Declan could see its ghastly form trembling and twitching in the shallow crater it had formed.

He was about to shout in triumph again when Bonner—stumbling and still clearly worn to nothing—bolted from his side, running in what could only have been pure madness towards the dying beast.

"ARE YOU INSANE?" Declan bellowed after him. "WHAT ARE YOU DOING? THAT THING MIGHT STILL BE ALIVE!"

For an answer, Bonner only pointed skyward. Following the motion up, Declan choked on his horror. In an instant his legs were moving of their own accord to hammer after the old man.

Above them, Ryn's massive form was dropping to the earth, tumbling headfirst, wings limp and useless as he plunged only slightly slower than the creature he had thrown from the heavens.

CHAPTER SEVENTEEN

Had he had the breath to articulate them, Declan was sure all manner of panicked profanity and prayer would have escaped his lips as he ran, chasing Bonner with every ounce of speed he could muster. His sword clattered against his legs, long hair getting in his eyes, but despite the risk of stumbling he couldn't look down, couldn't look away from the wheeling, falling form of Ryn. He didn't even see Bonner stop ahead of him, halting his haphazard dash some score of feet from the crumpled outline of the drey, and would have plowed over the smaller man if he hadn't heard the mage start to shout. The words, strange and incomprehensible to his ears, caught his attention in time to have him slide to a halt, and Declan watched as Bonner lifted dirty hands towards the clouds, voice still raised, like he was pleading to the heavens and hidden stars.

Whatever the case, he was answered with gusto.

Bonner's hands began to glow, a bright, rich emerald aura shimmering over his extended fingers like fire licking at dry wood. As Declan watched, the light solidified, slipping and collapsing inward onto itself, quickly forming into distinct tracings that shifted over the man's muddy skin. When Ryn was no more than a hundred feet above their heads, the aura flashed green, and Declan caught a glimpse of banded runes encircling Bonner's wrists like twin, glimmering bracelets. With the final bellowed word of whatever spell the mage was weaving, Bonner cast his hands downward, hands splayed in the direction of the ground some twenty feet before them.

The bracelets shattered with a *crack* of sound that could have been the world itself splitting in two.

Once again Declan felt the earth beneath his feet rumble. This time he managed to steel himself for the shattered shower of soil and grass as the roots answered their master's summons for a second time, lancing upward with such speed their rough surfaces sped by in a blur. They were less, this time, no more than a score in all rising in a rough ring, half racing towards the dragon while the rest bent inward and entwined themselves about one another. By the time the climbing roots reached Ryn fifty feet above them, the lower ones had formed a rough, thick net ten feet above a wide space of pitted, sinking earth.

Declan watched, unmoving, fear for the dragon snuffing out any astonishment he might have had at the sight. The higher roots wrapped themselves about Ryn's tumbling form one after the other, snaking around whatever part they encountered first. Legs, tail, body, even his neck. They stiffened and strained, Bonner's magic working to stop his descent before he struck the ground.

Unfortunately, this first barrier managed little.

With ten ringing *cracks* like splitting wood, the roots snapped in quick succession, unable to bear the force of Ryn's falling mass. The dragon tumbled through their lifted forms, momentum cut short but not completely halted. Declan screamed, howling his friend's name in horror, watching Ryn strike the net that awaited him too fast, far too fast. The dragon's weight tore through the wound shapes with only a heavy lurch of resistance slowing him once again. He continued downward, hurtling at the ground, striking the grass of the field with the force of a falling boulder...

And promptly vanished with a wet eruption of sound and muddy water.

Declan yowled in shock, but kept mind enough to launch himself forward and cover Bonner again as dirty rain splattered down around them, small stones and chunks of soaked dirt hammering his head and shoulders painfully after their violent launch skyward. When the chaos settled, Declan released the older man, wiping sludge from his own face and eyes while he blinked and cursed, looking around.

He understood what he'd missed, in Bonner's spells, had understood it the instant the earth had swallowed Ryn whole. He'd noticed the sunken earth beneath the netting, but hadn't thought anything of it in the moment. Now, spitting and swabbing mud from his week-old beard, Declan eyed the sinkhole before them critically, the murky well having materialized out of nowhere. He watched while a quartet of the least damaged roots bent down and slid beneath the recessed surface of the mire, fishing from its depths the still, massive form of the limp dragon.

"Ryn..." Declan breathed, leaving a sagging Bonner behind and hurrying forward, uncaring as his boots slipped and splashed through the dirty, soaked earth of the grass. The roots deposited the dragon along the edge of the hole with a wet, heavy *thud*, falling limp after they'd fulfilled the last of their tasks.

Ryn was a ruined, tattered mess of a creature. He was breathing, that much Declan could tell, but the heavy, labored lifting of his colossal chest did little more than accentuate the myriad of sickening wounds that colored his black scales red and brown as blood and mud trickled off him in equal measures. Long lacerations where the drey's claws had managed to pierce his hide revealed crimson flesh beneath. The markings of teeth were carved into his neck and around his face, and the punctured holes that were unfortunate souvenirs of the beast's wicked tail looked like the dragon had been skewered by half-a-hundred steel lances. Their ugly, ripped mouths were enough to make even Declan's strong stomach turn. When he reached the dragon, he traced the outline of one such wound with an extended hand, wincing as he found the scales and flesh loose about the hole.

It would only be sometime later that he would be grateful for the terror of that moment, the blind fear swallowing the trepidation Declan might have otherwise felt at approaching an unconscious—but still gargantuan—dragon.

"Bonner!" he called over his shoulder, not knowing what miracle the old man might or mightn't work around Ryn's ravaged body, but thinking of little else he could do. With the slosh of slow-moving feet, Bonner joined him, his weathered face strained and pale. With a ragged hiss he took in the dragon, then carefully knelt down by Ryn's side and put his hands on his wide, wet chest.

The silence of the several seconds that followed seemed to stretch into endlessness as Declan watched Bonner's brow furrow in concentration.

"He'll live," the mage finally said weakly. Even Declan—bottomless in his ignorance of the ways of magic—could tell he was approaching his limit. "But I can only do so much right now."

"How can I help?" Declan asked, not hearing the high note of concern in his own voice.

Bonner gave him a crooked, beaten smile, then inclined his head towards the smoldering ruins of his home. "Gather what you can from that mess. Food. Waterskins. Ester's weapons, if you can find them. We'll need them soon, I've no doubt."

Declan didn't have to ask why. He understood—to some small extent—the implications of this newest attack. Ryn had left him with the yr'Essels under the impression Bonner's wards would keep at bay whatever evils had followed them into the woods. The fact that they had failed brought to mind one simple, ringing truth.

They were no longer safe there, in the serene expanse of the open glen.

Swallowing his chagrin at the thought, Declan turned and hurried towards the house, pulling the collar of his muddy shirt up over his nose and mouth as he did. The dragonfire's lingering flames had largely abated with nothing but living wood and stone to feed on, but smoke lay thick all the same, and he had to watch his step as he vaulted over the ragged remnants of the east wall. Deftly he managed the smoldering rubble and ashes, kicking aside broken spruce limbs and cracked, seared rock. While he searched, he had to struggle to keep at bay the disappointment that followed him through the nearly-indistinguishable remainders of each room. Breakfasts with Bonner. Morning walks with Ester. All gone, now. Brought to a brutal end on the rush of a single monster's wings.

Ester.

That sudden concern, Declan didn't manage to hold back, and he paused in his one-handed rummaging through the ruins of what had been Bonner's kitchen and larder to glance towards the nearest tree line. The woman would have heard the fight, certainly, and was probably on her way back. He felt a faint relief, considering it now, that she hadn't been present during the attack.

Shaking his head of it all, he turned his attention back to his task.

It took him less time than he would have liked to gather what he could according to Bonner's instruction. The brevity of his undertaking, regrettably, had less to do with the ease of finding provisions and the like than it did with the fact that there was ultimately very little to be salvaged. Between the crushing chaos of the fallen trees and Ryn's consuming flames, all Declan managed to procure in the way of foodstuffs were a few apples and a single charred loaf of bread. When it came to drink, there was hardly an intact tankard to be found amid the smoldering mess, much less a waterskin. In the end Declan made do with a large flask he found in the outlines of a broken cabinet, the pungent spirits within sparking and catching brightly in the flames when he upended it

A drink for the Graces, he thought, offering a brief prayer to the Mother that she would see them through the coming trials he anticipated right along with Bonner.

By some miracle, the most untouched sections of the home were the living quarters, and Declan managed—with some difficulty—to squeeze himself through the space that had been the doorway to Ester's chambers, the roof only partially collapsed overhead. Ignoring the momentary flash of embarrassment as he pried open a half-collapsed dresser to gather some spare clothes for the woman, he was pleased to find a traveling satchel in one of the drawers, into which he promptly stuffed the meager rations and empty flask. Her sword, on the other hand, was nowhere to be found, and when the broken trees—already dangerously askew overhead—gave an ominous groan, Declan decided it was time to get clear of the wreckage.

It was as he shoved himself back out into the open, standing among the smoke and fire once again, that he heard the shouting.

Declan's heart plunged into his stomach. His sword was out before he could think to stop himself, the collar of his shirt falling from his face. In the next moment he was scrambling over the shattered timber and stone, boots kicking up sparks as he paid no heed to the embers underfoot. Through the shimmer of the rising heat around him, he made out the shapes. Ryn's great, dark form still limp on its side. Bonner beside him, on his feet now, shouting an incantation with a haggard resolve that betrayed his fatigue. And not far from them both, crawling towards the pair with agonizing determination…

Declan cursing himself, tossing the satchel of clothes and provisions over the last wall before clearing it himself, sprinting full tilt over the field again with steel bared.

The drey had survived its earthward plummet.

It was pulling itself, four feet at a time with each clawful of earth and grass it took, in the direction of the mage and fallen dragon, snarling audibly as it moved. Both its legs were clearly broken, and it was yet missing a wing and arm, but still the thing appeared utterly uncaring of its own condition, the one bloodshot eye Declan could see fixed on the prey in front of it. He watched, horrified, as it reached the pair before he could close the distance, the drey launching itself with a wet screech that sounded like one or both of its lungs were punctured. He shouted, his boots pounding at the earth, seeing the claws come down, flashing towards Bonner's clean-shaven head.

There was a *crack,* followed by a *sizzle* like the sound of insects flying too close to the campfire, and the drey screeched in pain as it tumbled to the earth again, knocked back several yards in a jumble of singed, broken limbs.

Declan didn't allow himself to think too much about what he'd just witnessed, barely even noticing the fleeting sheen of blue-green light that hovered around Bonner for a second or so after the foiled blow, like a dome of faintly colored glass. Instead, he howled a war-cry as he beat a sprint over the last short distance between himself and the struggling form of the drey. He thought he heard someone else echo his shout, but couldn't be sure, the entirety of his attention anchored on the twisted, ravaged horror before him. Demonstrating much of its earlier quickness, the drey righted itself with a nimble thrash of its body, awkwardly pressing up onto its one arm to face Declan with bared fangs.

That was when he knew his mistake.

He met its eyes, in that moment, *both* its eyes, one bloody and corrupt, the other a flattened, wet mess in a partially exposed skull. He saw the wolfish head, both horns cracked and broken. He saw the snout and lined, savage teeth, could smell the stench of rot and blood in its breath.

And there, behind and above it, a shape rose, tensing and readying with deadly patience.

The tail, he chided himself almost calmly, not slowing as he brought his blade up for a single, cleaving blow at the drey's throat he knew he wouldn't be given the opportunity to land. *I forgot about the damn tail.*

Shtunk!

Out of nowhere the drey jerked violently, head snapping back with an agonized squeal of pain. The barbed appendage that Declan was sure had been moments away from skewering him spasmed and flailed, and he had just enough time to make out the fletched end of an arrow buried into the beast's one good eye. He didn't care, didn't have *time* to care. Adapting for the positional change, Declan still managed to find the angle, sword arching in a two-handed swing that would have cleaved any man's head from his shoulders. In the drey's case, the strike was barely enough to find and cut to the bone of its spine, but all the same Declan knew it was a killing blow, watching dark blood spray from the wound to douse his arms and chest in a great sheet.

Then he heard Bonner's shouted warning.

"NO! The blood! Don't touch the blood!"

Too late.

Pain, bone-deep and lancing like a dozen sword points grinding into his flesh, arched across Declan body. He howled in dismayed suffering, releasing his sword where it had gotten wedged into the spine of the dead drey as the beast fell, not seeing the hilt tumble from the wound, the steel of the blade bubbling and melting. Declan's clothes hissed and smoked, tendrils of acrid fumes writhing about him as he felt the acetic ichor chew through to his skin, the leather and cloth garments offering no more protection than paper might have from a flame. It began to eat at him, digging into his arms and the muscles of his chest. In desperation he tried to fling the blackness from him, slapping at it with his hands, only to feel his palms and fingers begin to burn, hearing continued shrieks he knew to be his own.

There was the *crunch* of breaking earth, and an instant later Declan felt himself lifted off his feet. Had he been in his right mind he might have wondered at the single lash of thickened root that had sprouted behind him, entwining itself into his belt with the speed of a whip. All he knew, however, was the heavy tug at his waist, then the sensation of flying through the air.

Then, mercifully, the cool, dark relief of murky water as he was thrown headlong into the same sinkhole that still gaped, waiting like an open mouth not far away.

CHAPTER EIGHTEEN

Of all the terrors of the Endless Queen's army, the drey were always far and above the most fascinating to behold, and most horrifying to contest. Another of Sehranya's stitched creations, they—like their less-imposing wereyn cousins—were pieced together from the sentient fleshes of man and animal and elf. Where the two diverge, however, is the addition of another beast to the weaves that bind together the bodies of the drey.

One the Queen was only provided by the full, foolish force of man throwing himself against its home.

-private journals of Elysia Enus al'Dyor, Queen of Viridian, c. 325p.f.

Seated comfortably among the looped, gnarled roots of an elm, Gonin Whist felt fear trickle into him as the presence of the drey vanished from his split consciousness, winking out in an arching flash of pain. He gasped and opened his eyes, wizened hand jerking instinctively to the side of his neck where the final blow had claimed the beast's life before he could separate himself from the last fading fragments of the creature's mind.

When his senses were firmly back within the tired bones of his own decrepit frame, he let the hand drop with a weary curse.

The draugr had been one thing. A test. A prodding of defenses. He hadn't expected much from the shambling corpses, and had been thrilled when he'd felt them bring down the one of King's blood, nearly ripping him to pieces and forcing the dragon into his natural form.

But the drey...

This was not how he had expected things to go. He'd spent the better part of the last four days imbuing the beast with his own magic, casting his weaves of strength and speed over its already powerful limbs and body in patient, meticulous layers. By the time he'd been done with his castings, Gonin would have staked his life that the thing should have been a match for any pair of dragons, much less a lone example of the beasts aided by some common hedge mage.

The mage... Gonin considered in bitter frustration, pushing himself to his feet with a grunt.

He was wrong, he knew. He had witnessed the fight through the drey's eyes, had taken in the spellwork of that old man. His own magics, Gonin suspected, would pale in comparison were he not a bearer of the Queen's charm. That was no "common" wizard, something he supposed he should have suspected given the careful assembly of wards about the clearing. It had been a barrier Gonin hadn't even known was there, until the auras of the dragon and his rider faded behind them, hidden almost even from the talisman around his neck.

Gonin had miscalculated. Not by much, granted—the drey had downed the dragon, after all, and might even have overpowered the old mage had al'Dyor's bastard and the half-elf not been there to interfere—but enough. The advantages he'd been handed, the element of surprise and the power he had borrowed to temper the drey's strength, all wasted.

With a swallow of trepidation, Gonin turned east, summoning his mount from the sky with a muttered incantation even as he reached into his fur-lined robes to grasp the speaker's crystal, steeling himself for the imminent punishment his news would doubtless bring down upon him.

CHAPTER NINETEEN

"Of the common classifications of magic, auramancy has long been considered among the most trying schools to follow. The spellcrafting alone is initially more taxing than most other disciplines to begin with, as by the end of the third semester of study every student of the path is expected to be able to manipulate living flesh and bone, rather than simpler elements such as heat or light or water. Beyond that, however, is often overlooked the basic burden of anatomical knowledge required to be even competent in the field, much less a master of it. Auramancers are—when put plainly—arcane physicians, and I will personally attest that the understanding of the human body of the least among them is no less informed than that of royal surgeon."

-from a lecture by Archmagus Enton Da'Vor, c. 130p.f

Bonner's quick action, Declan knew, had very likely saved his life. The soaking coolness of the watery mud had washed away the drey's blood, ending the consuming gnaw of his skin and flesh. At the time, he'd been grateful for it, and suspected there would be a point where he would be so again.

For the present, on the other hand, all Declan could do was grind his teeth and curse the old man for not having let him drown in the sludge.

The pain was endless. A constant, eating burn that convinced Declan more than once that the better part of his upper body was on fire. He was aware, for those hours in which the agony was greatest, of people hovering over him, but their passings were as insubstantial and unimportant as the lazy drift of the clouds high overhead. All that existed for him, for too long, was the torment of his flesh, the constant, sheering ache that had him crying out frequently, his exclamations ranging from hard, pitching moans to lancing squeals as the pain fluctuated and spiked. He begged the Mother for reprieve—aloud as often as in his own head—asking to be released from this, to be allowed to slip off into oblivion, if only briefly. Miserably, she had no such mercy for him that day, and Declan was forced to stay as he was, bound by the torture that simultaneously pushed him towards unconsciousness while tethering him mere inches from its glorious ledge.

Eventually he realized that, at some point, night had fallen. The world was still bright around him, illuminated by what looked like a quartet of lazy, winged orbs drifting in an endless, formless circle above. He knew then, too, the outlines of Bonner and Ester on either side of him, the old man instructing his daughter in hushed tones as the pair applied what felt like cool, moist earth to his arms and torso. Declan was aware of Bonner's fingers dragging their way through the covering soil, and knew distantly that the mage would be scrawling some runic script across the surface of his body.

None of it mattered. The pain. The pain was what needed to end.

In that respect, whatever gods actually overlooked the world laughed at him.

■■

Declan came to with a start, his vision blurred and spinning against the confusing loop of the unearthly, illuminating orbs that still danced over his head. He'd fallen away, he realized, finally dozing off, waking up in the dark. Every inch of him ached, like his muscles had torn themselves to shreds in his spasms. Moving was a mistake, the smallest shift of his body sending a throb of nausea through his chest.

But the pain was largely gone, the stabbing sear of the blood reduced to a dull, thrumming discomfort.

Declan let out a sobbing laugh, a short, empty bark of bottomless relief. The sound might have been accompanied by tears, but as he blinked he felt the salty stickiness around his eyes, and knew that there were no more to be shed.

At his left, there was the faint crackle of dry, shifting grass.

"Welcome back," a woman's tired voice said. "I was worried you were going to drift off too far for even Father to reach…"

With some difficulty, Declan turned his head. Ester was there, easing herself up onto one elbow, loose strands of hair falling across her face. She'd been lying beside him on the ground, it appeared—sleeping, possibly?—but her green eyes were bright in the glow of the magical light that shined like a golden halo about her head. He graced her with as strong a smile as he could muster, which he suspected to be acutely lacking.

"Almost did," he muttered in response. His voice was hoarse from shouting, and all at once Declan realized he was parched, his throat dry and aching. He made to sit up, thinking of finding a stream in the woods in which he could quench his thirst, even if every step hurt along the way.

Mercifully, Ester stopped him with a firm hand.

"*Don't. Move.*" She punctuated the words with fervent individuality. "You're hardly done healing, and Father would be livid if he and I had to go through all this work again."

Declan, confused, glanced down at himself, tucking his chin against his chest to take in his body, ignoring the ache of his neck. What he saw made him laugh again, achieving at least the slightest bit of true amusement this time.

He was buried, from collar to waist, in a mound of damp, dark earth. Sure enough, in the shifting light he made out shapes traced into the dirt by a careful finger, even recognizing one or two of the runes from the scrying wheel Bonner had cast earlier in the day. He decided it didn't surprise him anymore.

Somberly, letting his head fall back to the grass with a faint *thump*, he wondered if anything would ever surprise him again.

"Did you want something?" Ester asked gently.

"Water," he croaked, his need outweighing his pride as absolutely as a brick might outweigh a feather. Without a word the half-elf got to her feet, fading for a minute or so into the dark beyond the dancing lights. While she was gone, Declan took the opportunity to look around as best he could.

His sheathed knife was nearby, he saw first, obviously pulled from his hip as the earth had been piled over him. It lay in the flattened grass not far from Ester's own weapons belt, as well as her bow and quiver. He felt a twinge of regret, noticing the hollow scabbard waiting by his dagger, recalling now the glimpse of the melting sword tumbling from the drey's cleaved neck. The weapon had been a good one, having seen him through the last few years of his and Ryn's adventures, and he would be hard-pressed to find another of its quality easily.

At the thought, he shifted his head and was relieved when the dragon's dark outline came into view, not having transitioned from his born form and still lying unconscious near the mouth of the sinkhole that had saved both their lives. It didn't take more than a glance for Declan to see Ryn had been made whole again. More scars now marred the silken sheen of his scales, but they were thin—like the faint mark Declan himself carried over his left elbow—and far come from the gaping, gory lacerations that had been weeping blood last he'd seen them. Beyond Ryn, east of the dragon, the glow of what looked like dying coals could be made out against the night, the last hints of what remained of the yr'Essels' woodland home.

The sight made Declan swallow a lump he didn't think he had the right to feel.

The quiet sound of boots announced Ester's return, and she reappeared in the ring of light not long after, a familiar travel sack in hand. "Father told me what happened," she answered his quizzical look at the bag, gesturing to the faint glimmer of orange beyond the light of their smaller circle. "I'm surprised you were able to find anything, in that mess."

"Where is he?" the question raked at Declan's throat. "Your father?"

Inexplicably, Ester smirked, taking a seat at his side again and starting to undo the bag's bucklings. "And they scoff at my *er'enthyl* blood," she said under her breath, almost to herself. "*I* wouldn't want eyes like yours, if given the choice."

Declan frowned, catching on to her meaning and looking around again. It took him several seconds, but at once he took back his assertion that he would never be surprised by anything again.

No more than five feet away, a shape he couldn't understand how he'd overlooked was distinct only in the shadows of the winged orbs of light overhead, a lump of camouflaged colors against the darkness of the glen. Its silhouette shifted with steady, slow breathing, and Declan could hardly believe his eyes when he recognized Bonner yr'Essel, curled up on his side with his back to them, hood pulled up over his bald head and knees tucked to his chest. The pattern of his strange robes looked to have reshaped itself, the original splotched markings—like fallen leaves—now striations that roughly matched the grass of the field, melting him against the backdrop with disquieting efficiency.

Magic, Declan thought with something akin to weary resignation before addressing Ester again. "Is he alright?"

"He's fine," Ester answered with a tired smile, tugging the last beltings loose and flipping open the satchel to reach inside. "He'll be like that until morning at least, after the power he had to pour into the two of you. Spells have their price, just like—"

She paused, eyes wide. Following her gaze, Declan choked when he made out what she held in her hand, the half-elf having just pulled a small wedge of stitched cloth free of the bag.

There was no mistaking women's undergarments in any light.

For a long, heavy moment, silence hung between them. The chirp of crickets and call of frogs and nocturnal birds could be heard off in the trees, and the wind made itself known again, teasing at their hair and drifting gently over the field.

Then Ester began to laugh.

The sound was warm and heartening, a faint light in the thickening shadows that had suddenly appeared in the world. She laughed and laughed, clutching the smallclothes to her breast like they were a precious thing thought lost and left behind. Her smile shined even brighter in her mirth, and Declan couldn't help but crack an unsure grin as he watched her.

"S-sorry," the woman finally choked out, not quite finished, while she wiped a tear from one eye. "I just—I very much needed that, I think."

"The laughter, or the undergarments?" Declan wheezed before he could stop himself, not wanting the clean sound to end just yet.

Ester gave him a smirk that hid none of her little returned cheer, reaching out to flick him in the side of the head in teasing rebuke.

"Both, ass," she chuckled, stuffing the clothes back into the sack and pulling out the flask Declan had retrieved that afternoon. It sloshed with liquid as she uncapped it.

"I hope you didn't fill that with water from the pit," he muttered, only half-teasing as she scooted closer.

"Maybe I should have," she quipped back, helping him lift his head and holding the mouth of the container to his lips. "But no. Father saw it full before he fell asleep. Drew a clean spring from whatever source he used to make that." She motioned to the sinkhole with her head.

Declan couldn't nod, too busy guzzling the water down greedily. When he'd had his fill, he let Ester ease his head back down again, watching her take a swig for herself.

"He's incredible, you know?"

"Father? I'm aware." She nodded, capping the flask and placing it by the sack. "Still... *that*—" she glanced over him, and Declan could imagine she was looking the hole and the thick, limp roots that likely encircled it like the ugly petals of a flower "—is new to me. I didn't see what happened. I can't believe I wasn't here to help..."

"You were there when it mattered," Declan grunted, shifting in an attempt to make himself more comfortable on the uneven ground. "That was your arrow the drey took in the eye, I'm assuming?"

"Best shot I've made in my life, I think." Ester's face was pale, like the thought scared her. "I came running the moment I heard the first scream, could see the two of them fighting through the canopy, but still... What *happened*, Declan? Father didn't have the energy to say, and Ryn's been unconscious since before I arrived. Where did it come from?"

"I don't know," Declan grunted, recalling the horrible sight of the drey diving from between the clouds, plummeting down upon them like black lightning. "Ryn had just returned. Told us that Estwyn had fallen to some wereyn horde."

Ester's eyes went wide at that. "Estwyn? The garrison of Karn's Gullet?"

"The same, but I don't know if anyone calls it that anymore."

"And the drey?"

"Ryn said he thought he'd felt something behind him, and your father had just scryed out where it was coming from when the thing reached us." Declan paused, drawing a shaking breath. "I don't think I've ever been so scared in my damn life."

Ester nodded slowly, taking in his recounting, staring off at nothing for a long moment before speaking. "I don't blame you. I've never seen anything like that." She waved an unsteady hand behind her, into the dark, where the body of the beast must have been waiting nearby. "What... *is* it? How does something like that exist?"

Declan tried and failed to shrug, ashamed of the relief he felt, not being the only one out of the loop anymore. "Your guess is as good as mine, and probably a hell of a lot better, if we're being frank. All I can say is it looked like someone stitched together all the worst parts of man, dragon, and beast, then set it loose on us."

"Horrible." Ester glanced over her shoulder. "And what its blood did to you... Like acid..."

"No need to remind me," Declan said, quicker than he liked, feeling a wave of nothing short of fear wash through him at the recollection of how he'd spent the last few hours. "Let's just say I won't be forgetting *that* little trait of theirs, if we run across another one anytime soon. Made rothwort feel like a hot bath."

"Mother forbid," Ester cursed with a shudder, reaching up to touch the back of her head absently. "It's bad enough if there are draugr and wereyn in Viridian now, let alone anything else." She met his eyes carefully. "Estwyn, though... You're sure about that?"

"It's what Ryn said. I wasn't convinced either, but he seemed to be. Heard it directly from the mouth of the Vigil, apparently."

Ester swore again, muttering something in an eloquent, twisted tongue, which managed to coax a grin out of Declan. She'd let slip a few choice phrases in elvish before, during their afternoon trainings.

"Indeed," he agreed with a dry snort. "Though I've no idea what the wereyn's mothers—nor where they stick their members—has anything to do with it."

Ester looked astounded. "You speak elvish?" she demanded, abruptly excited, making Declan immediately regret his jest.

"Only as much as that, along with a few more words that would get me in trouble in polite company," he said quickly. "The Iron Wind's quartermaster is half-*er'enthyl*. Old bugger who liked to explain every foul thing he called you, just to insult you twice over."

"Ah," Ester said with another laugh, doing a fair job of concealing her disappointment.

"Your mother's teachings?"

She nodded, then sighed. "All of which has little and less to do with the problem at hand," she said, bringing the conversation back on track. "Wereyn pressing into Viridian... When was the last time that happened? And the drey?"

"I never even heard of the latter before Bonner mentioned them," Declan answered with a grimace. "As for the wereyn... It was more than two decades ago, the last time Estwyn suffered an assault."

"And he's a learned man to boot," Ester said with a raised brow, feigning being impressed. "Am I to be trounced in sword *and* history in turn, good sir?"

Declan chuckled at that. "There's a good chance you'll always have the bow to hold over my head, so don't be too discouraged." Then he grew serious. "Estwyn was my birthplace. My parents and Ryn were there for the siege, as was I, but I was too young to remember any of it. Most of the town was burned to the ground, my mother told me. They've rebuilt and fortified since, little good as it seems to have done them…"

Ester deflated like a torn waterskin, her amusement vanishing. "Well there's me putting my foot in my mouth," she muttered apologetically. Then her eyes lifted from his, slipping off into the darkness again, finding the place where the remnants of her home still smoldered in the night. "But I think I have a sense of that, now… Seeing everything you know go up in flames before you…"

Once again, silence fell between the two of them, and Declan knew there would be no cheer to break its curse this time. He watched the half-elf's face as they sat, quiet in each other's company, barely detecting the strain of her lips and cheeks that he knew all too well.

Any man-at-arms who might claim that there was no place for tears in a swordsman's arsenal, after all, was nothing short of a liar and a braggart.

"I'm sorry."

The words, shy and subdued, left him before Declan knew they'd formed on his lips. Ester tensed, looking down at him.

After a moment, Declan decided it was best to press on, as he'd already let the greatest of his welling emotions slip. Again he felt that sadness, and again knew he had no right to harbor it.

Not when Ester and Bonner were sleeping in the dirt, so close to the ruins of their home one could see the ashes of it burning in the night…

"I'm sorry," he said again, his voice stronger now. "If we hadn't come… If Ryn and I hadn't been here… It followed *us*. I'm sure of it. Like the ghouls. It was after *us*, for some reason. If we hadn't come…"

He trailed off, discovering it much harder than he'd anticipated to get out the words he wanted to say.

"I'd be dead, probably, and the two of you very likely right along with me."

Ester's answer was so matter-of-fact, so nonchalant, it took Declan aback. He knew, too, the falsity of that confidence. The hidden pain had not left the half-elf's face as she'd spoken. For a time, she was quiet, not looking away from him.

Then she turned, reaching into the bag at her side again.

"I never thanked you, did I?" she asked, pulling out one of the apples from the meager bounty Declan had been able to salvage from the house. She wiped it on her sleeve, shining it as she got to her feet. "For rescuing me. I never thanked you."

Declan's brow furrowed, following her movement around his legs until she bent down to pluck her hunting knife—one of the only two blades they had left to them—from its sheath. "You did. The morning I woke up here."

Ester shook her head when she returned to his side, kneeling down again by his buried arm. Not looking at him, she dug the edge of the steel into the fruit and began peeling the apple distractedly. "No. I *acknowledged* it, but I don't think I ever thanked you. I think Father's doing that now, in his own way." She briefly tipped the point of the knife at the runes traced into the mound of dirt over Declan's torso. "He's been hoping for the opportunity to do so since he reached the three of us in the woods, not long after the ghoul attack."

"He'd been looking for you," Declan said with a nod, having been told as much by the mage himself during one of their morning conversations.

Ester nodded. "I'd been gone for three days by the time we practically waltzed back into the senses of the spell he was using to seek me out. In that time, there aren't many good options as to what could have happened to me, Declan. The best sounds like my wound would have eventually been my end, a slow death strung up like some scarecrow to tumble apart with the other corpses at my feet. *Worst* case—" her finger began to tremble ever so slightly, and Declan watched the knife in her hands with apprehension "—it sounds like I could very well have been fodder for that... thing."

The drey, Declan realized she meant, putting the pieces together for the first time. Hadn't Bonner said as much, on that first morning? That the clearing he and Ryn had dragged Ester from had likely been some feeding ground? Declan balked, his heart suddenly thudding anxiously against the sore cage of his chest.

We were that close? he thought, a shard of ice raking down his spine as he considered it, recalling the strange, ominous cave created by the great slabs of stone, one leaning against the other. *It was there? That close?*

Ester's continued words brought him back from his dark considerations, the effort she was putting into keeping her voice even now more apparent.

"As for you two," she said, cutting away the last of the peel with a *snick* of the knife to let it tumble across her knees and into the flattened grass, "you're probably right. It doesn't sound like whoever's behind these attacks gives two licks about *me*. They're after you. You or Ryn, or maybe both. The drey would have been set on you regardless, and if you hadn't been *here*, well..."

"We would have been done for," he finished for her this time, knowing he couldn't contest the point. On an even field, Ryn would have lost against the drey, he knew. It chilled him to the bone, turned his stomach, but he was sure it was true. The dragon had prevailed only with Bonner's assistance, and even *then* the damn thing had persisted, a fall from a distance that could be measured at the height of the lowest clouds not enough to break its body or quell its killing need.

"You would have been done for," Ester repeated in quiet agreement, starting to carve a slice from the thickest corner of the apple. For a few seconds there was nothing but the sound of the cutting.

"*So,*" the half-elf finally started again, firmly now, after she'd freed a sizable chunk of the fruit, picking it up delicately, "following that logic, I don't think you can say you have anything to be 'sorry' for, would you?"

Declan blinked at her in surprise. She was holding the apple out to him, at an angle that he could lift his head and accept it. He hesitated, looking past the offered food to meet the woman's eyes. She was forcing the strength in her gaze, he knew. She was fighting to keep herself together, to keep from tearing at the seams.

She'd lost everything she'd ever known. She'd said so herself. Her father lived, by the Mother's will, but aside from that miracle Esteria yr'Essel had nothing to her name but a knife, the clothes on her back, and the bow laying on the grass nearby.

He accepted the proffered morsel without complaint, chewing and swallowing as she cut him another piece. Again he took it.

It was when she offered him a third bite that he made his decision.

As the woman extended her hand, Declan forced his own arm to move. With a grunt and the rustling crack of caked dirt breaking, he pulled the limb free. Pain lanced into his shoulder and neck, and he saw that new, blotching scars painted his bare skin.

He ignored all of it, and reached instead for the woman.

At first Ester gasped, distraught as she saw the healing runes come apart, but when his fingers wrapped about her wrist the sound caught in her throat. She stared, her eyes first taking in his grip, then lifting to his face.

She started to shake.

"It's alright," he told her as gently as he could, sliding his hand up towards her palm, the knife going limp in her grasp. "Let it out. It's alright."

For a stunned moment, the woman could only look at him.

And then, with a wracking sob, she began to weep, the blade and apple falling each to the grass, both her hands moving to take Declan's proffered one, holding onto it with a desperate grief as her cries rang dully into the open night above.

They stayed like that for a long time, the two of them, neither speaking, each finding comfort in the other's grasp. Eventually Ester calmed again, and with soft words Declan guided her back down to lay beside him once more. Slowly, minute by minute, the woman's lingering, sharp inhales and spasms of empty sadness left her, and together they drifted off again, hands still held, still seeking that solace of the shared warmth of their touch.

Neither noticed Bonner, not so far away from them, shivering in much the same way as his daughter. With his back to them, they couldn't have seen the faint few tears that trailed down the old man's cheeks.

Nor the heartbroken smile lingering on his lips as he clutched at the clear crystal about his neck, whispering to it while the ethereal wash of the magical lights bounced and weaved above.

■■■

It was Ryn's thunderous groan that woke them all the next morning, a miraculous sound which immediately had Declan sitting up with an enthusiastic shout. Fortunately the dirt shell which had been his haven and cage alike the previous night appeared to have expended whatever life Bonner's magic had given it, and the soil fell away in a scattered shower as he jerked upright. He scrambled to his feet—Ester and Bonner mirroring his frantic movements to either side of him—finding himself bare-chested but caring little when the three of them hurried as one towards the shifting form of the dragon.

"Ryn!" Declan exclaimed, half-laughing, torn between relief, amazement, and even the slightest taste of awe, taking in the great black frame of his friend.

The dragon, in turn, let out a snorted, pained huff, managing to roll himself onto all fours with an audible shift of his lithe bulk. His massive head didn't leave the ground, and he made no attempt to lift himself onto his feet just yet.

W-what...? he started groggily, one white-gold eye blinking at them in an unfocused manner, batting away confusion and fatigue. *What happened? How...?* Abruptly, the eye snapped wide, the pale pupil constricting. *The drey!* His voice thundered across their minds, firmer now, and he struggled and failed to push himself up, dry, bloody mud cracking and tumbling from his form in thick flakes. *The drey! Where is the drey?*

"Dead, you oaf," Bonner said in a soothing, tired voice, raising both hands in a calming gesture. "Ease up. You're far from recovered, and it's done. It's been done for half-a-day, now."

Done...? Ryn sounded less convinced than he did merely confounded. *And...dead? Dead how?* His eye grew more focused, and Declan could almost see the gears of fierce intelligence begin to whir again, ridding themselves of the fog of what he guessed to have been an enchanted sleep. *Ah... It fell. We fell...*

"Aye, you did," Bonner grunted in agreement. "Giving Declan and I both the scare of our lives in the process, as well as forcing *me* to catch you.

I might add you're not exactly light in this form. I barely had any strength left in me by the time the bastard climbed back out of the hollow you made with its body. Think it no exaggeration when I say Declan nearly cutting it in two was all that kept you and I from being gutted by the thing."

What? Ryn asked, sharply. *It lived? And Declan...?*

His gaze moved away from Bonner, trailing over Ester to settle on Declan himself.

For some reason, Ryn made an audible, guttural sound, a true spoken word, hissed out with such fervor no one present could doubt it to have been anything other than a curse of disbelief in his race's own tongue.

On his left and right respectively, Bonner and Ester turned to see what it was that had drawn out the dragon's astonishment. Declan watched, momentarily perplexed, as the old man's face tightened in what looked like anticipated distress, while Ester's two hands rose to her mouth, the woman failing to stifle the gasp that escaped her lips.

With sudden, tight apprehension, Declan looked down on himself. He supposed that if he, too, had known any profanity in the dragon's language, *that* would have been the moment for it.

He'd seen the blotched discolorations the night before, trailing up his left arm as he'd held Ester's hand, but hadn't considered them further. It had been dark, and scars were scars. He had more of them than he could count already, so what were a few extra to add to the mix?

He'd forgotten, unfortunately, how thoroughly the drey's blood had drenched him.

His left arm *was* the worst of it. He swallowed with difficulty, witnessing the price of shunning Bonner's gift of the healing earth for much of the duration it had been offered. There, the pallid tarnish where the ichor had touched him was so distinct against his tanner complexion, he might as well have been grafted with some poor albino's stolen skin. The markings, each of slightly varied shades, splashed over and around the limb, like layers of colorless lichen across bark. They were tight, too, stiff even as he mutely flexed his arm, like healed burns.

Which is exactly what they are, he realized, taking in with a sinking heart what little was left of the company tattoos that had proudly graced his arm. The Grey Shield's starred kite shield was half-gone from his shoulder, consumed by a pale spray of blanched flesh.

The arrow of the Seekers, meanwhile, had been completely obliterated.

With a twisting of nostalgic panic, Declan looked down at himself. He breathed easier for the briefest of moments when he saw the winged sword of the Iron Wind glaring up at him from under his right collarbone, half of its outer wing and the end of the blade all that had been lost to the blood.

That was the greatest mercy he had received, however, and he gaped numbly, taking in the rest of his torso and right arm.

Bonner's weaves had worked their powers well, but there was clearly only so much even magic could do for such wounds. The new skin that patterned his chest, waist, and limb was darker, matching more closely to his natural tone, like aged scars. They worried at the muscled outlines of his body, leaving hardly more than any four square inches untainted. The crossed spears of the Holden's guard on his shoulder was largely untouched, but the crenelated band of Stonewall around his bicep was broken and muted, shattered by the discoloration. Declan felt a lance of true fear, and he clenched and unclenched his hand, flexing his elbow and moving his shoulder about in its socket as he did. He grimaced, feeling the skin stretch and pull, but it was far less of a hindrance than the joints of his left.

"Well..." he said weakly, trying his best to crack a grin at the three that were still standing around him, having watched him take in the ruinous markings in lifeless silence, "I can still swing a sword, I think..."

Ryn was the first to answer this, letting out a short, hard snort that eased the tension of the scene the slightest bit. Ester was next, taking a step towards Declan and reaching out a tentative hand, the other still lingering about her mouth. She was rumpled and disheveled from a night spent beneath the stars, silver-gold hair tumbling across her face, but her eyes shined with concern, tracing the bare form of his body from the waist of his pants up.

"Oh, Declan," she breathed, lightly touching the palest of the stains—part of the discoloration which had wiped away the Seeker's mark—on the inside of his left arm. She sounded remorseful, like she blamed herself for this devastation. "Does... Does it hurt much?"

Declan considered this question, flexing his hands again. "No," he answered with no small measure of surprise, realizing as he spoke that it was true. His left arm ached dully, but it was nothing worth making Ester feel any worse over. "My skin feels... tight? But it doesn't hurt. The pain is all but gone."

"The tension should fade as well, eventually." Bonner had joined the conversation, coming to stand on Declan's other side and peering at his chest with a curiosity that was near-academic. "That part of the recovery will be up to you, however. I can only recommend you resume your training with Ester as soon as possible, so as to keep the new skin from forming contractures. A pity the entirety of the wounds didn't stay within my healing spells, last night." There was a gleam of something that made Declan flush under the roguish smile the old man shot him. "What could possibly have possessed you to pull your arm free of the weaves, I wonder...?"

Declan ignored the comment, as he did the building suspicion that the mage may not have been as firmly ensconced in his previous evening's slumber as Ester had believed. To cover his deflection, he brought his hands to his face, wincing as he noted the blotching scarification twisting about his fingers. His father's gold ring on his left hand looked unblemished, for which he was grateful, but he couldn't help but berate himself for stupidity as he remembered his desperate attempt to wipe away the drey blood in the moments after the fight.

"Either way, I think I owe you a debt entirely beyond my ability to ever repay, Bonner," he muttered solemnly. "For the moment, regretfully, I can only offer you my deepest gratitude."

Bonner, in answer, scoffed. "You've saved the life of Ester *and* myself now, boy. I'd rather think that makes the debt still quite inclined in your favor, for the foreseeable future. If you hadn't intervened when you did… well…" He drew a thumb across his throat in a macabrely comical gesture, making clear his meaning. Then he frowned, looking over his shoulder at Ryn. "Which reminds me. Since when has a drey been a match for you— much less the *pair* of us—Ryndean?"

Ryn's grunt was commiserating, like the two were sharing a common thought. His roping muscles strained in preparation, and with a groan of effort he pressed himself up, more gently this time, and with greater success. After several second's struggle he got himself into a lopsided, half-sitting position. The top of his head lifted to rise above them, spined ears— the size of a small man's torso—clearing the nearby trees of the forest handedly.

Declan, for the first time, found himself appreciating the dragon's continued presence in his mind when he discovered he needed no more than a steadying breath to dissolve the pang of alarm that spasmed in his gut at the sight.

A question I have myself, as well as the likeliest reasoning, Ryn answered Bonner finally. *I'm not so out of practice for that encounter to have gone the way it did,* especially *with your assistance.*

"Imbued?" Bonner asked him, and Declan knew himself once again lost to the two's conversation. He glanced at Ester, but the woman wasn't looking at him. Her eyes were wide, listening to the pair.

Undoubtedly.

"Well, there's a simple way to confirm it." Bonner eyed the dragon critically. "Are you strong enough to call up your fire now, or shall we let you rest a bit longer?"

Ryn shook his head, standing a little taller, the new scars across his chest and shoulders straining against his scales. *We don't have the time to waste either way. I've enough for the task, and I can recuperate later.*

"Good." Bonner turned to Declan and Ester, catching the former's confused expression. "We'll explain in a moment," he said quickly, already moving past the pair, waving them back. "For now, get well behind Ryn, if you please."

This order, neither of them questioned. Declan—and Ester beside him, he suspected—had caught the gist of the last exchange, and they had no intention of staying in front of the dragon even if the mage hadn't ordered them away. They moved swiftly, around Ryn's looming form, until they stood behind a rear leg each, on opposite sides of the base of his thick, ridged tail.

You're sure you're alright?

Ryn's voice startled him slightly, and Declan glanced up. One golden eye was watching him, concern palpable in its depths. He got the impression the question had been only for him, seeing as Ester's attention was fixed on her father, who was moving towards the trees.

Declan smiled up at the dragon, then nodded, reaching out—with only the slightest hesitation—to pat the scaled flank on his left in reassurance.

Then there came a strange, rustling sound, like the wind picking up over the field, and he, too, turned to see what Bonner was about.

The mage was striding back towards them with slow, purposeful strides, one hand held out in front of him like he was pressing some invisible object along. At his feet, in a crumbled and broken pile of limbs and its one remaining wing, the body of the drey was keeping pace with him, sliding across the grass of the glen with disturbing fluidity. It moved like it was being toted on some low cart, similar to the ones Declan had seen the dock workers of the port cities of Vasteel and Sethylles using when loading and unloading heavy cargo. Only when Bonner got closer did he identify the trick of the mechanism.

The grass itself was bending to the mage's will, blades working together like ten thousand narrow arms to push the dead thing along and over them with alarming ease.

When the drey's body was some ten feet from Ryn's planted front legs, Bonner released the spell, and the creature settled into the grass with a muffled *thump*. Declan couldn't help but wince at the sudden movement, taking in the drey with measured fascination and disgust. In death the beast was hardly less terrifying than it had been in life. Its colorless eyes were gone, one crushed and one pierced by Ester's grey-fletched arrow, still protruding from its skull, but from so close the other details of the thing were impossible to discount. The matted, knotted fur of its wolfish head and face, dyed dark around its mouth by what could only have been bloody, long-finished meals. The yellowed teeth, some cracked and rotting to match the dirty, broken claws of its remaining hand. The stump of its missing wing was charred, and the torn flesh of its right arm was crawling with flies already, as was the great, cleaved opening in the side of its neck Declan himself had delivered. Animals had worried at it, in the night, ripping hunks of meat from its ribs and legs, and he felt sorry for the poor creatures, imagining their torment after they'd swallowed the beast's corrosive flesh and blood.

He shivered, forcing himself to tear his eyes from the horrid thing, just in time for Bonner to start hurrying in his and Ester's direction, motioning them even further back than they already were.

"Past his tail, at least," the old man chided, taking his daughter by the arm and giving Declan a look that said very plainly that he should follow. "Backs to the flames, obviously."

Declan trailed along dejectedly, having wanted to study Ryn's summoning up of the dragonfire for as long as was tolerable, but Bonner's tone made it clear he would bear no objections. With a twinge of disappointment he followed the yr'Essels further back, to the drying edge of the sinkhole itself. When they were ready, Bonner called a confirmation up to Ryn. Almost at once there was a deep, billowing intake of air, followed by a brief pause in which the glen itself could have been thought to be holding its breath right along with the dragon.

And then the blast of gushing flames rocked the morning, keening and howling as loud as the roar of a storm over a buckling sea.

The shockwave of heat caught their turned backs with enough force to make Ester and Bonner both stagger forward two steps. Declan managed hardly better, catching himself with an extended leg, and shouted in unexpected pain as the searing air stung the exposed, new skin of his scars. Fortunately the heat only lasted an instant, leaving the air almost chilly in its sudden absence and the world deceptively silent until the distant call of birds could be made out once more over the ringing in their ears. Together the three gathered themselves, turning back to the dragon and moving to stand alongside him again, eyes on the black crater he had made of the field before him.

The crater, and the charred, blackened shapes tumbling haphazardly to pile up in its smoking, smoldering center.

"Imbued," Bonner grunted in what could only have been dissatisfied confirmation, and Declan saw Ryn's head bob in acknowledgment overhead.

Not a hint of the drey's flesh remained, the fur and scales and muscles of its twisted form having burned and boiled away into instant ash. Its *bones*, on the other hand, had largely weathered the blast, and it was this fact that looked to have the mage and dragon so perturbed. Some of the more delicate among them were gone—the digits of its fingers and toes, some ribs, and those of the remaining wing—but Declan could identify the cage of the drey's chest, the vertebrae of its spine, and—especially—its skull, the latter leering up at them in a lopsided grin from among the assortment.

Abruptly, he understood, a detail of the fight coming back to him.

"Its arm," he said aloud, looking up at Ryn. "When you finally caught it. The bones survived the blast."

Ryn fixed him once again with a white-gold eye, looking impressed. *Full marks on that deduction, I think. That was when I knew, too. I'd suspected—from the first encounter, I must say—but not until I had to spit out the remains of the limb was I sure. I can't think of a beast in the world who can overcome a dragon's fire without arcane assistance. Even our own hide isn't completely impervious to it.*

"So it had help," Ester said from Declan's elbow, and he appreciated the tone of relief in her voice.

"Aye," Bonner answered flatly, squatting down at the edge of the smoking hole and extending a hand over it, wincing at what had to have been the bite of roiling heat. "And a lot of it, if I had to guess. For both of us to have had so much trouble with it…" He glanced up at Ryn, standing and pointing at the piled bones as he did. "Could you be so kind as to fetch me one of those, please? Any of them will do."

Ryn promptly bent down, nosing through the grisly stack until he gingerly plucked what might have been a femur—a three-foot-long femur—from among the mess with his jaws. He offered it to Bonner carefully, who reached out once again, letting his hand hover over the charred surface of the thing, then patted it carefully, clearly uninterested in burning himself.

Finally, he accepted it from the dragon's mouth outright, grasping it with both hands.

"As I suspected. Cool to the touch. Woven to withstand heat, if I imagine, among other things."

For once, Declan understood what that meant, and he was almost pleased with himself upon realizing that he was starting to follow along just the slightest bit. "Imbued," Bonner had said, and Declan knew now, what he had meant. Imbued. Infused. Fortified.

The drey had been strengthened with magic.

Declan felt an undeniable relief, at this revelation. It meant that Ryn and Bonner had *not* been as outmatched as one might have assumed, meant their ability was not lesser, but had rather been met pound for pound. His relief guttered, on the other, as he saw a dark look pass between the dragon and mage, some mutual understanding being shared in that brief exchange. Even as he watched them, the pair turned as one in his and Ester's direction, Bonner's braided beard creased into a frown beneath his bald pate, Ryn's massive head alone taller than the height the man opposite him.

"You two," the mage said to the both of them, casting the femur back into the burning hollow at his back and wiping his hands on the front of his robes. The ash stains he left vanished in the blink of an eye, swallowed by what Declan now understood to be enchanted cloth. "Gather what things you have, and quickly. We need to be away from this place as soon as possible."

"What's going on?" It was Ester who asked, voicing the question before Declan could get it out. "We knew there was a necromancer in Viridian. You said so yourself. Why is it important they imbued the drey?"

It takes enormous power to collar a creature like that, Ester, Ryn answered gently, lifting a great foot to point at the beast's charred remains without looking away from them. *They're made of magic, in their own way. Their blood alone is mostly ether, something human flesh can hardly tolerate contact with.* He glanced over Declan's scars again regretfully. *A strong mage might be able to control one, but to strengthen it... It would be like trying to fire-harden stone.*

Declan caught on, and a great weight fell into his stomach.

Ryn, apparently noticing the change in countenance, nodded in stiff condolence. *Declan has the bearing of it already, I think. There's only one spellcaster I've ever known who wielded enough power to achieve such a thing.*

The weight grew heavier.

"Time for you to voice those questions of yours again, lad," Bonner told him with a grim, morbid grin. "If the Endless Queen lives, you'll be needing every answer we can give you..."

CHAPTER TWENTY

Despite Bonner's statement, Declan had very little opportunity to voice any of the dozens of queries that looped in a blur across his thoughts for the remainder of the morning. He and Ester packed quickly, as instructed, gathering their paltry assortment of weapons and seeing to it the traveling pack was tightly clasped, protecting what meager rations they had and the flask that had become their sole watering can. To Declan's relief, Bonner had *not* thrown away the tattered remains of his shirt and hunting vest after removing them to tend to his wounds the night before, and promptly procured them on request from a patch of nearby grass where they'd been hurriedly cast aside. Regrettably, after a quick examination, Declan judged the cotton threading of the underlay to be beyond saving, and he tossed the shirt into the still-smoking pit to burn beside the drey's bones. His vest had faired only marginally better, sizable holes having been eaten here and there through the leather like some rodent treating itself to the hide, but it held together for the moment. With his only other option being to hike half-naked in the shade of the woods in the relative coolness of an approaching fall, Declan patted the vest free of dry mud with a stiff arm and pulled it on without complaint. He had a harder time buckling his belt about his waist, the new skin of his scars making the fingers of his left hand particularly ungainly. By the time the sheathed knife and empty scabbard hung at his sides, he'd vowed thrice over with profanity-laden grunts to do as Bonner had suggested. Ester would take up their daily training with him again as soon as they were able, even if he had to beg her on his hand and knees.

After all were ready, they took a minute for the yr'Essel's to look over their ruined glen one final time, giving Ryn the opportunity to shift into his familiar—but significantly smaller—form of the warped stallion.

Then, at last, the four of them were on the move.

They were quiet as they managed the woods, making north by east, Declan imitating the other three's relative silence with some effort. He understood they had to be careful, for the moment. His comprehension didn't extend much past the fact that something was out there, very clearly hunting them, but this alone was enough to help him hold his tongue, at least until he was given liberty to speak by Ryn and Bonner. For the length of the morning that pair led them, seemingly without any true direction, deeper into the trees. They ate as they traveled, saving the apples in the bag by breaking their fast on edible mushrooms the mage pointed out along their path, a bland meal that no one in particular found more than passably filling. Ryn tried twice to gallop down a hare, but his usual agility was largely absent, stolen by his still-healing injuries, and by the time Ester took pity on the dragon and wordlessly downed him a pair of squirrels with masterful

175

shots, Declan made his decision. The moment Ryn was done with the bloody meal, he offered him a rest with a quiet word, and the dragon only managed a murmur of thanks before transforming yet again, this time into the great black hawk. Hopping up onto his shoulder, Ryn promptly fell asleep once more.

After that, Bonner thankfully didn't keep them going long.

"This way," he said about an hour later, the first full words Declan had heard since they'd abandoned the clearing. His mind had wandered, chasing itself around as it tried to make sense of what few deductions he'd been able to make of their predicament on his own. He looked up to find the old man shifting them further east, along the ever-so-faint outline of a deer trail.

"Do you know where we're going?" he asked, taking Bonner's volume as leave to speak a little more freely. He was growing impatient with the silence, as companionable as it was, and the sun was breaking its high arc in the sky they could just see through the branches of the trees. They'd been walking for some five, maybe six hours, and he was equal parts hungry, tired, and thirsty.

Bonner nodded, ducking under the belly of a fallen oak that had been caught in the low branches of its siblings. "I've a friend not too far from here. His home should be spacious enough to accommodate the four of us in the short term, though I don't think it would be wise to linger long."

"A friend?" Declan asked dubiously, eyeing Ester askance.

She gave a weak grin, her delicate features sheened with sweat from the day's march. Deftest of them all in the undergrowth, she'd been scouting their flanks back and forth ever since Ryn had returned to his slumber. "I'd rather let you be surprised," she said with her best attempt at a laugh, grabbing his arm and tugging him sideways so he didn't catch his head on the very trunk Bonner had just avoided. "Father would be disappointed if I ruined it, anyway."

This answer being as far from satisfying as Declan could have imagined, he considered waking Ryn to ask him about it, but the dragon's horned head was tucked under one wing, taloned feet instinctively righting himself as they moved, clearly in need of the rest.

With a discontented shrug, Declan continued to trail behind the yr'Essels, considering that nothing—truly *nothing*, at this point—could be half-so-strange as the company he already found himself keeping.

A quarter-hour later, they deviated off the trail, true east now, and back into the thickness of the woods. Soon after, the sound of rushing water reached Declan's ears, and he identified the passing of a river not far off. Sure enough, they reached the flow's edge within minutes, and Bonner led them upstream at once, moving along the stony bank with confidence.

Taking a bend, Declan groaned as he made out the narrow mouth of a cave, dug out from the root of a massive, centuries-old pine, set high enough up the bank that even a heavy flood likely wouldn't drown out its inhabitants.

He thought he could guess what kind of "friend" Bonner had been referring to.

The old man reached the cave first, motioning for Declan and Ester to stay behind. When they stopped a respectable distance from the opening, Bonner hopped down like a rabbit into its hole, the sounds of slipping earth and rock vanishing as he disappeared into the earth. Exchanging a look, Ester motioned towards the river.

"He'll be a moment," she said, already moving down the embankment. "Care for a drink?"

Declan almost groaned in anticipation at the suggestion, sliding after her carefully, trying not to jostle Ryn more than he had to. The half-elf had taken the traveling bag from him when he'd accepted the dragon's weight, and she was already kneeling on a flat stone at the edge of the water, pulling the flask from within to dump its warmed contents into the flow. By the time he reached her she'd filled the container up again, offering it back to him first. He took it with a word of thanks, bringing the flask to his mouth hungrily.

"How's he doing?" Ester asked after taking the flask back and downing her own fill. She was watching Ryn with concern while bending down to sink the container into the water again.

"As best as can be expected, I think." Declan moved to join her, stepping onto another flat length of stone just to her left and squatting to dip his hands into the river. It felt cool and nice against his skin, and he made a mental note to take advantage and bathe later, if they had the chance. "He's been sleeping since he changed. I think the fight took everything he had."

Ester nodded. She hadn't yet heard all the details, and he thought to offer them, but before he could get the words out there was a hail from behind, and they turned to see Bonner's head peeking down at them from over the edge of the cave.

"All's well!" he shouted down at them over the rush of the flow. "I think we're welcome, for the time being!"

"He 'thinks' we're welcome?" Declan asked nervously, standing up and taking the broad step back to land before turning to present his hand to the woman. "And what's he mean, 'for the time being'?"

Ester laughed at that, gaining her own feet and accepting his offered assistance despite the fact he knew she could have managed just as well without.

"I'm surprised," she teased, hitching the pack up higher onto her shoulders before leading the way back up the hill. "I would have thought this sort of thing hardly more than an adventure for a man who'd so recently killed a drey."

Declan rolled his eyes, appreciating the opportunity to look anywhere but directly in front of him as Ester managed the incline at exactly the *wrong* height for his discretion. "I'm still not sure what that thing was, so the joke falls flat. Not to mention that to say it was half-dead by the time I got to take a swing might very well be the understatement of the year."

He caught her smile when she crested the embankment and twisted to offer her own hand, which he accepted gratefully. "Learn to take a compliment, Declan."

"*That*—" his sardonic exclamation was interrupted by the grunt-worthy strain of his stiff arm as together they got him over the edge "—was a compliment?" He looked at her ruefully, dusting his hands off on his pants. "On the contrary, I'm fairly sure you just very craftily attempted to call me a coward, if anything."

"Did I?" Ester asked with an exaggerated gasp, batting her eyes at him and covering her mouth in mock horror. Then she daintily took two steps in retreat and leapt backwards into the cave, grinning as she vanished, her voice coming out muffled from within. "I suppose you'll just have to prove me wrong then, won't you?"

Grumbling to himself, Declan followed, holding tight to his empty scabbard as he followed the woman down into the dark.

He didn't have far to go, but the loose earth of the entry gave under his feet, nearly sending him and Ryn both toppling to the flatter floor at the bottom of the hole. From there, he had to squat awkwardly to keep the dragon steady, crouching through a low, rough tunnel that had been dug straight between the heavy roots of the pine above, their rough lattice as struts in a mine. Ester was nowhere to be seen, the nimble half-elf having scampered off with nothing more than a lingering titter, and he found himself muttering again about cowards and drey and where she could put her "compliments", though he was smiling on the inside.

Not ten feet into the low space, Declan was forced to turn and follow the tunnel around a wide bend, the end coming into sight not a yard ahead of him. A surprising amount of light outlined the far mouth, and he found himself popping out into a wider, higher space, one in which he might have been able to safely stand had he been but two or three inches shorter. A second, much smaller tree looked to form the dense skeleton of the cave's ceiling, the spidering of narrower roots more delicate, but heavily entwined, allowing sunlight to stream through a dozen holes of varying widths in shifting rays that glimmered and shined with dust. The floor beneath his feet was hard-packed, almost as firm as stone, and the walls were concave, providing ample dry shelter for the days the pleasantness of the perforations overhead might have betrayed its occupant to rain or snow.

Not that said occupant looked as though a little precipitation would have done much to ruffle it…

Declan had been somewhat expecting the presence, but all the same he very nearly yelped when he caught sight of the bear, lounging on its back in a particularly thick patch of sunlight, off to one side of the cave. It wasn't the largest specimen he'd ever seen—the *er'enthyl* had trained red bears as border guardians along the edge of the Vyr'en that would have put this one to shame—but all the same it was a sizable creature, one that might have been of a height with him when it stood on its hind paws. He ogled it, and started yet again when he saw the animal's small, dark eyes on him, upside down as it warmed its stomach, studying him with lazy interest.

"Oh, stop staring and sit down," Ester's low, amused voice spoke up from his right, and he felt her slim fingers take him by the wrist and pull him earthward.

He complied without much resistance, finding himself seated on the woman's left along the wall perpendicular to the cave's mouth, her father on her other side. The mage appeared to be working on something in the air in front of him, and Declan leaned around Ester to watch, astounded, as Bonner drew rapid runes in the air with one hand over the outstretched palm of the other. With twisting fingers the man spun the rapidly building shape of a sphere this way and that, the hollow form comprised of the twisted symbols that flared into existence, deftly filling each space with what was obviously practiced order and deliberate care. Not long after, Bonner was done, and with a motion like he meant to pull on opposite ends of the orb it grew rapidly outward. The small runes kept their size while they moved, expanding away from each other in a rush, faint, gleaming tethers all that looked to bind them together. They reached the extent of the confined space, passing through their bodies and then the bear's harmlessly, until the symbols burned blue-green into the dirt and roots of the walls that surrounded them.

Then they vanished, leaving the cave as it had been, with no palpable change to be felt in the air.

"It's not much, but it will do for the moment," Bonner said with an expelling breath of ease, reaching up to pull his hood over his head with both hands before leaning back against the wall behind him. "It will make the job of anyone trying to track us that much harder, at the very least."

"You think that's probable?" Ester asked in a worried voice, looking to her father. "That we're being followed?"

Bonner shrugged not looking around. "Impossible to say. If Ryn and Declan have caught Sehranya's eye, I can hardly imagine she'd just give up on them because we took out a single specimen of her accursed pets. Where there's one such beast, there are undoubtedly more."

Sehranya. The Endless Queen. The very subject Declan had spent most of his morning mulling over. He found that he could not fear her the way Ester and Bonner and—to an extent—even Ryn seemed to. He knew next to nothing of whatever legend it was that she seemed to have sprung from, save for the small part of the conversation she'd dominated the first morning he'd woken up in the yr'Essel's home.

"Is she that much of a threat?" he asked, keeping his voice quiet as he glanced at the loafing bear not ten feet from them.

"Oh, ignore Talo," Bonner said with a snort and a wave at the beast. "He's agreed to let us stay, so long as we bring him a few fish from the stream before night's end. He won't cause us any trouble if we keep to our side of the cave."

Declan raised his eyes to the ceiling, shaking his head both at the name, and at the fact that Bonner could apparently communicate with the animal as he might a man.

He was kept from commenting on this by the old man's grave answer, which followed promptly.

"And yes, Declan. She is such a threat, and more. In all my days I've not heard of a fouler soul, much less come across one. She was dangerous on her own, even *without* her armies." He grimaced, correcting himself with a muttered: "*Is* dangerous…"

"Who is she?" It was as simple a deliberation as Declan could form from the maelstrom of suspicions he'd churned up in his head throughout their trek. "Or… *what* is she?"

Fair questions both, in their own way.

Ryn's voice was like a wash of warm water down Declan's back, easing a tension in his shoulders he hadn't even realized he'd been carrying. Ester made an abrupt, pleased sound at his elbow, and he looked around to find the dragon blinking himself awake.

"How are you feeling?" Bonner asked first, eyeing his companion's hawkish form.

Hungry, Ryn answered honestly, hopping down to Declan's knee, then the cave floor before eyeing the bear, who was watching him with almost genuine interest. *Will he be startled if I change? I've never liked this form much. It's always felt a poor replacement for my natural state.*

Ah, Declan thought with a flash of satisfaction. *One mystery resolved at last.*

Bonner, meanwhile, snorted. "Hardly. I saved his life after some drunken country knight tried to skewer him with a tourney lance. Had to transport him back to the cottage all my own. He's seen stranger magics, believe me."

Ryn offered the old man a blank look, but then gave his wings a brief shrug, and began to change. A few seconds later the dragonling sat before them, the shape Declan was starting to think was the dragon's preferred form when the functions of his others weren't needed.

I can tell you only so much of Sehranya's history before our encounter with her, Declan, he said, returning to the conversation at hand while settling his long tail about his crossed legs. *Her own people guarded the details of her past from us when we asked, or possibly knew no more of her history themselves. She presented herself in the guise of a young elven woman, but to think of her as anything other than ancient even seven hundred years ago would have obviously been underestimating the witch.*

"An elf?" Declan asked, surprised by this. For some reason, he had trouble justifying the image of a woman who looked a bit like Ester, with solid gold or silver hair, reigning over ranks of thousands of risen dead. "She came from the Vyr'en? Have the *er'enthyl* ever held that kind of power? If they were that strong I can't imagine them not pressing our borders more fervently…"

There was a short, almost awkward pause, in which Ryn and Bonner looked at each other.

There's more than one reason the wood elves don't push into Viridian, but… When it comes to Sehranya… The dragon looked to be having trouble finding the right words to explain. *She's not of the Vyr'en. She was—or is, it would rather seem—an elf, yes, but…* He broke off, chewing on his thoughts a moment. *Declan, have you ever heard of the 'er'endehn'?*

Declan blinked, not anticipating his own response to the word. It was odd to his ears, and yet distinctly familiar. After several seconds of being unable to place it, he looked to Ester and Bonner for help, meeting the half-elf's gaze first.

Her expectant, knowing gaze.

It hit him, then. He *had* indeed been made to know the word before, when he'd thought the woman to have misspoken the name of the *er'enthyl*. He hadn't given that particular confusion so much as a second's thought since, the limits of perplexion his mind was capable of consistently strained by the innumerable other uncertainties which had weighed on him in the last week.

"I… have…" he answered Ryn uncertainly, not looking away from the woman, recalling the other details of the exchange in question. "Ester mentioned it to me, in this very context. She told me the Queen was… 'er'endehn', was it?" He frowned at what he hoped was a correct pronunciation, turning his attention back on the dragon. "Are they a different breed of elf, perhaps?"

Ryn snorted. *I would be careful calling them a 'breed' of any sort, Declan. They're not likely to take that kindly, and as good as you are with a blade, I can't say I have much faith in you coming out on top in a duel with any er'endehn you might obliviously offend.* He sobered, meeting Declan's eye carefully. *I'm not surprised you haven't heard of them, of course. It's probably been six centuries since they locked themselves away in their lands. I suppose even some legends fade with time, given the short lifespans of your kind. Put simply—"* he paused, seeming to consider his explanation "*—the er'endehn are what you would call 'dark elves'.*

Declan's brow shot towards the ceiling, at this. He watched Ryn carefully for a moment, then looked to Bonner, and then Ester in turn. Neither of the others showed any sign of astonishment at the dragon's words, and he was left to swallow the facts by himself. In retrospect, he supposed he could have deduced as much at his own pace. 'Dehn' was the elvish word for 'black' or 'night', something he'd puzzled out given that the favored rebuke of the Iron Wind's quarter-master for anyone who lost a piece of gear was to accuse them of being "*t'wel syn'trev dehn*", or "unable to find the stars in the night."

"Dark elves?" he repeated after several seconds turning this revelation over. "No… I've not heard of them. And they're not of the Vyr'en? Where do they live? Beyond the southern forests?" It was the only position he could think to give them. To the west, beyond the Reaches, there was nothing but coastal ridges and an explored ocean, and to the east was Borel's Sea—so named for the explorer who had first charted its crossing some centuries ago—across which could be found the deserts of Sarahkan. He even considered, briefly, whether such a people might live underground, involuntarily looking down at the hard-packed earth upon which he sat.

This notion he discarded quickly enough.

Man has always had a talent for explaining away what he does not know, or what he does not wish to remember, Ryn said, tone tinged with just the faintest note of disappointment. *I suppose it's too much to hope that you might know why the ranges north of us are called 'the Tears'?*

Declan felt a little indignant at that. "Of course I know that," he said, not at all pleased with the assumption. "Some great war, long ago. Thousands dead. So many the Mother is said to have wept for grief. Any boy knows the tale."

"Not even the right *bloody* mountains," Bonner muttered in annoyance.

Declan look around at him, but Ryn reclaimed his attention at once, ignoring the old man.

But that's all they know? he pressed coaxingly. *Not the name of the war, nor the participants in that conflict? They couldn't even tell you*—he paused for emphasis—*what lies beyond those peaks?*

North...

The thought struck Declan so firmly, his eyes widened. He hadn't even *considered* Eserysh—the fabled lands beyond the Mother's Tears—an option worth thinking on. The realms passed the mountains were said to be nothing more than an uninhabitable tundra, a rolling wasteland of snow and ice and frozen lakelands, home only to feral beasts and unworthy creatures, the most civilized of which were the wereyn. Then again, no one in written memory had conquered those brutal ranges, or at least none Declan had ever heard of. Those who'd tried had never returned, always written off as having succumbed to the savage storms of the peaks, or the beastmen themselves...

"North," he said aloud, voicing the realization. "They... The elves live on the other side of the *Tears?*"

He could hardly wrap his mind around the concept, a familiar sensation he didn't like feeling he was growing accustomed to.

"And very well." Bonner spoke again, more firmly this time. "These tales of snow-covered barrens and endless white I've heard in this last century." He snorted. "Without magic I would have at least hoped to see Viridian move forward in its study of sciences and maths, and any learned observer of weather should be able to tell you such a drastic shift in climate with such little change in latitude is hardly plausible. I *mean*," he took on a distinct air of indignation, apparently offended by the very thought, "I grant that the winters are cold in our valley towns, but to think of the storm build-up it would require to cover the world in snow at all times of the year? One can hardly fathom the... the..."

He trailed off, at last taking note of the stares he was getting from the others, even Ryn. With a disgruntled huff he crossed his arms, muttering something about "seeing to their education in the important things", before settling back into silence.

Bonner is correct, in the essential, Ryn picked up. *As far as we know, the er'endehn live as well—if not better—than we do here, or the er'enthyl within the boundaries of their forests. They are an old people, and long-lived, longer even then their wood elf cousins. Theirs was a civilization well established long before mankind found his hold in Viridian.*

"Then how do we know nothing of them?" Declan demanded, truly refusing to believe now. "If such a-a *nation*—" he struggled to find the appropriate title "—existed, then *surely* we would have dealings with them? Trade? Border disputes? Even occasionally, if not on the regular! How is such an absence possible?"

"By desire of the *er'endehn* themselves." It was Ester's turn to answer, putting the response simply. "It was *they* who have cut themselves off from the world, Declan. *They* ended contact with the al'Dyor line. Father told me they even regularly drove the wereyn out of Eserysh and into the Tears, making the ranges essentially insurmountable."

"They did *what?*" Declan demanded, anger welling momentarily over his disbelief. He felt entitled to his outrage. Even if he couldn't recall any memory of Ertus Idrys, he *had* lost a father to the beasts.

Ryn attempted to cool him with a raised hand. *It's not what you think. The er'endehn have their own lands to protect, and have been waging something of a constant war with the wereyn since the race's creation along with the rest of the Endless Queen's brood. They would not deliberately press the beastmen into Viridian, but they have good reason—at least to their own logic—to segregate themselves from the world.* Particularly *mankind.*

"What 'reason'?" Declan demanded incredulously. He hadn't missed the rest of what Ryn had said—the "creation" of the wereyn?—but his anger was more pressing. "What logic could they possibly have, *especially* to push their enemies to the limits of *our own borders?* I have to tell you, Ryn, of *all* the things I've been made to swallow this last week, I'm having trouble understanding why—"

Sehranya.

The quiet way in which Ryn said it had Declan shutting up in an instant, and the dragon took his chance to continue.

Magic is a strange thing, Declan. We know very little of it. I won't weight you with the details now—Bonner would be able to better explain it, anyway—but magic is not so lifeless an entity as one might assume. It is… unpredictable. It has been known to pluck at the strings of fate, to set into motion events both wonderful and terrible, often in subtle ways, but occasionally simply by the manner in which it manifests itself. He looked Declan up and down, then, almost pensively. *You have an aptitude for it. Has Bonner told you that?*

Of all the things the dragon could have said, then, *this* was the last thing Declan might possibly have expected.

"W-What?" he stuttered, unable to craft any other response. On his right, he thought he felt Ester tense.

You have an aptitude for magic, Ryn repeated promptly. *Fire weaving in particular, if I had to guess, and a rather high one. But that isn't surprising. Mankind as a whole has always had an easier time manipulating the arcane than the elves of either race.*

"There was a theory going around, when I was at school," Bonner started to provide, clearly thinking he was being helpful, "that this directly correlated to our shorter lifespans. Of course, little conclusive evidence was ever found to back the idea, and judging from my own experience I can't say—"

He shut up swiftly, cowing under the sharp look Ryn shot him before looking away and whistling an innocent tune at the far wall.

The point I was attempting *to get at*—the dragon didn't look away from the reprimanded mage for a moment—*is that the ability to wield magic varies. As it might change the course of events and time, so too does in appear to select its vessels with equal prejudice, and with as little transparency. That variation can be drastic, too, even among those of human blood. Ester*—" he waved a claw to indicate the woman even as he offered her an apologetic look "—*has a lower aptitude, while yours is abnormally elevated.*"

Declan could not stop himself from feeling alarmed at this so-casually made proclamation, but Ryn placated him at once.

I misspoke, he said, raising both hands before him in an appeasing gesture. *I would have done better to say that your potential is* artificially *elevated. The gifts Herst was given by our primordial line affected more than his physical prowess. They expanded his ability to commune with the ley lines of the world—the heart of magic, stretched across every land, known and unknown—to an extent nearing our own ability.* Ryn grimaced. *In a twisted way, my kind have more akin to the drey then we do with any of the other sentient races. We are the elders of this world—some dragons believe we were born from magic itself, though I find that fanciful. Whatever the case, we are tethered to the lines almost directly, our ability to manipulate the currents of magic restricted only by the limits of our own bodies, as opposed to the reserves humans and elves draw from and rely on.*

An image of Bonner, weary and staggering as the fight with the drey wore on, flit across Declan's mind, and he thought he understood. He nodded slowly.

You share—in part, at least—with that power, much as you share Herst's memories. Ester, meanwhile, is of elven blood as equally as she is of human…

Ryn hesitated, looking to the woman, clearly desiring to offer her an opportunity to explain herself, which she did so promptly at a puzzled look from Declan.

"It's probably the reason my ability is so low," she answered with a half-grin, not bothering to hide what was clearly a healthy measure of disappointment. "Elves bear few children as is, and fewer still with any talent for spellwork. I've been through every book on the subject my father ever gave me a dozen times over, and I couldn't give you a rhyme or reason for it. It's just a fact. But—" she paused, exchanging a quick look with Ryn "—when one does come along…"

They are often exceedingly powerful, the dragon finished for her. *Like much of the scattered potential of an entire generation, condensed in a single individual. It's a trait of their kind, the wood elves and dark elves alike, and not always a blessing. That amount of power tends to consume the wielder, devouring the children sometimes even in their mother's wombs.*

"But not always."

It was Declan himself who said it, the words hissing out of him, comprehension finally starting to rise as the pieces fell into place.

Ryn nodded slowly. *No. Not always.*

"Sehranya." The name finally started to carry with it a measure of the fear Declan now saw it was due. "Born to the *er'endehn.*"

"A people who had little to no knowledge of the arcane arts, much less any means by which to train her." Bonner reentered the conversation, his tone serious. "And they *would* have wanted her trained..."

"Of course they would have." Declan had seen his share of battlefields. Minor rebellions crushed by the firm hand of the al'Dyors. Skirmishes at the borders of the Vyr'en, usually with poaching groups or trespassers. Outlaws forming raiding parties a hundred strong, thinking themselves far from the eye of the crown when they set upon the minor towns and villages at the extent of Viridian's lands. Just as well he had seen, too, Bonner's *prodigious* capability on the field, and it was more than a little obvious that combat was *not* the old man's specialty. A mage, particularly a powerful one, to bolster the ranks of any standing army, adding to its offensive, defensive, *and* support capabilities...

The larger picture was coming together faster now. "They would have wanted to see to her education. They would have sent her to the only kingdom with the means to do so, who bore enough mages to warrant that sort of training."

The others, even Ester, only nodded.

"*We* made her, didn't we?" Declan finished, his fingers suddenly numb. "Mankind created the Endless Queen..."

CHAPTER TWENTY-ONE

They spent the rest of the day in relatively tame company, going about basic tasks to make the cave even slightly more hospitable, though no one spoke as to how long they would be staying. Declan got his bath, as did Ester after him, but Ryn was still exhausted and his sleek scales never held filth well regardless. Bonner, for his part, shrugged off the proffered wash without comment. Seeing as the man was uncommonly spotless most any time Declan had ever laid eyes on him—*including* after their morning-long hike through the woods—he thought nothing more of it than to give the old man's robes a wistful glance.

They gathered dry wood for the evening, stacking it just outside the mouth of the cave—none of them imagining that Talo would have appreciated an open flame in the closed confines of his home—and set about scrounging for their dinner. Ryn was allowed to return to sleep, what little help he'd attempted to provide taxing his injuries to their limits. As a result, Ester set off alone with her bow and quiver to hunt, while Bonner went foraging for other edibles in the surrounding undergrowth. This left Declan to the fishing, looking to make good on their promise to the bear as much as he was hoping to catch enough to smoke and dry, ideally easing their next bout of travel.

For most of the afternoon Declan lingered in private contemplation, his mind distant while scouring the shallows for the flash of scales beneath the water, the four-pronged spear he'd fashioned for himself out of the straightest branch he'd been able to find at the ready. Their earlier conversation had kept on for a while after he'd come to see that *Viridian*— his own country—was at least partially responsible for the rise of the witch who would come to be called "the Endless Queen". He felt the chill in truth, now, whenever either of the dark elf's names were mentioned, a puzzling feeling given that he *still* had only little sense of what had made the woman so terrifying in her time, and even less what made her frightening now. The drey had been a terror, to be sure, as had the ghouls, but it was hard for Declan to connect those experiences with a being he'd only come to hear of mere days ago.

Still, he couldn't complain, knowing a good deal more now than he had even the day before…

Ryn had not been exaggerating the limited extent of his, Bonner's, and Ester's knowledge of the fabled necromancer. Once the connection had been established, the dragon had been able to explain only what Declan himself might have been able to eventually deduce on his own. Sehranya had been sent to the magical colleges of Aletha—the capital of Viridian centuries before Ryn himself was born, apparently—a consortium of schools now long-demolished. There she'd received the training her people had so desperately desired for her, making a name for herself among peers and professors alike. After that, though, she'd vanished for some unknown part of history, and Declan had begged to be excused of the details of her reappearance, if only for the time being. Ryn had wanted to say more, had very *badly* wanted to say more, but Bonner stopped him, recognizing that Declan was growing rapidly overwhelmed. The dragon eventually conceded, and settled on explaining a final, key point:

After the Queen's fall, the dark elves had shut themselves off from the lands of man, mistrusting the corruption their good faith had been repaid with.

Declan's eyes darted about the pool of clear, smooth water he was knee-deep in, having rolled up his pants and left his boots on the shore not far to his left. He'd picked the spot carefully, a narrow cut just beyond a pair of large, jutting rocks in which the current whirled back on itself, slowing the flow almost to a stop in certain places. He'd had good luck thus far, having speared and tossed two sizable yellow perch and a redfin of respectable girth up onto the bank already. Had he been of a clearer wit, he might have called an end to the chore some quarter-hour before, given the others were also out searching for food. But, caught in the depths of his own thoughts, Declan lost himself in the calming rhythm of the stalk, taking advantage of the mindless waiting to let everything sink in.

Even with the cool rush of the water about his feet and the soothing sound of the river all about him, he felt like his head was going to split in two.

Again Declan thought that it was too much. Too much. Dark elves. The Endless Queen. His own potential in the arts he'd witnessed Bonner yr'Essel wield to devastating effect. All of it pulled down on him like a heavy chain strung about his neck, and he was doubly grateful to the mage for having pressured Ryn into forgoing the rest of his recounting. Declan wanted to hear more, *needed* to, even, but with every new understanding he made, so too did the implication of it come to bear. He could scarcely believe, not needing to look back more than a few days, how the world presented itself to him now. He had felt he'd lived an intricate life, then, an adventurous path to be commended and even envied, in many ways. He'd been among the youngest ever to be counted in equal part with the grizzled former soldiers and renowned sellswords of Aletha's mercenary companies. He'd been a trusted hand of Cassandra Sert, guildmaster of the Iron Wind, and had carried out work for some of the greatest families of the Alethan royal court, his contracts shying just short of the King himself. Even that limit existed only because it had been years since the al'Dyors had seen fit to reach out to the companies for assistance, and not due to any shortcoming of his own. He had thought, from the perspective of any man—himself included—to have lived a boast-worthy, exciting life.

But now, casting back, Declan could see how linear his path had been, how absent of divergence and how plainly—if impressively—his years had truly passed. Magic, rare as it was, was reclaiming a place in Viridian. The undead were crawling from their graves, bidden forth by a cataclysmic power that Bonner himself swore he'd seen the end to seven hundred years ago. Dragons were anything but a legend, as were creatures of such fearsome ability they could meet the great beasts head-to-head, with the fight as easily decided on a toss of a coin.

There was no other way to put it. Declan felt like he had been playing the soldier with wooden swords his entire life, and only just been shown the gruesome reality of the battlefield he dreamed of fighting upon.

A glimmer of gold against the grey-green and blue of the riverbed. Declan lanced forward, but the perch slipped by in the current, and he stopped himself just in time to keep from dulling his spear against wet stone.

There were the wereyn, too, to consider. Estwyn had fallen to a horde, which meant the beastmen were possibly then-and-now spilling into the kingdom's borders. Declan had faith the Vigil would see to them in the end, of course. Aletha alone garrisoned some thirty-thousand troops, with thrice that number again stationed in various posts, cities, and patrols throughout the land. Called to bear, the crown could realistically muster a hundred thousand to face whatever threat the Tears let spill, not to mention the additional ten thousand in support if the al'Dyors opened their coffers to the guilds.

Still… It was more the fact that the wereyn were attacking at all, in any great number, that was concerning. It was anything but a coincidence. That much Declan was certain of, and had been from the moment Ryn returned from his scouting to inform them of the fall of the town. But did that mean Sehranya, wherever it was she had secluded herself, had *them* under her control as well? Hadn't Ryn implied as much, at the very least…?

'The Queen's brood', Declan considered again, mulling over the words the dragon had used. *And what did he mean, 'their creation'?*

Too much, he told himself again, lancing forward as the sheen of some darker fish he couldn't make out clearly swirled into view. Too much.

This time the four horns of the spear struck true, and Declan couldn't help but grunt in satisfaction as he heaved the animal out of the water. It was a small trout, a late shower for the season, but it was still the size of his forearm and would do well as someone's dinners at the minimum. With a careful snap of the weapon he sent the fish flopping to the shore to land with the trio of others. The movement shot an uncomfortable sensation of tension through his left arm, and he grit his teeth at the limb, flexing his fingers, wrist, and elbows without releasing the spear. He was fortunate he hadn't been fool enough to pull his *sword arm* from the healing mold, but just the same the impediment frustrated him. He'd been useless enough as it was for most of the fight with the drey. He had no desire to be dead weight to the group, particularly with wereyn making a push into the land…

Too much, he groaned, wishing for any means by which to distract himself from his vexation that didn't involve dunking his head under the cool rush of the river.

"Declan, I'm done. Do you need any help?"

Declan almost laughed aloud at the timing, turning to see Ester returned from her hunt. She was looking down on him from the top of the embankment, the unstrung staff of her bow in one hand, a pair of sizable rabbits held by the ears in her other.

"Yes!" he called back eagerly, sloshing out of the water. "Stay there. I'll come to you."

Reaching the shore, he set his spear aside and snatched up two fish between the thumb and forefingers of each hand. With bare feet he took the hill, finding purchase on the roots and stones, and came to stand beside the half-elf, looking her up and down hopefully.

"Your father hasn't come back yet?"

Ester shook her head, watching him glance around for the old man with a curious expression, clearly waiting on him to elaborate his previous statement.

"Good." He shot her a challenging grin, waving the limp tails of his day's yield in the direction of the firewood they'd gathered earlier. "Then what would you say if I told you I could use a spar?"

There was an instant—just an instant—in which what Declan thought might have been disappointment flashed across the woman's eyes. He probably imagined it, because not a heartbeat later she was answering him with an almost-savage smile. "I'd say I'll never need an excuse to beat you black and blue." She leaned her bow against a nearby tree and dropped the rabbits at its base without ceremony. "Come on."

Tossing his fish down in the grass nearby, Declan wiped his hands clean with a handful of leaves he stripped from a nearby bush before returning to the bank to don his boots. Taking up his spear again, he took the embankment again, he found Ester testing her own branch from the pile of kindling they'd gathered. They spent a few minutes clearing the wood of their makeshift weapons of any bark that might fly in their eyes on contact otherwise, then located the clearest patch of ground to be found within sight of the cave. The area was flat enough, if not completely level, and absent much of the brush that could trip them up.

It did the trick.

Their exchanges—disappointingly—could not match the cadence of the training they'd previously taken up daily. Their "weapons" were brittle, lacking the sturdiness of the practice swords lost to the destruction of Ryn's battle with the drey, and equally too light and poorly balanced. They had to take their time, more going through the patterns of their respective styles than actually fighting, but Declan didn't mind. It offered him an opportunity to study Ester's guile movements more closely, doing his best to learn what he could from the flowing dance of her mother's teachings. More importantly, the pallid skin of his hands, arms, and chest *was* tight, even along his *right* side, and the reduced pace allowed some much-needed acclimation to the uncomfortable stretch he felt with any extended motion. He caught himself, more than once, engaging Ester with only tight combinations, limiting the irritable sensation, and always willed himself back into the larger motions, pushing the scarring tissue. Ester, in kind, seemed to have equally recalled her father's words about Declan's rehabilitation, and was working him deliberately in much the same manner. Her strikes frequently came at odd angles and from unanticipated positions, forcing him to react and move every which way, and she often feinted her slash and thrusts, requiring quick corrections. He appreciated the half-elf once more as a sparring partner, grinning at her from between the interlocking of their makeshift swords when he could. She mirrored the expression, smiling through the sweat they were both building up, clearly as pleased as he was with the opportunity to vent some of the emotions he knew she—like him—was likely floundering under.

Bonner returned some half-hour later, arms loaded with a variety of fungal and floral discoveries, at which point both Declan and Ester quit their work to join the man, content despite the brevity of their session. Bonner was pleased to realize what they had been about, sweaty and sticky as they were, tossing his bounty down and prodding at Declan's left arm while asking how his movements had felt.

"Not sure," he admitted with a shrug, allowing the mage to examine the range of his fingers. "A little looser, maybe? But not much, if that."

"It will come," Bonner told him, his voice assuring, dropping the hand as Ester returned from where she'd taken her second dip of the day into the river. "It will be a slow process, but it will come. Keep me appraised of any changes, will you?"

He didn't encourage Declan to continue the training, apparently assuming—rightly so—that no pressure was needed on that front.

Talking between themselves about the various successes of their day, the three of them set about preparing dinner. Declan started on cleaning the fish while Ester broke the longest branches they'd gathered over her knee before stacking the cords with quick efficiency, forming a cone of tinder that would have impressed a practiced woodsman. As soon as she was done, she called for her father, and Declan paused in his scaling to watch with interest while Bonner reached into the hollow of the ready wood with an open palm. There was a *crack,* and flames rose from between the branches like a fire that had been burning merrily for hours. This time, something more than removed curiosity tugged at Declan, and he almost asked Bonner *how,* exactly, the man so easily conjured such power.

He got so far as to open his mouth before shutting it again. The throb between his temples—not completely resolved by the arduous exercise of the sparring—chided him into recalling that his head might very well explode if he opened himself up to being taught the intricacies of spell-crafting, just then.

Instead, he settled on a simpler, more pressing question.

"Do you know where we're going, Bonner?"

The old man had just taken a seat at the base of a young poplar on the far side of the fire, a rough stone held in one hand and a number of tubers he'd scrounged up tucked under his other arm, but he looked up at Declan's address.

"Ranheln," he said without hesitation, letting the roots tumble to the grass at his side before picking one up again and starting to polish away the clinging earth from its moist surface. "We're in fair dire need of supplies, and that's hardly considering that you and Ester both require new swords and—" he cast a good-humored look at Declan's ragged hunting vest "—new clothes."

Sitting almost knee-to-knee with Declan on his right, Ester perked up at this, knife in one hand and a rabbit in the other. He, meanwhile, only nodded, unsurprised. Their morning's bearing had indeed been north by east, and the only major settlement in that direction—assuming he'd correctly puzzled out a good sense of where Bonner's cottage might have been located on a map—was the lake city of Ranheln. It wasn't a fraction as large as Aletha, far further east and a ways south, but it was a municipality of respectable size and wealthy trade, thriving as the major source of fish and timber to most of its neighbors within a week's cart-ride in any direction.

"And after that?"

Bonner could only shrug, not looking away from his work this time. "The capital, if I have any say about it, lad. Ryn could give you a better answer, as things are, but the Queen's rise isn't something to be taken in stride. The al'Dyors will need to be told, if they don't know already. That being said… I've no idea how thoroughly you've been marked by Sehranya, or whatever ilk of hers has been tailing you these last days. If we can lose ourselves in the wilds for a time, it might be in our best interest to do so, even if it's as we move."

Declan would have answered in favor of this plan, of course. He and Ryn had means and connections in Aletha. Even if they *were* "marked", as Bonner put it, he imagined anything short of a hundred drey would be quickly overrun by the standing force of the city's Vigil.

Before he could say as much, Ester broke in enthusiastically.

"The capital?" She waved her knife eastward in excitement, through the woods. She'd hadn't touched the rabbit yet, having listened to the exchange with an odd intensity. "How far is it? When would we arrive?"

Declan blinked at her, not understanding the exuberance of her excitement.

"Six weeks on foot," Bonner, fortunately, answered for him, blowing dust away from his work. "Would be less than half of that riding, but I don't see us procuring mounts anytime soon."

Declan had to agree. He'd lost the reward he and Ryn had earned for the kidnapping job to the drey attack, and while he would have access to his old company funds in Ranheln, even poor horses were expensive when bought in pairs.

"Oh," Ester said, sounding a little disheartened. Then she perked up again. "But it's probably the safest place in Viridian right now, isn't it? I heard it's a walled city!"

"As well as the Vigil's primary stronghold, and home to a dozen different mercenary companies." Declan looked at her askance. "You've never been?"

It was hard to tell whether the pink on Ester's cheeks was from a flush of embarrassment, or the glow of the fire as the sky began to darken above them.

"No." Her silver-gold hair, cleanly braided in the familiar plait that swept across the top and back of her head, swayed with the shake of her head. "Not yet."

The words were quiet, and Declan frowned up at Bonner for clarification. The old man was busy with his work, however, and seemed to almost deliberately not meet his eye.

"Mother hated the cities," Ester explained after several seconds of silence, sensing Declan's disquiet and giving him a glance over her shoulder. "I've... never had the opportunity."

"To see Aletha?"

Another shake of the head. "To see any of them."

Declan's thumb slipped on the slick flesh of the trout in his hands, his knife barely missing the knuckle of his index finger. He stared at the back of the half-elf's head, seeing clearly now the tinge of blood in her pale neck and cheek, and understood her abrupt excitement.

Viridian was a wealthy country, as far as his own limited appreciation of economy and politics extended. There were some dozen cities across the expanse of its lands, the nation's High and Low Roads stretching east from the coastal metropolises of Dover, Sethylles, and Vasteel to the mountain fortress of Ebadon, built into the Reaches themselves far to the west. Some, like Kanrys and Edford, bordering the Vyr'en, were weeks separate from each other even by horse, but many others were within manageable distance of one another, even on foot. In the central country, Thenus and Perun were practically annexes of Aletha itself, able to be reached in no more than three days walking to the northwest and south respectively. It was uncommon enough for country peasants of no family and fewer means to have lacked *some* opportunity to visit any of them, and Declan could not easily bring himself to consider Ester or her father souls of such low circumstance. It astounded him, and he very nearly asked how such a thing was possible when he caught himself.

Ester's mother. A pure-blooded elf, he knew. He didn't know the conditions under which she had come to Viridian, much less met and married Bonner, but he could much more easily gather the woman's hesitation to be surrounded by bustling throngs brimming with a people who had not often, in anyone's memory, treated her kind with any sort of sympathy.

Noting Ester's chagrin again, bordering now on mortification as his obvious surprise weathered on, Declan swore to himself he would have nothing to do with furthering that impression.

"You're in for a treat," he said with as much genuine excitement as he could muster without sounding forced, going back to his fish. "Ranheln isn't anything as grand as Aletha, but if you've never seen a city…"

Ester flinched as he spoke—having very likely expected ridicule—but looked around at his words, the color fading from her cheeks. There was a moment in which her face passed from anxiety to relief, then settled on tempered delight.

"I've been to the villages!" she told him. "And *The Woodsman's Rest* isn't the only inn I've stayed in when I was away from home!"

Declan had to quell a laugh, gutting the fish and starting to scrape it empty. He didn't tell her the nameless hamlets that had posted the original bounty which had brought them all together were hardly anything to get excited over, and didn't want to comment on her last "stay" at *The Rest.* Unable to hide the grin at least, he hoped she would take it as a shared anticipation. "I'd raise your expectations a little, or you're like to faint on arrival."

He told her, then, of the sprawling buildings of the trade city, of the towering, colorful structures of the southern quarters that sometimes rose four or five stories tall. He described taking in Ranheln framed against the still water of the lake on a windless day, and told her of the north docks and the market square—the latter of which they would likely be spending no small amount of time perusing—as well as the variety of people that could be found in such places. She listened in rapt attention, the rabbit completely forgotten in her lap. He doubted he was the first to describe such things to her, but her enthusiasm was infectious, and after finishing with Ranheln, he spoke of Aletha herself. He painted for Ester the image of the vast, seven-story heights of her grey, weathered walls, from which banners in the Vigil's colors hung every fifty yards to bear the shield and crowned stag from their ramparts. He spoke of the palace of the al'Dyors, rising from the very center of the noble's quarters in the middle of the city, its towers and parapets like something out of child's fairytale, particularly the first time one took them in. He told her of the sprawling bazaars—the size of the city requiring several smaller districts across its expanse to be devoted to such markets—then the guildhalls of the companies, particularly the monolithic, timber-and-granite buildings of the Iron Wind which were practically a castle in-and-of their own. By the time he finished, the half-elf's eyes were so wide he thought he could have seen his reflection in their emerald depths if he'd leaned in far enough, and he smiled broadly.

At once, Ester scowled, catching herself and turning away to speak without looking at him. "Something funny?"

"No!" Declan said with a laugh, seeing her misunderstanding. "It's just..." He faltered, trying to find a way to put what he considered an endearing sentiment into words that could very well be taken otherwise.

Declan is thinking that he remembers what you're feeling, Ester. He used to sit and look at me like that himself, when we first set out for the capital, begging me every night to tell him more of the city.

Ryn appeared in the light of the flames then, black form taking shape over the edge of Talo's cave as he stepped into the light. Declan had been spinning his descriptions for so long that night was very nearly upon them, and the dragon's climb from the hole had been muffled by the crackling and popping of the fire in their midst.

Declan was about to ask him how he was feeling, pleased to see him up and about, when Ester spoke up indignantly from his side.

"I'm not a child! It's normal to be excited for something so new!" She looked around briefly, but received only grins from Declan and her father alike, and so hung her head and repeated, under her breath, "It's normal..."

Of course it is, Ryn told her consolingly, moving toward their side of the fire and plucking the sizeable redfin from where it lay waiting to be cleaned

195

at Declan's knee. Ignoring all protests, the dragon tilted his head back and dropped the fish whole, scales, head, and all, down his gullet. *Ah*, he sighed in apparent satisfaction after he'd swallowed. *Better.* He looked between the three of them. *What is it we're discussing? I've only just woken up.*

"Declan has been elaborating on the *wonders* of man's great cities," Bonner answered with a chuckle, waving the stone and a new root in his hands about in teasing exaggeration.

Fascinating, Ryn answered, equally sarcastic, eyeing with interest the last perch left to be scaled.

Declan snatched up the so-threatened fish with a glare. "We were talking—" he said poignantly "—about where it is we're going."

Ranheln, Ryn answered at once, turning his defeated attention onto the rabbit Ester had finally started to skin, the iron aroma of blood mixing with the heavy scent of burning wood. *We're short on provisions, and you both need new steel.*

"I've already told them as much." Bonner had returned to scrubbing his tubers clean. "We were speaking of *after* that. Aletha tops my own list, if it matters."

Ah, Ryn said, catching on. He'd given up on the hope for meat to sate what appeared to be the return of his typically ravenous appetite, and moved instead around the fire towards the mage. *I would say that's our best option, as things lie right now. Mathaleus will want to know what we've seen, even if he's already aware of Sehranya's hand in everything.*

"He knows of the Queen?" Declan asked, not expecting this piece of news. Bonner had said something to that effect as well, he realized then.

Ryn made a non-committal shrug of one shoulder. *Of her, I'm sure. There are measures in place to ensure the royal family stays informed on such matters, even if the common folk have long forgotten. Whether or not those around him have yet deduced her actual involvement, on the other hand...*

He settled down, taking up the thick stock of a mushroom whose head was the size of Declan's open hand, sniffing at it curiously. Giving it a nibble, he made a face—his reptilian features twisting in disappointment—and set the fungus aside in favor of crunching into a finger-sized root he must have recognized more readily.

Aletha is *a good idea, but I admit I'm hesitant to make solid plans until we can figure out more of the Queen's intentions, regarding us particularly. Our victory over the drey isn't a blow to be discounted, but Bonner had the right of it earlier: I'm hardly inclined to think she'll give up the hunt over something like that.*

Despite the lighthearted air with which he had spoken, Declan was put on edge by the dragon's words. It felt like the pair of them—Ryn and Bonner both—were trying to nudge he and Ester towards an understanding without wanting to outright alarm them.

The woman, it turned out, was thinking along the same lines.

"You two have no doubt we're going to be attacked again, do you?" she asked. Gone was the near-childish delight that had bloomed as Declan had related the interests of Ranheln and Aletha to her. She'd paused her bloody work to peer across the flames, expression set.

To their credit, Ryn and Bonner didn't do more than exchange the briefest of glances before the woman's father spoke.

"No, Esteria. None at all."

Ester nodded, saying nothing. After a time she went back to her skinning, her distress betrayed only by the barest shake of her knife hand.

"Can you guess when?" Declan asked in her stead.

If only. It was Ryn's turn to answer, taking advantage of his ability to communicate with no more than an extended thought while claiming another large bite of the carrot-like tuber. *Bonner's scrying requires specifics, and is still limited by distance, and my own senses are even more constrained, as you know. I'll be on the lookout, but I can't be on edge constantly, and forewarning can only go so far if Sehranya—or whatever second she's had tailing us—decides to put another drey on our scent.*

Nothing but the fire made any sort of sound after this, the party as a whole considering the implications of such an event. What would they do, now, in that moment, if one of the foul creatures descended on them, rampaging through the woods or plummeting down through the darkening canopy above? Ryn was hurt, Bonner's strength was limited, and Declan knew he and Ester were next to useless, even if they *had* had their swords. He felt helpless, a sinking sensation that drew away all confidence he'd long held in his own skills, and those of his companions.

It was an impression he didn't enjoy in the least...

CHAPTER TWENTY-TWO

It was another day before Ryn felt well enough to travel, and the group spent most of those two nights and the intervening hours of sunlight in the secure confines of Talo's spacious cave. Though he couldn't see the ward, Declan was sure he was able to sense its presence whenever descending through the thick roots of the pine, as well as its absence upon exiting. They discussed much of nothing, in that time, no one choosing to bring up the reality of imminent attack that hovered over their heads like a guillotine. Instead, they preferred to let their discussion linger about the subjects of provisions and the trek they had ahead of them, at the very least to Ranheln. Ryn added little to these talks, the dragon sleeping most of the time away on one of the softened pallets of moss and grass Bonner had conjured for each of them shortly after dinner the first evening. The rest of them, conversely, participated boisterously, eager for any excuse *not* to think of what could be waiting for them out there, beyond the relative safety of the bear's little nook.

Still, when morning of that second day rose and Ryn woke to announce that he felt strong enough to start the journey, no one was displeased. Better to keep moving, and not grow too attached to the illusion of safety holing up would eventually provide. In short order Bonner bid farewell to Talo while Declan and Ester saw to their supplies, packing dried fish in layers of clean leaves tight with a variety of fruits and vegetables they thought might keep a day or two. Ryn surprised them both by electing to take his wolf's form, presenting them with a creature that was almost more *dragon* than animal now that Ryn had dropped the illusions he'd held firm for so long. His back was scaled and ridged, ears spined over an angular, reptilian skull that had kept its fur. His tail was true to the beast, but his legs were each tipped with curved talons rather than claws, more raptor-like than mammalian. It took Declan and Ester each a moment to compose themselves—Ryn not even noticing their astonishment—but then Bonner appeared out of the cave mouth, calling loudly as to whether or not they were ready.

Shortly thereafter they were off, heading first upstream a ways to cross the river along a wide length of shallows Declan had found fishing the previous afternoon, then cutting a path northeast once more through the trees with Bonner in the lead.

The day's going was easy enough. The coolness of the coming fall allowed them to set as brisk a pace as Ryn could handle in his state of healing, and they made it till noon before the dragon requested a rest, at which point all settled in for their midday meal. Declan and Ester took the opportunity to spar again, managing a good hour of work with the branches the half-elf had held onto for them before the dragon called that he was well enough to move again.

Evening found them some hours later, and they set up a quick camp under the stars of a clearing Ryn located just when the colors of the sky began to change. Bonner denied them any sort of fire, but made up for it shortly by bothering Declan with a cryptic request to fetch him as wide and flat a stone as could be located. Declan provided—having noticed just such an appropriate specimen not a few minutes back along the path they'd taken. Returning to the clearing with it, Bonner had him set the thing down near the edge of the trees, giving only the most obscure of answers when Declan asked after his reasoning.

"Better for not being seen from above."

Then he put his hands on the surface of the stone, and in the space of a half-dozen breaths the thing began to glow a dull, hearty orange-red. Declan—to his own bemusement—found himself only momentarily speechless at the sight of the magic, now, and didn't have to be told not to touch it.

Seeing the dry grass along the base of the now-enchanted rock curl and smoke into a blacked ring was enough of a warning.

"Firestone?" he asked, remembering what Ester had said about the weaved rocks that had typically kept the yr'Essel's home warm and well-lit.

Bonner, for once, looked impressed. "It is indeed," he answered, giving Declan a curious look.

"Your daughter told me of them," Declan answered the silent question. "I didn't realize they were this big…"

Bonner chuckled, then bent down to snatch up a pebble from beside his boot. "They rarely are." He closed his fist about the stone, and when he opened it again, the pebble was glowing the same amber-red as the larger boulder at their feet. "And they weren't initially created for such mundane tasks as heat and cooking, mind you."

"Oh?"

The smile Bonner gave him then was so full of mischief, Declan knew what was going to happen before it did. With the slightest strain of the mage's fingers, the small firestone blazed white hot in his palm, only a few shades shy of Ryn's dragonfire, and erupted into open flame. Declan yelped, stumbling back from the old man and his burning handful, almost tripping on the rotten remains of a log strewn across the edge of the clearing behind him. Catching his balance, he straightened to find Bonner laughing uproariously, and eventually joined in, the old man's playful cheer too infectious to ignore.

Declan, though, hadn't missed the meaning of the lesson, as subtle as it had been, and his eyes followed the pebble—suddenly returned to its original temperature—into the woods after the mage had tossed it aside.

They dined on seared slabs of apple and fish that night, spiced with a variety of found herbs Ester crushed and lathered the foods with shortly before serving. It made for as good a meal as any Declan had ever had on the road, and for a time his thoughts drifted away from magic and dead things and the anxious weight that pressed down on all of them, dark and ominous in its presence. When dinner was done, he volunteered for first watch—his thoughts keeping him from feeling particularly tired despite the arduous day they'd had—and the others took him up on the offer with exhausted appreciation. When they were all asleep—Bonner's snoring probably loud enough to bring the Vigil from Aletha herself, much less any nearby drey—Declan took up a comfortable position with his back to one of the trees at the edge of the glade. He looked up at the sky, taking in the moon-lit, cloudless heavens in a bid for the beauty of the night to chase his mind away from his black contemplations. He stayed like that, finding solace in the clarity of the stars and the *snick* of sharpening steel while he ran a stone across the edge of his hunting knife, until it came time to rouse Ester for her own shift.

The next day passed much the same, as did the following. Ryn grew a little stronger with every night's rest, their overall pace improving steadily as a result. A rhythm to the mornings and afternoons set in, and by the fourth day the routine was so standard the group could have gone about their chores and habits without exchanging so much as a word. Rise with the sun, break their fast on the forest's offerings, then set out steadily north by east in search of the King's High Road, according to Bonner and Ryn. Eventually they would halt for a late lunch an hour or two after noon, at which point the mage and dragon willingly took care of meal preparations, giving Declan and Ester some time to themselves for sparring and training. After that, their second trek of the day usually lasted hardly half as long as the first, and they would set camp in whatever glen or clearing or plain Ryn found for them, taking turns on sentry duty. It became a pleasant pattern, and there was no shortage of conversation as they moved. Bonner and Ester both took advantage of the ample opportunity to test what Declan had learned from the half-elf during his earlier stay with them, as well as teach him plenty more. He learned to recognize a variety of trees which had looked to him previously to have been all one and the same, as well as a further range of plants and herbs with varying properties, both beneficial and malign. While he doubted he'd ever match Ester's sharp eye, he also grew rapidly more skilled at teasing out the trails and prints of a dozen different animals, from the crashing path of panicked deer to the subtle passage of foxes and forest hares. He, in turn, drew Ryn into regaling the yr'Essels with further anecdotes of the places they'd been and explored, as well as handsome retellings of some of the more memorable combat they'd seen in their time with and after their recruitment into the Alethan mercenary guilds. All were more than content with each other's company, and the mood held true all the more after they finally stumbled out onto the High Road following a morning of half-clambering up a steep set of outcroppings they had unfortunately been unable to avoid. Even the omnipresent threat of the Queen's wrath seemed far more distant and foreign than it had even some days prior.

Despite Declan knowing Ranheln was no more than a mere two-days' walk due east of them, they were bogged down for a full afternoon and night by a return of the late summer storms not long after reaching the causeway. Ryn's awareness saw them to a wide, planked bridge shortly before the rains caught them, but despite scrambling underneath it the shelter of the gapped wood was anything but ideal, and the overcast clouds sucked what little warmth had lingered in the already-cool day. Bonner got a shielding ward up for them as quickly as possible, but by the time the barrier expanded around them, cutting off the trickling fall of water from above, Declan and Ester were soaked to the bone. Already limited to what few mundane clothes they'd been able to take with them, the two resorted to huddling up against one another for warmth, their backs to a trio of glowing firestones the mage gathered up for them. Declan's arm was around the woman's shoulders, her hands tucked between their hips, each too miserable to bother with being embarrassed or awkward at the proximity.

With the Mother's good mercy, the storm at last quit sometime before the first light of the following morning. Declan was the one who roused the others, having drawn last watch as the heat of the enchanted rocks set everyone slowly at ease enough to sleep beneath the protection of the mage's sheltering weave. After taking the time to gather their things, it was with only slightly dampened spirits that the four resumed their journey, following the High Road at a steady pace.

Up until that point, they'd crossed with only a few other travelers, despite the breadth of the thoroughfare. Ryn had kept his wolf's form, tolerating the curious—and sometimes alarmed—looks of the waggoneers and King's messengers which had occasionally passed them going one direction or the other, but as they came within a day of Ranheln there was an exponential uptick in the traffic. Night saw them driving back into the woods deep enough to have their dinner away from the dirt and mud churned up by hooves and wheels after the passing storm, and to give the dragon a safe distance from prying eyes in which to transform. He elected the familiar figure of the handsome black stallion which had been his preference for so long, pointing out that he could act as a pack horse for whatever goods they made purchase of. No one voiced any complaint to this, though Declan couldn't help but stare for a time, once again taking in the oddity of the scales and split hooves and serpentine subtleties that undermarked his friend's equine features.

"That's really gonna take some getting used to," he'd muttered to himself, earning a grin from Ester sitting nearby, who had obviously overheard and understood his disquiet.

Still, by the time morning of what everyone hoped would be their last immediate day on the road rose, Declan found himself waking up cheerful and energized. It had occurred to him that Ryn was holding to his word from almost two weeks back, holding to his implication that he would allow Declan to see him as he was, rather than simply as the rest of the world did. Even having spent days in company with Ryn's dragonling shape, and then the twisted forms of the "hawk" and "wolf", *this* felt more to Declan a direct address of the confidence the dragon wished to rebuild, and was well on his way to doing so. He got more than one queer look from the others as they set off back for the North Road, not feeling any need to explain why he was whistling an old marching tune from his and Ryn's days with Holden's Guard.

Ester, of course, was the first to make out the high, angled roofs of the city proper, rising above a hill they found themselves climbing in the late afternoon. She gave a shout at the sight, racing on ahead of the other three to crest the incline, where she waited for them with energized anticipation, one hand held up to shield her eyes despite the sun being well at their backs. Declan smiled at her enthusiasm, and left Bonner grumbling to Ryn about "youths and their impatience" while he hurried after the woman, meeting her at the top.

"Is that it?" Ester demanded the moment she heard him coming up behind her. Her eyes were wide again, once more reminding him the smallest bit of a child being shown the wonders of the world for the first time. "Is that it?"

"That's it," he assured her happily, following her gaze to the outline of the town in the distance, indistinct against a backdrop of sprawling, still water. He couldn't recall the name of the lake—Tehrys? Or Tessys, maybe? —but he assented to its beauty from their high ground, and he couldn't help but be pleased that *this* was Ester's first impression of the place, even from a distance. They were closer to Ranheln than he might have anticipated, the rolling hills of the day's walk apparently having hidden its shape from them for some time. It was perhaps three miles off, well beyond Ryn's radius of awareness even if the dragon had been focused on looking for it, but they would certainly reach the city's border before nightfall, if not prior to the markets closing for the day.

Again, Ester's enthusiasm got the better of him.

"Come on," he told the woman eagerly, leading her down the slope and leaving Bonner and Ryn to catch up with them at their own pace.

Not an hour later, and still with a little light left in the day, he and Ester conquered the last bend in the High Road, forgoing the final line of trees that had swallowed up Ranheln's details again as they'd approached. The woman gave an audible exclamation of awe that made Declan feel quite pleased with himself as the city and lake—the Tessys, he was almost sure of after pondering it further—presented themselves more aptly in their proximity, and she didn't stop there.

"Gods above," Ester almost choked from his side, staring upwards while they approached the outskirts at a quick pace.

As it did with most townships that had sprung up along its length over the centuries, the High Road cut straight through the body of Ranheln, dividing the city proper into two distinct sectors. To their left, along the north side of the causeway and boarding the lake, the buildings tended to be humble, squat things, only a few examples of clay and timber structures rising a story or two here and there over the rest. These were the port and industry districts, the working quarters of the city, where its fishermen and woodcutters practiced their trades without end and often into the limits of any night and season that was allowed them. It carried its own sort of beauty, in its unassuming sprawl, tendrils of grey-white smoke trailing skyward from a hundred different chimneys and stacks over the plain roofs of slatted wood and folded clay.

All the same, the area didn't have so much as a prayer of stealing Ester's attention away from its counterpart.

Where Ranheln showed its wealth was in the southern portion of the city, on the other side of the High Road, demonstrating its success as a trading hub and exporter of goods in great demand beyond the heavy woodlands of the western and northern forests. Whereas the working quarters were low and blockish, along the right side of the road the buildings were almost uniformly no less than three stories tall, and often as much as twice that. The walls of the structures were bright, stucco-colored with paints and murals in shades of red and gold and green and blue, enunciating a festive air that lingered over the town year-round, tempting travelers within with an implied promise equal parts excitement and entertainment. The roofs were most commonly slate, and typically high and pointed, in the style of the northern valley towns despite the fact that Ranheln likely only ever saw two or three snow storms of any commendable strength over the course of its winters. It granted the entire southern half of the city a castle-like quality. Had there been banners of the nobilities' colors streaming over the district, Declan would have been strongly reminded of Aletha's tournament stadiums when the joust was on.

"Any recommendations on where we might stay the night?"

Declan turned at the sound of Bonner's voice. Ryn and the mage had caught up to them in good time, the latter having taken to the former's back, the dragon's hoofbeats swallowed by the dull clatter of the other carts trundling by and the more distant din of Ranheln itself. The man rode with the comfort of a practiced horseman despite his wrinkled hands having nothing more to purchase on than Ryn's inky mane. Behind the pair, Declan could make out the last line of the sun, a sliver of white haloed by rays of gold overtop the trees. It would be dark within the half-hour.

Declan, considering Bonner's question, exchanged a quick look with Ryn. "Will the outpost have us, you think?"

I don't see why we wouldn't be welcome, the dragon answered with a snort, trotting to a halt within arm's reach. *It hasn't been so long since we left that you won't be known, and we'll need access to your accounts regardless. Unless you plan on bartering for swords with warm water and wild onions?*

Declan chuckled, then nodded. "The Iron Wind has offices here," he explained to Bonner, who was looking between them curiously. "It's a small detachment, mostly just used to house company couriers and keep tabs on the local goings-on. Still, if they happen to have the rooms to spare we shouldn't have any issue claiming them. We'd have to go in the morning either way, to draw funds from the guild vault." He patted the empty loop of his belt sadly, where his coin purse had once hung. "Had almost ten levers and a handful of silver with me, payment for the kidnapping job, but it's gone with everything else."

Bonner grimaced, tossing a leg off Ryn's back and sliding to the damp dust of the road with a grace that continued to speak nothing of his age. "Had enough hoarded away myself to buy half the city, but I didn't even think to look for it in the aftermath." He patted Ryn's neck absently, approaching Declan. "Sure your funds will be sufficient? Good steel wasn't cheap, even in my day, and I doubt prices have *dropped* since I grew tired of the world…"

We'll have enough, Ryn answered with a note of pride, clomping forward in an indication that they should keep moving as the shadows of the trees began climbing up the painted faces of the buildings ahead of them. *Declan's services were of premium value by the time we resigned the commission.*

"The Wind pays well," Declan attempted to temper the claim with as much humility as he could muster, waving away the question Ester looked as though she wanted to voice. Ryn's statement had finally managed to draw her attention away from the city, if only fleetingly. "We shouldn't have any trouble, and if we happen to overspend, I'll have a letter sent to the guildmaster explaining the situation."

It'll give Cassandra the happy excuse to tear you a new one the next time we see her, Ryn said with a low whinny that could only have been a laugh at Declan's expense.

"I think she'd tell you she has enough reasons backlogged as is to last her through this life and the next," he muttered in response, internally wincing at the image of the woman seething over any missive from him that essentially begged forgiveness for emptying the Ranheln office's coffers.

Getting into the city was a little more tedious than anticipated. Six Vigil soldiers in the red and black uniforms of the King's army flanked either side of the High Road in split groups of three. They stood at rigid attention with left hands on the guards of sheathed swords as their commanding officers—a lieutenant and sub-lieutenant, judging by the gold insignias which adorned their shoulders—alternately stopped traffic coming and going from Ranheln. The line wasn't tediously long, but it was still more than Declan had anticipated, given the season. There were five carts and some dozen peddlers on foot in front of their group of four, and the officer's questions were heard to be pointed and stern, further slowing things down even with the sun setting rapidly to the west. It took some twenty minutes before they reached the front of the line, at which point the lieutenant—a tall, hard-faced woman with short-cropped red hair—motioned the four of them forward with an impatient wave.

"Purpose of your visit?" she asked, so brusquely it took Declan a moment to realize the words had formed a question.

Fortunately, Bonner was quicker on his feet. "We're in need of provisions and supplies, before making for Aletha," he answered with a polite, giving bob of his head.

Despite his manners, the officer's eyes narrowed.

"Where are you staying? Do you plan on trading for your goods, or paying in coin?"

This last question she asked with a disdainful look over the four of them, which Declan found irritating, if not-altogether without warrant. Bonner taking the lead had been a good idea, given how far and above the old man looked the cleanest of the lot. Declan himself was in the same tattered clothes he'd left the yr'Essel's clearing in—not to mention the odd scars left by the drey's blood not even *he* was near getting used to yet—and Ester wasn't all that much better off. What's more, neither of them had had any chance to bathe properly in days, and he had no doubt the grime and sweat of the week-long journey was prominent in their presentation.

Ryn, meanwhile, was… well… no more than a horse, to the lieutenant's blind eyes.

"One of our number is a member of the Iron Wind," Bonner said, allowing himself the small bend of truth as he motioned to Declan. "We intend to find housing in their outpost, where he'll also have access to his company wages."

The lieutenant's gaze moved smartly to Declan, taking him in more critically. He knew what she saw, in his relative youth, and almost sighed in exasperation. The suspicion had been the same in Brohn's case at *The Woodsman's Rest*, along with that of dozens of men and women in the time since he and Ryn had left the guild.

Still, Declan waited for the request, not wanting to seem overeager.

"Your mark, if you please, sir."

Despite the woman's stiff countenance, there was a note of hesitation in her voice now, and a bit more allowance. He thought slightly better of her for it, and as instructed reached up to tug back the collar of his vest, revealing the partially-blanched ink of the winged sword.

As soon as he was confirmed, the officer relaxed visibly, her voice softening significantly. "Looks like you've seen some action, judging by the state of that tattoo." She spoke of the Wing's mark to be considerate, but her gaze was on the discoloration of his arms. "Anything recent?"

The question wasn't modeled as an intrusion, but rather like the woman was deliberately seeking news, which piqued Declan's curiosity. The Vigil and mercenary companies were—contrary to what many outsiders might think—typically on amicable terms, each keeping their noses out of the other's business, the latter often handling jobs the former was too spread thin to address. It made for an affable sort of relationship, not infrequently to the benefit of either or both parties.

"Not so recent," Declan said, bending his own truth. He needed none of the sharp looks Bonner was surreptitiously giving him to understand the implication of telling a lower officer of the Vigil the details of the drey's or the draugr's attacks. "And elsewhere? We heard of Estwyn's fall…"

The lieutenant looked weary at the mention of the town. "Aye, but that was two weeks ago. Sevyll was razed not eight days later. Scouts say the bulk of the horde might be holding there for the time being, but we've contrary reports of wereyn sightings as far west as Therest, of late. Sometimes in large groups."

"*Therest?*" Declan demanded, stunned. He suspected Sevyll of being a major blow—the place was a sizable mining town almost due south of Estwyn, largely responsible for much of the country's gem trade—but it was the second bit of news that alarmed him far, far more. Therest was a small settlement, a farming commune he knew only because it had been founded successfully in his own lifetime, some four or five years prior. It wasn't anything of a kingdom keystone, but for there to be sightings even within a day or two of the place...

"Where is Therest, Declan?" Bonner asked him.

Of course... Neither he nor Ester were likely to have ever heard of the place.

"It's not even a week's ride north of here. Half that, if you go as the crow flies over the lake."

"*What?*" It was the half-elf's turn to hiss, taken as aback as he was. "That's not possible!"

"Not if they were part of the force that came through the pass, no..." her father agreed thoughtfully, exchanging a solemn look with Ryn, who looked equally pensive.

Declan had to agree. The pass—Karn's Gullet, as it had once been called—was a month's travel from Ranheln even in ideal conditions. The northern forests of Viridian were older, denser woods that would have taken the wereyn time to conquer. It wasn't feasible for even smaller packs to have made it this far in only two weeks...

Before them, the officer was clearly of like mind, nodding and eyeing the caravan that came rumbling up at their backs like she knew she couldn't delay with conversation longer. "We haven't even had time to get word back to Aletha that they're not *just* coming through the pass. It's not good news for us. The King's called most swords to bear in the flatlands north of the capital, trying to gather the Vigil before the snows come to mount a defense if the horde moves south. There's hardly a hundred of us left here, and I'll bet the Mother's favor it's the same in every township across the kingdom. If the bastards are coming over the Tears themselves..."

"It'll be trouble for all." Bonner too, was looking over his shoulder. "Mathaleus will find himself having to scramble to put out fires across Viridian." He grimaced. "But we won't keep you from your duties any longer, lieutenant. If you'll allow us to, we would thank you for the news and be on our way."

"Of course." The woman stepped aside to wave them through at once, signaling for the caravan behind them to advance. The four pressed into Ranheln a full block, the raptures of the rising buildings to their right temporarily wasted on them, before Ryn spoke up.

They're coming off the mountains themselves. That doesn't bode well for anyone, least of all us...

"Maybe the Vigil will rout the greater horde before winter?" Ester offered tentatively, her nerves betrayed by the hand playing with the pommel of her knife, her boot's leather soles clicking against the road that had shifted from wet dirt and grass to puddle-splashed cobblestone within the city limits. "There's a chance the wereyn will have to push early for

Aletha, isn't there? I can't imagine a host tens of thousands strong could feed itself easily for any extended period of time..."

You'd be surprised, Ryn said darkly, side-stepping a dirty pool that had lingered after the previous day's storm. *The wereyn can eat almost anything, putrefied meat included, and winter descends much faster in the lands north of here. With Estywn and Sevyll both overrun, now...*

He didn't press the point, and no one requested explanation. Declan could see in his mind's eye the innumerable corpses scattered about the ruins of the broken towns, soldiers and citizens alike, stiff and kept fresh by the cold.

Horribly, the creatures wouldn't be going hungry anytime soon...

"We can't ignore the fact that there's more than one reason the wereyn could be so close by, aside from a coordinated invasion," Bonner grumbled from the dragon's other side as Declan took them right, deeper into the southern district. "Not a few among them having something and more to do with *us*..."

Another silence, each of them contemplating the implication. First ghouls, then drey, and now packs of feral beastmen being put to their trail...

At his side, Declan saw Ester shiver, then get ahold of herself. "Nothing to do about it right now," she told the group, taking a deep breath before almost forcing herself to once again stare up and around while they moved, absorbing the striking sights of the city from the inside.

In the fifteen minutes it took Declan and Ryn working together to navigate their way through Ranheln, the sun's last true light finally set. It wasn't an unpleasant time to be out and about, however. Workers and citizens of the city were busy making their way home, giving the street a buzzing, bustling life that made it easy to ignore the occasional disapproving looks Declan caught thrown in Ester's direction. Lamp-lighters were about their labor, sparking the wicks of oil lanterns strung over the cobblestone from delicately hammered iron hangings. The flames illuminated their colorful surroundings with a different, calmer cheer than the day's light. By the time the party reached the Iron Wind's offices—a narrow, three-story building pinned between a quiet residence and a tavern that was so raucously audible they heard the shouting and bustle from half-a-block away—the four of them were in slightly better spirits.

I'll wait out here, Ryn told them, promptly making for a nearby watering trough over which a number of other company horses were already bent. The other three motioned their acknowledgment, then Declan led the way in through an already-open door, its archway crowned with a hefty wooden plaque emblazed with the winged sword and the Iron Wind maxim: "*Victory In All. Victory For All.*". He was pleased to find the inside of the outpost warm and well lit, but a little dismayed that the place was hardly any more subdued than its boisterous neighbor. He looked around, taken aback to find so many people gathered within the limited confines of the common area, most seated about a line of small, rectangular tables set in ordered pacing at their wall, with many more standing about or leaning against the room walls. A scattered few had even gone so far as to sit on the floor in small groups. Conversation was abound, and hardly anyone paid them any mind whatsoever as Declan excused his, Ester's, and Bonner's way towards the back of the building, angling for a wide, covered counter where he knew they would find the office-master.

He was nearly there when a drawling, hearty voice boomed out over the thrum of gathered voices.

"Grace's good love!" A man heaved himself to his feet with some difficulty from where he'd been lounging in a high wooden chair behind the kiosk. "Declan Idrys! Is tha' you, boy?"

"Vasser!" Declan was astounded—but hardly displeased—and he greeted the man warmly, each reaching over the counter to grasp the other's forearm with great enthusiasm. "What in Her name are you doing here? Last I heard, Cassandra had you getting cut to ribbons by pirates in Sethylles' harbor waters."

Before him, Vasser Timoth guffawed jovially. He was an older man, nearing his fiftieth year, and indeed looked much the worse for wear than the last time Declan had laid eyes on him. He had a new scar that cleaved a vertical dent through the tanned, Sarahkan skin of one side of his face, an ugly thing which split his hair and heavy beard line alike. It pulled the corner of his right eye down at an odd angle as it passed, giving his face a lopsided look which only accentuated an overall sense of imbalance in the man's posture. Glancing down, Declan identified the culprit of this awkwardness at once, the man's struggle to gain his feet explained by the fake leg he'd *certainly* not been sporting some three years back.

Catching the glance, Vasser grinned and gave his wooden thigh an almost-affectionate pat that *thunked* hollowly. "Aye, lost ta' the very pirates yer talkin' about, though I'm not so convinced I've born the years worse a' the two of us." He eyed Declan's scarred arms and chest with an expression somewhere between impressed and uneasy. "You dive into the camp soup-pot while it was still boilin', or somethin'?"

"Or something," Declan said with what he hoped wasn't too false a chuckle, the memory of the drowning agony Bonner and Ester had pulled him from hardly distant. "Still, arms are fine." He flexed them in demonstration, and indeed they were a good deal looser after the week of daily training. "Your leg, though…"

"Bah!" Vasser waved the apologetic comment away. "Long used to it, and I get around well enough, nowadays. Cassandra saw to me anyhow, moment she heard my days in the field was over. Been in charge a' this place ever since, if ya' can believe tha'!" He waved a big, hairy hand around his head, indicating the crowded outpost.

"Can't think of anyone more deserving of it," Declan said with genuine delight for his old friend. Then, realizing he'd forgotten himself, he took a half-step to the side and motioned Bonner and Ester forward, the two of them having waited patiently through the pleasantries. "Vasser, these are my companions. Bonner and Ester yr'Essel. You two—" he looked at the father and daughter pair "—this is Vasser Timoth, an old company friend. We used to serve together under the Iron Wind's guildmaster, before she sent him off to lead his own contingent."

"Aye, leavin' this runt ta' muck things up without end in my absence, I'm sure," the office-master finished good-naturedly, offering his hand out to each of the pair in turn, his eyes drifting over Ester's silver-gold hair for so brief a moment, one could hardly have called it impolite. "I hope he hasn't dragged you lot into any scrapes of his own doin'? This one's had a knack for findin' trouble that didn't need diggin' up, s'far back as I've known him!"

"Oh, much and more and then some," Bonner answered genially, giving Declan an amused wink as he leaned into the counter. "He's more hassle than he's worth, if you ask my coin purse."

This earned another belly laugh from Vasser, and Declan gave Bonner a favorable glance. He was quickly growing to appreciate the mage's quick tongue. Despite having separated himself from civilization for more than three times as many centuries as Declan had lived decades, in nothing more than a handful of words the old man had not only endeared himself to the resident commanding officer, but provided a viable reason for their shared company. There wasn't anything remotely odd about a freelancer working as a paid bodyguard. Viridian suffered outlaws and brigands aplenty, even along the High and Low Roads, and often one needed nothing more than the presence of hired steel to stave off most potential trouble.

"Well, all else aside, yer in good hands, the both of ya'," Vasser said with an encouraging nod, waving to Declan. "Don't be fooled by his years. You'd be hard-pressed to find any *three* fools who'd have a fightin' chance against this lug, even if he *does* look too young ta' know which end of the sword is sharp."

Declan gave his old companion a mock scowl, but allowed he and Bonner their banter, distracted as he was by a sudden subtle touch on his arm. He turned to see Ester not looking at him, a smile plastered thinly across her face while she pretended to watch the two men have their fun, but the smallest inclination of her head had Declan's eyes moving beyond her. A good portion of the crowd was watching them curiously, so it took him a moment to make out the scowling eyes between the bodies. A small group of men were seated at the farthest table, closest to the door, gazes as sullen and irked as they were steady on the three of them. It was a bit quieter now, conversations falling away as the curiosity of newcomers friendly with the local commander finally caught about the common room, and Declan suspected Ester's keen ears had overheard something she didn't like.

Trouble, he realized, sweeping his eyes away before the party had a chance to suspect he'd found them out. He reached up to touch his own ear with a questioning expression, hoping the woman would catch on while Bonner and Vasser continued to guffaw at his expense beside them. She did, and with a smooth motion reached up to tuck a strand of hair into the braids of her plait, hand lingering there only long enough to make a point.

Not a fan of half-elves, he deduced, turning to face the counter again so as to hide the scowl he couldn't hold at bay. Not an uncommon attitude in the general populace—they'd seen a few examples simply walking through the city—but such an outlook didn't usually last long in the Wind. Cassandra's only requirements when offering commission was that one's remarkable ability to wield a blade be on par with their willingness to follow orders. It was odd, in fact, to see such disdain blatantly on display, if the group was indeed talking loud enough for Ester to overhear them, even with her *er'enthyl* sensitivities…

"So, Declan," Vasser addressed him with a lingering grin that claimed his attention once more, the jesting with Bonner apparently having finally come to an end, "what can I help ya' with? Yer lookin' for lodgin', I'm assumin'?"

"And funds," Declan told him, setting aside his concerns for the moment and going with the same story Bonner had provided at the city entrance. "These two need to be in Aletha as soon as possible, and we need steel and supplies to get there."

Vasser's smile faded a little, eyes dropping to the empty scabbard at Declan's hip. "Thought it was odd, you without a weapon," he muttered, half to himself. "Beds ain't a problem, so long as you're all fine with common quarters. Got plenty a' room ta' spare, now that we're rentin' out the entirety a' *The King's Flag,* next door." He tossed a thumb at the wall to his right, in the direction of the inn whose continued bustle and clatter could just barely be heard through the wall. "Gold, though… Tha's not so easy a matter…"

"Are you short?" Declan asked, a little alarmed. He'd never known the Alethan branch to ever let any of its outposts run dry.

"In a way…" Vasser said slowly, looking like he was trying to figure out how best to explain the situation. After several seconds, he appeared to settle on the blunt facts. "Cassandra's opened up temporary recruitment to outside offices, at our discretion."

This brought Declan up short. The Iron Wind had always prided itself on maintaining the quality of its ranks above all else, influence and size included. It was what kept the reputation of the guild intact. Recruitment was almost exclusively handled in the headquarters, within the capital itself, and never trusted to anyone outside the company's lieutenants and managing officers. Declan—and by proxy Ryn—had been among these select for a short time, after his first two years with the group, and had counted it a great—if a little tedious—honor. For Cassandra to abruptly change such long-standing policies…

But of course, he knew very well what had pressed such a monumental alteration.

"This wereyn business has everyone from the Tears ta' the Vyr'en spooked, lad," Vasser continued, confirming Declan's assumption. "It's only short-term contracts, mind. No more than three-month cycles for the time being, and Cassandra was clear that *no one* gets inked unless they're particularly deserving. But there hasn't been any lack of response, as ya' can see." He indicated the room behind them, where most of the conversation had picked up again now that the onlookers' general curiosity was sated.

"And wages have to be paid," Declan finished with a nod, understanding well the priorities of the office-master. "How tight are you? Can you manage anything?"

Vasser considered for a moment. "I could get ya' maybe thirty levers worth in gold and silver without much trouble?" he offered tentatively. "Another five if yer willin' ta lug a bag a' copper pennies around for the day."

More than enough, Declan thought with relief. Had he been outfitting a full crew of five or ten, as was company standard, it would have been sorely lacking, but for their barer needs it was plenty adequate.

"Done. All thirty-five, if you're sure you can."

"Aye, if tha's all ya' need." Vasser sounded relieved. "Cassandra's sending guarded shipments weekly ta' keep up with recruitment demands, and some a' my boys 'ave just wrapped up a hundred-lever contract that will keep us afloat for a while yet."

"Perfect. Can you recommend a good smith, then?" Declan rapped a knuckle on the empty scabbard. "Our own priorities, and all that."

"I got a suggestion or two. If you've still got yer mark, they'll be sure ta' show ya' the best they got, and sell it at company price. We're the top clients to most of the local forges here, apart from the Vigil itself, and they're grateful enough for it when it counts."

"Much appreciated." Declan watched as the man reached under the counter to produce parchment and ink, scrawling the names down in a tight, confident hand that belayed his peasant's slur.

As he pulled out a second sheaf to pen out the transaction of funds, Vasser inclined his scarred head toward the set of stairs leading upwards, not far to their left. "Follow 'em ta' the third. Entire floor is the commons. Take any a' the made beds, so long as no one's things are on them. We been fillin' up the *Flag* ta' get our money's worth, so ya' shouldn't be short on space." He finished, turning over the note and quill to Declan. "I'll have the clerks gather ya' all by mornin'."

Declan signed the statement, then took the recommendations with another word of thanks and a promise to come back down to reminisce on long-gone days after they were settled. He'd just indicated the steps to the yr'Essels when a loud, confident voice rang out from behind them.

"Oy, Vasser! Are you *actually* offering terms to this sorry lot?"

Declan only caught a glimpse of the old fighter's features darkening with impatience before he, Ester, and Bonner all turned to face the figure who'd placed himself in the middle of the room, very deliberately blocking any easy route to the door. He was a tall, younger man, maybe a year to two over twenty, and he stood with the easy swagger of someone who knew how to use the curved saber at his side, or at least someone who was firmly under such an impression. At a glance Declan recognized him as one of the disgruntled recruits Ester had pointed out to him, and even as he thought this the woman stiffened, tensing more out of irritation than concern.

"Tha's '*sir*' ta' you, Owlet," Vasser rumbled commandingly from behind the kiosk. "And they're not here seeking commission. They're jus' takin' beds for the night, and you'll leave 'em in peace if you know what's good for ya'."

"That so?" the man—Owlet—asked with sarcastic impudence, eyeing Declan up and down, his greyish eyes, framed in a handsome face by black locks, lingering on the absence of his sword before lifting very shortly to Bonner, then finally resting on Ester's. "An old man, a half-breed tramp, and a lug who clearly can't keep track of his own weapon? I can't see any reason why we should let them stay."

"It's a good thing there's no 'we' in this conversation, then," Vasser growled in response. "*I* say they can stay, so they can stay."

"Why?" Owlet's face twisted into an amused smirk. "The mongrel, sure. I'm happy to offer her half my bed for as long as she likes. But the other two…"

From the corner of his eye Declan saw Bonner flinch involuntarily, and he reached out to take hold of the old mage's arm, feeling the tension in his thin muscles beneath the patterned sleeves of the robes. Any father had the right to be indignant on their child's behalf, but given that the mage could have brought the whole building down on their heads with a stray thought...

"Oh, is that a problem?" Owlet laughed, catching the motion and settling his hand on the hilt of his saber with lazy promise. It was a striking weapon, leather-threaded hilt entwined with gold weaving, and pommeled by an onyx counter-balance. "Is she your whelp, had by some she-elf you rutted in the woods when you could still stand without shaking? Don't worry." His grin widened, and he took a cool step forward. "Give her here, and I'll see to it she gets a roof over her head for the night. I'll even throw her a copper, if she's worth it."

There was a rumbling of laughter from the corner table, along with some like-minded individuals in the crowd now pressed largely out of the way to make space for the one-sided exchange. Some of the onlookers bore frowns at the swordsman's words, but more merely looked on with interest, the proceedings suddenly much more entertaining than whatever subject had been carrying along their evening's discussions. Declan could feel Bonner's arm shaking in his grasp, but it was Ester who he was watching, standing slightly ahead of the two of them, closest to Owlet and his foul suggestions. He could have stepped in—would have been happy to, even—but...

As anticipated, Ester half-turned, giving he and Vasser behind him a curious look.

Declan grinned. "Vasser," he started, also looking back at his old friend, letting the question play out on his face, "would it be a problem...?"

The crowd, apparently, didn't follow his meaning, not a few among them looking surprised, even a little disgusted, but the office-master was quicker than the lot. "Hardly," he snorted, loud enough for all to hear before lowering his voice to a grumbled whisper. "If anything, you'd be doin' me a *bloody* favor. This bastard and his friends have blessed me with more headaches in two weeks than all the rest of 'em combined. Despite the fact we ain't markin' the short-termers, they been struttin' around town showin' off their contracts like they was penned up by Mathaleus himself."

Declan, smile broadening, turned back and gave Ester a little nod. "Just give a shout if you need anything," he said with enthusiasm, drawing even more perturbed rumbles from the recruits.

The woman required no other coaxing.

Slowly, almost sensually, she approached Owlet, hands loose at her sides, not saying a word. This, very obviously, was not at all what the young man had anticipated, his smirk faltering and going so far as to take a surprised half-step back before catching himself. Then, slowly, the grin returned, and over Ester's head he met Declan's eye, giving him a disdainful, victorious look.

"Good choice," he snorted at the woman, not taking his gaze off Declan, basking in his triumph. The moment she was in reach, he took his hand off the guard of his sword to reach for her. "I can at *least* promise to be more enjoyable than that sorry—"

It was done in all of four seconds.

Taking the last step into his grasp with purpose, Ester did three things in the same moment. Her left hand plucked the hunting knife from her belt, her right took hold of the saber's now-freed hilt, and her knee slammed up into the recruit's groin with a hard *thud* that had every man in the room—Declan, Bonner, and Vasser included—wincing. As Owlet doubled over with a squawk of pain that was several octaves higher than it might ordinarily have come out, Ester sidestepped and drew the sword smoothly. The edge of her knife slid with a surgeon's precision between the man's back and britches, and with a quick jerk the steel split cloth and the threaded leather of his belt. Weighed down by an empty scabbard and a purse filled with the Iron Wind's coin, Owlet's pants slid promptly to the ground, revealing to all that he had chosen a *particularly* inopportune day to forgo donning underclothes. There was a great gale of mirth now from all around as he inadvertently revealed himself in unflattering entirety to the room.

The laughter spiked even higher when Ester twisted and brought the flat of the man's own saber across the bare cheeks of his uncovered rear, the sound of the smooth steel against pale skin a loud *crack* over the room's uniform hilarity. Owlet fell to the floor with a pitched yelp and a bare flailing of limbs, stumbling steps cut short by the cloth gathered about his knees and ankles, hands preoccupied with holding tight to the more tender parts of his insulted anatomy.

Ester, though, wasn't finished.

As the swordsman tumbled down, she whirled, borrowed sword swinging high. It froze, razored tip cutting short to stop with rigid precision not four inches from the twitching throat of one of the recruit's friends, who'd jumped to his feet and gone for his own blade the moment he realized what was happening. He stopped moving at once, letting the steel slide back into the sheath he'd only managed to draw it halfway from, taking several stumbling steps back as Ester pressed him slowly. When the back of the man's legs caught the edge of the chair he'd only just vacated, he sat back down with a firm *thump*.

All the while, Ester hadn't spoken a word.

With echoing yells of anger, the other members of the table clambered to stand, fiery eyes on the woman, but before they could so much as reach for their own weapons Vasser had them cowering with a booming bark.

"ENOUGH!"

There was a thunderous BANG of steel and wood. Declan glanced back to see the man had pulled his flanged mace out from behind the counter—a weapon for which he'd been well-known to wield with deft skill in his days as a fieldsman—slamming it down atop the wood with clear fury.

"If you lot want ta' bear arms against a guest for doing nothin' more than *defending her own reputation*, then ya' can bloody well do it under another company's roof!" he bellowed, misshapen eyes fixed on the back corner. "*Anyone* who draws another blade in my presence tonight will have their contracts terminated and be handed over ta' the Vigil for disruption and disturbin' the peace! IS THAT UNDERSTOOD?!"

Vasser's last question echoed clear in the suddenly-silent common room, broken shortly thereafter by a loud—if not entirely uniform— response of *"Yes, sir!"* from the recruits as a whole. Owlet's friends sat back down slowly, releasing the hilts of their weapons with resigned anger, though one or two refused to look away from Ester.

The half-elf, for her part, turned her back to them without so much as the hint of a care. "It's a fine sword, you've got here," she said to the huddled form of Owlet after she'd moved to stand over him, studying the unblemished steel with interest. "Hasn't seen much action, but I didn't much get the impression it would have, judging by its owner…" The subtle jab was awarded with another, if more subdued, round of laughter, and Ester turned her green eyes on Vasser. "May I keep this?"

The office-master didn't hesitate. "In exchange for forgivin' the rudeness one of mine has shown you, please do. The Iron Wind is better than tha', as Declan will tell you. We'll call it fair ransom, if you'd be so kind as ta' consider the matter settled."

"Done," Ester said with an inclination of her head before considering the scabbard tangled about Owlet's twitching knees. Grimacing at the ostentatious thing—lacquered wood dyed black and ribboned with more gold threading—she settled for sheathing her knife and letting the blade of the saber rest on her shoulder. Rejoining them, she eyed the stairs like nothing in all the world out of the ordinary had just happened.

"Shall we?"

Bonner, whose generally cheerful disposition had been buried under rigid, pale anger, seemed to come back to himself. With something that was almost a snigger he took his daughter by the arm, joining her as they made for the steps.

Declan was right behind them, held up only for a moment as Vasser stowed his mace away again and whispered at him: "Mother's word. The *bloody well* do they need *you* for, lad?"

CHAPTER TWENTY-THREE

They claimed a trio of clean beds in the far corner of the common quarters, that night. Once everyone was settled, Declan descended again to trade stories with Vasser for an hour or so over a glass of good brandy procured for them by the outpost staff. The night was deep before he bade his old brother-at-arms goodnight and farewell, not likely to catch him in the morning as the man had rounds to attend to about the city. Declan returned to Bonner and Ester to find that Ryn had joined them, having taken to his hawk's form and flown through an open window in the west wall, much to the astonishment of the handful of other men and women sharing the chamber with them. The yr'Essels had been busy regaling the dragon in quiet whispers of the evening's excitement, and Declan joined them eagerly, happy to repeat the tale from his own point of view for Ryn's general delight.

Treated to their first real beds in days, and with no need to post a lookout, the party slept so soundly they were only roused the following morning by dusty sunlight streaming in through the east windows over the neighboring buildings, several hours after dawn's rise. Waking first, Declan and Ester took advantage of a couple of screened-off bathing barrels set in a small courtyard behind the outpost for just the purpose. It felt good to be clean, even if they had to don the same clothes they'd worn into the city afterward, and by the time they made it back to the common quarters Bonner and Ryn had awoken to the smell of breakfast provided by the kitchens of *The King's Flag* next door. The four together dined on a filling breakfast of fresh bread, oatmeal, and bacon, Declan, Ester, and Bonner surreptitiously sneaking their meat portions to the dragon. As the trays were being cleared by office staff, their funds were presented to them by a clerk in dark robes adorned with the Iron Wing's mark across her left breast. Despite their protests, the woman refused to leave until she'd personally watched them count the coins down to the last, *including* the promised sack of one hundred copper pennies, four to the leht, twenty to the lever.

Once left to their own devices, it wasn't more than ten minutes before the four of them were back on the bright streets of Ranheln, Declan and Ryn taking the lead again. The dragon found an empty alley in which to transform back into a horse, and so the *clop* of hooves rejoined them while they walked, pressing through the morning crowd that only tightened with every step they took towards the market districts. The buzz of the city was abound, far more so than it had been the night before, and there was plenty to take in as they moved. Ester's head craned this way and that, mesmerized, and even Bonner's intrigue was apparent, the man muttering in interest at everything from the diamond-paned shop windows to the architecture of the buildings themselves.

It was nothing to what awaited them.

Ester positively *squeaked* in excitement when they turned a corner and the bazaar opened up before them, a sprawling cacophony of endless color and writhing people. Comprised of some hundred semi-permanent booths and more heartily established wooden stalls, the market swallowed up the massive rectangular square at the end of the sloping road they found themselves descending. Taking a note from the city itself, the place was even more vibrant and eye-catching than the walls of the greater buildings looming over it in a colossal perimeter, surrounding it almost like a park. Cloth overhangs were patterned and striped with myriad shades of greens and reds and blues, and banners—some simply hoisted to draw attention to their stalls while others showed the emblems of established enterprises— fluttered and danced over everything in the gentle wind of the day. There were no shortages of sights and smells, either. Despite having already eaten, Declan felt his mouth begin to water as they pressed into the bazaar proper, his nose teased by the scent of whole roasting chickens nearby, intermingling with the aroma of lavender and smelting iron and burning wood. The cacophony of voices was tumultuous, family and friends shouting out to each other through the crowd while peddlers and merchants hollered of the quality and value of the wares along every corner and line. Still, even over the controlled chaos, music could be heard coming from every-which-direction, here and there as a crafter demonstrated the fiddles or flutes of their trade, but more often when a troupe of street artists took up their performance to the accompaniment of partnered musicians. Ester—so calm and collected the night before—squealed in surprise and clutched at Declan's arm instinctively when a gush of flames shot out over the heads of the crowd to their left, spewed by some fire-breather who'd timed himself with the thunderous climax of heavy drum nearby.

Declan laughed, not pulling his arm from hers, then only harder as Bonner *whooped* and hurried to watch from a closer vantage. Ryn went after him with a roll of his white-gold eyes, the dragon's voice murmuring some unimpressed comment about "*parlor tricks*" as the fire billowed upwards again.

After the mage had been dragged back by the loose hood of his robes, protesting all the way, the four resumed their push into the market. As they walked, Declan was hardly displeased to find himself casually arm-in-arm with the woman at his side as they went about their business.

They found, first-and-foremost, a saddler to outfit Ryn with a packing-harness, a request that made the leatherworker's face fall in dismay, clearly having expected a grander order when presented with the handsome black stallion he undoubtedly saw. Regardless, the man did his job admirably, and Declan watched in amazement as he took height and girth measurements without flinching, his hands never seeming to feel the patches of scales they occasionally brushed over while he labored, the illusion encompassing and complete.

The saddler had a harness, it turned out, that fit Ryn quite well at his current size, and so not a half-hour later—and most of their pennies lighter—they were moving again, the dragon's new packs bouncing along his sides while they walked. After a short deliberation, it was decided the smith should be next to visit, provision and clothes being the easiest things to procure even if they were short on funds later. Ester caught the sleeve of a passing hawker, a boy selling apples from a wicker basket under one arm, and the lad was all-too-happy to point them in the direction of the first of Vasser's suggested forges when Declan pressed a copper into his hand. Together the group made their way in the indicated direction, slow and steady through the heartbeat of vibrant activity.

Declan knew instinctively, as soon as the shop came into view, that the office-master hadn't steered them wrong. The place, a smithy called simply *Stern's Anvil*, looked to take up the bottom two floors of one of the west buildings which looked down into the bazaar. Its massive doors, all three of them, had been heaved open to allow as much fresh air into the space as possible. From within Declan heard the breath of bellows and the ring of hammers striking hot metal long before he made out the orange glow of the fires themselves. Each opening was barred to the public, blocked by an assortment of mismatched tables upon which the establishment's works were in full display, and even from a distance Declan's hand began to itch, seeing the sheen of the steel in the morning light. A fire-tanned apprentice kept a careful eye on the wares, watching for thieves. He gave them a wary look as the four approached, breaking through into the narrow width of empty space many of the uninterested shoppers had left to be free of the thin haze of lingering smoke.

His attitude changed in an instant when Declan showed him the winged sword on his chest and presented the parchment in which the name of the *Anvil* was written in Vasser Timoth's own hand.

"Always happy ta' accommodate the company, sir," he said in a cracking voice that betrayed his age. "I've nothin' more than a few hand-and-a-halfers, longswords, and shields set aside for the Wind at the moment, but if you'll allow me, I'd be happy to fetch them...?"

"Just the blades would be fine," Declan said with a nod.

The moment the apprentice was gone, Ester gave a sigh of desire for which Declan couldn't blame her, slipping her arm from his elbow to bend over the closest of the tables.

A veritable arsenal was arranged in careful order atop a heavy layer of worn black cloth, the collection impressive enough to put any qualified garrison's stock to shame. There were blades of every shape and size, punch daggers and dirks laid out in the spaces between short-swords and bastard swords and claymores whose hilts and tips hung off the edges of the display. Combat lances and spears, their hammered points shining in the morning sun, were leaning in careful order against the nearby wall, and heavy axes stood against the corners of the table alongside flails and clubs and heavy awls, every one of meticulous quality. To their right, one display was devoted entirely to a presentation of dozens of different arrows, the innumerable uses of their varied heads as unfathomable to Declan as Bonner's alphabet of runes.

"I almost regret claiming this one, now." Ester was tapping the onyx pommel of her new saber, tucked carefully into the loop of her belt, a wrap of cloth salvaged from one of her more worn shirts acting as a makeshift sheath. She was examining a matching set of stilettos with a covetous eye, running her other hand over their silver guards in appreciative reverence.

You're better off with the sword, Ryn told her, pushing his head between Declan and the woman to himself examine a massive two-hander set in the very center of the table. The five-foot blade was so long Declan suspected the piece was meant more as an eye-catcher than a functioning weapon. *More versatile, at the very least.*

"And it makes for a better story, anyhow," Bonner chuckled from behind them, the only one to show little interest in the impressive assemblage.

At that moment the apprentice reappeared, assisted by two grimy-faced boys who couldn't have been more than ten. Each carried several sheathed blades in their arms, scabbards all of matching black leather and plain wood, with unadorned guards and pommels of brass and iron for sensible counterweights.

Declan accepted the first of them keenly as it was offered to him over the table, drawing the steel of the longsword halfway to examine the quality of the metal. Satisfied, he unsheathed it completely to test the balance, and was pleased with the feel of the weapon in his hand. Despite the simplicity of the design, it was masterfully crafted, and weighted towards the hilt as was his preference. It was shorter than he typically preferred his blades, but lightened by a wide fuller that extended from guard to tip. Pleased, he slid the sword back into its scabbard, then reached for the next one.

With Ester's help the pair went through the proffered arms quickly. In the end they settled on a hand-and-a-half that had fit Declan particularly well, choosing to also purchase the longsword he first tested, agreeing it a good spare for himself or the half-elf if either were ever in need. The cost of the blades was more than reasonable—something he thanked Vasser silently for as he dug through their purses for thirteen levers.

He was about to hand the gold over when Ryn's voice had him take pause.

Declan. The two-hander in the center. Can you tell me if it's well made?

The request was a puzzling one, to say the least, and Declan kept himself from looking back at the dragon by eyeing the massive sword dubiously. Ryn had never before expressed interest in a blade, aside from offering his opinion on Declan's own past purchases. Then again, as a horse, at what point would he have had much use for a weapon of any kind? With this consideration, Declan moved over and made a polite request of the apprentice to handle the claymore in question. The boy looked surprised, confirming the suspicion that the sword hadn't actually been forged to be wielded, but nodded his consent.

Declan gave an involuntary grunt as he hefted the weapon, his still-stiff left arm nearly giving in under its weight. Though it wasn't anything he himself would have been able—much less *preferred*—to carry, he knew enough of the type to deduce its favorable balance and secure tang. Despite the sword's decorative intent, it was a well-forged piece, and battle-sharpened, if requiring a monstrous strength to wield to any effect.

"Quality work," he announced, speaking to the apprentice with deliberate choice while very carefully easing the sword back onto the display. "Not so much as a shiver between blade and hilt, and a hammered edge to boot. Impressive."

The boy's appreciative response was lost to Ryn's private intrusion. *How much is it?*

Declan inquired, and the apprentice looked stumped, glancing back at his two helpers, who'd lingered to watch the testing of their blades. Neither could give him an answer. Clearly this was the first time anyone had actually asked after the cost of the sword. After a few seconds deliberation, one of the pair hurried back into the forge to exchange a few words with the large silhouette of an older man outlined against the light of the kiln, returning not long after.

"Master Stern says he ain't much liken ta' sell it fa' less tha' ten levers," the lad squeaked, his peasant's slur so thick it was almost beyond comprehension, "but since you's already bought two blades, he'll let i' go fa' eight an' three."

A hefty chunk of their funds, even if Ester's theatrics the night before had saved them replacing her own sword. Declan looked at Ryn apologetically, and the dragon seemed distinctly disappointed, his ears drooping just the slightest bit.

But, before Declan could regretfully turn down the offer, the older apprentice spoke up again, seeing the refusal coming. "Sir, if I might…" he motioned to Ester's hip, where the saber was questionably slung, most of the blade bare to the elements. "The lady looks in need of a scabbard. I'd be happy to provide one, free a' charge, if she'll lend me the sword for an hour or so. I'll also—" he glanced at the bow slung across the half-elf's back "—throw in two-score basic arrows, and knock off the three silvers from the two-hander personally, if it'll temp ya'. It's less than I'll make off commission for sellin' the thing, and you'll still have earned me half-a-week's wages with your other purchases as is…"

"Tempt" wasn't the word Declan would have used, his eyes going wide. The boy had just turned the offer from a questionable one into a steal of some proportion, if his calculations were right. The scabbard itself, even if it was plain, was likely to be worth a little under a lever, and the arrows on top of it…

Declan eyed the quiver slung across Ester's lower back. She was skilled at retrieval, but even so the journey had left her with no more than a dozen projectiles to her name. Making up his own mind, he glanced over his shoulder again.

Bonner nodded in Ryn's stead, patting the dragon's thick neck, having apparently exchanged a private word.

"Done, friend, and much appreciated," Declan said, looking back to the apprentice and reaching into their purse to retrieve the eight additional gold pieces. "One can see why Vasser Timoth put your forge at the top of the list, now."

"Aye, sir." The boy flushed with pride, the red in his cheeks barely noticeable beneath his bronzed skin as he accepted the levers and motioned to his helpers to see to the massive claymore. He himself handed over the bastard and longsword one after the other, but when the pair returned with the two-hander in a long, light sheath of leather rimmed with bleached wood, he seemed unable to help himself. "Can… Can I ask what you intend ta' do with the blade, sir? No disrespect intended, but I'm not thinkin' it's well fit for ya'…"

He trailed off, and Declan gave him a grin and a wink as he handed the smaller swords to Ester and took the claymore himself in both hands. His silence, of course, wasn't for any desire to leave the lad with some sense of mystery.

It was because Declan himself was at an utter loss for an answer.

He voiced this, too, a few minutes later, after Ester had given over her own saber with a deliberate request that the scabbard *not* be anything gaudy, and the group again moved into the market alleys in search of clothes and rations.

"Are you going to explain *why* we just spent a quarter of our gold on a blade Bonner has no interest in, and neither Ester nor I have a prayer of handling?"

Ryn, walking beside him, rolled one eye in his direction, a pleased expression apparent on the odd mix of serpentine and equine features, his mood much improved now that the claymore had been strapped securely atop his new packs. The weight of the thing was prodigious, but they'd managed to counterbalance it with their spare longsword and most of the forty arrows the forge helpers had gathered for them in bundles of oiled cloth to keep the delicate fletching out of the wear of rain and sun.

I've been teaching you for fifteen years how to swing a sword. Do you really think I never picked up a blade myself?

Declan took pause at this, having never considered the concept. Then again, *that* struck him as equally odd. "Another of the curiosities you suppressed?" he asked, working to keep his voice even despite the momentary irritation that flared up at the realization.

Ryn bobbed his head, sidestepping to avoid an empty, two-wheeled cart a pair of women were pulling along, shouting at the top of their lungs to "Clear the way! Clear the way!" Ester and Bonner had broken away from them, and were several paces ahead through the crowd.

One of many, Declan, for which you already have my apologies and regrets. But yes. Your forefather taught me himself. He was a prodigious swordsman—trained by the best the courts could offer—and I found the pursuit amusing. It was useful as well, at times. Taking to my natural body is draining and not always convenient, and there is only so much my other forms are capable of.

"'The courts'?" Declan echoed, curiosity suddenly peaked, keeping his voice lowered so no one might wonder if he was perhaps talking to himself. "What do you mean? Was Herst a nobleman? Or are you talking about somebody else?"

Ryn looked abruptly torn, like he'd slipped up and didn't know whether to press forward or retreat. Before he could get a word out, however, Ester shouted back over the heads of those that separated them, pointing upward to a black banner along a perpendicular lane that showed a needle and spool in gold threading.

That's an involved question, and one we can speak of later, Ryn said after Declan had waved a hand in acknowledgment. *Perhaps once we're back on the road. It's not a discussion to be had in whispers among the company of strangers. Bonner would tell you the same, and Ester, as little of the full story as she knows.*

Declan fleetingly considered arguing, but thought better of it after looking around. They'd been in the markets for well over an hour now, and the place had grown steadily more constricted. The fanfare and color had begun to lose its appeal in favor of a budding desire to be free of the entrapping throngs. Swallowing his curiosity, he conceded with a nod before following Ryn at an angle through the press to rejoin the yr'Essels, making together for the bright red tailor's tent Ester had spotted.

It took them longer than they would have liked to purchase their new vestments, the doting seamstress assigned to them keeping up a continuous torrent of comments that ranged from Ester's beauty to Declan's broad shoulders and scars to the horrid state of their current attire as a whole. They couldn't complain about the woman's work, on the other hand, and by the time they extricated themselves from her company the two were both bedecked in new threads that would hopefully last them any respectable journey. Ester, who at least still had *some* spare clothes, had opted for two new shirts, fresh britches, and a thin blue half-cloak that was treated to repel rain and mud. Declan, however, had nothing more than his boots, stained trousers, and the half-gone vest, and so ended up spending the bulk of their remaining funds on several pairs of new pants, shirts, and a proper coat to fend off the coming chill of fall. He would have called himself satisfied, but at the other three's insistence had also taken up a mantle of green and brown stitched cloth to replace his lost traveling cloak, light and treated like Ester's, but longer, hanging to the base of his calves.

Comforts and provisions were last. A small cooking pot. Waterskins. New bedrolls for Declan and Ester, as Bonner wasn't keen on the idea of depending on spellcraft for comfortable sleeping arrangements. Shortly thereafter, they'd finished stuffing Ryn's packs with a conglomeration of salted meats, dried vegetables, and the spices that significantly improved any roadside meal, and it was with no sense of disappointment that the group collectively decided it was time to be on their way. The thrum of the crowd had taken on a hollow, tedious quality that grated at one's patience, and even Ester voiced a need to be gone from the stifling crowd. They made one final round about the edge of the bazaar to pick up the promised scabbard from *Stern's Anvil*—a handsome, simple curve of leather stitched with silver wiring for rigidity. After that—and with a shared breath of relief—the party extricated themselves from the market's milling bustle via one of the smaller north roads. The calmer streets of Ranheln proper were almost empty in comparison to the organized chaos they were leaving behind, and the absence of the press of bodies was more than welcome. They moved at their own pace through the city for a time, talking lightly of their purchases and how long the foodstuffs might last, no one yet willing to address what had to be done next. After a quarter-hour or so, they reached the wide breadth of the High Road again, at which point the group took a united pause.

Behind them, the southern quarter of Ranheln rose, cheerful and lively, still inviting with its applauding colors and churning sounds of people.

Before them, the northern districts were quieter, but no less welcoming, smoke furling ever upward from the plain, low roofs, twisting about in the breeze that brought the clean smell of the Tessys' clear waters to them even from some distance off. To a one they felt the pressing security of the city all around them, the mute sense that they were safe, there, within the limits of its borders. Declan allowed himself a moment to think on whether they should leave at all, whether if perhaps it wasn't best to stay, to take advantage of the Iron Wind's hospitality and find some other way to get word to the Aletha.

The image of the drey, plummeting down upon them in the busy streets to ruinous results, set his thoughts to rest.

As one, without a word, they turned east, making towards the red and black uniforms of the Vigil guards, as distinct as the cobblestones giving way to the grass and earth of the open forests, beyond the warmth of Ranheln's walls.

CHAPTER TWENTY-FOUR

They didn't see so much as a new day before their combined fears bloomed into reality.

Despite all of Ryn's earlier promise to expand more on Declan's ancestry, they barely made it out of the city before the dragon's focus was justifiably required elsewhere. The first concerns welled immediately, at their exit from Ranheln, the departure far less tedious than their entry the previous night. The King's men stationed at the eastern mouth of the High Road were duly preoccupied, too taken in by dealing with the extensive flood of incomers to bother with a pedestrian handful of travelers making their leave. The line of carts, wagons, and families on foot was alarming from the go, stretching nearly half-a-mile long into the depth of the woods. Even upon reaching its end—where they might have expected to find some measure of privacy to converse—the four didn't spend more than a minute at a time alone on the path before crossing another group heading with all haste in the opposite direction. No one gave a word of protest when Ryn fell silent, eyes fixed on the road ahead, his senses very clearly extended to their limit.

They came across more signs of trouble as the day pressed on. While the passage of the fleeing country peasants eventually slowed, their presence was just as quickly taken up by Vigil messengers thundering by on courier steeds every ten or fifteen minutes, faces drawn and pale with whatever news it was they were carrying to and fro. As mid-afternoon arrived, patrols started to make their appearance, soldiers marching along the High Road in squads of as many as twenty, eyes set resolutely on the woods around them.

It wasn't hard to deduce what the men were on the lookout for.

Still, despite the dangerous atmosphere and Ryn's focused absence from conversation, Declan, Ester, and Bonner managed to distract themselves with their own discussions, talking as casually as any of them could manage about their plans. Aletha, in the end, was indeed the best option, they all agreed. If the army was gathering to hold back the wereyn holed up in Sevyll, there was a good chance the four of them would be able to safely manage the journey. Even given the news that the beastmen were coming over the Tears elsewhere, it would require little more than a detour to the south, off the causeway, to most likely avoid interaction with the creatures and approach the capital from the west rather than the north. It wasn't ideal, but it was a preferable option to the possible encounter with a horde of a size to put Mathaleus and the Vigil on edge. With this decision, a little of Ester's energy returned, her previous anticipation of seeing Viridian's greatest city only escalated by their visit to Ranheln. Her budding joy was contagious, an example Declan couldn't help but follow eventually. Before long the woman had him telling her of the place once again, green eyes shining beneath the hood of her new cloak while she listened. He described the Mother's Word cathedral, the grander details of the royal palace, and the flat grasslands surrounding Aletha which were responsible for the fascinating illusion of the city rising steadily from the earth itself no matter what direction one approached it from. Bonner had half-an-ear on the conversation as well, more closely paying attention to Ryn while they moved, offering only now and then a comment on how things sounded to have changed since his time.

All the same, these anecdotes—like the stories Bonner had shared during their pleasant mornings in and about the yr'Essel's lost home—frequently left Declan far more interested in the mage's tales than he was in his own.

They allowed themselves to be preoccupied in this way for the remainder of the day, forgoing the burden of nerves which had returned the moment Ranheln's colors disappeared into the trees at their back. Ryn hardly spoke a word throughout the entirety of the afternoon, so intent on their surroundings that he might have passed for a real horse had it not been for the dragonish traits mixed in with the hair and hooves. They took a late lunch on the move, and he barely allowed himself to be distracted long enough to thank Ester while she hand-fed him strips of dried beef and carrots.

The days were truly getting shorter, now. The sun began an early descent, and when the light started to fail and the steady chill of the fall evening crept over them all, Bonner said a quiet word to the dragon. Without answer Ryn shifted his course and led them off the High Road almost at once, into the thickets north of the path. For several minutes they made a plodding pace through the trees, watching their steps carefully while the shadows deepened around them. Eventually they reached a massive wall of solid dirt and broken stone, and Ryn led them along the cliff that was all that remained of a greater hill long split and washed away by time and the elements. There was plenty of shelter to be had among the outcroppings, the rocky juts extending out overhead here and there where the earth had fallen away unevenly, and eventually they found a large, removed chasm, a concave erosion so deep it was almost a cave. It seemed a precarious place to spend the night, and it took Bonner's pronouncement that all was quite solid after a moment's concentration with his hand pressed to the wall of the cliff before Declan and Ester could be convinced to step within.

The space was wide and open, the rough ceiling overhead hardly high enough for Declan to stand up in comfortably. The floor was dusty and scattered with loose rubble, but it was dry and easy enough to clear, and a far cry better than risking a night on damp grass beneath the coolness of the open sky. The familiar rhythm of evening set in almost at once, and without so much as a word the group began to make camp. Declan started unloading Ryn while Ester set to clearing a space for all of them to sleep at the back of the cavern, and Bonner began gathering an armful of scattered rocks from the edges of the space. There would be no fire, just as there had been none for the week-long trip to Ranheln, but no one minded. Bonner's firestones might have been wanting in light, but they provided ample warmth and were absent the smoke that would have been troublesome in such an enclosed, low area. By the time Declan had the dragon unpacked, the mage had a merry little pile smoldering silently nearby, in the center of the slightly-less dusty circle of ground Ester had just finished kicking clear.

"Anything?" Declan asked Ryn quietly while he pulled the leather straps over his long head. As soon as they were off his shoulders, the dragon began to change. By the time Declan had dropped the harness in a neat pile by the nearby wall, the horse had been replaced by the tall, bipedal form of his *rh'eem*.

At the question, Ryn seemed to shake himself a little from the intense focus he'd been consumed by all afternoon, going so far as to curse in his own tongue when he tried to stand tall only to have his spined ears scrape the low ceiling. *Nothing*, he admitted, brushing aside the breath of dirt fallen across the crown of his head. *Not a damn thing all day, other than more soldiers scouting the forests north of us. I'm almost regretting having let them put me so on edge.*

He sounded exhausted, for which Declan could only sympathize. He recalled the infrequent occasions in which the dragon had held a similar vigil in the past, when they'd been crossing through dangerous territory or knew to be wary of ambushes, and it had always seemed draining. He felt a little ashamed at the pang of disappointment that claimed him, then, realizing there was little chance he would manage to coax the dragon into much conversation for the remainder of the night.

"Take a rest, then," he said, resigning himself and motioning towards the cleared ground about Bonner's enchanted stones. "We can handle dinner. And don't even *think* about claiming the first watch."

Ryn, without the energy to argue, only did as he was bidden, easing himself down to sit in the warmth of the magic. Within five minutes he had slipped onto his side on the hard-packed ground, and was promptly asleep.

After that the evening's meal happened in quick order. Ester left the overhang for some twenty minutes, bow in hand, and returned dragging nothing less than a small doe behind her, leaving only the faintest trail of blood along the rock from the clean shot at the base of its neck. Declan made use of himself by dressing the thing down while Bonner kept busy warding the cove. Before long the three of them were silently roasting rough chunks of venison over the smoldering stones, Declan and Ester using their own blades while the mage borrowed the spare longsword from their things. They spoke quietly while turning the sizzling meat, not wanting to bother Ryn until the meal was cooked to their satisfaction. Only then did they rouse the dragon again, Declan shaking him gently and wordlessly offering him a full haunch of the catch when he cracked open a tired, gilded eye.

They ate in silence, each keeping company with their own thoughts. When they'd finished Declan saw to the rest of the deer carcass, dragging it a ways off into the woods, leaving the yr'Essels to clean the blades in a spout of water Bonner drew straight from the ground, then wash out and refill their half-empty skins. The evening's necessities done with, they set watches quickly, giving Ryn last shift with deliberate disregard to the dragon's protests, and settled in for the night. Declan made no complaint when Ester unrolled her bed mat by his—near enough for comfort but not so close as to be indecent—and fell asleep to the sound of her breathing nearby.

■■■

Up, you two! Up! Bonner, see to the light!

Declan was on his feet before Ryn's voice ended its alarm, his new bastard sword hissing from its sheath, taken up from where it had been carefully laid out beside him when he'd settled down after his lookout. To his left Ester was kneeling beside Ryn, looking like she'd just woke him to rouse he and Bonner more discretely, and across the glow of the enchanted stones the old man was clambering to stand. As soon as he found his feet the mage made a quick, slashing motion of one hand, and the warm light of the firestones died like a doused flame.

"What is it?" Declan hissed through the momentary blackness, eyes only slowly adjusting to the faint illumination of the moon and stars outside, framing the wide opening of their overhang. Ester had had the third watch, taking up her place after he'd finished his own shift, so it had to be past midnight, in the twilight hours of the morning.

Ryn didn't respond at once, and Declan saw only the barest shifting of shadows when the dragon's bleak shape moved along the back wall of the cavern. There was the *clink* and scrape of something metallic and heavy being lifted, and Declan suspected he knew what it was his friend had been fetching for himself.

Wereyn, Ryn answered, and it was odd not to know where he was speaking from, his form lost in the lack of light. *Two of them. A warg as well. Ester saw them tracing the path we took, along the cliffs.*

"*What?* But... Bonner's ward...?"

"Shields us from being found out by spellwork," the mage's voice answered quietly from the right, and Declan made out the outline of the man against the bare light of the night, hood up to stave away the evening chill while he braved a quick look around the edge of the cavern. "There's not so much I can do to keep us from being tracked by more conventional means."

Declan understood, then. Many of the wereyn were sure to have keen senses of one sort or another, and their damned warg—the wolfish, hulking creatures native to the Tears—most certainly so.

They were being hounded, like game in a fox hunt.

Quiet, both of you. They're nearly here.

Bonner's form vanished, slinking back into the shadows. There was a nearly imperceptible sound of wood on wood, and Declan knew Ester had knocked an arrow to her bow in preparation. Then all was still.

A minute stretched into two, then three. With patient trepidation the four of them held their place, not a one among them moving, barely daring to breathe more than was absolutely necessary. The sounds of the night grew deceptively loud as Declan's ears sought beyond them, straining past the soft hiss of the wind against the cliff and trees, marred only by the very few insects and frogs foolish enough to brave the cooling air.

Of course, it was Ester who heard the shuffling scrape across the rock-strewn earth first, her breath of warning lending itself to the more general awareness of the footsteps some time later.

Hold, Ryn's voice told them cautiously. *Hold...*

No one answered, the beasts too close at hand to voice their consent aloud. The sound of their approach was easy to make out now, the scraping noise of claws crunching over stone, unmuffled and quick. They couldn't have been more than twenty feet away, along the edge of the crags. Now ten. Now five...

And then, nothing more than a blot of darkness framed against the night, a figure appeared at the edge of the overhang, the sound of its movement almost echoing in the numb silence that took hold of the four within, their own heartbeats suddenly the only other things they could hear in the dark. Declan made out the shape of thick, looping horns and broad ears on a narrow head perched atop what might have been a man's body. The thing stood upright, but its legs were odd, twisted with the illusion of an additional joint, like the limbs of a horse. It stopped as it realized it had walked across the mouth of a deep, open space, and from behind it two more shapes loomed against the moonlight, one recognizable at once, the other as corrupted as the first, but equally different. The former of these trailing pair was the warg, a low, lumbering figure, moving on all fours, wide head crowned by a pair of narrow ears with a broad tail held stiff behind it.

The other was bipedal, with no horns to speak of and what looked to be the unassuming limbs of a naked human. Declan might have thought this last one *was* a man, in fact, until it turned its head to snuffle at the air, and the outline of a long, wolfish muzzle played against the evening glow.

Ester's bow *twanged* crisply just as the beast's mouth opened to snarl out a warning, arrow taking it through the throat with terrifying precision.

Declan charged with all silence, then, out of the shadows and into the somber light. At his side he heard Ryn's clawed feet pounding the earth, along with the screaming sound of steel being drawn from its sheath. Together they moved, powering forward.

Unfortunately, neither of them was fast enough.

Demonstrating animalistic instinct, the remaining wereyn and warg leapt back from the mouth of the overhang even as the other beastman fell, each of them bellowing out in surprise and warning. Their calls did not complement one another—the warg Ryn barreled towards roaring while the horned figure before Declan gave a growling bleat—but the sounds wailed out through the forest all the same. The two turned to flee, but the wereyn tripped on a rock and didn't make it two stumbling paces before Declan's blade caught it a vicious slash across the back of the legs, spraying blood over grass and stone. The blow brought it to the ground with a piercing shriek, silenced almost at once when the sword came around to drive down into its back, taking it through the heart.

Ending the thing's violent thrashing with a twist of the steel, Declan wrenched the weapon free and looked around. Ryn's prey had gotten farther, it appeared, vanishing westward into the tree line, but its lumbering pace could hardly have matched the dragon's. The shearing cry of metal cleaving into flesh rang out from the woods, followed by the uneven crash of something heavy falling and tumbling across the underbrush under its own momentum. For three seconds after this, there was silence again, not even the animals of the forest daring to make a sound now.

Then, almost expected, Ryn's voice rumbled out.

Back! Back to the cave! They're coming!

Declan—knowing very well who "they" were—turned and bolted without waiting into the looming cover of the outcropping. He nearly crashed headlong into Ester, who'd moved to the mouth to see what was going on, sidestepping her just in time. There was a curse, and from the depths of the space Bonner's face bloomed into existence, illuminated by a faint, blue glow he was clutching at with both hands.

Ryn came tearing in behind them, taking Ester unceremoniously by the arm and hauling her back, deeper within. Declan barely caught a glimpse of the azure light of the mage's weave shining against broad, bloodied steel before it was blocked by their retreating bodies.

The opening! Bonner—!

"And what do you think it is that I'm *doing*, exactly?" the mage cut in with a strained growl, obviously putting every ounce of his focus into the packed, swirling blue between his fingers. The magic had grown into a maelstrom of smoking, crackling energy. It hurt to look at it directly, brightening with every moment, but Declan forced himself to watch as best he could with his free hand brought up to his face to shield his eyes even a little bit. He noticed, as he did so, that his breath was misting against the outline of his fingers, and with a shock realized that the air was suddenly frigid, burning at his lungs like all the heat and moisture had been sucked from the space around them.

Abruptly, he thought he knew what Bonner yr'Essel was planning, and he leapt clear of the entrance just as the old man took the gathered spell in one hand and slammed it against the closest wall.

With a sound like shattering glass, ice formed in a thick, crystalline sheet from the place his palm lay against the stone. It ran up the wall and across the ceiling, following the arc formed by Bonner's other hand, like he was guiding a kite across the sky. Reaching the edge of the overhang, the mage brought the motion down, slower now, his face twisted in concentration.

With an open mouth Declan watched in stupefied fascination as the ice crept earthward, first in thin, frozen stalactites, then solidifying into a wall an easy foot thick as the protrusions broadened and molded into each other.

By the time Bonner was done, a vast majority of the opening had been blocked off, leaving nothing but a two-foot space at the very edge of the outcropping where the stone angled down into the earth, just broad enough for a single, stooped body to squeeze through. Unfortunately, no one had time to ogle the incredible sight, the marbled sheen of the ice glowing blue with the light of the night sky outside.

Even from only that limited opening, the thunderous sounds of gathered howls and barks and snarls had coupled with the rolling beat of a hundred clawed feet hammering in their direction.

CHAPTER TWENTY-FIVE

Declan, with me! Ester, as far behind us as you can get, but stay in front of the firestones! Bonner, when I say so, give us as much light as you can.

Ryn took charge with practiced efficiency, black outline sliding forward against the distorted surface of the ice beyond him like a shark through clear water. Declan didn't argue, the plan falling into place easily enough as he set himself some ten feet to the dragon's right, as close as he could get to the uneven opening left to them while staying well out of Ryn's range.

He had seen, silhouetted against the blue, the monstrous length of steel held in the dragon's right hand.

Behind them, he heard Ester and Bonner scrambling to take their positions, but he didn't dare look back. The sound of the approaching wereyn and their warg was nearer now, coming quickly, and he cursed the creatures' speed.

"How many are there?" he asked, eyes not leaving the opening.

Two score and more, Ryn answered calmly. *A good number of them are armed, too. Good steel.* He paused, focusing for a moment before continuing. *Vigil blades...*

Declan clenched his jaw, knowing what that meant. If they survived, it would be worth confirming, but there was nothing to be done about it for the moment. He set himself back to waiting, listening to the growing howl of the approaching beastmen. He knew that they were closer than they seemed, even now, the sound of their charge muffled by the trees. Sure enough, not half-a-minute later the noise erupted exponentially, and suddenly twisted shapes loomed out at them beyond the heavy barrier of the ice, dancing eerily through the spellwork against the light of the moon. There were howls of anger and dismay as the wereyn found themselves blockaded, then the first of them found the entrance Bonner had left, and with a roar of triumph ducked into the cavern at a run.

It barely made it two feet before Ester's arrow took the creature between the eyes, accurate even in the limited light.

The next two fell in the same way, bending to come through only to go down the moment they could stand. The fourth, smartening up, came in crouched but stayed low, and Ester's shot went wide over it, thudding instead into the shoulder of the creature closest on its heels. Unable to nock another arrow in time, Ester could offer no support as the pair barreled inside, the crouched wereyn taking the opportunity to rush at Ryn with clawed hands outstretched, the injured one bellowing as it charged Declan.

NOW!

There was an explosion of brilliant, rippling orange-yellow light, Bonner answering the awaited command with gusto. Even with his back to it Declan had to squint against the sudden illumination.

Their attackers weren't so lucky.

The beastmen screamed in panicked pain, hands instinctively thrown up in an effort to shield their eyes. Declan could see them clearly now, could take them in with the familiar distaste their kind had always elicited of him. They were corrupted things, ugly, disproportionate moldings of man and creature. The pair before them stood upright, on two legs, but that was the gross extent of their similarities. One—Ryn's opponent—was covering its face with thick, hairless arms ending in clawed hands. Its head was that of a bear, with blinking yellow eyes the same rotten taint as the vile, disorganized fangs filling its broad maw. Nothing more than a filthy strip of animal skin covered its waist, and its bare legs and feet were humanish, if dirty and scarred. The second, on the other hand—Declan's—was further disturbing. Its head was that of a stag, antlers broken and sharpened to cruel tips, but its teeth were of a shared kind, carnivorous and curved, the fur about its mouth stained with dried blood. It was wielding a longsword in clawless fingers, clean steel gleaming in the sudden light, but its arms were shaggy with ragged hair running over its shoulders and down its sides to cover double-jointed legs, like the scout's had been. It stood on black, muddy hooves, without even the barest hint of clothing to speak of, and it was bellowing deeply and without language, merely howling its discomfort and anger out to echo about the space.

Ryn's fell first.

The bear-headed wereyn went down in a single blow, its roars cut abruptly short when the massive claymore the dragon had taken up cleaved it in two from shoulder to hip. Declan wasn't long after him, leaping forward and ducking under a blind swipe from his own beast's longsword to come in low, catching it a horrible blow in the gut that sheared halfway to the thing's spine. It fell with a choking retch, weapon clattering to the floor, grasping at the putrid innards that spilled from its opened abdomen.

Declan left it to die without a second glance.

More of the things had followed on their comrades' heels, pouring in faster now as they realized they needed to overwhelm the narrow entrance if they wanted to get at their prey. Ester let off shots as fast as she could, but she had to be more careful now that Declan and Ryn were engaged. The beastmen fell in singles and pairs, some to swords and some to arrows, but just as quickly were their places taken up by others. Soon Declan and Ryn were being pressed back, forced to retreat step by step. The creatures started to pour in in truth, then, taking advantage of their gained ground.

There was the *snick* of fluidly drawn steel, and Ester was there, between the two of them, having abandoned the bow in favor of her new saber.

The battle held, for a time, their three blades enough to equal the wereyn's press, choking them through the corner between the wall of the cavern and Bonner's summoned ice. The beasts screamed and roared and died, often tumbling in pairs at Ryn's feet, and nearly as quickly at Declan's and Ester's. Steel cleaved in arcs and lanced through furred hide and humanish skin alike, parrying away rough blows from stolen Vigil blades and that of old, rusted weapons long-pillaged and well-worn. Before long the three of them were stained in blood, the black ichor splashing against the floor and walls and ceiling to steam and freeze in the frigid air. It made footing precarious, and eventually even three-strong they were forced back another step, then two, and the press began in earnest again.

"ESTER! AWAY!"

Bonner's bellow broke over the brutal sounds of the exchange, and out of the corner of his eye Declan saw the half-elf respond at once, riposting one last overhead blow from a driving club and allowing herself to drop to one knee. The onyx-pommeled saber flashed twice, cutting deeply into the tendons above the kneecaps of two separate beasts, and using their staggering forms as cover from the comrades behind them she rolled left, coming up sharply behind Ryn, well outside the reach of the great blade.

There was a flash, and with a familiar roar of fire the icy coldness of the space was swallowed by a broiling blast of searing, devastating heat.

A jet of ivory flames cut the gathered body of the wereyn almost in half. It was narrower than true dragonfire, a twisting, raging pillar maybe two feet in diameter at most. It burned, on the other hand, with the same intense hunger, and struck with no less force than Ryn's breath, splashing over the chest and bodies of the foremost beasts to spread like a cone through their shrieking ranks. Limbs and bodies and weapons vanished into ash and melted metal. Corpses fell half-devoured, and the creatures pushing Declan shrank away from the magic with howls of fear, vile eyes wide in terror. He took the advantage to glance back, seeing Bonner bent over cupped hands, exhaling into them as if he were blowing away gathered dust so that the fire spewed out overtop his fingers.

Then the flames died away, and Declan's focus was on the fight again.

The enemy was split, now, those who tried to trample into the smoldering lane of embers and smoking corpses screaming and leaping to one side or the other when their feet contacted the superheated stone with a *hiss* of burning flesh and hair. It made it easier to control their direction, Ryn on one side and Declan on the other, holding the two alleys of assault, and Ester took up her bow again to start loosing arrows rapid-fire through the space between them, downing creature after creature. Still, it made the press of the wereyn that much more intense, and while Ryn looked to be managing well with nothing more than his size and the sheer reach and weight of his massive blade, Declan could feel the fight start to pull at him, pushing him back inch by inch. The discipline born of so many years spent with a sword in hand kept him from dissolving into panic, but all the skill in the world could only do so much when they came at him again and again and again. With every passing breath the practiced, cutting patterns of his long blade—the only thing between him and a sudden, wretched death— grew more and more wanting under the flow of the onslaught.

When he went down, therefore, it wasn't completely unexpected.

The launching form was blocked initially from view by the coupled beasts that came at Declan barehanded and teeth bared. With a shearing blow he severed the reaching arms of one before back-stepping to be clear of the claws of the other. As the first screamed and the other stumbled under its own impetus, he darted in and brought the heavy bastard sword up and across in two arching swings, striking both heads—a wolf's and goat's—from their shoulders one after the other. As the bodies fell he started to pull the blade back into a defensive position.

The lumbering form beyond the slain pair didn't give him the opportunity to set himself.

With a roar that might have matched Ryn's, the warg broke through the tumbling corpses, dark eyes and yellowed teeth gleaming. It lunged with the force of a battering ram on broad, clawed paws, the bristling fur along its back of a height with Declan's chest. Before he could so much as think to bring his sword down between its exposed shoulders, the thing slammed into him, using its heft to send his smaller mass flying. The blow stole his wind, and he hit the ground heavily, head bouncing once against the stone. The thin hood of his cloak saved him from a truly ringing impact, muffling the back of his skull, but all the same he saw stars and slid several feet across the cleared space behind him. He came to a stop bare feet from the blazing pile of firestones, their outlines white-hot and flickering with real flames now as Bonner continued to pour his energy into them for light. Declan had managed to hold onto his weapon, but before he could bring it up before him the warg was overhead, pinning him to the ground by his sword arm with a clawed paw. Declan felt the bones of his forearm strain, and his shout only got lost in the sound of further fighting and Ester screaming his name. He scrabbled with his left hand even as canines bore down at his neck, finding and drawing his hunting knife from his side. With a defiant yell he lifted and drove the thing down at the creature's twisted face. The warg jerked its head aside at the last moment, accepting the blow in the shoulder, howling in furious agony when scarlet blood welled from the wound, washing over Declan's already splattered torso. Tearing the knife free, he made to drive it down again. This time, however, the warg was faster, gnashing at his hand. Nothing but luck had the savage teeth close around the blade of the dagger rather than flesh and bone, but cold fear flooded Declan's chest just the same when he felt the weapon pulled from his grasp. He scrambled with his now-empty hand, yelling and kicking up at the thing's underbelly as it tossed the knife aside in irritation, seeking anything—*anything*—that might buy him even a moment. His arms strained, the tight skin of his scars stretching beyond their comfort.

His fingers closed around the first solid object they came across.

There was the barest moment of searing, terrible heat, then it vanished, replaced by a strange, tingling warmth washing up his arm. Declan's mind didn't bother trying to make sense of the conflicting sensations, registering only that something heavy and hard had been taken up in his hand. With another yell he brought the object swinging up, aiming to land a solid blow to the side of the warg's head.

The trailing tail of sparks and light across his vision as the strike landed with a heavy *thud* finally clued him in to what it was he had seized up in his panic.

The firestone, a hefty, fist-sized rock with a mercifully jagged edge, collided with the wolfish-face, still glowing a brilliant orange-white. It struck with something of a small explosion of fire, flames washing across the warg's features like the flooding spread that followed the fall of a burning tree. The creature rocked under the combined force of the rock and outpour of heat, staggering to the side with a cracking scream, batting furiously at its ruined, smoking ear and eye with a paw. The moment he was free, Declan rolled sideways, not even thinking to drop the firestone, gaining his feet and preparing to launch himself in his opponent's moment of vulnerability.

Just as he was about to leap, he froze, finding there was no need.

In the time he watched, the warg collapsed to the ground, limbs twitching, half its face so badly charred he could see the sheen of a blackened, cracking skull beneath now-absent flesh.

"DECLAN! LEFT!"

Ester's shouted warning saved him. For a heartbeat he'd forgotten about the fight at hand, staring in horrified fascination at the convulsing form of the dying creature. Her shout brought him back in time to throw himself sideways, just avoiding being cleaved in two by the lunging blow of a heavy iron broadsword, half-eaten by rust and time. He scrambled to his feet, whirling on the wereyn only to find the fox-headed thing staggering into the wall, an arrow protruding from its temple. Others followed close behind, though, nearly a dozen who had pressed his side of the cavern when he'd been borne to the ground, and Declan hurled the firestone at them instinctively before lunging forward right behind it.

The moment the rock escaped his grasp, he felt that odd, shivering warmth vanish from his hand, leaving it clammy and cold. It missed the foremost two of the rushing line, sailing through the pair, but struck a body behind them with a *thunking* impact and another eruption of light and heat. More flames washed out of it like pouring water, splashing across the unlucky beast to shower the two over its shoulders with what was almost liquid fire. Declan didn't wait to see the outcome as the creatures started to howl in agony, rushing instead to meet the pair who'd been spared the torment. Only one of them was armed, and it was this one he angled for first, a bent, hunched form several inches taller than he, with a mountain-goat's head protruding hideously from heavily muscled shoulders. It carried one of the Vigil's longswords in one hand, but as it leapt with its partner its thick horns struck the low ceiling, cutting its momentum jarringly short. Sidestepping the suddenly lonesome lunge of the other—a boar-headed beast with striped fur running up its arms—Declan found himself between the two and didn't give either time to recover.

A flurry of spinning slashes shredded throat and exposed back respectively, cutting deep into the neck beneath the goat's head and severing the spine of its shorter companion.

They toppled, the larger of the pair sideways into the other firestones still piled atop each other nearby, scattering the glowing rocks and making the cavern dance with sudden, uneven light. Declan whirled to meet the rest, but found himself abruptly lacking in viable enemies. Ryn had carved through the last of his own opponents on the other side of the space, then leapt over the still-glowing lane of fire-blacked ground Bonner had burned down the middle of the group. The dragon was making quick work of the wereyn on Declan's side, having taken them from behind, wielding his massive claymore in one hand with no more apparent effort than a child playing at swords with a stick. With terrifying ease he ripped a swath through the group, his form rusty, but oh-so-familiar.

The dragon fought in the same style—with the same manners and balance—he had spent the last fifteen years instilling into Declan from the sidelines of his training.

"Mother's mercy," Declan himself choked, watching the dragon finish the last of the beasts with a spinning lunge that ran the doe-headed wereyn at an upwards angle through the chest, lifting it clear off its hooves under the angled force of the blow.

"Quite... Then again, we did tell you you had a knack for it."

Declan flinched and looked around. Bonner had moved to stand next to him, clearly worn by the power he'd drawn, but not in as a bad a shape as he'd shown after the battle with the drey. His eyes, however, were not on Ryn, but on something lower, closer to them, and Declan followed his gaze until a thrill of fascinated disgust shivered up his spine.

The dragon, it turned out, had not had to finish off *all* his remaining opponents. In a crumpled, smoldering pile that reeked of burned flesh and blood, a trio of wereyn lay one atop the other, trembling and thrashing. Had they been able to scream, Declan rather thought they would have, but as it was their voices appeared to have been stolen away by the acrid smoke which rose, thick and unforgiving, from their open mouths and gaping, consuming wounds. The creatures writhed in cruel silence, clawing at their chests and the charred holes that splattered their torsos, growing wider with every second, eaten away in expanding, glowing rings like the slowly burning edge of a dead leaf. The first of them went still after a few more seconds, the greater part of its body devoured and empty, leaving only a cave of blackened ash where there should have been ribs and muscles and organs. The other two quit their movements not long after, their torment mercifully ending. As they died, the life of the fire consuming them seemed to disperse as well, the burning glow fading and winking out.

Only then did Declan notice the firestone, fallen innocently to the floor before the dead, as cool and as plain as any of the other random rubble scattered about the space.

"Let me see your hand! Your *hand*, Declan!"

Ester had joined them, her bow slung haphazardly over one shoulder even as she'd leapt the charred lane. She was snatching at his left arm desperately—the one he'd swung the stone with—pulling it up so she could examine his fingers and palm. Feeling a terrible dread, Declan looked down himself.

Seeing the damage, all he could do was blink.

A scattered handful of mild blisters marked the skin, particularly around the tips of his fingers where he'd first grasped the stone, but that was the extent of it. It hurt, now that he had a moment to take in the pain, but was no more uncomfortable than the stinging aftermath of any other minor burn. Ester, at his side, was gaping at the unremarkable wounds, mouth agape and strands of hair falling across her bloody face from where they'd gotten loose of her plait in the fight. After several seconds she gave a gasping, cracking laugh of relief, and looked to her father.

"Not wholly unexpected." Bonner was peering over their shoulders to take in Declan's hand himself with a nod, speaking like he was observing some mildly interesting phenomenon. "Resonance with the pyromancy, undoubtedly. Still very impressive regardless, of course."

Declan himself would have had no words to respond with even if he'd known what the mage was talking about. He was stupefied, staring at the blisters, unable to comprehend. The firestone had eaten away the flesh and bone of the warg and wereyn almost as easily as dragonfire. How had his hand survived, practically unscathed...?

Is he injured?

Ryn was approaching now, having finished wiping the broad length of his claymore on the fur of some of the beastmen he'd cut down. He picked his way through the bodies as best he could, worried eyes on Declan's arm, still held in Ester's grasp.

"Hardly," Bonner said with a snort, pressing his daughter aside gently and taking Declan by the wrist. Without so much as a word he drew a quick rune in the air over the blistered palm, and before their eyes the damage faded to nothing, leaving the calloused skin unblemished.

Good, Ryn kept on, looking over their bloodied forms carefully. *Anyone else? Ester?*

"A few scratches, but nothing that can't wait." Ester frowned at Declan's other arm. "*That's* a nasty bruise, though..."

Declan's eyes barely flicked to the purpling contusion beneath the wet crimson splattering the inside of his sword arm, just below the elbow, where the warg had pinned him to the floor with most of its weight. He was still dumbstruck, struggling to catch up to the casualness with which Bonner and Ryn were treating what had just happened.

"I-I don't understand," he finally managed to get out, unable to look away from the now-healed skin of his left palm and fingers.

The mage looked about ready to explain, but Ryn cut him off. *Later,* he said quickly, repeating it when Ester started to protest. *No. Later. We have to be away from here. There's not a small chance there are more of these bastards nearby, beyond my awareness.* With a clawed foot he shoved the body of one of the fallen wereyn off the corpse of its brethren for emphasis. *Even worse would be if the Vigil heard that fight. Too many questions to answer, with their own swords scattered about the place.*

Bonner grumbled something in annoyance, eyeing one of the soldier's blades lying nearby, but Declan just nodded numbly. It was Ester's touch, returning to his arm, more gently this time, that brought him back to his senses.

"They'll explain," she promised him when he finally looked around at her. "I'll make them tell you at knifepoint if I have to, but Ryn's right for now. We need to leave, before anything else comes running."

Again, Declan could hardly do more than nod.

He wasn't much help as they broke camp, either. His right arm, it turned out, was likely fractured, and even after Bonner's tending to it the limb ached badly enough that Ester had to help clean his sword and get his weapon belt on to sheath it. They gathered their things as quickly as they could and slung them over Ryn's back, returned to his stallion's form. With a wave of his hand Bonner dispelled the ice, the wall turning to water in a sudden torrent that fortunately flooded down into the woods more than it did into the cave. Once they were outside, Declan offered his good hand to help Ester drag the bodies of the scouts they'd slain under the overhang, guided by Ryn to find the warg he'd caught deeper in the woods. This done, the dragon led the two of them farther east, along the cliffside, leaving Bonner behind with assurances from the old man that he would catch up shortly. After they'd been walking for a minute or so there came a thunderous *crack* of breaking stone, followed at once by the raging cacophony of a thousand tons of falling earth. Even in the night they made out the massive cloud of dust billowing up into the sky as the outcropping came down in the distance, blotting out a portion of the stars far overhead. When the sounds of the avalanche settled, they waited, and it wasn't long before Bonner caught up to them, brushing his hands clean and smiling in an attempt to mask his fatigue.

"Shall we?"

∎∎∎

Ryn, mercifully, didn't press them for long. They kept off the High Road—with Vigil patrols about, the blood drying on their skin and clothing was too conspicuous for the main fairway even in the dark—moving instead through the trees for barely more than an hour. Declan suffered the throbs of his mostly-healed arm in a shared silence. None of them had the energy to talk, all weighed down by the heavy exhaustion of interrupted sleep and the toll of the battle. They settled, eventually, along the bank of a wide stream running south. Only the sticky chill of the mess they were in convinced them to bathe despite the early hour, Ester a little ways up the flow, Declan and Ryn within view of their things once the dragon had changed back. Bonner—his robes having kept him in his typically pristine condition—went off to gather dry wood. No one—not even Ryn—protested when he built them a small, genuine fire, very-much needing the more substantial heat of true flames once they hauled themselves out of the cool water. The mage dried their clothes with a word—new garments scrubbed clean as best they could with stones from the riverbed—but all the same the dampness clung to them, forcing Declan and Ester to once more sit huddled together, close as either dared to the burning branches. The wash had shaken much of their exhaustion, and Declan was finding it hard not to keep his mind from racing as he stared into the bright glow of the modest flame, barely noticing even the warmth of the half-elf's arm on his.

"Here, boy."

Declan looked up to see Bonner standing over him, holding out a hand. Resting in his palm, a single firestone waited, hardly more than a large pebble, and smoldering only a dull, languid red. All Declan could do for a long moment was stare at it, then look up at the old man, unsure.

Bonner snorted before reaching out with his other hand to take Declan's own. "It's damn time you heard these answers, and you didn't suffer more than a few blisters when I was pouring as much will into the rocks as I could manage. I hardly think *this* is likely to leave so much as a mark."

Then, ignoring Declan's yelp of surprise, he pressed the stone between his fingers.

As before, there was a fraction of pain, a jolt of uncomfortable heat, and then the sensation faded into a pleasant, tingling warmth that ran like dull needles over the scarred skin of his hand and forearm. Feeling this, Declan managed *not* to hurl the pebble away instinctively, though he couldn't quite bring himself to curl his fingers around the thing when Bonner released it, leaving it with him. It felt pleasant, in his hands, like he was clutching a mug of hot drink. The mage stayed bent, peering at the firestone carefully, like he expected something interesting to happen. To Declan's eyes, nothing changed. The pebble merely flickered a little, fading slightly before regaining its dull brightness.

Apparently, however, this faintest sign of alteration was *exactly* what the old man was looking for, because he clapped his hands together like an excited schoolboy and gave a small "whoop" of delight.

"Ryndean, have you seen this? An intuitive balance! You're sure you haven't taught him anything, even in passing?"

The dragon, who'd been holding his clawed hands to the fire at Declan's left, looked around. Catching sight of the stone, he too gave an impressed grunt before assuring the mage. *Not a damn thing. How was I supposed to go about teaching him how to weave when I had my hands full enough not letting the world know what I was?*

Weave. That was a word Declan knew, and he clung to it. He stared at the glowing stone, feeling Ester's eyes doing the same beside him, forcing himself to comprehend, to piece together Bonner and Ryn's exchange.

"Is… Is this magic?" he asked tentatively, unable to keep his heart from skipping a single beat at the thought.

"Of a sort, yes." Bonner scooted over so that he didn't block the fire and sat with his back to the flames between Declan and Ryn. "It's not of the kind I have mastery over, mind you, nor one you're likely to find among any human or elf, outside your own line. Ordinarily, that stone would leave you with a nasty kind of burn, and the one you took command of in the cave should have scalded you to the bone, as it did the wereyn."

Declan reeled at this image, leaving Ester to voice the pressing question first.

"What do you mean, 'took command of'? Is that what he did? How? I've never heard of anything like that…"

"Resonance," Bonner said with a quaint nod, like this explained everything. Seeing their blank expressions, he sighed and elaborated. "Ryn's said before Declan has an affinity for this sort of arcana." He waved a hand at the firestone. "It used to be called 'pyromancy'—fire magics—but such delegations of subject are doubtlessly long abandoned in this day and age. The important thing is that that affinity very likely offers him a natural connection with spells of this sort, allowing him to take control of the casting despite he himself not having produced it. Resonance." He looked at Declan with excitement. "That King's blood of yours is something, I must say…"

There was a dense silence following this musing, Declan gaping at Bonner for several long seconds before managing to speak.

"'King's blood'," he repeated, astounded. "The Vigil adage?"

It was Bonner's turn to look at him blankly. Eventually the man turned to Ryn, obviously seeking to draw out an explanation, but the dragon addressed Declan instead.

Are you thinking of The Woodsman's Rest?

Declan nodded, recalling the conversation he'd had with Brohn and Dia, the innkeepers. Ryn grumbled something dissatisfied under his breath, but before he could continue, Bonner cut in.

"What does the Vigil have to do with bloodline?" he asked the dragon, distinctly perplexed.

Nothing and less, Ryn muttered in answer, allowing his tail to slink over his clawed feet and bask in the heat. *More warped history. Apparently 'the blood of Kings' is the rank-and-file's term for describing anyone who survives something they shouldn't. Bastardized it from how the al'Dyors have been viewed for so many generations.*

Bonner started to snort at this, but the sound died on his lips. "I suppose I can understand the confusion… They must appear a hardy line, with Elysia's gifts in their veins for hundreds of years now…"

Very hardy, Ryn affirmed. *I can't speak to any attempt on their lives succeeding, to my memory, save for a few who've married into the name.* He looked at Declan now, meeting his eyes intently. *To be of 'King's blood' did not always mean what those innkeepers would have had you believe. They were only half in the right, and even that much credit I'm loath to give them. Time has a way of warping the truth, as you've been shown already. It's no different, in this case, and barely a taste of the reason I kept you away from the army, when you were younger.*

"What does it mean then?" Declan asked with anticipation, feeling what might have been a throb of warmth from the stone, like the magic was responding to his excitement.

Ryn took a moment to gather the words. *To put it simply, it used to signify exactly what it spelled out, in a way. 'King's blood.' 'The blood of kings'. It had no more context, in the years before the Endless Queen, than any other way of saying that one was of royal lineage, some branch of the al'Dyors who ruled Viridian centuries even before Sehranya's rise to power.* He ignored Declan's widening eyes. *But after… it came to have a different understanding, at least for a time. It was the term used to describe only the most direct lines of royalty, the eldest descendants of Elysia al'Dyor, who claimed the crown some years after her father's—Igoric's—death. It meant one bearing the blessing and weight of the gifts granted by the primordial line of the dragons for their ancestor's efforts in the war against the Endless Queen.* Ryn took a breath, apparently needing to steel himself. *But history forgets. It forgets that there were* two *siblings who proved themselves worthy in that conflict. Elysia, Crown Princess of Viridian, eldest daughter of the King, was only one. The other—*

But he didn't have to finish. The name clicked into place, echoing up in the ripples of realization.

"Amherst al'Dyor," Declan heard himself say, his voice soft with shock.

Beside him, Ryn nodded.

Amherst Sehren al'Dyor, First Prince of Viridian, whom his friends fondly knew simply as 'Herst'.

CHAPTER TWENTY-SIX

At first, Declan couldn't help angry suspicion from boiling over, wondering if this was yet *another* realization Ryn had suppressed "for his own good". Almost at once, though, he let the notion drop, seeing clearly that—for once—the dragon had nothing to do with this missing piece of the puzzle.

Amherst.

He'd heard the name before. Twice at least, in fact. Dia had mentioned it at *the Rest*, but it was *Ester* who had granted him the greatest clue, who'd actually managed to give him most of Herst's name before Ryn had cut her off, that first morning waking up in the home of the yr'Essels. Considering it, he thought it likely he'd only failed to register the information under the pressure of the myriad wash of the other realities which had been pressed upon him, at the time.

Amherst. Amherst Sehren al'Dyor.

"*What?*"

Disbelief was the only concept that held firm in Declan's voice. It wasn't that he truly couldn't fathom the idea. He'd spent too long around Ryn and Bonner to so much as blink at the incredible, by now. It was more that the sheer heft of *this* illumination was enough to make his hands tremble so badly Ester had to reach up and close his fingers around the firestone just to keep it from tumbling to the ground. Her touch lingered there, reassuring.

"Listen to them, Declan," she said in a soft voice before looking at Ryn and her father and speaking more sharply. "It's past time you explained everything, I think."

Neither made any sign of denying this. On the contrary, Ryn nodded. *Tell us again what you know of mankind's war against my race, Declan. What have you been told?*

Declan, far from recovering, nonetheless didn't allow himself to hesitate. He spoke of how Brohn and Dia had recounted the tale for him, speaking of the dragons' attack on the capital, seven hundred years ago, of their kidnapping of the crown's heirs after the murder of the King. He repeated how innkeepers had told him the story of the Alethan nobility gathering the city's armies to lay siege to the Reaches, desperate to save the crown princess, Elysia al'Dyor, as well as her brother, Amherst. They'd rescued Elysia, but the prince had been lost to the war.

It was here that Declan stuttered and stopped, more pieces settling into place.

"He wasn't killed by the dragons..." he said slowly. "Amherst—Herst—he wasn't killed..."

Ryn shook his head in confirmation. *No. Quite the contrary, if anything.*

"But... Then what happened? I still... I don't understand why the dragons would have attacked Aletha in the first place...?"

"There's a very obvious answer to that, all things considered," Bonner spoke up bitterly, eyes on his clasped hands, elbows resting on his knees. "Put simply: they *didn't*."

Declan wasn't sure what to make of this statement, once more struggling to sieve out the truth from the muddle of history.

Ryn, kindly, came to his rescue. *I very much doubt those two had any intention of deliberately leading you astray. If anything, they very likely believe their version of events as accurate as any, given the time that has passed. But Bonner has the right of it, Declan: there was never any attack on Aletha. At least not by my kind. The tale that lingers in this age was spun a long, long time ago, and revolves around a single dragon.* He pulled a hand away from the fire for a moment to rest it against his corded chest. *Me.*

Declan stared at him, not for the first time grateful for Ester's stabilizing touch on his hand. Before he could voice his confusion, Ryn kept on.

Have you ever heard of the Accord of Four?

Declan frowned at the question, considering his limited knowledge of world lore, then shook his head unsteadily. "No... Should I have?"

"Damn well you should have," Bonner grumbled, irritation still thick in his tone, though Declan didn't think it directed at anyone in particular.

Ryn ignored the old man. *I would have been surprised otherwise. It's a relic of another time, buried along with the truth of those years. The reality of the war. The nobles' assault of the Reaches. The Endless Queen. The Accord, however, is where it all began.*

He reached out to grasp a narrow twig lying half-out of the fire, pulling it smoking from the flames to watch the grey haze twist and turn up into the darkness of the open sky by the stream.

Seven hundred years ago, these lands were a different place. Our races were not as segregated as they are now, and infinitely more aware of each other. Relations were good— between man, dragon, er'enthyl, and er'endehn alike. A balance was struck, in a way, one which had lasted for as long as the al'Dyors had held the throne in Viridian, some three hundred years already. Their rise marked the new age, in fact, your 'post-founding'. Man, with your plentiful populace and a command of magic rivaled only by my own kind, was the dominant power. But—penned in as you were, with the elves to the north and south and the dragons to the west—your strength largely allowed for no more than your security. To summarize it more dramatically than I would like: the world was at peace, and had been for centuries.

Ryn's expression changed, his reminiscent gaze on the wafting smoke hardening abruptly. *Then, in the year 309, she appeared.*

"The Endless Queen?" Declan guessed tentatively.

Ryn grunted in ascension. *The Queen. Sehranya. Taken in by man decades earlier for her education in the magical colleges of Aletha, only to vanish before she returned to the lands of her own people. Her disappearance—as powerful a presence as she would have been among the armies of the dark elves—corrupted relations for many years between the er'endehn and man, but the bad blood faded eventually. Even then Karn's Line—the mountains you now call the Mother's Tears—made for a dangerous passing, and Sehranya had long since been written off as lost to the ranges—a foolish traveler who'd insisted on returning home unassisted and without aid, overconfident in her own abilities. Time healed that wound.*

"For all the good it did us in the end," Bonner put in sourly.

Ryn made no effort to refute this. *When the witch reappeared, the first nation she fell upon was that of her own people. She'd spent the years gathering her strength, using her power as the strongest mage in living memory to create herself an army. The Tears were a graveyard—they still are. It's the reason they've been so dubbed. Failed expeditions to find safer passages through the mountains. Vigil patrols fallen prey to the perils of the ranges. Settlers who strayed too far into the foothills. She even had the bodies of the animals and beasts at her disposal. Thousands of corpses lost to the cliffs and snow over as many years, and she'd very clearly taken her time gathering as many as she could. She stitched together her own soldiers, crafting them from the dead of men and animal to form an army of creatures the likes of which the world had never seen. Savage, cruel things, and her magic was so potent many of the resulting monstrosities even regained the ability to breed.* Ryn pointed west, back through the woods, in the direction they had come. *You fought some of the bastard descendants of those corrupted beings tonight.*

This time, even Ester seemed taken by surprise. "The *wereyn?*" she demanded, her fingers tightening unbidden about Declan's hand. "The *Queen* created the wereyn?"

"And more." It was Bonner who answered, then. "There had been necromancers, mages who ignored the laws of the land to sate their dark curiosities, but Sehranya went further—much further—than any before her. She supplemented her ranks with those defeated as she swept across the city-states of the er'endehn. Ghouls were easy enough to raise, I'm sure, but the witch went beyond even that. Wights—faster and far more intelligent than their lesser draugr brethren. Liche—undead capable of wielding a portion of their master's magics. And later—when she had the bodies for it—" he glanced at Ryn, whose reptilian features were motionless in disgusted recollection "—she began to weave her spells into the fallen of the dragons, stitching them together with other beasts as she'd done with the wereyn, until the *true* terror of her armies took control of the skies."

"The drey," Declan said, understanding dawning on him.

Ryn took up the story, again, then. *They came later, however. At first, Sehranya struck with every ounce of force and speed she could into Eserysh, likely hoping to seize control of her own people with the advantage of surprise. The er'endehn are a martial race, though, and what the Queen had in power she lacked in strategy. After the first few cities fell, the others realized they could do little to withstand the assault on their own. They evacuated, nearly one and all, making for the greatest of their collective stronghold: the city of Ysenden.*

In his mind's eye an image formed for Declan, of a vast empire rising among the winter trees, like the tales he'd heard tell of the brighter metropolis of the *er'enthyl*, to the south.

*There, the standstill took hold, a siege that lasted the greater part of two years and gave the other races opportunity to answer. Igoric al'Dyor, King of Viridian at the time, was the first to rise to the need. He foresaw the disaster of the coming decade, anticipating the eventual fall of the dark elves if nothing was done, and did not assume that the Sehranya would be satisfied with the subjugation of nothing more than her own people. With no small effort the royal mages—including Igoric's own court mage—*Ryn glanced at Bonner, who grinned ruefully—*offered him an opportunity: the Accord of Four.*

Here, the dragon paused, still watching the old mage, who recognized the opportunity he was being offered.

"The Accord was—*is*, rather—a weave of immense proportions," he told Declan. Ester had returned her attention blankly to the fire, having clearly been privy to this explanation too many times before. "It's a binding magic derived from the minds and talent of a hundred of Viridian's greatest weavers of the time, myself among them. It was a covenant, of a kind. A contract, meticulously layered and crafted with a single purpose in mind: peace at any cost."

Declan waited for several seconds, following this, but once more Bonner demonstrated an almost-willful lack of understanding that his explanation was less than adequate.

Fortunately, as the pause started to grow awkward, Ester sighed and took matters in hand. "The Accord was intended to bring the four races into a state of 'enforced alliance'," she said, finally letting go of Declan's hand and the firestone grasped within it. "It was a magic designed to work itself into the sovereign lines of the elves, dragons, and men—a conditional binding that each kind would help the others if the need ever arose, and none could attack any of the Accord. It was a balancing act, specifically designed in response to the greater threat that was the Endless Queen. Igoric read the writing on the wall, and he wanted a way not only to raise a force sufficient enough to crush her, but also prevent the like from every threatening the balance of the four races again."

Declan's brow furrowed. "What was the condition? What would happen if one attacked another?"

"Death of the line," Bonner said with a casual shrug. "And not an altogether pleasant one, at that."

Declan blinked, taking this in. "The *entire* line?" he demanded. "Isn't that extreme?"

"Every eldest child, and any of their siblings," Bonner confirmed, his voice still even. "The Accord is thorough. It even binds those joined in wedlock and shifts priority of its weaves to the next oldest if the elder passes without an heir. And extreme was what was needed, Declan. You don't yet understand the implication of Sehranya's strength. To meet her in battle was to strengthen her forces. Even if she wasn't present on the frontlines herself, she had tricks to summon the fallen to their feet for her own purpose. Her liche. Amulets woven with dark power. The only way the dark elves weren't wiped from the world was by holing themselves up in Ysenden, hiding behind walls so well-defended even the drey were of little use in the siege. What was needed was an army that could overrun such power. Overrun it, and bull itself through to the very heart. Only by cutting off the head did the four races stand a chance of surviving. Sehranya herself had to be defeated, and in one single, fell swoop."

Declan followed, now, though it still made him uneasy. What was more, something still itched at the back of his mind. It took him a moment to place the thought.

"Was this... *Accord*... signed? Was it enacted?"

Ryn and Bonner exchanged a gloomy look, then nodded together.

Have you ever wondered why *the strain between Viridian and the Vyr'en has only ever been limited to minor scuffles and border disputes?* the dragon asked. *It's because all-out war would spell the end to the ruling line of the aggressors, either the al'Dyors or the house ehn'Vyr'en, of whom the sovereigns of the wood elves have been progeny for as long as their forest is old. It took time, of course. The politics of dragons are only slightly less tedious than those of man, I'm afraid, and the elves' arguably more so.*

"But then... If the dragons *didn't* attack Aletha... Does that mean mankind never assaulted the Reaches, either? If they had..." He hesitated, then waved his empty hand at himself in an empty, bewildered manner. "If Herst was what you say he was, and *I'm* what you say I am... I wouldn't be here, correct?"

If King Igoric or Elysia or Amherst had been the one to command the siege, that's correct. But that wasn't the case. Igoric was already dead by the time the nobility gathered the Vigil against the Reaches, and the heirs were long on their way to those same mountains, carried in my own claws.

This had Declan take pause. "Yours?"

Ryn nodded again, resuming the story where he'd left off. *After the Accord had been presented to him, Igoric called on the royalties of the other races to gather, to negotiate the pact, and plan assistance for the er'endehn. The dark elves themselves lacked a presence, obviously, to-a-one trapped behind the defenses of Ysenden as they were, but the er'enthyl came with a little coaxing. They sent a small delegation, the eldest son of their Matriarch, Elnaryl ehn'Vyr'en, and his personal retinue, which included a member of the Aveer al'En—the elves' High Knights—by the name of Arathia yr'Essel.*

Declan started, then looked between Bonner and Ester in understanding.

The mage's mood appeared a little mollified as he smiled. "My wife," he confirmed, motioning to the half-elf, "and Ester's own mother, yes, though it would be many years yet until such miracles came to be."

Before Declan could voice his astonishment, Ryn pressed on, which was all well and good because his next words struck Declan utterly dumb.

Of the dragons, he said evenly, *only I attended.*

Once more Declan began to feel the weight of too much. Too much. He was fighting again, gaping at his friend, struggling to cope with Ryn's words.

"You?" he got out after a few seconds battle to form the word. "You're... royalty?"

For the first time in what might have been Declan's entire life, Ryn looked discomfit. *No,* he said too firmly, then hedged himself. *Well... of a sort, perhaps. It's not so simple as—*

"It's simple enough," Bonner interrupted with a roll of his eyes before turning his attention to Declan. "The ways in which dragons interact with and view magic are different from mankind's—well... most of mankind, anyway." There was some of his old twinkle in his eye as he said this. "They have an innate capability for it, as do we, but their connection is... more substantial. Dragons are hatched with an intimacy of the ley lines, of the arcana, requiring only example and direction to master their abilities, much like you, Ester, and I needed only guidance to learn to walk. You could say they were born more *of* magic than *with* magic, I suppose." He glanced at the dragon for a moment, pondering in a distracted sort of way for a few seconds. "More importantly, parents don't treat their young with the same intimacy of that of man and elves."

He means we aren't seen as younglings of a pair, but rather as the responsibility of the race as a whole. It was Ryn's turn to clarify warily, noting Declan's look of incomprehension. *I don't have a 'mother' or 'father', as you might think of them. I was born to a female, of course—Thareneat was her name—but I didn't look upon her with any more or less affection than the other adults, my egg and my earliest years tended to by them all as a whole.*

This fascinated Declan, who had never so much as conceived of the idea of children of *any* kind being raised in any other way than by their own parents. Still, he kept his mouth shut, listening to Bonner again.

"For these reasons, dragons do not pass along the responsibilities of their leaders as we or the wood elves do, from child to child. Nor as the dark elves do, who—in Ysenden, at least—I believe elect a High Chancellor to their seat every half-century, and their lesser representatives every decade. Among dragons, those duties are tasked according to affinity and ability, the gifts of each of the Reaches' subsequent rulers passed along to a chosen successor directly, so that the next generation might bear the burden when the former is gone." Bonner waved a hand at Ryn, grinning. "Don't be fooled by this winged lug, boy. You're seated in the very presence of a sovereign of his kind: one of the primordial line."

Declan wanted to laugh, then, wanted to give up and throw his hands in the air and laugh. As it was he couldn't stop himself from cracking a strained, weathered grin, eyes on the lithe, reptilian form of his friend, who was refusing to meet his gaze. He recalled, now, the conversation they'd had, in the fields surrounding the yr'Essel's home.

An "ambassador", Ryn had called himself. Raised to the role.

Slowly, the story was starting to piece itself together.

Ryn's embarrassment was not altogether resolved when he spoke up with insistence. *There are hardly any dragons left in the world who consider me anything like a 'sovereign', and those few that* do *have lived separate from one another for centuries.*

"Only at your own instruction," Bonner managed to mutter, earning a raised eyebrow from Declan, but Ryn was already speaking again.

Regardless, it makes little difference. I was designated as the delegate to the conclave, chosen to be the voice of my kind in lieu of my sire when addressing Igoric's proposition. Tyrennus would not leave the Reaches, as equally wary of the events transpiring in Eserysh as the King was. I was young. Not even a century old. Tyrennus had little choice—given my selection had happened decades earlier—but I question to this day the wisdom of seating one so inexperienced at the table with the likes of Igoric al'Dyor and Elnaryl ehn'Vyr'en to discuss something as impactful as the Accord of Four.

Declan rather thought Ryn's definition of "experience" was measurably different than his own, hearing this, but he thought better of interrupting.

My youth came at a price. I had little patience for the negotiations of man and elves, and I sought distraction in those more my own equivalent when I could. The King's children were a gifted pair, I'd been told. The youngest, the son, was at his barely twenty years a great hand with the sword, and the crown princess was rumored to have a talent for magic only rarely seen among mankind. The spellwork of our races is very different, as you've seen, and I can truthfully say curiosity more than boredom had me asking her teacher—he waved a loose hand at Bonner again—*to introduce us. Elysia and I became fast friends*—

"Once she got over the claws and teeth of his *rh'eem*," Bonner offered with a chuckled aside.

—but it was her brother, *to my surprise, that I was more drawn to*, Ryn continued as though he hadn't been interrupted. He was still looking at Declan, but his white-gold eyes seemed to travel somewhere beyond the present while taking him in. *Not that I had met that many of man's numbers, by that point, but Herst was... something special, something more than one would have expected from his station.*

For once, Bonner made no indication of cutting in other than a slow nod of agreement.

Among dragons, there was a deference to the primordial line, and for good reason. Those chosen to take on the burden are superior in many ways to the common breeds, in brute power and magical ability alike. I had seen the same capitulation among the party of Elnaryl ehn'Vyr'en, as well as in the deference granted Igoric al'Dyor by even the greatest of his advisors and officers. Elysia was an even more firm example, never one to shy away from the preferred treatment. She could be caring, and often was, but she could be selfish as well, and hard in her own way. I imagine she was expected to be, as the next ruler of Viridian. Ryn frowned again, looking thoughtfully back in time. *Herst, though... You might have said Herst hated the obeisance to a dramatic point. I won't paint him out to be some fairy-tale hero. You weren't about to catch him sneaking out of the palace to feed the orphans or anything of the sort, but where he could ease the burdens of those around him, he always did. He was... the word is 'kind', I suppose. There was a softness to him that I found at first curious, given his position, a consideration of his lessers that transcended his station. At the time I was myself struggling over understanding how it was the leaders of man passed on their responsibilities, given their short lives, but I at least understood he was much like me in a way: an heir, even if only secondarily so. I think I may have even found him weak at the beginning, and there were certainly those in court who would have called him as much, if never to his face.* The dragon's lips turned upwards then in a reminiscent smirk, eyes focusing once more on his audience of one. *I've yet to meet a man more suited to the blade. Even* you *have a long way to go to catch up to your forefather, Declan.*

"He's the one who taught you," Declan remembered abruptly.

Ryn nodded. *I was bored, and he was interesting. He must have found me at least similarly intriguing, because he offered the lessons himself.*

"We had a damned time finding a practice sword of a size for you," Bonner recalled almost irritably, rubbing his temples with thumb and forefinger. "Had to have one specially made at the prince's request."

Ryn chuckled. *It paid off in the end.* He motioned to Declan without looking from the mage. *He's saved you and Ester's lives once apiece, and held his own against more than forty wereyn. I'd say you have nothing to complain about the lessons I received.*

Bonner grumbled good-naturedly, but didn't respond.

Declan took the chance to slip a question in. "But... if the Accord was enacted and you were friendly with the Kings' heirs... What happened?"

There was a sullen, distasteful pause.

"Vanity and greed."

Ester was the one to mutter the words, getting Declan to look around at her. She was grimacing, like she'd been chewing on something foul, the expression echoed in Ryn's answering voice.

I said the realm of man held the greatest power. His tone was hard, regaining Declan's attention. *You should consider that an understatement. Even to this day Mathaleus al'Dyor can gather a force of more than a hundred thousand men if given enough time, and four times that if he were willing to press the able-bodied of his subjects into rank. Your fertility is the one great blessing of your kind's abridged lifespan. You already know the elves breed more slowly, and that goes three-fold for us dragons. We were never that many to begin with—never more than a thousand in the entirety of the Reaches—but I was the only hatchling in the better part of a quarter-century. Shaldora was the next youngest, and she's twenty years older than I. Our populations do not grow vastly in any given space of time, whereas in the course of a handful of generations your people are able to sprawl and swell your numbers with nearly the same fervor of rabbits. I don't mean that as an insult.* He raised a quick hand to forestall Declan's wounded protest. *If anything, it is to your great advantage. It was the most substantial card Igoric had in hand, in fact. The only reason he ever convinced the er'enthyl and the dragons to consider a pact that threatened our sovereign lines, much less condone it.*

Declan caught on, then. "Security from mankind itself..." he said, following the reasoning better now.

Ryn nodded. *Even seven hundred years ago I don't doubt the armies of the al'Dyors could have waged war against any two of our nations to a draw. Igoric was aware of this, but just as aware was he of the storm on the horizon. Sehranya had the ability to make man's strength its weakness, you see. Even if his armies outnumbered hers ten to one, the fallen could be turned against him with nothing more than a flexing of the Endless Queen's will. He foresaw this disaster, foresaw the ruination of his race not so far behind the fall of the er'endehn, if the dark elves were left to their fate.* Ryn's expression soured, then. *Unfortunately, not all of his advisors and seconds felt the same.*

"Even *before* we'd weaved the Accord, Igoric was being pressured away from the idea." Bonner was staring at the ground now, watching the flecking sparks tumble earthward from Ryn's still-smoldering twig to wink out among the damp blades of the grass. "Sevus Kant, Tyrel al'Behn, Thana Vostyk. The heads of three of the four greatest Alethan families, all appalled by the idea of *willingly* putting themselves on keel with the other races when mankind had stood superior—even just in theory—for so long. They weren't the only ones, either. Many of the higher officers of the Vigil were of like mind with those three, and still more were happy to be convinced for a handful of gold or the promise of a grander future than they might have been born to. By the time everyone was seated at the negotiating table, even Tryvean Morne—Igoric's own First General—was on their side. Not that we knew that at the time..." Bonner sighed. "To their credit, the nobility started by trying everything they could to break up the talks peacefully—or what was considered peaceful among the circle of the court. It started small, with slander and rumors and mischief crafted to put pressure on the King's own guest. A *great* attempt was made to discredit Ryndean himself, Kant and the others apparently thinking him the easiest target for their machinations."

I recall that, Ryn said with the air of someone remembering something long forgotten. He sounded almost amused. *Stories started spreading that I was killing and eating the palace animals, the cats and dogs and the like.*

"Wasn't long before that grew into tales of you sneaking into the city at night to devour vagabonds, then pregnant mothers and infants in their cradles." Bonner snorted at the thought. "Fortunately Amherst and Elysia put a quick end to that, by keeping in your company. After though… That was when the real trouble started. Accusations of misconduct on the part of Elnaryl's party. Briberies attempted and failed. There was even an attempt on the elven prince's own life—belladonna in his morning tea, which had him bedridden for the better part of a fortnight. *That* nearly did the trick." To Declan's surprise, Bonner smiled then, wanly. "Arathia kept the peace, then, I remember. I was in love by the time Elnaryl found his feet again."

On Declan's right, Ester let out a groan somewhere between exasperated and resigning, leaning against his shoulder for warmth. The jostling of the limb made his forearm ache.

Just the same, he was quite sure he would have cut off his own hand before telling her that, and risking the woman shifting away again.

"But they failed?" he asked of Ryn, forcing himself to stay focused on the conversation. The firestone had pulsed again with the pleasant uptick in his heartbeat. "Igoric convinced you to agree to the Accord?"

The dragon bowed his head in slow acknowledgment, staring at the fire again.

He did. And he was dead before the sun rose the next day.

Silence fell again, and this time no one felt the urge to break it. Declan waited, impatient but sensing it wasn't his place to pull his friend from what appeared to be a painful memory. Finally, after nearly fifteen seconds in which the forest sounds of the early morning hours crept back over them, Ryn seemed to shake himself.

Despite everything—despite the rumors and the slander and even the attempt on Elnaryl's life—we none of us truly *anticipated how far they were willing to go. There had been inquiries, investigations, but the houses were clever, and between the care they'd taken in their plans and the sway they held over the Vigil, nothing was ever able to be lain at their feet. We* knew *who was responsible, of course. Kant, al'Behn, Vostyk. They made little secret of it in their own way, never going so far as to incriminate themselves, but making their implications clear enough just the same. I was of a mind multiple times to tear their heads from their shoulders and set them to spikes on the doors of the negotiating chambers, but Igoric wouldn't hear of it. He had much of the best parts of his children's qualities in that way. Elysia's stoicism, and Amherst's heart. It ended up being his unmaking…*

Ryn took a deep, uneven breath. *The binding—when it was finally agreed upon—was a simpler process than the elves or I had anticipated. An exchange of vows and a handful of rituals to chain our lines to the Accord's power, with plans to do the same with the leaders of the dark elves when the opportunity presented itself. Bonner and the other mages had done good work, and I think their efforts took the nobles by equal surprise, or they would have made their move earlier. As it was, it happened during the celebrations that evening, at the reveries thrown in commemoration of the agreement. I'd never seen anything like it. Herst and Elysia had taken me into the city when they could, and I'd become as familiar with your kind as one could in the months the talks had taken, but I remember being dazzled. Dancers. Musicians and singers. Food in every corner of the hall, and a hundred soldiers in ceremonial armor lining the walls.*

"A grand affair," Bonner put in quietly. "And the night we learned of the First General's betrayal…"

Igoric died at Tryvean's own hand. Ryn's tone had hardened again, and Declan could have believed the fury in his gaze was feeding the very flames he was staring into. *I didn't see it happen. None of us did. Herst, Elysia, Elnaryl, and I had been distracted, taken in by entertainers while the First General pulled the King aside for 'a word.' The fact that there was no screaming after the business was done will tell you enough of how thoroughly the nobility's influence had spread.*

"They'd even gone so far as to serve platters of raw meat," Bonner recalled bitterly. "I suspect just so you wouldn't smell the blood."

Ryn didn't disagree. *I'd been on alert for so long,* he muttered. *Ever since Elnaryl's attempt, I'd hardly let my guard down, even around Elysia and Herst. I thought the houses would have given up, with the Accord enacted. I'd assumed it. I didn't even* consider *they would go so far as to free themselves of it by cutting ties with the one thing that held them firmly in the weave's clutches.*

"The al'Dyors," Declan said, understanding coming faster now. "All of them."

He could glean how Ryn had been so fooled, *why* he had let his guard down. The dragon had been exhausted from a mere day spent on edge. He couldn't imagine what it must have done to him, to be wary and suspicious for so long, to have had to extend his magical senses for weeks on end.

All of them, Ryn echoed. *But they went further, too. It became clear to us, looking back, that Kant and his conspirators had had more reason than merely being wary of the ties of the Accord to desire its destruction, or at least its dissolvement. I think, if anything, they saw the Endless Queen as an opportunity, a chance to shift the power balance in the favor of man, while the dark elves were entangled in their own war. They probably imagined they would use the opportunity to expand themselves, to stretch into the Vyr'en and the Reaches, then turn whatever bounty and strength they gained in that conquering on Eserysh and whatever victor had risen from the conflict. I don't think they ever believed in the danger Sehranya posed to them, much less our four peoples as a whole. The houses were too secure, too confident in the superiority of man, their ways set and their path carved into stone by so many centuries spent wearing the crown of the world...*

Ryn quieted then, the memory momentarily taming his voice, the hardness in his eyes complimented by dark, dismal regret.

"They went after Elnaryl next," Bonner picked up in a low, sour tone. "If you're going to start a war, why not start by weakening the royal line of your opposition? The elves didn't number many to begin with—a dozen in all—and the soldiers of the banquet were in the nobility's pocket. They'd been hand-selected, undoubtedly, and if their armor was for show, their steel turned out to be very real. The King's death was the signal, the spark, and the *er'enthyl* were surrounded so quickly, most didn't so much as get the opportunity to draw their blades. Only the chance that I'd been standing nearby, sharing words with Arathia, kept it from being a complete massacre. Even then... Before I was able to put my power to use, most of the retinue had been carved through, and the prince already grievously injured." Bonner brought a hand up to the side of his throat, frowning. "A thrust to the neck. A nasty one. Arathia didn't even get a chance to fight, taking it on herself to see to Elnaryl while I and the others defended them. It happened so fast—*too* fast. By the time Amherst and Elysia were running to our aid, it was too late."

"What happened, then?" Declan pressed when the old man paused. He was riveted, taken in as little by little the puzzle formed a whole. "How did you survive?"

Bonner smirked—a humorless, grim expression. "Kant and the others had made a mistake, in their preparations. I imagine they wanted as many of their turned swords on hand as could be had. One does not take half-measures when plotting the assassination of a royal household, much less three."

Declan waited a moment, but when Bonner seemed uninclined to make his meaning clear, turned instead to Ryn.

The dragon grinned in hard satisfaction. *The room*, he said simply. *The fools thought it a good idea to hold their coup in the palace ballroom, the grandest and most spacious chamber in the entire city of Aletha.*

Abruptly, Declan understood, and at his side Ester gave a hoarse laugh as she, too, came to the same conclusion. The speed at which Ryn could take whichever of his forms he desired had always been nearly as astounding as the skill itself.

"Did they not realize?" Declan hissed, disbelieving. "How could they not have known?"

I don't think I'd ever given them reason to, Ryn answered with a shrug. *At the time, the only form I knew aside from my natural body was that of my rh'eem, and you can imagine the former wasn't likely to allow my entry into the palace unimpeded, physically or otherwise. I'd been as a dragonling for practically the entirety of my time spent within the city as a courtesy to Igoric, not to mention the palace staff.* He made a face. *It was miserable. I missed the open sky so much that I ended up begging assistance from the royal falconers in an effort to study the anatomy of their birds. I learned to take the form of a hawk just to fly again, as poor a substitute as it was.*

Bonner gave a small, pointed cough, and Ryn blinked as he was made aware of the tangent he'd taken.

Regardless. He cleared his throat in a not-so-subtle ploy to give himself a few moments to recall his train of thought. *Kant and the other nobles were never offered a chance to know me as capable of anything more than what they saw. It wasn't that they weren't aware that I could be more, but that awareness lacked the comprehension of my blood's distinction. Had I been anything less than a primordial, they might have indeed been in the right to assume they'd have an opportunity, even brief, to deal with me with sheer numbers.* His smile returned, sharper now. *I am not, however, and that ignorance resulted in them drawing steel against me and a good number of people I had come to care for very dearly in the months of their company.*

It happened, then. For the first time in weeks, Declan felt himself spinning away, felt the world inverse beneath his feet as he was ducked into a different time, a different mind. Before him the light of the fire and the outline of his friends were as twisting, pale ghosts over a brighter, bloodier scene. He hefted a sword in his right hand, its smooth metal sheened wet under the day-like glow of oil-lit chandeliers that reflected against the polished white marble of the floor, now spattered with streaking red. Men, in the colors of his father's court, surrounded him, and at his back he was aware of his sister's presence, gathering her weaves in preparation to join Bonner in the fight. Elnaryl was there somewhere, he knew too, the prince's life spilling out upon the ground with every passing second. He had seen the golden-haired elf take the blow which had felled him, had been unable to stop it even as he'd rushed to the *er'enthyl's* assistance.

Two of the soldiers darted forward in a pair, a third moving sidelong in an attempt to flank him. Declan's sword moved with a fluidity he had never known, an instinctive, easy delivery he'd only ever tasted after years of hard practice. He darted laterally, away from the man attempting to get in from his right, simultaneously dodging one thrusted blow while parrying the overhead slash of the third, left-most man. Disengaging his sword with astounding deftness, Declan spared no energy on wasteful movement, flicking the blade up to cut across the soldier's eyes with the same effort one might wave away a fly. The man screamed, tumbling back, but his comrades were already recovering, and more were moving to take their wounded comrade's place. Declan cursed, forced to take a step back and evaluate, seeing no other future before him but one which ended on the bloodied steel of the traitors closing in on him.

Then, just as the soldiers looked about to rush together, there was a roar of sound unlike anything Declan had ever heard before, imbued with such furious power that the chandeliers above tinkled and swayed threateningly overhead. Screams began to echo throughout the chamber, absent until that moment, and he watched with a convulsing mix of relief and terror as a shape seemed to erupt into existence over the heads of his attackers, scaled muscle and lashing, leathery wings swelling into being. The figure bloomed, expanding with such unnatural and astonishing speed that those soldiers standing closest to it were thrown bodily into the air under the sheer impact of the sudden presence. There was the clean gleam of white, hand-sized teeth and the flash of claws as the great beast—which had only moments ago been Declan's slighter, less-imposing friend—cleared the floor before him of men with a single sweep of his foreleg.

Then Ryndean opened his mouth, and all that was left to feel and see was a boiling, brutal assault of blinding white.

"Declan. Declan!"

Ester was shaking him, having noticed his absence before either of the others. Declan came back more smoothly now, either the brevity of the memory or the repetition of similar events in the past having made this slippage all that much easier. He blinked once, twice, then shook his head to clear his mind and looked up to find Ryn and Bonner watching him with a tense mix of concern and interest. For a moment Declan was distracted by the almost-amused consideration that—despite the pair's *very* different countenances of face and feature—he was so able to distinguish the same expression from both of them.

He decided not to keep them in suspense.

"I saw it," he told them all, the fading echo of the memory still fresh on his mind. "The attack. The ballroom. I saw you change." He met Ryn's gaze, and the dragon's eyes widened in impressed surprise.

I don't think I'll ever get used to that, Ryn muttered, and for some reason he looked down at his own hand. *To think it had the power to pull an entirely different time into our own…*

"Magic is without time, Ryndean," Bonner said sagely. "It does not exist as we do, living in the present and knowing only the past. Magic lingers in the very fabric of reality. It does not surprise me *in the least* that your blood could have carried this much of Amherst with it through the centuries."

"*Your* blood?" Ester asked, mirroring Declan's confusion. She was holding him again, this time by the arm, in such a position that made him suspect he had nearly toppled over despite the briefness of his departure.

I'm getting to that, Ryn said with the quick air of one who has caught themselves letting slip something they shouldn't. He grunted under Ester's suspicious eye. *I am, if only you would let me finish.* He turned his attention back on Declan. *What did you see? Exactly?*

Declan answered, satisfied for the moment with the dragon's word given what he and Bonner had already divulged so far that night—*Or morning, rather,* Declan thought to himself, noting the faint glow of orange over the eastern tops of the trees across the stream. He told them of the fight, of knowing of Elysia and Elnaryl and Bonner somewhere at his back. He described watching Ryn—or *Ryndean,* as Herst's mind had known him—take his true form to the immediate effect of a shift in the battle.

"And then… fire, I think?" he finished somewhat anti-climactically, giving Ryn an inquisitive look. To his surprise, the dragon appeared almost to pale.

The first time I'd ever set the dragonfire upon the likes of men… he muttered, partially to himself, clearly not relishing the memory. *I had no choice, of course. I had to get you—Herst—*he slid over the mistake as though nothing had been said amiss—*and the others out of there. Even then I was mostly too late. Only Arathia and Elnaryl were left alive of the elves, she and Bonner trying to see his wound while Herst and Elysia defended them. It was all I could do to grab them up and get away, taking down half the chamber as I fled…*

"Elysia was screaming for her father, even as we flew," Bonner recalled somberly, emerald eyes glassy beneath his heavy eyebrows. "And Elnaryl was beyond me the moment that sword cut into his throat. I don't think he survived more than a few minutes after we escaped… I still remember…"

Another flash, this one even shorter. The twilight darkness of a summer evening ripping past Declan at terrifying speed, his one arm pinned uncomfortably to his side by the great talons that had snatched him up from certain death. He could twist his head, could see his sister and Bonner held in the claws of Ryn's back legs. Across from him—caged as delicately as he thought the dragon might have been able to manage—he could just make out the gleam of tears trailing Arathia yr'Essel's pale face.

Those tears, and the limp, unmoving form of the prince the *Aveer al'En* clutched to, much of Elnaryl's white gown of elven silk stained black in the night with blood.

We waited two days to bury him, just inside the edge of the western forests. Ryn's voice spoke with what seemed almost forced calm. No one had noticed Declan's short departure, this time. *Arathia wouldn't have it any other way. She refused to put him to rest in the flatlands that surround Aletha and its neighbors, insisting she would see Elnaryl lain down beneath the trees, even if they weren't of the Vyr'en. She took his coronet, to present to his mother if ever there was the opportunity, and we left him there. There was no means by which man could have kept bodily pace with a dragon, but Bonner was hardly the only powerful mage in the kingdom, in those years, and I wasn't going to take any chances. It took us ten days more to make the Reaches.*

He snorted, then, caught by some odd memory. *Tyrennus didn't so much as blink when I showed up on his doorstep with the kingdom's heirs, a High Knight of the er'enthyl, and the greatest court mage of Aletha in tow. He was five hundred years the senior of any other dragon of the ranges, and three thousand years my own. I think he'd been alive too long to be surprised by anything, anymore. He took them all in with barely a word, and it was he who turned us all on to the very real possibility that we were hardly out of danger.*

"Because the Accord of Four still held?" Declan offered, for once managing to follow along. "Because the al'Dyors still lived?"

"Almost." It was Bonner's turn to answer again, his words bitter. Over his head, the morning's light was growing brighter now. "Though I suppose it amounts to the same thing, in the end. The nobility were hardly still bound by the pact, with Igoric dead and his children half-in-exile. The real trouble for them lay with the common folk of Viridian, the crown's lesser subjects. Farmers. Merchants and traders. Even the army regulars. No fortune in the world would have been enough to put a gold lever in every hand, and the al'Dyors—Igoric in particular—had been well-loved by the masses. The old King had kept a peace he might have pressed, and the nation was prospering under his rule, as it had his father's. Elysia was a handful in her own right, but she was hardly the bad sort, and had all the makings of her sires. There was little reason the larger populace would have lent their support to the nobility's coup."

"And if they found out about it, it would have been disastrous for the houses," Declan put in, catching on.

"Especially—" Bonner pressed the point "—if that news came directly from the mouths of the children of the murdered King, bearing the mark of the al'Dyors as evidence of their station."

"Their signets?"

It made sense, and knowledge of the King's seals was common enough. The signets of the al'Dyors. The rings of their office and rank. Trinkets that held all of the power of a member of the royal line in their presence. Declan had never seen one himself, having never crossed paths with Mathaleus or his Queen. The pair were yet childless, or the chances of him having run into some little prince or princess in the streets of Aletha bearing their own signet might have been higher. Still, Cassandra had received more than one missive pressed with the King's insignia, so Declan had had the opportunity to take in the shield and crowned stag up close on more than one occasion.

Instead of answering, however, Bonner hesitated, glancing almost tentatively at Ryn. The dragon, in turn, seemed to be considering something, watching Declan carefully.

Yes, the signets, Ryn said finally. *A ring of the al'Dyors held the same power then as one does now, Declan. It was an absolute presence, a mark of Kings. It denoted one as a member of the direct royal family, and was not intended to be passed along.* He stared and Declan pointedly. *Still... Circumstances of the world do not often allow for the petty laws of man to stand it their way...*

Declan stared right back into his friend's even gaze, perplexed. He had no idea what Ryn was trying to get at—and he was definitely trying to get at *something*—and could feel the old irritation begin to claw its way back into his thoughts.

He was about to coolly demand further explanation, when it hit him like a lightning bolt.

He looked down at his left hand, at the simple band of battered gold, set with a plain wedge of flat, black stone. He couldn't bring himself to accept it, couldn't even begin to contemplate it. And yet, Amherst *had* been an heir to the throne of Viridian, a prince of the line, if second to his elder sister. Perhaps, just perhaps...

And then Declan felt the odd sensation in the back of his head, the loosening, unclenching feeling of Ryn's magic falling away from his thoughts, releasing his mind to its freedom.

Before his very eyes, the ring changed.

The worn, dim luster of the metal vanished, replaced by a clean sheen of polished gold. The bland band became delicate, meticulously crafted, taking the form of paired swords behind matching shields, the blades bending around to encircle his finger. At its crown, set behind the hilts of the swords, the mundane stone took the form of a broad, polished black gem, emblazed with a coat of arms that was difficult to see in the dim light of their meager fire. As he peered closer, trying to make out the meticulously carved etchings, Declan recalled having known exactly such a ring before, flashing across his mind on the occasion Herst's memories had pressed forward with such fervor they had dragged him down into unconsciousness.

There was a *crack* and spark of the fire, the flames momentarily flashing brighter as the tinder resettled. In that chance of better light, Declan noted clearly the shapes at last, taking in the fine lines of the stag's head, crowned and regal atop its simple shield. It was not exactly the same as the arms one could find born upon the banners of Aletha's walls, perhaps having adapted with the passing of the years as new hands drafted its like over and over again.

But it was an unmistakable mark all the same.

Declan sat silent for a long, long time, gazing down at the crest of the al'Dyors. No one spoke. No one *dared* to speak. The others knew, he was sure, that it was not their place to break the stillness now, that such a step was his right to make, and his alone.

When Declan finally found his voice, he could only do so much to keep the anger from spilling out into every word.

"How much more are you yet hiding from me, Ryn?"

CHAPTER TWENTY-SEVEN

To Declan's mounting fury, Ryn didn't have the good dignity to look ashamed. On the contrary, the dragon held his head high and met Declan's gaze unflinching.

When his answer came, it was equally as unwavering.

This is the last of my secrets, Declan. There is nothing left for me to hide from you, nothing left for me to hold back. You're not even aware of the fact that you've been bearing the weight of your own mind for days now, unassisted. You've been free of my influence since before we reached Ranheln. This—he motioned to the ring, revealed from behind the veil of his magic—*was all that remained. And don't ask me why.* His hand stayed up in a halting gesture, foreseeing the demand even as Declan opened his mouth to make it. *Only stop and recall that Bonner and I would have gladly told you the truth of things already—we tried to, even. Remember that* you *were the one who wished us to hold back before you bare your teeth at me too fiercely. How would I have revealed this to you, given that request? What sort of conclusions would you have been left to make, having only heard a fraction of the story, and less of your family's history?*

The words rang hard and true. Declan's anger didn't dissipate, but rather turned inward, and he eased himself back again. He noticed then, Ester's restraining hand, her fingers having taken the loose cloth of his shirt sleeve tentatively, like she'd been prepared to reel him in herself. It was then that her words came back to him, that morning he'd finally learned the truth of the world, her demands and insistence on his behalf. He remembered her fighting for him, fighting for his right to be told, to know.

Just as sharply, he recalled Ryn's cutting answer. "*Almost a* millennia *of history,*" the dragon had said.

All at once, Declan felt the fatigue of their interrupted night once again, felt it press on him tenfold, along with every pain and ache Bonner had been unable to relieve after the fight. He wanted nothing more than to make his excuses, to be allowed to sleep and give himself a breath to accept the burden Ryn was casting upon him. Just as firmly, he knew he couldn't, knew he had neither the right nor ability to shy away from the dragon's words, now.

Steeling himself, Declan considered the ring more carefully.

He was *not* an al'Dyor, he knew, not in the real sense of the name. Even if this signet had passed down in a direct line, hand to hand, eldest to eldest, the centuries had undoubtedly diverged him from the royal lines too far to make any such claim. But to Declan, that distant relation was not what pulled on him so fiercely. The crest set into the black stone did not represent that chance, that sliver of possibility.

To Declan, it rather made whole the truth of his lineage, brought to bear an understanding of what it might mean to be the descendant of Amherst al'Dyor, heir to the blood of the second prince of Viridian.

"They framed you."

Despite every intention otherwise, Declan's voice came out hard and unforgiving, unable to quite shed the resentment that he could only redirect at his own weakness. He hoped instead that Ryn would take the offered chance, take the opportunity Declan was attempting to extend.

"They framed you," he said again, only slightly less severely. "The nobles. Kant, al'Behn, Vostyk. They threw the King's death at your feet."

It had not been a hard conclusion to draw. He'd never really reconciled the story Brohn and Dia had shared with the character of the creature that had been his truest friend and companion for the duration of his life, and Bonner had hardly made any attempt to conceal the bitterness of his memories, even before sharing them.

That, along with the other hints scattered for him along the way, brought Declan to the steps of comprehension.

They did. Ryn took Declan's offering graciously, not even blinking at the sudden return to his story. *And without much effort. Whatever clues of the reality of the coup might have been left for the uncorrupted to find must have been as nothing to the remnants of my own actions. I did not hold back when I understood what was happening, when I knew the King to be dead and my friends to be threatened. Between my flames and the violence of our exit, I don't imagine much of the ballroom was left untouched. I dare say the houses had nothing more to do than burn the bodies of Igoric and the elves to make the lie complete.*

"From there, it would have posed small issue to feed the tale to the masses," Bonner picked up with a sigh. "Even with a peace that had already lasted centuries, do you think it took much to convince the common man that a dragon had lain waste to the palace?" The old mage shook his head in disappointment. "There was no reason given to consider otherwise. Even if there *had* been rumors and whispers, what do you imagine was easier to swallow? That a beast of the distant west, mysterious and terrible in its power, had taken it into its mind to strike at the heart of man? Or that the great houses of Aletha—the very nobles now calling to arms the vastness of the Vigil to hunt after the creature and 'rescue' the King's heirs—had conspired together to see to the fall of Igoric for nothing more than their own ignoble intents?"

There was no argument to be made, and Declan saw it. He'd had a hand in quelling more than one rebellion, in his time. He knew well how anger could fuel the masses, even when said rage was fed on nothing more than half-truths and outright falsities.

"Is that what happened?" he asked, looking between Bonner and Ryn. "So the nobles *did* attack the Reaches?"

"They did, and without suffering the penalties of the Accord." The old man grit his teeth, staring at the ground. "A flaw in the weave I curse myself to this day for not having foreseen…"

Ryn reached out to put a comforting hand on the mage's shoulder. *You're hardly the one to bear the greatest guilt, I think*, he said quietly before turning his eyes on Declan again. *Kant and his supporters gathered the Vigil under the al'Dyors' own banners, all under the pretense that the full strength of mankind would be brought to bear against the Reaches in vengeance of a slain king and to chase the hope of rescuing Elysia and Herst. The mistake Bonner criticizes himself for is one that could not have been avoided given the nature of the men and women at the heart of the conspiracy, but* mine *was less forgivable. I offered the houses the perfect opportunity to set their larger plans in motion.*

"How?" Ester asked, apparently not following, and for once Declan was pleased to be the one to answer her.

"The nobility suddenly had a reason to launch an assault on the dragons." He was relieved to hear his voice had lost its hard edge. "By taking the al'Dyors in, Ryn provided the inducement to declare the war they were already angling for, with Sehranya preoccupying the black elves to the north."

Precisely. It was as ideal a scenario as they could have envisioned, I think. A cause to set themselves against the Reaches, and one that was whole-heartedly supported by the greater populace of Viridian. Tyrennus knew as much at a glance. It's why he saw no harm in taking Elysia and Herst in, as well as Bonner and Arathia. Mankind would launch their attack eventually, given only time, and there was more advantage in facing the threat with the assistance of those who could inform him on the strategies of a human army than to delay the inevitable. It was the right choice to make. Ryn's gaze drifted again, taking him back. *The Vigil was pressing into the foothills of our mountains within a month of our safe return. Fifty thousand men, with more coming every day from distant corners of the country. Meanwhile, our own gathered response numbered less than even the thousand mages that formed the real threat of the nobles' forces. As powerful individually as we may be, I have said it before: we are not gods. We are creatures of the world, as are you, and—when our advantages are stripped away—we are as susceptible to death as any man lain bear to the edge of steel and killing weave. One can assume we might have lasted months—even years, perhaps—by hiding away in our caves and holes, but that would have meant only a slower, more certain doom. Tyrennus made the decision that we would fight, and I don't recall any voice being raised in opposition.*

Ryn inclined his head towards Bonner, then, though his eyes were still distant and far away, glowing gold in the firelight while the sky shifted into the amber hue of true dawn overhead. *Bonner and Elysia proved invaluable to keeping what edges we had. Dragons know nothing of wards and charms and defensive magics apart from what lays innately within us. I think it gave the mages of the army a shock when they found their spells reflecting or rebounding, or when their traps failed because our kind had been taught to look for the signs of such work. Elysia was a frightening presence on the field alone, tearing into the ranks of soldiers that might otherwise have been her own as efficiently as any of us, and with even less mercy.*

"She wasn't the same, after her father's death," Bonner offered, almost under his breath. "She'd always been less even-tempered than her brother, but Igoric's assassination made that gulf much more distinctive, then and after the war…"

Ryn nodded. *Herst was less inclined to the butchery, even when it came to self-defense. He fought—he was no coward—taking to the field on my own back, but stayed his hand as needed.*

"I remember," Declan interrupted quietly, his own mind drifting back to the memory, to the spilling images of the dark shapes of dragons slipping from the ridges of the mountains onto the waiting lines of the army below. "He fought from the sky? How?"

"When he could, but not always." Bonner glanced at the ring on Declan's finger, as though recalling its first owner. "Elysia was the prodigy of the two, when it came to spellcraft, but Amherst wasn't without his own abilities. It was common, then, for the children of all noble houses to be educated in the ways of magic, and the al'Dyors were no different. Amherst was no great talent, but he knew when and how to strike to disrupt the enemy most efficiently. He may have had fewer deaths to his name than his sister, but I wouldn't credit him as being any less useful, especially when he took to the ground. That swordplay of his was as enough to make a full contingent balk on more than one occasion…"

"He wasn't recognized? The soldiers didn't know him?"

"Some did," Bonner answered with a slow bob of his head in acknowledgment. "The nobles could have hardly corrupted all fifty-thousand men, after all. But they'd cast their cards well enough. I think they assumed they would face the heirs themselves, on the field, and the answer came in the simplest fashion: playing on the dragon's strengths."

This time, Declan didn't follow.

Mind magics, Ryn answered his perplexed expression. *We found out later. The entire army was under the impression that the heirs—along with Bonner and Arathia—were under our spells, doing our bidding unwillingly. It was as clever as any other story they'd managed to spin. It gave answer to why they were fighting their own kind as fittingly as it gave a reason for my having taken prisoners in the first place.*

"They couldn't explain themselves?" Declan pressed, unconvinced. "They couldn't try to talk down the soldiers?"

"Elysia was too far gone for that, I'm afraid." Bonner shook his head sadly. "I think she found purpose in the bloodshed, for a time, found reason again. Her brother tried, once…"

"And?" Declan demanded. "What happened?"

He made it within twenty feet of the front lines, sword sheathed, before taking an arrow in the gut. Ryn's tone seethed, his eyes sharpened in hard, distinct anger. *They didn't even let him get a full word in.*

"Assassins?" Ester asked, more of a statement than a question.

Her father grimaced. "Throughout the ranks. Like I said, Kant and his compatriots had cast their cards well. They'd spread their influence carefully. You don't *need* fifty thousand hired killers when you have two or three skilled ones in each contingent. The trap was all-encompassing, and would have been Amherst's end if his wound hadn't cooled his sister's head long enough to help me tend to him, in the days after."

Declan flinched at the prospect, not envying the prince's condition. He'd seen more than one man die of such injuries, of arrows and thrusts to the torso, eaten away from the inside as acid and bile spilled into the abdomen.

It had always been kinder to make a quick end of it, and most begged for just that reprieve whenever the field surgeon had shaken his head to say there was nothing more to be done.

That event came out poorer for the nobles, though. Herst was less inclined to forgiveness, afterwards, and it was that wound that lent to Tyrennus' blessing regarding offering the heirs the greatest gift we had to give.

Ryn's words brought Declan quickly back. *This* was what he had been waiting for, more than anything. *This* was the explanation he desired above all else, the very reason he had been so violently dragged into the darker parts of reality.

"What was it?" He couldn't help himself leaning forward with anticipation, feeling Ester, too, crane around him to look at Ryn with equal suspense. "What did he give them?"

Almost immediately, Declan regretted the question. Beneath his gaze Ryn appeared to shrink away, drawing back into himself. He *gave them nothing.* The dragon's voice was low and wretched. *He had nothing to give when the time came. His condoning the act was Tyrennus' last wish, his very last hope for the survival of our kind. He gave me his permission as he died, broken on the cliffs of his own realm, brought down by magic and fatigue from a battle that seemed to have no end.*

There was a quiet moment, a stillness that held firm and heavy overhead. Declan knew Ester, like him, saw the weight of this particular memory lay itself over Ryn and Bonner, the pair almost sagging in weariness, borne by a pain that looked not to have fully healed in seven hundred years…

By the time the dragon broke the silence at last, Declan could almost feel the loss himself, like one of Herst's darkest remembrances scratching at the surface of his mind.

What I had to offer—Ryn said in a tone of only slightly too-fabricated calm—*was nothing less than the very same gifts Tyrennus had passed along to me. It had been done before, in the stories. The 'benediction of the dragons', handed on to examples of the lesser races who had proven themselves of particular worth and ability. They were tales, even to us, but they were enough to go by. In the end, Herst and Elysia both accepted, and took what I had to offer in the same fashion I'd taken it from Tyrennus a hundred years before, the very manner which allowed the Accord of Four to bind us so.* He lifted his left hand, palm up, and drew the claw of his other index finger across the dark scales of his wrist in an unmistakable motion.

Declan didn't know whether to recoil or lean even further in. "Your blood." The dragon's earlier words suddenly made sense. "You had them drink your own blood..."

Ryn nodded and shrugged, letting his arms fall. *Such was our way, and truth be told I can't think of a different fashion to go about it.* Here he glanced briefly at Bonner, who shook his head as if to say he had no better idea himself.

"What happened to them?" Ester's question was quiet, but urgent with curiosity. "To the al'Dyors?"

Ryn gave her a half-amused, half-exasperated look that returned a little of the warmth to his eyes. *Are you imagining them writhing about on the ground, my magics consuming and reforming them from the inside out?*

Ester blushed slightly, opening her mouth to answer to the contrary, but her inability to do so told Declan she must have indeed been thinking along those very lines. Bonner chuckled, and Ryn let out his own quick, exasperated laugh.

Why your kinds tend to always lean towards the dramatic, I will never understand.

"The drey's blood almost melted away the better part of me." Declan came to Ester's assistance, seeing the color in the half-elf's cheeks darken further. "You've already said they were part dragon, and you've told us before they weren't completely unlike you. I don't think it's an unfair deduction..."

This had Ryn take pause to consider, something between admittance and disgust playing across his features. *Yes...* he allowed slowly. *I suppose it's as inferable a thought as any, if that's the only experience you've had to go by.* He looked upon Ester with a more even eye. *No, then. Ours is not a magic of destruction, whatever my dragonfire may say otherwise.* He paused, searching for the right way to explain it. *If anything, you could consider it almost a weave of strength, one which accentuates the ability of its bearer. It's an... amplifier, for lack of a better term, though clearly there's more to it than I'd previously assumed.*

He gave Declan an appraising eye before continuing. *The effects were less immediate than they had been in my own case. For a time we'd even assumed the gifts hadn't taken hold, and the stories were proving themselves myth. The changes were merely slow, however, and once they began there was no denying them. It was most noticeable in Elysia first, her spellwork attaining a new potential for equal parts miracle and devastation after about a fortnight. Herst's magics, too, were so affected, but he being the less skilled of the pair in that field it was even longer before we saw the greater change. What Elysia held over his head in a new proficiency of the arcane, he made up for several times in physical prowess. He'd already been a master of the blade among his peers, but after accepting my blood…*

"He was a terror on the battlefield." Bonner capped the trailing implication succinctly. "Unlike anything you can imagine. In the old histories of Viridian, there were records of battlemages and warmancers— spellswords who used sorcery to imbue themselves with strength and inhuman ability. Amherst became something akin to this, I think, and more. It was otherworldly, the way he moved through his fights. Nothing touched him, not sword or arrow or even spell…"

He seemed unstoppable, at times, Ryn agreed, his eyes settling on Declan. *I wonder if you have the same potential…*

At once Declan started to splutter out a denial, but the dragon stopped him once again.

I do not mean to imply such ability is within your grasp this very moment. As I said, the gifts you bear are merely an intensifier. They reflect on your own strength, and to that end I cannot yet compare you to the likes of Amherst al'Dyor. He was an exceedingly rare talent, much like yourself, but the great fault lies again with me. I have been an unfitting teacher, unable to do more than instruct you from the sidelines. I won't say you haven't turned out splendidly despite, but in Aletha I'd hoped to find you the sort of talented teachers who might have honed you beyond what I could give. Cassandra and a few others filled those roles somewhat, but on the whole I should have known I'd be disappointed. I think much of the ways of war have been lost in so many centuries of peace, and even if they haven't been, Herst was a prince of the courts, privy to the finest masters Viridian had to offer, and some even from beyond its boundaries. We—on the other hand—were nothing more than a peasant boy with a knack for the sword and his horse, at least in the eyes of the city.

"We were lucky enough Kavel was willing to take a chance on us," Declan snorted in concession, speaking of the Seekers' guildmaster, the first to offer them a place among the companies. With a pang he looked down at the inside of his left forearm. The scars that patterned his skin had gained some color in the week since he'd fatefully buried his blade into the drey's neck, but the tattoo of the company's arrow had not returned even in outline.

It's possible I had something do with that, Ryn said with a smirk, earning himself a sharp look. He shrugged, clearly unrepentant. *It was a choice between guiding the mind of an old man in the direction of a mutually beneficial apprenticeship, or watch you either starve as an urchin in the street or take up some mundane craft I suspected you'd find as monotonous as it would have been unfulfilling.*

At Declan's elbow, Ester let out a girlish giggle that had him looking around with wide eyes.

"Oh don't pretend the idea of 'Declan Idrys, the tanner' isn't at least a *bit* laughable," she said with a snort that had her returning to a more mature air. "I see you about as content sitting at a workman's bench as I would be spending my days spinning cotton on a loom."

That image managed to steal a smile from him, and he couldn't help but chuckle as he gave his attention back to Ryn.

"Did it help, then? Did the al'Dyors manage to turn the battle?"

Just the two of them? Ryn frowned. *No. They had an impact, to be sure, mostly on the morale of the Vigil, but at that point we'd been fighting for months and hadn't made more than a respectable dent in the army's numbers. Of my own kind we'd lost hundreds. Some third of the entire population of the Reaches' dragons, Tyrennus among them. It left me—barely a century old—as the very last of the primordial line. We'd been marching steadily towards extinction—would have already suffered that fate without the help we had—and Herst and Elysia only managed to slow that pace from a tumble to a crawl. Still... we were losing. No one but a liar and a fool would have said otherwise, when Kant and the others had fresh troops arriving every week from the borders and the eastern coast.*

Ryn stopped again, drew a single, heavy breath, and spoke with such careful coolness Declan thought he might have been struggling to keep the fury from his words.

And then she *joined the fight.*

Once again, Declan could guess who "she" was. "Sehranya? From where?"

"North," Bonner answered simply. "Crept west over the Tears along the heights of the ranges so neither side could know she was coming, then down into the Reaches."

"But what about the *er'endehn?*" Ester asked in surprise. "Had she won? Did she break Ysenden?"

We'd feared so, at first, Ryn said, looking to the woman. *There were dark elves among her draugr—they made up the majority of her wights, too—but given she arrived with no more than a scattering of higher undead and ten thousand wereyn at her back, we eventually suspected otherwise. She'd grown tired, it appeared, of the siege. We all—dragons and men alike—had assumed her desire to conquer her own people would outweigh other reason, given how swiftly she'd launched herself against the er'endehn. She proved us all wrong in one fell swoop.*

"Ten thousand, though?" Declan was surprised that such a number could have had so great an impact. "Against fifty thousand of the Vigil and what remained of the dragons?"

Bonner showed a hard half-smile that lacked all amusement. "You assume a common enemy would have been enough to have the nobles seek a truce."

"It wasn't?" Declan asked, appalled. He couldn't fathom what sort of man wouldn't have set aside his own squabbles and ambitions, when faced with an army of undead. "Even against someone like the Queen?"

Hardly, Ryn answered. *Though, to be fair, this was true for both sides of the conflict, at that point. We made most of the same presumptions you did. What was another ten thousand when we were already being pressed steadily and consistently towards the end of our existence? We'd suffered too much ancient blood spilled to so easily turn a blind eye to the wrong humanity had dealt us.* His next breath came shakily. *Trouble was... It wasn't ten thousand for very long...*

"The corpses." It was Ester who made the realization first, her hollow voice a sharp contrast to the steadily blooming blue of the early morning sky.

Ryn only grunted to tell her she was right, letting Bonner handle the explanation.

"Despite everything—despite Igoric's conclave and the signing of the Accord—the base reality was we'd only had letters and reports, until then." The mage shifted his weight so he could bring his legs around to cross them more comfortably beneath him. "Even during the course of the negotiations in Aletha there had been voices of disbelief. To be frank, I'm not altogether convinced any man could have *wholly* believed in the power Sehranya was capable of wielding before witnessing it with their own two eyes, and by then it was always far too late." Bonner was staring at the ground once more. "Whether to our fortune or not in the end, the Vigil was struck first. Fall had come and gone by then, and winter in the mountains—even the Reaches—is a cruel thing. There were few places to bury the dead, and fewer ways still of carting them back to the lower forests of the valleys easily. The army had taken to laying their fallen down in whatever space they could afford among the cliffs, preserved by the ice and cold of the season, to be gathered and give their proper dues once the nobles had accomplished their goal..." Bonner lifted a hand slowly, almost thoughtlessly, like he was lifting some invisible thing from the ground before him. "They rose the very night Sehranya arrived on the field. She might have lacked for military strategy, but the witch was no fool. Before the bodies could be burned, she set them on the ranks of man. Almost ten-thousand of the dead, given a Purpose so as to suddenly take to life."

A thrill crawled its way unpleasantly up Declan's back. He was unable to keep himself from recalling his own encounters with the ghouls, in the woods far to the west of them now. Despite all desire not to, he saw again the dead, empty eyes, their reaching talons of bone and the black fire that echoed their final wail as they died. There'd only been a handful, when he and Ryn had faced them, but they had overcome him just the same.

He couldn't even imagine what kind of fear a thousand times their number would have brought to the hearts of the men and women of the Vigil…

"Ghouls are slow, though." Ester sounded dubious. "Even with the element of surprise, I can't image any force of them doing much in the end to fifty-thousand soldiers."

"Ghouls are," Bonner acknowledged, lifting his head to meet his daughter's eye, "but you forget that ghouls aren't the only thing Sehranya could manifest from the dead. Liche, for example. I imagine she'd had a hard time finding suitable corpses until then. She would have needed bodies capable of channeling magic in no small amount, and there would have been few—if any—among the *er'endehn* she'd lain waste to. Now, abruptly, here were more than a hundred slain mages, felled and ready with no effort in the least made on her part. Even those rent completely asunder by dragons' claws she made use of, patching them whole again, or stitching what parts she needed together as needed. She summoned wights, too, where she could, crafting more complex Purposes for those bodies which were the freshest, the most suitable. In the end, ghouls only made up the majority of the risen army that set upon the Vigil, serving as little more than a wall of flesh for the more dangerous factions of their ranks. One which could be summoned up again and again if they weren't properly slain."

That wasn't the worst of it, Ryn assured them sourly after Declan and Ester had exchanged a look of mixed horror and disgust. *Sehranya didn't set her eyes on man and leave it at that. We had done a better job of seeing to our fallen. There were fewer of us, and burning the dead was our custom already, so we'd disposed of most of those we'd lost. We couldn't see to every corpse, though. Many of us had been slain behind enemy lines, impossible to retrieve, and a few had been claimed by the winter storms that usually kept us in our caves until spring. We hadn't left her with much to work with, but what Sehranya had found she'd already corrupted in the most heinous of ways.* He spat—actually spat—then. *While the Vigil were fighting off their fallen comrades, the drey were set on us.*

Despite having known it was coming, Declan felt that clinging thrill redouble, made barely more bearable by Ester's hiss of angry fear from beside him.

Ryn, on the other hand, didn't even flinch. *I remember that night most vividly of any of those years, I think. More so than when I signed the Accord of Four, or even the fight and flight from Aletha. Abruptly, we were dying. Just… dying. Five, then ten, then twenty of us. The Vigil's mages had been able to mask much of their troops' movements from our senses before that, but this was something altogether different. We were falling from the* sky, *our patrols tumbling out of the heavens without cause or explanation. We could sense* nothing, *their presence completely shielded from us. I eventually called back all that remained, ordering everyone to take shelter within the caves until first light. When morning came, we were finally offered a glimpse of what it was that had been tearing us apart so absolutely.*

Ryn shuddered, like the memory was too much for even a dragon to bear without trouble. *I cannot explain the feeling to you, of seeing your brethren unmade, of knowing them torn apart and put back together into those… things. There weren't many of us to begin with, as you know.* His face went slack. *I could recognize the pieces of my friends, distinguish the parts Sehranya had used to create her beasts in the colors and patterns of the scales…*

Ester let out another sound, this time a soft "oh" of miserable empathy. Declan himself felt the urge to go to his friend then, to put a hand on his scaled shoulder, even if it meant offering only the barest of comforts against a horror long past.

Bonner, fortunately, did one better, giving Ryn a reprieve and taking up the story more succinctly.

"We fought like that for two more weeks, maybe three. Sehranya was the greatest threat—even the Vigil learned to set aside mages whose sole task it was to burn the dead—but it remained a three-way war, which must have suited the witch herself just fine. The more we killed each other, the stronger she became. Even as our sides grew more adept at dealing with her troops, so we also grew weaker as the battle devolved into one of equal attrition. The drey might have been *our* greatest trouble, but the Queen's wereyn ended up posing a threat of nearly equal magnitude to the Vigil. They were mostly-living things—only minimally less-so than their descendants are now—with no Purpose to make them vulnerable. No matter how many the soldiers cut down, Sehranya or her liche could raise them up again. It made their smaller number a negligible disadvantage."

"If given the choice between a hundred mortal men, or ten that can't be killed, I know who I'd pick," Declan muttered.

"As would any general worth their mettle," Bonner agreed. "For that reason and many others, it was a losing fight. Eventually the Vigil even quit their assaults on the cliffs, given little choice otherwise as their strength was steadily needed more acutely on their northern front if they were to keep at bay the Queen's mounting attacks. It allowed our own focus to be narrowed, allowed us to properly defend against the drey, and start pulling them apart one after the other. Sehranya could not so easily make those particular beasts, we found. Likely they required her personal attention, and could not be fabricated with a mere weave, despite her power. They were replaced, but slowly, and we managed to shed their overall numbers little by little, day by day."

At a steep cost. Ryn broke in then. *At the price of our own blood and lives.*

Bonner nodded. "Indeed. Even the Vigil had been decimated by then, a third of their remaining number lost to the Queen's army. In a matter of weeks Sehranya achieved what we had been unable to manage in *months* of defending and counter-attacking. Thousands—*tens* of thousands—of men dead or turned. Our numbers dwindled, while her own steadily increased, fed by our own losses."

"But… you won." Declan couldn't see hope on the horizon, had never glimpsed what had brought a close to such a battle through Herst's memories. "How? What happened?"

The er'endehn.

Ryn's tone was one of relief, like he was reliving the final days of the war all over again.

The er'endehn arrived. Theirs is a martial kind, a people raised from birth to fight and war, sometimes against the beasts of Eserysh, but more often amongst themselves and their individual states. He glanced at Declan. *Even among their lesser warriors you'd find better teachers than I, and certainly more to learn. The siege could not have done anything but rankle the pride and spirit of the dark elves, forced to cower one-and-all behind the walls of Ysenden under an onslaught they'd had no hope of defending against. They must have seen an opportunity when Sehranya turned her back on the fortress, a chance to rid themselves of tarnished pride and return in kind even some small measure of the suffering the Endless Queen had inflicted on them. They tracked her, followed the string of scattered bones she left behind as she fed her wereyn on the corpses of the army's ghouls. Barely half-a-moon after she'd set herself upon the battered forces of our own petty war, they arrived, having trailed the very same pass she'd taken. Sehranya had no scouts. Apart from the liche she kept on her front lines, she had no truly intelligent beings within her ranks that could be instructed to keep watch over her flanks and rear. She'd always depended on brute force to win her battles, with admittedly consistent results given her ability to regularly replenish her forces during and after most any fight. As a result, however, the dark elves struck her from behind with as much speed and surprise as she had taken our two armies with, and nearly equal in devastation.*

The dragon grinned, still without amusement, but there was a distinct pleasure in his eyes. *Where Sehranya had arrived confidently with a small force, the er'endehn made no such assumption. They'd set out en masse from Ysenden, every last man and woman among them who still had the will to fight taking up their swords and spears. They struck her rear with more than forty thousand blades, and fought with all the knowledge gained from two years battling the draugr through the snowy plains and forests of their homeland. Sehranya's arrogance proved her undoing. In a matter of a single morning she went from dictating a battle between two mortal enemies—a clash which would have undoubtedly had her emerge the victor, and all the more powerful for it—to fending off a three-sided assault she'd inadvertently positioned herself into. For the first time, our kind and the Vigil fought practically side by side, pressing her up from the south through the Reaches while the elves held their ground north of her, immovable in the opportunity to enact their vengeance.*

"Six days," Bonner picked up. "After months of ceaseless, back-and-forth slaughter, it took only six days to bring it to its end. Four of those were spent closing in, casting the undead from the cliffs and burning the rest where they fell to keep them from rising again. On the morning of the fifth, the will she had granted the wereyn broke, and what remained of them scattered, some thousands fleeing into the storms and crags of the mountains."

The last was spent pitched against Sehranya herself, Ryn said quietly. *Her, and the strongest dregs of the risen army she'd managed to gather about her.*

For the third time, Declan was taken away. On this occasion it was only a flash, a glimpse of a moment in a time long past. An overcast sky choked with hundreds of winged forms, some dragonish, some twisted and terrible.

And below them, the vice closed.

The black-and-red of the Vigil were pressing from the south, led by a torrent of flashing, fiery spellwork while to the north the dark armies of the elves in their gilded black armor held as a wall against the dwindling foe being crushed between them. Beneath him, Declan felt Ryndean tense, then dive abruptly with a roar of fury, making for the eastern edge of the remaining undead. Declan knew what he must have seen, knew in that instant what the dragon was plummeting after. He had to cast a ward before him to clear his vision enough to make out the details of the roiling, shifting masses below against the ripping force of the wind.

And then he, too, saw her. A small, ambiguous form standing near the great ledges her armies had been pressed against, distinguishable only by the glimmer of dull, iron-black magic flowing like smoke from upraised hands. A dozen looming figures hovered in an unliving, half-circled wall before her, frightening in their ragged robes and colors of what once had been the King's mages, their own spells shimmering outwards into the chaos. For a moment Declan met the witch's eyes, nothing more than flecks of grey flint beneath the raised hood of her tattered cowl.

Then he was wrenching his blade from its sheath and howling the Endless Queen's name as the familiar thrum of Ryndean gathering his flames built up beneath him.

Declan gasped as he came back, his physical body having been holding its breath while his spirit wandered. This time his journey—quick as it may have been—did not go unnoticed, and he felt Ester start at the sound of his return. Ryn and Bonner looked at him sharply, too, but he didn't give them the chance to ask.

"You reached her first," he said to the dragon, working to catch his breath while struggling to cling even momentarily to the subtler emotions of the memory. "You and Herst. You were the ones who found her."

Ryn blinked in mostly muted surprise. *We did,* he confirmed. *We had the advantage, in that. I'd forbidden the survivors of my kind to engage with the Queen even if they did make her out, and Elysia nor Bonner nor Arathia had ever been willing to go dragon-back. Herst and I caught her not long after the wereyn broke, all avenues of escape lost, short of casting herself from the very cliffs, which I very much doubt was a thought that would have ever crossed the mind of a woman like Sehranya. Eight hours.* He grunted at the memory with a shake of his head. *Eight hours at least we fought, until night came, the two of us facing off against her and the liche she'd gathered to her sides. Despite the fact that her strength lay outside of direct combat, she still made for a terrible opponent. We were a poor match for her, her weaves countering what fire and spells we could throw in her face while simultaneously making it essentially impossible for either of us to get close enough to strike at her with sword or claws. It was all we could do to keep her contained, to hold her attention while cutting down her guard one at a time, and even that we only managed because of our gifts, and not easily. We barely held out long enough for those better suited to the task to reach us.*

The dragon's eyes shifted to Bonner, who put on a smile marked with grim cheer. "Elysia and I were the ones who put an end to it," the mage said darkly, and Declan remembered he had already known this. "And not without great effort, even *after* the bitch had spent half-a-day engaged already. Amherst and Ryndean had seen to her liche, and the dragons, elves, and Vigil were dealing with the remainders of her other creatures. She was alone, and yet just the same it took the two of us—with the help of a handful of the bravest of man's surviving mages—to take her down. Elysia, in the final moments, became the hero of the war. She had a new talent for fire—an inclination you share, Declan—" he rolled his eyes pointedly at Ryn for a moment "—and the moment her chance came she took it. The instant the Queen broke—her wards shattering around her under our combined castings—Elysia weaved her into ash."

Declan *heard* rather than saw the spell, this time, the sound of it dragged to his ears. A roar, bearing ten times the force of Ryn's own dragonfire, and he could imagine a spiraling maelstrom of smoke and flame splitting the very heavens.

There was nothing left of her, the dragon himself finished. *By the time Elysia's spell had run its course, Sehranya was little more than scattered dust on the stones of the mountains.*

There were several seconds of silence, which Declan suspected was for his benefit, allowing him to soak in this tale that cast aside so much of the confusion which had plagued him these last weeks. Ester, however, was clearly not about to let the other two off the hook until they had explained everything to her satisfaction.

"You're not done," she said pointedly. "I admit I wasn't aware of much of that, but I know too that you're not done yet."

Ryn let out a long sigh. For all his earlier inclination to share, it was clear the story had stolen much of that will, the trip back through the centuries clearly more taxing than he'd anticipated. Bonner, too, looked weary, sitting across from the dragon with his back to a fire that had slowly burned down to embers while dawn broke overhead. Declan couldn't blame them. The heft of his own history was starting to make itself known, and he couldn't imagine what it must have been like to *live* through such a war, much less bear the responsibility of playing key roles in its outcome.

The noble houses were the first to take their leave of the field, drawing what was left of the Vigil away with them, Ryn picked up with a tired glance at Ester, and he spoke faster, like he wished to bring an end to the recounting as soon as possible. *Of the seventy-thousand who'd eventually mounted against us, less than half that number were returning to their homes. The er'endehn left not a day after, despite Herst and Bonner's attempts then and there to bring them into the fold of the Accord of Four. They mistrusted us, I think. All of us. If they'd been willing to listen to the wisdom of the pact before Sehranya's fall, they were distinctly of a different mind afterwards.*

"Can you blame them?" Bonner asked bitterly. "Of the three races that *did* take on the pledge, one had its crown prince murdered, and the others set to each other's throats barely a month after the signing. There was nothing more left than a vague assurance of future security to use as leverage, and with the Queen gone and most of humanity's army in tatters, what need had they of such a promise anymore?"

It was short-sighted, Ryn said. *In a few generations, man had replenished its ranks.*

"By which point the dark elves had already tricked the two of you into closing Karn's Gullet, effectively severing all lines of communication with the other races." Bonner scowled. "They knew what they were doing, just as you and Amherst apparently did when you refused to accompany Elysia back to Aletha."

"Wait... Tricked you?" Declan had momentarily gotten himself lost in the conversation again. "How did they trick you? And Elysia went back? But what about Kant and the others?"

Ryn let out a gruff laugh. *The er'endehn are as clever as they are powerful. All it took was a show of force—a threat some fifty years later of invading Viridian—for Herst and I to take it upon ourselves to close off the pass. The moment we'd done so, though, the elves turned around and marched right back to Ysenden like it had been their plan all along.* He shook his head, almost amused. *The played us like a damn fiddle.* Then he looked at Declan directly. *But as for the risk of Elysia's return...*

In all the years we spent in the city, can you tell me of a single time you heard the names Kant, al'Behn, or Vostyk?

Declan frowned, considering, then shook his head. He wasn't all that surprised, of course. Many of the capital's noble houses—the Seryns, Tholuses, and al'Vons just a few among them—claimed heritages that were centuries old, but it had been seven-hundred years since the ill-fated assault on the Reaches. Even noble lines had to die out eventually...

Of course you didn't, Ryn cut into his thoughts. *The heads of those houses took most of Viridian's standing army and led them into a battle that claimed the life of almost forty thousand of the nation's finest men and women, and with no victory taken to justify so much as a fraction of such a loss. Worse for them, the Vigil's survivors returned bearing the truth of the nobles' intents, many of the soldiers' eyes opened to the wrongs committed by Kant and the others in the aftermath of Sehranya's fall. The way it reached us later, it wasn't more than a week after the nobles' return to Aletha that their homes were set on by the city's population, men and women they had deceived and lied to with murderous results for the well-loved royal line. Among them: the families of thousands on thousands of the slain, robbed of their children, their husbands and wives, their parents and siblings.*

"Elysia left the Reaches not long after the army's departure." Bonner brought the conversation back to fill in the blanks for Declan. "I think the only reason she lingered in the first place was to try and convince her brother to come with her, after he refused her initial suggestion."

"He didn't believe the Queen was gone," Declan recalled, looking to Ryn. "Neither of you did."

The dragon nodded, but allowed Bonner to continue. "Sehranya's power was too far beyond what we knew, delving into a realm of magics none had tread before. Elysia—truth be told—was the *only* one of us convinced she'd indeed dealt a final blow, but Herst's disbelief struck her hardest. Her brother's refusal to accompany her home put a wedge between them, and Elysia left on her own in a rare rage. She arrived just as the population of the city was turning on the noble houses." He sighed, almost in disappointment. "I can't believe it took much effort on her part to reclaim her father's crown, given the situation. If anything, it was likely pressed into her hands by the lesser families of the court who sought any way to appease the masses. She took it, to be sure, but did nothing to rein in her people until the higher houses were razed to bloody rubble and dust."

He toyed with the clear crystal about his neck thoughtlessly. "The anger she had left the Reaches with stayed with her for a long time, I was told... I sought her out more than once, in the years that followed. At first in nothing more than an attempt to look in on her, then later in the hopes of talking her down from her decisions to abolish the magical colleges and ban spellcraft within the boundaries of Viridian. She never even received me..."

"She *banned* magic?" Declan demanded, astounded. "But... she was a mage! Why would she strip herself of her own abilities?"

"She didn't." Bonner shook his head. "Not to my knowledge at least. She went so far as keep her own children from learning the craft, but I don't believe she gave up her own powers. I'm not sure she could have, even *before* drinking a primordial's blood." His green eyes flicked quickly to Ryn. "But yes. Whether out of fear that someone like Sehranya would rise again, or for some other reason, Elysia barred all further education or apprenticeships, and punished mages who broke those laws severely. She had the people on her side, in this. The vaster population of Aletha and beyond who had suffered so greatly at the hands of the Endless Queen and the nobles whose magic was the one thing that truly set them apart from the common masses. Within a decade the prohibition was enacted, and within three the only weavers left in the world were of the old guard, far fallen from the respected guardians of power and secrets we had always been."

It got so bad, 'witchhunts' began to form, Ryn spat with a growl of frustration. *Even Herst and I were set upon on occasion, in our journeys, despite the fact he still wore that ring.* He nodded towards the signet of the al'Dyors on Declan's finger.

Something clicked into place then, and Declan scrutinized Bonner carefully. "That's why you went into hiding, isn't it?" he asked. "That's why you disappeared...?"

"That, and because there was as little place left for Arathia in the world as there was for me." The old man's voice took on a hard edge that went beyond his previous bitterness. Not a trace of his usual cheer could be found in the laugh lines that broke up the corners of his eyes. "Viridian's growing hatred did not fixate solely on us mages. It spread, building a mistrust of all the other races. Dragons were chief among them—fed on old stories of the attack on the palace that had spread too far to ever be completely cleared up, something you've already been witness to—but the elves suffered only minimally less resentment. The woman that was by then my wife was an outcast of the world as a whole, unwelcome in the forests of her homelands in the shadow of her failed duty to Elnaryl ehn'Vyr'en, and despised within the borders of Viridian. So yes, I left. *We* left. And I can honestly say I've not regretted it for a moment in the more than six hundred years since."

His tone was final, daring any to argue his conviction. No one spoke up, neither desiring such a confrontation nor possessing any justification to do so.

"What about you and Herst, Ryn?" Ester finally asked, leaning around Declan to cut through the lingering tension. "Obviously you never found Sehranya..."

The dragon flinched, like the bluntness of the statement was a jab to the ribs. *No*, he grumbled regretfully, jaw opening and closing while he chewed on his thoughts. *Not so much as a hair or hint of her in the fifty-odd years we spent looking. We eventually started to believe that she was gone—I think Herst even reached out to Elysia, to try to mend the rift our refusal to do so had caused—but we couldn't be convinced... Not completely, at least. It wasn't until he received word that his sister had died giving birth to her third child that Herst gave pause to think of what other joys of life he might have been sacrificing. He married, eventually.* The dragon smiled nostalgically. *Brilyn. A peasant woman whose vegetables we made the mistake of trying to steal in exchange for a gold piece left in the dirt.* He laughed aloud at the memory. *I remember her stomping out across the gardens in bare feet and nothing more than a nightgown to successfully make the greatest warrior of the age cower and apologize under the tongue lashing she gave him.* Ryn's cheer halted, then faded. *She died herself not two years later, giving Herst his daughter. He named her Elalyn, half for his sister and half for Brilyn, each taken by your Mother and Her Graces in the same brutal manner.*

Ryn sighed sadly. *Then... Herst passed himself. In the year 367. I... I had thought the gifts I'd given him might have kept him with me for some time more, but...*

He let the disappointment and grief hang in the air, his thought unfinished. No one pressed him. All knew the tale from there, even Declan. Ryn had stayed with his family through the generations that followed, had looked over Elalyn, then her son, Sehren, after her. Beyond that, dozens of men and women of Herst's line, centuries of a family that shared blood with the royals of Viridian and Ryn's own gifts. It made Declan's heart ache. He had never before considered the toll such a life must have taken on his friend. To see one's cherished charges born, live, and die over and over again. It seemed a cruel fate, bordering on the purgatory of sinners the priests of the Mother's Word cathedral could be heard preaching about in the streets of the city.

A thought bubbled up across Declan's thoughts, a question that *hadn't* been answered just yet.

"Why?" he muttered.

Bonner looked at him curiously. "What was that?"

Declan started and cursed himself. He hadn't realized he'd let the words slip out aloud. "Why?" he asked again, louder this time, looking to Ryn again. "*Why* have you been following us, all this time? After Herst died... What kept you with my family? Why didn't you return to the Reaches?"

Ryn, in response, stared back at him like he didn't understand the question. Bonner had to answer for him, in the end.

"Declan... By the time the war ended, there weren't more than fifty dragons to be spoken for in the entirety of the Ranges..."

Declan almost choked. *Fifty* dragons? He had thought the decimation of the Vigil had been extreme, but those had been soldiers whose lives had been lost on the battlefield. For any entire *race* to be all-but-eradicated...

As with Bonner, there was little left to me, in this world, Ryn finally managed, a waver in his voice betraying his emotions. *Many of even those few survivors refused to acknowledge me as their sovereign, some because of my age, and others because they blamed me for the evils that had befallen our home, and not altogether without cause. The few that pledged me their allegiance I had already ordered scattered, tasking them with protecting what tenuous vestiges remained of the Accord.*

Declan blinked at this, but Bonner foresaw the burgeoning question. "Oh yes, the Accord holds, boy. It's likely the reason Sehranya has seen fit to hunt us down like animals. Consider: man and the wood elves of the Vyr'en are at odds, and the dragons are but a shadow of what they might have been, but all three races signed the pact. Ryndean lives—" he waved to the dragon at his side "—and there are those that would rise to his call, if needed. Elnaryl ehn'Vyr'en was murdered, but the magic was bound to his *blood*, not his *life*. His mother is still Matriarch of the *er'enthyl*, as she has been for more than a thousand years. Even the dark elves could still be brought into the contract, should they be made willing to do so. As for man..." He paused to fix Declan with a scrutinizing look. "I cannot speak to whether your own line is bound by the weave. Even given the Queen's interest in your King's blood, too many generations have passed, and Amherst was—after all—only the second child of Igoric al'Dyor. But Elysia's line is strong, even today. This 'Mathaleus' you name as King is undoubtedly fettered and aware of it, as his children will one day be."

"He's aware?" Ester repeated, taken aback. "Do you truly think so, after so much time has passed?"

We do, Ryn answered. *We can be certain of it, in fact. I saw to that even before Herst and I left the Reaches.*

Declan watched him carefully, wanting to ask. He thought he could guess what the dragon meant, but the need for a more pressing answer still had hold of him.

"You stayed with us because... there was nothing else for you?" he asked tentatively, unpersuaded that this was all there was to the matter. The lack of conviction must have been distinct, because Ryn gave him a lopsided smirk.

Is that so hard to imagine? Do you think there would be another place for me, in the world? Unwanted in my homeland? Feared by mankind?

Declan felt himself flush. "I-I didn't mean—"

But Ryn held up a hand to stop him, the half-smile still lingering on his lips. *I know. And truth be told I'm being unfair. There was—is, rather—more to it than that. The gifts I granted Herst carried, first to Elalyn, then then to Sehren. I had not expected such a phenomenon. No such inheritance of the primordial gifts existed among us dragons, but I can't believe attempting to understand the intricacies of such a magic would be anything but futile in the extreme. I was as curious as I was concerned.* He pointed a clawed finger at Declan. *What methods had I at my disposal to ensure the abilities you harbor within that body of yours did not take seed in an unworthy soul? I could have killed Elalyn, or Sehren, ending your line myself, but I would have butchered anyone fool enough to make such a suggestion. I could have abandoned your family to whatever cruel or fortunate fate would come, but that would have involved turning my back on a problem I myself was largely at fault for creating, and I had seen first-hand what destruction men and women with more power than good judgment were capable of. Or*—the smile changed slightly—*I could stay.*

More emotions played across the dragon's face, in that moment, bright in the warmer light of the morning. True sadness, but mixed just as subtly with real joy. Pain and happiness in equal measure.

It was not a hard decision to make, Declan. I'd learned much, in Herst and Elysia's company, in the company of man as a whole. Yours is a people capable of great cruelty, but also of great kindness and affection. Before me, my kind bore little knowledge of the familial ties your race prides itself on, ties you have arguably built your empire up with. We knew enough to be equal parts curious and skeptical, inclined as we were in our own ways, but between the Accord's negotiations and the war, I had spent years with the al'Dyors, watching Bonner and Arathia grow closer, seeing soldiers weep over lost friends and lovers. I discovered myself capable of similar ties, similar feelings. Herst and Elysia were more than friends to me, more than comrades in arms. Their companionship became my most cherished possession, in many ways. Yes, I could have sought something else, somewhere else. But why? What greater purpose would I have found there than the one before me? The smile brightened, just a little. *In the end, your family had become mine, Declan.*

Declan stared at Ryn, taking in his words. He saw the dragon in a different light, then, one that was—if anything—more old than new. A space had grown between them in the last weeks, he realized suddenly. Not an impassable one, but a separation all the same. The knowledge and understandings imparted on him—not the least of which being Ryn's true nature—had been as roots pressing up to steadily crack apart a stone which would have ordinarily been without flaw.

For once it was Declan's own memories that made themselves known, that came to him one after another. Playing with Ryn as a boy. Working together to help his mother as he grew older. Training. Hunting with the creature in the dragon's wolf's form. Later, leaving home behind and struggling their way to the capital, where time had started passing faster and bloodier. For more than twenty years they had been on an adventure together. Twenty years, of which only not even the last month had been spent with this gap growing silently between them.

Family. The word struck Declan hard.

He matched his friend's smile, and at once a tension he hadn't noticed left Ryn's shoulders in a wave of acute relief. Across from them both, Bonner clapped his hands in almost boyish exuberance at the sight before casting a wary eye at his daughter.

"Are you satisfied now? Have we explained everything to your expectation?"

Ester shrugged. "That's hardly for me to decide, I think." She looked pointedly to Declan, but said nothing more, her hand still not having left his arm.

Declan, noting the opportunity, struggled for several seconds to decide whether or not he was content. He certainly understood far better now the nature of their predicament, the wider trouble they might very well be in, if they had caught the Endless Queen's eye. He understood, too, the weight Ryn and Bonner carried—had been carrying for centuries now. He felt, for the first time, like he had the chance to share even a little of that burden, even some measure of that labor.

To that end, his thoughts finally settled on one important question, bringing the conversation that had swallowed up the hours of the early morning full circle. Holding up the hand that still held the firestone, he looked to Bonner yr'Essel, former magician of the court of Igoric al'Dyor, and did his best to keep his voice calm despite the building hammer in his chest as he considered the implication of what he was about to ask.

"Can you instruct me? To use this? Can you show me how?"

For only a moment did the old mage look taken aback, blinking once, then twice.

Then his braided beard split into a wide, excited grin.

"Boy, that's the very *least* of what I plan on teaching you…"

CHAPTER TWENTY-EIGHT

If it had been up to Declan, he would have begged Bonner then and there to teach him everything he was willing to, starting at that very moment. It wasn't possible, of course. Declan saw now that they were well and truly on the run, and there was yet something about the previous night's encounter that didn't sit well with any of their number. Ester was the one to bring it up, and after a short discussion and the allowance of a few more hours rest—a poor attempt to make up for some of their collectively lost sleep—they broke camp shortly before noon in a tired, disgruntled fashion. Ryn took to his stallion's form to bear the load of their gear, and a few minutes later they were making west again, leaving behind the stream and the remnants of their little campfire in favor of retracing their steps back through the woods.

The going was quicker this time, their pace less treacherous under the light of the day. They found the ridgeline in less than an hour, and within five minutes more came across the dusty mass of broken and fallen stone that had only the evening before been the outcropping they'd fought for their lives beneath. Of the wereyn there wasn't any more hint than scattered stains of blood here and there among the rubble, and Declan couldn't help but whistle and glance at Bonner upon taking in the rockfall. The mage was studying the collapse with a critical eye, almost like a painter examining his finished work, and no one asked him about it after they pressed on.

Ryn began searching in earnest, then. He'd sporadically been extending his senses as a precaution, but after his exhaustion following the previous day's exertion, he was less inclined to push himself continuously to his limit. Now, however, he did so once more, what conversation he'd been carrying falling away as his ears lay flat and his white-gold eyes saw the world far beyond what the rest of them could make out only of the forest immediately surrounding them. Fortunately, he didn't have to maintain the magic very long. It wasn't more than ten minutes at a slower, more careful march up and down the winding hills beneath the trees that the dragon's neck went stiff and he came back to himself, swinging his long head to look north.

There, he said simply, indicating a narrow deer trail with his muzzle, and Declan and the others followed without more than a shared nod.

Even if Ryn hadn't filled them in as they walked, they would have had at least some idea of what to expect. The wereyn they'd encountered had been too well armed, too well outfitted, to have come across their steel anytime but recently and by any other fashion than violently. For this reason Declan's sword was drawn and Ester had an arrow nocked to her bow by the time they stepped out onto the sweep of the treeless hill the dragon had already described to them in detail. It would have been a pleasant scene, under any other circumstances. The grass had grown high beneath the open sun of the failing summer, and it swayed below the blue sky as the fall breeze began to make itself heard. Declan could imagine this would have been a known place to the local community, the sort of glade parents took their children for noon picnics, or where young lovers snuck out of their homes to meet beneath the evening stars.

It was with something like sadness that he took it in now.

The hill was a corpse-riddled massacre. The patrol had been a large one, twenty strong, surrounded and overwhelmed judging by the cyclical positioning of the uniformed dead. *Quickly, too,* Declan noted, eyeing the disproportionate colors of white and gold to the darker forms of the wereyn interspersed among them. There were fewer than a dozen beastmen to the Vigil's score, and curiously it was these corpses which had been fed on the most, rather than the men and women's. He even spotted the body of a warg, torn asunder with ribs ripped wide so that the clawed hands that had pulled it apart could have reached the fleshy organs within its chest.

From habit? Declan wondered to himself, thinking of the harsher conditions that graced the ranges that were the creatures' natural homelands while stepping forward to toe at the ravaged form of a fox-headed beast. *Maybe they're accustomed to feeding on their own kind.*

Thrum!

Ester's arrow sang and *thudded* into something with a shriek of pain. Declan didn't do more than glance up, seeing some sort of horned wereyn fall from where it had stood up near the edge of the hill, having clearly caught their scent. There were another ten or so of them around, he knew, the injured or dying long left behind. Ryn had even said there were a pair more of maimed warg near the far edge of the woods, on the other side of the hill. The unfortunate remains of the greater host the four of them had seen to the previous night, abandoned to whatever fate the Mother had in store for them by their kin. Declan wasn't much bothered by it. Even though the dragon kept to his horse's form, between his own blade, Ester's bow, and Bonner's spellwork, what little danger a handful of crippled enemies could pose to them was trivial compared to everything else they'd been through already. Indeed, Declan brought his eyes back down to the scene before him even as he heard the half-elf nock another arrow, returning to scanning the hill with a heavy heart.

They hadn't stood a chance, he saw. Counting the dozen dead and whatever more had likely been dragged off to be fed on, the less-than-twenty soldiers would have been facing a wave of beastmen over thrice their own number, with nothing more than their bare steel and discipline to protect them. The torches he saw lost about the carnage, black and long-extinguished, had likely only hindered them by stealing away their night vision. Declan couldn't help but feel a pang of sympathy as he imagined himself in their shoes, caught in the open beneath the moon and stars as black shapes darted out of the trees at them from every angle, howling as they charged.

"This was more coordinated than I would have expected," he said loudly over his shoulder, moving to stand over the closest of the fallen Vigil. She was a young woman, maybe a year or two shy of his own age, and her hazel eyes were wide and dim over a throat that had been torn half-open. "The wereyn aren't typically this organized. At least not in my experience."

"They have someone to follow, now." Bonner was moving to join him, navigating gingerly around the corpse of the fox-headed beastman, eyeing the Vigil girl with sympathy as he approached.

"Is it like this everywhere, you think? The messengers we were passing yesterday never looked pleased with the news they were carrying."

The old man didn't answer immediately, looking up the hill. Blood stained and streaked the blooming green of the grass, splashing where blows had landed and lining the paths along which bodies had been dragged off into the deeper woods. The flies must have been gathering since first light, their flight a ceaseless, unwavering drone, and Declan was glad for the wind blowing from their backs, carrying off the heavy stench of death they could taste in the air.

"I don't suppose we can hope for anything otherwise," Bonner finally answered with a shrug, navigating the corpses and starting to move up the hill, the orange glow of a spell gathering in one hand while he climbed. "With the sightings we were told of in Ranheln, I can't muster the courage to believe this group—" he gestured at the closest of the fallen beasts "—is anything but one of many. The Queen has the numbers for it, if the reports that officer gave us were true. Coming over the ranges and scattering makes more sense than standing and meeting the Vigil head-on in an open field."

Declan felt his gut twist at the thought, imagining the creatures running rampant across northern Viridian, likely moving south all the while. He was brought back by uneven shuffling and a croaking war cry, but Bonner's prepared weave flashed before the boar-headed wereyn—staggering under the weeping slash that had split open one side of its skull—got within ten feet of the man. A jet of fire—smaller than the one he'd used the night before—caught it full in the throat, and shortly thereafter it toppled over, allowing the charred remnants of its head to tumble free of its blackened shoulders.

"It's concerning, though," Bonner continued like nothing had happened, kneeling down beside another of the Vigil higher up the incline. "They seem to be taking great pains to preserve the bodies of their kills…"

Catching up to the mage, Declan made out the captain's insignia on the dead soldier's shoulder. His plain features were lax and marred by strains of blood that had trailed from his mouth, leaving his teeth red and drying along the collar of his black uniform and the leather thong of a necklace tucked into his shirt. "I'd noticed that, too," Declan said, studying the burned corpse of the wereyn with a pang of new jealousy. "Could they be so used to feeding on their own?"

Bonner shook his head slowly, not looking up from the body of the soldier. "I doubt it. If that were the case—and they reproduced fast enough to make such cannibalism sustainable—I don't imagine you would have ever seen them come down from their mountains before now."

"Is there any other point to doing so, then? Do they…" Declan had to pause, convincing himself to get the words out. "Do they make better ghouls, if they're less damaged?"

"Ghouls, no." The mages stood up again as he answered, still pondering. "I won't pretend to understand the nuances of necromancy, but I believe you don't need much more than bone and some minimal flesh to create their like."

"Then… the other kinds, maybe? The other… other draugr?"

Bonner frowned and said nothing, which was answer enough for Declan. After several seconds spent still studying the soldier at his feet, the mage turned to look down the hill, and there was a moment of silence before he spoke again. "There's that, at least. Ryn says he can't sense any other presence nearby."

Declan blinked, surprised at the exchange and looking between the old man and the dragon. Ryn was some fifty feet off from them, having moved with Ester around the western edge of the tree line, looking like they intended to circle the hill's base. He wanted to ask how Bonner had silently reached out, but refrained for the moment, stating the more significant fact. "He's been tricked before. Twice now, actually. Three if he's right in thinking he and I have already come across the necromancer that set those ghouls on us. Is that who you're worried about?"

Bonner grunted in concession. "Aside from the Queen herself, the necromancer would be the worst of it, but if Sehranya's found bodies suitable for liche and already has them in Viridian, we wouldn't be much better off." He knelt down by the soldier again and pressed a mottled hand over the dead man's heart, ignoring the gaping, fly-riddled hole some blade had carved through his lower ribs.

"We would have heard *that* news, wouldn't we?" Declan demanded, having to work to keep his voice strong as his earlier image of the wereyn overtaking the northern forests adjusting itself for the worst. He couldn't say he had a complete grasp of what a "liche" was, but he understood enough to imagine it meant trouble with the beastmen killing indiscriminatingly and leaving any and all bodies behind…

Below him, however, Bonner seemed to relax. "No sign of a Purpose," he said, starting to pull his hand away from the captain's still chest. "Whatever the reason is for the wereyn leaving these dead untouched, I don't think it has to do with—"

But then he froze, his fingers having paused over the center of the soldier's chest. Declan, witnessing this, tightened the grip on his blade instinctively, watching the mage's hand hover, twitching in place, then move to the dead man's neck.

"What is it?" he asked, hearing his own voice come out in a harsh whisper despite the only other sounds being the buzz of the flies and another *twang* of Ester's bow loosing from somewhere along the lapse of the hill.

In answer, Bonner hooked the leather braid about the soldier's neck with a finger, pulling the necklace up from under the shirt of his blood-soaked uniform to free it from the cloth.

Declan had only the briefest glimpse of the amulet dangling from the lowest loop of thong, but that moment was enough for him to know—even instinctively—that something was very, *very* wrong about it. It looked to have been made from a ring of bone, and Bonner didn't have to tell him the thing was of human origin. He had seen severed limbs before, both on the battlefield and on the surgeons' tables after, and the talisman had the distinct look of the white cross-section one could glimpse when an arm or leg fell to the blade. Worse, however, was the etched, carved intricacy of the thing. Rather than the smooth, sun-bleached surface one might have expected, the exterior of the bone had been hewn and engraved with meticulous care, the minuscule fissures flowing into each other in a pattern that was both familiar and utterly, horribly alien to Declan. They had the same angles and twists as some of the runes he had seen Bonner wield, but there was something off about these symbols in particular, something foul and cruel lingering in their design. He didn't know where that knowledge came from, where that assurance dwelled in his mind, but he was aware—positive of it—just the same. He bent down, wanting to peer closer.

There was a dull, thrumming tin, a sound that seemed to suck all other noise from the blood-spattered hill around them. For a lingering breath everything was quiet, the flies and the wind and the world as a whole having fallen silent.

And then, in the same instant, the amulet cracked with a flash of red light before Declan's eyes, and Bonner threw out a hand in his direction.

The force of the old man's spell hit Declan full in the chest, an invisible wave of sheer energy that carried him clear off his feet and out over the drop of the hill. He yelled as he fell, then again as he slammed back into the ground and tumbled head over heels down the bloody grass. He had just enough sense to let go of his sword to keep himself from ending up skewered as he rolled, sliding and bouncing until he came to a thumping halt near the very base of the incline.

"What in the *Mother's name* was that for?" he tried and failed to yell at the sky, his voice wheezing out in a weak grunt while his back flexed and writhed in involuntary response to the ache of having been slammed into the earth. When he could manage it, Declan rolled unsteadily onto his side and pushed himself up with a groan, intent on shouting at Bonner for a more deliberate explanation.

The demand died on his lips when he stood up to find himself face to face with a woman.

Horribly, he knew her at once. She wasn't Ester. The half-elf was out of sight, now, tagging along with Ryn around the hill. *This* woman had flat, hazel eyes, but the dimness that had claimed them in death was suddenly absent, replaced by a dark, burning gleam of hungry, wild intelligence. The savage wound that had torn open her throat rasped and bubbled as the body took in new breath, and for a heartbeat the two of them did nothing more than look at each other.

"Ah, shi—" Declan started, but didn't get the chance to finish the curse before the dead Vigil soldier lunged at him with a wet cry.

Had he not had a suspicion of what it was he was up against, Declan thought that first attack might well have been the end of him. The woman certainly didn't move like the ghouls he'd faced off with Ryn some weeks before, and the light, almost-living light in her flat eyes gleamed with something those lower undead had utterly lacked. There was cunning there, wit and thought in their own measure. The name came to him, though he hadn't recalled it earlier while speaking to Bonner on the subject. Declan threw himself into a sideways roll to dodge the heavy, deliberate swipe of the woman's arm that blew past him with such speed and force he felt the wind catch in his hair. He knew this strength, knew this creature, an echo of it resonating from a life that was not his own.

Wight.

Declan found his feet not far away, bounding up expertly, but the draugr was already whirling on him. The scabbard at her side was empty, the sword that had once been her soldier's lot having been pillaged by the wereyn who had taken her first life, but the glint of bloody white lining her outstretching hands made Declan suspect a blade was the last thing the creature needed. Sure enough, when she lunged next he was able to dart laterally behind the trunk of a wide oak along the edge of the forest, allowing the tree to take the wrenching strike that was meant for his chest.

It landed with an explosion of bark and splinters coupled with the ugly groan of wood, and a scattering of loose leaves fell down upon their paired head, shaken loose by the impact. It was only then that Declan got a good look at the woman's hands, had a moment to take in the ugly mess they had become. The flesh along the tips of her fingers had stretched and ripped, the bones beneath having elongated and sharpened under the work of whatever weave was playing the puppet-master with her corpse. They protruded from her torn skin as pointed, unsightly claws, and the parallel gouges in the trunk whose edges he could make out from behind the tree spoke enough as to their efficiency. It was clear—whatever the woman had become—that she would not be so easily handled as the ghouls.

Not that that changed what had to be done.

Declan's knife—the only weapon left to him after losing his sword—was out of its sheath and before him in a flash. He circled, keeping the oak between him and the undead women as much as possible, feeling out his footing among the grass and brush and roots while never actually taking his eyes away from the undead. She darted forward several times in the ten or so seconds they squared off, attempting to snarl in irritation and impatience at his tactics, the noise coming airy and harsh from her throat.

Declan had just made up his mind to take advantage of her next attempt when rushing footsteps from behind made him duck instinctively.

For the second time he felt the air rent above him when the blow that would have taken him in the upper back blew by just overhead. The poor tree that had been his sure barrier accepted a second series of long scores as the second wight stumbled by with a shriek, unprepared for its momentum to have carried passed him. A man, Declan saw when the thing righted itself and spun around, another of the Vigil's number. This one had a face half-crushed by what might have been a hoof or a mace, but his one good eye gleamed dull green with the same dangerous hunger as the woman's. Without exchanging so much as a glance the two draugr moved together, he coming at Declan straight on at a run, she moving quickly right around the tree to prevent him from ringing them around once more. Declan dodged yet again, left this time to keep the man between him and the woman, drawing the knife in a lingering arc under the lunging creature's belly as he moved. Unsurprisingly the thing didn't make a sound of protest when the blade dug into his flesh, but he did stagger back and away, clutching at his torso. The creature seemed to feel no pain, but when his clawed fingers came away stained with black blood, congealed from the long hours of death, the wight screeched in fury.

Faster and stronger, but more dependent on their bodies, Declan deduced, mind registering the details automatically from the depths of battlefog. He grinned grimly. *Something I can use, at least.*

And then he lanced forward himself, looking to take advantage of what little change the recoiling draugr had given him.

The undead man retreated yet again at the sudden assault, but it wasn't him that Declan went after. The female wight, her view having been temporarily obstructed by the maneuvering, rasped out what might almost have been a gasp of surprise when he came at her. She struck out with unnatural reflexes, but Declan anticipated the blow, sidestepping her claws before darting forward and driving eight inches of tempered steel between the ribs of her chest. He let out a hiss of triumph, waiting for the heat and the flash of black flames he knew would come.

Nothing happened.

For the space of an instant, time stopped. The wight's hazel eyes, like his, dropped to the knife, then together they lifted to meet each other's gaze. As he watched, the woman's mouth broke into a gleefully wicked smile, like she knew exactly what he had been planning, and found his attempt nothing short of comical.

Then she struck, and Declan was too close to do anything more than release the handle of his knife and attempt a desperate hurtle away.

He managed hardly more than saving his own life.

The claws caught in the folds of his tunic, then dug down deeper, ripping into the left side of his chest to tear through skin and muscle. He felt bone scrape against bone, and screamed while he stumbled away, taking his own turn to clutch at his body, right hand coming away wet and bloody. His left arm was numb under the shock of the wound, falling limp at his side. The pain of the blow made his eyes water, and he blinked desperately to clear his vision with little avail. The twin forms of the undead were blurry, indistinct against the agonized tears, and he thought he heard one or both of them laugh with cold, rasping enthusiasm as he made out their steady, confident approach. He saw the hands reaching for him, saw the outline of his knife still stuck firm in the chest of the woman.

Duck.

Declan didn't have to be told twice. He fell to his knees just in time to hear the shriek of a massive, keening blade scream through the air. There was the *shlunk* of metal catching into flesh, and his sight cleared enough to see, the woman's corpse topple—lifeless once again—with her head striking the ground almost two full seconds later. The fires came, this time, the bloom of black flames erupting from the bloody stumps of her split, ruined neck. The wail chased the inferno, the unearthly, eerie howl like some tormented soul being dragged forcefully back to its place of torture.

Then a dark shape obscured Declan's view, and he looked up to see Ryn's back to him, the massive claymore held in one hand, golden eyes trained on the last of the two wights.

Sorry, the dragon said, anger seething in his voice. *We should have told you it's no good trying to kill these things the same way you would a ghoul.*

Declan attempted a laugh, but the act only earned him a throbbing twinge into his shoulder and down his arm. "I... figured that out... myself... thanks." He heaved himself back up to stand behind his companion. Still grimacing away the pain, he joined Ryn in watching the male, who had retreated several yards away and was keening and snarling in fear and fury while his one eye darted between them and the charred mark of soot and burned grass that had been its companion. "Their Purpose is in the head, I gather?"

Ryn nodded. *The brain, to be precise. It's why they can typically only be fabricated from fresh corpses, or well-preserved ones. The weave actually takes over their bodies. It can even manipulate it, to some extent. Seems you're aware of that already too, though.* He braved a glance back at Declan's injury pointedly. *What happened? Ester and I were just about to engage with the last of the wereyn and warg when the corpses all came alive. There was* nothing *near us. I'm sure I would have sensed at least something if the necromancer had been watching, much less a liche. Even hidden as it was I had an idea that the drey was there, when it followed me to the yr'Essel's home.*

"It... wasn't a spell," Declan answered through clenched teeth, seeing the wight begin to gather itself, clawed fingers flexing and twitching. "At least nothing like... like what I've seen yet. There was some kind of... some kind of amulet? Bonner found it on the body of what.... might have been the patrol's captain."

Ryn stiffened, shifting his attention back to the draugr when the creature began to creep forward, low and with hands raised before it threateningly. *What was it made of? Wood? Metal?*

Declan winced, the gashes throbbing with his heartbeat. He suspected the dragon already knew the answer, but he gave it all the same. "Bone."

Ryn gave a rare curse in his own language, the sound rolling audibly out like a wave through his bared fangs. *No wonder I couldn't sense it...*

Then he lunged, the massive blade shrieking in a blinding arc, almost too fast to see.

The wight had not been without caution. The moment Ryn moved it dashed sideways, slipping just out of range, then made a leap at the dragon's exposed side. Not even hesitating, Ryn used the impetus of his failed swing to turn the move into a spinning kick, clawed foot coming to slam into the undead's chest with such force that Declan was sure he heard ribs snap. The creature gnashed its teeth and spat as it barely kept its footing, but had to duck when Ryn closed the gap between them in a blur, the claymore coming up diagonally this time. The wight escaped once more, but not whole, losing most of its left arm to the steel despite the speed with which it threw itself sideways. Not even noticing the abruptly missing limb it attempted once again to take advantage of the dragon's open flank. Ryn twisted a second time, but the creature had grown smart to the tactic, and sidestepped the kick it expected to follow up.

Unfortunately for the wight, it was obvious, in the light of the clear day, that Ryn had indeed learned his art from the best.

CRUNCH!

Instead of a leg, it was the dragon's fist that rocketed forward, catching the dead man with all the force of a swung mace. Scaled knuckles connected with ruined nose and forehead and, with the wet, violent sound of a collapsing skull, caved in the creature's face like it had been smashed between rock and wall. The wight's head snapped back, flinging trailing tendrils of gore, and even as it fell backwards the flame rose from the ugly ruin that had been its already-damaged features, pouring down its neck, chest, and limbs. The scream echoed once again, though the body did not flail as it burned, and then a second outline of blackened ash was all that remained to blink at.

A bone charm, Ryn growled like they'd never paused their conversation, flicking his bloody hand to clear it of the brain-matter and bits of skin that had clung to his scales. *Sehranya's own brand of black magic. This wasn't only the necromancer's doing, Declan. The Queen herself has played a hand here.*

CHAPTER TWENTY-NINE

Ester, it transpired, had bolted to help her father at Ryn's command the moment the wights had made themselves known. It wasn't hard to find the two of them after Declan had retrieved his knife and followed the dragon back to the base of the hill, doing his best to stem the blood seeping from his wounds.

Getting to them, on the other hand, was a different matter entirely.

The yr'Essels were just beyond the crest of the incline, spared from the lashing claws of the nine or ten creatures that still surrounded them only by a veritable cage of narrow, pointed tendrils. Declan recognized them at once as smaller versions of the roots Bonner had summoned to harass the drey. When he and Ryn came up on them, the mage looked to be focusing on keeping up the living barrier, on his knees with his hands sunk into the ground as they had been for the greater spell in the fields about his home. Ester, meanwhile, had slung her bow over her shoulder in favor of the more practical length of her onyx-pommeled saber. She'd clearly been instructed on the creatures' disposal, because she was thrusting the blade with masterful accuracy through the entwined roots where she could, catching the wights through the eyes or up under their chins. Her opportunities were few, however, given that the undead each had one or both arms shoved into the enclosed space, slashing and lashing at the father and daughter pair. A torn shirt and a pair of narrow cuts across her cheek spoke to the fact that the half-elf's attacks hadn't been without risk. For once even Bonner behind her wasn't completely untouched, blood dribbling along his nose and jaw from a wide gash across his wrinkled forehead.

Declan didn't argue when Ryn ordered him to stay put, well out of range. He'd put on a brave face climbing the hill, but the female wight had caught him a good blow, and he was having a hard-enough time between staunching the injury and not passing out from the pain *without* trying to fight off more of the beasts given nothing more than his knife and one good hand. Instead he watched Ryn rush the draugr on his own, the six-foot blade of the dragon's sword slashing indiscriminately to sever limbs, split skulls, and even sunder two of the wights clear in half at the waist. Those that were able to scattered at once, and at a signaling roar from the dragon Bonner let part of the barrier fall away, staggering to his feet. Distantly Declan registered the mage telling Ester to see to him, and only when he heard the woman hurrying in his direction did he realize his eyes had started to drift closed.

"Oh no." Ester's voice was a frightened groan when she caught sight of the bloody mess that was his left side. Without asking she looped her arm under his waist, letting him keep a good pressure on the injury while still accepting his weight. "Come on. Father will need to see to that."

"Wait…" Declan muttered, surprised at how tired his own voice sounded while he did his best to scour the ground from beneath heavy eyes. "My sword… My sword is around here somewhere…"

"And it'll still there be when your lungs *aren't* threatening to fall out of your chest. I can see bone, Declan. Come *on*."

Mollified, Declan allowed himself to be led up the hill. The roaring sound of more flames shook him into greater wakefulness, and he lifted his head to see Bonner wielding another jet of boiling white fire, dealing with two charging wights at once while Ryn took on another three not far ahead of him. Between the pair of them the other undead fell one after the other, but put up a good fight all the same. Declan hissed when he saw the dragon take a ripping blow to his lower back, and Bonner shouted once when a flailing claw caught an extended hand as he released a spell. They kept up their assault, though, hard-pressed as they were. After a minute, then two of the pair being pushed nearly to the point of being back-to-back, the last of the wights convulsed when Ryn's falling blade cleaved its head in two. The black fires split around the sides of the sword like the flames themselves were being cut in half.

Even then, the fight wasn't quite over.

"RIGHT!" Ester howled, and Ryn reacted just in time, whirling and lunging around Bonner. Declan watched the dragon catch the coming blade of one of a handful of injured wereyn that had been waiting on the heels of the undead. The beast howled in wolfish fashion when its blow was deflected, the sound cut short by Ryn's raking claws snapping out to make shredded meat of its throat. Another followed it, then a third, and as those who engaged the dragon fell, two bloody forms came bounding up the slope, aiming for Bonner. Declan tried to shout, but found he had neither energy nor breath for it. The warg were fast despite the slashing wounds that had cut up their sides and haunches, lithe bodies—the size of small horses—those of grey-white wolves, heavy heads the width and breadth of an average man's chest. Black eyes gleamed over those bared, yellowed, fangs that chomped and gnashed at the primitive iron bits between their wide jaws, reins held firm in the clawed hands of their matching, bear-headed riders.

It was Ester who managed to croak out the warning, but Bonner was already in motion, casting both hands out before him in a similar fashion to the spell that had sent Declan flying from the hill to the relative safety of the forest edge. Sure enough, the grass between the mage and the warg fluttered and flattened with a *whoom* of compressing air, and they were practically in midstride when the force of the weave caught them head-on.

For a half-second they froze, their momentum cut violently short, mounts and masters yowling in equal surprise.

Then the animals were catapulted back down the hill, wereyn still on their backs, hitting the ground in a muddled tangle of larger and smaller bodies crunching against the earth, skidding and tumbling until they came to rest halfway down the incline. The two warg whimpered and yelped in pain, struggling and failing to stand.

The wereyn, less fortunate, lay broken and still, crushed beneath the weight of the much larger creatures.

Ryn, meanwhile, was being truly pressed for once. He'd carved his way through the duo of wereyn who'd assaulted him, but now what looked like the last three had somehow managed to surround him, the trio having grown weary enough of his slashing claws and massive blade to not attack indiscriminately. They were hovering, waiting for the right moment. Ryn was spinning, the claymore in one hand threatening one of their number, his snapping teeth and outstretched hand keeping at bay the other two. Despite the effort, he couldn't quite engage any single or pair of them without leaving his already-injured back vulnerable.

With a *thump*, Ester planted her saber into the earth. Before his sluggish mind could contemplate what the half-elf was doing, Declan felt his knife tugged free from its sheath at his side.

Then it was ripping from her hand, steady as a thrown spear, to *thud* into the space between shoulder and spine of the closest of Ryn's opponents.

The dragon reacted to the thing's scream like he'd been waiting for the signal. Spinning away from the newly-maimed beast, he leapt with a roar at the other two, taking them on simultaneously as they met him. Ducking the club of another fox-headed beastman, he slammed its clawed feet out from under it with a low blow of his tail even as he carved its doe-headed partner's abdomen largely in two. Letting the latter fall, Ryn leapt clear of a second desperate blow from the former's blunt weapon, aimed at his knees. He landed with one foot on the wereyn's chest, pinning it down so the claymore could flash in a careful arc.

The fox head tumbled down the far side of the hill alone, cleaved free of its more human body.

The other two were already dead, or nearly so, Ester's throw having clearly taken the first through the heart. The second, meanwhile, was twitching out its final moments on the ground, narrow, feminine hands shaking miserably in the gore of its own insides while the creature's voice grew steadily quieter with each pitiful mewl of fear and pain. Not bothering to clean his blade just yet, Ryn looked about for other survivors, catching sight of the twin bodies of the warg Bonner had sent flying. The two had given up their attempts at rising in favor of struggling to pant in labored breaths under what might have been crushed ribs to compliment the older lacerations of the Vigil's blades.

To everyone's surprise, the mage brought him up short. "Wait, Ryndean! Leave them be!"

The dragon paused, quitting his thunderous approach on the two, but turned to give the old man a dubious look.

"They might be useful to us," Bonner answered his unasked question. "Leave them, for the moment. They aren't a threat anymore, and there are more pressing matters to attend to."

As he said this, Declan realized the man was moving swiftly towards him and Ester. Blinking away the ever-mounting fatigue of lost blood, the mage's face came into slow focus, and he got a good look at the wound that had split Bonner's forehead. An ugly gash that could only have been the work of a wight's claw, probably the captain's corpse they had been so closely examining together. His left hand, too, looked a mangled mess from where it had caught a stray blow.

Then Declan chuckled, spotting the scabs that were already taking over both injuries, torn and cut flesh knitting itself whole before his very eyes.

The next moment, unfortunately, he was hissing in pain while the yr'Essels worked together to ease him down to the grass.

"Is he going to be all right?"

Ester's voice, dim in the cloud of new ache.

There was a silence, Declan feeling confident fingers prodding about his injured side uncomfortably, then Bonner's relieved answer. "Yes. The damage is physical. Nothing like the mess the drey's blood made of him. Give me some room."

Can we help?

Ryn's voice, now, echoing more clearly than the others from the depths of Declan's mind.

"Water," came the mage's quick answer. "Get the skins from wherever you dropped our things. If we can get enough fluids into him, I can replenish his lost blood all the more easily."

There was the shuffling of retreating feet, coupled with a pleasant, blooming warmth that poured into Declan's burning chest and shoulder like mulled wine down a parched throat. He groaned again, but this time in relief, allowing himself to be lost in the pleasant numbness of what he knew was Bonner's healing weave. For a time there was nothing more to think about than the flow of the magic and the ceaseless drone of the flies, returning once again now that the fighting had come to a close.

Then he heard Ryn's heavy returning footsteps, and soon after the edge of one of their skins was pressed to his lips, paired with Ester's soft encouragement to drink.

He did so gladly, feeling the woman's careful fingers in his hair to help him tip his head back and guzzle down the lukewarm water.

It was like coming out of a heavy sleep. With every swallow Declan felt his awareness return to him a little more, his hearing and vision growing clearer and clearer, and before he knew it he had drained the bag, which should have lasted an ordinary man a full day and then some. As the last droplets slipped down his throat, Declan felt the magics pull away from his side, and he blinked yet again to clear the last lingering vestiges of dreariness.

Ester, Bonner, and Ryn were all watching him intently, the yr'Essels' faces closest to him from where they knelt on either side of him, the dragon's from between them as he bent standing above.

Swallowing the confusion that followed such a rapid return to what appeared excellent health, Declan felt at the left side of his chest, where the wight's claws had ripped into him. He found himself fingering the ruined tatters of his shirt, but beneath the shredded cloth was nothing but firm, whole skin covering knotted muscle.

"Mother's *fucking* mercy, old man," Declan wheezed in shock at Bonner, looking at him with wide eyes. "*That's* a trick I'd have you teach me too, if you would."

Bonner snorted, standing up and brushing non-existent dust from the knees of his robes. "Auramancy. We can try, but I doubt healing spells will be your forte, given the circumstances of your affinity. We're better off starting smaller anyway. *Much* smaller. He frowned down at Declan, eyeing him carefully. "Feeling better, then?"

"Feeling fine," Declan said with half-a-laugh, still astounded and looking down at himself. He was pleased they'd thought to purchase spare clothes in Ranheln, because on top of being shredded, his new shirt was stained almost-black with more blood than he had realized he'd been losing. "Absolutely fine."

On his other side, Ester closed her eyes and exhaled in relief, sitting back and covering her heart with a hand like she meant to steady it. Clearly he'd given her a fright.

When she'd gotten ahold of herself, she turned to her father. "What happened?" she demanded. "Ryn and I were making for the wereyn when the Vigil rose. And those *weren't* ghouls, were they?"

Bonner grimaced. "No. Wights, and as well made as any I've ever seen. This wasn't liche's work, at the very least. As for what happened…" He glanced at the dragon, who nodded.

A bone charm, Ryn said darkly, crossing his arms. His claymore he still held, sheathed now in one hand. *Declan told me. So it's true?*

"Unfortunately. This isn't good, Ryndean. Sehranya's reading our moves, or at very least her necromancer is. They knew we'd want to find out where the wereyn got their steel from."

Ryn nodded, but Declan cut in. "Wait. Explain, before you send me back down the hole I just started to climb out of. What's a 'bone charm'?" He thought he'd heard them mentioned before, but with everything else he'd had to intake since the previous evening…

"Black magic," Bonner told him at once, and Declan was relieved there would apparently be no more hesitation when it came to giving him the truth. "*Old* magic. Sehranya's own, and hers alone. There were some fools that tried to imitate the spellwork after the war, before *and* after Elysia banned the practice of magic, but with little success."

It's a binding weave, Ryn picked up. *Similar to the enhancement magics we saw used on the drey, but much more intricate, and much more dangerous. The charms were Sehranya's more subtle means of extending her power beyond her own body, how she often managed to turn great numbers at once without actually being present on the field of battle.* He met Declan's eye steadily. *Do you recall how we described her first assault on the Vigil? The way she raised the dead they'd been keeping preserved in the bluffs all at once?*

Declan nodded, hardly thinking he would ever forget the image that terrifying retelling had cursed him with.

Bone charms. Ryn said simply. *That blow and many others throughout the war she raged against her own people, then us. Done with bone charms.*

Declan would have liked to scream in frustration at this particular piece of news, if he'd thought it appropriate. It had been bad enough a *necromancer* had been dogging them—likely since he and Ryn had set foot upon what could only have been the drey's feeding ground—but if the Queen now involved *herself*…

"Does this change anything?" Ester asked aloud, standing up on Declan's right and offering him a hand. He took it even as she continued. "With our plans, I mean? Aletha is still the safest place in Viridian, even if Sehranya herself has her eye on us…"

Not for the first time, Bonner and Ryn exchanged a glance.

Are we still being scryed, do you think?

"Undoubtedly." Bonner's grunt was annoyed, and he frowned up at the sky. The cut over his eye was almost completely healed, now, leaving a wet sheet of fresh blood to stain the left side of his face with no apparent source. "It's the only explanation."

Can you detect it? Can you shield us from it?

"Not on the move, no, and I don't think hunkering down and finding a place to hole ourselves up in is an option anymore if Sehranya is sending wights after us." The mage frowned. "We're being too predictable, if they were able to foresee something as minor as this. We'll need to adjust, and certainly stay off the High Road." He looked out over the trees they could all make out from atop the hill, the vast sprawl of Viridian's woodlands sweeping out before them, with a dent in the distance that marked the far-off fairway. "Maybe south, back into the forest? Then east again after we've lost them?"

Ryn looked dubious. *How would we know if we'd lost them before it was too late? And that's exactly what they'll expect following this attack, if anything. I wouldn't be surprised if their intent is to* deliberately *take us off the beaten path.* He pointed towards the scattered bodies of the wereyn. *The Queen's made no secret of the beastmen pressing into the country, obviously, but we haven't heard anything of the draugr. Even this place is practically in the middle of nowhere. I don't think she's intent on letting the world know just yet of her return, and if she can't take us down with the wereyn...*

"She'll try again with the wights." Declan was the one who finished for the dragon, groaning at the idea and not-altogether pleased he was able to finally follow the thread of Ryn and Bonner's conversations.

"Or worse," the mage added with a slow nod. "If one drey survived the war, there are likely more. And that's only if Sehranya hasn't found a means by which to start fabricating them anew. Not to mention we've yet to see so much as a *hint* of the liche..."

"I see this is going to be a 'glass-half-full' sort of day," Ester said sardonically. "What are we going to do, then? Continue along the High Road and hope we've out-thought one of the greatest mages the world has ever known?"

"Probably *the* greatest..." Bonner added under his breath unhelpfully.

Still, no one else spoke, the four of them looking at each other without so much as an idea to share.

That is until Declan voiced the question he thought might have been teasing the tip of everyone suspicions.

"Is Aletha really our best option, then?"

Ester, Bonner, and Ryn all turned to look at him, and Declan winced under the combined intensity of their gaze.

"What do you mean?" the half-elf asked, her face set in something between confusion and bemusement. "Mathaleus is in Aletha. I thought we agreed he needed to be told what was happening."

Mathaleus is hardly without his own fonts of information, even in regards to the Endless Queen, Ryn offered, not for the first time. *There's a fair chance he's already aware of much of what we might tell him, and just hasn't spread it to the populace in order to avoid a panic. And Declan makes a good point: if it's likely we aren't going to live to see the capital, it may not be in our best interest to make for it. At least not directly…*

"But then where else would we go?" Ester asked with a touch of incredulity. "You two—" she gestured between the dragon and her father, who was now tending to Ryn's own injuries "—seem to be in agreement that we can't 'wait this out.' Is there some other human city I'm not aware of that would have even a fraction of Aletha's defensive value? One that could hold out if Sehranya comes after us in force?"

Ryn winced as Bonner's fingers prodded what must have been some nasty slashes along his low back. *No,* he said truthfully, his face slackening in relief when the mage began to mutter under his breath, and Declan knew the dragon was experiencing the same wash of magic he himself had earlier. *Ebadon might have held a candle to Aletha five-hundred years ago, but it's hardly more than a figurehead for the Viridian's western border anymore.*

"Kanrys and Edford are well-defended," Declan brought up tentatively, looking between the group. "South of us, along the Vyr'en. They're the only other walled cities in the country, and the al'Dyors have always kept them well-manned in case the elves… the elves push out of…" He stopped, his new awareness of the complexities of the world he'd grown up in suddenly catching up to his words. "Hang on." He looked at Ryn. "*Why* do we have a defensive line along the Vyr'en's frontier, if the elves are as bound by the Accord of Four as the al'Dyors are?"

"Perception, boy," Bonner answered from behind the dragon, still working on Ryn's back. "You think our esteemed royalty was going to let the people know of the Accord after it was so easily taken advantage of by the noble houses? No. If anything, Elysia squashed *that* knowledge even more thoroughly than she squashed the teaching of the arcane arts. And if the commonfolk were to think the southern borders of their nation were completely open to assault…"

Despite the only partial explanation, Declan followed. All-in-all there were four cities built within a dozen miles of the Vyr'en, with staggered outposts between them to cover the two-thousand miles of forest border. Kanrys, Edford, Sethylles, and Dover, the latter two having been raised along the coast of Borel's Sea to double as trading ports with each other and Vasteel, nine-hundred miles to the north. With how deep the distaste for elves could run in Viridian, Declan had no trouble imagining what sort of civil disaster might have budded if the line hadn't existed and the Vyr'en had been left—in the people's eyes—unchecked by their monarchs.

"It's the same for Ebadon, then?" he asked of Ryn. The mountain fortress *was* a figurehead, he knew, but he suspected now it may have stood for much more once, at least in the minds of the commoners.

The dragon nodded, breathing easier as Bonner finally came out from behind him. *It is. Or would have been, when the city was built in the decades after the war. One of Elysia's sons had it constructed, to convince the masses that the Reaches had been 'tamed'.*

Declan grit his teeth at the idea, realizing he was starting to feel some empathy for what he imagined was Ryn's own fury anytime the twisted history of his race was brought up and expounded upon.

"Does that help us?" Ester asked pointedly, dragging the conversation back. "Are Kanrys or Edford an option?"

Ryn grimaced, considering, then shook his head. *I don't see an advantage to it. We'd have to cut south, far south, giving Sehranya at least the initial opportunity she would need to try again for our lives. We might make it if she assumes we were then going to make east again, but what value would we have there? We could send a bird to the capital, but we could have done that from Ranheln, and it would have been met with equal suspicion and disbelief. I doubt such a missive would so much as make it to the steward, much less the King. We'd likely just be trapping ourselves like rats and...*

He paused, suddenly thoughtful, turning slowly to Bonner. The old man was wiping bloody fingers off on his robes, the stains he left behind vanishing into the patterns of the strange fabric almost as soon as they appeared.

What about the Vyr'en itself? Would the Matriarch have us, do you think? If we could make it?

The question had Declan's stomach jumping into his throat, and he was outright relieved to see Bonner's doubtful answering expression. He'd been told his entire adult life of—had seen with his own eyes—the contempt the *er'enthyl* held for mankind. He was about as keen on willingly stepping within the sacred boundaries of the wood elves' forest as he would have been facing off another hundred wights.

"I can't imagine so, no..." Bonner was saying, obviously pondering the words while he stared at the ground. After a few seconds his green eyes lifted to Ryn's. "Even Ester and I weren't allowed to accompany Arathia when she was called back. *You* might be welcome—I don't think the *er'enthyl* have any reason to resent the dragons—but I would be surprised if we—" he indicated himself and his daughter "—weren't thrown into chains and Declan wasn't killed outright the moment we crossed into their lands, even with the signet."

Ryn looked disgruntled, but unsurprised. *Of course. I suppose I should have assumed as much, but you'd think after seven-hundred years even the* ehn'Vyr'en *could get over a grudge.*

"If any descendants remained of Sevus Kant's, or Tyrel al'Behn's or Thana Vostyk's, would you so easily manage to set aside your resentment?"

Ryn bristled, then relaxed. *No. I suppose not.* He snorted, looking around at the corpse-strewn field like he was searching for something. *Then we keep making for Aletha? Perhaps swing north instead of south? It would add days, maybe weeks to the journey, but it might throw Sehranya's ilk off our scent…*

He looked at Declan and Ester, as though seeking their input, which Declan found both alarming and encouraging.

"Elghen is almost due north of here," he offered quickly, pleased to be able to provide any information that might be of use. "It's a small valley town, and it will be more winter than fall in the foothills, so we'd have to suffer a few days of the cold, but we can resupply there and buy warmer clothes. It would make the journey much easier, at the very l—"

"You're forgetting something, the both of you," Ester cut in sternly, eyeing them both with a raised eye. "Even if we lose the necromancer *and* Sehranya's own eye—assuming that's already upon us—there are who-knows-how-many wereyn coming off the Tears, and a horde numbering in the *tens of thousands* holed up in Sevyll, which we would be marching straight towards if we followed such a route." Her already pale features had lost what little color they had. "The Queen may not need to track us at all, if we find ourselves fighting for every mile gained towards Aletha…"

There was another silence, Declan suspecting Ryn—like him—was seeing the pitfall in their plan.

"Does she have us?" he asked eventually, quietly, considering each approach they could take towards the capital—even backtracking beyond Ranheln again—and seeing doom along every road. "Will it mean a fight any which way we go?"

"Not necessarily."

Declan, Ester, and Ryn all turned to Bonner. The old mage had put his back to them and was looking north, staring off into the distance with a thoughtful purse of his lips.

"When it comes to a fight, I think we can depend on that no matter what we do. Between the wereyn, the draugr, and the necromancer, I don't foresee whatever path we choose spending itself without incident. But as for Sehranya trapping us… I don't think that game is up just yet."

He looked over his shoulder at Ryn and Declan. "I think you both might be right. Aletha may be a foolhardy goal for us now, given what we know, but north—" he swept a hand before him, over the trees "—*could* well be the easiest direction to take."

"Heading *where*, then?" Ester demanded, definitely getting impatient at what even Declan felt was a conversation that was starting to turn in circles. "If there's no advantage to pressing south and at least having a *chance* at finding some stone walls to put between us and whatever the Queen throws our way, what's the point? I can't imagine there's much more along the slopes of the Mother's Tears than this 'Elkhen' Declan mentioned."

"Elghen," Declan corrected absently, his mind already moving ahead as he considered Bonner's words.

He had a nasty feeling he wasn't going to like where the mage was going.

"Elghen," Ester repeated with a curt nod, like he had somehow helped prove her point. "I don't know it, and I'd at least *heard* of Ranheln before we made for the city. I can't believe it could provide us more of an advantage than taking the risk and pressing south would."

"You're assuming I mean to suggest we hold firm there," her father said with a sly smile. "That's not the case. Even if Elghen *was* some grand, walled fortress Declan and Ryndean had both somehow forgotten to mention."

This had Ester take pause, the half-elf looking at her father in clear confusion. She hadn't yet followed the mage's thinking, an idea that Declan was himself only just starting to form, and dreaded putting into words.

Fortunately, Ryn beat him to it.

Bonner. The dragon's voice was a hiss of astonishment and doubt, like the concept he had just pieced together was simultaneously ingenious and deranged. *Are you... You're saying you want us to... to keep going?*

Finally, Ester caught on. Declan saw the understanding dawn even as the woman's father nodded with a calm confidence that would have fit well in the countenance of a madman who believed whole-heartedly in the verity of his own delusions.

"You suggested the Vyr'en because we can only assume the wood elves have as little love for Sehranya as mankind and the dragons do, neither of which is in a position to help us right now. There is another people, though, that we have yet to consider. One that despises the Endless Queen with every fiber of their blood and being."

He lifted his left hand—absent of any hint of the earlier wound that had split it, save for a little dried blood—to point north and slightly upward, like he was indicating something overtop the unseen peaks of the Tears, invisible to them in the hundred-and-some miles between themselves and the far-off mountains.

"If our ultimate goal is to see Sehranya cast back to whatever black hell she's somehow crawled out of, the *er'endehn* would have us without question. If anything, we should have thought of it before. To see to the final end of the Queen, I can only believe the dark elves would vie one and all to lend us their blades..."

CHAPTER THIRTY

The fact that no qualifying argument immediately came to mind following the mage's words was as alarming to Declan as the idea itself. There were the wereyn that undoubtedly lurked in the woods between themselves and the Tears, but Bonner was right in that respect as well: a fight was unavoidable no matter what path they chose. There were the mountains themselves, of course—commonly considered insurmountable and unconquered for hundreds of years—but somehow the potential dangers of the snow-swept crags seemed utterly mundane after the attacks they survived from ghouls, drey, wereyn, and now wights. That, and between Ryn's innate magic and Bonner's power, they would have a healthy advantage no traveler in the last seven centuries had certainly enjoyed.

A thought *did* occur to Declan, then, and his eyes fell from the distant horizon to the wheezing forms of the two warg the old man had seen spared.

Clever, he thought to himself with a smirk, suddenly suspecting the abruptness of Bonner's idea might just have been masking a well thought-out—and thoroughly considered—plan of action.

"The dark elves?" Ester asked in what was almost a moan, obviously not believing her own ears. "Father, you can't be…" She paused, gaping at the mage for a moment longer. "You *are*, aren't you? You *are* serious? Gods above…"

"Can you give a suggestion to the contrary?" Bonner asked her, though Declan felt the question was really meant to address the group as a whole. "South sees us likely fall prey to the necromancer, back west is only delaying the same, and any variation of east very likely means a slow and plodding fight for every day gained through the wereyn, who are likely to overrun us the moment they are told of our presence and ordered to converge." He indicated the distant horizon he was facing with a tilt of his head. "North seems our only option, in many ways."

No one argued this. No one had any *way* of arguing this. Still, just the same, Declan felt justified in staring at the back of the old man's bald head in open astonishment given that he knew Ester and even Ryn were doing the same within an arm's length.

You think they would take us in? the dragon finally got out. *That easily? You think they would join us?*

Bonner seemed, then, to deflate ever so slightly before their eyes, shoulders sagging under the pressure of the question.

"Truthfully… I can't say. I can hope as much, but I know no more of the *er'endehn* than you do, Ryndean. They may well take what information we have and imprison us in the same manner as their counterparts to the south would, and that's only *if* they believed us."

They would believe us.

It was Bonner's turn to look surprised, and he turned to look at the dragon with raised eyebrows. "They would? You're sure?"

Ryn hesitated. When he spoke, he sounded as uncertain as his expression. *Arrackes should be with them, if he's still alive.*

Bonner's eyes widened, his mouth forming into a quiet "oh" of comprehension.

"Who is Arrackes?" Ester asked, narrowing her eyes and looking between Ryn and her father.

A dragon, Ryn answered, not looking away from Bonner, but reinforcing Declan's relief that there would be no more secrets between them now. *Older than I by a thousand years, but one of a few who were still willing to follow my commands after the war ended.*

"You mentioned that," Declan interrupted, but paused, looking at Bonner. "Or was it you? Didn't you say there were others?"

"And that Ryndean was electing to live in isolation, away from his kind," the mage continued with a disgruntled shrug. Then his face softened. "I did, and it's true, but not without cause. There was a choice to make, after Elysia took down Sehranya—or thought she did. There *were* a handful of those dragons that remained who would have followed Ryndean, who would have bowed to him as a primordial and seen him redeem his place among their race with time. He could have stayed in the Reaches with them, could have seen to consolidating his own power and raising his kind back to prominence. Instead…"

Instead, Ryn picked up, looking somewhat pained, *I had those who would have followed me scatter themselves across the realms. As I've said, Declan, the Accord still holds, and I never quite believed Sehranya was gone for good. Not without a body to prove it. Then again, even if I'd had the proof, who knew when a threat like her would rear its head again? Elysia tempered the dangers of magic with her prohibition, but she also castrated your kind in doing so. The armies of man are still formidable in their vastness, but without its mages the Vigil is a shadow of what it once was. I had to consider what would happen if someone like the Endless Queen took hold of the world again.* He shrugged. *So I disseminated my dragons, the handful whose faith I still held, with orders to live their lives with one eye ever open.* He looked north almost wistfully. *Arrackes is such a sentry. If he still lives, he will have spent seven hundred years in Eserysh, likely among the er'endehn. He could vouch for us, assuming his word holds any sway with their High Chancellor.*

"'If,'" Ester repeated almost under her breath, clearly unconvinced. "'Assuming'. There are a lot of uncertain factors in this plan, you two." She was watching Ryn and Bonner with a mix of fear and trepidation. "Not to mention the Tears themselves. Between the two of you the climb would certainly be easier, but if the ranges are even *half* as barren as the stories I've heard, where are we going to find food?"

"We buy it," Bonner answered like this was the obvious solution.

"With what coin?" Ester insisted, face regaining some of its color, starting to flush with irritation. "We've hardly anything left of the levers Declan took from his accounts, and an ascent like that must take *weeks*. Even if Ryn bears the brunt of the load, we'll be weighed down beyond our ability."

"Money won't be an issue," Declan said over his shoulder, already turning away from the circle and moving a little ways down the hill.

"'Won't be an issue'?!" Ester hissed after him. "How won't it be an issue if what little gold we have to rub together—*your* gold, I might add—has to earn us not only warm clothes, but also the supplies enough for a fortnight of travel with no chance of resupply? And where are you going?"

Declan didn't answer immediately, kneeling down beside the closest of the wight's bodies. It was the captain, he saw the thong about his neck absent the horrible charm that has caused them so much trouble, leather dyed black now by the congealed blood of the ruin Ryn's sword had made of the man's head at some point during the fight. Ignoring the unappealing sight with a quick prayer to the Mother and Her Graces, Declan untied the object he'd seen from the body's belt with quick fingers, standing again before tossing it back up the hill.

The coin purse landed amidst his companions' feet with an audible *thump* and the faint *clink* of metal.

"Wereyn have no use for money," he said with a friendly grin at Ester, starting to climb again. The half-elf was looking at the purse with dawning understanding. "They took the steel, but left the gold."

There was a moment of silence, then Ryn snorted.

Ester glared at him briefly, then looked at Declan, fire in her green eyes. "Fine, money won't be an issue," she repeated like she didn't like the sounds of the words. "That only solves one problem, though, and the lesser of two. Now, if you would be so kind as to explain how you plan to carry *half-a-month's* provisions without turning our resident dragon into Viridian's most overburdened *pack mule*, I'm all ears."

"Your father's already thought of that," Declan said slowly, eyeing the mage. "Haven't you, Bonner?"

The old man paused, about to answer his daughter, to blink at Declan. He broke into a broad smile, chuckling. "You're a sharp boy, Declan. I'll give you that much."

What? Ryn, for once, was among those left behind now. *What do you mean? You already have a solution?*

Declan gave a low laugh which he hoped cloaked the nervousness of his answer. "The warg. Bonner thinks we can tame the warg to our advantage."

■■

It was a distasteful chore, collecting what purses they could find from the other dead. Declan wasn't bothered by the pillaging—one took what one needed to survive, in a war—but it turned out not *all* of the wights had been as cleanly killed as they might have liked. Several—generally among those who had fallen to Ryn's claymore—were in pieces and immobile, but with heads intact. It fell to Declan and Ester to gather the coin, and therefore in the same vein to see to it that the corpses in question wouldn't rise around them, even maimed as they were.

"Ugh," Ester groaned from nearby, and Declan turned to see her withdraw her saber blade from the eye of one unfortunate woman Ryn's sword had seen cleaved entirely in half, her legs and the lower part of her torso lying some five feet up the hill. "I don't think *this* is what the storytellers have in mind when they spin their tales of adventure and grand treasure."

Declan laughed, setting his own bastard sword against the nape of a man's skull and thrusting it in and up. He'd recovered the weapon shortly before, found not far from where he'd thought he'd lost it, and was grateful for the comfort of its plain weight back in his hand. "I don't know about adventure, but the 'treasure' part seems to be holding true." He held up the trio of purses gathered in his other hand with a grin. The smile faltered, however, when he noticed blood dripping from the soaked side of one of the burlap sacks. "Don't know about 'grand', though…"

Ester snorted, bending down to relieve the woman she had been seeing to of her own pouch and tossing it into the small pile she'd started nearby. She paused, arm falling slowly back to her side, listening to the yowling and growling which had drowned out the buzz of the flies for the last several minutes.

"Do you think it's going well?" she asked over her shoulder, not looking back at Declan.

He shrugged, moving on to the next corpse. "Your father can speak to bears and basically pull a drey out of the sky with living magic. If anyone can sway a couple of beasts like those, it's him. And—" he stopped over the body of a young man, who was absent both arms and a leg "—if he *can't*, Ryn will make short work of them."

Ester nodded, but even with her back to him Declan could tell she wasn't altogether convinced.

Finally, she resumed her task, looking discontent. "He should have just turned and fired the whole damn hill from the sky," she muttered. "Then we wouldn't have been attacked and no one would have gotten injured in the first place." She eyed Declan's chest with barely-masked worry. "You're *sure* you're all right? I wasn't kidding when I said I could see bone, you know?"

Declan gave her a truer smile this time, glancing down at himself. He'd taken the time to replace his ruined shirt with a new one, a grey garment of thinly-spun cotton he was particularly fond of. "I'm fine," he said for what might have been the sixth time, admitting to himself he didn't dislike being the subject of the half-elf's concern. "And I think you know that would have been a bad idea. He was exhausted for days after the last time, and we can see the fairway from the hill. I'm not sure even *Ryn* could create an illusion broad enough to hide his true form."

Ester mumbled something under her breath with a shrug, returning to her work. Declan followed suit, and within another five minutes they'd seen to the rest of the corpses, including the two wights that had nearly torn him limb from limb just inside the line of the trees. All in all most of the Vigil soldiers had been carrying some amount of coin when the wereyn had fallen upon them, and so the two ended up with more than half-a-dozen purses each, cradled in both arms when they set off around the hill towards the sounds of the warg's angry snaps and howls.

"I hope they hurry up," Ester said as they walked, glancing into the forest behind them nervously. "I know we're not *that* close to the High Road, but if someone hears them…"

"Ryn is probably keeping a lookout for that," Declan assured her as they came around the edge of the hill.

There would have been a time, not so long ago, in which the outlandish nature of the scene which unfolded before the pair of them as they cleared the rise would have left Declan bewildered and without words, and a not insignificant part of himself missed and longed for those simpler days. Now, it was with nothing more than mild curiosity that he approached the four figures. Ryn was largely at ease, leaning back on his clawed hands where he'd seated himself in a rare patch of clean grass, the sheathed claymore lying beside him while he watched Bonner's actions unfold. The mage, for his part, was standing closer to the two warg than any sane man might have found prudent, but given that the paired beasts were lashed securely on their sides by several knotted roots the thickness of Declan's arm, he appeared to have little cause to worry. The animals themselves were yowling and squirming, but their wounds—both old and new—had been healed, and their distress now was merely a manifestation of being immobilized and approached by a strange man who couldn't have looked or smelled anything like the riders they'd likely known all their lives.

"How's it going?" Declan asked of Ryn, dropping his gathered purses to the ground with mirrored *thumps* before claiming a place for himself beside the dragon. Ester did the same, sitting on his other side, watching her father.

Ryn grunted. *As well as can be expected?* He answered like he wasn't quite sure of the statement. *I think he's been talking to them, in his own way. They settled a little after he saw to their injuries, but I can't tell if he's had much luck since.*

Declan nodded, turning his attention on Bonner and the beasts. The old man was in the process of kneeling by the head of the larger of the two—a male, Declan believed—his hand reaching out, thumb and small finger extended. At first the warg growled and snapped its massive jaws at the limb, ugly stained fangs gnashing together, but as the mage's hand came down, the animal quieted. It continued to glare at him, black beady eyes taking Bonner in with dim suspicion. If the man was remotely afraid, he didn't show it, and with deliberate steadiness he brought the knuckles of his bent fingers down to rest gently between the warg's broad ears, hushing softly. Slowly he pet the animal like that, running his hand up and down the crest of the animal's muzzle slowly. For several seconds nothing more impressive than the warg's silence held.

Then the beast eased its head down slowly, resting it against the ground, allowing itself to be stroked with the same uncertain enjoyment of a stray dog being shown kindness for the first time.

From their safe distance away, Declan, Ester, and Ryn all gaped in astonishment.

"That was amazing," Declan finally got out in a low breath, not completely believing his eyes while Bonner yr'Essel continued to pet the calmed warg with as much care as he might have a housecat.

Ryn laughed beside him nervously. *Mind over matter, I suppose.*

Declan and Ester both nodded numbly, having no other words to answer with.

"Good lad," Declan heard the mage say under his breath. "There you go. There's a good boy."

He stayed like that for almost a minute. When the old man finally pushed himself up to his knees, Declan could have sworn he heard the male whimper, like he was asking for more, but Bonner was already moving cautiously towards the second of the creatures. This one—a slightly smaller female, Declan thought—had grown somber upon witnessing the taming of her companion, but it was with more rebellion than curiosity that she watched Bonner approach her. When he was within arm's reach, the growling and writhing started up again with a desperate fervor.

"Easy, girl," Bonner could be heard to say, kneeling beside the female's head in the same way he had the male's. "You'll hurt yourself like that. Easy. Eas—*ouch!*"

Declan, Ester, and Ryn alike were on their feet in a blur, going for their weapons, but Bonner waved them off with a bleeding hand without even looking around.

"Just a nip!" he assured them over his shoulder. "Settle. You'll only make her more nervous."

Declan thought the sizable divot in the meat of the man's outer palm looked like rather more than "a nip", but after a second's hesitation he relaxed the grip on his sword. Ryn followed his example, but it took some coaxing from both of them before Ester did the same, her saber having already been pulled half out of its sheath before her father had assured them all was well. Still, they didn't sit down again, and it was with a dose more trepidation that they watched Bonner work his magic—if indeed it *was* magic. Declan couldn't be sure. There were no runes, no flashes of light as he had seen with some of the man's casting. The roots held the beasts firm—even the calmed male—but he knew enough to believe he was seeing something altogether different take place, something more subtle than the weaves the mage so aptly used to manipulate the physical world.

Again, Declan felt a pang of anticipation, recalling the promise of instruction Bonner had made him earlier that very morning.

It took a good deal longer, but eventually the female settled, though even after she'd let her head to the ground she appeared restless, eyes blinking and ears twitching with every sound and motion around her. As before, Bonner stayed by her side several minutes longer, and it was only after her tail had quit its uneasy batting that he stood up carefully again.

"Alright. I'm going to release them."

You're sure that's wise? Ryn asked as he, Declan, and Ester all took up the hilts of their swords again, at the ready.

Bonner didn't answer, a fact that didn't lend itself to the group's confidence in whatever whisperings the man had managed to put into the warg's ears.

Bonner took several steps back, Ester moving aside so that he could slip in line with them between she and Declan, then carefully lifted his injured hand—the nip already having partially knit itself together—and lowered it. Heeding his command, the roots that were the beasts' cages shuddered, then began to pull away, slipping over and off the massive, shaggy bodies like earthen snakes to slide back into the coolness of the ground. Once they realized they were free, the warg regained some of their earlier energy, thrashing and snorting until they rolled themselves onto wolfish legs and stood up.

The first sign that things might work out—or so Declan hoped—was that the beasts neither outright attacked them nor turned tail and fled into the open forest that waited for them not ten feet further down the hill. Rather, the pair trotted to each other and sniffed at one another's sides, licking the dried blood about their faces and eyeing the conspicuously absent spaces of empty fur and new scars that had been gaping lacerations not long before. Only once they appeared assured they were each indeed unharmed did the warg turn to look at Declan and the others, black gazes not completely without malice, but overcome much more greatly with what might have been curiosity and—to no one's surprise—hunger.

"Ryn, toss them the body of that wereyn behind you, will you?"

Ryn did as Bonner asked, keeping tight hold of his weapon and moving to retrieve the corpse of a goat-headed beastman and launching it one-handed in the warg's direction. It tumbled to a halt almost directly between them, and the animals snorted at it for a time, unsure.

Then the female—apparently the bolder of the pair—put a clawed paw the size of a small buckler on the thing's chest and promptly tore off its right arm with a single clamp and wrench of her jaws.

"Devouring their former master before our very eyes," Ester said sidelong to her father, voice dripping with sarcasm while they watched the animals dig into the wereyn with clear relish. "As their *new* masters, I must say I am *overcome* with confidence in this plan."

"These are animals, not monsters, Esteria," Bonner reprimanded her firmly, looking on the feasting with clear approval. "Whatever stories you might have been told, whatever tales you might have heard, they are more akin to the wolves they descend from than any beast of Sehranya's ilk. The wereyn treat them with less disdain than they do our own kind only because the warg are *useful* to them. I can assure you there is no love lost between these two and their handlers."

Declan wondered if he could argue that point, watching the pair tugging at the beastman's torso until it ripped in two with the ugly sound of tearing flesh and separating joints, but nothing came to mind. He had seen only a handful of warg in the eradication assignments the Iron Wind had given him, and the creatures had always seemed more untamed mounts handled by brute force than any sort of domesticated companion.

Then again, who would recommend trying to befriend a wolf? he couldn't help but consider while their warg ripped into their won halves with bloody relish.

Now what? Ryn asked, also watching the pair with suspicious eyes. *Do we approach them? Do we load them with our gear?*

Bonner made a sound that would have been a scoff had he not caught himself and turned it into a cough. "I've barely convinced them of the fact that they will be neither harmed nor abused if they follow us, and will both be kept well fed. You'll have to bear the brunt of the supplies for some time yet, I'm afraid."

Ryn shrugged in response. The load wasn't too great—his own sword comprising most of the weight of their traveling things already—but Declan wondered if he would have the same nonchalance once they reached the foot of the Mother's Tears.

The Tears…

Declan cursed silently. He'd forgotten—if just for a brief few minutes—the marginal *insanity* of their new intentions. Coaxing a couple of warg to their side seemed quite reasonable when compared to the idea that they would be making the most treacherous crossing known to modern man. Not to mention doing so on the slim hope that an ancient civilization of elves—*which his own race didn't even know existed*—wouldn't turn them away to the cold or lock them up in some barren dungeon beneath their great city.

We're mad. Every last damn one of us.

"In fact—" Bonner was still speaking, studying the animals thoughtfully while they finished their grisly meal "—I wouldn't recommend approaching them at all just yet. They're skittish, for the time being."

"And none of the rest of us can miraculously grow back half-a-limb," Ester added, still cynically.

Bonner sighed in exasperation, but didn't deign to answer. Instead, like a man looking for a change of subject, he turned his back on the beasts and took in the hill behind them. "We'll need to do something about these corpses," he muttered, taking in the scattered dead with pity and distaste. "Half of them are still ghoul fodder, and one never knows what else Sehranya or her lackey could do with fresh flesh." He looked to Ryn. "Can you see to it they get another body?" He tossed a thumb over his shoulder at the warg, now licking the blood from the ground. Nothing but a few larger leg bones remained of the wereyn. "I can only venture a guess at how much they eat regularly."

Ryn grunted in assent before moving towards another dead beastman not far away.

"When you're done with that, come help us!" Bonner called after Ryn's retreating form before turning his attention on Declan and Ester. "Meanwhile, you two are going to help me pile the others. We'll need a pyre."

Declan and Ester shuddered together, but nodded, at last releasing the grips of their swords to set about the grim work with less than enthusiasm.

It took them the better half of an hour—even after Ryn joined in—to finish the ugly work. Huffing and grunting they dragged and carried the corpses of the Vigil soldiers and wereyn alike to the chosen spot, far enough up the hill to avoid risking setting the forest alight, but not so high up to make the task harder than it needed to be. After the thirty or so corpses left had been piled atop one another—the men and women with a great deal more respect and care than the beastmen—they all stepped back to observe their work, grimacing as a group at the pile.

"Well... that's that," Bonner said awkwardly after a moment. Then, to everyone's surprise, he looked to Declan. "Do you still have the firestone I gave you this morning, boy?"

Declan started, staring at him like he couldn't believe his ears. "I-I..." he stammered, wrapping his head around the mage's implication. "I do. Here... somewhere..."

He scrambled at the pockets of his pants, then jacket, finding the pebble near his left breast, somehow having miraculously avoided being rent free by the wight that had very nearly separated his arm from his body. He pulled it out, but with a sinking of his heart found the stone dull and cold, utterly absent the dim warmth it had sustained for him that morning.

"Hmm," Bonner mused over the thing, peering at it analytically. "Well, I suppose we shouldn't be surprised. I know it might not seem so, but it's impressive enough you were able to keep the weave intact for as long as you did, particularly going on nothing by intuition."

"I-I didn't do any—" Declan tried to stammer out, but Bonner waved the words off.

"Yes, yes, I can't imagine it would appear that way as of yet, but you'll know the difference soon enough, I think. Here, I'll give you a hand." Taking a single finger, he tapped the stone lightly. There was an ochre flash, followed by a now-familiar spark of pain that vanished as quickly as it had come, anticipated this time. By the time Bonner pulled his hand away, the firestone glowed orange-red once again, the color dimming slightly, then blooming forth again as Declan felt the tingling sensation crawling up his skin like needles.

"I *was* planning to get you started on our evening fire, but I suppose this is as good a place to begin your instruction as any." Bonner gave a grim smile, glancing at the piled corpses. "If you would be so kind as to see to the bodies, we would all be grateful."

Declan stared at Bonner, not quite sure he had understood. The buzzing of the flies was incessant now, gathered as they were, and somewhere out of sight beyond the edge of the hill he could hear what sounded like the warg gnawing at the femurs they had saved as a last treat.

"S-sorry?" he managed to get out. "See to them... See to them how?"

"Burn them, of course," Bonner answered like this were the obvious answer. Of course, it *was* the obvious answer, but that fact made no more difference on Declan's incomprehension than if the man had suggested splitting the hill in two to let the earth swallow the dead whole. He looked at the mage with continued perplexion, feeling a mix of embarrassment and confusion burning up through his neck and into his face, until he noticed the curl of Bonner's lip behind his beard.

The old man was toying with him.

"Ass." Declan wheezed out a laugh, hoping the explosion of relief he felt wasn't made visible on his face, and Bonner chuckled.

"Sorry, I felt the mood required a little lightening. Come here."

He beckoned Declan forward, stepping close to the pyre so that the closest of the bodies, a grey-haired wereyn missing its head entirely, was within arm's reach.

Bonner didn't look at the creature, his eyes intent on Declan. "Tell me what you feel, boy. *Exactly* what you feel."

For once, he didn't have to expound on what he was talking about.

"A-a tingling," Declan said after a breath of contemplation, holding the stone up a little higher so they could both take it in. "Sort of... like needles, prickling along my arm."

"A good comparison." Bonner nodded in approval. "But you say 'along'... Can you feel the direction then? Can you feel the flow?"

The flow? Declan thought to himself, not comprehending.

Then he considered it, considered the sensation, the steady, rhythmic, passing sense. Yes... Yes, it *did* flow, he realized now. Like the faintest touch of water across his skin, a streaming with no beginning and no end, moving outward, towards the stone.

"I *can*..." he said, not believing he had missed it. It was obvious, now that Bonner had put the image in his head. The motion was there, *there*, faint, but so distinct. "What is it?"

"Magic, boy. The threads of the weave your body is maintaining unconsciously, instinctively. I imagine you felt something similar, in the cave last night?"

Declan nodded slowly, thinking back. He *had* experienced such a sensation, though it had been exponentially more intense. In the moment he hadn't noticed any flow—he'd been more preoccupied with not getting his throat torn out by the warg—but he recalled it enough to suspect the feeling must have been comparable. An outward movement of something fluid, absent and intangible, and yet unmistakably present.

"Magic..."

The word tumbled out of Declan's mouth in a whisper, unable to hold it in. He watched the glow of the stone with wide eyes, seeing it ebb and flare in minute asymmetry, each variation accompanied by just the faintest shift in the sensation he felt along his hand and arm. He understood, then, what Bonner had been talking about. His body was adjusting the weave for him, the blood in his veins—the "blood of Kings", as Ryn and the mage had continued to call it—adapting to maintain the balance of the spell without conscious thought.

Like shifting footwork in a duel, his swordsman's mind made the comparison.

"Bring the stone closer." Bonner took his scarred forearm and guided it towards the corpse until the stone was inches from the headless beastman's arm. "There. Good. Now… You can feel the flow, yes? Can you change it?"

Though his first instinct was to snort, Declan swallowed the response and said nothing, concentrating. It was like flexing a muscle he didn't know he had, or had at least never thought to use. Like bending a single joint of a single finger, rather than the whole. He felt his face twist in focus, engrossing himself in the feeling of the magic he now knew was there. He felt it more keenly, as one feels one's heartbeat only when they pause to think about it. He sensed its movement. Not a pulse, but a true, constant flow that shifted only to balance the heat of the firestone in his hand. He felt more too, felt the stone itself, and the spell within it. As the weight of the rock pressed into his palm, so too did the weave touch against his own magic. It made it easier, gave him something distinct to set his mind against, trying to flex that single joint in his mind's eye in order to—

Pop! Sizzle!

Declan yelped and nearly dropped the stone. It had blazed for only an instant, flashing white-hot and sparking a thin tongue of flame that had taken him by surprise despite the assumed goal of the exercise. He held onto it only by catching it with both hands, which in turn nearly had him miss Bonner's *whoop* of excitement.

"Oh!"

Declan started. He hadn't noticed Ester approaching them, but the half-elf now had her head bent low, between him and her father. She wasn't looking at either of them, however, nor was she looking at the stone. Instead, she was scrutinizing the body of the wereyn Bonner had clearly intended Declan to set alight.

The bare patch of curled, blackened fur over the beast's bicep made Declan's heart sink in disappointment.

Sink, that is, until Ester turned her emerald eyes on him, bright with fascinated surprise, and Ryn's voice echoed in the back of his head as the dragon's clawed hand came down on his shoulder.

Bonner wasn't wrong, it seems. You have a talent for this, to be sure.

Declan looked between his friends dubiously, not understanding. "I just singed a few hairs," he grumbled, looking down at the firestone in disappointment. "Can't imagine that'll do us much good in a fight…"

It seemed that Ryn was about to say something more, but Ester beat him to the punch. "Declan, give me the stone."

Declan frowned, hesitating. "You're sure? It's hot…"

Ester rolled her eyes. Before he could stop her, she had plucked the firestone from his palm with the same delicate speed he found so intriguing in her fighting style. Her face contorted for hardly a moment, then relaxed, and the pebble blazed orange between her fingers. As he watched, she held the stone up to the wereyn's arm, face set. After several seconds, the heat blazed, fire blossoming out to fill most of Ester's hand.

Then it was gone as quickly as it had come, vanishing in a wink that left behind several square inches of blackened, charred skin and flesh.

Declan whistled at the burn, dutifully impressed and feeling all-the-worse for the display. "That's better than I could do…"

"Yes," the half-elf said in a voice that was almost out of breath, like the effort had claimed a good deal of energy. Handing the stone back quickly, she rubbed her fingers against her hip as though to soothe them. "With twenty years of practice more than you, I would damn well hope so."

Declan started, head snapping to Bonner for confirmation.

The mage nodded somberly. "It's true. Ester has no real talent for weaving—which in no way changes the fact that I love her dearly!" he added quickly when the woman glowered at him. When she appeared appeased, walking away from them and flexing her fingers tentatively, the mage continued. "What she just showed you is the extent of decades of attempts, of daily repetition abandoned only a few years ago. Her elven blood is strong in that respect, a deterrent to the magic she might have had from my own side. But Declan," the old man met Declan's eyes with a nearly-alarming fervor, "what you've just achieved is no small feat, even for a pure-blooded human. Energy manipulation—the basis of pyromancy—was among the essential basics taught to fledgling mages in the arcane colleges of the past. It took the average student *weeks* of patience and practice under the tutelage of the greatest masters of the age to demonstrate the level of control you just did, and years after that before most of them could manipulate any amount of magic into something functional."

"But… But the bodies?" Declan asked, his perplexion not remotely alleviated. "You wanted me to burn the bodies…"

"I wanted you to *try*." Bonner grinned at him. "And try you did, boy, with magnificent results. I can't think of a man who grew up to be master of their arts who could have done what you just achieved in the same amount of time, as trivial as it seems to you. It usually takes a breadth of knowledge and awareness—not to mention the study of theory and arcane physics—to even *begin* the process of weaving anything even so simple as a basic spell of heat."

It's more of a dragonish quality. Ryn's hand squeezed reassuringly on Declan's shoulder before falling away. *We're born from the shell bonded to the ley lines, born breathing fire. It's an affinity of blood more than a gained skill.*

"So I... I don't need to practice?" Declan asked, unsure if he was following the conversation. Would his ability simply grow on its own?

Though she was still turned away from them some ten feet away, Ester gave a bark of laughter like the comment were well and truly absurd.

Bonner ignored his daughter with a frown. "Would that that could be the case," he answered with a shake of his head. "But no. Quite the opposite. To put it into words you might find more familiar: if you were the materials one could forge into a sword, Declan, what you are now is merely an ore of the finest quality. Potential. Potential a skilled smith could only dream off, but a cold lump of metal all the same. Ryndean has seen you polished and hammered in some ways, but—having witnessed Amherst al'Dyor's ability with a blade first hand—I can only hope you take it as encouragement when I say that even your *physical abilities* have far yet to come. As for magic..." the old man gave Declan a pained sort of smile, "I think it goes without saying that you and I have much, much to work on."

And then Bonner reached out with two fingers to draw a single, simple rune over the charred flesh of the wereyn. The shape traced itself into the beast's blackened skin in a smoldering line of burning red. When he was done, the mage winked at Declan, then put his palm over the rune like he was pushing it down, into the depth of the piled bodies.

There was a *whoosh* of fire, and an instant later the pyre was in flames, smokeless heat rising to shatter the quiet morning sky.

Point made, Declan thought, stepping away from the broiling force of the spellwork, his fingers curling about the small firestone at his side with new determination.

CHAPTER THIRTY-ONE

After weeks spent in the sole company of Ryn, Ester, and Bonner, to consider themselves six-strong when they set off north was strange to Declan, especially in the next few days of their travels. The paired warg that skulked in their shadows were unnaturally quiet companions, swift and silent even through the woods that were not their customary environment, and Declan found himself often forgetting the beasts for hours at a time as he conversed with the other three.

Then he would catch a glimpse of grey-white fur slinking through the trees, or a long shape slipping over the edge of a shadowed hill, and the reality of the newest additions to their party would be brought back to him with almost physical abruptness.

The warg, however, proved swiftly to be anything but a hindrance. While it had been assumed that the responsibility of seeing them fed would be taken on by Ester and her skill with the bow she kept constantly strung by her side, the animals appeared quite content to hunt for themselves whenever the opportunity presented itself. Further intriguingly, they more often than not brought back whatever they killed, usually deer—though the larger male once downed a black bear that must have weighed some four-hundred pounds—and seemed as perplexed by Bonner's refusal of the meat as the mage was by the original presentation of it.

"I think they're accustomed to eating second, even of their own kills," the old man had whispered to the group after the third time this happened, by which point the warg had begun happily digging into their prizes at the first indication that the meal would be refused.

"Not unlikely," Declan had agreed, eyeing the beast's thin forms. The wave of ribs beneath the mottled fur had not been unapparent. It seemed the wereyn hadn't gone to any great pains to see to the care and welfare of their mounts.

Declan had almost felt sorry for the beasts, until the female looked up at him suspiciously from the doe she'd just wrenched half-a-ribcage from, chewing on the bones slowly while staring him down with cold black eyes.

Still, despite the moments of unpleasantness, the warg demonstrated themselves not only self-sufficient, but equally useful in a fight, and fight the group did. Not two days into the trek north they came across their first band of wereyn, fortunately no more than ten strong. Declan was sure he and the others would have proven more than a match for the group, but even as the beastmen howled out their excited war-cries and charged them through the trees, the warg were snarling and meeting them head-on. By the time any of their original four entered the fight, two of the wereyn were dead, with half of the remainder fleeing in terror from the creatures they must not have been accustomed to bearing such defiance from.

Declan thought better of the warg after that, and a little bit more each encounter that followed with the beastmen of the Tears.

But despite the skirmishing—hardly any two nights in a row passing without some battle to be had with larger and larger parties of the beastmen—it wasn't the fighting that Declan found most grueling about their journey. Nor, infuriatingly, was it the seemingly endless toil of managing the thickening verdure of Viridian's northern woods. Indeed, Declan thought he would have climbed every hill and forded each consecutively colder river thrice over if it meant a day away from the grinding training he was starting to regret having coaxed out of Bonner. What was more, the mage was only *half* the strain in that department. *Ryn* appeared to have taken the comments regarding Declan's physical prowess to heart, and rose to the challenge they implied with a passion born of something between regret and anticipation. As they walked, Bonner would work with Declan on his mastery of the firestone he still kept pocketed over his breast out of habit, answering any complaint that attempting to learn magic while on the move was practically impossible by pointing out that one did not *fight* while standing still. In turn, every evening Ryn would take Declan and Ester to find as clear and flat a space as they could in the denseness of woods, then proceed to give them what quickly became a nightly thrashing. Now that he had his own sword and was free to move about in a form that allowed him to use it, the dragon proved a terror with the blade. It wasn't that he was markedly *skilled* with the weapon. He was capable, to be sure, *more* than capable, but he fought with the rigidity of one whose ability was in every way born from effort and study rather than any nascent skill. Then again, his quite-*literally* inhuman speed and strength balanced out any stuttering in his form, and when it came to teaching what Ryn lacked in personal proficiency he made up for with a dragon's memory and a long habit of instruction. Gone were the days of verbal beratement and correction by a horse who stood outside the range of the sword. Gone were the regular trials of swinging sticks at trees on their way to Aletha for the first time. In their stead, Declan found himself and the half-elf being put through skills and techniques carried through time from an older world. There was no denying it was swordplay of a royal teaching, one he saw clearly had been handed to Ryn directly by one of the—if not *the*—greatest swordsman of an era long gone from the memories of man. Within a week Declan was looking back with reminiscent fondness on the training of his early years, missing what—in retrospect—seemed a comparably lazy regiment of daily tutelage. Bonner even had opportunity to attempt to instruct him on the basics of auramancy, applied to the blisters and torn callouses of his and Ester's hands.

The mage appeared unsurprised by Declan's complete lack of success in that particular college of weaving, though having his ability summarized as "about as much skill as a rock" did little to lift his worn spirits.

Fortunately, Ester's good-natured laugh at her father's aside made up for the slight.

And so each day passed, the training as exhausting as the instructors were unyielding, but Declan's energies were bolstered and maintained by the equally-constant awareness that he was—very clearly—improving. Of the two of them Ester was one who showed the most change in her bladework under Ryn's eye, but as she'd had a greater opportunity for advancement, Declan didn't begrudge the woman her growing strength. He, too, could feel his progress, could note the changes in his strength and speed in small increments, even by the time a week had passed them by. Ryn was yet the most formidable opponent he'd ever had the misfortune of crossing blades with, but each night Declan felt his repeated defeats as they sparred came a little less easily to the dragon, taxing him just a touch more with every match.

It was under Bonner's wing, however, that Declan saw the much greater change.

He finally had a sense, within five days, of the true potency of his "blood of Kings" when he managed to summon a fistful of flames from the firestone of a likeness with the one Ester had demonstrated to him. He held it longer, too, for several full seconds, and while the conscious weaving of the energies to maintain the spell left him sweating and mentally exhausted, the heat did not pain him as it seemed to have her. Bonner had given another one of his delighted *whoops* at the success, with Ryn grinning in equal pleasure and even Ester herself giving an impressed nod that did a good job of hiding the glint of sad envy in her eye. Declan had felt a disheartened stirring in his heart at the visible disappointment.

Then, not a day later, the woman managed to disarm and down him in practice with a technique of Ryn's demonstration, and Declan decided he had little enough reason to feel sorry for her.

The week passed, followed by another day, and then two. At the dawn of their tenth morning headed due north, Declan awoke shivering on his bedroll, sitting up to find his breath misting in the air before him, a thin sheen of frost teasing the grass that surrounded their little campsite in pale accents. He blinked sleep and surprise away, feeling his teeth chattering as he instinctively clutched at himself for warmth.

Cold snap. The abruptness of Ryn's voice helped hound away the last of his lethargy. *Fell about an hour ago. Sorry for not waking you. I was hoping it wouldn't get this bad.*

Having drawn the night's last watch, he was sitting with his back against a thin elm that stood nearby, sheathed sword by his side. Astoundingly the warg were there, too, asleep within arm's reach of the dragon, each half-wrapped around the trunk of the tree on either side of him like mirrored boulders splotched with white lichen. Ryn glanced at the closest of them—the male—when Declan eyed the beast with lingering mistrust, but shrugged and reached out to very carefully run his clawed hand along the crest of its neck.

The warg didn't do more than twitch an ear at the touch, apparently content enough in its slumber.

They came into camp around the same time the temperatures dropped. Settled right down next to me, too. Probably looking for a little warmth. Ryn gave Declan a bemused smile. *I've named them, if you'll believe it. They made better company than talking to myself, that way.*

"You named them?" Declan repeated with doubtful amusement, reaching over to pull up the furs that had started to slip off the shoulder of a still-sleeping Ester—her bedroll laid up near his as was her habit—before sliding his own pelts atop her, too. This done, he heaved himself up with a grunt and moved to kick some life into the bare embers of the fire Bonner had finally started to allow them. With more than a week gone without a sign of anything worse than the wereyn, the mage and Ryn had decided together it was likely they'd finally slipped the scrying eyes of Sehranya and her necromancer.

They were, for a time at least, free and clear, lost in the expanse of the northern woodlands. They could count themselves safe, so long as they made sure to kill each and every one of the beastmen they came across so no word could get back to the greater horde of their movements.

Ryn nodded, looking to the male again. *This is Orsik. After your great-great-great*—he paused, looking like he was trying to count in his head before giving up. *It doesn't matter. He's named for another one of your ancestors. Bear of a man, but as kind as any human I've ever known. I was very fond of him.* He chuckled, still petting the warg. *I think I might be hoping to force a little of his character into this one.*

Not sure whether he was supposed to balk or laugh at the fact that a *warg* now bore the moniker of one of his forefathers, Declan instead looked to the other animal. "And the female?"

Eyera. Ryn glanced around at the slighter of the pair, curled tightly about herself so her black snout was hidden in the crook of her back leg.

Though to give credit where credit is due, it was Ester's suggestion. Some er'enthyl warrior from a story her mother used to tell her, apparently. I just stuck with it.

Declan raised an eyebrow at that, and Ryn chuckled. *You haven't noticed? While you've been busy letting yourself get worn to the bone by her father, she's been getting friendly with these two.* He reached out his other hand so that he could gently pet both of the beasts together. *It's quite entertaining to see them slink off into the woods together, given how opposed she was to the idea hardly more than a week ago.*

"She does have a thing for animals," Declan muttered in response as he scrounged around in the cold grass for a few twigs to feed the fire with, recalling the walks he used to take with the woman into the forests about the yr'Essel's former home.

Once he had a small blaze going again, he stood and stepped over Bonner's snoring form—the old man apparently oblivious to the frost—to approach Ryn and the warg. The crunch of his boots had the female— *Eyera*, Declan corrected himself—perk up, and she brought her head out from its warm nook to look around at him. Her teeth were only faintly bared, and after a moment's hesitation Declan continued his advance at a slower, more considerate pace, hands up to show they were empty. The habitual growl came, as expected, but lower and without much energy for once. Ryn, too, raised a hand and made a vocal hushing noise at the female, who looked at him with a puzzled expression like she was equally confused by their proximity and the sound he had just made. Either way, it provided the distraction required, allowing Declan to close the last few feet. Choosing the safer bet, he knelt down just within reach of the male's— *Orsik's*—head. In sleep the warg had more the look of an overgrown dog than any terrifying, wild beast. Declan managed half-a-grin, convincing himself to reach out and—with a level of caution that would have made his old Iron Wind guildmates laugh and question the existence of certain aspects of his anatomy—run his fingers between the animal's ears. Orsik gave a throaty sound that was almost a purr of pleasure this time, rolling his head to one side slightly to offer what appeared to be a preferred angle, stealing a quiet laugh from Declan. The warg's fur was coarse and dirty, matted with mud and dirt and what was undoubtedly blood the two hadn't been able to lick off each other, but it was a pleasant sensation all the same.

"We should find a way to bathe them, if we get the chance," he said to Ryn after he'd had his fill. "Can't imagine there will be much opportunity once we reach the foothills. If it's this cold two days out, I suspect most of the smaller streams will be frozen around Elghen."

Are we so close, you think? Ryn asked, looking around Declan's legs as the sound of Bonner's snuffling breaths told them both he, too, was waking. *Only two days?*

"Maybe three?" Declan turned to watch the mage sit up and rub at his eyes. "Even that isn't much more than a guess, given the route we're taking. There was a road to Therest, not far out of Ranheln, which would have seen us all the way if we'd followed it, but given our predicament I don't imagine that would have been our brightest idea."

Better to take our time and suffer the chill for a bit than risk the mainways, yes, Ryn agreed, picking up his sword and using the tree behind him to stand himself while Bonner did the same by the fire. *Not that I have much to complain about, mind. It's you lot who will suffer the worst of it.*

Declan nodded, looking over the frosted ground again. Even when he'd known him as nothing more than a horse, Ryn had never seemed much bothered by the cold, or *any* great variation in temperature, truth be told. "Another of your primordial gifts?"

More just a trait of my kind. I'm sorry to see that particular attribution wasn't passed on through my blood.

Declan snorted. Given everything else the dragon's gift to Amherst al'Dyor all those centuries ago appeared to have left him with, he wasn't about to complain that he remained as vulnerable to the climate as any other man.

"What is it you two have been muttering about?"

Bonner was yawning, rounding the fire to join them. Eyera's head picked up on Ryn's other side, and she looked to be considering whether to growl or not when the mage shot her a look. The warg recoiled ever so slightly, clearly thinking better of it.

"We were trying to gauge how much farther we have to Elghen," Declan answered, barely fazed by such odd exchanges anymore. "I was telling Ryn I think we're no more than two or three days off, and I think a little east, but—"

"Two," Bonner interrupted, reaching them and waving west. "And you're correct about our heading as well."

It took him a moment to register the blank expressions Declan and Ryn were treating him to. When he did, the old man rubbed at his bald head and pulled his hood up, looking around with obvious displeasure. "I spent some time scrying during my watch last night. If we keep up this pace, we'll reach town sometime the day after tomorrow." He frowned in particular distaste as a breeze shifted the icy air about them. "Wish I'd had a thought to look into the *weather* while I was at it..."

Is that wise? Ryn asked uncertainly. *Scrying in general, I mean? You don't think it will make us more noticeable?*

Bonner shook his head. "Not unless Sehranya or her lackey *happen* to be in Elghen, and just *happen* to be weaving a counterspell when I *happen* to be looking." As though struck by a thought, he turned to Declan. "Which reminds me: we'll be reviewing the Six Essentials of the Arcana, today. You've been progressing so well it utterly slipped my mind, but learning the basic laws of casting is *extremely* important if you're going to progress and…"

After Bonner had had his meandering fill and Declan had promised several times over that he would pay particular attention during the day's lessons—which seemed ironic, given that they had been *literally* playing with fire for the better part of two weeks now—they set about their morning's tasks. Ester was woken—muttering and cursing at the cold that had flushed her pale cheeks to rose—and together they broke camp. Ryn took to his stallion's form and accepted their gear without complaint. After coaxing Orsik into wakefulness with half-a-slab of venison left over from their meal the previous night—the other half going to Eyera in order to avoid a fight—the six of them set off through the cold of the woods.

As threatened, Bonner spent the entirety of the morning doing his utmost to drill some dozen dictations and limitations on the art of magic into Declan's mind, much to *everyone's* eventual fatigue. By the time they took a short break a little past noon—the temperatures having risen only mildly since daybreak—Declan's head was swimming with words and phrases like "amorphic" and "solipsism" and "arcanic disillusion". Only the sight of Ester on the other side of the fire Bonner had conjured for them— shivering and pulling at the thin cloak that was all they'd thought to buy for themselves in Ranheln—was enough to lift him from the headache and beg a moment's reprieve from the old man. Pulling free the firestone from the pocket of his jacket, he tugged free his own cloak and moved around the flames to toss the mantle over the woman's shoulders, flashing her a wink when she looked up in surprise. Moving back to Bonner's side before the half-elf could give a word of protest, Declan summoned his will into the stone, feeling it flare into life in his hands. Sitting back down and preparing himself mentally for the continued onslaught of magical methodology, Declan sighed in relief as he pushed the firestone's weave beyond its vessel, enveloping as much of himself as he could in an orb of weak-but-steady heat. It was a simple spell, one he'd practiced a thousand times as Bonner had been working on getting him to summon true fire, but it did the trick, and he looked around at the old man expecting to be greeted with a look of mild annoyance.

What he did *not* expect, on the contrary, was to find one of the history's most powerful mages, a man of over eight hundred years of age, grinning at him like a schoolboy with a secret.

"What?" Declan asked, taken aback.

"Oh, nothing," Bonner answered too-quickly, his eyes flicking only briefly to his daughter. "It's just... Do you realize this is the first time you've used magic of your own deliberate creation?"

It took a moment for Declan to understand what the mage meant, but once he did he looked down at the firestone, held in both hands as he leaned over his legs, with some small shock. It was true, he realized. It was the first time he'd crafted any spell of his own volition. Even before Bonner's lessons there had been the warg and wereyn he'd seen burned in the cave, but that had been inadvertent, a fortunate circumstance that had happened to play into his hands and his King's blood. *This*, indeed, was the very first time he had willfully summoned up the weaves of heat and binding without deliberate instruction.

And he had done it with so little thought to the act...

He couldn't help but return Bonner's grin with genuine enthusiasm, feeling the stone in his hands flare hot at the excitement that sharpened in his heart.

■■

Unfortunately, it took them longer than the assumed two days to reach Elghen. They lost most of one morning to a ravine none of them had expected until Ryn warned them of it a mile out. From late dawn to noon they traced its ledges after a quick deliberation and decision *not* to have the dragon turn and carry them over the gorge, gear, warg, and all. In the end they found a wooden bridge that Bonner reinforced before crossing, having once more need to bribe Orsik and Eyera along with meat before the pair would do more than sniff and paw doubtfully the wooden slats that ordinarily might indeed not have held their weight. Beyond that, the wereyn chose those last legs of their journey to make themselves known in force, descending on their party no less than six times over the course of half as many days. Declan didn't know if it was because they were nearing the Tears, or because the beastmen were merely denser the closer they got to the ranges, but he was growing tired of the frequent assaults. Bonner's weaving saw to their wounds and some of their fatigue whenever possible, but resting became paramount, and even Ryn agreed to put their training on hold so they could all get an extra hour's sleep each night without the fatigue of their evening bouts.

The mage was less merciful, choosing instead to lean further into his instructions, stating again and again how important it could be for Declan to master the basics of even simple pyromancy if they were to challenge the northern ranges. If he'd expected to hear any complaint from his pupil, however, he found none. While the magical training was arguably *more* exhausting than sparring with Ryn and Ester had been, the fruits of

Declan's labor in that realm were also that much more tangible. With each passing day he felt his control of his abilities solidify ever so slightly, to the point where he'd even traded his hunting knife for holding onto the firestone in his offhand when they fought. He could see, now, how manipulation of even the basic weaves of heat and light might eventually prove more versatile than a second blade in combat. What's more, Bonner had assured him that the stone was nothing more than a tool of the moment, a channel through which to focus his crafting, and one he would not need to cling to forever. This news had brought with it more flashes of memories that Declan knew were not his own, brief glimpses of another man's hand casting flame and hellfire over the field of battle even as his sword carved a path through the enemies directly before him.

When he'd told Ryn of these recollections, the dragon had only nodded and confirmed that they were more of Herst's lingering presence before his white-gold eyes had glazed over, brought once more back into the past.

Finally, not long after a midday break and meal on their thirteenth day of travel, Ryn's ears perked up from behind the reptilian shape of his warped horse's head. His neck straightened, and his gait faltered, earning glances from Declan, Ester, and Bonner alike as they followed alongside him, interrupting their lively discussion regarding the merits of magic in warfare.

He did not, though, say a word to any of them.

"Ryndean?" Bonner ventured after nearly ten seconds of quiet, but Ryn silenced him with a flick of an ear. Another few breaths paced by, and it was in that time that Declan heard a faint growling, and he turned to see Orsik and Eyera come slinking out of the woods on either side of the path they were cutting for themselves. The warg's attention was not trained on any of them, however, and Declan followed their black eyes, finding himself looking in the same direction the dragon was.

"Smoke."

Ester's voice was tight, and when Declan and her father looked around at her she had reached around to draw an arrow from the quiver slung along her lower back. "Smoke," she repeated, knocking it swiftly and drawing the give out of the string. "Blood as well. I can smell them both."

"Which means they can, as well," Declan muttered, glancing at the warg again. "No wonder they're so on edge."

There's fire. Ryn finally spoke up, still not looking around at them. *At the very edge of my senses. Buildings too, maybe?*

Declan's insides went cold. "Elghen?"

Undoubtedly.

"What do we do?" Bonner asked the dragon, himself peering along the same direction. "If the town's fallen, it means there's a larger arm of the horde, here. I can't imagine the wereyn making an assault on a full municipality with a few scattered groups of tens and twenties."

"Ryn, how much closer do we need to get before you can tell us more?" Declan asked in a low tone despite the danger obviously still being a ways away.

Half-a-mile. Maybe a little less.

"And we'll still be at least another half-mile away from whatever's going on?"

Ryn nodded.

Declan glanced at Bonner and Ester, and the three of them nodded together. "Then let's get closer."

Only Orsik and Eyera appeared to hesitate when they began moving due west at a clipped pace, hurrying as best they could through the woods. Declan wondered if the scent of fire and death might scare the warg off completely, but thought he should have known better after glancing back and seeing the pair loping alongside them with ease over the frozen ground.

He was starting to find it hard *not* to appreciate their company, in situations like this…

It took them less than five minutes to close the distance, Ryn pressing a little ahead when he clearly sensed no threat in their immediate surroundings. They caught up to him on the ridge of an open outcropping, the break in the trees not offering any hint of the town, but providing a clear view of the heavens. The dragon's head was upturned, looking to the clouds, and Declan's lesser eyes took a moment to identify the faint, curling plumes rising from beyond the canopy.

He could make it out too, now that they were near. The ashy smell of steady fire.

"Whatever happened, it's long over," he muttered to the group even before Ryn could fill them in, pointing upward with the hand he'd found himself holding the firestone in instinctively. "That smoke is waning. I'd expect to see a lot more if Elghen were actively burning." He looked to the dragon. "Am I wrong?"

Ryn shook his head slowly. *No. Yesterday, or the day before, possibly.*

"Are… Are there any survivors?" Ester asked quietly, the grip on her bowstring slackening as her face fell.

Ryn paused, every inch of him going still while he reached outward with what Declan imagined was every ounce of his will.

Then he shook his head once more.

Declan heard Bonner take a shaking breath beside him, steadying himself.

"Nothing to be done, then." His voice was low, almost like the words were meant only for his own ears, green eyes on the rising tendrils high,

high above them. When he spoke again, it was with his usual confidence, marred only by a slight shake that betrayed his true feelings. "What of the wereyn?"

Half-a-hundred in the town itself. Many of those injured. Probably left behind like the ones we came across off the High Road.

"Any others in the woods beyond us?"

A pause. *A dozen more in scattered groups, with an equal number of warg. Foragers, I think. We'll have to hunt them down, but I doubt they'll pose much issue.*

"You want to go in, then?" Declan asked. He had no doubt of his own resolution. They were only four—*six*, he corrected himself, glancing sidelong at Orsik, who'd taken a seat on Ester's right and was looking up at the sky with hackles raised—but they were anything but defenseless. Between their number Declan was sure they had enough tricks to handle the remnants of whatever greater force of beastmen had fallen upon the town, so long as they could use Ryn's senses to their advantage.

Yes.

The firmness with which Ryn said the word had everyone looking around at him in concern. Declan almost stepped away out of instinct, his heart clenching in nothing less than fear as the dragon's equine form shivered and swelled. The day seemed to grow darker around them, like Ryn was sucking away the light, and Declan recalled the only other time he had witnessed such a distortion, almost a month passed now.

At *The Woodsman's Rest*, when Dia had sent the dragon into a towering fury Declan hadn't understood at the time.

He suddenly feared what it was the dragon could see within Elghen's ruined borders that was so beyond their own mundane sight…

Getting control of himself, he lifted a hand and rested it on his friend's shoulder, atop a patch of scales that hadn't transition into true horse hair. The touch was all the dragon needed. The light returned, bending away from him like he was releasing his grip on the cold sun above, and his form solidified. He half-brought his head about to give Declan a grateful look, then turned his attention to Bonner.

Can we leave the foragers to you? None of them can be left to escape.

The mage considered the question, eyes falling to Orsik and Eyera.

Then he nodded. "If I take the warg, it shouldn't be any issue. Give me their general locations. The forest will tell me the rest."

Declan watched and listened to Ryn provide the mage with the requested information with a knot in his stomach. He hadn't been thinking Bonner wouldn't be with them, when they took the town, and his confidence in their success dipped as he watched the old man nod and make for the two warg. To everyone's surprise, Bonner took a handful of Eyera's neck fur in hand and leapt nimbly atop her, discolored robes setting about her sides as he made himself comfortable on her back.

"Oh hush," he told the female impatiently when she rolled her large head around to snarl in confused displeasure. "You've had much less pleasant riders, I'm sure, and we'll move much faster like this. It's about time you two make yourselves more useful than a pair of oversized attack dogs anyhow."

Eyera's protest ended like she'd understood every word of the mage's retort—which she might very well have, Declan considered—and she looked forward again with a sort of resigned annoyance lingering about the hunched muscles of her shoulders.

His mount somewhat settled, Bonner looked around at them, attention on Ryn in particular. "Stay calm," he told the dragon specifically. "Recall that we will still need to salvage everything we can for our ascent. Don't torch whatever's left of the town just for revenge."

Torch whatever's left? Declan repeated to himself in alarm, his trepidation mounting. What was it that had riled the dragon so? And with Bonner seeing to the scattered beastmen in the forests about the town, would they have the strength to—?

A clatter of tumbling gear from behind him interrupted his thoughts, and he understood all at once why Bonner was so utterly unconcerned with leaving them on their own.

Declan felt the presence before he even had a moment to look around. Ryn must have shifted into one of his smaller forms first, so as to discard the carrying harness before he shredded it. Now, however, he was growing, swelling at an alarming pace, stepping away from Declan and Ester even as he drew himself up to his full height so as not to inadvertently bowl them over with the change.

Not a handful of seconds later, the full mass of Ryndean, primordial of the dragons of the Reaches, towered like a black monolith against the clear blue of the cloud scattered sky.

And his eyes, burning with an anger Declan couldn't quite resonate with, were fixed on the wisping trails of smoke in the distance.

CHAPTER THIRTY-TWO

Despite the misconceptions of the rest of mankind, I am of the rare opinion that the wereyn are not an unintelligent race—though I admit to difficulty calling them "a race" at all. In granting them will through the process of their creation, the Endless Queen enabled the greater mass of her army in many ways. They could think independently, react to an enemy's tactics—if primitively—and exist as a self-sustained branch of her forces without the constant need for her power or one of her cursed charms or liche to maintain any Purpose. However, in doing so, Sehranya also created a space in her armor, a gap in the wall that was her barrier of unfeeling, emotionless defenders brought forth from the grave. This is evidenced by the final collapse of the last of the wereyn under the joint assault of the dragons, Vigil, and elves, in the Queen's final stand among the cliffs of the Reaches. The stitched beasts broke and scattered, and it is this fact that leads me to believe above all else that the wereyn are truly intelligent—if simple—creatures.

Fear, after all, is a concept which exists only in the soul of the self-aware...

-private journals of Elysia Enus al'Dyor, Queen of Viridian, c. 325p.f.

To the beastkin of the mountains, the idea of language—vocal or otherwise—was an absent notion. Theirs was a primitive, feral race, lacking in the essential capacities that would have allowed such a concept to take seed and grow despite the centuries the creatures had spent in relative seclusion among the snowy, frigid crags they had come to call home. They lacked even such simple identifiers as unique names, discarding the need for individuality in favor of the cold intelligence that allowed them to move and react as a single unit. They were much like the wolves that were their rival hunters among the ranges in that regard, or the warg who had come under their bonds through cruel force and hungry necessity.

All the same, though an animal can lack developed language, no such level of communication is required to convey the terror evoked by the strangled, shrieking screams of one's own kind.

It was this kind of stirring fear that eventually settled over the once-open space in the middle of the human's now-conquered community, what the beastkin would have thought of as a gathering ground amidst the walled enclosures the fragile race used as dens. At first the cries were distant, hard to make out over the crackle and snap of the flames that were still dying out from the previous night's raid. They might have been taken for anything, and many feeding among the vanquished prey they had gathered in that open place looked up with anticipation from their grisly meals, wondering if the hunt would resume again so soon. There were still those among the injured capable of hounding whatever response those few who had escaped the butchery would have managed to gather in so short a period. Perhaps the strongest among the beastkin would once again feast on fresh meat that day, aiming to regain enough strength to set off after the larger pack that had kept moving south along one of the wide, cleared paths man made for himself from settlement to settlement. Indeed, with this building anticipation, those among their kind still capable of doing so discarded their food and made to set off in the direction of the cries, slaver already dripping from red-stained mouths.

Not a one among them *didn't* take pause, therefore, when the sounds grew closer, and the understanding dawned that the howls and screeches were not those of the gathering hunt.

They were the screams of the dying.

In the few moments it took for this realization to settle in, for fear to take hold of the beastkin of the mountains, a shadow of unfathomable proportions erupted from over the tops of the walled dens that surrounded the space where they had built up their feast. The screams came from the very throats of those that had been standing nearest their gathered kills, now, erupting as their eyes tracked the great shape circling in a wide arc overhead, black against the blue of the mid-day sky and the grey of the smoke. They would have scattered, likely, had they been able to. The quickest among them did, those still with the strength in their limbs to escape, and the great creature let them go with the cool confidence of a predator who could run down its prey at its own leisure. Those with less ability to run could do nothing more than shriek and scramble out of the way as the colossal form descended, so massive that even in making for the largest clear space it still crushed two of the burned-out husks of the human's ruined homes. As it landed, the broad, sky-swallowing wings that had kept it aloft stayed splayed, keeping it reared on its hind legs long enough for it to drop two smaller shapes onto the ground in front of it before it fell onto all fours with mirrored *thuds* that shook the earth.

Then the creature opened its great, gaping maw, and roared with such terrifying, resonating anger that the world itself seemed to shiver in fear.

■■

As Declan found his feet, he worked hard to keep his focus, to keep his mind on anything—*anything*—apart from the horrible sight that lingered in his periphery. He thought about the terrifying thrill that had swallowed his stomach the moment Ryn had taken him up in one clawed hand, of Ester's helpless shriek when the dragon had launched himself upward. Declan thought of the blinding speed at which they had moved, the forest sweeping by below them so quickly he'd been able to make out nothing but blurred streaks of green and fall colors. He thought of the tear he'd had to blink away, blooming in his eyes as they were met with the howling of the frigid air.

Now, sword in hand and the half-elf only feet to his left, he thought instead of the twisted, cruel creatures scattered about what remained of the town square before them.

The wereyn who'd been left behind by their quicker comrades made no move to attack immediately, which wasn't unexpected. Most were frozen in terror at the sight of Ryn's natural form looming before them, while others clearly largely immobilized by wounds suffered in the destruction of what had been Elghen.

Will you be able to manage here? the dragon's voice asked in a voice of forced calm, and Declan suspected that if he had looked around, Ryn's attention would have just as fixedly been set on anything but the center of the square. *The quickest are making a run for it, and there are a handful already fleeing along the southern road.*

Declan took in the wereyn before him quickly. There were a good number of them, maybe two dozen in all, but they generally looked to be the worse of the abandoned, dragged to the middle of the ruined town to feed and regain some of their lost strength.

He grit his teeth, feeling the firestone in his left hand blaze with an intensity he doubted he could have managed in any calmer state of mind.

"Don't worry about us," he told the dragon over his shoulder. "Go."

In answer there was a *crunch* of shifting stone and earth, then Declan and Ester both were buffeted forward a full step under the *whooshing* gale of Ryn's beating wings as the dragon got himself airborne again. They didn't watch him depart, the entirety of their attention set on the beasts before them, many of the wereyn appearing to find their senses as what they must have perceived to be the greater threat left the scene.

The firestone throbbed once again in Declan's hand, and he would have felt sorry for the few creatures who started limping towards them with howls of glee had he not been so horrendously, bottomlessly *angry*.

He discovered, in that moment, that he and Ester required no words to find their rhythm. The *thrum* of the woman's bow sang twice, downing two of the closest creatures with pinpoint accuracy. She shifted then to take up a position at his back, the bow ringing again and again as she sighted on what must have been more of the foul beasts coming up behind them. By the time Declan made out the slipping sound of her saber being drawn from its sheath, the slower of their forward opponents had reached him.

He made sure it was known to each and every one of them that the absent dragon was only *part* of the retribution that had fallen upon them that day.

Declan moved more now as he fought than he had just two weeks prior. Without his knife in his off-hand, defending attacks from multiple sides was made difficult, and as a result his fighting became more of a dance than it ever had before. He kept close to Ester's back all the same, twisting and turning and lunging this way and that while still shielding her rear from his share of their enemies. The Iron Wind bastard sword cut left and right, up and down in ringing strikes that fell in single, deliberate sweeps and thrusts. He saw, in those exchanges, the true improvements the hard efforts of the last fortnight had wrought on his blade-play. He had noted minor changes during the smaller skirmishes they'd overcome on their way north, but their victories in those exchanges had always been quick and absolute, made swift usually by Bonner's overwhelming power, or Ryn's oversized blade. Now, faced with his own pool of enemies and challenged in truth for the first time since battling the wights, Declan witnessed his improvement.

Particularly—and to his own amazement—in the control of his own small magics.

The knuckles of his left hand thudded into the exposed gut of a stag-headed creature whose rusted sword he'd ducked under, the fist he'd made around the firestone erupting with red and orange flames as he willed his built-up weave outward. There was a *whoom* of distorted air, and in an eruption of rippling heat the wereyn flew backwards into a pair of its own kind, dead as stone, the flesh of its chest and stomach charred to a crackling black. Not allowing his focus to falter, Declan brought his blade up to cleave into the throat of another opponent, flicking his left hand out in the opposite direction as he adjusted the spell into a more solid form. He was far from being able to conjure anything remotely like the jet of all-consuming fire Bonner could summon up with a thought, but the firestone responded to his desire in a spray of molten, clinging flames, like lit alcohol cast from a bottle. It rained down over an unfortunate trio of wereyn who'd been attempting to skulk around his left, going for Ester's open flank. As one they recoiled with agonized screams, weapons tumbling from their hands as they swiped and clawed at the molten fire that clung to the fur of their chests, shoulders, and faces.

Serves them right, Declan thought, already whirling to deflect a thrusted knife, willing himself to stay focused, to stay present.

Willing himself not let the horrible outline of what lay in the center of the square, silhouetted against the fires all around them, pull him away from the task at hand.

Between the pair of them, Declan and Ester ripped through the assaulting wereyn with stunning efficiency. They never exchanged a word as they fought, the matching sounds of their blades cutting and thrusting through skin and flesh speaking enough of each other's continued wellbeing, which was all either needed to know. Five had died to the half-elf's arrows before the fight had so much as begun, and more than another dozen fell too in the first minutes of the engagement, nine or so to Declan's flames and steel, five or six to Ester's saber. They had the distasteful task, after that, of chasing down the beasts who made an attempt to turn and flee, and one or two would indeed have escaped into the smoldering ruins of the town had the woman not tossed Declan her sword and unshouldered her bow in a blink.

It would have been hard even if the wereyn *hadn't* been injured to outrun the arrows that took them in rapid succession between the shoulder blades.

It was almost hard, finally, to stalk down the handful of beastmen who had been the more grievously wounded of the group, those who hadn't been able to gain their feet and attack in the first place. Declan took no pleasure, after handing Ester back her saber, in pacing after the crawling forms of the half-dozen such creatures who were desperately trying to make their escape from the square. Then again, nor did he feel much pity for them as he cut each down one after the other, straddling them from behind and slitting their throats even as they squealed and shrieked in panic.

The anger was still there, after all, and when the last of the wereyn finally lay dying in a pool of its own blood, Declan finally allowed himself to look, to take in the sight of what lay in the center of the square.

There had been no mercy for the people of Elghen, he saw. No quarter offered. No kindness given. He couldn't fathom why he would have imagined there might have been, given the nature he had come to know of the wereyn, but just the same the slaughter before him seemed cruel even by the standards of the wildest of animals. There was hardly a whole body among those piled into the side of the hill that he could see. The corpses of the women, children, and men of the town looked like they had been fought over, ripped into for whatever choicest parts had been taken by what must have been the greater body of the horde, long departed. They were broken, tattered pieces of what once had been life, a nightmarish mound piled eight feet high, the wereyn having stacked their food all in one place for easy access. In the center of the square, away from the heat of the fires, frost had built up over the topmost layer of bodies, the grisly details of the limp hands and wide, frozen eyes outlined in icy white. The grim colors of the coming winter melted when one's eyes fell, vanishing into black and red where the remaining beasts had torn into the side of the hill to feast. Looking now, Declan could make out the dragging, crimson streaks that marked the paths along which the bodies had been hauled. Even the cobblestone around the base of the hill was hard to look at, sketched in black by spidering veins of long-dried blood…

Ester's shaking breath told him the half-elf had joined him in his observance, and he was grateful for her comforting warmth when he felt her reach out and loop her arm into his, pulling herself close against him as they took in the horror together.

He began a silent prayer to the Mother and Her Graces, unable to tell if the shivering he felt in the woman's touch was hers, his, or theirs both to share.

How long they stayed like that, Declan didn't know. Horror and grief transfixed them both, equally muddled by the sight before them and the heavy weight of wondering. Could they have helped? Could they have done anything to stop it? They couldn't, they both knew, but it was an awareness as empty in its existence as it might have been in its absence.

That was how Ryn found them, sometime later, when his own hunt had come to an end. The sheer power of his attendance in his natural form was the only thing that finally managed to break their trance, the two of them looking away together to take in the dragon's colossal frame when he descended as delicately as his bulk allowed some dozen feet to their right. They didn't notice the frozen tracks on their cheeks, cutting lines through the blood and ashen dust that had built up during and after their fight, and Ryn made no mention of it. Instead, he, too, took his moment of vigil, tyrannical features dark and still, golden eyes on the gathered mound of desecrated dead. Declan felt a piercing pain in his heart as he registered, then, that the dragon had known what they would find within the wreckage of the town, had witnessed this very sight through his mind's eye long before he or Ester had been forced to face it.

Power at a price, he thought to himself numbly.

After a long moment in which neither Declan nor Ester made any move to interrupt whatever entreaty the dragon might have been casting into the wind, Ryn finally stirred again. He looked to the pair of them, indicating with his head a heavy shelving of wall that still stood erect a ways behind them.

Get to cover. I'll see to their rest.

Neither Declan nor the woman said anything in response, turning together to do as the dragon suggested. They didn't even break apart from each other, their shared touch an anchor to the understanding that the world was not an utterly abyssal place, that there was more to their existence than the black evil over which Ryn now towered alone. Declan allowed himself a peek over the wall after he and Ester had settled firmly behind it, but looked away quickly again when he saw that the dragon was swelling, taking in the massive, heaving breath that precluded the foreboding glow of brilliant white light building in his maw. Declan hunkered down, pulling himself over Ester instinctively as the thundering roar of the dragonfire ripped through the more subdued sound of the slower flames still eating at what was left of Elghen around them.

When they looked over the wall again, together this time, Ryn was standing, great head bowed in silent misery, over the massive, ashen stain that was the only rest he'd been able to offer the broken dead.

■■■

It took several hours—once Ryn assured them that the wereyn had been eradicated—for the three of them to salvage the supplies they'd come for, food and gear and clothing they would have all preferred to have the opportunity to purchase. The dragon's senses proved indispensable to the endeavor, discerning the minute details of what lay beneath the ruin and rubble the beastmen had made of the town, but all the same it was heavy work digging through the mess to haul out what they could find. Declan didn't mind. The labor gave him the opportunity to lose himself in the strain and sweat. He was even conscientious to take every opportunity to enforce his will over the smaller fires they came across, doing his utmost to nullify their heat by attempting to draw their energies into the firestone he kept palmed in one hand.

Still, even when he succeeded—thus making their work a little bit easier—Declan was unable to feel anything more than a mute sort of satisfaction, overhung by the black mood of their slow parade through the still, soot-covered streets.

They managed eventually, though. Provisions were the easiest, as they discovered an ample supply of salted meats the wereyn appeared to have disregarded in favor of fresher sources in a butcher's shop that miraculously had been left mostly standing. They found sacks of nuts and grains in a few homes Ryn pointed them towards, and even a small bushel of potatoes that somehow hadn't been spoiled in the heat of the fires. Next came clothing, which they gathered piecemeal, over the course of the early afternoon collecting a heavy winter cloak and gloves for Declan and Ester both, as well as new, thicker boots they were lucky enough to salvage from the ruins of a tanner's shop. Ryn—returned to his dragonling's form—also gathered several long straps of leather he found buried under a drying rack, muttering something about a carrying harness for the warg.

In that vein, the half-elf also took the time to find several spools of thick thread and matching needles. It gave Declan the opportunity to look out upon the town again, absent the distraction of foraging now that they had practically everything they needed to attempt their foolish journey. He felt his heart still, felt it falter and sink, upon looking out over the smoking destruction, the blank, lifeless ruin that was all that remained of what must have been a bustling haven of quiet existence not a few days before. He wondered, helplessly, if the townspeople had been forewarned of their impending doom, if they had even had time to mount what small defenses might have been gathered, or they had simply been fallen upon in the night, like the Vigil patrol from near two-weeks prior.

"Declan."

Declan started, brought back to earth from his empty wanderings. Ester and Ryn were waiting for him, both loaded down with their salvaged things, looking as though they had been making their way north up the road when they'd realized he wasn't following them. He thought they must have called for him and he hadn't heard, because they were both watching him with wretched understanding. He realized, then, the wetness that stung at his vision, and he turned away long enough to wipe his eyes on the wrist of one dusty sleeve before joining them.

They found Bonner twenty minutes later, waiting for them outside of town, just short of the tree line that continued to sweep north. He was sitting quietly on an old stump, whistling a tune that was too cheerful for the threesomes' shared mood while watching Orsik and Eyera playing a bloody game of tug of war with the furred torso of what must have once been a wereyn of exceptional size. The warg quit their roughhousing upon Declan, Ester, and Ryn's approach, wet, crimson muzzles lifting to sniff in their direction. For the first time the animals showed no interest in threats or growls, but their sudden shift in attention had the old man glancing around.

"Ah, there you are!" he called out, jumping to his feet and lifting a hand in greeting as he started to jog towards them. Their things, they saw, were already gathered beside the stump. "Another ten minutes and I was about to come looking myself. Did you find everything? What took you so—?"

His questions faltered upon getting closer. The mage must have registered the trio's shared expressions, because his own face fell, and he looked to Ryn. "That bad?"

That bad, the dragon confirmed with a dull dip of his head. *We could have used you, I think. I wasn't able to give them much of a proper burial.*

Bonner's shoulders sagged briefly. "I'm sorry. It took us longer than I would have liked to see to all the foragers. A few of the warg were in fair health, and one group must have made it halfway to the Tears before Orsik managed to catch them and bring the beasts down. Apparently there's not much love shared even among their own kind. I'm starting to think these two might have been siblings, or perhaps a mated pair..."

Declan barely heard anything the old man had to say. At the mention of the mountains, his eyes had lifted, looking up, over the canopy of the forest that waited for them not far away.

For two weeks now the heavy overhang of thick evergreens had done much to hide the sky from view. Now, though, standing in the cut clearing the settlers of Elghen had tended for however many decades or centuries their families had been residents of the valley town, the heavens opened up to them.

And there, lingering over the horizon Declan still couldn't see, the Mother's Tears loomed with like a cold, hulking threat, a hundred snow-tipped blades thrust up into the blue of the sky to scrape at the clouds themselves.

It wasn't the first time Declan had laid eyes on the ranges, and even then, he'd always disliked the look of those peaks. Somehow, however, they were different on this occasion. There was a solidity to their presence, a weightiness to the towering heights he hadn't been conscious of before. They felt... absolute. Like a wall, raised at the edge of the world, marking the place beyond which no being of mortal flesh had the right to venture. He felt his breath catch in his throat, taking in their wide, stabbing outlines, the serrated edge of a single massive blade that seemed intent, somehow, on seeing him cut in two...

"I suppose we're really doing this..."

The hesitant statement was offered to him so quietly, it took a second for Declan to discern Ester's voice from his own thoughts. When he did, he brought his eyes down to where she had come to stand beside him, finding the woman's attention transfixed—as his had been—on the distant caps of the ranges. There was a tension in her face, an excitement melded with fear, that he understood well.

He himself was experiencing it in kind.

"Seems like it, doesn't it?" he answered under his breath, lifting his gaze again so that they could look together on the peaks. "Madness... I feel like the Mother and all Her Graces aren't going to be enough to watch our backs in those cliffs..."

"Then we'll just have to watch each other's, I suppose."

For the second time that day, he felt Ester's arm slip into his. He might have flushed, might at least have given Bonner a sheepish grin if he'd caught the mage's smug glance in their direction, but Declan's awareness was limited to nothing more than the pressure of the half-elf's touch through his new cloak, and the comfort it offered him. He again felt the world stabilize, if only just a little, and the overbearing resonance of the far-off mountains retreated the slightest bit.

When Ryn called for them to get moving, Declan was able to do so with nothing more than a clench of his jaw and a quick prayer as they stepped back into the last breadth of woodland that separated them from the edge of the only world he'd ever known.

A Mark of Kings

CHAPTER THIRTY-THREE

It is only natural to fear the end of one's existence. Death is a concept beyond even the most brilliant of minds, a state of nothingness existing far past all we—as living beings—could ever know so long as we still draw breath.

Of course, there are many who would claim an understanding of what lies beyond the veil of ends, who would claim to have glimpsed the other side. Priests of "the Mother", who preach of a better place waiting for those living in virtue and consideration, are most common in this nation of ours, but you will hear ravings of equally wanting intellectual value muttered by not a few of the drunkards and addled beggars of the slums of any sizable city. Even if there should be a god of any shape and form, who are we to profess so much as the slightest understanding of what awaits us on the other side, to allege a grasp of Their intention for us once we shed flesh and pass into "the beyond"?

If it is not blasphemous, it is—at the very least—impetuous…

-*A Study of Mortal Ardor*, Archmagus Kyla Tha'ren, c. 275p.f.

It was not uncommon for shivers of awareness to permeate the Endless Queen's restless mind. There was little she could not see within the borders of her harsh domain, after all, the edges of her mountains layered with weaves and wards that had taken more decades than she would have bothered counting to establish. Everything flickered across her thoughts, in its own way, and she had long since learned to drone out the passing of the lesser beasts. The wild wereyn and the humans of the valley towns were as uninteresting as the flight of the cliff falcons or the passing of the wolves and deer through the lower crags, and she treated each with equal inattentiveness. They were as nothing to her, as inconsequential as the drafts of air that wove through the darkness of her audience hall, unfelt across her desiccated skin.

Other presences, on the other hand, she had known, had registered and contemplated with the mild attentiveness of one who has seen too much of time and the world. Her own beastmen, fifty thousand strong, had been as a current across her mind when they had begun their press south, smaller packs chasing them over the mountains in the following weeks. Gonin Whist flicked in and out of being on occasion too, when he was close, and the *er'endehn* had begun their skulking into the borders of her realm for the first time in more than five hundred years. This last group she had contemplated seeing too, but eventually settled against it. It was not yet the moment to strike at the black elves. Not yet. The forces she had left herself with upon dispatching the beastmen from her subterranean halls was limited, and she wished not to waste her greatest prizes by throwing them against the darkened blades of Ysenden's ilk. She had settled back into the recesses of her awareness, satisfied with the knowledge that her strength was growing, and that the iron black walls of the *er'endehn's* last great city *would* eventually fall.

Then *they* passed into the borders of her domain, and the thrum of shock to the Queen's mind was enough to drive her out of the depths of that omniscience absence from her immediate surroundings.

For the first time in what must have been many moons, the Queen felt her face shift. Dry, dead muscle pulled at her cheeks, and with the audible crack of flaking skin she knew herself to be smiling. Her eyes were next, heavy lids lifting fraction by fraction, blinking slowly, then again, then a third time. The chamber was pitch dark, she knew, beyond the reaches of the world's light far above, but what was such a blackness to the weaves of old magics? She could have seen her surroundings, had she chosen to, could have observed the basalt pillars rising from the broad expanse of the slate floor to bear the weight of the rough-hewn ceiling of stone. She could have taken in the polished seat that was her throne, cut right into the rock of the chamber wall atop a three-tiered dais of black obsidian. She might even have paused to observe the stained marks of dried blood splashed about her feet, all that remained of the last meal she had thought to call for, likely more than a year ago now.

But the Queen's eyes were elsewhere, taken away, far beyond the confines of that shadowed room she had long since locked herself away in.

"There you are..." she heard her own voice rasp from a throat gone dry and stiff with disuse.

As though through a rusted looking glass she took in the curious party, smile broadening over rotted teeth when her suspicions were confirmed. There had been no other potential answer, of course, but even to the mind of the all-powerful it was a settling thing to see one's hopes upheld. She forgave herself her moment of confusion, as well. It had been strange to feel *six* presences pass within the confines of her wards. According to Gonin, there should have been no more than four, and of those only two she might have felt as more than ruffles in the winds of her weaves. It would have appeared, however, that her apprentice had yet again proven himself inept. Briefly the Queen took in the mirrored shapes of the two warg who lurked about the other four forms as they managed the slighter foothills along the southern base of her mountains. She examined, amused, the harnesses and gear that looked to be hanging from the animals' broad, loping shoulders. Satisfied with the resolution of that mystery, however, she focused on the other curiosity, feeling the listless skin of her forehead crinkle and crack as her eyebrows rose in surprise.

"Oh..." she croaked at nothingness. "Amherst *would* be proud..."

The Queen's vision warped and bent, magnifying as she manipulated her mind's eye. There was physically little left of the son of Igoric al'Dyor in the descendant she saw before her. Seven-hundred years come and gone, and the only resonating echoes of Amherst Sehren al'Dyor in the youth she took in now were the steady confidence of the man's stride, the broad shoulders of a body built with hard labor, and the thick arms of a born swordsman. Whereas the prince's eyes had been brown, however, *this* youth's were a deep, penetrating blue, and the blond, cropped hair and beard of the ancestor had been superseded by the more common, darker hues and week-old stubble. Their features, too, were different, both faces handsome, but the narrower, delicate lines of Amherst's jaw and cheeks were nowhere to be found in the stronger outlines of this man's.

But it was what lay beneath the flesh that intrigued the Queen the most, the spark that flickered and guttered and shined, like a newborn flame, within his very core.

The blood of Kings. The King's blood. She suspected the potential of the dragon's gifts must have been dormant until recently for Gonin not to have taken more note of the man's presence when they'd crossed paths. Indeed, compared to the thrumming, overbearing aura of the other two struggling evenly with the man while they attempted the first pitiful inclines of her ranges, there was little of note even now.

But the Queen could see the possible, could note the vastness of the empty space that pitiful flitting of light might one day fill within his soul. It was almost a shame. His was a body she could have done much with, a mostly-empty vessel into which she might have poured her own power. It would have been useful, to have a right hand absent the mind and will of her apprentice. She had considered more than once whether Gonin would have been more use to her dead than alive, but it was practical to possess at least one pair of eyes capable of openly traversing the realms of man.

This body, though... Oh, the things she could do...

With no small effort the Queen set her desires aside, pushed away the curiosity and fascination which had blessed and plagued her for more than seven hundred years. Had the man been on his own, it would have been different. Had he merely happened to wander into her domain, as he was now it would have been as nothing to see him snatched up and brought before her.

But he was *not* alone. He was anything *but* alone. The very beast which had centuries ago seen to it that none of the eldest bearers of the blood of Kings was ever far from the eyes of his kind stood on the man's left. On his right, another familiar being struggled, one of such striking power it made her head hurt to focus on him more than fleetingly. All the same, for a long time the Queen took in this pair, studying them as sad, bitter memories of a lost life itched at her consciousness.

Then these, too, she set aside.

With a thought the Queen pulled her eye away from the group, studying instead their surroundings, their position, their speed and bearings. It had been clever of the old man—for who else could have had such a notion?—to tame the warg as he had. No cart or wagon would slow them down even when they reached the snows of the higher altitudes. They would make good headway, and with the majority of her own wereyn long gone for the peaks, her options for dealing with them quickly were limited.

Then again, when time was a currency one could spend without limit, there was hardly ever a reason to do things "quickly".

Tracing the likeliest course the group would have to take, the Queen smiled again to herself. With Karn's Gullet long blocked off, there were few ways to penetrate the sheer cliffs of the mountaintops. All she had to do was see to their direction, and she would have them. They might well try to *fly* over the highest parts of the ranges, but that option too could be mitigated if she started her work right away. A week, she estimated. A week would she need to sow and bind the magics.

Releasing her scrying eye, the Queen allowed her presence to soar, to drive upward, far beyond her hidden chamber within the belly of the mountains, beyond the forests of the world, beyond the sheer slopes of the ranges. She became one with the endless sky, feeling the shift of the air and clouds, feeling the coolness of the ripping winds and heat of the sun. She allowed herself a moment, a single moment, to bask in the freedom of the flight, soaking in the blissful lack of the corporeal form which would ever chain her physical being to the world.

And then the moment passed, and the Endless Queen began to craft her spell, began to draw into herself the very currents of the heavens, weaving them with steady, slow care into a force that would bring even the powerful presences of the beings far below her to their knees.

CHAPTER THIRTY-FOUR

Know yourself capable.
Never believe yourself unconquerable.

-Cassandra Sert, Iron Wind Guildmaster, 1067p.f.

By the time Declan and his company reached the final edges of the northern woods, they were all, each and every one of them, unanimously grateful for Bonner's presence of mind to have brought Orsik and Eyera into the fold. Ryn in particular had no complaints when Ester took his old traveling harness and—with a few minor adjustments using some of the leather they'd salvaged from Elghen—fit it to Orsik's thicker neck and chest. The dragon had made no mention of it in their weeks on the road, but Declan suspected playing the part of the group's glorified pack animal might have indeed wounded his friend's pride, if even just a little.

Once half their things had been hitched to the male's sides without complaint, Ester promptly saw the rest of the loose straps turned into a second, rougher tack. Declan had watched her quick fingers make short work of her heavy needle and thread even as they walked, smiling as he faintly recalled the skillful stitching which had once repaired the sleeve of a torn shirt. Eyera, regrettably, had proven herself less amiable to being harnessed than her brother—for Bonner was apparently sure now that the two were siblings—and required some coaxing from the half-elf. Ester had—at some point lost to Declan—become the only of the four of them who could approach the female without Eyera at least turning up a lip in annoyance.

In the end, the animal had to be bribed with a bit of salted meat while Bonner distracted Orsik with a stick the size of his arm. Amusingly enough, when she was finally laden with the rest of their things, the warg made no additional comment aside from snorting hopefully at the bags of provisions hanging behind her shoulders.

In comparison to their overall mass, the extra weight proved small hindrance to the creatures, even after the party reached the foothills and began climbing as the trees thinned around them. The pair managed the rocky, frosted slopes with ease, and seemed particularly animated upon returning to what must have been more familiar territory for them. It was oddly satisfying, watching the laden siblings nip and bark at each other like dogs at play, and Declan had found himself largely enjoying their antics, going so far as to occasionally laugh out loud into the echoing emptiness that were the blooming cliffs overhead. For a time he was able to forget the

346

dread of the coming days, able to ignore the looming presence of the mountains rolling overhead, the waves of some great, violent ocean of stone and snow.

They had left the forest proper long behind when the unfortunate nature of their course was brought back to him all-too-abruptly.

It was the fact that Ryn and Bonner paused and looked skyward *together* that had Declan immediately on the alert. Ester would have noticed too, he was sure, but she was some fifteen feet above them already, her nimble, elven form keeping pace with Orsik and Eyera as they climbed. Instead, he was left alone to tense when the dragon and mage paused in unison, turning to peer up over their shoulders like queer mirrors of one another.

"What is it?" Declan had to ask, looking between the two, one on either side of him. Neither answered immediately, but their shared frown told him there was indeed something worth being concerned about.

When their gazes finally fell earthward, they sought each other's eyes for confirmation.

"You felt it?" Bonner asked.

I did. Briefly. It was there, then it was gone.

"What was?" Declan pressed them.

"A spell of some kind," Bonner told him, looking up again. "More powerful than the scrying weaves I can conjure, or else we wouldn't have sensed it at all. It was like… an eye, watching us from above."

A stone dropped into Declan's gut. He wasn't sure what bothered him more: the knowledge that something had so effortlessly spied on them, or the fact that said "something" had done so with a magic more powerful than *Bonner* claimed to be able to conjure up.

Then he put two and two together, and the stone turned into a weight that would have liked to see him dragged him to his knees.

"Sehranya?" he asked, hating that he was unable to keep the hush out of his voice.

Ryn and the old man nodded together.

Likely, the dragon said with what seemed to Declan an alarming lack of concern, restarting his climb. *It would appear we've stumbled into some sort of warning ward.*

"*What?!*"

Declan's half-hissed demand was alarmed enough to have Ester and even the warg quit their ascent and glance back down on them in concern.

"Stay calm." Bonner's hand came to rest on Declan's arm. "Recall that it was always a possibility we'd be found out. Whether they discovered us by chance or by this misfortune makes little difference. We've no choice, either way, but to keep on as we've planned. If that was indeed the Queen's eye, I don't imagine turning around would help us in the least. Elghen was sacked by a force far larger than the pittance we all saw to. If that arm of the horde had their attention turned on us, I doubt there would be much any of us could do about it."

The weight hadn't yet left Declan's stomach, and he found it hard to swallow as he stared at the old man. His words were logical—of course they were—but they still rang hollow in Declan's ears. He couldn't stop himself from turning and casting out over the northern forests, taking in the sweeping woodlands they had spent the afternoon traversing. In the distance he could still make out the waning tendrils of smoke that marked the town. He found himself suddenly doubting, suddenly questioning as he hadn't before, that they were indeed making the right choice. It wasn't just the Queen's gaze on them—which, though he hadn't sensed, was already itching at the back of his neck. That clawed on him, to be sure, but Bonner's words had brought about a sudden sense that he was abandoning something, some duty that would go unfulfilled if he turned tail and ran…

There's nothing you can do.

Ryn's voice shook Declan from his depressed considerations, and with the crunch of loose stone the dragon slid back down the slope to come to a stop on his right, joining him once more in looking out over what small part of Viridian they could see from their vantage.

"In my head again?" Declan asked, only half-joking.

Ryn chuckled dryly, shaking his reptilian head. *Hardly. I just know a doubting mind when I see one.* He pointed south, towards the faint smoke. *As you are now, there's nothing you can do. Rather, I should say there is little you can do. You're a good sword, Declan. Better than good. And with what little Bonner has taught you, I admit you're more a force to be reckoned with now than ever before. But I've known times when there is no choice but to stand and fight.* He frowned, and for some reason his white-gold eyes fell to the gold signet on the middle finger of Declan's left hand. *I've known men who have lost their lives in such moments. Not needlessly, I can say to my small comfort, but wastefully all the same.*

He turned and took a step upwards again, nudging Declan's shoulder with his own in suggestion that he should follow this time. *And turning around now would be a waste. Even if Sehranya has us in her sights, we aren't defenseless. Have faith in your companions. I don't know about you, but I've no intention of letting some witch without courage enough to face us head-on dictate our decisions from the shadows.*

The dragon's words were fiery, and Declan felt a little warmth return to him, budding in his heart like the firestone in his breast pocket had responded to Ryn's encouragements.

He turned, and forced himself not to glance over his shoulder at the clouds as they began to climb once again.

For the rest of that afternoon and half of the next day, the ascent went smoothly. It was cold, their panting breaths coming in heavy billows of mist after any particularly arduous effort, and the ground beneath their feet had long since turned from grass and loam to loose earth and broken slate, requiring particular attention to one's footing. Still, the initial climb proved only slightly more laborious than managing the rooted hills and rivers of the woods had been. Trees were sparse, but those that still clung to the unfriendly earth were tough, thin things which offered excellent handholds when available. Jutting boulders and outcroppings, too, provided ample opportunity to rest, as well as shelter from a growing wind that tossed their hair and the loose edges of their clothes about them while they climbed. For some time Declan managed to stay in high spirits, or as high-spirited as one can manage when bearing the awareness that the Endless Queen herself could fix them in her gaze at any time she saw fit…

Then, though, the shale began to disappear, their footing firming up into packed earth and hard stone, and the incline of the world tilted drastically beneath them. By the time dusk fell on their first full day beyond the woods—the painted colors of the sky cast in awkward shadows around them as the sun sank almost directly to their left along the ranges—Declan knew they had reached the mountains true.

They were within the Mother's Tears, ascending the great peaks he had been raised to believe—as any child of Viridian was—marked certain death for any man or woman fool enough to test them.

That night, during his watch—spent huddled under the layers of his salvaged cloak and bed-furs with the firestone clutched to his chest for warmth—Declan found himself repeating his conviction of their shared madness until it sounded like a mantra on his lips.

The pace slowed exponentially, after that. Orsik and Eyera continued to prove themselves by instinctively taking the easiest paths up the slopes, the clinking of their shifting pack harnesses making them easy to follow even when the breaking juts of rock and cliff hid the pair from view. Ester was always second behind them, with Ryn third. It hadn't been more than an hour into the true climb before the dragon had given up on his *rh'eem* and transformed into the massive, loping wolf, taking up his claymore in his mouth to chase after the half-elf and warg on a steadier foursome of legs.

After Ryn, Declan usually came next, with Bonner most often bringing up a straggling rear. The old man, like the animals, was usually audible even when out of sight, though his telling sounds were more often curses and mumbled seethings about the mountains and the blasted wind that continued to buffet them about like leaves on a sparse branch.

The ascent was, on the other hand, not without its silver linings. For one the fact that they had to keep a close eye on their footing at all times meant that there was little energy or thought to spare to daily training. Declan was excused from all weave practice other than some evening repetition of the arcane laws across a summoned fire, over which they warmed their meat and roasted slices of potatoes for supper. Ryn had considered putting them about their swordplay, but Ester put her foot down on this idea with a pointed commentary that if the dragon wanted them to fall asleep on their feet the next day, then *of course* she and Declan would draw steel for him. She'd indeed looked exhausted, lounging back into the crook of Eyera's swelling, furred sides for warmth while the warg slept soundly, half-curled about the woman.

Declan could have kissed her for joy when Ryn had—somewhat sheepishly—bowed to this sardonic wisdom, and didn't bring up the idea again.

That was not the only benefit, however. Whether because they had left Viridian behind or because Sehranya had summoned all her own beasts to her cause, the attacks and ambushes they'd suffered daily in the last half-week of their trek towards the mountains came no more. There *were* wereyn about them. None of them needed Ryn's occasional words of warning to know that. Declan put the skills Ester had once taught him in the woods around her home to use, noting infrequently an overturned stone or freshly furrowed earth which outlined the marks of clawed feet. They'd even seen one or two of the creatures outright, but for whatever reason *these* beastmen did not launch themselves into any furious assault, as had their brethren in the woods. Bonner put forth the hypothesis that these were wild wereyn, possibly moving in smaller packs or even alone, and so lacked the confidence that had led so many larger groups to gleefully leap upon the party's claws and teeth and steel. It seemed a plausible theory, particularly when Declan had opportunity to observe the exceptionally haggard state of one pair, showing themselves for longer than the rest as they hesitated, thin forms clearly torn between hunger and caution.

To the benefit of all, the latter won out, and the beasts had left them to seek out less troublesome prey.

Aside from these few sightings, there was hardly a living soul to be found among the uneven, arid terrain of the crags, the environment growing drier and colder as they climbed. Declan saw on occasion a diving cliff falcon—the bird they'd always claimed Ryn to be in his hawk's form—chasing after what must have been some small rodent among the rocks, and once or twice thought he caught the slinking forms of wolves peeking at them from the shelves high above. Given that this was the extent of any and all contact they had with the fabled dangers of the ranges, Declan felt himself growing more confident as one day passed into two. Without the threat of attack ever-present in the back of his mind, he found himself sleeping better than he had in weeks, though this was certainly partially due to the ardor of their daily journey.

Indeed exhaustion, if anything, would have been the most dangerous of their enemies, but Bonner was their saving grace in that respect. They took frequent rests, stopping every hour or so, in which time the mage would see to any scrapes or bruises any of their number might have incurred, and weave spells of vitality into their bodies. He was sparse with his magic, providing just enough to assist their aching muscles and lungs in adapting to the altitudes, but it was enough. By the time the morning of their third day came, Declan found himself waking feeling refreshed and ready, like he had spent weeks adjusting to clambering up the Tears, rather than mere days.

Alas, where fatigue failed in seeing them defeated, the elements put up a greater fight.

Declan rather thought that they might have ordinarily managed relatively well without spellwork for the first two-thirds of the climb. His and Ester's heavy cloaks, gloves, and boots were godsend, and Bonner and Ryn were initially as bothered by the chill as they might have been by a mild drizzle on a summer's morning. Had it been any other mountain range, they might have been fine until they reached the true bluffs still high above them.

But these were the Tears, and they did not bear trespass lightly.

The cold was bad enough. By the time Declan ventured to guess they had managed half the ascent, the slickness of the stone underfoot had turned to true ice, as frequently smooth and glassy as it was rough and manageable. He and Ester had taken to wrapping spare clothes about their faces every morning to ward off the bite of the air, and even Bonner joined them on their fourth day in doing so, as well as tucking his hands into make-shift mittens from some of his spare socks which Declan hoped were warmer than they appeared. Orsik and Eyera were less affected, their heavy fur keeping them content on the move, but at night they always curled around each other for warmth, leaving only enough space between their two massive, shivering bodies for Ester to slip between. By the time they reached the snow-shelves, only Ryn appeared yet unperturbed by the cold.

Even the dragon, though, could do little against the *wind*.

In the first days, it had been noticeable, but hardly concerning. At worst a particularly strong gust would throw back one of their hoods, exposing faces and ears to the winter-worthy chill while costing them a few seconds of cursing and scrambling to cover themselves. But, as they got higher, the blasts worsened, arriving in an almost timetable fashion while a steady, unrestful zephyr pressed at them constantly in between. Their pace became crawling, their movement upward every hour feeling like it could be counted in body-lengths rather than any valuable measurement of distance. The wind tore at them, scouring them and buffeting their bodies first this way, then that, more than once almost costing someone the already-precarious purchase they had on the slick rock and ice. It was unrelenting, and by the time they settled for camp on the evening of their fifth day on the slopes, Declan had noticed Bonner and Ryn both glancing up at the clouds more times than he was comfortable with over the course of the afternoon.

"Is something wrong?!"

Exhausted by the day's climb, the yr'Essel's had taken to their rest the moment the group had finished scarfing down a meager dinner. Ester had clambered between the warg while her father huddled atop one of the beds of thin roots and small firestones that was all he was able to summon up for he and Declan to sleep on this high up the mountain. Declan, for his part, had found himself awake despite his own fatigue, a nagging doubt prodding him away from his bedroll.

Ryn's twisted, wolfish head bent around at his voice, the question yelled over the buffeting scream of the cliffs. The dragon had somehow backed his large body into a crevice formed between two smaller boulders, settling down in preparation of the first watch of the night.

We'll have to teach you to mind-speak, if this keeps up, he said with something like a laugh. *And what do you mean?*

In answer, Declan pointed skyward, not trusting his words to reach against the wind picking up even more.

Ryn looked once at the clouds, then back down, his expression inexplicably fascinated.

Don't tell me you can feel it, too? I'm impressed, Declan. I don't think I've been giving the old man enough credit as a teacher...

"No!" Declan yelled and waved his hands in an attempt to get his point across. "No! I've just seen you and Bonner watching the sky all day! What's got you both worked up?!"

Ah. Ryn frowned, his white-gold eyes lifting a second time. The very last light of the sun was all that illuminated the heavens now, dim beyond the overcast blanket of the storm.

There was no mistaking, this close, the brief flash of worry that passed across the dragon's face.

Whatever that is, it isn't natural. Ryn sounded uncertain. *Bonner thinks the same.*

Declan felt a now-familiar fear scrape at the back of his neck. They were high, five days up the incline of the mountains, and some part of him felt like he wouldn't have had to do more than reach up in order to touch the dimming sky. Even had that been possible, though, he didn't think he would have. He'd never seen clouds move like those above them now, churning and dipping fast enough for the eye to follow. It gave new meaning to the idea of a "brewing storm", and he supposed he should have guessed there was more to the tempest if he'd really been willing to consider the alternative. He forgave himself the neglect. Declan had never before had the opportunity to witness anything remotely like such a phenomenon from such proximity. It had allowed him to cast the fear aside, to ignore it in favor of assuming the roiling cloud cover was nothing more than a trick of proximity and the cruel nature of the Tears.

Ryn's words, of course, snuffed out that small spark of hope.

"Is it her?!"

He *despised* the fact that it had become even the least bit difficult to say the witch's name. He'd found himself avoiding it during what conversation they'd been able to maintain as they climbed, like voicing it would give cause for Sehranya—obviously close, now—to summon herself to them once more.

If Ryn noticed Declan's trepidation, he made no comment of it.

Who else? Either she's preparing something she hopes will take us out in one fell swoop, or she's using the winds to herd us into some other danger.

Mercifully, if only for a moment, the howl of the storm faded enough to speak normally, and Declan eased himself down to sit in a small nook of the rocks beside his companion, eyes still on the boiling clouds.

"And there's nothing to be done about it?" His voice, at a normal volume, sounded dull to his ears.

In the immediate moment, I don't know what we could *do.* Ryn, too, was yet watching the sky. *All we have left is to prepare ourselves. She's making no attempt to hide her weaving. Then again, she might not have a choice, given the amount of power in that storm. But the fact that she isn't* trying *is what's most concerning. Whatever she has in store for us, she's confident it will be enough.*

Declan didn't ask what the dragon meant. He could figure it out on his own.

It was apparent, staring into that storm, that the Endless Queen had no intention of letting any of them off those mountains alive.

■■

The snows started the next day.

At first it was hardly noticeable, the flecks of white little more than added annoyance to the pebbles and ice dust the wind kicked maliciously about their heads. By the time mid-morning arrived, however, the blizzard had started in truth, and soon what little security they'd had in their footing was betraying them to the slickness of a half-inch of piled snow, built up in barely an hour. It was getting worse, too. Declan had his fair share of experience with winter storms, having grown up not a few hours south of these very ranges farther to the east. Now, old memories of his childhood's more brutal tempests pricked at him every time he lifted his gaze from his feet to look upwards. First they'd lost the sky, then the outlines of the peaks above. Now he could barely make out Ester and the warg some twenty feet up the slope, with Ryn distinguishable from the larger rocks about them only by the distinct darkness of his fur and scales. The winds, too, had mounted once more in their fury, and as they pressed on towards noon Declan finally understood what the dragon had said the previous evening about being "herded". Orsik and Eyera, more than once, had nosed at paths and lesser inclines only to be buffeted back onto their previous course like some eye in the storm was shunting them away from any easy climb. Orsik had lost all balance on one such occasion when a particularly vicious blast caught his long body length-wise, sending him yelping and tumbling back down the mountain face. Only Bonner's quick thinking—and even quicker spellwork—kept the warg from plummeting on without end, the mage shifting and angling a sizable slab of jutting stone to cut the animal's fall short. Even then, Orsik hit the rock hard enough to make every one of them wince, and they'd broken for their noon meal early so Bonner could tend to the beast's wounds and recuperate himself from the toll the abrupt weaving had taken out of him.

Despite those misfortunes, it wasn't until the afternoon that the Queen's power lashed out with more deliberate intent.

CRACK.

The lightning seemed to strike out of nowhere, lancing down from the grey and white of the falling snow like a blade of brilliant, blue-etched light. It caught the jutting end of an outcropping not a hundred feet to their left, outlining the stone's silhouette through the blizzard when it struck with such force the crag exploded in an eruption of rubble, smoke, and dust. Without time to take up the firestone in his pocket, Declan could do nothing more than throw himself to the ground, stomach twisting when he found nothing but slick ice beneath him. He slid a good three feet before one boot found a hold in some break in the shelf beneath the snow, and the moment his momentum was cut short he jerked his knife from its sheath and jammed it down for another point of purchase. When he knew he wasn't about to slip off to his doom, he lifted his face, squinting through the flecked frost about his eyes.

He could make out Ryn picking himself up from what looked to have been a similarly frantic flattening. The dragon was lifting his great blade out of the snow with his mouth to look west, where the place the lightning had bit into the mountain face had vanished again behind the endless curtain of the blizzard. Bonner, too, Declan could hear cursing somewhere behind him, and with Ester even further away than the three of them with the warg, he relaxed ever so slightly.

Then a second incandescent bolt descended, this time much closer, and Declan actually felt the discharging buzz of static through the handle of the blade still stuck in the ground.

EAST! Ryn's voice reverberated in his mind. *MOVE! FIND SHELTER!*

Declan was on his feet as fast as the ice beneath him would allow, not letting go of his knife and using it to aid his scramble laterally along the slope. He heard, from somewhere above, the howls of the warg—something between terrified and furious—and paused to look up, desperate to make out Ester's form through the snow.

"Move, boy!" Bonner bellowed up at him from somewhere close to his feet. "She's fine! Quick as she is, she'll outrun the damn storm while you and I are left to cook!"

Too full of adrenaline to be embarrassed at having been caught—and hardly disagreeing—Declan did as he was told. He couldn't see the mage through the narrow slit of the cloth about his face—what limited vision it offered already so often crusted with snow the wind seemed to kick up deliberately into his face—but he could make out a hint of the man's panting breaths and grunts not far at his rear. Then Declan's own heavy breathing filled his ears within his wrapping, and all he could do was focus on the blurred black shape of Ryn, who appeared to keep with their slower pace, leading them east. He ignored the sound of yet another lightning strike at his back, ignored the sting of what must have been shrapneled rock thudding into the heavy coat over his spine and shoulders. After two days of struggling foot by foot upward with meticulous deliberation, Declan suddenly found himself moving almost at a run, casting caution aside while he sacrificed sure-footing for even the barest chance of escaping the arcing bolts.

He was so desperate to move, in fact, he almost missed the second sound when it came, so similar to the break of the lightning, and yet distinctly different.

This sound, after all, came not from the sky, but from beneath his very feet.

CRACK.

Despite himself, despite every ounce of his being telling him to run, to flee, Declan froze. He found his legs unwilling to move, his muscles tensing up with a palpable fear that was more primal even than the terror of what it was he was trying to outrace.

"What in the *name of all the gods* are you doing, boy?!"

Bonner had caught up to him, and Declan felt a hand on his back shove him forward with that familiar deceptive strength, beyond the body of any ordinary man. Just the same, he took one stumbling step forward, then halted again, throwing an arm out to block the mage himself from going around.

"Stop! Wait!" He lifted his gaze, heart hammering, seeking the black outline of the dragon through the bounding snow. "Ryn! RYN!"

There was a moment of terrifying silence.

Then the wolf's form melted back into view.

Declan, you have to move! What's—?!

"Beneath us! *Beneath us!* What's there?!"

There's no time to—!

"WHAT'S THERE, RYN?!"

The desperation in Declan's voice must have rung clear, because the dragon took pause even as another strike erupted what couldn't have been thirty feet behind them. His body went still, and Declan knew he was extending his sense, digging downward.

The look of horror that played across his canine features told Declan he had been right to fear.

IT'S A TRAP! Ryn bellowed just as the bare forms of Ester and the warg appeared beyond him, apparently having turned around when they realized they were alone. *BONNER! YOU NEED TO—!*

Whatever it was that Bonner should have done, however, was lost to the brilliant eruption of light and ringing of their eyes as the lightning struck a final time. The ripping geometry of its flaring descent seared itself across Declan's eyes as it bit into the snow-covered ground barely ten feet behind Ryn, almost directly between their group and Ester's not far away. There was a sound like a hundred breaking mirrors.

Then Declan felt the shelf of ice beneath their feet shatter, and they were all plummeting into nothingness.

CHAPTER THIRTY-FIVE

Bonner's drilled lessons proved themselves, in that moment. The instant he knew himself to be falling, Declan's free hand wrenched up to grab at the pocket of his coat. No inhuman reflex would have been enough to pull the firestone out as he tumbled, however, and so Declan simply *willed* the magic of the vessel into being, seeking it even through the leather and cloth between it and his fingers. Whether due to his own power, or the stone somehow responding to the hopelessness of the situation, the weave came into being in the space of a breath. It wasn't anything he'd ever practiced before, but he had the gist of it. Turning fire into force was something he'd been able to grasp well enough to blast opponents off their feet more than once, and so in the only moment of clarity before gravity took control of him Declan pictured just such a magic, pressing it outward all around. At once the cold of the mountain vanished, replaced instead by a broiling, consuming heat that enveloped him completely. It was so shocking that Declan took in a sharp, short breath, regretting it immediately when his lungs screamed in protest at the searing air that filled them. Still, he held on, mentally gripping the spell with all his will.

When the floor of whatever space awaited them found him some twenty feet below, that field of blistering force was all that kept Declan from smashing backwards into cold, icy stone.

As it was, even the spell could only do so much. He felt it accept the weight of his fall beneath him, felt it warp and bubble away from him. He tried to hold it, tried to maintain the integrity of the weave, but the fall had been too great, the impact bending the magic out of proportion. It flexed, taking what it could.

Then, without a sound, it fractured into oblivion, leaving Declan to slam into frozen ground at only a significantly reduced speed. His head snapped back, cracking against hard rock through the hood of his cloak.

The impact of it felt like he'd been clubbed by a mace.

"Aaahhhh...!" was the only sound he could make, knife tumbling forgotten from his hand as he reached out to clutch at the back of his neck and skull. His vision went black for several seconds, even the seared imprint of the lightning strike disappearing, and when it came back it was so full of stars it looked like the blizzard—still raging above—was raining diamonds upon them.

Declan blinked, trying to clear his head, but the world was spinning, and his thoughts along with them. What had happened? What had...? How...?

Declan! Declan?!

Ryn's fear cut through his confusion, bringing with it its own throb of discomfort. Declan held onto it, clung to his friend's soundless words, ignoring the discomfort. It cost him, and he rolled onto his side to curl helplessly over himself, still grabbing at his head, stomach convulsing involuntarily. He retched, like his body was trying to expel the dizzying pain through his stomach.

He felt a cool, clawed hand pulling at the wrappings of his face.

Hold on. Hold on! I can help.

The moment the shirt cloth was out of the way, Declan gulped in a clean breath he hadn't been aware he so desperately needed. As he inhaled, his mind cleared with almost alarming speed, and he blinked again, surprised to find himself on his side and hunched over his knees. Ryn was kneeling beside him, having returned to his dragonling's form, the claymore in the hand that wasn't currently holding Declan by the shoulder.

Clearly the dragon hadn't had any trouble weathering the fall.

"Ryn, where—?" Declan began to ask, trying to sit up, but Ryn held him down.

Don't move. Your clarity is an illusion of my making. I'm substituting some of your cognition with a few of my own. It's not a terribly useful trick, but if it keeps you from vomiting up your day's lunch, I'll call it a win.

Declan froze, understanding coming to him. The dragon was in his head again.

Yes, I am, and I will be until Bonner can take a look at you.

Declan felt his entire body tense, and he stared up at the dragon's golden eyes, wondering if—

If I can read your mind? Yes, but only for the moment. That blow wasn't anything to joke about. Your natural defenses are down, which is the only thing letting me go this deep right now. I won't pry, but if I'd left you as you were you'd be likely to pass out. Now, I need to help Bonner. Stay here, alright?

Declan realized, then, that this bizarre new connection went both ways. He didn't so much "read" anything of Ryn's thoughts, but something else came through, slipping along with the dragon's words. Emotions. Fear. Anxiety. Need. An image, too, of flailing arms and silver-gold hair.

"Ester," Declan hissed seeing the faintest glimpse of the woman falling from the dragon's eyes. "Go!"

Ryn was gone in a flash of black and gold, and his hand pulling away took with it a little of whatever barrier he had weaved into Declan's mind. Some of the pain returned, duller this time, and his concentration grew muddled again.

Not enough, however, to drag away that image of the half-elf's tumbling form.

CRACK!

Lightning flashed above them, and Declan winced and lifted his gaze to find himself staring up through a massive, broken hole twenty feet or so above their heads. They were in a cavern of some kind, made half of ice and half of stone, and the snow was chasing them into that pit the Queen had very clearly led them to. It drifted lazily down to settle over the black and grey rock of chamber floor, steadily building up upon the otherwise-untouched ground.

Declan hardly registered any of it. Ryn and Bonner would have been able to see to their own safety. Orsik and Eyera would have tumbled along with them, but he couldn't spare the warg more than a thought.

If Ester had plummeted from that height without any way to break her fall…

Then he heard the woman screaming, and the horrible sound was like music to his ears.

He brought his attention earthward again, and from among the shattered debris of ice and rubble he saw Bonner dragging his daughter, kicking aside loose rocks as he yelled for Ryn's assistance. The dragon was there at once, dropping his sword to take up the half-elf's legs, and Ester screeched again when he touched the limbs. Ignoring her, Bonner hurried backwards, past Declan, to settle her well beneath the overhang of what was left of the ice shelf they had fallen through.

That was when Declan noticed the tunnel.

He'd be wrong, he realized. The "pit" was less a hole than it was a cave, or an open cavern. Behind him, in whose mouth Bonner and Ryn were struggling to calm Ester down, a tunnel passage gaped, wide and unwelcoming. Following its line, Declan looked to the other side of the space, finding the wall similarly absent, descending down into dark nothingness. It was like some great *thing* had dug a massive channel through the mountain, barely breaching the surface long enough to form the broken hole the party had fallen through.

"All Her Graces…" Declan cursed, staring at the opening of the far tunnel with disbelief.

On your feet. Bonner needs you.

Declan's attention was successfully diverted by Ryn's clawed hand looping him under one arm. He started, then allowed himself to be lifted carefully to his feet, suppressing a groan as his headache protested the motion. He could only imagine what state he would be in if not for the dragon's intervention, and begrudgingly offered Ryn some silent gratitude for the intrusion as he led him slowly out of the falling snow and into the shadow of the overhang. When they reached the yr'Essels, Declan's astonishment at the place they had found themselves in was cast aside in favor of horrified fascination upon taking in Ester's state.

Both of her legs were broken. That much was obvious at the very least. The cloth of her pants was darkening before his very eyes with seeping blood, and here and there he saw bone stick out, jutting and sharp where it had torn through. One arm, too, looked to have snapped above the elbow, and her normally-elegant face was a mess of red from a gash that had been torn into her scalp over one eye. She was screaming, still, clearly lost to the agony of her condition, the sound reverberating through the icy walls of the chamber to echo horribly all about them

"Declan, I know you're hurt, but I can't do this all on my own!" Bonner was struggling as his muffled shout rose over his daughter's keening wails, pinning her one good arm to her chest to keep it from lashing out in agony while drawing a rune over her face with his other. The symbol drew itself out in the air in glowing blue threads, flashed, then vanished, and Ester's cries came to an abrupt end. She went limp, and Bonner looked up to meet Declan's eye with grave severity through the slit in the cloth he still had wrapped about his head. "The ground. Can you warm it? The air, too. She'll freeze to death before I can finish fixing her, and I can't do everything myself."

Declan mouthed at the air, the ache in his skull spiking, trying to will his confused mind to understand, to process.

"Can you do it?!" Bonner demanded, already reaching over to tear open the legs of the woman's pants.

Finding he lacked the means by which to answer efficiently, Declan instead let himself fall roughly to one knee, pulling off a glove as he did to wrench the firestone from its pocket. Ryn left them, moving back towards the smashed remnants of the ice, and Declan let him go without a word, closing his eyes, too focused on summoning the magics into life.

He discovered over the next few minutes that he had to work in the opposite order of Bonner's request. Despite their contact with the stone, the first problem was his own fingers, which were numb within seconds in the churning air of the cavern. He summoned the familiar weave of heat first about himself, then pressed it out, expanding it until it warmed the space around him, Bonner, and an unconscious Ester. Only *then* could Declan pursue the mage's initial request of applying his magic to the ground.

It was the first time he'd attempted any such thing, but he understood the theory of it at least well enough to try. Manipulating the energies within a solid posed a different challenge than the gases Bonner had taught him comprised the air they breathed. He had to delve deeper, had to weave his mind first *into* the ground. Declan felt the thrumming of it as he pressed his will downward, through the mountain itself, felt the faint, distant flow of power coursing slowly—so, so slowly—through the earth. He wondered if this wasn't the resonance of the ley lines Ryn and the mage had spoken of, but he cast that distraction aside in favor of seizing on the power, of wrapping his consciousness around it.

Declan didn't count the minutes, knowing it would serve no purpose to rush. It took him a long time, but eventually he felt the coursing of his own magic melt into the stone, allowing the weave to expand. Immediately he began spinning the familiar threads of the spellwork for heat, feeling the rock respond at once. Even Bonner let out an audible sigh as the cavern floor began to respond, warming steadily within the sphere of magic Declan had already produced among them. When he'd finished the weave, assuring himself thrice over that it was solid enough to hold with only minimal conscious effort, Declan finally allowed himself to open his eyes.

He must have been deeper in his own mind than he'd thought, because his mouth fell open at the sight before him. Bonner was still leaning over his daughter, but he was working quickly with both hands now, drawing runes into... the *stone*?!

Declan, despite everything he had seen so far in his time spent with the mage and Ryn, had to blink and shake his head to convince himself the blow he'd taken wasn't deluding him. Ester lay as she had, still insensate, but the floor around her had changed. Declan had seen Bonner *move* stone before, had witnessed it only that morning when the old man had saved Orsik from plummeting to his doom, but he had never witnessed it *growing*. As he watched, the black rock of the floor between his knees and the half-elf appeared to be stretching, inching up and over the woman in alternating layers from either side in sharp, curved arches. She looked like she was being enclosed within the ribcage of some earthen golem, and it was into these black bones that Bonner was busy tracing his symbols in rapid succession.

It looked, of a fashion, all-too-familiar...

Bonner caught him studying the structures with interest, and nodded.

"You recognize it?" He had, at some point, tugged free the lower half of the cloth from his face, revealing his mouth and beard. He looked strained, but not so much that Declan felt any fear for Ester's life. Something in him relaxed, at the realization.

She was going to be all right...

"I do," he got out after a moment. "Reminds me of the... the shell...? The one you had me in after the drey attacked."

"That's because it's the same spell, or something very similar." The mage worked even as he spoke, and Declan got the impression he was pleased to have anything to think about other than his bleeding, broken daughter. "I've never used solid stone before as the vessel. Fresh earth is better, I think. We may be here for some time." He paused just long enough to give Declan an appraising look. "Will you hold up?"

Declan considered. His head hurt something awful, but it was still far come from the blinding pain Ryn was keeping at bay with his mind magics. The weaving of the spells of warmth had taken their toll, too, but not so much that he was straining under their burden. The firestone felt vibrant in his hand, responding to his conscious adjustments as much as to his subconscious.

He nodded, but glanced over his shoulder, up at the hole that still opened up into a pelting of snow. Every now and then lightning would *flash* again, shaking the world with following thunder, and the wind screamed down in a billowing spiral to reach them even twenty feet below. "I'll manage for now. Are we alright here, though? Aren't we a little... exposed?"

"Better here than out there," Bonner answered at once. "Even if it *is* the Queen's intention."

"Why didn't she just strike us down above? Does she not want us dead? She obviously had the power..."

"The power, yes, but not necessarily the control." Bonner squinted, working with particular care on the runes over Ester's fractured legs. "A spell of that magnitude... It wasn't intended to be *precise* as much as it was to be *overwhelming*, I think. Whatever Sehranya is up to, she has it thought out." As though to give Declan a hint, the old man glanced over his shoulder at the tunnel leading deeper into the mountain.

Declan felt a shiver down the back of his neck as he, too, took in the passage. It was vast at the mouth, but tightened even in what limited light was offered to them by the grey of the storm outside. He had *no* inclination whatsoever to delve deeper into the Tears, but just as equally did he have the distinct notion none of them had been given any choice in the matter...

"I guess trying to climb out isn't an option, then?" he muttered half-heartedly, looking forlornly back up into the blizzard.

Bonner laughed darkly, now at Ester's knees. "If *you* want to brave that, you'll be doing it on your own, boy. I don't think even Ryndean could fly us out of here with those winds, and—if by some miracle of any of our gods we made it airborne—he's a much bigger target in the sky than we were as individuals on the ground. The witch might have a plan for us down here, but I doubt she's so desperate to see it through she'd be willing to let us free otherwise."

Declan only managed a resigned grimace in return, looking around again. Bonner was correct, of course. It might have been no issue for Ryn to get them *out*, per se, but after that they would be stranded again, with nowhere to go as they waited for the storm to finally strike them down.

Which means, Declan thought miserably, *that there's only one way left.*

Well, *two,* but the orientation of the passages had the way at their back digging south and down through the incline of the slopes, while the one before them looked to tunnel more north and *through.* Declan considered it as critically as he could, doing his best to model his attitude after the mage's and swallow his fear.

"You think that'll lead us out?" he asked, studying the arch of the cave behind the old man, hoping his voice sounded calmer than he felt.

In answer, Bonner lifted one shoulder in a half-hearted shrug, scooting over slightly so that he could see to Ester's fractured ankles. "Ryn or I will be able to get a better sense of it once we're done here, but either way I don't know what choice we'll have."

"Food could become an issue…" Declan frowned. "Even water, if this ice doesn't extend deeper." He eyed the sheen of the walls dubiously.

"Water won't be a problem. I can see to that. As for rations, we'll just have to be careful. We've enough for another eight days or so, and if we portion that I think we can make it last a while longer. Worst case scenario, we have the warg."

Declan almost recoiled, a little surprised to find himself somewhat disgusted by Bonner's suggestion, and only minimally because he didn't fancy eating *warg* meat. He'd grown a little fond of the animals over the last weeks, and didn't in the least want to entertain the thought of butchering them for sustenance.

"If we have to," he muttered unenthusiastically, looking around at the thought of the beasts. Ryn had pulled the pair out of the debris, he found, and Declan was relieved to see the two were largely unhurt. Eyera was keening near the far wall—the sound mostly stolen away by the howling of the wind—licking at a paw that hung too-limply from a raised leg. Around her, Orsik was prowling almost nervously, alternating between nudging at his sister and baring teeth at the storm that continued to rage overhead. He was favoring his left side, his right back leg apparently unable to bear his weight, and Declan saw blood slicking the grey-white fur of the male's haunch. Ryn was still with them, and looked to be doing his best to comfort the pair. For once, not even Eyera complained about his clawed hand running gently between her ears.

They'd all survived. There was that at least. Ester was the worst off of them by far, but they'd made it. If the Queen had intended to do more damage with her trap, she had failed.

Declan felt a little of his courage return, at that.

When he'd been drenched in the drey's blood, he only had vague recollections of the work the yr'Essels had put into his recovery, but he was sure it must have been hours. Fortunately, with Ester's injuries being only physical, Bonner's initial spellcrafting took a mere twenty minutes more, and when he was done he sat back with a groan that for once made him sound of the age he looked. He spent a little time like that, eyes closed and leaning back against his hands, as though trying to catch his breath, and Declan didn't bother him. He had a better understanding, now, of the toll magic could take on one's body. His own will was starting to tire, and if it had been two weeks prior he was fairly sure he would have long since collapsed from exhaustion while trying to keep up even those simple weaves of heat that were keeping them all from freezing.

"Right," Bonner finally grunted, shoving himself to his feet. "She's out of the woods. Your turn."

With a bit more of his usual energy the mage moved around Ester and—without preamble—took hold of Declan's head with both hands. Declan did his best not to let out a markedly-unmanly squawk of pain when the sudden pressure through his skull brought with it a wave of nausea.

"Sorry," Bonner muttered in apology, tugging off the rest of the wrapped shirt so he could lean down and sift through Declan's long hair to examine the spot where bone had struck stone. "Bear it for a moment, if you would."

Declan did as he was told, though he had to work harder to maintain his grip on the magics he was upholding when Bonner's fingers started prodding and poking. Soon after, he felt the tingling of a weave settling itself against his mind, the sensation not-unlike the occasions where Ryn had slipped his presence between Declan's thoughts.

"Hmm. Concussed. Badly, too. Nothing to worry about, though. Ester won't be able to move for a few hours, so you might as well sleep while you can as well." Declan felt Bonner turn at his back. "Ryndean! Release him. I'll see to it now."

Declan tensed, knowing what was about to happen. Sure enough, the alien sensation of something *detaching* itself from his mind followed shortly. This time—instead of the fear and confusion and anxiety that the dragon had once let loose in this very manner—what returned was a throbbing, soul-deep ache that immediately had Declan's vision spinning for a second time.

"Aaaah...!" he moaned again, bringing one hand up to his face like covering his eyes might help the pain, but before he'd done so the tingling of Bonner's weave intensified, and much of the discomfort faded into a pleasant, empty haze. Declan breathed easier, the respite outweighing the perturbing sensation that something was being pieced back together *inside* his head, like a surgeon might stitch close an open wound. A minute passed, then two, and finally Bonner's hands came away, leaving Declan with nothing but a faint echo of the nauseating throb that had sent his world tumbling.

"Thanks," Declan said with an easing sigh, looking over his shoulder at the mage. Bonner was tired, he could tell—the cost of all this spellwork adding to the physical tax their day's climb had claimed of them—but he waved the comment aside all the same.

"I'm going to see to the beasts. Shouldn't take but a few minutes. Can you keep up your weaves a little longer?"

Declan's heart skipped a beat. As Ryn's shielding magics had fallen away, he'd lost track of his own spellwork. He reached out, through the firestone in his hand, fearing that the weaves would have fallen apart, but with equal surprise and relief he found the tethers intact, if somewhat faded. He willed them back into steadier being as he answered.

"I can. We'll *all* need rest, after this, though."

Bonner gave a bleak laugh, like Declan had made an excellent joke, and started making his way towards the warg. Left on his own, Declan forced himself to focus solely on the task at hand, on Ester's steadily rising and falling chest he could make out through the lattice of stone, on the thrum of his own power. At some point he reached into the shell to brush free the hair that had gotten plastered over the left side of the woman's face, stuck to the blood of the gash that was sealing slowly before his eyes. He studied her, taking her in, losing himself in the half-elf's features.

It kept him from dwelling on the gaping maw of the tunnel beyond her, wide and waiting, like the patient gullet of a hungry leviathan eager to swallow them all whole…

CHAPTER THIRTY-SIX

Ester's groans of tired confusion shook Declan slowly from a fitful rest. He opened his eyes, blearily registering that the stone he'd fallen asleep on was still warm. It wasn't *his* magic, he knew, reaching out with his mind as he pressed himself up onto one arm. Sure enough, the flow of power was not tethered to himself, but behind him, and rolling over onto both elbows he found Bonner leaning against the nearby wall, chin lolled to his chest and eyes closed. A series of complex runes smoldered in the icy rock by his shoulder, and Declan could only assume them to be some more-lasting source of heat than his meager weave had been able to provide. Orsik and Eyera, too, were nearby, scarred chests rising and falling in near-unison while they slept curled about one another to the right of the mage, free of the gear and harnesses that were neatly piled not far away. They looked better off than they'd seemed before Bonner had finally given him leave to sleep, the female's paw intact, while her brother's flank no longer wept with blood.

"Declan...?"

He started, looking around again. Ester was squinting at him sidelong through the stone ribs of the healing cage, her weariness apparent, her continued discomfort spelled out in the stiffness of her neck and shoulders.

"Welcome back," he joked with as firm a grin as he could manage, hoping she would recall. It took her a moment, but Ester eventually returned the smile.

"Oh..." she half-laughed, eyes focusing to take in the underside of the arches that curved several inches above her face. "I feel like we've done this before, haven't we...?"

"Our roles were a little different, but yes," Declan answered, pressing himself up to sit cross-legged next to her. He took in the enclosure for himself, noting that many of the runes still tremored with a faint, green light. "Looks like your father's spells are still doing their work, so don't try moving." He met her eyes, feeling a weight lift from his chest when they opened a little wider for him. "How are you feeling?"

"I'm... not sure." Ester's voice came a little stronger, but still faint. "Everything hurts, but..." She shut her eyes tight and gave a groan, like she were trying and failing to recall something. "What happened? I remember running, then the lightning strike, but then..."

"You fell," Declan explained gently, reaching through the stone to wipe some dried blood from the half-elf's cheek. "We all fell." Withdrawing his hand, he gestured upward. "Can you see the hole?"

Ester followed his finger, then nodded, promptly wincing when the motion triggered some obvious spasm of pain.

"Try not to move," Declan reminder her softly. "You were a mess, but Bonner's seen you right, I think. He's sleeping now. He and Ryn managed fine, but the rest of us were in rougher shape. I think the old man will be out for a while."

"Ah," Ester said in understanding this time, smartening up. Then she did her best to look around without moving her neck. "Where... Where *is* Ryn, by the way?"

Declan paused, then cast about himself in surprise. Sure enough, the dragon was nowhere to be seen.

Given that he doubted Ryn would wander far while the three of them slept, he settled on the mouth of the tunnel on Ester's other side.

"I imagine he's close by," he dodged deliberately, not wanting to alarm the woman and have her crane trying to get a peek at the passage she hadn't seemed to have noticed yet. "Probably trying to find us a way out of here. Are you warm enough?"

He was a little relieved when Ester took the bait, giving a muttered confirmation and closing her eyes again. Her brow pinched together, however, and Declan knew the woman's discomfort to be far from over.

Pulling a glove off with his teeth, he reached through the lattice again and took Ester's hand in his own scarred grip. She accepted it without a word, squeezing his fingers until whatever ached passed, and didn't let go after.

Unwilling to try for more sleep despite Declan's encouragement, the woman instead pressed him on how the warg were doing, and if they'd lost any of the gear. As the beasts were clearly on the mend and it didn't look like anything had been lost from their harnesses in the fall, it was easy to reassure her, and they spent the next quarter-hour or so in quiet conversation. They were discussing the storm—he filling Ester in on her father's suspicion of Sehranya's involvement—when Ryn reappeared, climbing up out of the dark of the shaft just as Declan had expected, his claymore sheathed in one hand.

Good, you're awake, the dragon said with a mix of surprise and relief, coming to stand over the pair of them and looking down at Ester. *How are you?*

"I'll be fine," Ester answer with a brave face, and Declan said nothing to the contrary as her gripped tightened against another wave of pain. "Where were you?"

Exploring, the dragon answered before Declan could stop him. *There's a network of caves descending north of us. I expect the intention is to force us into the mountains, rather than allow us to pass over them.*

"Caves?" Ester asked with interest, suddenly a little more awake. Declan pressed her hand in his before she started looking about again.

"You'll see what he's talking about when you're healed," he said firmly, and Ester took his point, settling after straining only a little to try and peer around Ryn. When he was sure she wouldn't hurt herself for the sake of curiosity, Declan looked to the dragon. "Find anything?"

It's definitely not a dead end. There's an air flow—Ryn gestured to his webbed ears, which indeed looked sensitive enough to pick up even the slightest breeze—*but I couldn't tell you if the tunnels go* through *the ranges, or open up further below us on the south face. I'm inclined to think it's the former, though. I couldn't sense any passages paralleling this side of the slopes, aside from some branches off that one.* He indicated the mouth across the cavern from them, and Declan only briefly turned around to glance at it.

Back isn't an option, he told himself for the hundredth time since they'd started the infernal climb up the Tears.

"Nothing else?" he pressed, hoping he didn't come off too anxiously. "I'd toss myself off the cliffs before I believed we'd been forced down here for little more than a detour."

Nothing. Ryn shook his head, moving around Ester to where the warg lay beside Bonner. Orsik, hearing him approach, cracked open an eye before lifting his head expectantly, happily accepting the scratch of the dragon's claws behind one ear. *But there are miles of tunnels down there, and my magics don't extend so well beneath the earth. I don't know if we can trust my senses regardless, given how often the Queen and her ilk have fooled us thus far.*

Declan nodded, glad he didn't have to voice that shared opinion.

"Will our provisions last?" Ester asked, getting both Ryn and Declan to look around at her. She'd closed her eyes again, but her words were growing stronger with every passing minute. "If we have to go through?"

"Your father and I already talked about that." Declan tried to inject some reassurance into his answer. "He says we have eight days of food at least, and more if we ration them."

Ester grunted, face taut. "That's less than it might seem. If we get turned around down there, we'll be wandering around until our legs can't carry us anymore. And that's only *if* we survive long enough to lose our way." She cracked a tired eye up at him. "I've heard it's not a pretty way to go…"

Declan had no words for that, having considered the same consequence already. He'd never witnessed true starvation himself, but in Ranheln, Vasser Timoth had shared some troubling stories of sailors lost at sea in his time spent in Sethylles, rescued on a mere chance only to return home as nothing more than fleshless mannequins of skin and bone.

It was anything but an encouraging image.

"We'll get through."

As one, all three turned to see Bonner lifting his head from his chest, wiping his mouth with a sleeve of his colored robes and grimacing up at the greyish white of the snows still tumbling through the hole above them like the light was too bright. He'd pulled free the rest of the shirt he'd borrowed to shield his face from the elements, so when he reached up to push back his hood his bald head shown orange in the glow of the runes by his ear. He stretched, indicating with his chin the passage Ryn had been exploring as he did so.

"If there's a current, we need only follow it. It just means we have to be careful, in case the Queen has some method by which to manipulate our direction, like she did on the slopes. We'll at least mark our path as we move, so we can always find our way back here if need be."

"How would that help us?" Declan asked, unconvinced.

Bonner shrugged. "Might not, and probably won't, but having *any* point by which to plot our direction is better than nothing, don't you think?"

Declan shrugged. "I suppose," he conceded without much enthusiasm, looking to Ryn. "You think you can follow the air flow?"

The dragon looked uncertain. *It's strong up here, at the mouth. The tunnel narrows, so it's easy to make out. If it broadens again lower down, it won't be so distinct. If there are caverns, or any larger open spaces, I might not be able to detect it at all...*

"Wonderful," Ester muttered sarcastically from the ground.

"There are ways to mediate that," Bonner assured them, grunting as he used the wall at his back to push himself to his feet. The sound woke Eyera, who looked up blearily for a moment, then settled her head back under the crook of her brother's leg for warmth.

I think we would all feel better if you would tell us how before *we throw ourselves down that hole, Bonner,* Ryn said with just the faintest note of tired impatience, still rubbing Orsik behind one ear.

"It's simple enough," Bonner said with more than a hint of his typical smile. *How* the man could be amused by anything, given their situation, the Mother only knew. "Declan will demonstrate."

There was a moment of silent confusion, at these words.

"*Me?*" Declan finally spluttered. "If you think *I* have a way of getting us through these damned—!"

Bonner cut him short with a single raised finger.

"Summon us up a flame, if you would. Nothing extravagant. A small one. Like a candle."

At once, Declan understood, and the quick noise of comprehension Ryn made told him the dragon had followed the idea as well. Ester, for her part, was busy weathering another spell, her grip so tight about Declan's digits it hurt, and didn't look to be listening.

With his left hand, Declan awkwardly pulled the firestone from where he had stowed it in its habitual pocket. A focusing thought, and he condensed the heat within it, then allowed the energy to expand in a small burst. It took flame in his palm, licking harmlessly at the leather of his glove, and Declan weaved it into a single point at the tip of one finger, just as Bonner had suggested. The red-yellow fire burned low, but the mage's plan was proven in a heartbeat. It danced in the wind that still rolled down the walls at them, but when the storm gave them a moment's respite the flame flickered and bent away from Declan, shimmering in some unseen flow he couldn't make out.

It bowed, bouncing and bobbing, in the direction of the tunnel.

"So?" Bonner asked in his ear, and Declan jumped to find the man had approached him while he'd been crafting the simple spell. "Am I not a clever man?"

"Too clever by half," Declan muttered back, repressing a laugh and releasing the weave to stow the firestone away again. "But yes. I credit you with some fraction of brilliance, in this case."

"Are we going to make it through?" Ester murmured wearily. Declan looked down at her to find her eyes slightly open again, her grasp relaxed.

With an *actual* smile, this time, he nodded at her between the stones.

It was another hour before the magics imbued in the woman's cage ran their course—time Declan, Ryn, and Bonner put to use making what few preparations they could for their inevitable descent into the mountains while the storm continued to flash and rage high above them. The old man checked and rechecked Declan's head, then Orsik's and Eyera's injuries, and when he announced them all fit to move they saw the warg harnessed again. A needless count of their gear and provisions followed—Ryn's senses had already confirmed that nothing was lost in the fall—but it provided a good reminder of their provisions, which Bonner claimed responsibility for partitioning over the coming days. By the time this was done, the runes had finally faded from the black arches, and Ester declared herself well enough to try standing. Bonner spent several minutes pulling the stonework back into the rock from which it had come, and the moment there was space enough to do so Declan had reached down to help the half-elf up, careful to keep her steady as she found her feet. She was haler by far than the broken mess of a woman she'd been only hours before, but a long way from completely recovered, and staggered against him the moment she attempted to take a step. Deaf to all protests, Declan bent and pulled the woman's arm over his shoulder to half-guide, half-carry her to where Eyera and her brother were sniffing at the darkness of the tunnel mouth.

"It'll be fine if it's her, right?" he asked of the female, shifting some packs on the animal's back to make room. He hadn't, of course, expected any response other than a growl.

He was taken aback, therefore, when the warg looked around at them, took in Ester's trembling form for a long moment, then proceeded to ease her considerable bulk down to the ground like she knew exactly what he intended.

More appreciative than words could entail, Declan first rummaged about one-handed in their things until he found a spare pair of pants for the half-elf to replace the torn remnants of her current coverings. He allowed her the dignity of struggling on her own to don the clothes while he averted his gaze, listening to her curse under her breath as she fought to kick off her boots. The moment she was decent again, on the other hand, he practically lifted her slender body up onto Eyera's back—still ignoring Ester's insistence that she "only needed a moment"—then gratefully snuck the beast a small piece of dried meat he pilfered from their provisions while Bonner and Ryn weren't looking.

"Sorry, boy," he had to tell a hopeful Orsik sadly when the male came padding over to lick at his fingers in request. "That'll have to be the last treat any of us get for some time, I think…"

Further feeding into his growing suspicion that the warg were more intelligent creatures than he'd ever given them credit for, Orsik made no sound of complaint. Instead, he settled for shifting his head so that Declan could pet him between the ears in the fashion he appeared to prefer.

All set, you two?

Ryn and Bonner were rejoining them, having put themselves through one last fruitless examination of the cratered hole they'd all fallen through, just to be sure they were making the right decision.

"I can *walk*, you know," Ester complained, earning herself a raised eyebrow from her father.

"Aye, and you'll be allowed to do so," the man said dryly, pointing to her new pants. "The moment those legs stop shaking just trying to keep you upright *as you are now*, that is."

That had Ester quieting down, ending the conversation with the woman responding in nothing more than half-hearted mumblings of dissension, and Bonner turned his attention on Declan instead.

"Ready?" the old man asked, and there was only the faintest tremor in his tone, the barest hint of shaken confidence.

It made Declan—if anything—feel better, knowing he wasn't the only one scared as Ryn, too, met his gaze with just a slivered gleam of apprehension in his golden eyes.

Not trusting himself quite yet to speak, Declan nodded and turned.

Then, all together, the six of them stepped into the maw of the passage, and began to descend.

■■

They weren't more than a hundred feet down the tunnel before the dim sunlight of the cavern behind them grew too faint to see by. Without a word Declan and Bonner both summoned themselves a light, his flowing through gloved fingers from the brightened firestone, the mage's taking the shape of one of the winged orbs he'd conjured up the night prior to their departure from the yr'Essel's clearing. A single source of illumination might have served the purpose just as well, but no one complained of the little extra brightness, especially after even the sounds of the thunder and lightning faded into the empty nothingness at their back.

None of them spoke, as they walked. Not at first. There was an eeriness to the passage that swallowed all courage, that made one feel small despite the fact the space had narrowed quickly until Orsik and Eyera couldn't so much as trot side-by-side without rubbing shoulders. The sounds of their footsteps were hard and loud in their ears, boots scraping the dry, icy floor like claws against the stone. The walls shone, glimmering with frozen streams and spills of water, but there was no beauty in the sight. On the contrary, Declan felt like he was being constantly watched by a hundred different eyes at any given moment, each of them blinking and winking out with every shift of the light.

It brought back the itching feeling, reminding him of the Endless Queen's gaze...

It was almost twenty minutes before anyone spoke a word, and even then their conversation consisted of nothing more than a quiet deliberation between Declan, Bonner, and Ryn when they reached a split in the tunnel. The path they'd been following continued, but another passage, a little broader, diverged down and westward—or at least what any of them could guess was westward, without the sun overhead to guide them. Ryn thought the draft pressed more firmly down this new direction, and even Ester coaxed Eyera closer to watch over the three's shoulders while Declan summoned up a flame to test the dragon's theory. Sure enough, the fire danced here and there along both paths, but more frequently and aggressively to the left, towards the steeper pass. After an exchanged nod of agreement, Ryn drew a claw across the closest wall in the shape of an arrowhead leading back, up the way they'd come, the raking sound piercing in the silence.

Then the six of them took their first divergence in their descent into the Tears.

It had been afternoon already when Sehranya's storm saw them shepherded to the pit that had swallowed them, but having taken a rest while Declan, Ester, and the warg recuperated from their injuries, no one was particularly tired. What was more, while the floor of the caveworks often proved slick and slippery, the going was a far cry less laborious than *ascending* the mountain slopes outside had been. For this reason Declan suspected it must have been a good six hours—well into the night, and some half-dozen changes in direction later—before Ryn called for their first halt.

Due to the limited breadth of the path, making camp for the evening proved itself a bit of an unwieldy ordeal compared to the weeks past. Declan left Bonner and Ryn to prepare a meal for them at one end of the relatively flat measure of passage they'd selected to settle in, choosing himself to see to their sleeping arrangements. Willing his weaves into the cave floor was a little simpler, this second time around, and now he pressed the magics more firmly, threading a spell of slightly greater complexity together. The *hiss* of evaporating water rewarded him after several minutes of work, and he summoned a little more light out of the firestone to watch the rivulets of ice they had been navigating crack and boil away into wisps of steam. He had to repeat the process several times—he could only fabricate this significantly more intense heating for a few feet in every direction at once—but it got easier with each attempt. By the time he was done, some five or six yards of the tunnel's width were dry and clear for them.

Satisfied, Declan stowed away the firestone and moved to have Eyera bring herself down to her stomach so he could help Ester slide off the warg's bony back.

"You're getting better," the half-elf commented after she'd found her legs capable of bearing her own weight with only a little help. "At your weaving, I mean. When did you learn to do that?"

She was eyeing the cleared space of ground while Declan tugged free her bedroll from Eyera's harness with his other hand. Without its wet sheen of ice, the passage floor was more grey and brown than black. It looked almost welcoming, especially compared to the bleak rock that still arched several feet over their heads.

"While you were unconscious," he answered, guiding her to the center of the space, where he tossed the mat down and unrolled it with a kick before helping her to sit. "Figured it out for myself, if you can believe it."

"I can," Ester said with an amused grunt, laying back without protest on the padding. "Compared to the histories Father's had me read of the old magical colleges, you're a bit of a star pupil, I think."

Declan laughed. "Considering some of my blood comes from a creature that can manipulate minds, transform at will, and melt steel with a glorified belch, I think we can all agree I might be cheating a bit." He reached up to pull the shirt that was still wrapped about his neck free, tucking it under the woman's silver-gold hair with care to form a makeshift pillow. "Get some rest. I'll bring you something to eat when Ryn and your father are done making supper."

Ester only nodded slowly, eyes already closing again. She was yet stronger, but Declan suspected Bonner's auramancy had only been able to do so much for the extent of the damage she'd suffered in the Queen's trap. He left her to grab what sleep she could, pausing only when he passed the warg, who'd been watching him and the woman from where they'd been seated at the edge of the cleared ground.

"Keep an eye on her, will you?" he asked of the two, patting both gently on the shoulders. Whether the animals understood the particulars of the request or not, Orsik and Eyera both stood and pawed over to Ester at once. The female even made a huffing sound as she got up that any human might have meant as an indication of the obvious.

Declan smiled, watching the beasts settle on either side of the half-elf, heads in the direction of the darkness from which they'd come.

Ryn and Bonner, it turned out, had decided on a clever way to make the rationing of their supplies a bit more filling. Their cooking pot, purchased in Ranheln, was filled to the brim with a brothy mixture as it sat on the most level part of the floor the pair looked to have been able to find. The stone beneath it was glowing, a circle of heat encased in a trio of simple, equidistant runes, bringing the food within to a boil while the dragon and mage alternately tossed in small chunks of salted beef, potatoes, and pinches of grain. A trickling of not-yet-frozen water ran from a crack in the nearest wall, and Declan could guess Bonner had summoned up a spring from some unknown source within the rock itself.

"Stew," Declan said, coming to sit between his companions. "Clever. That'll certainly help things last."

"Or give the illusion of it," Bonner said without looking around, using what appeared to be his daughter's dagger to slice another spud into chunks. "It'll be filling, at the very least."

How's Ester? Ryn asked after Declan had taken up a potato and drawn his own knife to help.

"Better, but still weak."

"Healing magics can only do so much," Bonner offered, confirming Declan's early guess. "It's better to let the body heal what it can, when possible."

Ryn grunted, but said no more on the subject, choosing instead to ask after the old man's sense of how far they had descended into the mountain. Their conversation after that was solemn, each of the three distinctly content to have anything to discuss, but simultaneously aware of the continued pressure of the Tears above and around them, the glimmering winking of the icy walls ever-present in their periphery. When the stew was cooked to satisfaction, they ate in silence, and Declan excused himself quickly to bring a bowlful to Ester, who woke up eagerly enough to eat. Orsik and Eyera were fed what meager portion of meat Bonner thought they could afford, and the group settled down to sleep, Declan, Ryn, and the old man splitting the watch after the half-elf had fallen asleep again. Declan ended up with first lookout, and it was with gratitude for both their company and warmth that he settled between the heads of the slumbering warg. He did his best to ignore the unnerving new depth of the silence that descended as the others all took to their rest, distracting himself by fidgeting with the gold signet of the al'Dyors, whose true form he had yet to get accustomed to. He tried praying—several times, in fact—but each attempt choked off before he could get the words out.

Something in the bleak, dead quiet of the tunnels told him that not even the Mother and Her Graces above would be able to hear him down there...

CHAPTER THIRTY-SEVEN

"The Witch has no place in this world. Betrayer. Corrupter. Blasphemer. Her actions—even had she not turned on our people—have long put her beyond the reach of redemption. She is a disease, an infection which has scarred our hearts and history, and must be cut away.

Justice, now, can only be served off the end of a cold blade."

- translated from the private journals of Ciriak as'ahRen, 311p.f.

Three days spent in the bowels of Karn's Line, and Lysiat ay'ahSel had long since grown tired of the dark.

The silence of her unit, executed with a military precision drilled into them from the day they'd been old enough to lift a sword, was equally oppressing company. As per her own decree, not a word had been spoken between their number from the moment they'd descended into the ranges, chasing their ancient prey. The creature had been spotted by one of the regular patrols some week prior, hunting about the southern edge of the Vyr'esh, and it was only the bravery and speed of the scouts that had allowed them to track it back to its hole. The grotto, unfortunately, proved itself connected to the mess of caveworks known to hive beneath the mountains, and so Lysiat and her command had been tasked with rooting the monster out.

She allowed herself a glance back at the nine forms of the company following her. She and her brothers made up the officers of the unit, and it was in their hands that the moonwing lanterns were carried, the faint glow of the white moths—fed carefully each day on preserved oak leaves they'd brought with them for the purpose—more than enough for their sharp eyes even so far into the passages. Aliek held the middle with his usual tall confidence, head unmoving while his gaze flit about them to every nook and shadow they passed, the grip of his free hand about his spear firm and ready. Tesied, at their rear, gave off an only slightly less stiff air, his own spear—a mirror image of his twin's—cast over one shoulder. Just the same, even decades of discipline apparently couldn't keep him from turning about every now and then to scrutinize the darkness at their backs, the light of his lantern dancing and waning every time he did so.

Lysiat didn't bother rebuking him. She was the oldest of her siblings, true, but even *she* only had a broad sense of what it was they were hunting from the dark words offered to them by Ciriak as'ahRen. Those warnings had been almost unnecessary, of course, given the implications of the Lord Commander setting *ten* of the army's finest to the task of hunting it down.

Worse still, it was now known to them all that this duty they'd been handed was likely more complicated than even Ciriak had assumed.

The sound of a tongue clicking quietly.

At once every member of the company stopped, Lysiat among them, and she looked back a second time. Unsurprisingly it was Aliek—with his particularly keen sight—who had sounded out the warning. He was already moving, silent as the wood wraiths of song, stealing forward up the line to stoop over a spot on the ground Lysiat had only just been about to pass. Moving to join him, she saw what had caught her brother's attention at once, kneeling at his side for closer inspection.

The earth beneath their feet had been solid stone for most of their hunt, carved out of the mountain itself here by trickles and thin streams over millennia beyond fathoming, there by some shifting of the world or some monstrous, tunneling behemoth that must have existed long before the dawn of the modern races. Every now and then, however, water would gather in a crevice or smoothed pool, collecting with it what little dust and dirt and debris came loose of the tunnels over time. It was such a puddle that had caught Aliek's attention—a cool sheen of still water that cut into the side of the passage—and for good reason. As her brother held his moonwings over its surface, Lysiat made out the shapes in the silt, distinct and only slightly blemished by the careless movements of whatever had made them as it likely stooped to drink.

Footprints. Clawed footprints, as broad across as Lysiat's hand was long.

No, she realized, slipping her fingers into the pool to make this exact measurement, taking deliberate care not to disturb the fragile impressions. *Broader. Much broader.*

She forced herself to take a steadying breath, withdrawing her hand gently. Water dripped from her sleeve and skin, sending trembling ripples across the reflection of her silhouette, but Lysiat's thoughts were already away. She contemplated for a moment, taking in this confirmation they'd been seeking for what had to have been most of the last day. Their company had come across hints before, small signs even *they* couldn't be sure of, but nothing so damning as this. Convincing herself, Lysiat looked up to find Tesied had joined them, standing over Aliek to offer the light of his own lantern to the scene.

She signed her question in the silent language of soldiers, taught to every child with the same deliberateness as the spoken word.

Two?

Aliek grimaced, and shook his head. With a stiffness that betrayed his unease, her brother motioned with his spear to the far side of the pool, lifting his moths high.

This time it took a moment for Lysiat to make out the prints, hidden among some scattered pebbling that had long ago tumbled into the water. They were mirrors of the ones at her knee—as well as those they'd found over the last three days—but smaller than either previous set by far. She didn't have to measure to see that. The couldn't have been more than half-a-hand across, distinctly different than the other two.

Giving herself time to think, Lysiat studied the rest of the pond's edge, but found no other signs of yet more of the beasts. She looked to Aliek, who affirmed her thoughts, putting his weapon down carefully to free up one hand so he could sign his agreement.

Three. These make three.

Tesied nodded as well, looking to be scrutinizing the loop of the pool.

Lysiat stayed kneeling for a long moment, considering. Turning around was an option, and not without value. Ciriak would likely send them back in with reinforcements and greater provisions as quickly as possible. She considered it, glancing at the other members of her company, nothing more than patient shadows while they waited in the dark for their officers to return.

Still… It had been a near enough thing to track even *one* of the beasts. What if they missed an opportunity, and lost the creatures in the mountains? If what the Lord Commander had said of the things was even *half* true, Lysiat had the dark feeling leaving them to risk an escape could spell far greater trouble down the road…

In the end, she made her decision on practicality.

We hunt one, she signed to her brothers, pointing briefly to the slightest footprints across the pool from them. *The smallest, if we can. When that's done, we hunt the next, or retreat, depending on what we learn from the fight.*

Aliek nodded at once, taking up his weapon again, but before he could stand Tesied tucked his own spear under his elbow.

And if they're all together? he asked with his now-freed hand.

Lysiat gave him a grim smirk, pushing herself to her feet.

Then we hope the Lord Commander has learned to exaggerate in his old age, or we pray to the Spirits for a miracle.

CHAPTER THIRTY-EIGHT

"It has been suspected, by men learned in the matter, that the Mother's Tears have hidden multiple avenues of passage from the eyes of humanity for as long as the curious have been looking for them. The eastern pass—guarded by the walled town of Estwyn—must have been one such channel, though to what purpose or end I cannot say. The Virisian courts of old saw fit only to start keeping records some six-hundred-and-fifty years ago, a heartbreaking reality to a scholar such as I. Still, those centuries of archives provide enough of an image to form the educated conclusion that man has ever held a curiosity on the subject of what lies beyond those northern ranges. The commonfolk are quick and content to brand Eserysh—a name for those unknown lands whose origins I cannot seem to track—a godless realm of ice and snow and emptiness. It is possible, certainly, but doubtful, and similarly pointless an argument to hold when time has so consistently proven attempting to conquer the mountain an equally reckless and useless endeavor.

One can only imagine, after all, the dangers lurking among those peaks which have failed to return even a single foolish soul after swallowing them up…"

-*The World Unknown*, by Kentan Vale, 1051p.f.

"Aye!" Bonner exclaimed excitedly. "That's it, boy! That's it! Stay focused!"

Declan grimaced, half in annoyance at the mage's words, half in effort. He *was* focused, concentrating as hard on the fragile weave in his palm—his *empty* palm—as he had on anything in his life. Then again, it was at his own request that Bonner had started to instruct him on spellcrafting without a vessel, so there was no real room to complain. Declan could feel the firestone thrumming in his breast pocket where he'd left it, responding to his calling of the magics, but he ignored the tempting heat. Instead, he struggled to keep his mind on the tiny, guttering pinpoint of fire caged in his half-open fingers.

They were three days into these lessons, now, and Declan had a whole new appreciation of Bonner's ability to control his own power. Whereas using the firestone to channel his weaving had been like filling a waterskin with the assistance of a funnel, Declan found that doing so without was more like trying to alternately fill that same skin under the torrent of a waterfall. He had no lack of strength, he realized quickly. If anything, this new tutelage was granting him a greater and greater awareness of the lingering song of magic in his veins, the music of his "King's blood" more distinct with every passing day. The trouble, rather, was *controlling* it, tempering the force of the flood so that the skin wouldn't overflow, or burst, or be swept away in the current.

Three days, and this was the first time Declan had managed to conjure up so much as a single flame for more than a few seconds at a time.

Unfortunately, that was the moment he found his limit again.

"Guuh!"

Air erupted into Declan's lungs as the spell broke with a flash of red-gold light, and he realized—not for the first time—that he had been holding his breath. Bonner's glowing orb kept the path before them illuminated, but all the same Declan almost tripped as a healthy fatigue settled over his mind after the summoning.

"Steady," Bonner told him, taking him quickly by the arm to stabilize him. "Give me a moment."

A warmth spread from the spot above Declan's elbow where the old man's hand had ahold of him, and after a few seconds his head cleared somewhat.

"Ever a pity I've no talent for healing," Declan muttered with a nod of thanks, standing straight again and stepping over a scattering of broken stone which had come loose from the left wall to tumble across their path. "Still… That was the best I've done, I think?"

"By far!" Bonner answered with his typical gusto, grinning broadly as he let go of Declan's arm. "I know it doesn't seem like it, but you *will* get there. A vessel like that stone I gave you is merely an implement of focus. With practice it can be just as easy to use your own body in the same way."

"So you've said," Declan groaned, reaching up with one hand to rub at his temples with thumb and forefinger. The old man's auramancy hadn't quite shaken the fatigue away completely.

Bonner seemed unperturbed by this lack of responsive enthusiasm. "Aye, and so I'll *keep* saying. You're advancing marvelously, boy, but you can't be depending on having that stone in hand every time you're in need."

"I have to be able to focus my weaves on my own. I know. That's why I asked you to teach me."

It was true, despite the frustration he was putting himself through. Ever since the fall, when he'd tapped into the energies of the firestone without touching it directly—saving his own life in the process—Declan had been aware of two distinct facts. The first: he had the ability to go beyond casting with a vessel in hand. He was sure of it, now.

Second: he wouldn't always have a moment's notice to seek any greater tool to depend on than his own body and mind.

Still… There was a limit to what said implements could handle in any given day.

"Do you want to try again?" Bonner asked, to his credit doing a fair job of hiding his eagerness behind a tone of attentive concern.

Declan shook his head. "No. Enough for now. I'm afraid if we keep going it will end up with me slung over Orsik's back like one of our grain sacks."

At his given name, the warg's ears perked up, and he looked around at them from some yards ahead, earning a chuckle from Declan and Bonner both.

"Mind your own business, you walking gullet!" the mage chided the animal good-naturedly. "Not every mention of you means it's time to be fed."

The male gave low bark in answer, then turned forward again and sped up his trot to make up the few feet his distraction had cost him between he and his sister. From Eyera's side, Ester glanced back to glare at her father. Three days had done wonders for her health, and she'd flat-out refused to ride the warg any longer starting the morning before.

"Don't tease them," she rebuked the man. "It's unkind. They're hungry, and you know it."

"What's unkind is those two wolfing down *half* our combined provisions," Bonner rebutted with a twinkle in his eye, earning another laugh from Declan.

He was grateful—and not for the first time—for the character of his companions. The first hours of their descent into the black had been hard, as had the next day, but by the time what all assumed to be their second morning within the tunnels had come around, Bonner in particular had very obviously grown tired of being worn down by the blank darkness of the Tears. He'd woken them all up, jovial as he might have been in the full light of a mid-summer day, and got them packed and moving with frequent jests and encouraging quips that had had them all grinning by the time they'd broken their small camp. Declan suspected part of the man's display had been a charade. It was impossible, after all, *not* to feel the colossal weight of the place, of the monotonous walls and the imposing quiet. Even false cheer, however, could do something to fill a void in a place where there was otherwise no joy. Before long, what might have initially been pretense took root, making the going easier as each of their party managed to cling to some small sanity in the company of the others.

Are you two done back there? Ryn's voice came with its usual absence of direction, but Declan and Bonner knew the dragon was well ahead of them, separated by Ester and the staggered forms of the laden warg. *If you've the energy to banter, then you've the energy to light our damn way. This thing's about reached its limit.*

Over the outlines of the beasts, a clawed hand could be seen lifting up, displaying a faintly glowing stone the size of a fist in its palm. Early on, Declan and Bonner's practices had had several explosive results when Declan discovered himself unable to remotely throttle his own ability. Addressing this—and mitigating the risk of singeing any clothes or hair or fur—he and Bonner had taken to having their lessons at the back of the group, trailing the others by some distance. As Ester was incapable of anything but the faintest control of even basic spellwork, it had fallen to Ryn to see to their path, guided by the light of a firestone Bonner provided him. The dragon was abler than the half-elf, and had the strength to spare, but the magics of his kind and those of man appeared different enough that even his own considerable ability could only manage to balance the stone's weaves for so long.

"Yes, yes, we're coming," Bonner said loudly, taking the lead so that he and Declan could move between the warg, Ester joining them as they passed. Declan patted Orsik's head when he stepped by, earning himself a pleased rumble from the back of the male's throat.

How'd it go? Ryn asked after the three convened on him at the front, tossing aside the dying firestone when Bonner's glowing orb subverted its meager illumination. The moment it left his grasp, the heat within the rock faded, leaving nothing more than a strewn piece of debris to clatter off and rest along the side of the path.

"Marvelously," Bonner said with an excited bounce in his step. "With any luck, he'll have some measure of control by the time we're out of this infernal hell hole."

Assuming we get out, the dragon muttered, though more ponderously than anything. *I can't feel the current, but the air isn't stale and there haven't been any offshoots in the last hours, so I know we're still headed in the right direction. But we've... what? Four days' worth of food left?*

"We can make it five or six well enough, though the beasts will have to go a day or two without." Bonner's green eyes were scanning the ceiling overhead. "I'd estimate we're well over halfway through regardless, so long as we haven't gotten ourselves turned around."

I can't suppose we have. As best I can tell we've been moving generally north, if occasionally west, too.

Bonner clapped his hands like that settled the matter, the sound echoing queerly in either direction along the tunnel before and behind them. "Then we should have no issue, assuming we aren't short of game once we're free and clear of these caves."

Ryn, beside him, nodded in a satisfied sort of way, but Declan— standing slightly behind the pair with Ester as the passage was yet too narrow to walk even three abreast—thought he heard something odd in the old mage's tone. He hadn't failed to notice that Bonner was still peering up at the ceiling of stone above their heads, but when he tried to follow the man's gaze, he saw nothing out of the ordinary.

It was Ester, of course, who voiced the distinction first.

"Ryn, can you make out what's ahead of us?"

The dragon looked curiously over his shoulder at her, but before he could pose the question, the half-elf pointed upwards.

"The ceiling is rising."

Ryn and Declan together followed her finger, and while Declan couldn't make out in the slightest change in the incline of the stone, he *did* notice some faint difference in the texturing of it this time. It was pocked, almost, pitted and lumpy, like gooseflesh.

He knew the change at once, the signs of condensation streaming down an incline

"Stalactites," he muttered in recognition. "The start of them, at least. It's definitely rising."

So it is, Ryn said distractedly, his white-gold eyes unfocused. Then he was back, frowning in irritation and peering into the blackness ahead of them. *Damned stone... I can't make out much of anything in these caves. I think there might be a space ahead?*

"A space?" Bonner asked, his tone abruptly serious. "A cavern?"

Ryn didn't answer for a moment, clearly attempting again to concentrate, then he grunted and shrugged. *Likely. I can tell you the way opens up, at the very least.*

This clearly did nothing to appease the old mage, because he, too, glanced back at Declan and Ester. "On your guard, the pair of you."

The warning was completely unnecessary. Thus far, their journey had consisted of nothing but endless tunnels with nothing more alarming than frequent splits in the path or the occasional patch of ice that had sent all but Ryn and the warg tumbling onto their rears more than once. Of Sehranya's purpose in seeing them guided into the mountains, there had been no hint, and—despite the morale they'd had managed to reclaim second to Bonner's efforts—*none* of them had forgotten the lingering threat the unlit blackness ever-posed before and behind them.

And now, for the first time, they appeared to be coming upon something more than merely another length of the endless caveworks...

Silence fell between their number, and the eeriness of their footsteps through the emptiness returned with a sharp fervor. Declan eased his bastard sword from its sheath, doing his best to dampen the sound of steel sliding against wood. When the blade was bare, Ester eyed it for a second or two before falling back to where Orsik and Eyera padded along behind them.

When she took up her place at his side again, her strung bow was in hand, and a full quiver of arrows knocked lightly against the small of her back.

It was five minutes later before Declan more distinctly made out the change in their surroundings, this time because it wasn't only the ceiling that bent up and away from them. The walls, too, were distancing themselves on either side of them. It was a steady expansion, slow at first, the glimmering of the ice and stone fading as they pulled further and further away. While this happened, the ground became steadily harder to navigate, the stunted stalactites above starting to be mirrored by the humps of stalagmites beneath their feet.

Then, seemingly all at once, they were walking through true blackness, the glow of Bonner's spell shining off the rounded bodies of pointed pillars which had sprouted abruptly about and before them.

Halt.

Ryn's order was almost a whisper among their thoughts as the dragon stopped at their lead, everyone else doing the same at once. Behind them, Orsik and Eyera were navigating the rising forest of wet and frozen columns, the female snarling in quiet annoyance when she had to go around a pair of stalagmites of particular girth.

Ester clicked her tongue in the warg's direction, however, and the animals stilled at once.

"More light?" Bonner whispered after a moment's silence.

All of them nodded. Declan drew out the firestone—he wasn't anywhere near comfortable with the idea of casting without it—and as he himself summoned as bright a glow as he could from its depth, Bonner reached out a hand to his orb. It drifted to settle on one wrinkled finger, as a butterfly or small bird might have, and the mage brought it to his lips to whisper some word of power into the spell.

Then he flicked his hand as though to send the light off, and it erupted outward into a hundred copies of itself in all directions with the sound of scattering leaves caught in an autumn wind.

The first thing Declan thought, in that moment, was that he had never seen anything half-so-beautiful in all his life. The winged weaves drifted like floating lanterns this way and that all around them, momentarily stealing away their sight like clouds shifting to expose a heaven of stars in a clear night. His breath caught in his chest, and wasn't even surprised when he felt Ester's hand grip his shirt sleeve. He couldn't look down at her, couldn't bring himself to tear his eyes away from the sight overhead, but he doubted it would have mattered. He knew that she, like him, would be staring upward, mouth agape, taking in the wonder of the magic.

Then the woman's touch fell away, and with it much of the lingering magnificence as their surroundings came into sharp, well-lit focus.

They were standing in a *massive* space, a chamber that might indeed have been called a "cavern", if the word hadn't been so conspicuously inadequate. All around them the stalagmites rose head-high and well-beyond, obstructing their path like a dense forest of slick, grey-black teeth. The walls had vanished, aside from the faintest hint of those at their backs, expanding beyond even the range of Bonner's conjured lights. The ceiling was only slightly less obscure, shadowed and looming until the old man waved a hand upward, and the layer of orbs lifted in response like on a rising wind. When the stone overhead came into focus, Declan cursed at the sweeping blanket of stalactites that painted the uneven swell of the ceiling, some slim and no longer than he was tall, others four feet thick and five times that in length, their forms dancing and twisting in the shifting glow.

He felt like he was standing at the mouth of some horrible beast of myth, waiting for it to close its jaws to crush them all within the fangs of its endless maw...

"Anything?"

Bonner's question, even said under his breath, echoed a dozen times in the vastness of the cave, and Declan started, finally looking down. The old man's eyes were on their surroundings, but it was obvious who he'd been addressing.

Ryn's answer was measured. *I don't know... I can sense more now, but something's... off.*

"Off how?" Declan probed quietly, turning his back on the dragon and mage to watch their rear, Ester doing the same at his side. His voice called back maddeningly to him over and over again, fading a little with every repetition.

Like... I'm not getting the whole picture. I can sense it, now that I know what to look for. The dragon's head was turning slowly as he spoke, scanning the rising stones like he was trying to peer through them.

He stopped, looking west, to his left. *There. Something's masked.*

"How close?" Bonner demanded, taking a quick step towards the closest column.

A brief pause, then...

Close! Ryn snarled, the claymore ringing out of its sheath in his hand.

The mage didn't hesitate. With a string of incomprehensible words he reached out and took hold of an uneven protrusion of rock along the side of the stalagmite. His entire arm pulsed with a faint green light, and with a *crunch* he tore away a piece of rubble the size of Declan's head. At once his words shifted, coming harsher, and the stone started to glow as the old man enchanted it with heat.

"Cover your eyes!" he shouted.

Then he hurled the small boulder into the air, in the direction Ryn had indicated, throwing it with no more apparent effort than a child lobbing a toy ball.

Declan, Ester, and Ryn did as they were told in the nick time, shielding their faces with raised arms just as the thing arched and fell. There was a flash of light, then the *BOOM* of an explosion that shivered across the air and shook water and dust free of the ceiling above. Declan dropped his hand, watching with a jolt of fear as a rain of white-hot gravel *thudded* and *plunked* in a wide spread into the darkness.

The echoing sound of the eruption did nothing to hide the screech of surprised pain, sharp as a sword drawn against solid ice, nor the clambering scuffles of something large scrambling away into the depths of the cavern.

There was no mistaking that call, that keening, piercing shriek. It rang through Declan's ears, bringing with it a cold spasm of terror that had every muscle in his body tense in fearful anticipation.

None of them spoke for a long time after the sounds of the creature disappearing into the blackness faded. They stood, unmoving, to a one straining to make out any sign that the thing was turning around, was coming back to challenge them. The only noise came from Orsik and Eyera, whose throaty growls rumbled in the stillness, the warg's hackles lifted and yellowish teeth bared in the direction Bonner had thrown his heat-woven stone.

"Well, I suppose we know why the witch wanted us down here, now," Ester finally managed weakly, trying and failing to infuse some light-heartedness in the statement.

No one answered her. Declan would have liked to, would have liked to meet her attempt at keeping their disposition positive, but he couldn't bring himself to do it.

All of you, step away. Ryn was next to speak, and he made no attempt at hiding the gravity of his tone as he sheathed his great blade again with a snap and held it out for Bonner to take in both hands. *I'm going to turn.*

Not a word of protest arose, and Declan, Ester, and the old man all hurried away from the dragon, the half-elf coaxing the warg along with them. The moment they were clear, Ryn's form shifted and expanded, heavy, corded muscle boiling into being, wings sprouting from his back like sales from some black ship. Stone columns cracked and shattered under his swelling bulk, the closest stalagmites giving way to crumble beneath massive, clawed feet.

Within seconds, Ryn's *rh'eem* had been replaced with the gargantuan presence of his born form.

We need to get moving. Quickly. The dragon's great head rolled around to fix them with a single eye, white-gold depths gleaming among the floating orbs they were now almost level with. *If it comes back, it won't be to observe us.*

"Which way, though?" Declan called up. "I doubt we'll find *any* kind of current, in a place as big as this."

In answer, Ryn lifted a leg to point with a clawed toe the diameter of a strong man's thigh. *I can sense the east wall. It's not as far into the dark as it might seem. The only way is forward, unless any of you think it's a good idea to go west?*

As one the other three all looked to the left, in the direction the sounds of the beast had vanished.

"Lead on," Ester managed to get out first, this time achieving the faintest hint of false cheer.

Ryn didn't bother trying for stealth, as they moved. Declan supposed it was for the best, given the dragon's size and the sheer impossibility of him managing the confines of the cave quietly in any fashion, but he still flinched every time the huge, surging form knocked down another half-dozen columns of stone with every lumbering step. It made the going easier than it might otherwise have been, though, especially after Bonner's shouted suggestion they take to Orsik and Eyera's backs. As it was Declan's first time doing so, he wasn't displeased when Ester clambered up first, then lent him a hand to help him mount the pack-laden male and settle into the space behind her. Given the circumstance of their situation, however, he found himself regretfully only faintly capable of enjoying the pressure of the woman's upper back against his chest. If anything, he was aware more of the tension in her shoulders as Orsik bounded after the dragon, and of the nervous glances she kept shooting off to their left.

She, like him, knew all-too-well the company they now kept in the dark…

Despite the added weight of riders, the warg demonstrated themselves indeed more adept at managing the ruinous path left in Ryn's thunderous wake than Declan, Bonner, or even Ester would have been capable of on foot. A lifetime among the ragged crags of the Tears proved their worth as the animals leapt and bound nimbly over the scattered rubble, clawed paws finding purchase even on the slick stone. They kept pace with the dragon without much trouble, and Declan was surprised to find the experience not at all inferior to riding a horse. Orsik's ribs were narrower, the ridge of his spine a little prominent in places that would have done better with more padding, but this mild discomfort was made up for by the male's agility and deftness. It was a different sort of ride, Orsik's loping gait swelling up and down more than the stable pace of a stallion's, but it was one Declan thought he could get used to.

Then Ester looked west yet again, and he remembered what it was they were running from.

For whatever reason, nothing leapt at them from the forest of stalagmites in the time they kept moving. For a good ten minutes Ryn continued his cacophonous rampage through the chamber, Bonner—riding a little ways behind them on Eyera—carefully keeping his floating orbs of light even with their progress. The crushing falling of the stone became monotonous, and Declan eventually tuned it out, focusing instead on studying the unchanging panorama of their surroundings. It bothered him—more than he was willing to say out loud—that the beast hadn't fallen upon them yet. They'd caught it unawares, finding it out despite its masked presence, and the shock of Bonner's spell showering it with molten shrapnel *might* have explained the thing's initial fleeing.

But now... Declan would never have expected patience from such a creature. Not without a specific purpose.

"It's a trap," he grumbled, voicing the suspicion he'd been developing for several minutes.

Unsurprisingly, Ester nodded from her place in front of him, not even bothering to turn around. "Without a doubt. Otherwise it would have been on us by now."

Declan grunted in agreement, not bothering to ask the woman if she thought Ryn and her father were aware of it. If he'd figured it out, he was damn sure those two had done so the moment the beast ran away in the first place.

"Think they have a plan?" he asked instead, fingers kneading the hilt of his bastard sword—still bare in one hand at his side while they rode—as he sought any way to calm his nerves.

"Damn well hope so!" she half-shouted back as the crashing sound of Ryn sweeping a smaller line of pillars out of his way with a clawed foot drowned out most all sound in its echoes. "If not, at least we know we're less likely to starve to death!"

Declan snorted at the black humor. "There's more of your father in you than meets the eyes, if you're going to start making jests like that."

Ester laughed hollowly, shifting her weight with him to accommodate a swift turn from Orsik as the warg managed the newly felled rubble with ease. "It comes out when I've nothing left to lose."

Declan chuckled, and would have said more, but stopped himself when the male came up short beneath them. Ryn had quit his advance, and with something between relief and apprehension Declan saw that they had reached a sort of narrowing in the cavern, a place where the entirety of the ceiling shifted drastically downward in a single, colossal slab of broken earth. The ground before the dragon, too, was equally changed, falling away drastically into blind shadows. Before anyone could ask it of him, Bonner brought down some score of his lights, guiding them through the narrowed gap, illuminating a line of heavy stalactites which had fused with the closer stone of the ground to bar their path.

"Shall I clear the way?" the mage asked of the dragon.

Ryn snorted an almost-amused refusal.

Then he made a heavy turn and, with a barreling sweep of his ridged tail, smashed several of the obstructing columns aside to leave a wide, jagged opening for them in the settling dust.

Get through. Quickly. I think it's following us.

The dragon's words had the hairs on Declan's arms standing on end, and neither he nor Ester managed to keep themselves from shifting around to peer into the darkness at their back. As though to confirm Ryn's words, Orsik himself half-turned beneath them to growl in the direction they'd come, his sister joining in a moment later.

"I'd say the beasts would agree," Bonner said in a strained voice. "I'll go first. You two—" he gave Declan and Ester a pointed look "—follow as close behind as you can. Ryn will watch our rear."

They nodded in understanding, Ester bringing Orsik's attention around again with a click of her tongue and a calming pat to his side while Bonner led Eyera carefully around Ryn's foreleg, approaching the breach. There was a pause, then he and the female vanished over the edge of the cracked ledge, the sound of the warg's claws digging against more unseen stone. Ester coaxed Orsik forward next, and after they'd passed the dragon they found themselves looking down over a steep incline of some twenty feet, ending where a waiting Bonner looked up at them from Eyera's back in the glow of his lights.

Orsik only took a moment to paw along the lip of the rise, finding some ideal path invisible to human eyes, then leapt down in three loping bounds.

They came to a skidding halt by Bonner, along the slick slant of a wide expanse of relatively clear stone. It was as though the world had been broken and shifted by some incomprehensible force of god or nature, the entire space around them—ceiling included—angled like part of the earth had shifted an untold time ago. The moisture that had formed the wall of caging stalactites Ryn saw too had not held firm, here, carving instead *into* the rock as the condensation of millennia ran along the slant. Shallow channels had formed, for which Declan was immediately grateful, because they offered Orsik some purchase on the wet surface.

Otherwise, he had a sinking feeling they might just have slipped and slid right into the black, gaping chasm that waited, like the entrance to a hellish abyss, not twenty feet down the incline.

"Gods above," Ester hissed, catching sight of the massive pit as well. Declan sympathized with her alarm. Without the bristling presence of the stalagmites rising all around them, even the bare few winged orbs Bonner had drawn through onto this side of the break offered decent lighting, but within their glow the great opening did not end. It extended, a sea of nothing, into absolute emptiness, as if whatever earth might once have been there had been consumed in a dreadful, devouring void.

"Earthquake," Bonner told them, voice reverberating nightmarishly in this new, more-open part of the cavern. He'd pulled Eyera up carefully beside Orsik, and was himself eyeing the chasm. "Terrible one, at that. Only thing that could create a place like this. Looks like it swallowed half the damn mountain." He looked up, cupping a hand over his mouth to call out to Ryn above them. "Be careful coming down. I'm not sure how stable this shelf is."

Declan had never heard of an "earthquake" before, but he could deduce the concept, and Bonner's statement offered no soothing of his rapidly-fraying nerves. He glanced down, eyeing the stream-cut ground beneath them until the *crunch* of stone lifted his attention in time to see Ryn struggling to pull himself through the opening in the break. The space was just wide enough to accommodate his massive bulk with his wings tucked tightly to his side, and the remnants of the broken stalactites gave way as he wriggled and jerked, tearing furrows five feet long into the slope and ceiling while he fought to gain traction.

Then, with a final snarl and heave, a good chunk of the ledge beneath him broke off in a torrent of shale and gravel, and Ryn half-scrambled, half-bounded down the slope to join them with several heavy *thuds* of his clawed feet. Coming to a stop, the dragon pulled himself up to look around at their five. He seemed rather pleased with his success, right up until he caught sight of Bonner's bone-white face.

What? he asked in alarm, looking down at the stone beneath him, where the others were staring in unified horror. *What is it?*

None of them answered, Declan, Ester, and Bonner all holding their breath in fear.

When they *didn't* plummet into oblivion, there was a collective exhalation of relief.

"Bloody oversized *reptile!*" Bonner seethed, some color coming back to his cheeks. "How, under the eyes of *any* god, did that constitute 'being careful'?!"

Ryn snorted, and looked about to answer when he froze. His head swiveling to face the darkness further along the angle of the shelf, to the north. He stilled, his focus distinctly aimed.

People? he asked after a moment, turning a little and taking a step towards the edge of the light. *I feel like there are people nearb—?*

Every inch of the dragon stiffened, then. His head flung back in their direction, white-gold eyes wide as they looked down the slope, spined ears suddenly spread. In the same instant, Ester gasped and groped for an arrow, bringing her bow around Declan and leaning out to draw it in the direction of the open lip of the chasm behind them.

The dragon's howled warning came only an instant of a second later.

AWAY! AWAY FROM THE EDGE!

It was likely only Orsik and Eyera's instincts that saved them, following this. They, too, must have heard whatever sound had given away the ambush, because together the siblings leapt and flung themselves about-face just as a dark, twisted shape pulled itself over the edge of the abyss with terrifying speed. It surged up onto the incline so quickly that Declan at first caught only the merest glimpse of clawed hands and large, leathery wings in the glow of Bonner's light, his mind struggling to register the other details of the monster.

Then the drey was lunging for them with that familiar, horrible screech, and Declan had a fraction of a second to take the beast in in truth.

It was simultaneously much like the horror he had watched Ryn and Bonner fight to the death over a month ago now, and yet completely different. *This* drey did not bear the oversized wolf's head of its vanquished kin, sporting instead the features of a massive, antlered elk. It was heavier than the other had been, too—*much* heavier—its manish chest five feet broad and striped with brown fur that descended to cover its hoofed legs, behind which curled that horrible, barbed tail. Scaled arms of a blue-red sheen rippled with muscle, each limb more than a foot thick as it reached with its taloned fingers for the group, and its cruel, savage teeth were the same as the wereyn's, uneven fangs that were too-large for its mouth.

Despite the differences, however, in the drey's eyes Declan saw the same hungry evil, the same pale, colorless savagery.

WHAM.

Ryn, moving with what could only have been all the speed in the world, slammed into the beast with a sound akin to flesh striking stone. In one moment it had been feet away from crushing Ester's head with an outstretched hand, then in the next it was flung aside, smashing into the sloped wall of the break nearby with a chilling scream of angry pain.

There was the rumbling warning of Ryn taking in a flooding breath, and Declan got a hand up just in time, covering his eyes and shutting them as tight as he could.

The rumbling howl of the dragonfire, so close the heat struck them all with enough force to send their clothes rippling, was deafening in the echo of the chamber. It set Declan's head to pounding, and he cursed as he blinked away the blinding light he hadn't quite been able to block out, struggling to regain his vision in the hopes of finding the drey's bones tumbling along the shelf into the chasm.

There was no such luck, of course.

Despite its size, the beast proved as quick as its long-dead brethren. It had managed to take flight, the fur of its legs barely smoking, and was darting and dipping away until it spun to hover tauntingly over the emptiness of the pit.

BONNER, PROTECT THEM! Ryn bellowed, barreling forward while his own wings stretched and spread. *I'LL HELP YOU AS SOON AS I CAN!*

Then he was off, taking to the air after the elk-headed creature

"Help us?!" Declan shouted in confusion over the reverberating keen of the monster as it dove to meet the dragon. "Help us with wha—?!"

And then the crunching clatter of falling stone reached him through the ringing in his ears, and Declan whirled on Orsik's back to look up, up the incline, where a new presence had knocked loose some of the rubble left in Ryn's destructive wake. Too late he recalled that their hurry through the cavern had not been one of choice, but of necessity. They'd been running, after all, struggling to put as much distance between them and the creature which had been stalking them through the dark.

And now that second monster was gazing down on them, pallid eyes affixed on their grouped forms from within a massive ram's head, crooked fangs bared in wicked anticipation.

CHAPTER THIRTY-NINE

"MOVE!" Bonner howled, and Declan felt Orsik respond to the mage's command like it had been meant for the warg's own ears. The male flung himself sideways, nearly tossing off both his riders, but his incaution paid off when he threw himself, Declan, and Ester clear just as the drey moved in a blur of white and yellow. It launched itself down on them with a screeching leap, slamming into the ground right where the five of them had been standing, Eyera having taken Bonner away in the other direction with similar reflex. The flashing swipe of its slimmer arms—angled with lines of ivory fur—caught the striated stone with a *crunch* and eruption that sent shattered rock flying. The force of the strike was so dauntingly violent, Declan felt the grip on his sword grow weak. His mind reeled, drowning itself in panic even as Ester shouted in alarm before him, shielding her face from the explosion of earth.

What do we do?! his thoughts demanded of no one in particular, tumbling into confusion. *What do we do?! What do we do?!*

Shlunk!

The drey howled, a pained, agonized cry this time, shaking Declan from his moment of madness. He saw, with a surge of hope, the thin, brittle spike of solid black stone that had lanced out of the slick cavern floor to spear it through the shoulder. The beast writhed and keened, clawing at the shaft, trying to pull itself from its end. Black, acrid blood flowed over the rock and splattered the ground, hissing and smoking. Only when it dripped over the thing's clawless, humanish hands and the amber scales of its great, dragon-like legs did it not sizzle. Beyond the creature, Declan saw Bonner tracing rapid runes in the air around him with both hands as Eyera kept moving, keeping well out of reach, and as he watched a second spine of rock cracked upward to take the drey in the gut.

Abruptly, Declan recalled that he, too, was no longer as defenseless as he'd once been.

Fight, the answer to his panicked question came to him, settling his terror.

Almost in response to this gathered conviction, he felt the firestone in his left hand thrum with a budding warmth beneath his fingers.

"Ester, can you get Orsik to take us behind it?!" he demanded, already pressing his will into the vessel. To her credit, the half-elf only gave him the barest look, the one cheek he could make out bloody from a shallow cut below her right eye.

Then he felt her shift in place, pressing the warg's sides with her knees as she reached back to draw another arrow from its quiver.

Orsik was less inclined to respond accordingly than Declan might have liked, but he answered after only a brief hesitation. With a *clack* of claws he took off over the wet ground, refusing to get as close as might have been ideal while he circled around behind the struggling drey, but it did the trick. Ester's shot thrummed, the arrow taking the beast in the flesh along the back of the neck, and Declan focused on his weave, struggling to call on and bind the powers. He still couldn't summon up the sort of jetting flames Bonner had demonstrated before their trek north, but the practice he and the old man had put into manipulating his King's Blood over the last few days came through in the spell he gathered then. The power felt rawer, more malleable, running through the firestone. He molded it into shape, feeling the weave come together.

When the opportunity came, Declan whipped his casting hand with a shout of effort in a diagonal arc, willing the fire to take form.

It responded with an intensity he had yet seen.

The molten flames didn't so much as *spray* this time as they did *spout*. Like heat made liquid, the weave congealed and splashed in a blade of burning, fluid orange and red across the back of the drey's knees, clinging and catching alight to lick at the yellowish scales. The creature screamed, its ram's head thrashing, fighting harder as it suffered this new, unexpected attack. With mirrored *cracks,* the two stone spikes that had been holding it in place finally broke.

"Not the legs!" Ester shouted as Orsik fled the freed creature. She was bent almost all the way around to draw and send another arrow flying in the monster's direction. "They're dragon flesh!"

Declan cursed his foolishness, looking back as well. Indeed, while the spell clung to the struggling drey's golden hide, boiling and gnawing at the scales as it wrenched the shattered spines of rock from its shoulder and torso, the fires had done far less damage than he would have hoped. He didn't let the disappointment shake his resolution.

It just meant he'd have to be more careful next time.

"The wings, boy!" Bonner called out when he and Eyera crossed them, sprinting by in the other direction to make full-tilt for the creature. "Go for the wings! Keep it from getting airborne!"

Declan saw the sense in *this* idea immediately, taking the chance to cast about for Ryn and the other drey. The dragon was still fighting, he saw with some relief, he and his opponent flitting in and out of the range of Bonner's lights over the waiting mouth of the chasm, slashing and tearing at each other with every pass, light up the black now and again with blasts of white fire. Ryn seemed to be holding his own, for the time being, but if this second beast managed to join the battle…

No. They couldn't allow it.

Having survived one pass unscathed—and likely seeing his sibling charging in without so much as an ounce of apparent fear—Orsik was easier to coax around this time. They thundered directly at the drey not a few seconds behind Bonner and Eyera, Ester managing a brilliant shot that took the thing in the back of the throat when it opened its mouth to shriek at them. It had to reach up and rip the arrow from between its jaws, and that moment bought the five of them the time they needed to close the distance. Bonner's shouted spell boomed with power, and more spines of stone lanced upward—four or five smaller ones, this time—to impale the thing's left leg below the knee from as many angles, skewering it into place. The creature keened in pain again, swiping at the spears to shatter half of them with a blow, but by that point Orsik was on it as well, and this time Declan's second summoning of the molten weave was much more particularly aimed.

The fire splashed against the fragile-looking membrane of the drey's left wing, splattering its length in waves of rolling, blue-orange flame.

The shrieking reached a new level, the echoes of the beast's agony as piercing as the distant sound of clawed and sheering flesh. It thrashed, whipping its wings about like it was trying to cast off the fire, but the spell clung to it with stubborn intent. Declan watched—relishing this small victory—as the weave tore into the black skin, eating holes into the taut membrane.

The admiration of his own success nearly cost he, Ester, and Orsik their lives.

"DECLAN!"

The half-elf's scream snapped his attention down again, just in time to see a dark, lashing blur coming at them. Instinct took over again, and with the firestone in hand, on this occasion the boiling shield of heat he summoned was denser, more focused.

It still shattered when the drey's sectioned tail smashed into it, driving through the spellwork with a crashing distortion of light and fire.

The jointed appendage collided with Orsik's side, crushing Declan and Ester's legs against the warg's ribs. He felt bone strain and something *pop* in his left knee, felt the woman falling away from him as they were thrown bodily sideways. Time seemed to distort, and he reached for her, thinking he might just grab hold of her, securing her to himself. He caught only air, feeling Ester's fine hair slip through his fingers.

Then they hit the ground, tumbling and rolling all until they slid to a final halt at the base of the slope leading up to the higher cavern.

Everything was a scattered jumble. Every thought, every sense and feeling. Declan groaned, struggling to sit, and found himself having difficulty registering which way was up and which way was down. When he managed it at last, it occurred to him that both his sword and the firestone were gone from his hands, a fact which might have frightened him more had he been able to think straight.

Then the heavy, scraping footsteps of something large limping towards him swallowed all other considerations.

His vision still spinning, Declan struggled to lift his gaze. The ram-headed drey, all fifteen feet of it, was moving towards him. Orsik, whimpering and struggling to get up, was between them, and when it reached the warg the beast kicked the four-hundred-pound animal aside with no more effort than it might have a stone in its path. Orsik went tumbling a second time, yelping and rolling, and appeared unable to do more than spasm and tremble when he finally came to a halt on his side.

Declan could barely spare the poor creature a thought. He was too busy watching his own death looming down on him with uneven steps that covered six feet of the slick, slanted ground at a time, a smoking patch of acidic blood trailing every step of its injured leg.

Had his mind been of a condition to register anything else, Declan might have made out other sounds in the ongoing battle. He might have heard Ryn scream in pain as his opponent caught him a savage slash to the face. He might have caught Bonner's distant shouting, his incantation fueled by desperation, knowing he was too far away to make it in time. Declan might even have noticed Ester's uneven breathing not a few feet to his right, might have thought to reach out and touch her, to take some last moment of comfort in her presence at his side.

All there was, though, was the drey.

It seemed to grow exponentially huge as it approached, white fur and the golden scales of its legs losing their detail when it's extended wings—the left smoking and patched with holes—started to blot out the glowing orbs high above. Before long the monster was nothing more than a lumbering silhouette, pale eyes mere flecks of colorless flint in the shadowed outline of its horned head. Declan saw the hand lift—clawless fingers somehow more terrifying for their lack of talons—saw the muscles tense for the brutal blow which would crush both he and Ester as it swept them down the slope and over the edge of the chasm. Strangely enough, fear did not come, did not summon itself appropriately to heel in Declan's ringing head. Instead, he felt only something like sadness, or perhaps regret. His eyes closed of their own volition, giving in to the loss. In the bright darkness he waited, hoping only that the end would be swift.

The strike never came.

After several seconds, Declan opened his eyes again.

The drey had stilled, arm yet lifted overhead, half-turned to look behind it, deeper into the cave. At first Declan thought Bonner had somehow stolen its attention, winning he and Ester a few bare moments more of life, but he saw through the beast's legs that the mage, too, had stopped short, Eyera sliding and slipping over the rock as she fought to scramble around. For a long moment more, Declan sat in confusion, not sure what was going on.

And then a shape moved out of the darkness north of them and into the light, sliding from the black like the thing was stepping through some impenetrable smoke, and he felt his heart skip a beat, then another. Two had been enough, he knew. Two had seen them defeated.

Sehranya, though, had sent *three* of her unholiest children.

The third drey took to the battlefield slowly, eyes fixed and unmoving in its overlarge fox's head. Black scales patterned its neck, chest, and torso like spilled water, and broad wings extended from behind its shoulders. It was smaller than either of the others—likely not more than eight or nine feet tall—and otherwise stood as no more than a towering, naked man save for slight claws at the tips of its hands and feet. The beast approached, covering a quarter of the distance towards them steadily, like it was taking the time to assess the situation. Declan could feel his heart hammering, watching it close on Bonner, pinning the mage between it and its larger kin.

And then, with a rattling breath that could be heard echoing across the cavern, the drey collapsed facedown onto the stone, and didn't move again.

Only then, as Declan watched smoke begin to rise from about its body, did he realize that its scales had not been black at all. Indeed, they shone pale grey in spreading patterns over its shoulders and back.

The darkness, rather, had been the stain of sheeting, spilling blood.

That moment, as he registered this incredible fact, was when the shadows beyond the light spilled like silent death from the emptiness of the blackness.

There was nothing to be done but watch as the figures made themselves known, dashing over the uneven ground without fear, as sure-footed on the wet, icy stone as one might have been on a dry, cobbled road. For a few seconds Declan was convinced his addled mind was playing tricks on him, but as the new arrivals closed the distance between them and the ram-headed drey—spinning around Bonner and Eyera without so much as a glance at the pair—he saw that they were indeed men and women of flesh and bone.

Well... men and women of a sort, at least.

The figures appeared, initially, to be clad from head to foot in all black, but as they dashed beneath the shifting spells of light, Declan caught the glint and glimmer of gold inlaid in what looked like smoke-darkened leather-and-metal armor. Long, inky plumes trailed from closed helms that covered all but the strangers' mouths and eyes, and in their hands they wielded a collection of weaponry unlike anything Declan had ever known. Each had either a pair of swords or a spear to their name, but instead of steel, the blades looked almost to be made of polished, carved glass. The strange material was crystalline, opaque and black, and years of experience screamed that such armaments were folly to lift against opponents like the drey.

Then, however, the first of the figures was on the monster that had been moments from crushing his life into nothingness, and Declan knew nothing more than awe.

She—for it *was* a "she", he judged by the slenderness of her armor—moved as Declan could only dream of, engaging the drey. The beast turned to meet this new threat, but the blur of its tail struck uselessly, the figure having sidestepped a half-second before the attack with a twirl that would have made the royal dancers of Mathaleus al'Dyor's palace ballrooms green with envy. As she spun, the twin blades of that strange, glass-like metal cut through the air in paired, audible shrieks, and Declan knew the value of the weapons the moment they bit into the drey's inner thigh, just above its knee. Blood splashed to the ground, hissing and burning, and the drey itself screamed when the joint half-gave beneath it, but the stranger had already ducked and slid as gracefully as water through the beast's legs, skillfully avoiding the dangerous splattering.

Her swords, Declan saw, dripped with acid ichor, but did not smoke themselves.

It doesn't hold, he realized in dawn understanding, gaping at the sheen of the blades from the depths of his muddled consciousness. *The blood doesn't hold.*

Before he could get a better look, however, the weapons' owner was moving again, quick as thought itself, this time joined by the half-dozen other shadows who'd caught up with her in a blink.

The fight was quick and brutal. Without the means to get airborne, the drey could only lash out with arms and tail. Unfortunately for it, despite its unfathomable speed its strikes were largely ineffective, every blow landing a fraction of a second too late, every thrust of its barbed appendage catching only the air where a moment before a figure had stood. Declan didn't know if it was magic, or merely some superior consciousness of their enemy's movements, but to a one the black-clad newcomers were as wraiths haunting much larger prey, cutting it down little by little. They darted in and out in the same breath, sometimes slipping through the drey's legs as the figure in their lead had, other times simply dancing away with lissome steps that seemed always to find the clean rock among the growing spots of acid-eaten ground. The drey screamed and thrashed, turning this way and that, howling in fury as every attempt to catch one of its attackers left it open for slices from two or three more. As it steadily weakened it grew more desperate, and in its panicked rage luck did more than focus had managed. In the space of ten seconds, one of the figures was sent flying as the tail spasmed and caught them unexpectedly in the side, and a second body tumbled to hiss in the pooling blood when a thrashing hand caught and took hold of her helmeted head, crushing it into metallic, bloody pulp with an instinctive flexing of the drey's fingers.

Though horrible a death to witness, that was when the one who had led the charge, the female who'd dealt the first blow, saw her opening.

There was nothing grand about the execution, but the simple ease of it took Declan's breath away. In reaching for the kill, the drey overextended, bending low on legs already weakened by twenty gouging lacerations. Even as it crushed the life from one of her own, the swordswoman was moving, stepping into the shadows of the beast, twisting and sweeping upward in a twin flurry of blades. Dark, shining metal dug into the drey's neck, cleaving through muscle and flesh, but as blood bloomed in a gush from the wound the killer was already gone, having twisted and rolled bodily over the drey's bent knee, using the thing's own scaled hide for cover. The beast tried to snarl, tried to scream, but only more blood came, spilling through its crooked fangs. It choked, breath bubbling from a severed windpipe, then staggered, clawless hands coming up to its neck while its pale eyes widened. There was a moment of realization in the monster's expression, something almost like confusion tainted with fear.

And then it, too, collapsed, spasming and drowning with gagging coughs while its lungs filled with its own blood.

That, though, was the moment Ryn screamed.

Despite the incomprehensible sight before him, despite the beauty and the terror and the disbelief of the moment, Declan looked around at the anguished sound of his friend's shriek. To his horror he saw that the elk-headed drey had somehow latched itself to the dragon's shoulder, one hand holding tight to a horn overhead, the other arm looped about Ryn's throat.

With the sound of ripping flesh, Declan watched the drey bite into the side of Ryn's neck, tearing away a mouthful of sinew skin and muscle. He saw the dragon's entire body spasm, his wings jerking and failing to beat on the shock of the pain.

Then they were falling, tumbling down together into the black of the abyss, the drey ripping at scale and bloody flesh again even as they vanished over the edge of the void.

"RYN!" Declan choked, fighting his addled mind to get up, to run to the lip of the chasm. He tried to stand, tried to get his feet under him. His left knee screamed in protesting pain, but he ignored it, knowing only the violent need to hurry, to run.

He'd almost managed to stand when something hard, smooth, and inexplicably sharp hooked him beneath the line of his jaw.

Declan stopped cold, instinct overpowering every other desperation. He looked down slowly, trailing the curved edge of the dark blade to its hilt, along with the gloved hand that held it without so much as a hint of a tremor. He followed the slender arm up, tracing the layers of gold-gilded armor until he found the still, hard face beneath its plumed helm. Declan had known what he would find, had glimpsed the reality the moment this very figure had led the devastating charge against the drey.

All the same, it was hard not to stare at the black skin of the swordswoman's face, nor the white eyes, hinting at irises of red, that held his gaze firm.

When she spoke, the strange syllables were as cold as the edge of the sword at his throat.

"Yl vas ah'ren, veht?"

Though he knew only a little of the language—and a dialect entirely different at that—Declan could guess well enough at the meaning of the question.

"What are you doing here, human?" the dark elf had demanded of him.

Thank You All! Please Read!

After months of effort, back-and-forth, and editing, the first installment of this crazy collaboration that is *The Shattered Reigns* has finally hit the shelves! We are so grateful to you—yes you, reading this right now—for making the investment in and taking the time for *A Mark of Kings*, joining us on this wild adventure. It's your support that makes it possible for writers like the pair of us to practice our craft, and your involvement that makes this journey so enjoyable for us.

On that subject, a few notes:

First: Please, *please,* consider rating and reviewing *A Mark of Kings* on Amazon, or any of your favorite book sites. Many people don't know that there are thousands of books published every day, most of those in the USA alone. Over the course of a year, a quarter of a million authors will vie for a small place in the massive world of print and publishing. We fight to get even the tiniest traction, fight to climb upward one inch at a time towards the bright light of bestsellers, publishing contracts, and busy book signings.

Thing is, we need all the help we can get, and that's where wonderful readers like you come in!

Second: If you want to join our growing communities, be sure to like us on Facebook! If you'd rather hit either of us up directly with thoughts, feedback, or anything else that peaks your interest, our contact emails are bryce@bryceoconnorbooks.com and LyrianRastler@gmail.com respectively!

Even better, consider joining our Patreon pages on Patreon.com! You'll be the first to know of any news, artwork, and announcements! What's more, by joining Bryce's page (patreon.com/bryceoconnor) you'll receive chapter-by-chapter releases of the rest of *The Shattered Reigns* series *months* in advance, and on Luke's page (patreon.com/LukeChmilenko) you'll have early access to books from his incredible *Ascend Online* series, and other upcoming releases!

Regardless of whether or not you choose to review, reach out, or support us elsewhere, thank you again for taking the time to read *A Mark of Kings,* and we will see you in the sequel!

Your biggest fans,

Bryce O'Connor & Luke Chmilenko

39157118R00251

Made in the USA
San Bernardino, CA
17 June 2019